Paul Doherty was born in Middlesbrough. He studied History at Liverpool and Oxford Universities and obtained a doctorate at Oxford for his thesis on Edward II and Queen Isabella. He is now the Headmaster of a school in North-East London, and lives with his wife and family near Epping Forest.

Paul Doherty's Hugh Corbett medieval mysteries – SATAN IN ST MARY'S, CROWN IN DARKNESS, SPY IN CHANCERY, THE ANGEL OF DEATH, THE PRINCE OF DARKNESS, MURDER WEARS A COWL, THE ASSASSIN IN THE GREENWOOD, THE SONG OF A DARK ANGEL, SATAN'S FIRE and THE DEVIL'S HUNT – are also available from Headline, as are his other novels of mystery and murder – AN ANCIENT EVIL, being the Knight's Tale, A TAPESTRY OF MURDERS, being the Man of Law's Tale, A TOURNAMENT OF MURDERS, being the Franklin's Tale, and GHOSTLY MURDERS, being the Priest's Tale, all told during the evenings on a pilgrimage from London to Canterbury.

Acclaim for Paul Doherty's medieval mysteries:

'Medieval London comes vividly to life . . . Doherty's depictions of medieval characters and manners of thought, from the highest to the lowest, ringing true' *Publishers Weekly*

'I really like these medieval whodunnits' Sarah Broadhurst, *Bookseller*

'. . . this is one of those books you hate to put down' *Prima*

'A powerful compound of history and intrigue' *Redbridge Guardian*.

The
Rose Demon

Paul Doherty

HEADLINE

First published in 1997
by HEADLINE BOOK PUBLISHING

First published in paperback in 1998
by HEADLINE BOOK PUBLISHING

10 9 8 7 6

ISBN 0 7472 5441 9

Typeset by Palimpsest Book Production Limited,
Polmont, Stirlingshire
Printed in England by Clays Ltd, St Ives plc

HEADLINE BOOK PUBLISHING
A division of Hodder Headline PLC
338 Euston Road
London NW1 3BH

Dedicated to the memory of
Colonel Gilland Wales Corbitt (U.S.A.F.) D.F.C.

'The Rose is the Perfume of the Gods'

Anacreon, Ode 51C, 6th Century BC

'Quantum Mechanics suggest that consciousness,
or mind, may be independent of the body it inhabits'

Hans J. Eysenck & Com. Sargent,
Explaining the Unexplained' Prion, 1993

'The same Evil Spirit may serve as a succubus
to a Man and an incubus to a Woman'

Charles Rene Billuart, *Treatise on Angels*, 1746

HISTORICAL NOTE

In 1453 the great Byzantine civilisation was extinguished when the Ottoman Turks broke into Constantinople, killing the Emperor and bringing his empire and what land he ruled firmly under the control of the Ottoman Turks. Despite the help of Venice and the military religious orders such as the Knights Hospitallers, as well as the fighting skills of Western mercenaries, Constantinople ceased to be.

In England such a disaster made little impact as the country was divided between the Houses of York and Lancaster. A bitter civil war raged which, in 1471, culminated in the destruction of the Lancastrian cause, the death of their king, Henry VI, the exile of his queen, Margaret of Anjou, and the execution of most of the Lancastrian commanders. York remained in the ascendant until the Battle of Bosworth in 1485 when Henry Tudor defeated the Yorkist king Richard III. Henry VII's victory, however, was not complete and, for years afterwards, his reign was plagued by a series of powerful Yorkist pretenders.

In Spain, Aragon and Castile were to be united by the marriage of Ferdinand and Isabella. The successful union of these kingdoms led to the implementation of a much-treasured dream: the removal of the Moors, the capture of their great city of Granada, and the emergence of a Catholic Spain.

In Italy, meanwhile, a Genoese explorer and map-maker, Christopher Columbus, dreamt of sailing across the great Western Ocean to find a safer and more direct route to the Indies . . .

THE PROLOGUES

1

Constantinople 29 May 1453

The Rosa Mundi,
Its heart is cankered.
Its petals drop like a fallen angel
From the fields of heaven.

'Oh day of wrath,
Oh day of mourning!
See fulfilled the prophet's warning.
Heaven and earth in ashes burning!'

The opening lines of the Dies Irae echoed along the marble
naves of the churches. The priests in their gorgeous vestments, shrouded by clouds of incense, lifted their hands and
beseeched the Almighty to help against the tide of terror
which had broached the massive walls, towers and fortifications of Constantinople. Mohammed II, self-styled God's
Vice-Regent on earth, had brought his fleet across the Golden
Horn. Just after dawn, his yellow-coated janissaries had made
their final assault. The walls had been breached, the last home
of the Caesars was about to fall. Already the purple, imperial
banners were retreating deep into the city as cries of desolation
rang out along the streets and alleyways of the Emperor's city.
Soon, the horses of the conquerors would ride in triumph into
the palaces of the Byzantine nobles.

The calamity had been foretold. Hideous portents had
filled the skies. Satan, like some great bat, his shadowy wings
extended, his talons like those of a huge eagle, had been seen
hovering over the city. And had not demons appeared in the
hippodrome, red-clawed hands turned up towards the sky,
whilst sepulchral voices at midnight, sounding like hollow

bells, prophesied horror upon horror: Constantinople was about to fall.

In his private chamber at the Blachernae Palace, only a short distance from the fighting, Constantine Palaeologus, the last Roman Emperor, was about to leave and die on the walls of his city. In the antechamber, his housecarls, their long, blond hair falling down to their waists, now rested against marble walls, loosening the straps from their chain mail byrnies. They sipped wine and knew they would not taste it again until they met in the kingdom of God. They too were to die. Each had taken the blood oath. They would fight until their master fell, and beyond. They would never bend the knee to the Ottoman Turk. They were impatient for death and whispered amongst themselves what could occupy their emperor at such a fatal hour. He was closeted behind the ivory-plated doors of his private chamber with the old priest Eutyches and the two Westerners, the Hospitaller knights, Raymond and Otto Grandison. The brothers had come from Rhodes to offer their swords in the Emperor's last stand. The housecarls agreed that the Grandisons were sturdy fighters – unlike the Western mercenaries, who had fled through the night, seeking shelter and succour from the Venetian fleet waiting so helplessly beyond the harbour.

Inside his privy chamber, Emperor Constantine slouched in his purple, gold-embossed throne. He stared down at the two knights kneeling before him. Their hair was thick with grease, dark faces unshaven, their armour was blood-spattered, their leather leggings stained with sweat. They both leant on their great, two-handed swords whilst between them stood the venerable Eutyches, dressed gorgeously in the full pontifical robes of a Byzantine priest. A gold-encrusted cape hung about Eutyches' thin, bent shoulders, clasped by a silver chain at the front. Beneath this, in his white gloved hands, he held a pyx bearing the Sacrament.

'I am going to die,' the Emperor declared, breaking from his reverie. 'Before noon I will be dead. I will die like a Roman general, my face to the enemy, my sword in my hands.'

'Then, Excellency, let us die with you,' said the elder of the knights. 'That is why we entered our order, what we live for. To die for Christ, His Holy Mother and the Christian faith.'

Constantine shook his head.

'My empire is to fall,' he murmured. 'It will never rise again. This city is twelve hundred years old.' He smiled thinly, wiping the dust from his face. 'Our conquerors will find secrets – they are welcome to them – but, one they must not discover. I have sworn a great oath, on holy relics, as my father did before me, that, if this city falls, my last act must be to destroy a great evil.' He stirred in his chair. 'That is why you are in Constantinople. You are to help me.'

The two Hospitaller knights stared at him. They were young men, their soft faces sunburnt, eyes gleaming with the light of battle. They looked so alike – black hair neatly cropped, well-spaced, honest eyes. The Emperor allowed himself another smile. He had chosen well: these men, sworn to celibacy and obedience, would carry out his commands.

'Stand up!' he ordered.

The knights got to their feet.

'Place your hands on the Sacrament!'

The knights took off sweat-stained gauntlets. Each placed a hand gently over that of the old priest as he stood, face impassive, eyes closed, murmuring his prayers.

'Swear!' Constantine insisted. 'Swear on the Sacrament that you will carry out my last order! Swear that you will do so, whatever the cost!'

'We swear!'

Constantine opened the purple filigree pouch on his war belt and took out a ring on which seven keys hung. The clasp on each was strangely carved and the handle of every key was shaped into a cross, in the centre of which was a small glass reliquary.

'These are special keys,' the Emperor explained. 'Each holds the relic of a great saint.' He handed them to Sir Raymond. 'Follow Eutyches! He will take you, by secret passageways, down deep into the bowels of the palace. The way is already lighted.' The Emperor paused, his head slightly sideways. 'Listen!' he whispered.

The roar of battle was now not so faint.

'I must hurry,' the Emperor continued. 'In the vault the five silver keys will open a chamber. The two golden ones will unlock whatever that chamber contains.'

'What is it?' Sir Otto asked hoarsely.

'A casket,' the Emperor replied. 'You are to open it. Once

you have done so, do whatever Eutyches tells you to. You have sworn an oath.'

The Emperor got to his feet, his chain mail jingling as he walked across to a huge, golden rose painted on the blue marble wall. He pressed the centre and a door swung open. Otto flinched at the cold blast of air which swept into the chamber. Both knights, seasoned warriors, felt a deep sense of fear, blood chilling as if a dagger were being drawn along the napes of their necks. They looked at each other, then back at the Emperor.

'You feel it as I do,' Constantine declared.

'Every man does.' Eutyches opened his rheumy eyes. His voice was low, grating, and he talked the lingua franca, the language understood by everyone in Constantinople. 'Your Excellency,' Eutyches bowed, 'we must go, time is short. You must die and, when I have done my task, I, too, must prepare for death.'

Constantine came and knelt before the priest.

'Then bless me, Father.'

The priest raised the pyx before the Emperor in the sign of the cross. Constantine got to his feet. He kissed the priest on both cheeks and exchanged the kiss of peace with the two Hospitaller knights, then, without a backward glance, left the chamber, shouting for his guards to follow.

The knights heard the door being closed and locked; the shouts of officers as furniture was piled against it.

'If the Turks break in,' Eutyches explained, 'that will give us more time. Now, come.' He walked towards the secret passageway, stopped and gestured for Otto to precede him. 'Sir Raymond, you will follow behind. Close the door after us.'

Sir Otto and the priest disappeared into the darkness. Raymond waited for a few moments then, drawing his sword, followed. He found himself at the top of steep steps which swept down into the darkness. On the walls above him, cresset torches fought hard to keep out the darkness. Raymond studied these curiously. He cursed his imagination. The fire itself seemed frightened. The flame was weak and the centre of each had turned a strange bluish tint.

'Come!' Eutyches ordered.

Raymond fumbled in the darkness. He found a clasp and

pushed the door over. It closed like the lid of a tomb. He followed the other two down the steps. The walls on either side were cold marble. Raymond had to fight against the shivers which racked his body.

'Do not think!' Eutyches' voice sounded hollow. 'Just pray! Make the sign of the cross to ward off any evil!'

Raymond began praying. Peering through the gloom, he could see that his brother, just in front of the priest, was faltering now and again as if unsteady on his feet, and would only continue at Eutyches' hushed entreaties.

Following, Raymond felt so cold. Suddenly he started back, his sword coming up. He was sure an ice-cold hand had trailed its fingers across his throat, freezing the beads of sweat which laced his skin. He walked on, trying to ignore the sensation of hands clutching at his shoulder or his arm. On one occasion he dropped his sword. It fell with a clash and he scrabbled in the darkness to pick it up. Suddenly a face, grey like a puff of smoke, with grinning gargoyle mouth from which bare fangs protruded, came up before him. Sir Raymond wiped his face on the sleeve of his jerkin. Eutyches was now praying aloud, his words booming like the knell of a bell, urging them both to continue, to ignore what was happening.

At last they reached the bottom of the steps. In the torchlight the old priest looked more ancient and wizened: he, too, was soaked in sweat whilst Otto stood as if he had been running for his life, chest heaving, mouth open gasping for air, sweat dripping down his unshaven cheeks as if he had doused his head in water.

'How much further?' Sir Raymond asked.

The priest pointed along the passageway, which seemed to stretch into eternity.

'Continue!' he urged. 'Whatever happens, don't stop!'

This time both knights followed him. They were too frightened to speak. Now and again they clasped hands, fighting the urge to leave this venerable priest and flee for their lives.

'When your task is done—' Eutyches spoke up, 'and it will be done quickly – leave the chamber. Don't come back this way but flee further along the gallery. It will bring you out beyond the city walls.'

'We thought to die at Constantinople,' Otto replied.

7

'Why are the young so interested in dying?' the priest said wryly. 'In the end, die you will and die you must!'

His grim jest seemed to lighten the tension. Just as the shadowy fears were closing in again, they reached a bend in the passageway where it turned abruptly to the left. Eutyches, however, ignored the gloomy, dark-filled gallery. He stood before a doorway, one of the most extraordinary the brothers had ever seen – not made of wood or steel but of sheer marble with a mother-of-pearl cross in the centre.

'Unlock the door!' Eutyches called.

For a while Raymond fumbled with the keys. There were five locks along the side of the door. It took some time to find the key for each lock but, as he turned them, Sir Raymond could hear some intricate mechanism click. At last he finished and pushed the door hard. It swung open smoothly and both brothers gasped: if the door was a work of wonder, the octagonal chamber it guarded was even more so. It was lighted by shafts which came down from the roof and filled the chamber with sharp rays of sunlight. The walls were covered in gold-fringed, velvet drapes, the marble ceiling was concave, whilst each slab of the marble floor had a small glass case embedded in the middle.

'Reliquaries,' the priest explained.

'Why?' Otto whispered.

Eutyches pointed to the centre of the chamber which, because of the angle of the light, was shrouded in a veil of darkness.

Raymond narrowed his eyes. He could see the casket about a yard high and three yards long. He lifted his head and sniffed the air.

'Roses!' he whispered. 'I can smell roses!'

The air was growing sweeter by the second; a subtle fragrance, which provoked bittersweet memories of luxuriant gardens at the height of summer around the Priory of St John of Jerusalem in London.

'Where are the roses?' Otto asked. 'Why does the chamber smell so fragrantly?'

'Ignore it,' Eutyches almost snarled. 'We have a task to do!'

They followed Eutyches across to the sarcophagus. Made out of costly wood, the casket was sealed with two locks, one at either end. Again, at Eutyches' urgings, Raymond opened each lock and lifted back the lid. The smell of roses grew even richer, more cloying. He and Otto stared down in amazement. Beneath the gauze cloths lay the body of a beautiful young woman.

'Do not tarry!' Eutyches urged. 'Lift the cloths!'

They did so. Both men stared open-mouthed, the woman was so extraordinarily beautiful. Her dark hair was framed by a cloth-of-gold veil; her body hidden beneath the silver damask dress of a Byzantine princess; her velvet-gloved hands lay by her side. Raymond felt her cheek, soft as down-feather, slightly warm.

'She's sleeping!' he exclaimed.

'You are to open her mouth,' the priest ordered. 'I will press in the host, then you must seal the casket.' Eutyches pointed across to where huge earthenware jars stood. 'They are filled with oil. Once the casket is resealed, you are to tip them over. Take a torch from the wall outside and let the room burn!'

Raymond stared aghast at the priest. 'This is murder!' he rasped. 'I am a knight of Christ, not an assassin!'

'Open her mouth!' Eutyches shouted.

Both knights backed away. The young woman was moving, her eyes fluttering. Eutyches put the pyx down and drew a bejewelled dagger from his robes. Sir Raymond stepped forward: those lovely eyes were open, smiling up at him. The Hospitaller lashed out, intending to block the thrust of the raised dagger. Instead, he struck Eutyches a powerful blow on the side of the shoulder. The old priest staggered and fell; his head hit the marble floor, cracking open like an egg. The blood seeped out. Sir Raymond stared in horror but turned at the warm, soft touch to his cheek. The young woman's eyes were so lovely, so entreating her hands stretching out . . .

9

2

Masada, above the Dead Sea, July 1461

In the beginning:
The Rosifer, Lucifer's great henchman,
Took a rose from the gardens of heaven
And rode down to Paradise to pay court to Eve.

Sir Otto Grandison was much changed. No longer the fiery young knight, he was clothed in a cloak of camelhair with rough sandals on his feet. Yet the greatest change, at least to the eye, was his face: no longer smooth and olive-skinned but deeply furrowed, burnt by a fiery sun, whilst his hair had turned grey, and an unkempt beard fell in a tangled mess to his stomach.

Sir Otto Grandison, now a hermit, stood on the cliffs of Masada. Narrowing his eyes, he stared out over the shimmering mass of the Dead Sea. It was just after dawn. The sun had sprung up like a fiery ball and already Grandison could feel the blast of heat from the desert below. He shaded his eyes and stared down the precipitous cliffs. He had slept badly, his mind racked by nightmares, the fears and terrors of the night. He looked back over his shoulder at the small cave built into the rock. A hermit's dwelling: nothing but rough sacking for a bed; a battered pair of saddlebags hung on a peg; and a stone jar, the gift of a kindly Arab, to hold the water he drew from the well.

Grandison looked up. Vultures hung black against the sky, hovering, keen-eyed for any prey or for those about to die. Sir Otto crossed himself. Usually the vultures would preen their great feathered wings and fly out over the desert but, recently, they had begun to stay, hovering above him. He wondered whether they, too, sensed that death was near.

He stared round the ruins built on the top of these cliffs. A traveller, a seller of perfumes from whom Sir Otto had begged scraps of food in the valley below, had told him about these ruins. How Masada had once been a great fortress built by Herod the Great, he who had slaughtered the innocents at the time of Jesus' birth. Later it had become a stronghold for the Jews in their violent struggle against the Roman legions, and its last defenders, determined not to be taken prisoner, had poisoned themselves, their wives and their children. Otto often wondered if their ghosts haunted this eagle's eyrie or if Herod the Great, bound by chains in his own fiery hell, walked the ruins of his former greatness.

During the day, all was well. Sir Otto would stay in his cave, sleep, pray or pore over the battered copy of the Scriptures he had bought before leaving Rhodes. Sometimes, if he saw a camel train or merchants on the road below, he'd go down to beg for coins or food, assuring his would-be benefactors of his prayers to God Almighty. He was always treated gently by Christian, Turk or Jew. Some saw him as a holy man, a hermit; others a madcap fool to live in the heart of the wilderness and haunt the ghostly ruins of Masada.

Sir Otto, feeling the heat of the sun, walked back to the coolness of his cave. He knelt down and stared at the makeshift wooden cross placed on a ledge beside his bed.

'I cannot blame them, Lord,' he murmured. 'I am what I appear to be: a sinner, a lost soul.'

Otto combed his iron-grey, straggling beard. His brother would not recognise him now. He drank a little of his precious water and lay down on his bed.

'God bless you, Raymond,' he whispered. 'Wherever you are.'

He knew they'd never meet again, yet, sometimes, whether it was a temptation from the devil or not, he just wished he could clasp his brother one more time, especially now, before he died. Otto, deep in his heart, realised the Demon had found him. Turning on his side, he stared at the tangle of wild roses, now decaying, where he had thrown them into a corner of the cave. Otto had found these about a week ago, after he had come back from the road below, placed on a stone outside the entrance to the cave. Wild roses! He didn't know where they had come from or how they could survive for so long in the fiery heat, yet they were a token, a warning: the Rose Demon was, once again, about to enter his life.

Otto rolled back and clasped his hands. He was ready for death. He had atoned for his terrible sin. He had spent seven years here: a life of atonement, for breaking his oath and, above all, loosing the Rose Demon into the world of man.

Otto could never forget Eutyches lying on that marble floor, the blood seeping out of his hoary, cracked head. Raymond and he had taken the princess out of the sarcophagus; so beautiful, so delicate, her body exuding the most fragrant of perfumes. She had not said much but thanked them softly and asked for their protection, which they had solemnly pledged.

Then the Turks broke into the Blachernae. He and Raymond, the princess between them, had fled along the gloomy gallery and up steep stairs which took them out on to a hillside just beyond the walls of Constantinople. They had hoped to reach their ship but a squadron of Sipahis, Turkish light horse, had cut off their escape. He and Raymond were threatened with a violent and bloody struggle. God knows why or how – perhaps in their souls they realised what they had failed to do – but Otto and his brother had allowed the Sipahis to seize the mysterious princess. In return, the Hospitallers had been permitted through.

Bloody and bruised, Raymond and Otto had secured passage on a small boat. By dusk that day they were on board a Venetian galley and, like the rest of the refugees, could only stare helplessly at the shoreline, watching columns of smoke float up from the city. To the Venetians the fall of Constantinople was a disaster but, to the two brothers, it was a personal shame. They had broken their oath. Eutyches had been killed – and the princess? Otto could never forget the hateful look she threw at them as the Sipahis seized her.

'We did not mean to hand her over,' Raymond later told the Grand Master of the Knights Hospitallers when they reached the island of Rhodes. 'The Sipahis took her. It was impossible to rescue her.'

The Grand Master, however, had sat grey-faced, open-mouthed, staring at them. At last he shook himself and rose slowly to his feet.

'You should have killed her,' he whispered.

'Why?' Raymond had asked.

12

The Grand Master sat in a window seat and put his head in his hands.

'Why?' Raymond followed him across the room. When the Grand Master looked up, his face was suffused with a terrible anger.

'In his last letter to me,' the Grand Master jabbed a finger at Raymond, 'His Imperial Highness, the Emperor Constantine, asked me to name two Hospitallers, two of my most trustworthy men for a task which only a priest and a soldier could perform. I chose you. You took your oath and you broke it. Now, because of your perfidy, not only is a good and venerable priest killed but a terror, much worse than any Ottoman army, has been unleashed on the world!'

Raymond had fallen on his knees before the Grand Master, head bowed, hands clasped. Otto had done likewise.

'Father,' Raymond confessed, 'we have sinned before Heaven, before earth and before thee.'

'Yes you have,' the Grand Master retorted, turning his back on them. 'And, in all justice, I must tell you about your sin. For years there has been a secret held by this Order. I shall not tell you the details.' He shook his head. 'There is a woman in England who knows the full story, a devilish tale of horrible evil. In the vaults of the Blachernae Palace at Constantinople a great demon, the Rosifer or Rosebearer, was held fast in a human body.' He sighed noisily. 'This Rosifer is both an incubus and a succubus, one of the principal demons of Hell. This Duke of Darkness can move from one body to another, be it male or female, and possess it to its fullness. Only the Sacrament and fire blessed by a priest can destroy its hold and send it back to Hell.'

Otto had just knelt, open-mouthed, whilst his brother had put his face in his hands and began to sob quietly.

'The Emperor's letter called on our help,' the Grand Master continued harshly. 'According to him, years ago this Great Demon Rosifer, Lucifer's henchman, was brought unwittingly by Westerners into Constantinople and possessed a Byzantine princess. The Emperor of the time would have burnt her as a witch but her father and others pleaded for her life. Somehow, I can't explain, she was put in a drugged sleep and placed in the vault. The Emperor decreed that she would be safe there as long as the Empire was safe. His successors took a great and secret oath that if the city were ever to fall, what should have been done at the beginning would be done then.'

'And we failed?'

'Yes,' the Grand Master snarled as he turned round. 'You failed!'

'Father, what can we do?'

The Grand Master refused to answer then. However, a week later, he called them into the Priory church. He was calmer as he walked in silence between them, up and down the transept. At last he stopped and stared up at a picture of Christ in Judgment. On the Saviour's right the saints, on the left, the damned being driven off to Hell.

'Every so often—' the Grand Master began, 'and I am a man of sixty years, a priest and a soldier of Christ – every so often our humdrum lives are broken by something extraordinary such as this. I have reported as much to His Holiness in Rome as well as our Vicar General but there is little they can do.' He held a hand up. 'I have already told you all I know. A great evil has been unleashed on the world and only the Good Lord knows where it will end. You two are responsible. So this is my judgment and there is no appeal. You must leave the Order.' He silenced their gasps. 'One of you must spend a life of atonement, prayer and fasting, the life of a solitary hermit well away from the affairs of men. The other, well, the other must spend his life hunting for this demon.' He paused. 'It's now Sunday. Your answer must be with me within fourteen days, the Feast of St Peter and St Paul.'

The two brothers had conferred, their decisions made. Raymond had left for Europe. Otto had come to Palestine on a pilgrimage and founded his own hermitage here on the rocky slopes of Masada. Now and again he had travelled to one of the ports – Sidon, Tyre and even into Acre – but never had he heard anything about his brother. Only once, when he made enquiries from a merchant who traded between Cyprus and Constantinople, had he learnt about a Byzantine princess being given to one of Mohammed's commanders in his harem. Otto could never discover whether this was the same woman he and his brother had taken from the vaults beneath Constantinople.

'But she has not forgotten me,' he murmured. 'Who else would climb a rocky path to leave roses outside my cave?'

14

He closed his eyes and cleared his mind. Every time he dreamt, he was back in that vault, the air rich with the smell of roses and, recently, even here, he had caught their fragrance. But no one was ever seen round here apart from an Arab boy tending some goats. Otto had considered returning to Rhodes, to seek the help and assistance of the Grand Master but, the last time he had been at Acre, a pilgrim had told him that the Grand Master had died in rather mysterious circumstances.

Otto sighed and got to his feet. He left the cave and stared down into the valley. The goat boy was moving his herd towards the nearby oasis. Faintly, on the breeze, Otto heard the chime of bells and boyish shouts. He returned to his cave, opened the Scriptures and, once again, turned to the Apocalypse. He read the lines about the Great Beast, the Devil from Hell who wandered the face of the earth determined to destroy God's creation. Otto closed his eyes.

'I find it so hard to believe,' he whispered. 'So difficult, Lord. She was so young, so beautiful, so serene. Her skin was soft as shot silk. And those eyes, so blue, so innocent.'

He recalled how, when they had hurried along the underground passage, the princess did not lose her dignity but kept up with the knights. When they paused so Raymond could scout ahead, she had simply leant against the wall and begun a song softly in French about a rose, a beautiful rose, which bloomed before Creation ever began.

Otto opened his eyes and stared at the crucifix. Recently, at night, he had begun to hear that song again and he did not know whether it was the wind or his stupid mind playing tricks on himself. Yet he had gone out and stood at the mouth of his cave and seen shapes and forms moving amongst the stones. He had called out, crossed himself and, putting his trust in Christ, returned to sleep.

Otto returned to his study of the Scriptures. For a while he dozed and then, as customary, walked round the ruins. Once the sun began to dip, he took his precious tinder and, gathering the kindling he had collected together and some of the camel dung he had taken from the road below, he lit a weak fire.

For a while Otto just sat and warmed himself, and then he stiffened. The voice was so pure, clear, lilting.

'In Heaven's meadows before the world began
The mystic Rose grew there.
But I plucked it as a gift
For the daughter of God.'

Otto whirled round. In the firelight he could see a young boy dressed in a simple white tunic with a stick in his hand.

'Who are you?' he stammered.

The boy moved forward. Otto caught the smell of goat but then stood up in horror as the heady fragrance of a rose garden seemed to envelop him. The boy was now walking slowly towards him, tapping his stick on the ground, his dark face broken by a grin. His teeth were pearl white, his eyes full of laughter. He dropped his stick and held out his hands towards Otto.

The hermit could only stare and, as he did so, in that Arab boy's eyes he recognised the look, the same glance, the same soul he had glimpsed so long ago in the eyes of the Byzantine princess.

3

St Paul's Graveyard, London, May 1471

Rosa Mundi, rapta excoelo non munda:
The Rose of the World,
Stolen from Heaven,
Is not pure.

The crowd thronged about the gaudily garbed herald who stood on the step of the towering cross of St Paul's. He lifted his hand and a shrill bray of trumpets silenced the clamour, bringing to the foot of the cross traders, journeymen, tinkers, priests, monks, friars as well as the rifflers, the bawdy girls, the strumpets of the city. All were eager to hear the latest news. The herald raised his hand and again the trumpets brayed.

'Come on!' a burly tinker bawled from the back of the crowd before shaking his fist at a pickpocket coming too close to his wallet. 'Come on! What news?'

The herald ignored the tinker. He lifted one gloved hand, drawing in his breath. He knew his trade: here, at St Paul's, news of the kingdom was always proclaimed and people would wait for his message. He would proclaim it here, and again at the cross in Cheapside before taking a barge downriver to make the same announcement before the cross at Westminster. A hush descended over the crowd. Even the whores took off their scarlet wigs, stretching their necks to catch the cool breeze and allowing their shaven pates some relief from the constant itching of their flea-infested hairpieces.

'Know you this!' the herald began. 'That Edward IV, by the grace of God, King of England, Ireland, Scotland and France . . .'

'Aye, and of every woman in this city!' someone shouted from the back of the crowd.

'Know ye!' the herald continued relentlessly. 'That the King and his two brothers, Richard, Duke of Gloucester and George, Duke of Clarence, having destroyed the traitor's army on the field at Barnet, have now moved west to seek out and destroy the rebel Margaret of Anjou. Yes, she who calls herself Queen, together with her coven of foreign mercenaries, outlaws, wolf's-heads and other traitorous subjects who have withdrawn their rightful allegiance from the said noble Edward. Know ye this! That any man, giving sustenance to the said rebels, or who refuses to give sustenance to the King's rightful subjects, will himself be declared a rebel and suffer the full rigours of the law!'

The herald raised his hand again and the trumpets brayed. Then the royal messenger and the trumpeters mounted their horses and rode across the graveyard into Paternoster Row.

The crowd, however, did not disperse and the water-tipplers, their leather buckets slung round their shoulders, did a roaring trade as they moved amongst the crowd, slaking dusty throats and wetting dry, cracked lips.

'I hope the bloody war ends soon!' A journeyman pushed his way to the foot of the steps. He placed his sack of goods on the ground, his eyes fiercely sweeping the crowd. 'It's no good,' he continued, 'to walk the lanes and trackways of England when armies are on the march with soldiers who steal from any honest man. Not that Edward of England's men would do that . . . !'

The crowd nodded. The war between the Houses of Lancaster and York did not really affect them but they always listened avidly to the doings of Great Ones. Not far from here, in the Temple garden near Fleet Street, or so popular legend had it, the Dukes of York and Lancaster had each plucked a rose, white for York and red for Lancaster, as badges for their opposing armies. All because their king, Henry VI, was feckless. Oh yes, a living saint but too weak to rule effectively. The two great factions had fought the length and breadth of the kingdom. Now York was in the ascendant, led by the golden Edward and his two warrior brothers, Richard and George. Having smashed a Lancastrian army at Barnet, to the north of the city, they now intended to sweep west to bring to battle

18

and kill weak Henry's French wife, Margaret of Anjou, and her young son.

The journeyman continued his harangue, extolling the prowess of Edward of York. A black-garbed preacher, standing with his back to a buttress of the cathedral, smiled bleakly. He studied the journeyman's clothes, his broad leather belt, well-fashioned boots, the dagger in its embroidered pouch.

You are no journeyman, he thought, but a Yorkist spy, travelling the length and breadth of the kingdom on your master's work.

The Preacher's smile faded. He, too, was on his master's work. He pushed his scrawny, black hair away up above his ears. He wetted his lips, calling across to a water-tippler to bring him a stoup. The man did so: the water tasted brackish, but at least the tippler refused the Preacher's penny.

'No, no, brother!' he declared. 'I can see you are a holy man.'

The Preacher did not contradict him. After all, he was a messenger from God, a man whose skin had been scorched by the sun and wind of Outremer.

A lay brother in the Order of the Hospitallers, the Preacher had travelled the roads of Europe seeking out that great opponent, the Demon, described to him in hushed tones by Sir Raymond Grandison, his commander in the Order of the Hospitallers. The Preacher had become accustomed to his task. He had delivered the same sermon on the banks of the Rhine, in the piazzas of the great Italian cities, even under the towering gibbet of Montfaucon in Paris. Now he would give it here. The Preacher's eyes wandered to a buxom young courtesan. She was dressed simply in a costly blue samite dress tied at the throat by a pure white cord. She moved her hips provocatively and, sensing she was being studied, glanced over her shoulder and smiled enticingly at the Preacher. The self-styled man of God swallowed hard and looked away. The temptations of the flesh, he thought, were ever present. But, oh, the woman was beautiful: soft, golden skin, mocking eyes, lips meant to be kissed and hair like fire. She made to move towards him but the Preacher, seeing the journeyman, the Yorkist spy, had finished his declamation, moved quickly to take his place on the steps.

'Listen to me!' he shouted, arms flung wide. 'Listen to me, people of God, because I am His messenger!'

The crowd, on the point of breaking up, now clustered together again, congratulating themselves on a good morning's entertainment, a welcome break from the humdrum of trading. The Preacher did look interesting. Dressed in black sackcloth, bound round his waist by a dirty cord, wooden sandals on his feet, he had a face which attracted attention: wild, staring eyes in a dark, seamed face, like one of the prophets from the Old Testament which they had seen painted on the walls of their parish church.

The Preacher dramatically lowered his hands.

'The Rose of the World,' he began in a hoarse whisper, 'is cankered and rotten to its core!'

The people strained to listen. The Preacher caught their collective sigh as if savouring what was coming.

'The Devil walks!' His voice rose like a rumble of thunder. 'I have seen his stallion, black and swift as a storm cloud. Satan has come to ransack the treasures of the earth!' He spread his arms out. 'I have seen at night the horned goats of Hell and, on their backs, flesh-shrivelled hags. I have, in the howling of the wind, heard the squawking of crows and the hiss of serpents!'

The crowd nodded. Nothing was more interesting than the workings of the Devil and his legions of demons who ran through their world turning milk sour, causing fire in hay ricks, plague in the streets or pollution in the water.

'I have seen one too!' an old man shouted out. 'A grotesque shape with goggling eyes which burnt like fire!'

'You've been drinking again!' someone shouted.

'No, the good citizen is right!' the Preacher shouted back, hands clawing the air. 'Look around you! Kings go to war! Battles rage but these are only the precursors of things to come!' He stared in satisfaction as his audience, gape-mouthed, stared back. 'Oh yes,' he continued in a loud whisper, 'a great demon has been loosed upon the earth. Terrible will his work be. So be on your guard!'

'How do we know?' a man asked.

'This devil drinks human blood!' the Preacher replied, and paused, one finger pointing to the sky. 'For sustenance and strength he must drink our blood, a travesty of the Mass.'

The Preacher felt his stomach clench in disappointment. He glimpsed the disbelief in their eyes and knew that, at least in London, the great Demon, the Rosifer whom Sir Raymond had described, was not known. Only twice on his travels around Europe had the Preacher's claims ever been vindicated by a witness who could describe, in graphic and horrifying detail, some corpse found in a ditch or alleyway, its throat slashed from ear to ear, drained of blood like an ox slung above a butcher's stall. It was ever the same. The Demon seemed to stay well away from great cities. The Preacher added a few more phrases, telling the people to be on their guard. He sketched a blessing in the air and wandered back down the steps.

'Is that really true?'

He turned. The red-haired, pretty-mouthed courtesan was standing, arms folded, staring coolly at him.

'It's true, my child.'

He would have walked away but she caught him by the hand.

'Come,' she invited soothingly. 'A drink of ale to clear the throat and sweeten the mouth?'

The Preacher smiled and squeezed her fingers.

4

The Woods of Sutton Courteny, Gloucestershire, May 1471

In Paradise, in the glades of Eden,
Eve was tempted twice: first by Lucifer
Then by Rosifer who offered her
A rose plucked from Heaven.

Edith, daughter of Fulcher the blacksmith, sat in a sun-filled glade half listening to the voices of the women washing the clothes in the brook at the foot of the hill. She really should be with them but, as her father said, Edith was for ever a dreamer. This was her favourite spot: a small wood which stood on the brow of a hill. The trees were the walls of her castle, the grassy glade the most velvet of carpets and the flowers which lined the edge of the brook – teasel, bird's-foot, mallow and elder – the ornaments of her solar. She stared around. The glade was now covered in a carpet of bluebells, dog rose, mercury and primrose. A quiet, restful place where she could hide and dream. Edith was now sixteen summers old, three years since her courses had begun and her mother had sent her out into the garden to lie down naked to enrich the soil. Edith was a woman, or so her mother kept repeating, and Edith marvelled in her new-found power. Only weeks ago a troop of Yorkist horse had stopped in the village, hiring all the chambers at the Hungry Man tavern. Of course they needed their horses shod and seen to. Edith had been there when the young squire, Aymer Valance, or so he called himself, had come down to watch her father heat the furnace and turn the iron red-hot. He had paid sweet but secret court to her and she had brought him here. They had lain beneath the trees naked as worms, wrapped round each other. He had promised to come back but her father, sharp of eye, must have sensed what had happened. He cuffed her round the ear, shouting, 'Such men come and go, girl. We mean nothing to them!'

Edith ran her hand across her stomach and down the folds of her simple linen dress. Perhaps tomorrow, when the village gathered on the green after sunset to carouse and dance around the maypole, she might meet someone else. Her mother was now washing her best smock before laying it out along the fence at the back of the smithy to dry in the afternoon sun.

Edith heard a twig snap and her head came up, the buttercups in her hand slipping between her fingers.

'Who's there?' she called.

She sniffed the air and caught a fragrance: she had smelt it before, of roses. Once at Easter, when her mother bathed, Edith had been allowed to use the water afterwards. She still remembered the rose petals floating there and the sweet fragrance which tickled her nose. The scent was stronger now. Edith, a little alarmed, got to her feet. She'd heard stories, travellers' tales, of horrid murders in lonely places. Of corpses found, the blood drained, like the loving couple found in a meadow outside Tewkesbury.

'Who's there?' she repeated.

A voice began to sing softly. Edith was confused. The words were French. She had heard Aymer use the same tongue but, strangely, now she could understand it: about a rose which had bloomed in heaven before the world had ever begun. Edith took a step backward but the man who stepped out of the trees did not frighten her. He was tall, his face dark, his mouth merry. When he smiled, his teeth were so white and clean, he reminded her of Aymer. Edith smiled and stretched out her hands towards him.

PART I

SUTTON COURTENY, 1471

The pure light of dawn is only the pale glow from the rose gardens of Heaven.

1

Matthias Fitzosbert made sure the belt round his tunic was fastened tight, then crawled quietly over the weather-beaten gravestone in the cemetery and through a gap in the hedge. He scuttled like a mouse along the earth trackway and on to the highway of Sutton Courteny village. On the corner, beneath a large, overspreading oak tree, he turned and stared back. He clawed nervously at his black, shiny hair, licked his lips and scratched a spot high on his olive-skinned cheek.

Above the trees soared the spire of his father's church. Matthias hoped that he would not be missed for some time. His father, who had been weeding around the graves, had taken a stoup of ale and was now fast asleep in the shadow of the lych-gate. Christina, his woman, Matthias' mother, was in the small herb garden at the back of the priest's house tending the camomile, mint, thyme and coriander, which she would later pluck, dry and store in small jars in the buttery. All was quiet. Not even the birds chirped. They were hiding under the cool, green leaves well away from the surprisingly hot May sun. Somewhere a bee buzzed angrily in his search for honey. A snow-white butterfly came floating by. Matthias went to catch it but missed his footing and fell on the trackway. He yelped but then froze. He must remember he was only seven. He had no right to be out by himself, going through the woods to the derelict village of Tenebral.

Matthias ran on. Thankfully the houses of the cottagers and peasants were all quiet. Men, women and children were out in the fields, driving away the legion of birds and small animals which plundered the corn and anything else that the villagers had sown. Matthias crouched in the shadow of a house and stared further along the highroad. He studied the entrance to the Hungry Man tavern where the loungers and the lazy would squat with their backs to the walls, supping ale or quarrelling quietly amongst themselves. Such men were to be watched. They were always curious about Parson Osbert and his illegitimate by-blow.

Osbert was a priest and, according to Canon Law, should lead a chaste and celibate life. However, when he had come to Sutton Courteny fourteen years ago, Christina, daughter of Sigrid, a prosperous yeoman, had caught his eyes as he preached in church. They had fallen in love, become handfast and Matthias was their love child. Most of his parishioners accepted this; however, they were still curious and might go running up to the church to ask Parson Osbert why his son was stealing out of the village again.

Matthias stiffened as the burly, hard-faced blacksmith, Fulcher, lurched out of the tavern with a tankard in his hand. The man should have been out in the fields with the others but his daughter, Edith, had been found barbarously murdered in Sutton Courteny woods: her throat had been torn, her blood drained. Edith's poor mangled corpse now lay in the parish coffin at the door to the rood screen of the church. Fulcher was mourning her in the only way he could.

'Drunk as a pig!' So he announced. 'Until the pain has passed!'

Matthias' eyes softened. Fulcher looked so distraught, and Edith, his dreamy-eyed daughter, had been so kind. Whenever a corpse was laid in the coffin, Matthias always helped his mother to make sure that all was well before Requiem Mass was sung and the corpse was buried in its shroud beneath the outstretched yew trees in the cemetery. Corpses did not frighten Matthias. They were all the same: stiff and cold, lips turning blue and eyes half-open. This time, however, Osbert had been insistent that he himself tend the corpse. He wrapped it in a special canvas sheet and screwed the coffin lid well down till the poor girl's remains were buried.

'Edith!' Fulcher cried up at the sky, swaying backwards and forwards on his feet. 'Edith!'

Piers the ploughman came out, caught Fulcher by the arm and took him back into the tangy coolness of the Hungry Man taproom.

Matthias ran on, slipping like a shadow past the doorway of the tavern and up through the village. He stopped at the gallows stone from which Baron Sanguis' gibbet stretched up, black and stark against the sky. No corpse hung there but, now and again, the Manor Lord gibbeted a victim coated in tar, bound with old rope, as a warning to the outlaws, wolf's-heads and poachers to stay well away from his domain.

At last the line of cottages ended. The trackway narrowed as it entered the dark wood. Matthias paused: his father and mother had warned him, on many an occasion, to stay well clear of this place.

'Men as violent as wolves,' the kindly parson's face had been serious, 'wander like demons. These horrid murders!' Parson Osbert had shaken his balding head. 'Moreover, there are armies on the march and, where there are soldiers, murder and rapine ride close behind. Isn't that right, Mother?'

Christina had brushed her thick, blonde hair away from her face and stared, white-faced, at her son. Matthias, being so young, did not know what murder and rapine were, though they sounded interesting. What concerned him more was how tired and grey his mother now looked. Usually merry-eyed, laughing and vigorous, Christina had, over the last few weeks, become quiet, withdrawn and ever anxious. Only last night Matthias had woken and found her in her shift, a blanket about her shoulders, staring down at him. The tallow candle in her hand had made her face look even more gaunt. When he'd stirred, she had sat down on the edge of his pallet bed and gently stroked his face.

'Matthias.'

'Yes, Mother?'

'You go through the woods, don't you? You go to see the hermit? . . . In his refuge at Tenebral?'

Matthias had been about to lie but his mother's eyes looked so strange, so full of fear, he had nodded slowly. Christina had turned away. She had told him to go back to sleep but, as she'd turned to say good night, he'd glimpsed the tears on her cheeks.

Matthias now gnawed on his lips; the wood was a dark and secret place. He remembered the stories the villagers liked to tell when they all gathered around the great roaring fire in the taproom of the Hungry Man: about the pigmy king who lived beneath the tumuli, the ancient burial mounds, deep in the woods. Of Edric the Wild and his demonic horsemen who hunted along the banks of the Severn.

A bird stirred noisily in the branches above him. Matthias recalled other stories about the Strigoi, the ravenous birds with hooked feet, grasping talons, eyes which stared fixedly – fowls from hell who preyed on the young. Or the hag whose carcass was clothed in feathers and whose belly was swollen with the blood of her victims. Yet he had to go on! The hermit would be waiting for him and Matthias loved the hermit, with his magic and his stories, his merry mouth and laughing eyes. The boy took a deep breath, closed his eyes and, hands flapping by his side, ran into the shade of the trees. He tried to ignore the sounds from the undergrowth. He mustn't think of Old Bogglebow, his name for Margot, the evil-eyed hag who lived in Baron Sanguis' manor house and who, so the villagers whispered, practised the black arts on behalf of her master. Matthias did fear Old Bogglebow, with her sunken cheeks, twisted nose and sharp dog teeth scattered in rotting gums like tombs in a moon-lit churchyard.

Matthias opened his eyes and smiled. He had run so fast he was sure he was near the edge of the woods. He turned a corner and ran on, his eyes fixed on the trackway before him. He found breathing difficult, even more so when he tried to hum a song Christina had taught him. His fears only increased for, when the wood ended, he would be in Tenebral.

Once a village, its inhabitants had been wiped out by the Great Death, which had raged along the Severn valley a hundred years previously. The ancient ones still talked about it, of the dead lying in their beds, or at a table, or in the fields, their hands still fixed to the plough. Tenebral was a place for ghosts, haunted and eerie. Matthias paused and drew in his breath. Yet the hermit would be there: he would protect him. He ran on, then stopped, searching the trackway carefully until he discovered the secret path the hermit had shown him. Matthias followed this carefully. The trees gave way and suddenly he was on the edge of Tenebral. Some of the houses still stood along the highroad, their plaster cracked, the rooms inside open to the sky. The wooden doors and windows, anything which could be salvaged, had been plundered a long time ago.

Matthias crouched down like a little dog and stared around. The highroad was overgrown, ivy crept around the cottage walls. A silent place, a village where life had suddenly stopped.

Even the birds seemed to avoid it. At the far end Matthias glimpsed the ruined steeple of the church. He hurried on but hesitated beneath the remains of the lych-gate, staring down at the main porch. The wooden doors had long gone; the church walls were covered in ivy and lichen. Matthias would go no further. He was proud of having come so far, but now he would wait.

'Hermit!' he called. 'Hermit, it's Matthias! You asked me to come!'

Only a crow, circling solitary above the church, called raucously back. Matthias forgot his fears and ran up the path to the church porch. He stood within the entrance. To his left was the baptismal font. He glanced up. The roof had long gone, but the sanctuary at the far end was partially covered by bushes, both inside and outside the church, which had sprouted up to form their own canopy. The boy swallowed. The hermit should be here. He jumped as a rat scurried across the floor, then walked on. He was about to call the hermit again when a warm hand touched the side of his neck. He gasped and spun round. The hermit was there, crouching down, face wrinkled in amusement, eyes dancing, lips parted in a smile.

'You scared me!'

The hermit grasped him by the arms and squeezed gently.

'You tricked me!' Matthias accused.

The hermit threw his head back and laughed. He drew Matthias close, putting his arms around him, gently crushing the boy against him. Matthias let his body slacken. His father never did this and the hermit was always so warm, smelling so fragrantly of rose-water.

'I saw you come into the village,' the hermit murmured. 'I have been behind you all the time.'

'I was frightened,' Matthias confessed. 'It's so lonely.'

The hermit gently stroked his hair.

'*Creatura bona atque parva!*' he murmured.

'What does that mean?'

The hermit held him away: he stared in mock seriousness. 'It's Latin, Matthias. It means you are my little and good creature.'

'I am not your creature. You make me sound like a bat.'

Again the hermit laughed, rocking gently backwards and

forwards. Matthias watched him intently. If the truth be known, Matthias could sit and watch the hermit all day. He was tall and strong, his iron-grey hair carefully cut, like that of a monk, up around his ears. His face, burnt dark by the sun, was clean-shaven, open and fresh. He had a gentle smile and his eyes were always full of merriment. His hands, broad and brown, were warm and, whenever he touched Matthias, the boy felt soothed and calm.

'How long have we known each other now, Matthias?'

'You came here in March,' Matthias replied slowly. 'Just before the Feast of the Annunciation.'

'So, you've known me two months,' the hermit replied. 'And when you come here you are still frightened. Never let fear rule you, Matthias. It is a dark worm inside your mind.' His voice dropped to a whisper. 'And the more you feed it, the fatter it grows!'

'Aren't you afraid?' Matthias accused.

'Of some things, yes. Of people and creatures, never!'

'But that's because you are a soldier. You were a soldier, weren't you?'

'I was a soldier, Matthias. In the beginning I was a soldier.'

His face, as it sometimes did, became not serious but sad. Matthias watched his mouth, lips half-parted.

'Did you kill many men?' Matthias asked.

The hermit sighed and got to his feet. 'Killing is part of nature, Matthias. The hawk kills the hen: the fox the rabbit, all things feed upon each other.'

'If you are not frightened,' Matthias continued, 'why don't you come into the village?'

The hermit crouched down and touched the tip of Matthias' nose with the point of his finger.

'You tell me, Matthias Fitzosbert. Why don't I go into the village?'

'The people be frightened of you.'

'Why? How can they be frightened of something they don't know?'

'They said you had been here before,' Matthias replied. 'About eight years ago, before I was born.'

'But I was kind to them. I tended some of their sick. Yet, when I asked them for food, they drove me away.'

'So, why did you come back?'

In answer the hermit scooped Matthias up in his arms. 'I came back because I came back,' he announced. 'Now, Matthias, I am going to show you something.' He put the boy gently back on the ground.

'A trick?' Matthias asked, his eyes round in wonderment.

'A trick? What kind of trick? That's sorcery,' the hermit replied. 'As it is to have white doves in your ear!'

'Don't be—'

The hermit stretched his hand out. Matthias felt something feathery and warm against his ear. The hermit dramatically drew his hand back. Matthias stared in astonishment at the small white dove nestling in the palm of the hermit's hand. The hermit stroked its down feathers gently with a finger. The bird quietly cooed.

'Watch it fly, Matthias,' he whispered.

He threw the bird up and, in a flash of white, the dove climbed, wings outstretched, speeding up against the sky. Matthias watched it go but screamed at the black shape which seemed to strike out of nowhere: white feathers floated gently back into the church followed by one, two drops of blood. When he looked up again, the hawk and its victim had vanished. The hermit, however, his face impassive, glared up at the sky. He said something in a language Matthias couldn't understand and made a cutting move with his hand.

'Life preys upon life,' he declared. 'Come, Matthias, let me show you something else.'

He took the child by the hand and led him out of the ruined church along the old high street. With the hermit holding his hand, Matthias wasn't at all frightened. Now and again they would stop and the hermit would crouch down and point out different flowers: lilies, cowslips, the deadly belladonna and the blue-belled monkshood.

'Be careful of these latter two, Creatura. A deadly venom runs in their veins. But look!' The hermit pointed towards a bush. 'See, a goldfinch and, further down, a kingfisher rests before it returns to the mere. But, today, you must see this.'

He led Matthias into the ruined courtyard of what must have been Tenebral's tavern. The hermit put a finger to his lips.

'Shush now!'

They walked on tiptoe towards an outhouse. Matthias peered in: at first he could see nothing but then, against the far wall, in what must have been a recess for store jars, he glimpsed movement – small, reddish bundles of fur – and realised the hermit had brought him to a fox's den. The vixen, apparently oblivious to these spectators, licked one of the cubs whilst they, full of mischief, pounced and darted upon each other. Matthias had seen many a fox. He had heard the villagers after Sunday Mass loudly moan that one had taken a cockerel or goose from their pen. This, however, was different. He had never seen baby foxes so close up, so full of life. He would have stepped forward but the hermit gripped his shoulder.

'No, no, let it be.'

For a while they stood and watched. The vixen abruptly looked up, staring towards the door, and a look of pure fear crossed her face. She knocked her cubs back into the recess, then curled up at the entrance, head on her front paws, whimpering quietly. The hermit led Matthias away.

'Come on, Creatura, it's time we ate.'

On the way back to the church the hermit stopped to search amongst the bushes. He gave a cry of triumph and brought out a rabbit caught in his snare. He slung the carcass over his shoulder and, whistling softly, led Matthias by the hand, listening carefully to the boy's chatter.

Once more in the church, he took Matthias into the old sanctuary. The boy stared round. There was no sign of any altar or any vestige of the sacred mysteries which had been celebrated there. In the corner was a bed of flock and a wooden peg stool. The floor was clean, though scattered around were pots of paint and, whilst the hermit gutted and skinned the rabbit, Matthias stared in awe at the huge rose his friend was painting on the wall. It was like no rose he had ever seen: the leaves were red-black, the heart was gold, the stem silver. The boy put his hand out. He was sure that if he touched the rose, he would feel its soft texture and catch its perfume.

'Do you like it, Creatura?' the hermit asked.

'It's beautiful,' the boy replied. 'It's so large.'

'It's the world,' the hermit explained. 'Each leaf, each petal closing in on itself. That's why I paint it.'

'But there are no thorns?'

'The rose is the flower of Paradise,' the hermit said. 'When it grew in the meadows of Heaven it had no thorns. It only sprouted them when it fell into the hands of wicked men.'

Matthias heard a tinder strike. He looked over his shoulder: the rabbit was skinned, gutted and pierced through by a small spit which the hermit now placed over a bed of glowing charcoal. Matthias blinked. He had seen his mother and father light a fire but never with such speed. The hermit could do everything so quickly, so skilfully. The hermit winked at him and began to turn the spit: as he did so, he sprinkled herbs and a little oil from a small jug along the rabbit's flesh.

'Look at the rose, Matthias. What do you feel?'

'I feel as if I could smell it.'

'Then do so . . . Go on!' the hermit urged.

Matthias, laughing, put his nose up against the wall.

'I can smell the rabbit!' he giggled, wrinkling his nose. 'And the plaster's damp.'

'No, no, think about the rose, Matthias. Smell it now!'

The boy did so and exclaimed in surprise: the sweetest, most fragrant of perfumes seeped from the painting. He clapped his hands. 'I can smell it! I can smell it! It's beautiful!'

The hermit laughed and went back to turning the rabbit on the spit. Matthias, however, studied the wall. This time, at the hermit's urging, he touched one of the petals and felt its soft wetness against his fingers.

'It's a trick, isn't it?' he exclaimed.

'Yes, Creatura, it's a trick!'

The boy noticed a series of marks on the wall, strange carvings, like the letters of his hornbook, but jumbled up and broken.

'What are these?' he asked.

'Runes,' the hermit replied. 'An ancient writing.'

'And what do they mean?'

'Too many questions, Creatura. In time, in time. Now,' the hermit pointed across the sanctuary to a small pannier. 'Enough questions, we must eat. Go over there and see what you can find.'

Matthias opened it up and gasped in surprise: wrapped in a linen cloth were fresh manchet loaves, a small pot of butter and a jar of honey.

'Where did you get these?'

'In Tredington,' the hermit replied. 'I went across there.'

'Do you know a boy there?' Matthias asked.

'I know no boy, Creatura, except you. Now, bring the food across.'

'You shouldn't go to Tredington,' Matthias declared. 'Father says they are our . . .'

'Enemies?'

Matthias shook his head.

'Rivals?'

'That's it: rivals! We have disputes with them over the great meadow and pannage rights in the woods.'

'And yet there's enough for everyone,' the hermit replied. 'Do you love your father?'

Matthias, crouching before the fire, nodded solemnly.

'But he's a priest,' the hermit teased. 'He has taken vows never to know a woman.'

Matthias just blinked owlishly back.

'Will you . . .' the boy pointed further down the wall to the faded paintings of angels, 'will you paint them as well?'

The hermit, crouching, looked over his shoulder at the faded portraits: a group of angels each with a musical instrument: lute, flute, sackbut, shawm and rebec.

'What are they supposed to be?' he teased.

'Angels, of course!' Matthias replied.

'Are they now?' The hermit's eyes looked sad. 'I tell you this, Matthias, they look nothing like angels.'

He took the rabbit off the spit, broke the flesh with his fingers, and handed over the most succulent pieces. Matthias gnawed the sweet, soft flesh.

'Do you know about angels?'

The hermit's eyes were now very sad.

'In the beginning,' he replied, 'before the Spirit moved over to the darkness, only the angels existed before the face of the Almighty. Think of them, Matthias, an army of brilliant lights, genius, pure will. However, in beauty and power, they were nothing compared to the great five.' He put the piece of meat down and counted the names off on his fingers. 'Michael, Gabriel, Raphael, Lucifer . . .'

'And?' Matthias asked.

The hermit was staring at the fire. Matthias shivered at the cold blast of wind which blew through the church.

'And who?' he whispered.

'The Rosifer.' There were tears in the hermit's eyes. 'All beautiful,' he whispered. 'Magnificent as an army in battle array. Glorious leaders of a glorious host.'

'Lucifer's the Devil,' Matthias broke in quickly, wanting to break the tension as well as display his knowledge.

'Lucifer is Lucifer.' The hermit was now rocking gently backwards and forwards on his feet. 'Brother and soul mate, great friend and comrade-in-arms to the Rosifer.'

'Who's he?' Matthias asked.

'Oh, Creatura, he was the rose-carrier. God's gardener who laid out Paradise for Adam and Eve.'

'They committed a sin, didn't they?' Matthias asked, remembering a painting from the parish church. 'That's why,' he continued in a rush, 'Jesus came from Heaven to save us from our sins. Do you believe that?'

The hermit looked up towards the sky, scored by red flashes of sunset.

'See, Matthias,' the hermit whispered. 'See Christ's blood streaming in the firmament.'

Matthias watched him curiously and recalled never seeing the hermit pray or attend Mass.

'So, you do believe in Jesus?'

'The Beloved,' the hermit replied. 'Oh yes.'

'And Mary, his mother?' Matthias was now repeating the catechism taught him by his father.

'God's pure candle,' the hermit replied. 'Who brought forth the light of the world.'

'Do you believe,' Matthias asked, half-imitating his father's sermons, 'that the Lord Jesus came to save us from our sins?' The boy nibbled on a piece of rabbit flesh.

'He didn't come to save you from your sins.' The hermit was now half-smiling. 'In the end, Creatura, remember this. All begins and ends with love. All things are done for love. All things go right for love. All things go wrong for love. Heaven and Hell are not places, but states of mind and will.' His voice sunk to a whisper. 'Love eternally offered and eternally refused. Pardon eternally issued but never accepted. In Heaven because of love or driven out because of love.'

'What are you talking about? Do you want some honey?'

The hermit blinked. Stretching across the fire, he ruffled Matthias' black hair.

'I love you, Creatura. But come, soon it will be dark. I have something else to show you. So, finish your food.'

Matthias did so, staring warily around the ruined church. The sun was beginning to set. Soon it would be dark and he had to return to Sutton Courteny. He pushed more rabbit into his mouth, followed by the butter and honey. He tried to talk but the hermit laughed and pressed his finger against his lips.

'Shush, you chatter like a jay!'

The hermit got up, brushing the crumbs from his brown robe. He walked down the church. Matthias looked at the rose on the wall – it seemed to glow as if a great fire burnt behind it. He shook his head, got to his feet and scampered after his friend. The hermit grasped him by the hand and led him out of the village, walking vigorously. Matthias stumbled and had to stop to catch his breath. The hermit, laughing, picked him up and put him on his shoulder, reminding Matthias of a statue he had seen of St Christopher carrying the boy Jesus. They reached the top of the hill. The wind caught at their hair, making Matthias gasp as the hermit lowered him to the ground. The boy stared down into the gathering darkness.

'What is it?' he asked.

The hermit crouched beside him. 'Follow my finger, Matthias. Tell me what you see.'

Matthias narrowed his eyes and peered carefully. At first nothing, but then he caught a flash of colour. Concentrating carefully he saw that, protected by the trees, a great troop of horse, men-at-arms and carts were making their way along the valley below. Now and again, in the fading rays of the setting sun, he caught the shimmer of armour or a brave banner fluttering in the evening breeze.

'Margaret of Anjou's army,' the hermit explained. 'The Lancastrians are in retreat. She and her generals – Edmund Beaufort, Duke of Somerset, Lord Wenlock, and Lord Raymond Grandison, Prior in the Order of the Hospitallers, are fleeing for their lives—'

'Oh yes,' Matthias interrupted. 'She is the Red Rose, is she not?'

'Aye, you could say that. They flee from the followers of the White Rose.' The hermit pulled Matthias around and pointed further back along the valley. 'In hot pursuit comes Edward of York and his war band.'

'What will happen?' Matthias asked, his stomach clenching with excitement.

'Margaret Anjou and her army are tired. They have tried to cross the Severn but the bridges are either held or destroyed. They can go no further. Ah, these men of war and their armour, their proud banners of azure, gold bars, martlets, ruby-red chevrons; tomorrow they will all be drenched in blood.'

'There will be a battle?' Matthias asked.

'Yes, there will be a battle. Queen Margaret will have to stop at Tewkesbury.'

Matthias recalled the great abbey which nestled on a small hill overlooking the market town.

'How do you know that?' he asked.

The hermit winked. 'I could say,' he whispered, eyes staring, 'that I am a sorcerer but I was a soldier, too, Matthias. The Queen's army is exhausted. They will stop to take provisions from the abbey whilst Beaufort, her leading general, will think it's good to fight with the Severn at his back.'

'I have never seen a battle.'

'Would you like to see this one?'

Matthias' eyes rounded. 'Could I, really?'

'Tomorrow, at dawn, come back to me.' The hermit held Matthias' arms and squeezed gently. 'Before first light, steal out of your house and meet me.' He smiled and, drawing Matthias closer, kissed him on the brow. 'This time I won't play games. I won't hide or play tricks upon you. I'll be waiting for you.'

'Why do you want to see the battle?' Matthias asked.

The hermit's face suddenly became grave, even angry. He looked over his shoulder, staring down through the darkness at the retreating army.

'Edward of York will come on fast,' he murmured, 'like the horsemen of Asia. The ground will shake with the hooves of his cavalry. A man born for killing is Edward of York. The Lancastrians are dead.' He looked back at Matthias. 'I have a friend I wish to see. Someone who has been looking for me for many a day. I want to see him and I want him to see you, Matthias. So, promise me—'

'They say it's dangerous.'

'Now, why is that, Creatura?'

'Oh, not the battle, the people who have been killed outside Tredington and Tewkesbury.'

The hermit rose abruptly to his feet.

Matthias pulled a face. Adults always dismissed you when they didn't want to talk any more.

2

The hermit took Matthias back through the derelict village to the edge of the forest. He stopped and crouched down.

'Remember what I taught you today, *Creatura bona atque parva*. Life feeds on life. The rabbit feeds on grass and we fed on the rabbit. The dove feeds on corn and the hawk kills it. Even in the spiritual life, only life itself can make the spirit fresh and strong.'

Matthias nodded solemnly. The hermit smiled, his eyes bright with mischief.

'You don't understand, do you, Creatura?'

'I am sorry, I don't,' the boy stammered.

'Go.' The hermit kissed him on each cheek. 'Go on now, Matthias. Run like the wind and, if you remember my second lesson, for you there can be no fear.'

Matthias trotted down the path into the wood. He was so engrossed in what the hermit had said, so puzzled, he was deep into the darkness before he fully realised where he was. Then he stopped. Why didn't the hermit come with him? He stared up where the branches formed a canopy against the sky. Surely he could have come to the wood with him? Matthias became aware of a stirring in the undergrowth, the flutter of birds' wings and those mysterious, indistinguishable sounds of the night. His fears came flooding back, about the witches who hung like bats in the trees from dusk till dawn. Or the ghosts of women who dropped on the necks of the unsuspecting.

'You can only tell them,' Joscelyn the Taverner had loudly intoned from where he sat in an inglenook in the corner of the Hungry Man, 'oh yes, you can only tell them because their feet are back to front.'

Matthias hurried on, his mind now full of stories of Black Vaughan and his ghostly henchmen who prowled the forests of the Severn valley. Matthias closed his eyes, but he stumbled so he opened them again. The moonlit trackway lay ahead of him and he grew fearful of what his father and mother might say about where he'd been, and at this hour. The bracken cracked and the shapes sprang out of the darkness: two men, soldiers, stinking of sweat, urine and stale wine, their boiled leather jackets hard and coarse, their dirt-smeared leggings now cut and torn by the brambles. Yet, they were armed, broad leather war belts round their waists. They seized the boy as swiftly as the hawk had the dove. A dirty, smelly hand across his mouth stopped Matthias screaming. He was dragged off the track into the trees. The two men, as they carried him, lashed his hands and feet. They threw him on to a bed of bracken. All Matthias could see were dark shapes, bearded faces framed by torn chain mail coifs.

'Now, now, let's see what we have here?'

A tinder was struck and a piece of candle flared into light. Matthias preferred the darkness: in the candlelight the soldiers' faces, unshaven and dirty, were twisted and evil, their eyes glittering. One of them grasped Matthias' genitals.

'We have a boy! We have a boy, Petain, fresh and soft!'

Coarse fingers pulled at Matthias' legs and cheeks. The other soldier turned him over on to his face. Matthias, rigid with terror, moaned softly as the man dug a finger between his buttocks.

'Soft and pert,' he whispered. 'Any port in a storm eh, comrade?'

'Hush!'

Both soldiers stopped. Matthias could now hear it. Someone was running towards them.

'Matthias!' The voice was low, unmistakably that of a young girl. 'Matthias, where are you?'

'Oh, twice fortunate!' one of the soldiers whispered. 'Keep him there, Petain!'

Matthias was rolled over on his back as one of the soldiers, knife drawn, disappeared in the direction of the voice. The soldier left holding the candle leant down and jabbed Matthias' chest.

'Your sister?' he whispered. 'Your sister come to join the fun, has she?' His teeth were yellow and cracked, his breath foul. 'We will play Pass The Fardel. We'll get some pleasure out of this!'

A soul-chilling scream cut the silence.

'In Satan's name!'

The soldier slapped Matthias and hurried into the trees. The boy just lay there whimpering like a puppy. He heard the soldier crashing and stumbling. He turned on his side. Something like a shadow, moving dark and fast as if some giant hawk were flying over the trees, caught his eye. The noise of the retreating soldier stopped. Again a blood-chilling scream shattered the night air and Matthias began to shake. Closing his eyes he tried to pray. He felt something warm press his cheek. The hermit was crouching over him. He carried the piece of tallow candle the soldiers had dropped. He lit this, his eyes and face a mask of concern.

'Did they hurt you, Creatura?' he whispered. 'Did they hurt you, little one?'

'They touched me,' Matthias stammered. 'They said they were going to!' He began to shake.

The hermit put the candle on a crook of a tree. The ropes round Matthias' hands and feet were slashed. The hermit picked him up like a mother would a baby. He held him close, rocking gently to and fro. Then the hermit lifted his head. He spoke sharply to the darkness in a tongue Matthias could not understand, like a wolfhound growling against the moon. Matthias stared up in alarm.

'Don't worry, little one,' the hermit whispered. 'I've cursed those evil ones. They will do no more terror in their journey to wherever they are destined. But, come now.'

He lifted a water bottle to Matthias' lips. The juice it contained tasted sweeter than water. It cleansed Matthias' mouth and brought the warmth back into his body. He felt invigorated, like he did when he splashed in a pool on a bright summer's morning with the rest of the boys.

'I must go.' Matthias struggled to his feet.

'And this time I shall go with you.'

The hermit extinguished the candle, took him by the hand and led him back on to the path. Despite the attack, Matthias now felt calm and refreshed. The hermit was telling him about the stars as Matthias hopped and skipped beside him. When they reached the edge of Sutton Courteny, the hermit crouched down and embraced him again.

'Go on, Creatura,' he whispered. 'Go through the village.

43

But, remember, tomorrow, just after dawn, I'll be waiting.'

The boy sped away like an arrow. The door to the Hungry Man was shut but candlelight and music poured through the unshuttered windows. Here and there a dog barked but Matthias was not afraid. He reached the church, opened the lych-gate and took a short cut across the cemetery. Usually he would never take such a path at night. The villagers were always telling stories of the ghosts and spirits which lived there, especially about the bell.

Years ago, Maud Brasenose, the widow of a wealthy peasant, had a great fear of being buried alive. So the priest at the time agreed that a bell be fixed in a small holder on the top of her tomb, attached, through a hole in the coffin, to her hand. Accordingly, if she woke and found herself buried alive, she only had to ring the bell. The stone still stood, the bell and chain now rusted. However, at midsummer or Samhain Eve when the fires were lit, some fool, full of ale, would always come down to the cemetery and try to ring the bell even though it was encrusted with rust. Or again, there was the black angel which adorned the tomb of Thomas Pepperel, a wealthy spicer who had moved from Tredington and spent his last years at Sutton Courteny. Parson Osbert had declared that, when the angel had first been carved, it had been white as snow but Pepperel had been cheated: the stone was of poor quality and had turned a horrid black so it looked as if some demonic imp, rather than an angel, guarded poor Pepperel's tomb.

Matthias' route took him over the wall and into the small vegetable plot which lay in front of the priest's house. The windows were shuttered but he glimpsed chinks of light. Still full of courage, he knocked on the door, there was a slap of sandals, the door opened and his father stood staring down at him.

'Oh, Matthias, where have you been?'

'I've been to Tenebral.' The boy decided it was best not to lie.

'Come in. Your mother and I . . .'

Parson Fitzosbert seized his son's hand and led him down the stone-paved passageway into the small parlour. Matthias' courage began to ebb. Oh, he was pleased to be home. The straw on the passageway floor was crisp and clean, sprinkled with fennel and rosemary. Small rushlights burnt in their shiny metal holders. The parlour was warm and inviting. Oil lamps hung from the great beam which ran down the length of the chamber. A fire leapt in the great hearth and the cauldron, hanging up on a hook above it, gave off the fragrant smell of freshly cooked meat.

Christina, his mother, was sitting at her spinning wheel under the light of a lantern. She looked busy but Matthias saw her face was still white, dark rings round those lustrous eyes. She put down the spindle and held out her hands. Matthias ran to her, snuggling his face deep into her woollen dress, savouring her lovely smell, a mixture of cooking, sweat and the fragrant herb water Christina always used to wash herself. Her fingers, long and cool, stroked his hot cheeks.

'I was worried, Matthias, so very, very worried.'

Christina let him go and he stood up to face his father. Parson Osbert stared sadly down at him. Matthias abruptly realised how his father was beginning to age. Folds of skin hung loose on his neck; his cheeks looked a little sunken, those gentle eyes now lined with care.

'Now you are home, Matthias, perhaps we can eat!'

He caught the reproof in his mother's words and stammered an apology. He was only too pleased to be caught up in the preparations for the evening meal. He washed his hands in the water tub which stood outside the buttery. He then set the wooden pegged table with trenchers, knives, horn spoons, pewter mugs and the large jugs of strong ale drained from the barrel, a cloth cover tied round the rim, which stood on a small stool beneath the window.

His father muttered something about going to the church, and left.

Christina opened the small cupboard built next to the fire and brought out a tray of freshly baked manchet loaves, which filled the parlour with a spicy smell. She rolled these in a linen napkin and put them on the table, then went to sit at the fireplace, stirring the stew with a ladle. Matthias, all his tasks done, sat at the table and looked mournfully at her.

'You've been out to Tenebral, haven't you, to see the hermit?'

Matthias nodded.

'Your father was worried,' she continued, and she pointed to the hour candle where it burnt in its niche. 'One more ring and he'd have had to go down to the Hungry Man for help.' She turned, ladle in her hands. 'He was very worried,' she insisted. 'There are soldiers in the area, mercenaries, wolves in human clothing.'

'I was safe,' Matthias stammered. He was shrewd enough not to fuel his mother's fears.

'And the hermit?' she asked softly, turning her back on him.

'He was very kind.' Matthias had long learnt that to tell his parents what they wanted to hear was the best way to calm their anxieties. 'He showed me flowers.'

'Did he talk about the rose?' Christina grew rigid. She stopped stirring the cauldron.

'What's this about a rose?' His father came into the kitchen. He took off his boots and tossed them into a corner. Neither Christina nor Matthias answered. 'The church is all locked up.' Parson Osbert smiled and clapped his hands. 'And no lovers lie in the cemetery's long grass. God's acre, as I keep telling my parishioners, is for those buried in the peace of Christ, not for wanton lust.'

On any other occasion this would have been the signal for Christina to quip back but tonight she remained silent. The parson's smile faded.

'Let's eat. Matthias, tell me what you did today.'

Once the benediction was said, Matthias was only too happy to fill the silence with his chatter, especially about the foxes. He mentioned nothing about the rose or the hermit's sayings and, bearing in mind what was going to happen tomorrow, certainly nothing about the two soldiers who had accosted him in the wood.

'Can I go back tomorrow?'

His mother dropped her spoon. She smiled apologetically and picked it up.

'Please, can I go back tomorrow?' Matthias persisted.

'Why?' His father asked.

'The hermit is going to show me a kingfisher.'

Matthias blinked to keep back the tears. He was lying to this gentle man who was his father, and to his mother who looked so careworn. He fought the guilt, the lies slipped so

46

smoothly from his tongue. He had to go. But how could he tell them the truth? It would only hurt them.

'No, you can't.' His father wiped his bowl with a piece of bread and popped it into his mouth. 'It's dangerous.' He grasped his son's hand, continuing in a rush, 'A journeyman has told us the news. Queen Margaret and her army are in full retreat along the Severn. The King and his forces are hurrying behind, breathing threats and slaughter. God knows what will happen when the armies meet!'

Matthias was about to protest, lie again that he would go nowhere near the battle, but found he could not do that.

'Let the boy go.' Christina raised her head and stared across the table. 'Let the boy go,' she repeated.

Matthias noticed how her face was even paler than before, those generous lips now one thin line. Her eyes looked dull.

'He'll be safe,' she said. She got up from the table and began to collect their pewter bowls. 'The hermit's a soldier, isn't he? Or was one. Now he's a man of God. He'll keep the boy safe.' Her voice was devoid of any emotion.

Matthias noticed how she kept her back to him whilst she spoke. His father released his hand and leant across.

'So, you can go,' he whispered. 'But you are to be back before dark.'

Matthias, pleased that he had obtained his father's permission, fairly skipped down from the table. Determined to put things right by being as helpful as he could, he took the rest of the pots into the buttery, swept the floor round the table, arranging everything as it should be. His mother came over and, crouching down, caught him in her arms. She held him close, speaking over his shoulder to his father who sat at the table, his Book of Hours in his hands.

'I'm going to bed,' she said softly. 'I feel tired.' She kissed Matthias again, then her husband on the brow, and left the room.

Once she had gone, Matthias sat on a stool, all his gaiety seeming to have drained away. The fire looked weak, the light of the candles and oils mere splutterings whilst his father, eyes closed, lost in his own devotions, was distant, rather cold.

'What is wrong with Mother?' Matthias asked.

Parson Osbert opened his eyes. He sighed and put the Book of Hours down.

'I don't know.' He paused, half-cocking his head for sounds from their chamber above. 'I don't know, Matthias. When I came here I was a young priest.' He ran his hand across the smoothness of the table. 'The day I climbed the pulpit to give my first sermon I saw her sitting beneath me. She is beautiful, Matthias, but, on that morning, with the sunlight streaming through the window and catching her face, I thought she was an angel.' He beckoned his son across and grasped him by the wrists. 'As you grow older, Matthias, you will hear whispers in the village. I am a priest. I was not to become handfast and what I did is condemned by the Church. I live with a woman but, God be my witness,' his eyes filled with tears, 'I love her more than life itself and I would leave Heaven for Hell to find her there.'

'But what is wrong with Mother?' Matthias found he couldn't stop trembling. 'Is she sickening?'

'I don't know.' His father rubbed his eyes. 'Sometimes she wonders if we did wrong. Whether this place is accursed.'

He smiled wanly and pointed across to a small aperture built below the window. Inside it was a yellowing, aged skull. Nobody knew why it was there. The priest's house had stood since the reign of the first Edward, almost two hundred years ago. The skull had been built into the brickwork: all Matthias could ever see were the teeth, face bones and dark holes where the eyes had been. Parson Osbert chewed his lip. Christina had strange fancies. She now believed the skull was a source of evil. He had remonstrated with her, explaining that, from the little he knew, the skull was really a sacred relic, the remains of a priest who had been killed here many centuries ago by marauding Danes.

'Father, Father, what's the matter?'

The priest looked at his son's pale, attentive face. He felt a great surge of affection. Perhaps I've not been a good priest, he thought, but in Matthias I have been truly blessed.

'Your mother is tired, Matthias, just tired. Come now, let's say our prayers.'

Matthias brought his hands together and bowed his head, his lips moved soundlessly as he recited the Paternoster and Ave Maria.

Parson Osbert stared across at the black crucifix against the wall. What was really wrong with his wife? She seemed agitated, constantly dreaming as if her body were here but her mind elsewhere. The parson's face became grim. He knew he had enemies in the parish council. Fat Walter Mapp, the local scrivener – he was not above, during Sunday Mass, circulating a piece of vellum filled with malicious questions, such as why their priest preached to them but kept a woman and his bastard son as a burden on the parish. Osbert closed his eyes and prayed for forgiveness. A gentle soul, he had never really hated, but Mapp, with his pig-like eyes, fleshy nose and slobbering mouth . . . Parson Osbert crossed himself and quickly said a prayer for Walter Mapp.

'Father, I've finished my prayers. Shall I go to bed?'

The priest smiled. 'And what is the last thing, Matthias, you must say before you go to sleep? And the first thing you must repeat when you wake in the morning?'

Matthias took a deep breath.

'If you get it right,' his father added, 'there's a sweetmeat in the buttery . . .'

Matthias closed his eyes. 'Remember this, my soul, and remember it well.' His voice grew loud and vibrant. 'The Lord thy God is One and He is holy.' Matthias paused to recall the words. 'And thou shalt love the Lord thy God with all thy mind, with all thy heart and all thy strength. And thou shalt love thy neighbour as thyself.'

The parson kissed him on the brow. 'Oh, holiest of boys,' he grinned. 'Take the sweetmeat and go to your chamber.'

Matthias, the sweetmeat firmly in his mouth, scampered up the stairs. These were narrow and winding: Matthias always pretended he was a knight climbing a castle to rescue a maiden. He was most fortunate. Unlike other boys of his age, he had a small chamber, a little garret to himself under the eaves. It contained a cot, a desk, a battered leather chest and some pegs on the wall for his clothes. The small casement window, which overlooked the cemetery, was covered in horn paper. His mother had left it open. The room smelt fragrant but rather cold. Matthias climbed on to the bed. He was about to close the window when he glimpsed, in the moon-dappled cemetery below, a shadow beneath one of the yew trees, as if someone were standing there staring up at him. Yet, when he looked again, the shadow was gone.

*　　*　　*

49

In Margaret of Anjou's camp, pitched within bowshot of the great Abbey of Tewkesbury, the Lancastrian Queen and her generals were holding counsel late into the night: Sir Raymond Grandison, Prior in the Order of the Hospitallers, with Sir Thomas Tresham, John Wainfleet and the Queen's two principal commanders, Edmund Beaufort, Duke of Somerset and Lord Wenlock. They all sat along the trestle table hastily erected in the Queen's gold-fringed, silken tent. On the floor around them were piled chests, coffers and panniers, lids thrown back or buckles undone, their contents spilling on to the muddy floor. Sir Raymond Grandison stared at these, then at each of his companions. They were arguing feverishly amongst themselves on what steps they should take next. Deep in his soul, however, Sir Raymond knew it was all finished. At the top of the table Margaret of Anjou, once a renowned beauty, sat slumped in her chair, her veil awry, her famous blonde hair now faded and mixed with iron-grey streaks. Her long face was haggard, eyes so bright, the Hospitaller wondered if the Queen were ill with a fever. She kept playing with the rings on her fingers or moving the pieces of parchment around on the table. On a chair beside her, her son Prince Edward, his blond hair uncombed, sat with a sulky expression on his smooth-shaven, spoilt face. Wenlock Sir Raymond dismissed with a contemptuous look. He did not trust that little fat soldier who, over the years, had fought for both York and Lancaster. In reality, the only person Wenlock served was Wenlock himself, and the Hospitaller wondered if he could be relied on tomorrow. Now and again the Queen would stretch across the table and grip Beaufort's arm. Grandison wondered about the rumours that Beaufort was also her lover and, possibly, the true father of Prince Edward.

Beaufort coughed to catch his attention.

'Sir Raymond, what do you advise?'

The Hospitaller took the piece of parchment Beaufort pushed across: a roughly drawn map which showed the abbey behind them and, to the west, the River Severn. He fought against the growing feeling of despair as the rest of the council waited.

'Well, Sir Raymond, you are a professional soldier, what do you advise?'

Beaufort pushed his red hair away from his brow, fingers drumming on the table. Clearly agitated, he kept licking his lips whilst a nervous tic twitched a muscle under his right eye.

Raymond picked up the makeshift map. 'Our situation is parlous, my lord. In the east the Lancastrians under the Earl of Warwick have been destroyed. The towns and cities between here and London are firmly in the hands of York. To the west the River Severn is swollen, the bridges destroyed or closely guarded so we cannot cross to our friends in Wales. Our men are too tired to march north. They are deserting in droves and our supplies are few. To the south Edward of York and his army pursue us like a pack of hunting dogs.'

'You offer us no sympathy.' Margaret's voice was harsh, and, eyes half-closed, she glared at this Hospitaller commander who had chosen to tie his fortunes to those of her house.

'Madam, I can only describe things as they are, not how they should be.'

'And your advice?' Beaufort demanded.

'Whatever we decide,' Sir Raymond replied, 'Edward of York will come on.'

'And lose?' Wenlock squeaked.

Raymond stared down at the piece of parchment. He himself needed more time, just a little. All his searches, all his travelling had brought one result. The Rosifer, the great demon he had released so many years ago from the vaults of the Blachernae Palace, was somewhere in England. Raymond had a legion of spies throughout Europe, a flow of constant information and all this pointed to England, possibly a village in the south. He prayed the Preacher would reach him before he was swept up in the maelstrom of bloody battle.

'Sir Raymond, we are waiting.' Beaufort tapped the table. 'You say we should stand yet, at the same time, that our men are tired and cannot be trusted.'

'What I suggest,' the Hospitaller replied slowly, 'is that in this countryside broken by woods and small hills, where hedgerows cut the land, we make it look as if we were preparing for battle. Leave a token force whilst the rest of us retreat, go north, find a bridge over the Severn and force our way across. Once there, we are only a day's march from Wales. Tudor and the Queen's other friends will give us succour and refuge. We can rest, obtain fresh supplies, more men, and fight another day.'

'Pshaw!' Wenlock just waved his hands. 'Run like children before Edward of York!'

'If we fight tomorrow,' the Hospitaller replied hotly, 'we will lose!'

'I am inclined to agree,' Beaufort said. 'Madam, if we left three or four hundred foot, some light horse . . . Sir Raymond is correct: we could dilly and dally till nightfall, then slip northwards through the dark.'

Others intervened. Sir Raymond sat back, so immersed in his own thoughts, he jumped when a servant touched his shoulder.

'Sir Raymond,' the man whispered, 'a messenger, he calls himself the Preacher, awaits outside.'

Sir Raymond rose and excused himself, bowed to the Queen and followed the servant out into the darkness. All around him rose the sounds of the camp: horses neighing; armourers busy pounding and hammering at their makeshift forges; the cries of the sentries. Sir Raymond's despair deepened as he passed each campfire. The men were sprawled out on the ground, sleeping like the dead. Those who were awake crouched dourly over their cold food or cups of watered ale from the supply wagons. In the flickering firelight their faces were grey, eyes heavy with exhaustion. Few raised their heads as he passed.

He found his visitor in his own makeshift tent. The Preacher was sitting on an overturned cask, eating noisily from a bowl of dried meat and scraps of bread.

'Christ's greetings to you, sir.' The Preacher pushed more food into his mouth and noisily swallowed it down with some wine.

Sir Raymond pulled across a camp stool and sat opposite.

'I've travelled from London,' the Preacher began. 'I was heading for Gloucester. The good monks there would give me shelter and sustenance, but then I heard that Margaret of Anjou was coming north. I knew you would be with her.'

'Yes, yes,' the Hospitaller replied testily. 'But what news do you have?'

'I have found him.' The Preacher took the cup away from

his lips. He smiled at Sir Raymond's surprise. 'He was in these parts seven or eight years ago posing as a recluse, living in the ruins of some deserted village.' He ticked the places off on his fingers. 'Stroud, Berkeley, Gloucester, Tredington, Tewkesbury. Now, I believe, he hides in a deserted village near Sutton Courteny.'

'What proof do you have of this?'

'What do you expect?' the Preacher replied. 'People like him. Even the brothers at Tewkesbury remember him: a man of prayer, a former soldier, clean in his ways, personable in his manners.'

Sir Raymond looked at the filthy fingers of the Preacher and bit back his tart observation.

'But there's something else, isn't there?'

'Oh yes.' The Preacher sipped from the wine. 'Over the last eight years corpses have been found, their throats cut, their cadavers drained like slashed wineskins. In most cases the bodies were those of travellers, journeymen, traders and tinkers. Now and again a villager, the same bloody death.' He sighed. 'Other people have been blamed. At Stroud they burnt an old man, claiming he was a warlock, yet the murders have continued. A bailiff at Berkeley told me he had met our adversary on the roads: he was going to Sutton Courteny. A few weeks afterwards a young girl was killed in the usual bloody way.' The Preacher leant forward, his eyes bright with excitement. 'He is the one, isn't he, Sir Raymond?'

Sir Raymond stared through a gap in the tent.

'He is the one,' he replied.

'Then why not leave and come with me?'

Sir Raymond got up. He poured himself a cup of wine and refilled that of the Preacher.

'I am here in the camp,' he said, 'of Margaret of Anjou and the Lancastrians. God be my witness, I couldn't give a fig for Lancaster – or York!'

'So why not flee?'

'I gave my word. I made a decision. Once I learnt my quarry was in England, I knew that I would need the authority of the Crown to pursue my searches to a successful end. It's like a game of hazard. England was divided between York and Lancaster. I chose Lancaster and I am going to lose.'

'So why not flee?'

'It's too late,' the Hospitaller replied. 'Beaufort has issued an order: any man who tries to desert is to be killed on the spot. I doubt if I would get far. Even if I were successful the Yorkists would show me no mercy, whilst if a miracle occurs, and Margaret of Anjou wins tomorrow, my name would head the list of proscriptions.' He sat down. 'No, no, there is a slender chance, my best, that this time tomorrow night I will be across the Severn in Wales.'

'And me?'

Sir Raymond dug into his purse and took out two coins.

'This is good silver, the best the French can supply. Go to Sutton Courteny, seek out our enemy and do what you have to. But act wisely.' The Hospitaller stared at the Preacher's wild eyes and wondered if his advice would be heeded. 'Do not be carried away by the force of your own eloquence. He is to be watched. Only move against him when you have proof.' He went across to a small writing desk and scribbled a few words on a piece of parchment. 'Show this to the captain of the guard. They'll let you through the lines.'

The Preacher took the silver and the warrant, finished his wine and slipped into the night.

Sir Raymond sat for a while, wrapping his cloak around him, for the night had grown cold. On the one hand he was pleased that what he had been searching for so many years he'd almost found. On the other hand although he was so close, he was yet unable to do anything about it. He wondered about Otto. His brother had elected to become a hermit, travelling to Outremer where eventually he took refuge on the great rock of Masada overlooking the Dead Sea. Seven years ago Sir Raymond had made careful searches, not knowing whether his brother were alive or dead. The Hospitaller Order had merchants friendly to their interests in the area, and Sir Raymond had been numbed by the news. Otto had, some years previously, mysteriously vanished from his cave. At the same time a young shepherd boy had been found dead amongst the rocks at the foot of the cliffs. The finger of suspicion had been pointed at his brother but Raymond could hardly believe that. Otto would never hurt a child. Nevertheless, any attempts by Raymond to discover the whereabouts of his brother ended in mystery as if he had vanished from the face of the earth. Raymond had concluded his brother had died in some lonely place, and he returned to his hunt for this sinister being, the spirit he had released from the vaults of the Blachernae Palace.

By now the Grand Master, who had helped Raymond since the brothers' escape from Constantinople, was dead in mysterious circumstances, a fall from a horse whilst out riding alone. To the rest of the Order Raymond had become an eccentric, enigmatic figure. They could not understand his absorption with the past, in finding some mysterious Byzantine princess. Over the years, piece by piece, Sir Raymond had built up a picture, done careful study, yet it was years before he accepted the truth about the Rosifer.

He took a key from his pouch and unlocked the coffer where he kept his papers. He plucked out a piece of yellowing parchment and studied the faded green-blue ink. It was dated some ten years previously from an Armenian slave-dealer who had been paid by the Order to search for this elusive Byzantine princess.

The merchant had made careful searches and discovered that a Byzantine princess, singular in her beauty and strange garb, had been sold to a Sipahi commander. None of the other captives could recognise her or say which family she had belonged to. The Turkish commander had taken her to his palace at Adrianople. About three months after the fall of Constantinople, the Sipahi commander and his entire family had been mysteriously killed: throats cut or pierced, blood drained from their cadavers. Of the Byzantine princess there was no sign. Search parties had been organised and, eventually, the princess's corpse had been found in a cypress wood close to the house: she bore no mark of violence, or any indication of how she had died. Only on hearing of this some years later from the Armenian had Sir Raymond fully accepted that it was no longer flesh and blood he was hunting, but the most cruel and subtle of spirits.

3

Sir Raymond put the parchment away. He felt tired after the wine. He lay down on his camp bed, promising himself a few minutes' rest before he returned to Margaret of Anjou's council. He had scarcely made himself comfortable when he fell into a deep sleep, only to be roughly shaken awake by a royal messenger.

'Sir Raymond, come! The Queen is waiting!'

The Hospitaller groaned and struggled from his bed. He took a water bottle and splashed the contents over his face, then, having dried himself on his cloak, he followed the man back through the camp to the Queen's pavilion. As soon as he entered and glimpsed Wenlock's triumphant smile, he knew his counsel and advice had been rejected.

'Sir Raymond,' Beaufort refused to meet his eyes, 'Her Grace the Queen has decided. We will deploy before dawn, our backs to the abbey. Our army will be divided into three divisions. Devon will command the left, myself the right, Lord Wenlock here, together with Prince Edward, will hold the centre.' He pushed across the map which had been drawn during Sir Raymond's absence. 'You, Sir Raymond, will stay with Lord Wenlock.' Beaufort explained. 'I shall take my force,' a stubby finger traced a line, 'and try to go behind York's left flank. They will think they are being attacked in the rear as well as the front. Wenlock will then charge.' He smiled bleakly. 'Panic will ensue, the Yorkists will flee.'

'It's foolishness!' Sir Raymond snapped, glaring down the table at the Queen. 'Madam, Edward of York, whatever you think of him, is a capable general. He has smashed your armies at Barnet: he will have scouted the terrain of this land and be prepared for any ambuscade or surprise.'

'We can't retreat!' the Queen snapped. 'Sir Raymond, I have never really understood your reasons for tying your fortunes to my banner. However, you have seen our star rise and fall. We have lately come from France.' Her shoulders sagged. 'I am tired of being King Louis' pensioner. Every day York grows stronger.' She jabbed at the piece of parchment. 'We must bring him to battle and destroy him and his entire house once and for all!'

'And what if it goes wrong?' Sir Raymond asked desperately. He tried to control the panic seething in his stomach. 'Only a few miles away lie Edward and his brothers, Richard of Gloucester and George of Clarence. They, too, have been fighting the length and breadth of this kingdom and are bent on total victory.' Sir Raymond drew himself up. 'If we lose tomorrow, then we lose for ever!'

The Queen, however, got to her feet, one hand resting on the shoulder of her sulky, spoilt son. The commanders also rose to leave. Sir Raymond looked around. We are dead men, he thought. We should commit ourselves to God and our bodies to our enemies. I am to die, my task unfulfilled.

'Gentlemen,' the Queen folded back the voluminous sleeves of her dark murrey dress, 'our deliberations are finished. We should be moving before dawn.' She swept out of the tent and her commanders followed.

Sir Raymond sighed. He stayed for a while staring at Beaufort's crudely drawn map, then he heard a commotion outside, men shouting for the captain of the watch. Sir Raymond went out. In the flickering firelight he could see two horses, each with a corpse slung over it. A throng of men stood around. Officers arrived, beating them back with the flat of their swords. Sir Raymond pushed his way through: the corpses were unroped and laid next to each other on the ground.

'What's the matter here?' Raymond demanded.

The officer lowered his torch. Sir Raymond's heart skipped a beat. The throats of both soldiers had been neatly pierced on either side of their windpipes, the fronts of their jerkins were soaked in blood. Their faces were white-blue, eyes staring: a look of terror frozen on their dead faces.

'In God's name!' a soldier muttered. 'They are two of our scouts.' He pointed into the darkness. 'They went hunting for food, as well as information, in the woods near Sutton Courteny.'

'I found them,' another voice replied. 'They were lying in the woods, faces down, about ten yards apart. Each had drawn his knife but I couldn't find anything.'

'What do you mean?' The Hospitaller looked up at him.

'Well, six of us went out,' the soldier replied. 'We all agreed to meet at a certain place and return to camp. These two went into the woods. I went to a deserted village but there was nothing there. When they failed to return, I went looking for them.' He scratched his chin. 'They were just lying there, no sign of any enemy.'

The officer tapped one of the corpses. 'What weapon could cause such wounds? Just look, are they dagger holes?'

'Or teeth marks?' another added. 'Like those of a large wolf.'

Sir Raymond stood up. He felt unsteady, his mouth dry with fear. He had seen such marks before in his haunting journey around Europe. While the officer made arrangements for the men's bodies to be tossed into a pit, Sir Raymond, breathing deeply to control his fear, walked slowly back to his tent. He pulled aside the flap and went inside. He was pouring himself another cup of wine when he noticed two white roses lying on top of a chest. They had not been there when he left the tent. On each were sprinkled small drops of blood. Sir Raymond drank greedily but he couldn't stop shaking. He knocked the roses to the soil and ground them into the earth under his boot.

'The Devil is very close,' he muttered. 'And so is my death.'

Throwing the cup into a corner of the tent, he went out and searched for a friar to hear his confession and give him final absolution. Sir Raymond did not sleep that night but spent the early hours before dawn deep in prayer and preparing his affairs. He wrote letters to his superior, arranged with the friar who had shriven him to sing Masses for his soul and then distributed all his possessions amongst the poorest of the camp followers. He then shaved, washed, attended Mass and received the Sacrament before breaking his fast on some dry bread and wine.

Sir Raymond was armoured and ready for battle when the trumpets blew, the banners unfurled and the sergeants-at-arms began to marshal the men into their divisions. Sir

Raymond collected his destrier and, with his war helm lashed to his saddle horn, made his way through the camp looking for the gold leopards rampant of the young Prince Edward.

Despite his foreboding, Sir Raymond felt a thrill at the coming battle. His horse neighed, shaking its head restlessly, ready to charge. Sir Raymond leant down and stroked it gently on the neck, whispering quietly to it. He felt his sword, making sure it slid easily in and out of its scabbard. One of Wenlock's retainers grasped his reins and led him to the massed men at the front where Wenlock and the other commanders were grouped round the young prince. The sky was brightening, the cool dawn breeze already beginning to fall under the growing heat of the rising sun. The men chattered and laughed to hide their unease. Raymond looked to his left where the white-coated men of the Earl of Devon, foot soldiers and archers, were mustering. In the centre before them, knights were massing behind their wall of archers and men-at-arms; to the right he glimpsed the black crosses of Somerset's Trinity banner.

Sir Raymond stood high in the stirrups. The river mist which had curled in just before dawn was beginning to dissipate. The Hospitaller could see how broken the land was, fields and meadows dotted with ditches and hedges.

Suddenly there was the crack of bombards, and huge stones began to fall amongst the archers, sending them whirling like bloody ninepins. Wenlock, surprised, rode forward. Sir Raymond stared in horror for, through the fading mist, coming much faster than they had expected, was Edward of York's army. Bombardiers pushed their cannons, behind them lines of archers. The Hospitaller was astonished as the guns opened up again. The Yorkist archers came quickly past them, some standing, some kneeling; the order to 'Loose!' rang out and the air became black with whirring shafts which fell like deadly hail. Here and there, a knight, still unhelmed, took an arrow in the face or neck. Their own men-at-arms and archers tried to reply but confusion had already been caused. Sir Raymond hastily put on his helmet and drew his sword. He pushed his horse through the struggling mass alongside that of Wenlock.

'For God's sake, man!' he screamed through the slits in his helm. 'We are to advance!'

'The Duke of Somerset,' Wenlock murmured, 'has taken a force. He will circle the enemy. We have only to stand our ground.'

'We are to charge!' another commander said.

Wenlock, however, his visor raised, looked like a man caught in a deadly fear, his face pasty-white. He fumbled at his reins and pulled his horse away. Sir Raymond again lifted himself up in his stirrups. He could already see that their left flank was beginning to disintegrate, the men either running towards the centre or back across the fields in the direction of Tewkesbury. Somerset's right, however, still stood firm: Tresham, Somerset's principal commander, turned his horse and galloped up towards them, helmet raised. He was screaming abuse at Wenlock, pointing his arm towards the enemy. Suddenly Tresham's horse stumbled, its front legs caving in. Tresham was thrown from the saddle, his body bouncing on the ground like that of a child's toy.

The Yorkist archers, now emboldened, were running forward, taking up a closer position; behind them, the massed ranks of Edward of York's cavalry and men-at-arms, their banners flapping, blue, gold and red; the black lion of Hastings, the white lion of Howard. Wenlock still dithered. A roar came from the right, Sir Raymond stared in disbelief. Somerset's lines were crumbling. Throwing down their arms, the men were running back up the hill behind them. A messenger came riding through, an archer covered in dust and sweat, eyes red-rimmed and staring, voice nothing more than a creak. He flung his arm towards the disintegrating ranks on their right.

'The Duke of Somerset,' he gasped, 'is in retreat! He did not encircle the enemy but ran straight into Richard of Gloucester. Look, his banners can be seen!'

Wenlock's commanders, lifting their helms, looked to their right. Somerset's men were fleeing the field and, in the distance, they could see the huge war banners bearing Richard of Gloucester's insignia, a white boar rampant. Sir Raymond grasped Wenlock's arm.

'Stand!' he shouted. 'Stand if not charge!'

As if in answer, Raymond heard a fanfare of trumpets from the front. He turned his head and knew the battle was lost. Edward of York had ordered a general advance and a wall of Yorkist steel, solid and impenetrable, was coming in an armed mass towards them. Wenlock turned and fled, the others, including Sir Raymond, followed suit. Behind them they heard the screams and yells, the shimmering clash of sword and armour as the Yorkists met what was left of the Lancastrian front line. At the top of the hill Wenlock reined in, took his helmet off, mopping his face with his hands. He stared around.

'The Prince!' he cried. 'In God's name, the Prince!'

'He did not retreat,' a voice called.

Sir Raymond and others were about to ride down, when pounding along the brim of the hill, their banners held high, came Beaufort and others. The Duke's rage was terrible. He had lost his helmet, his hair was matted with blood, which ran in rivulets through the dust which masked his face. He did not bother to rein in; his horse crashed amongst them and Beaufort, bringing his axe back, smashed Wenlock's head, turning it into a bloody pulp. He then lifted his boot and kicked his erstwhile commander's corpse from the saddle. Beaufort, his eyes mad with fury, glared at the other commanders.

'So die all traitors!' he screamed. 'Wenlock has lost us the battle!'

A shout went up from the mêlée at the foot of the hill: 'The Prince is down! The Prince is down!'

Raymond stared back. The dust of battle cleared momentarily in a puff of wind. The gold leopards rampant of Prince Edward's banner had disappeared. The pennants of York were now clear and the remnants of the Lancastrian army were breaking.

'We must flee!' Beaufort shouted. 'Seek sanctuary in the abbey!'

The Hospitaller, however, just stared open-mouthed towards the battle line. Someone was walking towards him, tall, erect, steel-grey hair cropped, face burnt swarthy by the sun. The man, unnoticed by the men dying and struggling around him, was moving slowly, arms raised in friendship. In one hand he carried a white rose, in the other a red.

'Otto,' Sir Raymond whispered. 'My brother? My brother, what are you . . . ?'

He felt his arm shaken. One of Beaufort's squires was staring beseechingly at him.

'Sir Raymond, we have to flee!'

The Hospitaller looked back. His mind was playing tricks. The vision had vanished: all he could see was a line of men hurrying towards him. Grasping the reins of his horse, he dug his spurs in and followed the rest, galloping across the meadow towards Tewkesbury.

Matthias had woken just before dawn: the house was quiet, his mother and father still sleeping. He dressed hurriedly and, remembering the attack the night before, put on a belt which carried a small sheath knife. He stole down to the kitchen where he ate some bread and salted bacon, and gulped at a cup of watered ale. He stood listening: nothing, except the birds chirping under the eaves. He went across and pulled back the shutter. The day looked set to become a beautiful one. Matthias bit his lip. He felt guilty. He really should wait for his parents but permission had been given, and sometimes adults could change their minds. He stared across at the crucifix, finished the rest of the ale and, still feeling guilty, went across and knelt down, staring up at the face of the crucified Christ. He would, at least, say his prayers.

'Remember this, my soul, and remember it well. The Lord thy God is One and He is holy. And thou shalt love the Lord thy God with all thy mind, with all thy heart and all thy strength.'

Matthias paused as he heard the floorboards creak above him and, grabbing his small leather bag in which he had placed some bread and fruit, he rushed down the passageway and out of the front door. He slipped over the cemetery wall and ran through the long grass, relishing the wet dew, which splashed his hands, and the morning breeze, which cooled his brow.

Within a short while he was in the village. The high street was empty. A dog ran out barking but, recognising Matthias, slunk away. Two fat sows, rooting amongst the midden-heap, looked up, great ears flapping, before they returned to their work. The doors and windows of the Hungry Man were shuttered and locked. A few of the peasants were already up, ready to leave for the fields. Fulcher's younger daughter,

Ethelina, went by with a yoke across her shoulder from which hung two pails of milk: the blacksmith was a wealthy man and had his own small pasture with a few fat-bellied cows. Any other time Matthias would have stopped to beg for a drink but he was frightened that someone might learn where he was going and decide it was best to check with Parson Osbert.

Matthias sped on, only slowing down when he noticed the old woman sitting on the gallows stone, a basket of herbs in her lap. Old Bogglebow: the hag, Margot, from Baron Sanguis' manor house. No one really knew why the manor lord kept her but the gossips whispered that Baron Sanguis, interested in the black arts, had used Margot to divine the future. Indeed, or so Parson Osbert had whispered, Baron Sanguis had asked Margot to discover whether York or Lancaster would be victorious in the war. Only then did the Sanguis family make its decision, pinning its hopes to Edward of York. Six weeks earlier the baron, accompanied by his son, twelve yeomen and six men-at-arms, had marched east for the great road to London to place their swords at the disposal of the Yorkist princes.

Old Bogglebow rarely came into the village – sometimes to beg. Other times she'd wander in the forest to collect flowers and herbs for her potions and elixirs. No one dare insult this ancient, one-eyed crone with a face as lean as a hatchet, twisted mouth and a tongue steeped in bitterness. Matthias had occasionally glimpsed Margot as she moved like a spider through the village. Now he walked slowly: he did not want to show he was frightened of Old Bogglebow. He meant to pass her by and had almost done so when she called out.

'Matthias, isn't it? The priest's brat. How is your father, and the fair Christina?'

Matthias stopped and turned. The old woman studied him, her one good eye gleaming like a freshly washed, black pebble, the other hidden by loose flaps of skin. Her face was snowy-white, her hair too, and the boy wondered if she had rubbed some powder into both; her bloodless lips parted in a half-sneer. She was holding one of the flowers the hermit had pointed out yesterday. Matthias recognised the venomous monkshood.

'Aye, Matthias,' she declared. 'So, where does Matthias go?'

'About my own business.'

63

She got up and hobbled towards him. Matthias recalled how she was supposed to have been born with a club foot.

'Clever, clever boy,' she declared. 'They say,' her head came forward, scrawny neck now tight, 'they say you are a clever boy.' One hand, thin and cold like a claw, reached out and touched him gently on the cheek. Matthias flinched but held his ground. 'I know where you are going, boy. To the village of the dead, to meet your friend the hermit.'

She was trying to be sweet but Matthias caught the venom in her words. She was now watching him closely, her one good eye studying his face as if she intended to remember every feature.

'Can't I go with you?' she simpered.

'The hermit's not your friend,' Matthias replied. 'If you want to see him, you should go yourself.'

'One has to be invited into a great lord's presence,' she cooed back. 'But remember me to him, won't you, boy? Say sweet things about poor Margot. Tell him how fond I am of you.' She drew closer and Matthias caught her stink. 'I am your servant, Matthias. Anything you want, a potion, an elixir . . . ?' She grasped him by the shoulder, her nails dug deep into his skin.

Matthias squirmed. 'Let me go!' he cried. 'You are hurting me! I'll tell—' He was going to say his father but he stopped short because the change in Margot was so dramatic.

She clasped her hands together, bowing, making small jigging movements like Matthias had seen other old women do in front of the sanctuary lamp.

'Oh, don't tell the hermit,' she whispered. 'Please, I never intended to hurt, only to serve you. Look!' Again the clawlike hand came up.

This time Matthias didn't wait. He ran like the wind along the trackway into the wood. He went as fast as he could. Only once did he stop, where the soldiers had attacked him last night. He looked fearfully into the undergrowth: he could see where the grass and plants had been beaten down but nothing else. He hurried on. The hermit was true to his word. Matthias found him waiting outside the old, crumbling lych-gate.

'I thought you wouldn't come.'

The hermit crouched down. He drew the boy to him, hugging him gently, softly stroking the back of his head.

'It's good to see you, Creatura,' he whispered. 'You are well?'

'Those soldiers,' the boy blurted out. 'Those wicked men last night—'

'I followed you,' the hermit replied. 'I wanted to show you that you had nothing to fear.'

'But the soliders? That voice!'

'They have gone.' The hermit grinned. 'And I am the best of mimics.'

'Did you kill them?'

'They have gone.' The hermit stood up. 'And they'll never trouble you again, Creatura.' He stared down in mock anger. 'You are later than I expected.'

'I met the witch. Margot, Old Bogglebow. She wishes to be remembered to you. She was strange. She wanted to meet you. She said she was my servant but I don't think she is.'

'No, she isn't.' The hermit picked up a staff leaning against the wall. 'Such people, Creatura, are nothing but meddlers. They crawl into the darkness and take to themselves powers they should not, and cannot have. I do not like Margot. But, come, we must be in Tewkesbury soon.'

'Are we walking there?'

'No, no. I've got a surprise for you.'

He led him along a trackway. Matthias didn't understand how he knew his way but, just before they left the wood, the hermit took Matthias into a small clearing where a horse, saddled and harnessed, stood hobbled, eating the grass. It was a fine, smooth, deep-chested bay. The hermit stroked its muzzle and whispered gently in its ear.

'Where did you get it from?' Matthias asked as the hermit swung him into the saddle and climbed up behind.

'You ask too many questions, Creatura. I found it wandering. It's probably from one of the armies. You are comfortable?'

Matthias enjoyed the ride. The trackways were hard, the horse fresh and strong, and it moved along in a fine canter. The hermit was silent. Now and again he'd pause at the top of a hill and stare down, murmur to himself and then ride on.

As they skirted Tredington and took the road to Tewkesbury, Matthias began to realise something was wrong. His parents had taken him here on market days. He was used to the carts and barrows, the hucksters and the traders, the cheerful banter of men looking forward to a good day's trading. Now the people on the roads were different: grim-faced, heads down, they hurried along as if they wished to be indoors, well away from what might happen. On two occasions they met parties of soldiers, horsemen galloping hither and thither, their clothes stained with mud, white flecks of foam on their tired horses. Two foot soldiers, probably deserters, drew their swords and approached the man and the boy, but when the hermit turned to face them they slunk away.

They entered Tewkesbury just as the bells of the great abbey were tolling for morning prayers. The streets and lanes were strangely empty. No stalls or shops were open. Journeymen and traders stayed in the taverns with the doors closed and windows shuttered. No children played in the streets, even the wandering hogs and dogs had been penned in. A funeral cortège passed them, the mourners walking quickly, and the old priest who preceded them gasping and stammering at his prayers.

'What's the matter?' Matthias asked.

'It's the battle,' the hermit replied. 'As I told you, Matthias, blood will be spilt, armies will shatter. Princes will topple. The ravens will feast well tonight. Women will be widowed and children made fatherless. This is a dreadful day.' His voice grew grim. 'Remember, Creatura, all life preys on life. Now, I have someone to see.'

They rode through the small town and up into the abbey close. They dismounted and the hermit led the horse around into the monastic enclosure. A lay brother, followed by the guestmaster, came out to greet them. The latter apparently recognised the hermit and shook his hand warmly as his companion led the horse away to the stables.

'It's good to see you.' The old monk's tired face was lit by a smile. 'And who's this?' He pointed down at Matthias.

'My friend and companion, Matthias Fitzosbert. His father is priest at Sutton Courteny.'

The man's smile faded. 'Yes, yes, quite. And what do you wish here?'

'To pray in the abbey.'

The guestmaster blinked and wetted dry lips.

'It is not safe to be in Tewkesbury today, my friend. Father

Abbot has received news from the battlefield. A terrible and bloody struggle has taken place. Edward of York carries all before him. Men from the Lancastrian army have been deserting all night, stopping at our house, begging for alms.'

'I just want to pray,' the hermit replied.

'Yes, yes, of course.' The monk led them forward. 'Morning Office is finished and Mass has been said. Do you wish food, drink from our refectory?'

The hermit shook his head and, clasping Matthias' hand, he went through a side door into the soaring nave. Matthias stared in disbelief: great columns marched the length of the church up to a gloriously painted sanctuary whilst the carved roof above him looked as if it were held up by magic. He stared in amazement at the shafts of light pouring through the multicoloured, painted windows.

'I have loved, oh Lord,' the hermit whispered, 'the beauty of Thy house, the place where Your glory dwells. This, Matthias, is the gate of Heaven and, indeed, a terrible place.'

'It's beautiful,' Matthias whispered.

His father had never brought him here and, caught up in wonderment, Matthias did not know where to gaze first. The wall paintings drew him, striking in their glorious vigour: angels swooped, satyr-faced demons were spat out of the fire of Hell, the just were carried by Christ in judgment; St Anthony preached to the fishes; Lazarus was swept up into the bosom of Abraham.

'Look!' he cried, but the hermit had walked away. He was staring at a painting on the far wall. Matthias, curious, ran across, his sandals slapping on the hard paved floor. Matthias gazed at the painting: a beautiful woman, her naked body white as alabaster, hair of spun gold, stood beneath a tree: one hand covered her breasts, the other the secret place between her thighs. She was staring at the figure of a glorious young man clothed in the sun. Olive-skinned, lustrous-eyed, he was holding a rose towards the woman. Matthias noticed it had no thorns. When he looked at the hermit, his friend's face was tragic and sad, silent tears running down his cheeks. The hermit extended his hands and touched the painted rose, then the beautiful woman. He muttered something Matthias didn't understand then, folding his arms across his chest, went and sat at the foot of a pillar lost in his own thoughts.

4

The Lancastrian retreat into Tewkesbury had turned into a bloody rout. Most of Margaret of Anjou's army fled across the open countryside, only to be cut down in the great meadows which stretched down to the Severn. Somerset and the other commanders, Sir Raymond included, decided to seek sanctuary in Tewkesbury Abbey. They had to fight every foot of the way into the town. The Yorkists, moving fast, tried to cut them off in a ring of steel. Sir Raymond fought like a man demented, with all his fury, rage and frustration, not only at the defeat, but in the certain knowledge that he would never fulfil his vow. On the edge of the town they ran into a party of Yorkist horse but the Hospitaller led his companions through. Tying his reins to his belt, Sir Raymond wielded his sword, cutting and slashing at the contorted faces and eager hands ready to pluck him from the saddle. His sword scythed the air, slicing through armour and chain mail, biting deep into bone and flesh. The cobbled streets ran with blood, turning the town into a butcher's yard. At last they were through, though three of their party were down, two killed, one a prisoner.

By the time they reached the abbey they were splattered in blood from head to toe. Edmund Beaufort, Duke of Somerset, had lost all his hauteur. A weary, dispirited man, he slid from his horse and almost ran through the small door into the abbey nave. He threw his sword on the ground, wrenching off pieces of armour, throwing his bloody gauntlets into the dark transept. Others joined him, not only from his own party but other Lancastrians who knew that the sanctuary of the church was their only refuge and defence against summary execution. The nave began to fill with injured men, some groaning over terrible wounds in their stomachs or shoulders, others seeking news about companions or relations. They cursed Somerset – one even spat in his face – though others took comfort that Wenlock's cowardice had received its just deserts. Men sprawled about, lying on the floor or resting against the pillars. Sir Raymond stood in the centre of the nave and stared down at the gorgeous rood screen which sectioned off the sanctuary. He knelt, crossed himself, closed his eyes and was halfway through the Ave Maria when he heard the sound of hoofbeats on the cobbled close outside, followed by shouts and yells. One of Somerset's squires came running into the church, blood seeping from a cut on his left arm.

'Yorkists!' he screamed.

The tired Lancastrians picked up whatever weapons they could, forming themselves into a shield wall. A party tried to bar the door but the Yorkist soldiers burst in. The battle began again and the cathedral filled with the sound of scraping steel and the shrieks of wounded and dying men. No quarter was asked and none given. Sir Raymond, with his back to a pillar, fought off two Yorkist bowmen. Their quivers were empty but, armed with spear and sword, they came at him like two wolves snarling and jabbing. Sir Raymond despatched both, one with a thrust to the chest; the other stumbled over his companion's corpse, and Sir Raymond took his head off like a gardener would snip a rose. The head rolled down the nave whilst Sir Raymond drew away from the blood-gushing, severed neck. The fighting was frenetic. Individual duels and hand-to-hand combat now ranged the whole length of the nave.

Sir Raymond was about to help Somerset when the great bell of the cathedral began to toll. From the sanctuary came a procession of monks led by their abbot carrying his crucifix in one hand, a handbell in the other. He banged the steel cross on the paving stone and began to clang the bell. The sound of fighting died away. Men locked in deadly combat stepped back and stared in awe at the might of the Church. The Abbot was dressed in full pontificals – a gold chasuble inlaid with mother-of-pearl and, on his head, a mitre of the same texture. He rang the bell again.

'This is God's house!' his voice boomed through the church. 'And you have stained it with the blood of your brothers. So, hear this. Any man who lifts his hand in anger is accursed, bound and tied under the most dreadful sentence of excommunication!'

His words created a chilling pool of silence.

'Cursed be he,' the Abbot intoned, 'who disobeys my decree! Cursed be he in life! Cursed be he in death! May he die unshriven and remain outside the pale of Christ's mercy!'

He handed the bell to one of the monks. Beaufort came forward and knelt before him.

'Father Abbot, we seek sanctuary.'

'The abbey does not have the right to give sanctuary to rebels and traitors!' a Yorkist shouted.

The Abbot stared down at Beaufort. Sir Raymond, who had walked across to join the Duke, heard the Abbot's whisper.

'He speaks the truth. My Lord of Somerset, for I know it is you, I cannot give you sanctuary here. Edward of York has won the battle. He is our crowned king. His lawyers will say you are traitors and have no right to shelter here.'

'Are we to be slaughtered like cattle?' Somerset snarled.

The Abbot lifted his head. 'Sanctuary or no, no man has a right to draw his sword in God's house. My Lord of Somerset and his party are my guests here. The rest will withdraw or suffer the rigour of excommunication!'

The Yorkists protested but the Abbot's stern face, as well as the realisation that the Lancastrians would fight to the death, gave them wiser counsel. Muttering threats, the Yorkists collected their wounded and dead, then left. At the Abbot's request, the Lancastrians piled their own weapons in a heap in one of the transepts. Lay brothers brought wine and bread from the refectory whilst the infirmarian and his assistants moved amongst the wounded. Somerset went to sit on a bench just near the rood screen. He put his head in his hands. Sir Raymond sat beside him.

'Father Abbot was right,' the Hospitaller began. 'Edward of York will show us no compassion.'

Beaufort lifted his head. 'The Queen must have been captured,' he declared. 'The Prince is dead. Warwick is dead, the House of Lancaster is finished. Sickly, white-faced Henry Tudor, what hope does he have?' He offered the wine cup cradled in his hands to the Hospitaller. 'Sir Raymond, before we die, I would ask you one question? Why did you, a knight of the Church, support Margaret of Anjou?'

'I thought you'd win. I really did and, if you had, my Lord

of Somerset, I would have asked for your help in hunting down a demon.'

Sir Raymond got to his feet and walked into the lonely Lady Chapel. He was kneeling on the prie-dieu before the statue of the Virgin when he felt a tap on his shoulder. He turned and almost fainted as he recognised his brother, Otto. Further down the transept, crouching in the shadows, was a small boy, fist to his mouth, dark eyes rounded in a pale face.

'Otto!' He clasped his brother. 'Otto!'

He felt his brother's arms but his brother stared impassively back.

'Look at me, Sir Raymond! Stare into my eyes!'

The Hospitaller did so, his heart skipped a beat, his blood ran cold. The hair, the face, the arms, the body, these were his brother's – but those eyes! The same hateful stare as that Byzantine princess.

'You!' he whispered. 'You!'

He would have collapsed but the hermit helped him to sit on the cushioned kneeler of the prie-dieu.

'You have been hunting me,' the hermit declared. 'Otto has gone. I am here. I see through his eyes. I speak through his tongue and his heart beats for me.'

Sir Raymond turned away.

'How?' he asked weakly.

'Have you not read your Scriptures?' the hermit mocked gently. 'How the demons can enter a man and make their home there?'

'But why?'

'That is not for you to know.'

'No, why do you hate us?'

'I do not hate you, Sir Raymond. Truly, I thank you. You rescued me from the vault but then you failed me. You broke your pledge and let me be taken. What is worse, you pursued me and sent others hunting me along the highways and byways of Europe. I will not be interfered with!'

Sir Raymond saw the fury blazing in the hermit's eyes.

'I am not some rabbit or fox to be hunted. Always remember, Sir Raymond: when you declare war on Hell, Hell declares war on you.' Lifting his finger he brushed some of the blood from Raymond's face and licked it carefully.

71

'Here in God's house!' Raymond felt his courage return. 'You dare to come into God's house!'

'Have you not studied your Scriptures, Sir Raymond?' the hermit taunted again. 'Read the Book of Job. Satan is allowed to come before the throne of God and, according to the Gospels, even into the presence of Christ.' The hermit gestured at the paintings on the wall. 'Do you think we are like that, Sir Raymond? Dirty little imps with the faces of monkeys and the heads of goats? Don't you realise we are pure spirit, powerful, brooding for all eternity? We have not withdrawn from Heaven, Heaven has unjustly withdrawn from us.' He would have touched Sir Raymond's face again but the Hospitaller flinched. 'Heaven and Hell are the same. Think of that before you die.'

'And the boy?' Sir Raymond asked. 'Another of your victims?'

'More sacred than life itself,' the hermit replied. 'He is nothing to you.'

The Hospitaller got to his feet, refusing to be cowed.

'There are others,' he said.

'Ah, you mean the Preacher?' The hermit shrugged. 'I will take care of him as I have taken care of others. Once he is dead the hunt will end. Farewell, brother!'

The hermit, turning on his heel, walked back through the shadows and collected the boy.

Sir Raymond went back to his prayers. He felt cold as if his heart had turned to stone. He did not care about his companions or their endless speculation. Instead he prayed, preparing himself for death. When the Yorkist captains returned later in the day with warrants for their arrest, Sir Raymond did not struggle as the others did, but allowed his hands to be lashed behind his back. He was pushed out of the main door, blinking at the strong afternoon sunlight.

Just beyond the abbey close a great table had been set up, covered by a green baize cloth. Behind the table soared a black-draped scaffold. On it stood the executioner, his face masked, a huge two-sided axe in his hand, one foot resting on the block and, beside that, a great wicker basket. The townspeople thronged about, held back by a line of archers wearing the royal livery. Each prisoner was taken before the table, Somerset first. Two men were seated there. Richard,

Duke of Gloucester, and his henchman John Howard of Norfolk, their faces still bearing the marks of recent battle. They shouted questions, jabbing their fingers at the fallen Duke. Somerset just shook his head. Gloucester, his pale, pinched face framed by red hair, sprang to his feet, screaming how the Beauforts were responsible for the death of his father. Somerset brought his head back, hawked and spat, the globule of phlegm hitting Gloucester on his cheek. Gloucester bent down and picked up one of the captured standards of Margaret of Anjou and wiped his face. He made a dismissive gesture with his hand. The soldiers hustled Somerset away, up the steps to the scaffold. He refused the blindfold offered by the executioner, lay down and placed his head on the block.

Sir Raymond saw the axe lifting, a flash of sunlight, the blade fell with a thud. He looked away as the executioner picked up the head and showed it to the cheering crowd. Other trials followed. Some prisoners pleaded for mercy and were taken away. Others, Sir Raymond noticed with wry amusement, were greeted as long-lost friends, their bonds cut, and he realised there had been traitors in the Lancastrian ranks. A few, like Somerset, refused to bend the knee and the scaffold behind the makeshift court dripped with blood.

Eventually his turn came. His arms pinioned by two archers, he was pushed up against a table and stared into the catlike eyes of Richard of Gloucester. The Duke's prim lips formed a thin, bloodless line; his face bore cuts whilst his right hand was swathed in bandages.

'A Hospitaller.' John of Norfolk lounged in his chair. He scratched a blood-veined, red cheek, his blue, watery eyes staring contemptuously at Sir Raymond. 'What's a Hospitaller doing amongst the forces of Lancaster?'

'What's a farmer from Norfolk doing amongst those of York?' Raymond retorted.

Norfolk sat straight in his chair. He took his dagger from his belt and dug into the green baize cloth.

'You are in no position to taunt, Hospitaller.'

'What position is that?' Sir Raymond replied.

'Come, come, come!' Richard of Gloucester forced a smile. 'Sir Raymond Grandison, is it not? You'll bend the knee and accept the King's pardon?'

'From now on,' Sir Raymond replied slowly, 'I'll bend the

knee to neither York nor Lancaster. A curse on both your houses!'

'You want to die?' Norfolk jibed.

Sir Raymond smiled. 'Yes, yes, I do.'

'Why?' Gloucester asked curiously.

'I broke my vow,' the Hospitaller replied, staring up at the executioner. 'I broke my vow to a prince better than you, to my superiors, to my God. I have failed. I deserve to die. I can do no more!'

Richard of Gloucester sat back in his chair and flinched at the hostility in the Hospitaller's gaze.

'You and your sort,' Sir Raymond added softly, 'are soon for the dark. You squabble about the fold whilst the sheep are ravished by wolves.'

'Enough!' Gloucester banged on the table with his fist. 'Sir Raymond Grandison, you are a traitor taken in arms against the King. You have offered nothing in your defence.' His face lost some of its hardness. 'God knows why you want to die but, God knows, I will not stop you. Take him away!'

Sir Raymond was hustled up the steps of the scaffold. It was higher than he had thought and, above the crowds, he could catch the breeze coming in from the meadows. He gazed up at the sky.

'It will be a beautiful evening,' he murmured as the executioner forced him down on his knees.

Sir Raymond closed his eyes and said a quick prayer. He heard his name called. He looked up and stared into the crowd. The hermit was standing in the front row, staring across at the scaffold, beside him the boy whom Sir Raymond had only glimpsed in the shadows. The hermit had his hand on the lad's shoulder. Sir Raymond stared at him and felt the sweat break out on his body.

'It cannot be!' he whispered.

'It is,' the executioner replied.

He forced the condemned man to lie down. Sir Raymond closed his eyes but all he could see was the hermit's face and that of the young boy. He heard a roar and the axe fell.

'Why did you take me there?' Matthias twisted round in the saddle and stared up into the hermit's face.

'I told you, I had to see someone before he died.'

'But how did you know he would be in Tewkesbury, in the cathedral? Are you like the crone Margot? Can you see into the future?'

The hermit laughed, a merry chuckle deep in his chest, and he gently stroked Matthias' hair.

'Creatura, Creatura, I would love to tell you that I can see the future and all its glory as well as what present you will receive on your birthing day.' His voice became grave. 'But that's not true. Margaret of Anjou was doomed to lose. The House of York is strong as long as Edward its prince rules but, there again, that might not be as long as they think. I knew the Lancastrians would lose the battle and, if they did, though it was foolish to fight, they would have nowhere to flee for sanctuary but the abbey. So I went there to wait.'

Matthias closed his eyes. He would never forget today. He would not dare tell his parents what he had seen. That terrible bloody fight up the nave, men hacking and screaming at each other. And then the executions, though he had seen men die before; poachers and outlaws jerking and dangling on Baron Sanguis' gallows, but nothing as bloody as that!

'I know what you are going to ask me, Creatura,' the hermit said, guiding his horse along the woodland path. 'Why did you have to see it? But that's the nature of life. Struggling, fighting, dying. In the trees around us, life struggles for existence. The death of one animal is the life of another. The world of man is no different.'

'And will you take me to Tenebral now?'

'No, not tonight. You were home late yesterday; that must not happen again. Will you tell your parents what you have seen?'

Matthias shook his head.

'I suppose it's best,' the hermit replied drily.

'And who was that man?' Matthias asked. 'The one you were talking to, who later died?'

'Someone I knew from my past,' the hermit retorted. 'I had to say farewell before his end.' The hermit pointed further up the forest path. 'Look!'

Matthias peered down the long tunnel formed by the overhanging trees and glimpsed a small wayside tavern built of wood and wattle. Two horses stood tied to a post outside.

'We'll stop there,' the hermit said. 'A tankard of ale, something to drink. Would you like a sweetmeat, Matthias?'

The boy immediately forgot about Tewkesbury and clapped his hands. When they reached the tavern, the hermit lowered him gently from the saddle and told him to sit on the bench. He dismounted and tied the horse, then walked into the little taproom. He came out a short while later carrying a small trencher of sweetened bread baked in honey and a delicious drink of herbs mixed with watered ale. He placed these on to Matthias' lap.

'Stay there,' he said. 'I will not be long.'

The hermit went back inside. Matthias leaned against the wall of the tavern and slowly chewed on the honey-drenched morsels. He sipped at the pewter cup, staring across the trackway, watching the squirrels scramble up the trunks of trees whilst, above them, a magpie chattered noisily. The sun was still warm. Matthias felt his eyes grow heavy but, curious why the hermit had not returned, he put the trencher down and stared through the unshuttered window.

The taproom was gloomy but, as Matthias' eyes grew accustomed, he saw the hermit. He was sitting at a table in the far corner, his back to him, talking to two people. One looked like a monk, cowled and hooded. The other was a beautiful young woman, the fairest Matthias had seen. She had lustrous, flaming red hair. Large earrings glittered in the darkness, a gleaming necklace hung round the swanlike neck. She was whispering earnestly to the hermit. Now and again the woman would pause and lean across to her hooded companion as if to ask for confirmation. The hooded one would simply nod. She said something to the hermit, who laughed. She turned and saw Matthias staring at her through the window. She raised her hand prettily. Matthias blushed, looked away and returned to his sweetmeats. After a short while the hermit came out and, without a word, untethered his horse and lifted Matthias into the saddle. They left the tavern.

'Before you ask, Creatura,' the hermit laughingly teased, 'they are friends I know.'

'Who was the woman?'

'Her name is Morgana. She is part-English, part-Spanish.'

'She's beautiful.' Matthias chattered on. 'She's like a princess I saw. It was in a Book of Hours Baron Sanguis loaned

Father. A beautiful princess being attacked by a savage dragon. She was defended by a brave knight.'

'And am I the dragon?' the hermit asked.

'No,' Matthias replied. He leant back against the hermit's chest. 'You are the knight.'

Matthias stared at the trackway; the jogging horse, the warmth of the hermit's body and what he had drunk at the tavern made him heavy-eyed. He fought against it but eventually he was in a deep sleep full of dreams: beautiful princesses, knights covered in blood fighting to the death, dragons, executioners, wolf's-heads and forest outlaws garbed in Lincoln green. He woke with a start. It was dusk, they were in the woods leading down to Sutton Courteny. The hermit reined in.

'Are you well, Matthias? You should have slept on. This is dusk, the Watching Hour.'

'I want to pee,' Matthias replied. 'If I don't, I'll wet my breeches.'

The hermit laughed and let him down. The boy ran into the bushes and undid his points. When he had finished, he shivered. He was glad the hermit was taking him home. It was growing dark and cold. He had seen enough. He wanted his mother, to say his prayers, to sit by his father near the fireside and chatter. He glanced over at the hermit. For the first time ever Matthias felt frightened of him. In the dusk he looked taller, more sombre, as if horse and man were one creature.

'What's the matter, Matthias?'

The boy just took a step back. He couldn't understand his fear.

'I want to go home,' he said weakly. 'I'm frightened!'

The hermit dismounted and walked towards him. When Matthias stood stock-still the hermit crouched down. The boy relaxed at those friendly, twinkling eyes and merry mouth.

'You are not frightened of me, are you, Matthias?'

'It was strange.' The boy drew closer. 'It's dusk and the wood is quiet.'

'This is the most dangerous hour,' the hermit replied, catching Matthias' hand and stroking it gently. 'This and the hour before dawn.'

'I've heard of that,' Matthias replied, recalling a sermon his father had given last Palm Sunday. 'They say just before dusk Christ was buried and just before dawn he rose from the dead. So, about these times, ghosts walk.'

The hermit led him back to the horse. 'Then it's also time little boys were home and in bed,' he remarked.

They continued on their journey. The hermit tried to make him go back to sleep but Matthias was now too alert.

'Then close your eyes,' the hermit said, 'and do not be frightened by what you might see.'

The horse jogged on. Matthias, of course, kept his eyes wide open. He felt the night breeze spring up, rustling the trees around him, then, through the gathering gloom, he saw a figure coming towards them.

'I wonder who that is,' Matthias murmured.

The boy peered again. It wasn't one, it was two, no three, four, five figures walking in single file, slowly, in step. Matthias began to shiver. There was something dreadfully wrong with them. They didn't walk, they shuffled. He felt the hermit tense.

'Look away, Matthias,' he whispered. 'Do not look at them as they pass. They can do us no harm.'

He tried to cover the boy's eyes with his hand. Matthias knocked it away: these figures approaching posed danger. He'd played in these woods and he knew no one ever came here after dark unless they had to. Journeymen and pedlars always stayed in the village, and why would any of his father's parishioners be walking here at this hour? And why were they walking in single file like mourners at a funeral? And the wood was so quiet . . . It should be full of birdsong, with rabbits, foxes, stoats and weasels scurrying about. The horse became restless, neighing and whinnying. The hermit leant down, gently pushing Matthias aside, and whispered some strange words. The horse became more docile though it still remained tense, ever ready to shy. The line of figures grew nearer. Matthias looked up at the hermit's face, it was passive, eyes half-closed. Then the figures were upon them. Matthias looked quickly, his mouth went dry, his heart began to thud.

'Edith!' he exclaimed.

The blacksmith's daughter was one of the line, face white as snow, eyes rimmed with black. She walked, eyes sightless, behind her a face Matthias didn't recognise. He also glimpsed the features of the man the hermit had been talking to in the abbey at Tewkesbury. Again the face was as white as a coffin cloth, dark staring eyes. And weren't those the two soldiers? The ones who had attacked him the previous night? But they looked more dreadful, they had their chins up and he could see the cuts in their throats. The horse began to shy, then reared up as Matthias covered his face and began to scream.

For a while all was confusion: the horse whirling round, the terrible faces staring at him. The hermit remained calm, talking fast. This time Matthias recognised he was speaking in Latin.

Abruptly all went quiet. The horse stopped, its head drooping with exhaustion. Matthias couldn't stop shaking but he felt the hermit's hand on the back of his neck, stroking him gently. Birdsong broke out high in the trees. Matthias took his hands away from his face. The trackway was deserted. He could see nothing. A rabbit loped across the path and, above him, a nightingale began to serenade the setting sun. The hermit was talking softly, gently stroking him. Matthias calmed down, the sick feeling in his stomach disappeared. He twisted, the saddle horn catching his thigh, and stared up at the hermit.

'What was that?' he asked. 'I saw Edith, but she's dead. That man, that man in Tewkesbury, he too is dead. Edith's body lies before the altar. It is to be buried tomorrow!'

'Open your mouth, Matthias.'

The boy obeyed and the hermit popped a sugared almond into his mouth. Matthias chewed it, his throat became wet whilst the sweetness seemed to fill his mouth.

'Do you like it?' the hermit asked.

The boy smiled and nodded.

'It was nothing,' the hermit continued in a matter-of-fact voice. 'Nothing at all, Matthias. The day has been long. Perhaps I should not have shown you the things I did. And, when you are half-awake at this time of shadows, the mind plays strange games.'

'But the horse was frightened . . .'

The hermit gathered his reins and urged the horse on.

'That's because you were frightened, Matthias,' he replied soothingly. 'Creatura, you screamed loud enough to wake the dead.' The hermit laughed quietly to himself.

'Will I see you tomorrow?' Matthias asked.

'Perhaps. But tonight, Matthias, sit by your fire, chatter, fill your stomach with bread and soup. Enjoy the warmth.'

They rode on. At the edge of the village, the hermit reined in and lowered Matthias to the ground.

'Run home, Creatura!'

The boy stared up. He knew the hermit had tears in his eyes. He could see them glistening and was ashamed at what he had felt when he had first woken up in the wood.

'I love being with you,' he stammered. 'I really do. It's exciting.'

The hermit leant down and gently stroked the top of Matthias' head.

'And I love you, Creatura. Now run like the wind. Your mother is waiting.'

5

As soon as he entered the village Matthias sensed something was wrong. It was quiet, the doors and shutters of the Hungry Man were firmly closed, though chinks of light peeped through the slats. Matthias heard a creak and, peering into the gloom, saw a corpse hung from the scaffold, twirling and turning in the evening breeze. He closed his eyes and ran past this. Further up the street, near the small cesspit covered by wooden boards, his foot caught on a piece of armour lying near the raised rim of the pit. He ran on but stopped as he approached the cemetery wall. He could hear voices and glimpsed torchlight amongst the trees. He took the long way round. The front door to his house was off the latch. He pushed this open and ran down the passageway.

'Mother! Mother!'

Christina was sitting by the fireside. She looked better, more colour in her cheeks. She scooped him into her arms, her lips brushing his cheeks. Matthias felt the wine on her breath and noticed how bright her eyes were.

'You should have stayed here!' she exclaimed, pushing him gently away towards his own stool. 'There has been a great battle.'

Matthias bit his tongue before he gave away how close he had been to it.

'A great battle,' Christina continued excitedly. 'Horsemen, soldiers coming out of the woods, some wounded, others without a scratch on them.' She put down the piece of embroidery, an altar cloth for the Lady Chapel. 'And then others followed. The first ones caught one of Queen Margaret's men and hanged him on the gallows. At the far end of the village, just near the great meadow, they trapped three more and killed them out of hand. Your father and the Preacher are now busy digging the graves.'

'The Preacher? Who's he?' Matthias asked.

Christina's smile faded. 'A wandering monk, friar or priest – I don't know what.' She waved her hands irritably. 'He arrived about three hours ago and has been closeted with your father. Simon the reeve and John the bailiff have also been here.' She laughed behind her hands. 'We drank some wine, a little too much. Now, go and wash your hands in the rain butt.'

Matthias did so, slightly alarmed at his mother's mood, her air of frenetic gaiety. She set the table and served him a platter of dried pork, onions, some leeks covered in cream, and bread which tasted hard. Matthias ate slowly. His mother said she was tired and would lie on the bed. Matthias heard her go upstairs. After he had eaten he cleared the table and sat in his mother's chair in front of the fire, half-dozing. He jumped as his father pushed back the front door with a crash and came down the passageway. Matthias leapt out of the chair. His father embraced him carefully.

'I haven't washed yet.' He gently pushed his son away, lifting his hands, flecked with clay and mud.

Matthias, however, was staring up at the Preacher, who stood just within the doorway. The boy's heart skipped a beat. He forced a smile but he did not like this man. His black, greasy hair hung in ringlets down to his shoulders; his face was lean and swarthy with cruel eyes and a hooked nose. He reminded Matthias of one of Baron Sanguis' kestrels.

'Good morrow, Matthias, Christ's blessing!' The Preacher held out a hand and gently squeezed Matthias'.

The boy thought his face would ache with the smile. He was glad when the Preacher let go, although the man's eyes followed him as he went back to his chair.

'What's the matter, Father?'

Matthias, eager to break the Preacher's gaze, wanted his father to stay, not go out to the rain butt in the garden.

'Why, hasn't your mother told you? Men from the battle fled here. They were killed, one still hangs on the gallows. John the bailiff will cut the body down and bury it later tonight.' Parson Osbert's face looked tired. 'We are men, not dogs. The corpses can't be left to rot in a filthy ditch. God knows, I buried them without knowing their names. Tomorrow I'll remember them when I celebrate the Mass for poor Edith.' The parson gestured at the Preacher. 'Our guest here helped me. You have a strong arm, sir, but now we must clean off the dirt.'

The Preacher followed the parson out to wash his hands and face. Christina came downstairs, heavy-eyed. She sat in a chair. Matthias' unease deepened. Something was about to happen, but what? His father and the Preacher returned. More wine was poured, Christina using their best pewter cups. They sat for a while in a semicircle round the fire, discussing the battle, the Preacher praising Parson Osbert's generosity.

Then he began to tell tales of his wanderings. Matthias sat open-mouthed as the Preacher described the great cities along the Rhine, Turkish galleys in a sky-blue sea, the white marble palaces of kingdoms in the middle of golden deserts. All the time he kept watching Matthias, studying him carefully.

'Now,' he concluded, 'I have come to Sutton Courteny.'

'The Preacher,' Parson Osbert explained, 'has learnt about Edith's murder. He knows of similar deaths in the neighbourhood, across the valley outside Tredington. Also around Berkeley, Gloucester, even as far south as Bristol—'

'Tell me about the hermit,' the Preacher interrupted harshly. 'You know the hermit, don't you, Matthias?'

The boy nodded.

'Then tell me about him. What does he do?'

Matthias glanced at his mother, who sat slumped in her chair, staring into the fire. He realised he had to be careful.

'Come on, boy.' Parson Osbert squeezed his son's shoulder.

'He's a holy man,' Matthias declared. 'He lives in the old church in Tenebral. He paints on the walls: a large rose. He cares for animals and birds. He showed me foxes and he knows where the badger digs his sett.' Matthias did not like the look of disdain on the Preacher's face.

'And has he done you any harm, boy?'

'Of course not. He lets me go with him. We talk.'

'About what?'

'About God and Christ.'

Matthias licked his lips, his mind now racing. What did the Preacher think they did? What did they talk about? Matthias suddenly realised the hermit was his friend, closer to him than any of the village children – he felt a pang of guilt – even closer than his mother or father. They had always been distant, more involved with each other than him. Oh, they loved him but it was as if he were a second thought.

'And what does he say?' the Preacher insisted.

'That the Lord God,' Matthias recalled his own lessons, 'that the Lord God made Heaven and earth and that He sent His Son to redeem us.'

'Does he ever practise magic, sorcery, the black arts?'

'Pish!' Parson Osbert spoke up. 'The boy would know little about that.'

'The Devil casts his net wide,' the Preacher retorted.

'He is only a child.' Christina suddenly sat upright in her chair. 'And a very tired one at that. Matthias, it's time for bed.' She stared defiantly across at the Preacher. 'He is my son. He is only a child. He is very tired.'

Matthias was only too pleased to escape. He kissed his mother and father, nodded quickly at the Preacher and almost ran from the parlour.

Matthias was awoken the next morning just after dawn by the sound of the church bell tolling, and got up in alarm. Hastily wrapping a horsehair blanket round him, he hurried downstairs. The kitchen was clean and swept, his mother, rather pale-faced, was standing over a bowl of oatmeal bubbling above a weak fire.

'What's wrong?' Matthias cried.

'Your father has decided to call the villagers to a meeting in the nave of the church, before he celebrates the Requiem for Fulcher's daughter.'

'What about?'

'Hurry up and get dressed, Matthias. You and I are both going.'

Matthias obeyed. He washed, put on his Sunday robes and went down to the kitchen to break his fast. His father and the Preacher came in. Parson Osbert was now dressed in his dark brown gown, fastened round the middle by a white cord. He had washed and shaved but the Preacher appeared no different. His sallow, dirty features had a look of excitement as if he savoured what was about to happen. They ate in silence, interrupted now and again by knocks on the door, as villagers enquired what was happening. Parson Osbert quietly told them to meet in the church. He and the Preacher left. Christina doused the fire and, taking Matthias' hand, walked across the cemetery and through a side door into the nave.

Matthias slipped away, back into the cemetery – God's acre, as his father always termed it. He went to stand under a yew tree and watched as the villagers came into the graveyard. Many of the peasants mumbled and protested at being called away from the fields but, after yesterday's events, they were frightened of other occurrences. The law of the village was very clear: if the church bell was rung in alarm they all had a duty to assemble. They left their scythes, hoes and mattocks in a pile in a corner of the church wall. The women went straight in but the men stamped their feet and looked up at the brightening sky, bemoaning the waste of a good day. They fell silent as Fulcher, followed by his wife and family, came up the graveyard path. The blacksmith's family were all dressed in their Sunday best with pieces of dyed black ribbon sewn on their tunics and gowns as a mark of mourning. The other villagers let them through, murmuring their condolences, before following the blacksmith into the church. Matthias stared round the cemetery: he glimpsed the fresh mounds of earth where his father had buried the unfortunates killed the day before. The boy chewed on his thumbnail. He did not know whether to stay or flee to Tenebral. The Preacher meant his friend the hermit no good and shouldn't he be warned? Matthias stood up. Surely he wouldn't be missed?

'Matthias!'

The boy turned. Christina was standing in the church porch.

'Matthias, you are to come, your father is missing you.'

Matthias sighed and followed her into the church. Christina's firm grip on his hand showed she would stand no nonsense and the way she kept looking down at him made him wonder. Did she know? Did she suspect what he had been planning? The nave was packed. All the families of Sutton Courteny, the old as well as the young, filled the small nave. Fulcher and his family sat at the front, grouped around the parish coffin, which stood on black-draped trestles guarded by six purple candles. The church bell began to ring again. The chattering and the gossip died. The bell ceased its tolling. Parson Osbert, dressed in the black chasuble of the Requiem Mass, came out through the rood screen followed by the Preacher. The villagers watched with interest. Any desire to go out into the fields or gossip outside the Hungry Man was now replaced by a thrill of excitement. Something was about to happen, to shatter the tedium of their lives. Parson Osbert climbed the steps into the pulpit.

'Brethren!' His voice echoed round the church. 'Today we intend to sing the Requiem Mass and perform the funeral obsequies for a child of this village, Edith, daughter of Fulcher our blacksmith.' He paused as Fulcher's wife put her face in her hands and sobbed noisily. 'The events of the last few days have shattered the peace and harmony of our village. There has been a great battle outside Tewkesbury. Once again the roads are full of soldiers but there are other evils. Edith is not the only person to have died, been murdered, in such terrible and mysterious circumstances. I have news that similar deaths have occurred throughout the shire. I have agreed that the Preacher here—' Parson Osbert gestured to where the Preacher stood at the foot of the pulpit, staring down the nave, his eyes moving slowly from one face to another – 'this man of God has news on this. In normal circumstances I would have gone to see Baron Sanguis but our lord is still absent, and these affairs cannot wait.'

Parson Osbert made the sign of the cross and came down the steps. The Preacher now mounted the pulpit. Matthias watched expectantly. This mysterious stranger seemed taller, broader, more powerful than he'd been the night before. For a few moments the Preacher just stared round the church.

'Satan!' His voice thundered, making Matthias jump. 'Satan, as the Good Book says, goes about roaring like a lion, seeking whom he may devour!'

The villagers stared up at him. The reference to the Devil or works of Hell always caught their attention.

'The murder of this child,' the Preacher continued, 'is not the bloody-handed work of anyone who knew her. These deaths, as Parson Osbert has told you, have occurred elsewhere. I ask you now to search your memories. Have such deaths ever occurred before?'

With his hands clasped on the pulpit, the Preacher reminded Matthias even more of a hunting kestrel on its perch.

'There were deaths eight years ago.' Joscelyn the taverner spoke up. 'Not in the village but between here and Tewkesbury.'

'Horrible murders!' another cried. 'Throats gashed, corpses drained. Even then we thought it was the work of night walkers!'

The Preacher stilled the growing clamour with one wave of his hand. 'And I ask you,' he was now enjoying himself, 'who was here in your village at that time?'

Again silence. Matthias tensed. He looked up at his mother. She was now white as a ghost. She sat as if carved out of stone, her eyes never leaving the Preacher. Matthias closed his eyes to pray.

'The hermit!'

Matthias opened his eyes with a start.

'The hermit!' Joscelyn the taverner shouted. 'He was here, where he is now, in the ruined church at Tenebral!'

'But he's a holy man.' Simon the reeve got to his feet.

'Holy?' the Preacher retorted, glaring down at the reeve. 'No one is holy but God!'

'I mean . . .' Simon the reeve swallowed hard. He was used to holding his own at such meetings and refused to give up so easily. After all, he knew his letters and could write, was skilled in the hornbook and the ledger. He did not like this stranger entering their village and telling them what to do. Yet the Preacher's eyes seemed to burn into him. 'I mean,' he stammered, 'he did no one any harm, except beg for food.'

'Hush! Listen now!' The Preacher's voice dropped. He leant against the pulpit, then lifted one hand, fingers splayed. 'Eight years ago,' he jabbed the air, 'these murders occurred, the hermit was here. Eight years later,' he continued, holding another finger up, 'and the murders begin again. The hermit can wander hither and thither. No one knows where he goes or what he intends.' He pointed up to the crucifix behind him. 'And if he's a man of religion why does he not come here to church? At Christmas? At Easter? On Lady Day? At Pentecost?'

The Preacher's voice was now booming through the church. Matthias felt like crying out. He could not believe this. His friend the hermit? Who could make doves appear in his hand? Who was so gentle and kind? Matthias would have screamed out, but his mother, sitting so still, put her hand across his mouth and looked down at him: in that look Matthias knew something was dreadfully wrong.

'Then let's arrest him now!' Simon the reeve shouted.

'We have no power,' John the bailiff pointed out, getting to his feet. 'Baron Sanguis is Lord of the Manor. He has the right of the tumbrel, axe and rope!'

'Well, it's too far to go to Gloucester!' another shouted. 'Whilst the sheriff could keep us hanging about until Michaelmas!'

The Preacher held up both hands. 'But you do have the right,' he intoned. '*Vox populi est vox Dei*: the voice of the people is the voice of God. This is not a matter for the Crown. It is a matter for Holy Mother Church. As the Bible says, "Thou shalt not suffer a witch to live." We can arrest him.'

By now the villagers were nodding and whispering amongst each other. Fulcher the blacksmith got to his feet. The great burly man bowed to the Preacher and turned to face his neighbours.

'The Preacher speaks the truth,' he declared. 'Think now, good people, who would murder poor Edith in such a barbarous way? No woman would, and every man was in the fields preparing for the harvest.'

Fulcher's words drew a chorus of agreement. Matthias felt himself sweating, heart beating faster than he had thought possible. His mother's grip on his wrist grew even firmer.

'However,' Fulcher continued, 'my daughter lies here in the parish coffin: her soul is with God but the earth waits for her body. Let us complete what we have begun. I say the funeral Mass should be said, our plans laid and tomorrow, just after dawn, we go out to Tenebral.'

The villagers clapped, getting to their feet. The Preacher smiled and nodded, proud at how quickly he had gained mastery over these strangers.

'But what happens if he's warned?' a voice shouted from the back.

'But who will warn him?' the Preacher retorted. His gaze slid quickly to Matthias. 'I say this: let your young men guard the path through the woods to Tenebral. That is enough.'

His words won general agreement. Parson Osbert returned to the sacristy to don his vestments and the people stayed to hear the Requiem Mass for poor Edith. After this was completed Fulcher and five other men carried her coffin out to the cemetery. The lid was unscrewed, the sheeted corpse taken out and lowered quickly into the earth. Parson Osbert blessed, sprinkled with holy water and incensed Edith's last resting place. The soil was then thrown in. A wooden cross was driven deep into the earth. Afterwards most of the parishioners streamed out of the graveyard back into the village to break their fast and gossip at the Hungry Man.

Parson Osbert and the Preacher joined them. Christina hurried back to her house, her hand still gripping that of Matthias. Once inside she locked and bolted the door. She took Matthias into the small parlour where again she sealed the room, shutting and barring the windows and door. Matthias was now frightened. The chamber was dark. His mother seemed so agitated, muttering wordlessly to herself. Now and again she would stop to scratch the side of her face. Then, as if she were too hot, she snatched the wimple from her head and undid the clasps of her dark burgundy dress. A small jug of water, used to freshen the flowers in their wooden boxes, stood on the window sill. She seized the jug and started dabbing at her neck. Matthias ran up.

'Mother!'

Christina stared at him.

'Mother!' Matthias insisted. 'What is wrong? What is going to happen?'

Christina clutched her stomach and breathed in deeply.

'Matthias, your father and I talked about this last night. You are not to go out to Tenebral again. You are not to meet the hermit.'

'Why?' Matthias asked. 'The Preacher is wrong. He lies!'

'Just do it!' Christina screamed at him, the skin of her face drawn tight. 'Oh, Matthias, just do it! Leave him alone!'

She hurried to the door, fumbled with the lock and, throwing this open, ran down the passageway. Matthias, shaking, went to follow her. He could hear her sobbing in the small solar so he quietly left the house. He slipped across the cemetery to his secret place, the small stone death house at the far side of the church. Matthias crept in. He crouched, thumb in mouth, trying to make sense of what was happening. He knew the hermit was strange. He said things which Matthias did not understand. But a murderer? A man violent like those soldiers? Matthias closed his eyes.

'Remember this, my soul,' he murmured, 'and remember it well. The Lord thy God is One and He is holy.' Then he finished the prayer. 'And thou shalt love thy neighbour as thyself.'

Matthias' eyes flew open. He should remember that. What would the hermit expect him to do? What would he want?

Matthias heard his mother calling, her voice carrying faintly across the cemetery. He lay down on the bed of soft bracken he'd once made there, crossing his arms, bringing his knees up. He felt tired, a little cold. His eyes grew heavy and for a while he dozed. He woke with a start, some bird crashing in the bushes outside.

The boy stole out of his secret place and stretched, enjoying the warm sunlight. He had made his mind up. He climbed the cemetery wall but, instead of taking the highroad, he took a narrow trackway which snaked behind the houses of the village. He ran furtively, pinching his nose now and again at the sour smell from the cesspits which stood at the bottom of each plot of land. When he approached the rear of the Hungry Man, he had to be more careful. Joscelyn and two of his sons were there, raising new casks from the cellar. Once they had gone Matthias continued on his way. Soon he was in the woods but this time he wasn't afraid. He saw the guards the villagers had sent out. However, they had brought a small tun of ale with them and seemed more keen on emptying that, laughing and teasing each other. Matthias scrambled through the bushes, his hands and face stung by the nettles, and scratched by the prickly holly. At last he was past them and, forcing his way through the undergrowth, made his way back to the path which led to Tenebral.

He approached the ruined church, calling his friend's name but there was no reply. Matthias slipped in under the crumbling doorway and stared. The hermit was kneeling in the sanctuary, hands extended, before the rose painted on the wall. Matthias held his breath. A strong red light, like that of the sky just before the dawn, came from the painting and bathed the hermit in its mysterious glow. And the hermit? It seemed as if he were at least a good yard from the ground, kneeling in midair, hands extended. There was no sound.

Nothing but this bright, rose-coloured light and the hermit embracing it. Matthias stepped back. His foot caught on some dry wood, it cracked, shattering the silence. Matthias stared down in horror. When he looked up again the light had gone, the hermit was just standing on the edge of the sanctuary, smiling down at him.

'Matthias, I did not know you were coming. Creatura, you move so softly.'

'What was that light?' Matthias asked, coming forward.

'What light?' the hermit teased back. 'Matthias, you'll make a great poet or troubadour.' He saw the puzzlement in the boy's face. 'A troubadour is a singer of songs,' he explained. 'A dreamer of dreams. A teller of tales.'

'Are you a murderer?' Matthias asked harshly.

'Creatura!'

The hermit sat down at the foot of a crumbling pillar, resting his head against the ivy which wound round it. He tilted up his face and, from under heavy-lidded eyes, studied the boy.

'They say you are,' Matthias blurted out, coming forward. 'They say you killed Edith and others. Now and eight years ago.'

'Who says that?'

'The stranger, a preacher.' Matthias now ran towards him. He tugged at the hermit's robe. 'They are going to come here tomorrow morning. They are going to arrest you. They call you a witch. They've put guards on the path through the woods.'

'And you came to warn me?' The hermit stretched out his legs and patted his lap. 'Sit here, Matthias.'

The boy did so. The hermit put his arms round him.

'I'm not supposed to be here. My mother, she told me not to come.'

'But you came, didn't you, Matthias?' The hermit was now whispering in his ear. 'I can see the cuts on your hands and face. You came here to warn me, didn't you?' He stroked Matthias' hair. 'Oh Creatura, come.' He got up and led Matthias into the sanctuary.

Matthias stared at the rose on the wall, brighter, more breathtakingly beautiful than ever. There were now more runes or strange marks carved beneath it. The hermit told him to sit down on a stone. He himself sat on the floor opposite and studied the boy.

'I'm going to tell you things,' he smiled, 'that you may not understand now, but in years to come you will. Look around you, Matthias. All you see is a ruined church. However, as I have said before, there's more to reality than your life or what you see, feel or touch. In the heavens,' he looked up towards the sky, 'I have seen souls, as many as snowflakes, yet each is a brilliant flash of lightning. I have seen spirits of the great nine circles: cherubim, seraphim, angels and archangels. They wheel and turn before the throne of God.' He touched Matthias' cheek. 'I said you might be a poet. A long time ago, in Italy, there was a great poet.' He leant forward, his eyes bright with excitement. 'A man called Dante. He wrote a poem about earth, Hell and Heaven.' The hermit pointed over his shoulder at the rose. 'According to Dante, just before you enter the presence of God,' he held his hand up, 'He who is All Holy, you go through the Paradise of the Rose on which the Trinity – Father, Son and Holy Spirit – meditate and reflect for all eternity—'

'Have you seen this?' Matthias broke in. He couldn't fully understand what the hermit was saying. Yet his words evoked memories. His father's sermons and the paintings in the parish church showed the great angels of God going about their divine work.

The hermit was now looking at a point above Matthias' head.

'Like Dante,' he replied slowly, 'I have seen the Paradise of the Rose. Like him I have glimpsed the love of God.' He paused. 'They say God is love but the preachers and the priests don't know what love is. A Greek writer who lived centuries ago, Dionysius the Areopagite, he came close to the truth. He said love was the search for harmony.' The hermit's eyes now filled with tears. 'The priests have it wrong, Matthias. They prattle about love but they don't understand the first thing about it.' He held the boy's gaze. 'You can lose Heaven for love, be damned for love, and for all eternity turn your face against the Lord God because of love. It's the one thing, Creatura, which the intellect and will makes its own decision about. You can force a man to hate you. You can break him on the wheel, hang him on the gallows or bribe him with gold and silver. Take him into the seventh heaven and show him all the mysteries but you cannot make anyone love you.' He sighed, it was like a breeze echoing round the sanctuary. 'And if you love, even if it's not requited, even if it creates an eternal hunger in you, no one, not even the Lord God, can force you to give it up. So, *Creatura bona atque parva*, do you love me?'

'Yes,' Matthias said in a rush. He wanted to ask questions but sensed this was not the time or the place.

'Then remember what the apostle Paul said.'

Matthias caught the humour in the hermit's voice.

'Love covers a multitude of sins.' He rose to a half-crouch and stretched out his arms. 'So come, Matthias, here in our secret place, one last embrace.'

This time the hermit squeezed him tightly, holding him so close the boy could feel the man's tears wet on his cheek. The hermit released him.

'Go now, little one. Go on!' He clapped his hands. 'Show me how fast you can run.'

Matthias did so. He felt a lump in his throat. He wanted to stay. When he reached the ruined lych-gate, he stopped and turned round but the hermit had gone. Matthias ran into the woods, following his secret way, creeping past the guards, now shouting and laughing as they filled their tankards and discussed, yet again, the Preacher's strange sermon. Matthias returned to the village, slipping back into his house. He fled to his chamber and, lying on his bed, wondered what would happen to the hermit.

At Tenebral the hermit, who had taken the name of Otto Grandison, was already preparing for what would happen the following morning. He lay face down in the sanctuary, the tears streaming down his cheeks, his body trembling with sobs as he whispered into the darkness.

'I have loved and I will not lose,' he said. 'I have tried one way and I have failed. I will return!'

He lay stock-still waiting for the answer but the only image which filled his soul was of the beautiful woman, hair bright as the sun, her hands stretched out to take the thornless rose.

Then another image followed: the small, dark face of the boy, proof that, at last, if he searched long enough for love, love would respond.

6

The chronicler at Tewkesbury described the villagers' attack
on the hermit at Tenebral in the most colourful language.
According to the old monk, who blew on his knuckles and
scratched the parchment with his quill, the night before was
riven with protests. A blazing comet was seen in the sky,
the stars dripped blood and a screech owl was heard in the
woods around the village. Strange beasts appeared, plodding
through the night: men with the heads of dogs; ghostly hunters
speeding through the trees. Black Vaughan and his demon
riders pounded along moonlit trackways. An angel perched
on the spire of the church and, in the graveyard, ghosts were
seen, their grey empty shapes moving amongst the tombstones
and lichen-covered crosses. Strange knockings were made on
doors. The patter of invisible feet was heard in passageways.
When the sun rose, Tenebral was bathed in a fiery reddish
glow of Hell.

Of course these were legends. The arrest of the hermit
was a simple, even pathetic affair. Matthias, forbidden to
leave the house, had spent the previous evening avoiding
both his father and mother as well as the sinister, chilling
presence of the Preacher. The men of the village, armed to
the teeth, with arbalests, longbows, spears, hatchets, dirks
and daggers, marched towards Tenebral like a phalanx across
a battlefield. The hermit was waiting: standing under the
ruined lych-gate, he did not struggle when they bound his
hands. Some of the younger men beat him with sticks and
drew blood from his nose and mouth yet he offered no
objection. They tied the other end of the rope to Fulcher's
great horse and dragged him like a sack of dirt into the
village.

The Preacher was in charge. Parson Osbert bleated about
compassion and the rights of the prisoner but the peasants'

blood was up: they were determined to try this hermit for his life.

Christina did not come down that morning but stayed in bed. Matthias heard the uproar as the men dragged the hermit into the nave of the church. He slipped out of the house and joined the women and children of the village as they thronged the church, eagerly awaiting the trial. A jury was empanelled, twelve good men and true symbolising the apostles who followed Christ. There was, however, nothing Christlike about the Preacher. Parson Osbert could only stand flailing his hands, bemoaning the violence of his parishioners. The Preacher acted as both judge and prosecutor. The jury sat on the benches facing each other across the nave. The prisoner was bound to a pillar whilst the Preacher dominated the proceedings from the pulpit. Walter Mapp the scrivener had a small table brought from the sacristy as he would act as clerk. He pompously laid out the parchment, ink horns, quills, pumice stone and the keen little knife which would keep his pen sharp.

The Preacher clapped his hands three times.

'*Vox populi, vox Dei!*' he intoned. 'The voice of the people is the voice of God!' He pointed to a vivid scene painted on the church wall: Christ in Judgment at the parousia, the last day, dividing the people into sheep and goats. 'Christ is our witness,' the Preacher began. 'We are here in the nave of the church to try this man for the crimes of witchcraft, devilish practices and murder. What say ye?'

A roar like the howl of some great beast filled the church. Men, women and children stamped their feet and held their hands out, a sign they always used in the manor court when petitioning for justice.

'What is your name?' the Preacher demanded.

'What is yours?' the hermit coolly replied, bringing back his head.

The Preacher looked nonplussed. 'My name is not your business!'

'Then neither is mine yours!' the hermit retorted.

The Preacher, his face flushed with anger, looked down at the scrivener. 'Take careful note of what the prisoner says.'

'I am glad you will,' the hermit replied, 'for the record will condemn you, your own words and actions.'

95

The Preacher drew himself up. He was disconcerted by the cool mockery in the hermit's voice.

'What do you mean?' The Preacher could have bitten his tongue out.

'By what authority do you try me?' the hermit demanded. 'You are not a member of this village. You are not a tenant of the manor. You hold no warrant either from the Crown or the Church. So, by what authority do you try me? By what right do you hold this court? What warrant gives you the role of judge and prosecutor?'

A murmur of approval greeted the hermit's words. The villagers peered anxiously at each other, then at the Preacher. They accepted the power of the prisoner's words. The villagers had a reverential awe of the written word, the sealed warrant, the rites and ancient customs. More importantly, what would Baron Sanguis say when he returned? Manor lords were very jealous about their rights.

The Preacher in the pulpit was also concerned. Unless he reasserted his authority, these proceedings would end like some mummers' farce. He dug into his wallet and drew out a scroll of parchment, dark and greasy with age. He unrolled this, holding it up so the villagers could see the indentations down the side and especially the great purple blob of wax at the bottom, an official seal.

The villagers sighed with relief.

'What is that?' the hermit mocked.

'The warrant of Holy Mother Church!' the Preacher snapped. 'Permission from the great Order of the Hospital to preach God's words, extirpate heresy and bring wrongdoers to justice.'

'It has no authority here,' the hermit declared.

'Hasn't it?' the Preacher replied silkily.

He came down the steps of the pulpit. He now realised standing there was a mistake. Too aloof, too distant from the people he wished to manage. The Preacher handed his warrant to the scrivener, who studied it carefully and nodded wisely.

'It has the authority of Holy Mother Church,' the scrivener lied.

'Then why am I bound?' The hermit seemed determined to fight the Preacher every step of the way.

The Preacher nodded and gestured at Simon the reeve.

He must not allow the prisoner too much sympathy. The cords were cut. The hermit, rubbing his wrists and flexing his arms, walked into the centre of the nave. Matthias, who had managed to worm his way to the front of the crowd, squatted open-mouthed. The hermit caught his eye, smiled faintly and winked.

'I accuse you,' the Preacher decided to waste no more time, 'of the murder of Edith, daughter of Fulcher the blacksmith!'

'What proof do you have?'

'So, you don't deny it?'

The Preacher now walked up and down, more intent on the parishioners than the prisoner.

'You have accused me of a crime,' the hermit retorted. 'And I ask you for the proof. If I see the proof then I will reply.'

The Preacher decided to shift his ground, to move on to other cases, only to receive the same incisive reply. Matthias stared at his father but Parson Osbert, his face haggard, shoulders drooping, had lost all control over the proceedings. He sat on the steps of the small Lady Chapel, eyes down, refusing to lift his head. For the first time ever, Matthias felt ashamed, scornful of his father's cowardice before this stranger. Now and again the Preacher would look to the priest for assistance but there was none.

The Preacher, fingers to his lips, walked up and down, silent for a while: this was not going the way he wanted it. The hermit, instead of protesting his innocence, kept bringing his questions back to matters of legal principle, evidence, witnesses. The Preacher realised that, indeed, the hermit knew more of the law then he did. What, therefore, had Prior Sir Raymond Grandison advised? He paused in his pacing.

'You ask about rights and evidence,' he snapped. 'Are you a true son of Holy Mother Church?'

'It is up to you,' the hermit replied, 'to produce evidence that I am not.'

'Recite the Creed!' the Preacher snapped.

The hermit turned to face the villagers.

'Credo in Unum Deum, Patrem omnipotentem, factorem caeli et terrae.'

The Preacher made a cutting movement with his hand.

That was a mistake, he realised. The hermit had launched into the Nicene Creed, which was always intoned in Latin every Sunday by their priest: the Church's eternal hymn of belief to the Trinity, to the Incarnate God and to the Church.

'You don't pray,' the Preacher taunted.

'How do you know that?' the hermit replied.

'You consort with lewd women.'

'I didn't know there were any in Sutton Courteny,' came the quick reply, causing a ripple of mirth amongst the villagers. 'This is Sutton Courteny,' the hermit continued smoothly, 'not St Paul's churchyard.'

The Preacher stopped his pacing. He tried to hide his confusion. He glanced quickly at the hermit. His opponent's eyes mocked him: I know you, his gaze said, your secret sins, your weakness for soft flesh, for the pleasures of the bed.

The Preacher swallowed hard and glanced quickly at the jurors. He did not like what he saw: not one of them would meet his eye. Two or three of them were shuffling their feet. The Preacher went to the mouth of the sanctuary screen and stared at the crucifix, then at the red lamp glowing beneath the pyx which contained the Blessed Sacrament. The Preacher recalled the words of Sir Raymond. He cursed his own impetuosity as he watched the flickering red lamp.

'Do you go to church, hermit?' he asked, not turning round.

'I live in one,' the prisoner replied, causing a fresh outbreak of laughter.

'Do you attend Mass?' the Preacher continued. 'Do you take the Sacrament?'

Without even looking round, the Preacher knew he had hit his mark. For the first time the hermit was silent.

'Well? Well?' The Preacher walked back, arms folded. 'A hermit who lives in a church, who constantly asks for evidence for this and evidence for that. Do you take the body and blood of Christ?'

The hermit was staring at the floor.

'Well, do you?'

'I am unworthy.'

'In the eyes of God we all are,' the Preacher replied tersely. 'But the Church encourages the faithful to eat the sacred species. Why don't you?'

'I have answered that question. I will say no more.'

The Preacher stared at the villagers, walking slowly towards them, arms raised.

'Belief in the Eucharist,' he declared, 'is the heart of our faith. Moreover, the prisoner talks about law. It is an ancient custom that a man can prove his innocence by partaking of the Body and Blood of Our Lord. In the time of King Edward the Confessor, the traitorous Earl Godwin, being offered the host, choked and died. I now appeal,' his voice rose, 'to Heaven!'

And, swinging on his heel, the Preacher strode into the sanctuary. He ignored the protests of Parson Osbert and the murmur from the villagers. He took down the pyx, placed it on the altar and genuflected. He opened it, took out the host and walked purposefully towards the prisoner.

'*Ecce Corpus Christi!*' he intoned.

The prisoner turned his head away.

'Behold the Body of Christ!' the Preacher repeated. He turned to John the bailiff. 'Take some men, seize him, open his mouth!'

'You cannot do this,' the hermit protested. 'It is against God's law to force the host upon any man!'

'He speaks the truth.' Parson Osbert got to his feet, his hands hanging by his side. He had been rubbing his eyes until they were red-rimmed. 'Enough is enough,' he whispered to the Preacher. 'If he will not partake, he shall not partake, that is the law of the Church. If you press him further it will be a blasphemous sacrilege.'

The Preacher glared down the church. The victory was his. He returned the host to the pyx and walked back into the nave. He stopped before the jurors.

'How do you find him?'

'Guilty.'

'And you?'

'Guilty.'

The other ten replied the same.

'And how do you find him?' he appealed to the congregation.

'Guilty! Guilty! Guilty!'

The chant rose, echoing round the church. The Preacher clapped his hands.

'And what sentence?'

'Death by fire!'

The response came loud and clear, men stamping their feet as they repeated the words, relishing the sombre threat of their verdict.

Matthias felt cold, stricken to the heart. He could not believe what was happening. The Preacher, his lips curled in a sneer, turned towards the hermit.

'Do you have anything to say?'

'Yes.' The hermit's face was pale but he held himself upright, head erect. He walked towards the villagers. 'You have condemned me without evidence. Let me remind you – yes, I came here eight years ago. And, since my first arrival to this moment, has not Sutton Courteny been spared? No soldiers, pillaging or burning? Your crops have been rich and plentiful? Your cattle grown fat?'

The villagers stared back.

'Fulcher the blacksmith, are not your profits so great that you are planning to build a better house? And look to provide a good marriage dowry for your remaining daughters? Simon the reeve, do you not have plans to purchase more meadow land? Even Baron Sanguis is thinking of allowing you to be a partner in the profits from his sheep. John the bailiff, Fulke the tanner, Watkin the tiler, have not your businesses prospered? Joscelyn, your beer and ale is now sold as far afield as Stroud and Gloucester, is it not?'

The villagers heard him out. One or two of them were nodding, others stared narrow-eyed. They could not understand how the hermit knew so much about their affairs yet he spoke the truth. In the last eight years Sutton Courteny had prospered and become the envy of its neighbours. No war, no famine, no pestilence.

'And you?' The hermit spun on his heel and pointed to the scrivener. Matthias caught a look of venom in his friend's eyes. 'Are not your storerooms full of good hides? Do you not have a lucrative trade with the scriptorium at Tewkesbury Abbey?'

The hermit walked closer. The scrivener, quill raised, was fearful at how this man's eyes seemed to search his very soul.

'Plenty of money,' the hermit declared in a loud whisper. 'The joys of the tavern, the bodies of lithe young women thrashing beneath you.' He wiped the spittle from the corner of his mouth. 'But even that does not satisfy you!'

'You have proved your own witchcraft,' the Preacher intervened, fearful of the hold this man might have over the villagers.

'No, sir. You have proved it!'

The Preacher refused to answer but shouted at the villagers, 'Is there anyone here who will speak for him?'

A deathly silence.

'I ask you now, before God, is there any man, woman or child who will speak for the prisoner?'

'I will!'

The words were out of Matthias' mouth before he could stop them. He was on his feet, walking forward. His father, wringing his hands, just shook his head. Matthias didn't care. He didn't like the Preacher. He felt sorry for the hermit – like when he and the other children gathered here in the church to study their hornbooks, would go out into the cemetery and play a game: 'Who will play with him?' 'Or who will play with her?' Matthias always felt sorry for the boy or girl left alone. It was no different now. He walked over and looked up at the hermit. His friend gazed back, the tears rolling down his cheeks.

'*Oh, Creatura bona atque parva!*' he whispered. 'Brave little man!'

'You are a child,' the Preacher declared.

'He was kind,' Matthias replied. 'He could hold doves and knows the names of flowers. He showed me young fox cubs, he caught a rabbit and roasted it.'

Matthias blushed at the laughter from the villagers.

'It's true! It's true!' he cried.

He stamped his foot and the Preacher, mimicking him, stamped his. The villagers burst into laughter. Matthias, face burning red, fled the church, across the cemetery and into his house. He ran up the stairs and burst into his mother's room. She was lying on the small four-poster bed, face buried in the bolsters. He ran up, tugging at her hand.

'Mother, they are going to take him out and burn him!'

Christina lifted her sleep-laden face from the bolsters. Matthias could see she had been crying.

'It's finished,' she whispered. 'There's nothing you can do. May God help us all!'

She let his hand drop and fell back on the bolsters, staring at the blue and gold tester over the bed.

'Did your father speak?'

'Some.' Matthias bit back the insults he felt. 'It made no difference.'

He walked slowly out of the chamber, closing the door silently behind him, and went down the rickety stairs. He sat for a while poking the cold ash in the fireplace with a stick. From the cemetery came the shouts and cries of the villagers. The door opened and his father came down the passageway. Matthias did not look up. He sat jabbing at the ash, wishing it were the Preacher's face.

'They've put him in the death house,' Parson Osbert said. 'The Preacher and others are guarding him. They . . .' Parson Osbert licked his dry lips. 'He says sentence must be carried out by dusk. Fulcher and the rest, they are piling brushwood around the bear-baiting post. You know,' he continued in a matter-of-fact voice, 'it's near the gallows. Matthias?'

The boy kept jabbing at the ash. His father came and knelt beside him.

'Matthias, why did you speak?'

His son turned to him. Parson Osbert had grown old that morning: cheeks sagging, eyes constantly blinking.

'I don't know,' Matthias replied.

'He wants to see us,' his father continued. 'He made that last request: to see me, you and Christina before he died.'

'I thought he would.'

Parson Osbert whirled round. Christina stood in the doorway, a woollen coverlet round her shoulders.

'I thought he would,' she repeated.

'Christina, are you well?'

The parson went across and pressed his wife's hands: they were lifeless and cold like those of a corpse. Her face had an unhealthy pallor. Her hair, usually so lustrous, now hung lank and untidy.

'You don't have to see him,' Parson Osbert said.

'He's going to die, isn't he? We'll take him some wine, some bread.' She went like a dreamwalker back up the stairs.

Parson Osbert went across to the small podium where the

church missal was put. He opened this, pretending to study the gospel from the Mass of the day. He felt sick, anxious about the Preacher's actions. Matters had proceeded far too fast. On his return, Baron Sanguis would not be pleased.

Christina came back. She'd put a dress over her linen shift, tied her hair back and covered it with a veil, wooden sandals on her feet. She took a small jug of wine from the buttery, some manchet loaves and, without saying a word, walked out of the house. Parson Osbert and Matthias hurried after her. The scene in the cemetery was like that of an armed camp. Women and children sat on the grass or on fallen headstones sharing out the food they had brought. Their menfolk strutted up and down, boldly showing off their rusty swords, daggers and spears and bent shields. A group of young men, under the direction of the Preacher, stood on guard outside the stone death house. As they approached, the Preacher held his hand up but Parson Osbert had regained his courage.

'This is my church! This is my cemetery!' he declared. 'I must protest at the proceedings: the prisoner needs some spiritual comfort.'

The Preacher shrugged and stepped back. One of the young men pulled back the bolts. Parson Osbert stooped and went in. He wasn't long and came out shaking his head. Christina took the bread and wine in. Matthias looked around the cemetery. He saw a wild rose bush and, using his small dagger, cut a shoot off. The rose was full-blown, still wet from the morning dew. The door to the death house was flung open; Christina, her face soaked with tears, came out. She brushed by her husband and ran across the cemetery.

'You'd best go in, boy,' Parson Osbert whispered. 'But don't be long.'

'Will the lad be safe?' a villager asked.

'If the hermit wished to hurt him,' Osbert snapped, 'he would have done so already.'

The death house was dark. Matthias waited until the door slammed behind him, then he ran across. The hermit, sitting in the corner, embraced him warmly.

'You spoke for me, Matthias,' he murmured. 'You spoke for me!'

The boy gave him the rose. 'I thought you'd like this. It's not as good as the one you drew in the church.'

The hermit took the rose. He laid it on the ground and, moving like a cat, he went and knelt before the boy.

'Do not cry for me, Matthias. Promise me you won't cry for me. Now go!'

The boy stared at him in puzzlement.

'Go on!' the hermit smiled. 'Don't worry, Matthias. Death is never an end to anything. Please! They will listen at the door. Please go! They'll only become suspicious.'

Matthias left. His father had also gone. Someone said he was in the church. Matthias groaned: some of the village boys were coming towards him. They would only tease and taunt him about what had happened so, like a rabbit, he scuttled amongst the gravestones, climbed the cemetery wall and ran to the other end of the village. Here the lane snaked past the hedgerows towards the great road south to Bristol.

For a while Matthias hid in a ditch, thinking about what had happened. Now and again he would look at the sky and notice the black smoke rising like a plume from the village. He felt hungry so he stole back to his house. The kitchen was untidy, the platters unwashed, there was no sign of his parents.

Matthias ate some salted bacon and bread from the buttery then went into the cemetery. The place was now empty, the door to the death house flung open. Matthias walked into the village. He caught the smell of wood smoke and something else, like fat boiling over the fire. He turned the corner and stared in horror down the high street. Fulcher had done his job well. The old bear-baiting post had been taken out and put on a small makeshift platform. The hermit had been lashed to this, dry brushwood piled high around: the flames had already caught hold. As Matthias pushed his way through the crowd, he could just make out the hermit's face behind the wall of flame. Yet something was wrong. The fire roared but the prisoner bound to the stake did not squirm or cry out. The villagers, too, were silent.

'Is he dead?' someone asked.

'Has he fainted?'

Matthias sniffed, wrinkling his nose. He could not understand it: the fire must have caught the hermit's body.

'Has he swooned?' someone shouted.

As if in answer, the hermit started to sing, his voice loud and clear through the flames. A chill swept through the assembled villagers. Men who had served in the King's wars and seen others die in different horrible ways, stared aghast. The flames roared higher, hiding the hermit's face. Still the song was sung, the words clear and full on the air: at first in French, '*La Rose du Paradis*', the second verse in English. The voice was strong and vibrant like a man sitting on a summer afternoon carolling his heart out. Some of the villagers ran away. Others crossed themselves. A few fell on their knees. The singing died away. The stench of burning flesh became unbearable. Matthias, whose shoulder had been gripped by Joscelyn the taverner, broke free and fled up an alleyway.

Matthias ran blindly, not stopping till he found himself in the woods. He crouched at the foot of a tree, then made his way along the trackway to Tenebral. He went into the church. The sanctuary was full of sad reminders of his friend: a piece of leather, scraps of bone and meat from his cooking. Any meagre possessions had already been stolen by the villagers. Matthias gazed in awe at the beautiful rose painted on the wall: the runes, the strange marks beneath, had grown in number, as if the hermit had spent his last night etching out these signs. Matthias walked slowly out on to the porchway. The breeze caught his face. He heard the whisper: '*Oh Creatura, bona atque parva!*'

He stared around, no one was there.

Matthias left the church, vowing he would never return, and hastened along the trackway. He turned the corner and almost ran into the Preacher who, with his scrip on his back and a stout ash pole in one hand, was striding along.

'Murderer!' the boy screamed.

The Preacher hawked and spat, narrowly missing Matthias' face.

'Your friend is dead. I am off to Tewkesbury where the good brothers will give me sustenance!'

Matthias made an obscene gesture at the Preacher's receding back. The boy didn't know what it meant but he had seen the men at the Hungry Man make it when tax collectors or royal purveyors were about. Matthias hoped the Preacher would turn but the man strode round the bend of the trackway.

By the time Matthias returned to the village, the fire was out. The platform against the bear-baiting post had crumbled under the searing heat. Simon the reeve was piling the ash into one great mound.

'We'll throw it into one of the cesspits,' he declared, not lifting his face.

Matthias went across to the grassy verge. He picked some of the wild flowers growing there and tossed them on the top of the burning ash. The flowers began to scorch. Matthias thought of throwing on some more: he glimpsed a bone, yellow and blackened amongst the cinders, so he walked away.

The Hungry Man was full of customers, the villagers carousing, celebrating as if they had won a great victory, drinking deeply of the taverner's newly brewed ale, eager to forget the memories of the day. Matthias spied his father amongst them, his face flushed, eyes glittering. Parson Osbert beckoned his son over. Matthias glared back, then hurried on.

The following evening Thurston the tinker and his pretty wife, Mariotta, left the town of Tewkesbury. Their small barrow was full of scraps, pieces of armour and other items they had collected after the battle. Mariotta pulled the cart, the ropes biting into her shoulders, whilst her husband, full of ale, staggered beside her. Mariotta didn't mind. The day had been a prosperous one. They could take the armour to a forge, have it beaten flat and make a good profit. Mariotta was pleased to be out of the town. The corpses of those killed in the battle were now laid out on the steps of the churches, naked as white worms. Around the town, corpses hung from the signs of inns or on the gallows near the market cross, whilst severed heads adorned the pikes above the gates.

'The place stank of death,' Mariotta declared, stopping to rest her shoulders. She smoothed down her brown smock. She admired the new sandals on her dusty feet, then glanced sideways at her husband. She had bought these when he had been asleep, snoring his head off in an outhouse. That young squire, who had caught her eye in the tavern, had been ever so grateful. Mariotta closed her eyes. Thank God, her red-faced, irascible husband never discovered the secret source of such wealth. He, however, was now swaying on his feet, burping loudly, patting his stomach.

'We'd best stop for the night,' Mariotta declared.

Her husband went to release the large fardel he carried on his back.

'Not here,' Mariotta scolded.

She pushed him on and, grabbing the ropes, pulled the barrow. Further up the lane, Mariotta espied a gap in the hedge: sheep grazed in a meadow which ran down to a stream glinting invitingly in the rays of the setting sun. Cursing Thurston under her breath, Mariotta pulled her barrow into the meadow; he staggering after her. The sheep hardly lifted their heads. Mariotta found a suitable place to camp and went off amongst the trees looking for kindling. Thurston sat, head drooping, eyes heavy. He heard a sound and got up. He felt cold.

'Mariotta!' he called. Getting no answer, he released the burden on his back and staggered into the trees. 'Mariotta!' he yelled. 'Where are you?'

Suddenly the ground dipped. Thurston found himself on the rim of a small dell. He couldn't understand what he saw. Mariotta was lying on the grass, head turned away. A figure crouched over her. The figure moved. Mariotta's throat was all gashed. Thurston screamed and ran towards her. The squire Mariotta had met turned and poor Thurston ran straight on to the dagger he held.

7

The news of Thurston and Mariotta's murder, as well as others in the wooded, secret places along the River Severn, seeped into Sutton Courteny. It chilled the hearts of those involved in the hermit's death. In the corners of the Hungry Man people began to whisper how they had been responsible for spilling innocent blood. Neighbours drew apart. Friendships failed and a sense of guilt haunted the village. Parson Osbert, although many said his hands were clean of any man's blood, only felt more guilty. Not that he had done anything wrong, but that he had failed to do anything right.

The gossips and the whisperers were quick to point out how God's hand seemed to have turned against the village. Christina, Parson Osbert's woman, fell ill. She kept to her bed, a pale ghost of her former self. Fulcher the blacksmith was kicked in the groin by a horse and, for days, his smithy lay cold at a time when everyone wanted to have their horses tended. Simon the reeve was gored by a bull, not grievously, but enough to put him ill in bed so he could lie and reflect on what he had done. John the bailiff was no more fortunate: he was attacked by outlaws, soldiers from the defeated Lancastrian army, who badly mauled him. Joscelyn the taverner became a little too fond of the ale he sold: one night there was a fire in his cellar which destroyed his best madeira sack, mead and ale. Other mishaps occurred. The sun proved very strong; the crops began to burn, mysterious fires being started in the long meadow and in other places around the village. Tempers became short. Knives were drawn in the fields, in the tavern and even, on one occasion, outside the church.

A violent thunderstorm broke at the beginning of June. Lightning, jagged bolts of fire from heaven, split trees and fired a hay rick. The heavy rains afterwards beat down the corn and turned the fields, ripe for harvest, into a soggy mess. Oh yes, the gossips muttered, God's vengeance was making itself felt. Matters were not helped by young girls having dreams of devils coming out of the earth; by goblins and elves turning the milk sour; whilst a strange howling was heard from the woods at night which frightened the children and stampeded the cattle and sheep.

Worse was to come. In the second week of June, Baron Sanguis and his hatchet-faced son returned from the King's war on the eastern shores. The Manor Lord rode through the village, his standard-bearer going before him, his son a few paces behind. Following in their dust, retinues of armed men, not to mention the clerks, bailiffs and scriveners from Baron Sanguis' household. The Manor Lord, with his iron-grey hair and hard, sunburnt face, looked neither to the left nor the right. Dressed in his half-armour, despite the heat, and slouched in the high saddle of his destrier, Baron Sanguis progressed like a conquering hero along the village high street.

The villagers gathered at the hanging stone, brought presents to greet their lord. Baron Sanguis rode on, not even deigning to look, and the villagers' hearts sank: Sanguis knew that something dreadful had happened during his absence. The manor lay to the north-west of the village, a sprawling, moated mansion protected by its high curtain wall, a small village in itself. Baron Sanguis had been away since the previous autumn and, on his return, the manor quickened into life. Other retainers followed him, carts full of possessions. For three days there was silence, then Sanguis' clerks and bailiffs moved into the village. Monies were owed: tolls were due: levies to be raised on this or that. Who had been picking apples from Baron Sanguis' orchards? Who had allowed pigs to forage in his woods? And what about the tithes owing to the Church? And were the villagers prepared, according to ancient custom, to work this autumn in the Manor Lord's fields? What marriages had taken place? What births? Had all dues been paid? The flint-eyed clerks knew their master's rights, as they moved from house to house with quill, ink horn and the manor accounts.

Parson Osbert stayed in his house, Matthias with him. A great chasm had grown up between the boy and his father since the hermit's death. They hardly ever talked. The priest seemed to have caught some of his wife's languid torpidity and, if it hadn't been for Blanche, a merry-eyed widow from the village, clothes would not have been washed, food cooked or the house cleaned. Christina was now a recluse, lying in her bed, only eating when forced by her husband or Blanche. She hardly talked but sat staring like a madcap, lips moving wordlessly, lost in her own private hell.

Now Baron Sanguis had returned, Parson Osbert's fears only increased. On the Sunday, two weeks after the Baron's return, the summons came. Parson Osbert made a special effort.

'Soon it will be the feast of Corpus Christi,' he announced, smiling at Matthias. 'So, I might as well bathe and change my clothes for that, as well as meeting Baron Sanguis.'

He did so, carefully shaving his face, even rubbing a little oil into his thinning hair.

'Will you go with me, Matthias?' Parson Osbert's face was almost pleading.

'Of course, Father,' the boy dutifully replied.

Parson Osbert sighed with relief. Matthias knew the reason why. For some strange reason Baron Sanguis had a liking for the priest's son. If he was present, perhaps the Manor Lord's fury might be curtailed.

By the time they entered the great hall of the manor, Parson Osbert was in a state of fright: he clasped Matthias' hands so tightly the boy winced in pain. The priest stood inside the double doors of the hall. The Manor Lord sat behind the great table on the dais at the far end. His face was hidden by the great, ornate silver saltcellar. The tables down either side of the hall were empty; the Baron sat in solemn majesty: his one and only son, Robert, on his right, seneschal Taldo on his left. Parson Osbert could see that his lord had profited in his support of the Yorkists. Glaziers had put glass in the windows on each side of the hall – these gleamed like freshly fallen water in the bright sunlight. The walls had been freshly washed in pink paint. The banners which hung from the rafters glowed in their brilliant colours, whilst the shields and weapons which decorated the walls had all been newly cleaned and painted.

'You'd best come forward!' Baron Sanguis boomed.

The priest, still clutching Matthias' hand, walked quickly

up the hall. He felt strange. There were no rushes but thick Turkey carpets on the floor, which deadened any sound. Parson Osbert felt as if he were walking in his sleep. If that was the case, he thought, as he paused before the dais and bowed, then Baron Sanguis was a nightmare. The Manor Lord sat erect in his high-backed chair, elbows resting on its arms: his hair had been freshly cut, shorn well above the ears, but this only emphasised the harshness of his face: black-pebble eyes and a nose which seemed to cut the air. The Baron smoothed his long, grey moustache, which fell at least two inches beneath his chin. He played with the rings on his fingers or tapped the gold medal which hung on a silver chain round his neck. His son, attired like his father, gazed just as bleakly, though seneschal Taldo, a friend of the priest, smiled weakly and raised his eyes heavenwards. Baron Sanguis looked up at the banner bearing his arms, three black crows on a golden field.

'My son carried a banner like that at Barnet.' His voice rose. 'When I was fighting for my king and lord!'

Parson Osbert bowed. 'Sir Henry, I am so pleased you have returned safe and sound, rightfully covered in honours and glory.'

'Yet, while I'm gone—' the Manor Lord was now leaning across the table – 'while I'm gone,' he bellowed, 'my villagers take rights unto themselves, acting like the Manor Lord! Seigneurs of the soil, are they?' He banged the table with his fist. 'By what right,' he shouted, 'did they hold a court in your church and condemn a man to death? By what right did they lay claim to the power of the axe, the tumbrel and the rope? Did you know that, according to the law, they and you have committed murder? You could all hang!'

'My father didn't agree with it!' Matthias spoke up.

Baron Sanguis turned his head and breathed in deeply, nostrils flaring. His face softened and his hand went out as if he wanted to stroke Matthias' head. Even Robert smiled, whilst Taldo beamed, relieved at the break in the tension.

'My father didn't agree to anything!' Matthias repeated. 'It was the Preacher!'

'You!' Baron Sanguis jabbed a finger in mock anger at Matthias. 'You should be a soldier, a knight!'

Parson Osbert closed his eyes and quickly thanked God

that he had brought Matthias. Baron Sanguis liked to act the bully but the priest knew that he had a good heart and could be quickly mollified. The Manor Lord dug into his purse and pushed some pennies across the table.

'That's for you, boy,' he declared. 'Buy some sweetmeats. Ah,' he waved his hand, 'I know, I know, I know, you, Parson Osbert, objected and your boy was the only one who had the courage to speak up.' He pulled a face. 'So stop quivering!' He pointed to the end of the table. 'Sit down. Let's have some wine.' He smiled at Matthias. 'The boy can have a cup of apple juice.' His voice fell to a whisper. 'It's been in the cellar, it's cold and strong so, not too much.'

Once they were settled, Parson Osbert told his lord exactly what had happened. The Manor Lord heard him out, steepling his fingers on the table, now and again whispering to his son. Robert always gave a curt reply. When Osbert had finished, he sat sipping the white wine which Taldo had served. The Manor Lord beat his fist on the table as if it were a drum.

'This is what I've decided, priest. The villagers will pay a fine of twenty shillings. You will not pay it. I have also sent a messenger to London. I have friends.' He preened himself. 'At court, my Lord of Hastings.'

Parson Osbert bowed. Hastings was the King's personal friend. After the royal brothers, George and Richard, he was one of the most powerful men in the kingdom.

'I have asked him to send down a royal clerk, someone to investigate this business. The real culprit is the Preacher.' Baron Sanguis ticked the points off on his finger. 'He had no right to hold a court. He had no right to condemn.' His hands fell away. 'And, for all we know, boy, the Preacher himself could be the assassin?'

Matthias' heart leapt with joy. For the first time since the hermit's death, he smiled. He also forgot Baron Sanguis' advice, drank his apple juice a little too fast and had to be carried home by his father.

Rahere, the royal clerk, swaggered down the King's Steps at Westminster and into the waiting barge. The wherrymen, dressed in the royal livery, took one look at the chancery ring on his left hand and the red sealed warrant in the other and ushered him to the cushioned seat in the stern as if he were the King himself. Royal clerks ruled the roost. They were the King's lawyers, his money-men, the searchers out of his prerogative. They had the power of the Chancery and, on their advice, a man rose or fell. This clerk looked the part: tall, elegantly dressed in a soft, woollen tunic, hose of the same colour and texture and high-heeled morocco boots, he gathered his cloak about him and lounged in the stern. Now and again he'd turn his head to study a Spanish caravel, a two-masted ship of the Hanse or the long, wolflike galleys from Venice as they made their way up and down the Thames.

Rahere was young and ambitious; with his black-raven hair, smooth, olive-skinned face and lustrous eyes, he had even caught the attention of the Queen, Elizabeth Woodville. Rahere was one of her henchmen, being sent hither and thither on royal business. Now he had received a fresh charge. He had been appointed the King's Commissioner in the Western Shires, with powers of life and death. He was to search out the person responsible for the dreadful murders which had been committed outside Tewkesbury and bring the culprit to summary justice.

Rahere played with the hem of his pure wool cloak, deftly brushing off some crumbs which were clinging to his thick, burgundy-coloured tunic. I will act the part, he thought. I will take the swiftest, sleekest horse and sumpter pony from the royal stables and ride through the shires like a King's Justice. Rahere smiled. Like a King's Justice! He would *be* the King's Justice, girt with sword and carrying a royal pennant. Every knee would have to bow.

Rahere looked up at the sky. The summer sun was beginning to set. He would celebrate his good fortune in Southwark with a tasty meal; good wine, venison soaked in claret – and afterwards? Beneath his cloak, Rahere's hand stole to his groin and plucked at his protuberant codpiece. A fresh whore from one of the stews: some young palfrey he could strip, mount and ride through the night. A young girl who would be fresh and quick beneath him. Rahere smacked his lips.

'You'd best pull harder!' he snapped.

The wherrymen bent over their oars, quietly cursing this pompous young lord. Their barge turned, making its way through the little bumboats which always thronged around

113

the great ships, offering the sailors everything: fruit, almonds, sweetmeats, roasted chicken, apples, pears and, if the officers didn't mind, some of the painted whores who always paid to tout their services from such boats. Rahere studied these surreptitiously. Now and again he'd turn to admire one of the King's cogs; the royal men-of-war beginning to assemble in the Thames. Now the war was over, Edward of England was determined to teach the French not to support his enemies.

At last the royal wherry reached Southwark, just between the inn called the Bishop of Winchester and the Priory of St Mary Overy. To his left, Rahere could see the mass of London Bridge and the long, jutting poles bearing the severed heads of Lancastrian traitors. Rahere smiled. That was what was so good about being a clerk. Whoever won, men like himself were always valued: scholars from the Halls of Oxford or Cambridge who knew the law and the secrets of the Chancery. Rahere tossed a coin and went up the water-soaked steps and into the crowds milling along the quayside.

Rahere loved Southwark, thronged with every villain under the sun: cutthroats, naps, foists, apple-squires and a glorious profusion of whores of every age offering all forms of delicacies for a young lord like himself. He arrogantly pushed his way through them and into the Grey Goose tavern. The landlord and tapsters greeted him like a prince. They knew how he liked his dishes served: venison cooked though left pink in the middle; the sauce had to be thick and full of mushrooms and onions. No watered wine or vineyard dregs but the best Gascony.

Rahere was shown to his table next to the window. His meal was served piping hot, not on a dirty trencher but clean pewter plates with a special horn spoon in a leather purse.

Rahere ate well and drank deeply. He was staring out over the garden, picking at his teeth, when he heard soft steps. He turned and his wine-filled belly clenched in excitement. The young woman was ravishingly beautiful, hair as red as a burning flame, skin like alabaster, light-green eyes slanted at the corners. Her rosebud mouth parted in a half-smile . . .

Matthias sat in the ruined sanctuary of Tenebral church. He gazed at the rose painted on the wall and let the tears stream down his cheeks. Above him a wood pigeon cooed, breaking the silence of the summer afternoon. Matthias felt truly alone. At that moment, he realised how, apart from the hermit, he always had been by himself. As long as he could remember he had been only tolerated by the village children. They resented his knowledge of letters, his ability to read his hornbook. Matthias didn't recognise that. He just felt their cruelty, their dismissive taunts as the 'priest's brat'. At home it had been no different. His father and mother were engrossed in themselves. Sometimes he felt they were embarrassed by him. His father was kind and generous but Christina was aloof; so much so that in his private dreams and games, Matthias considered her a fairy-tale princess locked up in an ivory tower. The hermit had been different: his friendship had been the first time Matthias had ever experienced such closeness. Now he was gone, everything was changing, including himself. Matthias was upset, yet he felt stronger whilst his parents seemed more like strangers. Christina had now totally drawn into herself whilst his father fumbled like an old man. Despite their visit to Baron Sanguis ten days ago, the parson had not improved whilst matters in the village went from bad to worse.

Sigherd, a lonely crofter who owned two messuages of land, became drunk and, one night, stumbled into the millpond where he had drowned. Peterlinus, one of the baker's sons, had fallen from a tree and broken an arm. An outlaw band had crossed the Severn and were now plaguing travellers and journeymen on the Sutton Courteny road. Despite the best efforts of Baron Sanguis, this small band of wolf's-heads were driving journeymen and merchants away from the village. At night, so it was said, devils danced around Sutton Courteny. Death, astride a purple horse, had ridden slowly through the village, a death's-head helmet over its skeletal face, a huge scythe in his hand. Behind him, so rumours alleged, trailed a legion of imps to plague the villagers of Sutton Courteny.

Matthias folded his arms and pricked up his ears. He was sure he heard a horse's hooves yet no one came this way. Sometimes when he was here, particularly just before dusk, he sensed the hermit's presence, his voice calling him *Creatura bona atque parva*. Matthias had ruefully recognised this must be his own wishful longing.

He went back to contemplating the rose and reflecting on what had happened in the village over the last few days.

People knew Baron Sanguis had honoured Matthias. Now they respected, even feared him. People recalled how only the boy had spoken for the hermit. Baron Sanguis had also been affected by the ill fortune which afflicted the village. Margot, Old Bogglebow, had been found dead at the foot of the tower of the manor house. Some claimed she had slipped and broken her neck. Others claimed a devil, a great dark shape, had been hunting her for days. The demon had seized her by the neck and flung her down the steps. Baron Sanguis' carp and stew ponds had also been broken into. People pointed the finger at the wolf's-heads who, besides poaching the King's venison, were not averse to helping themselves to a fat carp or a succulent tench.

Baron Sanguis had vowed retribution but his main quarry had been the Preacher who had dared to usurp his seigneurial powers. In this he had been more successful. The Preacher had taken sanctuary with the monks at Tewkesbury where his conduct had alarmed Father Abbot. He had become witless, a madcap who kept proclaiming he had been possessed by a devil. This hadn't saved him from the Baron's vengeance. He had been dragged, a halter round his neck, through the village, and thrown into one of Baron Sanguis' dungeons. Now the villagers waited for a new arrival: a royal commissioner, armed with special powers, was coming from London to investigate the matter – a royal justiciar who would make a tally of the corpses and put the Preacher on trial.

Matthias started: that was the clop of a horse! He stole down the church and peered out. Near the lych-gate a horseman sat, tall and erect, in the shiny red leather saddle, his great cloak about him, the sword belt around his waist beautifully embroidered. The horse was a destrier, a noble-looking animal with arched neck and glossy hide. Its housing and harness were those of a great lord, the leather soft and gleaming, the buckles glittering in the sunlight. The rider was looking back at a sumpter pony piled high with possessions under a clean canvas sheet. The man dismounted, the spurs on his high-heeled leather riding boots jingling like little bells. Matthias noticed how the man's oiled black hair was tied back in a queue. He went to check his sumpter pony, lifting one of its forelegs. Matthias heard him talking quietly to the animal.

The boy, intrigued, stole out of the ruins and down the weed-filled path. The destrier snickered, its hooves pawing the earth. The sumpter pony drew back its head and brayed. Something skimmed over Matthias' head and smacked into the wall of the church behind him. He looked back but could see nothing except a puff of dust where something had hit the wall.

'You shouldn't steal up on people like that, boy!'

Matthias whirled round. The man was now standing at the lych-gate, in his hand a small arbalest. He was putting a second bolt into the groove. Matthias' heart lurched. He extended his hands.

'I'm sorry!' he shouted. 'I was hiding here. I often do. No one ever rides by here!'

The man came towards him. He moved elegantly, like a cat, fluid movements: a man certain of himself, arrogant in his power. He stopped before the boy, his dark-blue eyes studying him carefully: the arbalest cord was still pulled back, though the crossbow was held down.

'How do I know,' the man asked, 'that you are not an outlaw brat?'

'And how do I know you are not an outlaw?' Matthias retorted.

The man smiled. He gently loosed the cord, removed the bolt and put it into a small pouch on his belt. He crouched down so that his face was level with that of Matthias. A kind, handsome face; the eyes crinkled when he smiled and the smooth-shaven cheeks showed dimples, as if the man loved life but found everything slightly amusing.

'Well, if you are not an outlaw brat, who are you?' He took off his leather, gold-fringed gauntlets.

Matthias noticed the ring on his finger. It bore the arms of England. He had seen similar insignia when he had been in Tewkesbury with the hermit.

'I'm the priest's brat,' Matthias replied. 'Matthias, son of Osbert the priest at Sutton Courteny.'

The man stood up and extended his hand.

'And I am Rahere, the royal clerk.' His hand was soft and warm. He gripped Matthias' gently.

'You are the clerk?' Matthias exclaimed.

'I am the clerk,' Rahere mimicked back. 'Sent by His

Grace the King, at the request of Baron Sanguis, to carry out the King's justice.' He looked around. 'I thought I'd come by this way.' He pointed to the church. 'One of the old villages, I suppose, wiped out by the plague? And this is your hiding place?'

'No, it was the home of a friend,' Matthias replied. 'He was a hermit. He was taken prisoner and burnt as a witch by the villagers. Now Baron Sanguis has caught the man responsible.'

Rahere nodded, slapping his gauntlets against his thigh, though he gazed at the church, smiling faintly.

'And did you like the hermit?'

'He was my great friend,' Matthias replied. 'He was strange, very strange, but kind to me. I come here because I miss him.' His voice trembled. 'I am a little sad.'

Rahere crouched down again. 'You shouldn't be sad, Matthias, not on a summer's day like this.'

'He showed me foxes,' Matthias continued, his lower lip trembling. 'He did no one any harm. He used to live there.' He pointed with his thumb back over his shoulder towards the church. 'He drew a beautiful rose.'

Rahere stood up. 'And I have come to do justice for his death,' he declared, his voice harsh and low. 'So, little Matthias, the day is drawing on. Show me the path to Sutton Courteny.'

'I thought your pony was lame?' Matthias chattered as they walked back towards the lych-gate.

'Oh, just a pebble in his shoe.'

Without asking, the clerk picked Matthias up and put him on the saddle and climbed up behind him. He gathered his reins, clicked his tongue and the horse moved on, the pony trotting behind. The clerk wore a perfume, a faint fragrance. Matthias felt warm and secure, though he wondered why such a clerk should come by forest paths.

'Before I arrive anywhere,' Rahere spoke up, as if he could read Matthias' mind, 'I like to ride around, speak to people, acquaint myself with the place in which I am going to work. I learn a lot that way. So, Matthias, this ride is not free. Tell me about Sutton Courteny.'

The boy began to chatter. How his father was the priest, that Christina, his mother, was ill. About the different accidents which had occurred since the hermit's death. How he hated the Preacher. How Baron Sanguis was kind and how Bogglebow, the witch woman, had died so mysteriously.

The clerk listened. Now and again he would interrupt with a question. Matthias was so engrossed in this series of questions and answers, he hardly noticed the wolf's-heads until they were upon them. Just where the path narrowed, before it turned the corner, the outlaws, seven in number, came like shadows out of the trees. Armed with sword and dagger, they blocked the path: two carried longbows, arrows notched to the string. Their leader, dressed in dirty green, his head covered by animal skins, swaggered forward.

'A traveller and a boy.' His voice was harsh. 'Get down from your horse!'

'Stay still,' the clerk murmured to Matthias.

'We could have shot you from the forest,' the outlaw continued. He moved sideways and whistled under his breath. 'But that horse looks expensive and it's the horse we want to save, and your clothes, of course.' He laughed over his shoulder at his companions. 'Nothing like a bloody arrow wound to ruin a good shirt. So, down you get, fine sir, you and the boy. We'll take your clothes, your purse, your weapons, your horse. If you are good and do what we say, you can keep your lives.' He spread his hands. 'I am all compassion.'

'You promise our lives?' Rahere replied.

'On my mother's honour. Or rather your father's.' The outlaw laughed aloud. 'That is if you have one!'

'When I put you down,' Rahere whispered, 'run like the wind!'

He lowered Matthias gently to the ground. The boy scampered into the undergrowth. Even as he did so he heard the horse behind him neigh. He stopped and turned round. The clerk had moved with lightning speed, digging his spurs in savagely. The great war horse had leapt forward in rage, its hooves scything the air. The outlaw leader was knocked over like a twirling ninepin. The bowmen were unable to loose but now they closed. Matthias, fingers to his mouth, saw them slice the clerk's body with sword and dagger and heard the yells of expectant triumph. These faded as the clerk just turned his horse and came back. Sword raised, he struck the outlaws like an avenging angel. The horse, trained to war and quickened by the scent of blood, struck out with iron-shod hooves. One outlaw, hands to his face, staggered away screaming, the blood pumping between his fingers. Matthias stood stock-still. He had seen Baron Sanguis' mounted men practise at the tourney but never anything like this. For a short while the stillness of the forest was shattered by the scrape of steel, the cries and oaths of men locked in mortal combat.

And then it was over. The clerk still sat on his horse, face sweating, chest heaving, his sword covered in blood from tip to hilt. Five of the outlaws lay dead; one knelt whimpering, still holding his face. Another groaned in agony, twisting on the ground. The clerk nudged his horse towards them. Twice his sword was lifted, coming down in cutting scythes and the two surviving outlaws died. Rahere dismounted. He cleaned his sword on one of the outlaw's cloaks, took a water bottle from his saddle horn and splashed his hands and face. He then inspected the horses.

'They are fine,' he called over his shoulder. 'They are trained for war, Matthias. Notice how the sumpter pony stayed stock-still and how the destrier fought like a warrior.'

Rahere picked up his sword where he had placed it against a corpse, resheathed it and walked along the trackway. He pulled the small, red ribbon from his hair, shook his hair loose around his face like Matthias had seen Christina do. Then he took a comb from his wallet and began to comb his hair, all the time staring at Matthias.

'A bloody day's work, eh?'

The boy just stared at the corpses. It had happened so quickly. One minute these were living men, dangerous, now they lay scattered about like hunks of meat.

'Life and death,' the clerk declared.

'But they cut at you,' Matthias said. 'I saw them cut you with sword and dagger.'

'You probably saved my life,' Rahere replied. 'They may have been after the horse but one of them, with a spark of kindness, balked at killing a child.'

'They struck at you,' Matthias repeated.

The clerk now retied his hair at the back of his head. He brushed the dust and stains from his cloak, jerkin and hose.

'Two things, Matthias. First, if you strike at a man on a horse, your sword is going upwards: it loses a great deal of its force. Secondly,' he threw his cloak over his shoulder and pulled up his jerkin. Matthias glimpsed the bright steel mesh beneath. 'Milanese steel,' the clerk explained. 'Light as a feather but stronger than iron. Now come, boy. Let's ride in triumph to your village. I'll leave you at your house and then I'll go to Baron Sanguis. I'll tell our good lord to clear his forest paths.'

They continued on their journey. Only as they entered Sutton Courteny did Matthias remember the clerk's words: '*Run like the wind!*' That's what the hermit had always said to him.

8

The Chronicler of Tewkesbury, when he came to describe the bloody and horrific events which occurred in Sutton Courteny around the Feast of All Saints 1471, noted that the beginning of the end was the Preacher's trial in the nave of the parish church of Sutton Courteny on the feast of St Benedict. The proceedings were much different from the last time. Baron Sanguis sat enthroned in a chair placed just before the entrance to the rood screen. On his right, his grim-faced son, on his left Taldo the seneschal. In a corner, perched on a stool, quill in hand, one of his scribes. Before him a new jury had been empanelled.

The proceedings were dominated by Rahere the clerk. He stood, dressed in black from head to toe, a silver gilt war belt round his slim waist. The sword and dagger hanging there slapped threateningly against his thigh. On his black leather boots he had the affectation still to wear his spurs, which clinked and jingled at every step. The high-collared tunic with the white linen bands beneath came up just beneath his chin: his black oiled hair hung down to his shoulders. As he moved backwards and forwards, turning now and again to address Baron Sanguis, sometimes the jury, sometimes the crowd, they all watched fascinated. Matthias thought he was beautiful. The clerk reminded him of a black, languorous cat holding court over a group of mice. The women of the village gazed hot-eyed and whispered amongst themselves how this handsome young clerk from London had an eye for a pretty face and was already known for his sweet words. Rahere seemed to sense this. Like an actor in a play, he pitched his words and spun his web. At first he described himself, showing his commission on creamy-coloured parchment, the red wax still bearing clearly the imprint of the King's Great Seal. He'd reproved the villagers for taking the law into their own hands and paused to allow Baron Sanguis to announce the fine. The villagers nodded. In the circumstances, they whispered, their manor lord was being compassionate. Matthias stared at his father, crouching in the same place he had during the previous trial, on the steps of the Lady Chapel. Parson Osbert had made an effort this morning to wash, shave and change his clothing though he still looked pale and woebegone.

Rahere the clerk now took up the story again, listing the dreadful deaths which had occurred in the area. He spoke in clear English, now and again lapsing into figures of speech common in the area. Matthias could tell Baron Sanguis and his son were fascinated. At last the clerk stopped speaking and jabbed a finger towards the corpse door.

'In my view,' he proclaimed, 'the man we are about to confront is the true murderer: the spiller of innocent blood. Bring him in!'

Taldo got up and hurried to the door. A short while later the seneschal returned followed by Baron Sanguis' burly bailiffs. The Preacher, his arms pinioned, was dragged between them into the church and forced to kneel facing the villagers. Matthias stared. Was this the man who had frightened him? The Preacher's hair was tinged with grey, his hard face slack, globules of spit smeared the unkempt beard round his half-open mouth, his eyes were vacant as he gazed around. He was forced to kneel whilst Rahere summarised the accusations laid against him. When he came to answer, the Preacher could only shake his head.

'I have been ill!' he whimpered. His hands, released from their bonds, tapped either side of his head. 'I cannot remember where I have been or what I have done. It's as if I've been asleep.'

'Do you deny the charges?' Rahere asked crisply.

'I don't know who I am or where I have been.' He coughed. 'I have done ill, great evil.'

'The man you condemned, the hermit, was innocent.'

'Oh yes, oh yes, but I am confused.'

Rahere shrugged and glanced at Baron Sanguis.

'What say ye?'

The Baron turned to the jurors.

'Guilty!' they chorused.

'And the sentence?' Rahere asked.

'To be hanged on the common gallows!' Baron Sanguis snapped. 'Let his body be gibbeted as a warning to others who think they can come here and usurp my power!'

The villagers clapped and cheered.

'Sentence to be carried out immediately!' Baron Sanguis added.

The Preacher's head went down. He started to sob. The jurors stood up, congratulating themselves. Matthias, squatting in the front, watched Rahere crouch down and drag back the Preacher's head. He pushed his face only a few inches from that of the prisoner. Perhaps only Matthias heard the word 'YOU!' come from the Preacher's lips before he dropped on all fours, head down like a dog.

Baron Sanguis' bailiffs came forward. The prisoner was dragged out through the cemetery. A horse was waiting with a leather-covered sledge attached by wooden shafts. The Preacher was forced to lie on this. He was stripped naked except for his linen breeches, and the horse, its bridle held by Rahere, made its slow journey up the high street towards the waiting gallows. Parson Osbert stayed in the Lady Chapel, face in his hands.

Matthias decided to follow the crowd. They were throwing rubbish, dung and dirt at the Preacher stretched out on the makeshift sledge. The rutted tracks of the highroad scarred his back and made him scream in pain. At the Hungry Man Matthias stopped. He did not wish to go any further. Instead he stood on a table outside the tavern. The crowd reached the gallows. The Preacher was released, his hands lashed behind his back. The bailiffs pushed him up on to the horse. A noose was fitted round his neck.

'Let it be done!' Rahere's voice broke the stillness. 'Let the King's justice be done!'

The horse was led away. The Preacher danced, jerking like a doll at the end of the rope, twisting and turning, his legs kicking. Matthias fled inside the Hungry Man and sat in the darkened taproom. He was still there when the men returned from the gallows. He was about to slip away when a hand caught at his shoulder. He glanced up. Rahere was smiling down at him.

'It had to be done, boy,' he murmured. 'It had to be done.'

He leant down. 'Enough of royal justice,' he whispered. 'Will you show me the woods?'

'Tomorrow.' Matthias stepped back. He felt weak, slightly sick. 'Tomorrow morning,' he promised. 'But my father needs me.'

Rahere tapped him on the shoulder. 'An obedient son,' he murmured, 'brings pleasure to all!'

Matthias left the Hungry Man and ran up the highroad. Matthias found his father in the kitchen at home, sitting before the hearth, staring into the ashes. He was already on his second goblet of wine. Matthias tried to talk to him but his father just shook his head. Matthias stole up the stairs. The door to his parents' bedchamber was open. He went inside. It was dark and stale. He narrowed his eyes. His mother was lying on the bed. She had her back to him. He went across.

'Mother, Mother, it's Matthias.' He tapped again but she didn't stir. 'Mother, it's Matthias. Are you well?'

Again no reply. He tiptoed out and went up the stairs to his own little garret. He lay down on the bed. Images flitted through his mind. The hermit, arms extended; the Preacher, dancing at the end of the rope; Rahere smiling down at him. Matthias drifted into sleep. He was awoken violently: his mother, grasping him by the shoulders, was shaking him up and down, banging his head against the feather-filled bolster. Matthias stared in horror. Christina's face was white as a sheet, a blueish tinge high in her cheeks. Her eyes were red-rimmed and dark circled. She was glaring sightlessly at him, lips moving.

'Mother!' Matthias moaned. 'Mother, what is wrong? You are hurting!'

Christina had a madcap, vacant look. Her nails were digging deep into his shoulder. Matthias closed his eyes and started to cry. He heard a pounding on the stairs and his father was dragging Christina away, arms locked tightly round her. Christina struggled. She began to cry and then went limp. Osbert let her slip gently to the floor, placing her back against the wall. She sat, legs out, her bare feet dirty, her hands crossed. Her head went slack, a trickle of saliva coming out of the corner of her mouth. She lifted her face, her eyes puffy with tears.

'I am sorry,' she whispered. 'Matthias, I am very sorry.' She held a hand out to her husband. 'Take me back to my bed,' she murmured. 'Some food. Hear my confession.'

Matthias, alarmed, swung his legs off the bed.

'Stay there, Matthias!' Osbert ordered. Picking his wife up, he stumbled out of the room and down the stairs.

Matthias waited for a while, looking through the window. He had slept longer than he had thought. He felt hungry and went down to the kitchen. He ate some fruit and cheese, finished his father's wine, then returned to his own room. The wine and the shock made Matthias feel depleted. He'd never felt such tiredness before. His legs and arms seemed to weigh like lead and, throwing himself on to the bed, he fell fast asleep.

Matthias awoke cold and stiff just after dawn. He felt stronger, refreshed. He went downstairs. His father sat on his mother's chair. Matthias' heart lurched: Osbert had aged, his face was pale and drawn and he was rocking himself backwards and forwards, his hands pushed up the voluminous sleeves of his gown. Matthias became frightened. He didn't want to be here any more. He just wanted to flee.

'Your mother is dead.' Osbert didn't even turn his head. 'I heard her confession last night. She died in the early hours!' He drew his hands from his sleeves. 'Gone!' he added, fingers clawing the air. 'Like a candle going out!'

Matthias began to tremble. His world was falling apart. His mother was dead, his father was sitting there like a madcap, talking to himself.

'Perhaps she's just asleep.'

Matthias couldn't think of anything else to say. Osbert turned his head, lips curled in a sneer.

'Asleep? You stupid little boy. She's dead! My Christina is dead! Your mother is dead and all you can say is that she's asleep!' Osbert's shoulders began to shake. He put his face in his hands, sobbing uncontrollably.

Matthias backed towards the door. He couldn't make sense of this. His mother would never die. He was in a dream.

'Where are you going?' The priest staggered from the chair and pounced threateningly on him. 'Where are you going, brat? You little bastard!'

'Father!' Matthias screamed.

The priest blinked.

'Father, I don't know!'

The priest breathed in deeply, closing his eyes; he crossed himself three times.

'This hermit of yours? This hermit of yours?' he repeated.

'He's dead,' Matthias whimpered.

The priest muttered something to himself. Then: 'I want to go there,' he declared. 'Go on, boy! Get your cloak, put your boots on and don't run away!'

Matthias hurried to obey. When he came downstairs his father was all ready; a water bottle filled with wine in one hand, a greasy leather bag in the other. 'Food and drink,' he explained.

They went to the stable. Parson Osbert brought out the little palfrey he kept there. Matthias thought he'd lift him up into the saddle but the parson hung the leather bag on the saddle horn and mounted.

'Run beside me, brat!'

Along the high street Parson Osbert stopped, hammering at the door of Widow Blanche. He told her, in harsh, halting sentences, what had happened, and would she dress the corpse and watch the house until he returned? After that the parson rode on. He stopped at the gallows and stared at the Preacher's body, now coated with pitch and tar. It hung, head askew, neck still clenched by the rough, thick hemp. Again Parson Osbert muttered something to himself and, with Matthias trotting beside him, entered the woods, following the path to Tenebral.

Matthias did not know what kind of morning it was. He did not seem to be able to hear or see anything. His mother was dead. Christina would never talk to him again. Now his father rode like a madcap, while he himself scampered along like some mongrel dog.

Matthias' head and stomach pained him. He was aware that it had rained the night before. There were puddles on the trackway. The trees overhead still dripped water. He had to pause to catch his breath, to relieve the stitch in his side but his father rode on. Matthias, sobbing and gasping, followed. He didn't bother to keep up but left the forest path, making his way along his secret trackway into Tenebral. The tendrils of the morning mist still seeped through its broken-down houses, hanging like a cloud around the old church.

Matthias waited at the lych-gate. His father came up and dismounted. He gripped the boy's shoulder.

'I told you to stay with me!' he snapped. 'Now, mind the horse!'

The parson strode up the pathway to the church. Matthias didn't follow. He was frightened. He'd caught a look in his father's eye of something he had never seen before. He must have stayed an hour until his father came out of the ruins.

'Matthias, come here to me, boy!'

Matthias stood stock-still. Parson Osbert stepped forward. Matthias cringed at the look on his father's face.

'I am not what I appear, boy.' The parson was trying to keep his voice sweet and low yet Matthias sensed a terrible danger. He was sure that if he went into the church, he would never leave alive. He noticed his father had taken off his belt, this was tightly wrapped round his right hand.

'It's the runes,' Parson Osbert explained, as he began to edge forward. 'I am not as simple as people think, Matthias. I am a scholar. I can read French and Latin. But that rose and the runes, you must know what they mean?' He held his left hand up, fingers splayed. 'Do you know what they mean, Matthias? Do you know what they say? Come and tell your father.'

Matthias couldn't move. His mouth was dry. He edged backwards. The docile palfrey caught his fear and began to tug at the reins.

'We'll look at the pictures.' Parson's Osbert's head came forward. Matthias could see how tight his throat was, the Adam's apple bobbing there. 'We'll look at the pictures and then I'll go to Tewkesbury.'

He hurried forward, head rigid, eyes intent on Matthias. The boy found it impossible to move.

'Good morrow, Parson Osbert.'

At the side of the church, behind his father, stood Rahere the clerk. The priest paused. Rahere walked slowly towards him. He was dressed for hunting in a dark-green jerkin and hose of the same colour. As he moved, his hand went to the dagger in his belt.

'Good morrow, Parson Osbert. Good morrow, Matthias.'

He moved between them, his back to Matthias. Parson Osbert's fingers went to his lips, eyes flitting left and right, as if he suddenly realised where he was and what he was doing.

'I heard the news in the village,' Rahere said. 'My condolences on the death of Christina. She was a good woman.' He smiled over his shoulder at Matthias. 'She must have been, to have a son like you. So, Parson Osbert, if your wife lies dead at home, why are you both here in this ruin?'

Matthias couldn't exactly see what was happening but his father seemed frightened, moving his head backwards and forwards, blinking as he tried to break free of the clerk's gaze.

'We are on our way to Tewkesbury,' he gabbled. 'I called off to see, well, to see Matthias' secret place.'

'Why Tewkesbury?' the clerk asked softly. 'Your wife's corpse is not yet cold.'

'I have business there.' The parson was now agitated, licking his lips, moving from foot to foot. 'Yes, I must go there.'

He moved sideways but the clerk moved with him.

'And Matthias?' Rahere asked. 'He doesn't have to go to Tewkesbury, does he?'

'No, no, he doesn't have to go to Tewkesbury,' the parson echoed.

'So you had better leave now.'

The parson nodded his head and, brushing by the clerk, snatched the reins and clambered on to his palfrey. He kicked his heels in, hurrying off along the trackway which would take him down the road to Tewkesbury. Rahere watched him go before turning to Matthias. The boy noticed how the clerk's face was pale, a coating of sweat on his brow.

'I'm frightened,' Matthias said. 'I'm cold and I'm very frightened.'

Rahere took his cloak off, wrapped it round the boy, picked him up and carried him round the old cemetery walls to where his horse had been hobbled in a cluster of trees.

'You are coming back with me to Sutton Courteny,' the clerk said. 'I have the best room at the Hungry Man.'

The journey back was silent. When they arrived at the tavern, the scullions and tapsters were still heavy-eyed, the fires had not yet been lit. Joscelyn the tavern master came hurrying up, curious about the bundle Rahere carried in his arms. The clerk whispered an explanation. Matthias didn't hear and he

129

really didn't care. He was shivering so much, his stomach was curdling and he felt a burning sensation in the back of his throat. Rahere had taken the large and spacious chamber on the first floor overlooking the high street. He put Matthias on the bed, went across to his saddlebags and took out a phial. He poured its contents into some wine and forced the cup between the boy's lips. Matthias tried to protest. He was sure his stomach wouldn't hold it but the clerk held him tight.

'Don't worry, boy,' he said. 'Just look in my eyes.'

Matthias did, saw two dark pools . . . felt a sensation similar to when he stared into the dark mere in the woods around Tenebral. His own eyes grew heavy. He was falling into darkness . . .

Matthias must have slept for hours. When he awoke he felt refreshed and very hungry.

'It's three hours past midday,' Rahere declared, sitting on a stool next to the bed. 'You've been snoring like a little pig. How do you feel now?'

'Warm,' Matthias replied.

'Good. Then it's time you ate.'

He left. A few minutes later he returned, carrying a tray which had a pewter bowl of venison stew, cheese, soft-baked white loaves, a pot of butter and a dish of sugared pears. Matthias ate until he felt his stomach was going to burst. All the time the clerk watched him intently.

'I'd best go home.' Matthias pushed the tray away.

'I don't think so,' Rahere answered. 'Not yet anyway. You can help me. I have letters to write: I will show you the secrets of the Chancery.'

Matthias spent a fascinating afternoon helping the clerk draw up letters reporting to the Chancellor what had happened at Sutton Courteny. The clerk showed him how to take a fresh, virginal roll of parchment, brush it lightly with a pumice stone until it was silky to the touch, then how to cut it with a special knife, using a slat of wood to ensure the line ran straight. Then there was the ink: the proportion of water to powder, the mixing and heating over a candle. The quills, delicate to the touch, needed to be sharpened. Matthias broke at least three before he learnt how to prepare them. The clerk was very patient. Never once did he show any irritation, but praised Matthias.

130

'You have a quick mind, lad. You'll make a good clerk. Now, I'll show you how to write.'

The clerk sat at the small desk, dipped the quill into the ink and began to write. His pen fairly skimmed across the page.

'Can you read it?'

'I only know Church Latin.' Matthias shook his head.

'It's not Latin,' Rahere grinned. 'It's Norman French, the language of the court. That's the tongue the great ones speak.'

And, getting to his feet, the clerk spoke in French whilst imitating the affectations of the courtiers, both men and women. He was such a good mimic that Matthias laughed until his sides ached. Rahere sat back on his stool.

'It's marvellous to watch them, Matthias,' he declared. 'They carry their heads as if what was in them were sacred. Yet they are all noddle-pates.' His face became grim. 'Most of them have one strength and one strength only: they know how to kill – but the same could be said of any savage animal.'

'Surely the clerks are different?' Matthias asked.

'They are no better nor worse,' Rahere replied. 'Time-servers; they carefully watch who is about to rise and who is about to fall. Well, the parchment has to be sealed.'

He took a small copper spoon and a finger of wax out of his chancery bag, showing Matthias how the wax had to be melted, poured on the parchment to receive the imprint of the seal he carried.

'Now,' Rahere left the parchment on the desk, 'we let it dry then I'll roll it up, tie it with a piece of ribbon and we'll hire some honest journeyman to take it down to Westminster. As for you, my boy,' he went to the window, 'it's nearly evening. Your father will be home.'

Matthias did not want to return to his house, but the clerk insisted on accompanying him. Widow Blanche opened the door, her face all concerned. In the kitchen Parson Osbert sat in a chair, head lolling. The cup he had been holding had rolled on the floor, the flagon of wine beside him was empty.

'He only came back a short while ago,' the widow woman whispered. 'I've never seen him like that before: bad-tempered and cursing. He asked where his brat was.' She glanced pityingly at Matthias. 'He had a stick in his hand.'

'And Christina, the boy's mother?' Rahere asked.

'She's upstairs. God save us! I've dressed her for burial. But this?' She shook her head, mumbling under her breath.

'We'll see her,' Rahere declared. 'I'll take the boy up. He should see his mother, at least once.'

He led Matthias up the stairs. Christina was laid out on her bed. She had been dressed in her best gown, her hair was combed, falling down to her shoulders, her face was serene, hands placed across her chest. Matthias felt that if he stretched out, he could shake her awake yet he did not want to. He felt guilty. She looked younger, at peace with herself. Matthias caught a glimpse of the mother he wanted to remember. He stood, the tears streaming down his face.

'Say your prayers,' Rahere whispered.

Matthias tried to think of one but he couldn't. All he could remember were the words his father had taught him to say every morning.

'Remember this, my soul, and remember it well. The Lord thy God is One and He is holy. And thou shalt love the Lord thy God with all thy mind, with all thy heart and with all thy strength.' He looked up at Rahere. 'That's all I can say.'

'Kiss your mother,' Rahere said.

Matthias climbed on the bed. He kissed Christina on her cheeks and brow. He clambered off and watched in surprise as Rahere also bent over the dead woman and kissed her gently on the lips. He ran his fingers gently down her face.

'It's finished, Matthias.' He stared down at the boy. 'Only the shell remains. The spirit has long gone.' Rahere whispered something, staring up at the ceiling. 'She has gone,' he continued to the boy. 'She suffered much, yet, despite her sins, she was good. No objection has been made: she has been allowed to pass into the light.'

Matthias stared, puzzled: Rahere shrugged and took him downstairs. Widow Blanche was still clucking like a hen over the sleeping parson.

'You can leave the boy with me,' she said. 'I'll get him something to eat.'

'I don't think so,' Rahere retorted. His eyes held those of Blanche. 'I am sure you'll agree it's best the boy stay with me for a while.' He held his hand out and pressed silver coins into Blanche's.

'I would agree, sir,' she replied. 'Parson Osbert's mind is turned with grief.'

Matthias did not object: he did not want to stay here.

'Will he get better?' he asked as they left.

'I don't know,' Rahere replied. He looked up at the sky. 'I don't think so. Some sicknesses cannot be cured.'

The clerk's words proved to be prophetic. Parson Osbert was so incapacitated that Baron Sanguis had to bring a priest from Tredington for Christina's funeral Mass. Matthias attended with the other villagers. He felt a pang of compassion for his father, who sat on a bench supported by old Blanche and Simon the reeve.

The day of Christina's burial was a dismal one. The sky was overclouded. Once the sheeted corpse had been lowered and the dirt piled in, the mourners ran for shelter from the fat drops of rain which began to fall. Matthias went back with Rahere to the Hungry Man. He felt comfortable there, either assisting the clerk or doing jobs round the tavern for Joscelyn.

The villagers grew accustomed to the clerk's presence and, as the days passed, they accepted him as their leader and counsellor. Parson Osbert, constantly in his cups, was dismissed as a madcap who, before long, would be relieved of his living. In his turn, the clerk seemed unwilling to leave and, when questioned by Sanguis and others, dismissed any notion of returning to Westminster just yet.

'I need to be sure,' he explained, 'that there are no more deaths in the locality. The Preacher's corpse might be rotting on the gallows but there may be more than one killer. He might have been a member of a coven.'

He told the villagers this when they all crowded into the tavern late at night after the harvest had been stored. The villagers gathered round him.

'It's true what you say, sir,' Fulcher declared. 'So many corpses, yet no one has given the reason why.'

'I beg your pardon?' Rahere sat back in his seat, putting his arm round Matthias.

'Well, my Edith,' the blacksmith hastily explained. 'Why was she killed? Why were these corpses drained of blood?'

'Perhaps you should ask the Preacher?' Rahere joked.

The assembled men and women laughed self-consciously.

'And what about the boy?' Scrivener Mapp pointed at Matthias. 'I mean, when you go, sir?'

'Oh, he'll come with me.'

Matthias hid his surprise but he found it easy to do so. Over the last few weeks he'd grown more secretive: he had already decided that, if the clerk left, he would not stay, though where he would go was, until now, unresolved.

'Will you stay long?' Piers the ploughman asked.

His voice was anxious though he forced a smile. He and the other men were becoming increasingly concerned by this handsome, elegant clerk's attraction for their women. Rahere leant his elbows on the table, steepling his fingers over the lower half of his face.

'I'll tell you what,' he declared. 'I'll stay until Samhain evening. Yes, to the Eve of the Feast of All Saints.' He chuckled deep in his throat. 'I promise you, it will be a Samhain that will be remembered for years!'

9

In the scriptorium of Tewkesbury Abbey, the Chronicler did not know how to describe the horrifying events which occurred at Sutton Courteny in the autumn of 1471. The old monk scratched the quill against his face. He had talked to his brothers. Baron Sanguis had arranged for the survivors to be brought into the abbey where he'd met them in the refectory. They were all white-faced, haggard-eyed. Some were uncertain, others too shocked. A few had lost their reason, wandering in their own black pit of madness. Those who could speak mentioned the meeting in the taproom on 14 September, the Feast of the Exaltation of the Holy Cross. Rahere the clerk was there, laughing and courteous. He generously bought stoups of ale and goblets of wine for the villagers when they met to prepare for All-Hallows and the Feast of Samhain Eve.

Samhain was the night when the door between this world and the other was thrown open and the spirits of the dead were allowed to wander the world. The villagers agreed to a great feast being held at the Hungry Man tavern. Work on the land would pause. Cattle would be sheltered in preparation for winter. They would deck their houses with the branches of rowan and elder. Of course, they would also light bonfires around the village, as was ancient custom, to keep the evil spirits away. The villagers were relaxed and happy. The evils which had oppressed them since the death of the hermit seemed to have been lifted. True, Parson Osbert wandered his churchyard like a madcap, keening over poor Christina's grave, but his boy seemed in good spirits, now looked after by Rahere the clerk. The villagers had grown accustomed to seeing him around the Hungry Man.

Matthias, however, kept his own counsel. His mind was confused. He still could not understand or accept his mother's death, whilst his father had become a dishevelled, wild-eyed stranger, neglecting his duties, lost in mourning for his dead wife. Rahere, however, kept the boy busy. They'd go out into the woods where Matthias would show off his forest lore whilst Rahere introduced him to the secrets of the Chancery and filled his mind with vivid stories about the King's gorgeous court. He even hinted that Matthias might become a clerk, attend the abbey school and, if he showed wit and sharp intelligence, enter the schools of Oxford and become a master of learning. Matthias nodded when he heard this. He felt oppressed by Sutton Courteny. The villagers were strangers and he did secretly worry what would happen to him if Rahere abruptly left.

Autumn made itself felt. Cold winds blew along the Severn, stripping the trees of their leaves: these were cold, hard, bleak days under an iron-grey sky. If the villagers thought their troubles were over, they were mistaken. Simon the reeve's was the first tragic death. He was out ploughing in the great open fields, his boy walking behind him, scattering the marauding crows with his slingshot. Simon leant on the great plough and watched the iron hook rip open the dark brown soil. Simon liked this part of the year, when the earth opened to receive new seed. Yet, today, he felt uneasy. The trees which bordered the field had now lost their leaves in a violent wind storm a week before. They stood like sombre grey sentinels. The reeve was sure some-one was watching him. Simon paused and scratched his head. He had drunk too deeply the night before but that was because he was worried. His young wife, Elizabeth, she with her black hair and warm, brown skin, merry eyes and kissing mouth, seemed a little too fond of the arrogant young clerk Rahere. Simon had heard whispers: how Elizabeth was absenting herself from the home for this reason or that, going hither and thither, with no real explanation or excuse.

'I really should question her,' he muttered to himself.

Elizabeth was his second wife, much younger than he, and Simon was cunning enough to realise that there was nothing more amusing to everyone than a man showing his cuckold's horns. He grasped the handle of the plough and savagely whipped the ox. But, if it was true . . . ?

Behind him, the boy was whistling. Simon wished to be alone.

'Go back to the house!' he shouted over his shoulder. 'Go to Elizabeth and tell her to bring me some bread, cheese and a jug of ale. If she's not there, find out where she is!'

The boy ceased his whistling. He could see his father was angry. Moreover, Simon was free with his fists when he lost his temper, so the boy loped across the furrow like a hare, quietly planning that he would take as long as he could. Simon returned to his ploughing. He could not bear the thought of Elizabeth playing the wanton with that young fop from London. Elizabeth was a merry bed companion: her legs wrapped round him, Simon enjoyed her smooth, slim body writhing beneath his, her face twisted into pleasure, her mouth urging him on. What if the clerk had experienced these pleasures?

The oxen suddenly stopped. Simon looked up. It was late in the afternoon and a mist was beginning to seep in through the trees. He brought his small whip down across the oxen's rumps but the animals didn't move. Simon sighed and undid the cords around his waist. Perhaps the great blade of the plough was stuck. He stepped between the plough and the oxen, crouching down to dig at the earth, then he heard the whistling. Simon remembered that tune. He'd heard it before, but where? The whistling grew clearer. The reeve remembered. It was the song the hermit had sung from the fire!

Simon stood up and looked over the heads of the oxen. A figure was moving towards him out of the mist, a man hooded and cowled. Simon blinked. He could not understand it. The figure was not walking but gliding, its feet not touching the ground. The figure drew closer. The oxen grew restless. Simon's heart began to beat faster as the figure pulled back the cavernous cowl. Simon moaned in fear.

'It can't be!' he whispered, making the sign of the cross against the evil one. The figure was the hermit, the man he had seen burnt to death! Now he was coming to greet him, eyes staring, mouth open in a fixed smile. Simon crouched down behind the oxen like a child, believing it was all a figment of his imagination. The oxen moved back. Simon gave a terrible scream which grew to a groan of strangled terror as the oxen then lurched forward. They dragged the plough out of the soil. Simon was knocked flat. He tried to roll but, in his panic, exposed his neck and the sharp iron blade cut deep into his throat. When Elizabeth and the boy arrived an hour later, they found the oxen still terrified. They'd moved backwards and forwards in terror and, in doing so, had turned Simon's corpse into a bloody, mangled heap.

Three days later Joscelyn climbed up on to the roof of the Hungry Man tavern. He was angry. He could not believe that tiles, freshly laid the previous spring, had grown loose, allowing rainwater to seep into the garrets. Joscelyn was determined that he would not pay good silver for the tiler to make a second mistake: this time he would do it himself. He ignored his wife's protests and climbed to the very top of the sloping roof. He edged along, looking for the loose tile. When he found it, he gave a shout of exclamation.

'The bastard!' he muttered.

The tiler had laid it wrongly and the slate had slipped, knocking others loose. Joscelyn stretched out, leaning precariously down. He heard a flutter of wings and looked up. A raven, black feathery wings extended, was gliding through the air towards him. Joscelyn raised his hand to fend off those cruel claws aiming straight for his face. He lost his balance, slid down the roof and fell from the tavern. He should have survived the fall but his head came down: it hit the sharp iron bar near the front door of his tavern where travellers scraped the mud off their boots. The iron sliced deep and Joscelyn died immediately.

The same day, late in the evening, Walter Mapp the scrivener was plotting lechery. The scrivener had not yet recovered from his previous injury but he now felt in good fettle. He'd promised himself that, before the weather changed and the roads became clogged, he would travel to Gloucester. He'd spend a few nights in the Merry Hog tavern which lay under the shadow of the great cathedral. Mapp was not too well known in Gloucester and he could play whatever part he liked. He would take his carefully guarded pile of silver coins and live the life of a lord, feasting and drinking and hiring the services of the flaxen-haired chambermaid there. Mapp scratched his stomach in pleasure, thinking what he would do with her this time. In his mind, he carefully undid the laces of her bodice, stripping her roughly of her dress and shift and then, in that little chamber, made merry and warm by a glowing charcoal brazier, he would take his heart's delight. Still engrossed in such thoughts Mapp took a taper to the fire. His chamber had grown dark and more candles had to be lit. He caught a flame and lit the three-branched candelabra on his desk under the window.

At first Mapp did not know what was happening. He tried to blow the taper out but the flame grew stronger, eating away at the wax, racing towards his fingers. Mapp tried to drop it but found the wax was stuck to his fingers. For a while he just stood transfixed in terror, his wits numb. He could hear someone singing outside, close to the window, a song Mapp recalled, but now the flame of the taper was almost near his fingers. The scrivener remembered the small pitcher of water he kept in the buttery. He hastened across but his foot caught a saddlebag. He slipped, rolling on to the floor, screaming as the flames reached his fingers and caught at his woollen mittens. He tried to dash his hand against the floor but the flames caught the dried rushes and, before he even realised, the flames were dancing around him. His cloak was on fire and, within minutes, Mapp the scrivener, so intent on his pleasures, was turned into a blazing torch.

The following evening Fidelis, wife of Joscelyn the taverner, went into the lonely, cold parish church. Her husband's body now lay in the parish coffin at the entrance to the sanctuary. Fidelis had not yet accepted that her husband had died so quickly. She knelt on the prie-dieu left out for anyone who wished to keep the corpse watch. Putting her face in her hands, Fidelis began to cry. Not so much for Joscelyn but for herself. Things had been going so well. The arrival of the clerk had increased their profits and village life was now centred round the tavern rather than this dirty, bleak church whose parson's wits were always wandering. Fidelis also felt guilty. A small, buxom woman, she knew her neighbours described her as wet-lipped and hot-eyed but Rahere had been so handsome, his touch so smooth and soft, his words and kisses sweeter than honey. On many an occasion, in a chamber just under the eaves, she had given herself to him. Now she blushed with shame at how beseeching she had been. Was her husband's death God's punishment?

Fidelis heard a sound and looked up. She blinked. She couldn't believe her eyes. At the top of the coffin a figure now stood, its back to her. Despite the gathering gloom, Fidelis knew it was her husband. She sprang to her feet and ran towards him. She wasn't frightened, at least until he turned. Fidelis gave a gasp and stepped back, hand to her mouth. Joscelyn's head was strangely twisted and, in the poor light, his ghastly colour and red-rimmed, staring eyes made him terrifying. The lips moved. 'Adulteress!' His hand went out towards her. Fidelis, realising the full horror of what was happening, staggered backwards. The vision, the phantasm followed: staring, popping eyes, the lips opening and shutting like those of a landed fish and those splayed fingers, stretching out, trying to catch the side of her face. Fidelis bumped into a pillar, her hand dropped away. She couldn't stop shaking. The ghastly vision drew closer. She caught the reek, the stench of the grave.

'You are dead!' she whispered. 'Oh Lord save us, you are dead!'

Her husband's ice-cold hand brushed her cheek.

'And so are you!'

Parson Osbert made a valiant effort to break free of the demons which seemed to haunt his soul. The deaths in the village, particularly that of Fidelis, made him realise that his parishioners, whom he was supposed to serve, were under deadly threat. He washed and shaved. He brought Blanche back into the house to clean and polish. One evening he did not drink but sat by the fire. He would love to walk down to the Hungry Man, embrace his son, tell him all would be well. He prayed quietly for the grace to do so but, in the end, he only reached the door of his house before his will failed and he returned morosely to sit before the fire.

Outside night was falling. He closed his eyes. Today was the Feast of the apostles Saints Simon and Jude. In three days it would be All-Hallows Eve when, as in former years, he good-naturedly allowed his villagers to partake in the pagan rites of Samhain. On 2 November was the Feast of All Souls, when the villagers would pray for their dead. He should pray for Christina. He should pray for himself and Matthias.

Parson Osbert got to his feet. He took his Ave beads out

of their pouch and wrapped them round his fingers. He, by his drunkenness, by his arrogance, had sinned and, before he made his peace with his son, he really should make his peace with God.

Parson Osbert walked out of the house and across the graveyard. He unlocked the corpse door and went inside. God's house had not been cleaned. The flagstones should be washed and scrubbed, the benches polished, cobwebs removed. He drew himself up and breathed in. He would clean God's house. He would put matters right in his own soul. He would reconcile himself to his son and face the future, whatever happened. Parson Osbert went round the darkened church, lighting the candles in their iron holders. He came back and knelt before the rood screen but his mind was too distressed to pray. He kept drifting back into the past when Christina was alive, joyful, merry and winsome. Now? Parson Osbert bitterly regretted the Preacher. It had all begun here, when he had sat like a frightened rabbit, and allowed the Preacher to climb into his pulpit. Parson Osbert got to his feet and climbed the steps to the pulpit. He glanced at the stark crucifix fixed to the wall above him.

'I'll have a meeting tomorrow,' he whispered. 'I'll gather all the people here. I'll confess my wrong!'

He heard a sound and whirled round. People were standing in the shadows at the back of the church.

'Who's there? Come forward!'

Dark shapes shuffled towards him, slowly, stumblingly. Parson Osbert's hand went to his throat. He stared in horror. Eight, nine persons all in their shrouds, all people buried in his graveyard: Edith, Simon the reeve, Joscelyn the taverner! Parson Osbert screamed and, running down the steps, fled out into the darkness.

The Eve of All-Hallows dawned gloomy and damp. Black, heavy rain clouds massed over Sutton Courteny and, by mid-morning, a heavy downpour had begun. Not even the oldest inhabitant of the village could recall such heavy rains. The water fell in drenching sheets. The small brook, already swollen, broke its banks. Trackways and paths were turned to a muddy morass and the village was effectively cut off. All hopes of any festivities planned for the evening died with the downpour. The bonfires and beacons which ringed the village

141

were reduced to nothing more than a soggy pile of wood and kindling. No fires were lit to ward off the evil spirits. By noon the situation had become even worse. No work was done in the fields. Everyone was confined to their homes.

In the taproom of the Hungry Man, Matthias realised matters were coming to a climax. He could sense the tension. Rahere sat brooding in a corner, cloak wrapped about him, just staring out of the window. He'd hardly murmured a word since he had risen early that morning. Matthias tried to engage him in conversation but the clerk just shook his head and returned to staring at the sky.

Over the last few weeks, Rahere had distanced himself from the villagers. Once their leader, even their hero, the peasants now distrusted him. Rahere didn't care. Matthias knew the clerk looked forward to this day but never understood the reason why. The boy himself had been kept busy. He'd heard about the strange deaths but any desire to return home had been quickly curbed by fresh reports of his father's strange behaviour and drunken ways. Something was about to happen and Matthias realised all he could do was watch and wait.

As the day drew on, the occasional villager called in to buy some ale but the atmosphere remained bleak. Fulcher, who had taken over the running of the tavern, had none of the welcoming charm of Joscelyn. Indeed, the tavern was a stark reminder of the tragedies which had befallen the villagers over the last few days.

Rahere abruptly stood up. 'The rain is going to get worse,' he decided. 'Fulcher, the covered wagon?'

The blacksmith came out of the scullery, wiping his hands on a dirty cloth.

'It's out in the yard,' he retorted.

'There'll be no festivities tonight,' Rahere declared. 'But I have arranged with Baron Sanguis that the children will not be disappointed.' He plucked a gold coin out of his purse. Fulcher's surly face became more lively. 'I want you to go round the village,' Rahere told him, 'before the trackway to the manor becomes too clogged. Collect all the children, take them to Baron Sanguis. He will give them a treat; mummers' games, entertainment, apple juice and sweetmeats.'

He tossed the coin at Fulcher. The blacksmith caught it deftly.

'Will the boy be going?' Fulcher pointed across to where Matthias sat, wide-eyed in expectation.

Rahere smiled. 'No, no, he won't!'

Fulcher lumbered out of the room. Matthias heard voices out in the yard grumbling and complaining as grooms hitched the horses to the traces.

'Do come back, Fulcher!' Rahere called. 'I have another surprise for you!'

'Why can't I go?' Matthias walked across the taproom.

Rahere grasped his shoulders. The clerk's eyes glittered.

'Sleep, Matthias,' he urged. 'It's best if you slept for a while.'

Rahere went to the buttery and came back with a goblet.

'It's watered wine,' he explained and, before Matthias could object, the clerk held it to his lips.

Matthias sipped. He wanted to sit before the fire and ask Rahere what was happening but his eyes grew very heavy. He clambered up the stairs, curled up like a puppy in the clerk's chamber and fell fast asleep.

Whilst Matthias slept, Fulcher returned. The blacksmith was in a hurry. He had delivered the children to Baron Sanguis and had just about been able to urge the horses to pull the covered cart back into Sutton Courteny. The blacksmith was frightened. It was only mid-afternoon yet the clouds hung black and low. Daylight was fading and, as he unhitched the horses in the yard, he realised the wind was rising. Doors to the outhouses creaked; bits and pieces left in the yard tumbled about as if driven by some unseen hand. Within the hour the wind storm was driving full force. The villagers were terrified. The rain continued to fall in sheets whilst the wind, which had sprung from nowhere, rattled their houses, howling like a lost soul as it beat against the shutters.

Accidents began to happen. John the bailiff, going out to ensure the tiles of his roof were secure, was hit by a piece of flying masonry, the stone smashing like a crossbow bolt into the back of his head. In the ploughman's house the wind fanned sparks from the fire, which caught the rushes. The crackling flames quickly spread, trapping Piers and his wife where they were hiding in their bedchamber. Fulcher saw an ostler, trying to run for shelter into one of the outhouses, sent flying by a piece of lead piping the wind had dragged loose.

Similar scenes occurred throughout the village and, despite the rain and driving winds, the people braved the elements; some, the fortunate ones, made their way out to the manor. Others began to throng into the Hungry Man. They were soaked to the skin; clutching a few paltry possessions, they huddled like sheep in the taproom.

'You can't stay here,' Fulcher declared. 'I have an ostler seriously injured upstairs.'

The villagers gathered there trembled as they heard the wind. It howled round the tavern like some terrible beast which had hunted them and was now determined to break in. The clamour of the wind and the noise downstairs awoke Matthias from his deep slumber. He gazed heavy-eyed: the clerk sat at the foot of the bed watching him intently.

'What's the matter?' the boy muttered, drawing his knees up.

'It's a storm,' Rahere replied softly. 'A wind storm. The villagers are fleeing. A few have stayed in their homes.' He played with the ring on his finger, his eyes never leaving those of Matthias. 'Some have gone to the manor house but the rest are downstairs.'

'And what will happen?' Matthias asked. He chewed at his lip. He felt as if he should be frightened but he was half-asleep and drowsy.

'We are going to the church. Don't worry, Matthias. Nothing is going to happen to you. Put your boots and cloak on.'

Matthias noticed the clerk had his cloak already wrapped around him, fastened by a chain at the neck. It covered him completely but, as he moved, the boy heard the clink of weapons and the jingle of the chain mail shirt beneath. The clerk helped him dress and they went down to the taproom. Rahere's arrival stilled the clamour and the acrimonious dispute about to break out. The clerk clapped his hands and stood on a stool.

'None of us can stay here,' he declared.

He paused as the door was flung open and a dishevelled, wide-eyed Parson Osbert staggered into the taproom, wiping the rain from his unshaven face.

'You should come to the church.' Parson Osbert swayed on his feet. 'I confess I have failed you. I have drunk too

144

deeply.' His eyes caught those of Matthias. 'I have sinned before Heaven and before you but this storm is not the elements. It is God's punishment and we should shelter in God's house.'

'The priest speaks the truth,' Rahere said. 'The church is built of stone. Fulcher, gather provisions from the buttery.'

The blacksmith hastened to obey, then Parson Osbert led them out into the high street. The journey to the church, taken so many times by all of them, proved to be a veritable calvary. The wind shrieked and howled, knocking and buffeting them. One of the tapsters from the Hungry Man was knocked senseless by a flying tile but no one went to assist him. An old woman was hit by a sign and she was left bloody-headed, crouching in a doorway, hands flapping. The others dare not stop. The wind made them turn their faces for it caught their breath. Parson Osbert, however, determined to do his duty, led them on.

Matthias was carried by the clerk. He then realised something quite terrible was about to happen. Now and again the clerk would look down at him. Matthias caught the same look he had seen in the hermit's eyes: soft, tender, sad. He also noticed how the wind did not seem to trouble the clerk. Rahere walked as if it were a summer's day, effortlessly, the wind scarcely touching him.

They entered the lych-gate, and the parishioners saw how the storm had flattened crosses and gravestones. Fulcher, despite the wind, stopped and stared across the rain-soaked cemetery. He opened his mouth to speak but the wind caught his words. The blacksmith staggered on, terrified by what he had seen. He was sure the black angel on top of old Pepperel's tomb was now standing like some infernal imp, its wings spread. Fulcher cursed the wine he had drunk: like the rest, he threw himself through the main door of the church, into the shelter and sanctuary of the nave.

Parson Osbert locked and bolted the doors behind them. He then went round the church and, assisted by Rahere, pulled the shutters across and barred them, plunging the church into darkness. Parson Osbert, overcoming his fears, lit the candles in the nave, those in the Lady Chapel as well as the tall ones on the high altar. At first the villagers lay around the nave, gasping, recovering their breath and their wits as well as trying to dry their hair and clothes. They welcomed the candlelight until the wind seeped through cracks and vents and made the flames dance. The church became an eerie vault, filled with flickering light and dancing shadows.

Fulcher had brought wineskins and leather panniers full of bread, dried meat and cheese. The food was shared out, and gave some momentary cheer. The villagers congratulated each other on their safe arrival: how they were pleased their children were in Baron Sanguis' manor and that the storm would soon abate. It did not. The wind now howled and lashed the church, rattling the door, buffeting the shutters. Even the bell in the steeple began to toll, driven backwards and forwards by the raucous gusts.

Outside darkness fell and then, abruptly, the storm subsided, the wind abated. The villagers helped themselves to more food and began to talk of returning to their homes.

Fulcher the blacksmith, full of wine and determined to relieve his bladder, opened the corpse door and went out into the cemetery. He undid the points of his breeches and gave a sigh of satisfaction. He heard a sound, glanced around, then staggered back, not caring that he was wetting his own boots and clothing: shadowy, cowled figures stood like statues around the cemetery. One under a yew tree, another on a fallen headstone. Fulcher rubbed his eyes but, when he looked again, the figures were still there, hidden in their crumbling cloths. The blacksmith, whimpering with terror, fled back to the church, locking and barring the door.

Parson Osbert saw the man's fear and opened the door grille and looked out. He, too, saw the figures and realised that the villagers would never leave this church alive. He snapped the grille shut. He didn't bother to comfort Fulcher, who crouched sobbing at the foot of a pillar. So far, the others had not noticed the blacksmith's terror. Osbert went to kneel before the sanctuary screen. He looked over his shoulder and glimpsed Matthias further down the church. Rahere the clerk was giving him something to drink. Osbert closed his eyes and made the sign of the cross.

'I confess,' he began, 'to Almighty God and to you, my brothers and sisters, that I have sinned most grievously in thought, word and deed.'

He paused as Rahere the clerk swept by him, crossing the

sanctuary into the small sacristy. Osbert closed his eyes. He was ready. The work he had done over the last three days he would give to his son. He made the sign of the cross, took out a piece of parchment from his pouch and went where his son now sat at the base of a pillar. The boy looked pale and sleepy-eyed but he didn't flinch when his father knelt beside him.

'Matthias.'

The boy looked up. He saw the softness in his father's eyes but he was too tired, too drowsy.

'Matthias, I love you.'

The boy smiled weakly.

'I am sorry.' The priest chose to ignore the tapping on the shutters outside. 'I am sorry for what I have done but I love you and Christina loved you. I do not know what is going to happen now.' He ignored the clamour of the people, who were exclaiming in horror at the tapping on the shutters. 'You will survive,' Parson Osbert continued. He thrust the piece of parchment into Matthias' hand. 'Keep that safe. No, don't look at it now, put it in your pouch.'

Parson Osbert took his son's face and kissed him on the forehead.

'May the Lord keep you in His peace.' He blessed his son, got to his feet and walked towards the sanctuary.

Fulcher came running up.

'Can't you hear it?' he demanded.

Parson Osbert stopped. The tapping on the shutters had increased but he also heard the tinkling of the corpse bell fastened over old Maud Brasenose's grave. Parson Osbert swallowed hard. He turned to face his parishioners. Even as he did so, the tapping grew louder, more insistent. Similar knocks and raps could be heard on the side door and the main door of the church. Peter the cobbler stared through the window. He shrieked and drew away, fingers to his mouth.

'They are in the graveyard!' he whispered. 'People in shrouds! The dead are all about us!'

The knocking and clamouring rose in a crescendo. The villagers in the church screamed and, as if of one mind, they came to huddle before their priest.

'I can do nothing,' Osbert declared. 'But I bid you—' he looked round the church: Matthias was now fast asleep –

147

'I bid you say an act of contrition. I will give you absolution.'

He ignored their cries and protests. He recited the words to shrive them from their sins. He had barely finished when he saw Fulcher staring in horror at something behind him. Osbert turned slowly as if in a dream. Rahere was standing in the mouth of the rood screen: his cloak was doffed, his hair tied in a knot behind him. In one hand he bore a sword, in the other an axe. Osbert drew his own knife and ran screaming towards him . . .

PART II

1486–1487

The Rose keeps its secret
Old English saying

Before they wither,
Let us crown ourselves with roses.
Book of Wisdom

10

Amasia, slattern of the Blue Boar tavern near Carfax in Oxford, rolled over on her narrow cot bed. She stared down at the man sleeping beside her. He lay on his back, head slightly tilted, breathing deeply. Now and again his lips moved, lost in some dream or nightmare. Amasia clutched the soiled bedsheet around her. She sat up and ran a finger gently down the man's face. She would have to admit, Matthias Fitzosbert was a handsome student, a dark, lean face, clean shaven. When awake, his eyes were light green, sometimes sad, but when he laughed or smiled, the crinkles transformed his rather sombre face. His hair was jet-black and oiled, though Amasia noticed tufts of grey about his ears. She stared down at the silver cross Matthias always wore round his neck on its strong copper chain. He never took that off. Amasia touched it gently.

She was only seventeen summers old, so she thought, and she was in the habit of entertaining many students: Matthias and his friend, the young Frenchman Santerre, were her favourites. She made a face and puckered her mouth. No, that wasn't right! Santerre, with his devil-may-care smile, snow-white skin and shock of red hair? Well, she could take or leave him. He was too cutting and she felt he was always laughing at her. Amasia could not stand people who secretly laughed behind their hands but never shared the jest with her. However, one thing she had learnt from Matthias was that, though she was a slattern, she had a dignity she should defend. He had told her so on that night four months ago when he had hit the drover, drunk as a sot, who pushed his dirty hand down her smock and grabbed her breasts. Matthias, not the tavern keeper, had come to her aid. He'd given the man a beating he would never forget before throwing him on to the muddy cobbles outside.

Amasia sat with her back against the cracked, plastered wall. It cooled her sweaty skin. She looked round the garret Matthias called a chamber. Not much dignity here, she thought, with its crumbling walls and rush-covered floor. On a table in the far corner stood a cracked bowl and jug, beneath it a large, dirty piss-pot. Amasia closed her eyes. She wondered if Matthias, when he became a Master, would take her out of here. He'd sometimes hinted at it. But where to? She knew so little about him. She often teased him about the mystery yet she'd learnt very little. He had been a scholar in the abbey schools at Tewkesbury and Gloucester before his patron, Baron Sanguis, had paid for him to come to the Halls of Oxford. More importantly, Matthias didn't know what he was going to do. Sometimes he talked of being a clerk, even a priest. Then he became tight-lipped, narrow-eyed: his jaw would stick out as if he had made a decision but stubbornly refused to tell anyone about it. Amasia sighed and opened her eyes. If only he would talk more . . .

'Will they miss you in the taproom below?'

Amasia jumped and looked down. Matthias was staring up at her.

'How long have you been awake?' she snapped and, leaning over, pinched his nose.

The student laughed and pushed away her hand. He sat up beside her.

'Do you want to go?' she asked archly.

'I have to,' he replied. 'There is still enough daylight left.' He pointed to the narrow window at the far end of the room.

'Ah!' Amasia threw the sheets back. She swung her long legs off the bed, stood up and stretched, looking coyly at Matthias. She knew men liked that: her body turning, her breasts thrust out. She smiled as Matthias moved and teasingly took a step backwards.

'I have to go,' she simpered. 'I really must. Agatha isn't—'

'Oh yes,' Matthias interrupted, 'Agatha Merryfeet.'

'That's not her real name,' Amasia snapped.

'Oh, I think it is,' Matthias replied, keeping his face straight as he caught the note of jealousy in her voice. 'Whatever she is, Agatha can dance.'

'Aye!' she snapped. 'On the tables, flaunting herself.'

Angrily Amasia picked her shift up and pulled it over her head. 'Well, she'll dance no more. She's dead! Dead as a worm,' she continued. 'Her corpse has been taken to the death house at the Crutched Friars. Found in Christ Church Meadow she was,' Amasia trilled on. 'Pinch marks on her neck. Like two holes, the bailiff told us, as if someone had taken a nail—'

She was spun round. Matthias clutched her shoulders, his fingers biting deeply into her flesh. Amasia struggled but she forgot the pain: it was Matthias' face which frightened her. No longer the soft, calm student. His face was pallid, skin drawn tight, eyes fixed and staring. He opened his mouth but then swallowed hard.

'Matthias!' She slapped at his wrist.

The student's grip still held firm.

'Matthias, you are hurting me!'

He let go of her and slumped down on the bed. Amasia stepped away and watched him carefully. She had heard stories about men like that. Quiet ones but, when they were in a chamber alone with a woman, they became violent, taking their pleasure out of pain. But was Matthias one of these? She noticed a trickle of sweat running down the side of his face, his chest heaving as if he had been running. He was staring at the floor. Now and again his mouth would twist into a grimace or he would shake his head as if he were carrying on a conversation with someone she could not see. She picked up a bowl of wine he had brought and, sitting beside him, raised it to his lips. He drank like a babe, then he coughed, retched and, with his hand covering his mouth, ran across the room to the piss bowl where he vomited. He crouched there like a dog, cleaning his mouth with his fingers.

'Matthias, are you sickening?'

Amasia became frightened. Last summer the sweating sickness had swept through Oxford. They said it had been brought by Henry Tudor's soldiers when they had marched through the city after their victory over Richard III at Market Bosworth. Amasia knew all about that battle: two of the pot boys had fought on the Yorkist side and had never returned. Amasia got to her feet. Perhaps she should go downstairs to Goodman the taverner.

'I'm all right,' Matthias muttered. 'Don't be afeared.'

He got to his feet, poured some water over his fingers and cleaned his mouth. He came back to the bed.

'You look pale, Matthias!'

'No, no.' He shook his head and, taking her by the arm, forced her to sit next to him. 'Tell me again,' he said. 'Tell me what happened to Agatha.'

Amasia did so.

'You are always lost in your books, Matthias,' she concluded. 'Haven't you heard about the other deaths? People like Agatha and myself, slatterns, maids. No one misses us. No one makes a fuss. No one except you,' she added. 'Why, did Agatha dance for you?'

Matthias got to his feet and began to dress.

'And where did you say the body had been taken? Ah, yes, the Crutched Friars.'

Amasia, with the sheet up about her, watched as the student put on his hose, linen shirt, his tabard, which bore the arms of his college, Exeter in Turl Street. He pulled the hood over his head, tied the leather belt around him, his fingers going to the hilt of the dagger in its embroidered scabbard.

'Don't forget your boots!' she teased.

Matthias was not listening. He picked these up, pulled them on, then walked out of the room without a by-your-leave or a backward glance.

'Time for your studies?' Goodman the taverner, filling a tankard from a tun near the door, hailed the student as Matthias crossed the taproom. Goodman would have loved to have drawn this young man into conversation. One day, when the time was ripe, Goodman hoped to have his own tryst with Amasia. He wished to savour the pleasures yet to come.

'How long was Agatha missing?' Matthias asked harshly.

'Three days.' The taverner got to his feet. 'We'll all miss her dancing. I mean in . . .' The filthy remark he was going to make died on his lips. The student's pale face and hard, watchful eyes frightened him. 'I'm busy.' The taverner turned away. 'And I'm glad the slut Amasia can return to her other duties!'

Matthias went out into the alleyway, along Northgate and Oxford High Street. He walked purposefully, hood pulled over his head. He did not acknowledge the cries and shouts of those who knew him. Matthias was blind to anything but the direction he was taking. A sow, flanks quivering, careered across his path. Chickens pecking at the dust scattered before him. A dog, which came yapping out of a runnel, hoping to draw the student's attention to his master, a one-footed beggar, slunk away. Nor did the stall-holders, journeymen or tinkers catch his glance. Matthias shouldered his way through, not caring whom he elbowed out of his way: the well-dressed burgesses, lean-faced scholars in their shabby tabards, even the Masters and lecturers, the lords of the schools, whom every scholar had to treat with reverence, at least to their faces.

Matthias kept staring ahead. He felt like screaming, running, hiding in some dark hole, trying to make sense of what Amasia had told him. Images floated through his mind; Edith, daughter of Fulcher the blacksmith, in her coffin before the high altar of his father's church; those ghosts shifting along the path of Sutton Courteny; the hermit singing as he died; Christina screaming at him; Rahere, ever present, ever watchful; his father's last sad words; that dreadful sleep in the parish church. Matthias paused, closing his eyes. He breathed in deeply. Maybe he should go back to his hall? Seek out Santerre? Matthias rubbed the side of his head. He felt as if his mind were about to explode. That trap door he had closed so firmly on the nightmares of the past was forcing itself open.

'You are blocking the way!'

Matthias opened his eyes. A market beadle, an official of the Pie Powder court which governed the prices of the city market, was staring at him: his white wand of office held erect like a spear.

'You are blocking the way!'

Matthias' hand went to the dagger in his belt.

'Get out of my path,' he snarled, 'and I'll continue!'

The beadle hurriedly stepped sideways. Matthias continued up the High Street, past St Mary's church and the stone and timber dwellings of All Souls. The street became broader. Matthias walked on to Magdalen Bridge and stared down at the stream which swirled amongst the rushes. The weather being fine, scholars sat on the grass sleeping, talking, drinking and eating. On any other day Matthias would have joined them. He could only hope Amasia was wrong.

He walked on and stopped before the narrow greystone

church of the Crutched Friars. He went through the open door, down the nave and out through the side door of one of the transepts. A friar, poring over a manuscript in the cloisters, pointed across the garth.

'The death house is over there,' he declared. 'But you must get permission from the infirmarian.'

Matthias continued, impervious to the curious looks of the good brothers who bustled about. He left the cloisters and walked through a small garden towards a large half-timbered building at the far end. Oxford was a shifting city, visited by strangers from Italy, France, Germany and even further east. Unnamed corpses were often found and the friars saw it as their pious duty to afford church burial to these strangers. Agatha would be one of these, a mere slattern with no family. Her corpse would lie in the death house for three or four days awaiting recognition. The coroner would sit and deliver his verdict. Agatha's corpse would then be buried in the old Jewish cemetery which stood in Paris Mead, a broad, derelict expanse of land which stretched down to the River Cherwell.

Matthias walked down the path and tapped on the door. A small grille slid open.

'Your business? Your business?' the voice asked.

'There's a corpse,' Matthias replied. 'A girl called Agatha.'

'She's to be buried tonight,' the voice replied.

'I knew her,' Matthias said haltingly. 'I wish to pay my respects.'

The grille was closed. Bolts were drawn and the doors swung open. Matthias stepped over the threshold into a long, cavernous chamber: its white-washed walls and broad beams reminded him of a barn. Despite the herbs scattered along the freshly scrubbed paving stones, Matthias caught the stench of putrefaction and corruption from the corpses which lay in rows either side of this barnlike chamber. He stared down at the lay brother.

'Agatha?' Matthias repeated.

'Poor girl.' The friar scratched his unkempt beard. 'So young, so beautiful. Cut down like the flower of the field.'

Matthias dug into his purse and took out a penny. The friar snatched this and, snapping his fingers, led Matthias halfway down, stopping before a makeshift stretcher. He pulled back the dark woollen rug. Matthias fought hard against the dizziness and nausea. In life, Agatha had been a happy, winsome girl. Matthias had seen her dance, bracelets on her arm, blonde hair flying. She could whirl around lighted candles, her bare feet never touching the flames whilst customers clapped their hands and shouted encouragement. Now she lay, a pathetic bundle of flesh. She still wore her dark-blue smock but her face had lost all its beauty. A greenish pallor tinged her sagging cheeks, head slightly twisted, eyes half-closed, her lips tinged with blood. It was the mark in her throat which repelled Matthias – two large gaps on either side of the windpipe.

'That's how she was found,' the friar explained, kneeling at the other side of the makeshift bed. 'Those who found her,' he continued, 'said she had been pierced like a plum and drained of her blood.'

Matthias flinched and fought to keep his own nightmares under control.

'Something else,' the friar got to his feet, 'there were rose petals all about her, as if she had been playing "He loves me, He loves me not" with the flowers. It would appear,' he continued cautiously, 'he loved her not, or perhaps too much.'

Matthias could take no more. He sprang to his feet, threw a penny at the surprised lay brother and fled the death house. He was across the bridge, back in the city, before he recovered his wits.

The sun had disappeared. The sky had turned a leaden grey, the clouds pressing down, threatening rain. The stall-holders were already pulling sheets over their goods. Matthias loosened the clasp on his shirt. Pulling down his jerkin, he allowed the cool breeze to bathe the sweat on his neck. For a while he wandered amongst the stalls, past the clothiers, the baturs, who smoothed the coarse cloth: the cuissiers with their cushions heaped high on the stalls. An apprentice came running out, trying to clasp a spur on Matthias' boot, but he caught Matthias' glance and fled back into his shop.

Matthias wanted such commonplace things to soothe the turmoil in his soul but a young man with a falcon on his wrist reminded him of the hermit. A priest leading a funeral cortège recalled Parson Osbert. Matthias was sure that the young woman in front of him with a child holding a pig's bladder was Christina. And was that not Fulcher the blacksmith sitting at a table staring through a tavern window?

Matthias turned into Ivy Lane, a broad alleyway which led down to one of his favourite ale houses, the Pestle and Mortar. Yet, even here, Matthias felt he was in a nightmare. A makeshift gallows had been erected halfway down: the corpse of a felon swung there, neck awry, face turned a purplish hue. The placard round his neck proclaimed he was a thrice-caught housebreaker. Some drunken students stood around, carolling the corpse with a favourite goliard song 'Jove cum laude'. They tried to entice Matthias to join in but he shouldered by them. The students, led by a golden-haired, baby-faced young man, screamed obscenities back. Matthias hurried on into the taproom of the Pestle and Mortar. He drank two cups of wine before he felt the panic recede.

Across the tavern a physician, a quack, his vein-streaked face coarsened by alcohol, his silvery-grey hair shrouding his face like that of a woman, was trying to sell his potions to the saggy-faced, bleary-eyed customers. To one old woman, her skin a blotchy, purplish grey, the quack offered a potion to cure toothache: a copper needle steeped in the juice of a woodlouse. To another a piece of Spanish jade, a sure remedy for pains in the side. When he failed to sell these, the quack brought his tray across and offered Matthias a whole range of herbs: nasturtium, sour thistle, wood sorrel, wood sage, liverwort, fennel.

'And,' the fellow screeched, thin fingers snaking out, 'milk of roses: a love potion . . .' He stopped gabbling and stared down at the tip of the dagger only an inch from his nose. The fellow's mouth cracked into a smile. 'The young sir does not want to buy?'

'Piss off!' Matthias retorted. 'Take your rubbish and piss off!'

The quack seized his goods and scurried like a squirrel through the doorway. The rest of the customers, who had grown tired of the charlatan, applauded Matthias, but the student resheathed his dagger, already lost in his own thoughts.

The nightmare had returned! He thought he had locked it into the darkness of the past, ever since that morning when he had woken in a chamber in Baron Sanguis' manor house and those young women, maids of the household, clustered round his bed. He could tell by their eyes that something horrible had happened. Matthias felt inside his pouch and pulled out a piece of parchment. It was not the same one his father had given him that last, dreadful night in the parish church but it was a fair copy. Time and again he had studied the citations Parson Osbert had scrawled on that greasy piece of parchment.

The first Genesis was from Chapter 6, Verse 2: 'The sons of God saw the daughters of men that they were fair; and they took them wives of all which they chose.' And a text from Chapter 14 of the prophet Isaiah. 'Art thou also become weak as we? Art thou become like unto us? Thy pomp is brought down to the grave . . . How art thou fallen from heaven, O Lucifer, son of the morning! how art thou cut down to the ground.'

The next text was from the Book of Tobit, Chapter 3, Verse 8, about a young woman Sarah: 'She had been married to seven husbands whom Asmadeus, the evil spirit, had killed before they had lain with her.' Finally, there was a quotation from the Gospels, which had very little to do with the ones which went before. The words of Christ to his disciples: 'If anyone loves me, I shall love him and my Father will love him. And my Father and I will come and make our home with him.'

Matthias sighed, rolled the parchment up and slipped it back into his pouch. He had never really understood what his father had meant by these messages. Over the years Matthias' interest in demonology, the activities of witches and warlocks, had deepened. In his heart he recognised that the events which had occurred at Sutton Courteny during those few months of 1471 could not be explained in human terms. During his years of scholarship, where he could, Matthias had consulted the secret books of writers on demonology. At Oxford he attended the schools, listened to lectures and studied the works of Peter the Lombard, Abelard, Bonaventure, the great commentators on philosophy, theology and scripture. In Duke Humphrey's library, however, Matthias read the works of authors which, if the University authorities found out, would certainly bring him under suspicion of being a heretic or a warlock. The writings of the alchemist John de Meung, the 'Opera' of

Arnaud de Villeneuve the occultist. The treatises of Simon bar Yokhai, master of the secret cabal. These scholars, as well as the orthodox ones such as Aquinas, Augustine, Origen and Tertullian, provided a bleak perception of man's reality: a constant battle between good and evil; of Satan and other demon lords waging eternal war against man and all God's creation.

Matthias had remained both cynical and confused by what he read: most of it was the work of fertile imaginations. Even at Oxford, students were only too keen to become involved in secret rites, a pretext for dancing naked in some wood under the stars and fornicating freely with whores. Moreover, these writings did little to explain the events at Sutton Courteny. Why did they happen? What was so important about a sleepy little hamlet in Gloucestershire that could provoke such terrible events and lead to so many hideous deaths? Stories and legends abounded yet Matthias had found no one who could really explain such events. Everyone in that church had died, apart from himself. He had been heavily drugged and slept during the entire massacre.

No one had explained why he'd survived. Many believed Parson Osbert had given him a potion and so saved his life. Matthias had always wondered about the friendship shown to him by Rahere and the hermit. Why was he singled out for such tenderness? Were they really responsible for the blood-drained cadavers and, if so, why did they kill in such a barbaric fashion? How was it the hermit and the clerk, complete strangers to each other and so contrasting in their appearance and background, were reflections of the same personality? What had turned the minds of his parents in such a turbulent way? What was their relationship with the hermit? Such questions vexed Matthias' mind, nagged his soul, yet the passing of time and all his studies had yielded no real answers.

Once Matthias had entered the household of Baron Sanguis nothing else mysterious had happened, except when he had lodged with the monks at Tewkesbury, just after his fourteenth birthday. The brothers had gossiped how, in the gallery outside the boys' dormitory where Matthias slept, they could smell, even though it was mid-winter, the rich, heavy aroma of roses. Matthias had kept silent, as he always did, during those few weeks in the winter of 1478. He had fallen ill but then the phenomenon had passed and his life had continued. Indeed, only his youth and the humdrum tenor of the years after the sinister events of that All-Hallows Eve had kept him sane. Matthias dare not mention his fears to others and, in time, he half-believed that night was just a horrifying phantasm, something dreamt in a nightmare. He had held on to this; his way of keeping the door to that dark past of his soul firmly locked, until today.

Matthias closed his eyes: why, he wondered, why now?

He opened his eyes and drained his wine cup. He stared through the open doorway. He felt slightly drunk but more comfortable. He would seek out Santerre, his friend and companion. Perhaps there was some rational explanation of what had occurred? Matthias went out to the alleyway. It was darker than he thought, the place now empty, the drunken students long disappeared, only the corpse still hung from its makeshift scaffold, twirling in the brisk evening breeze. Matthias closed his eyes and said a prayer, the same one his father had taught him.

'Remember this, my soul, and remember it well. The Lord thy God is One and He is holy . . .'

Matthias opened his eyes and walked purposefully down the alleyway. Somewhere, deep in the city, a bell tolled for Compline. A dog barked and Matthias jumped as a screeching cat scampered across his path. He passed the scaffold, averting his eyes.

He was scarcely by it when he heard a voice whisper: '*Creatura bona atque parva*: Matthias, my little one.'

The voice of the hermit! Matthias broke out into a cold sweat. He turned slowly, one hand going to the crucifix round his neck, the other to the hilt of his dagger.

'*Oh, Creatura bona atque parva . . . !*'

Matthias stood rooted to the spot. He stared at the corpse. Had the dead man spoken? Matthias rubbed his eyes and stepped back. He breathed in and, as he did, instead of the fetid alleyway smell, he caught the fragrance of roses as if he were standing in some woodland glade.

'Who's there?' he called.

The smell of roses disappeared. Matthias became aware of the dirt and muck of the alleyway, the corpse dangling at the end of its rope. Turning on his heel, Matthias fled down the alley. He ran blindly, head down, straight into a group of scholars who came round the corner laughing and shouting.

Matthias apologised and stepped back. The scholars would have let him by but one came forward. Matthias recognised the golden-haired, baby-faced young man who had cursed him earlier in the day.

'Well, well, well.' Golden Locks pushed Matthias up against the wall. 'What do we have here? A man who hurries and scurries about? Shouts abuse, shoves and pushes and won't even join in a little sweet singing?'

'Leave him be!'

'No, no.' The scholar drew his knife; its tip pricked Matthias' chin. 'I think this young man needs to be taught some manners.'

'I am sorry,' Matthias mumbled. 'I meant no offence.'

'He meant no offence!' Golden Locks mimicked.

The other students now crowded round. Their faces were sodden with drink, the ale heavy on their breath.

'I know what we'll do,' Golden Locks declared, his blue eyes rounding in mock innocence. 'This impudent boy wouldn't sing to the corpse on the gallows. Now, that's bad manners, isn't it?'

'True,' another replied.

'He should respect the dead. So, what we'll do is this,' Golden Locks continued. 'We'll take you back there and introduce you. A few hours tied to our dead friend will teach you manners and proper decorum. Would you like that?' he lisped.

Matthias knocked away Golden Locks' knife and drove his fist straight into the man's face, battering his nose so violently, the blood squirted out. Golden Locks staggered away, hands to his face, crying and screaming. Matthias tried to draw his dagger but the others were upon him, kicking and beating him. They laughed cruelly at their companion's discomfiture and, leaving him to hold his face, dragged Matthias back up the alleyway. One of them found a piece of old rope and another took off Matthias' belt.

'Let's tie them together like lovers!' one of them shouted. 'Remember Villon's poem? About being bound to the corpse of a friend, lips to lips, nose to nose?'

162

The others agreed but Matthias, desperate with fear, struggled, lashing out with his feet. Golden Locks joined them, smashing his fists in the side of Matthias' head. Slowly they dragged him towards the scaffold. The students leapt about like imps, determined on carrying out their punishment. Above them a window opened: a woman's voice shouted that she'd call the watch. The students picked up clods of dirt from the midden-heap and flung them at her, and the window promptly closed.

Matthias could now smell the rottenness of the corpse. He could not bear the thought but he knew it was impossible to beg. Even in the dusk, he could make out the dead man's features. He closed his eyes, tightening his lips, not conscious of the pain which racked him.

'That will be enough of that!'

Matthias sighed and let his body sag. The students turned, staring at the dark figure, cloak thrown back, sword and dagger drawn.

'Go to hell!' Golden Locks shouted.

The figure darted forward: the tip of Santerre's sword bit into the fleshy part of Golden Locks' shoulder. The Frenchman danced back, sword and dagger swishing the air. The students recognised a street-fighter, a born swordsman. They let go of Matthias.

'Go on!' Santerre lunged forward, his sword snaking out. 'Leave my friend and go!'

The students dropped Matthias and took to their heels.

Matthias felt his friend's arm lifting him up, then he sank into a faint.

11

Matthias woke early the next morning. He felt sore and stiff; the side of his face hurt. He struggled up, pushing back the bolsters. He groaned and carefully made his way down the ladder from his small bed. Santerre was fast asleep on his palliasse under the window, red hair splayed out, mouth half open. The Frenchman had not even bothered to take his boots off but lay sprawled over the blankets, his sword belt on the floor beside him. Matthias staggered over to the lavarium. A piece of polished metal above it served as a mirror. Matthias was pleased to see his face was not too bruised. He washed and shaved, wincing as the razor scraped his tender skin. He dried himself, glancing round the chamber to make sure that he was no longer dreaming, that the chamber was his. The crumbling masonry hearth; the wall above blackened with soot; the small windows covered by a pig's bladder; a low ceiling of rough beams, sparse furniture, a table, wooden-peg stools, chests, coffers and hooks on the walls with various garments hanging from them. Beneath the loft was a cupboard to hold provisions, pots, jugs, cups and a tankard Santerre had stolen from a tavern. Matthias went across but the bread and cheese he had left there were gone. He sat down, recalling the horrors of the previous day.

'I really should go to the schools,' he whispered. 'Perhaps that is best.'

'There'll be no lectures for you today, *mon ami.*'

Matthias looked over his shoulder. Santerre was sitting on the edge of the mattress; his long, white face was heavy with sleep but his sharp green eyes watched Matthias intently.

'Thank you for last night.' Matthias staggered across to him.

Santerre clasped his hand and grinned.

'I've been busy on your behalf.' The Frenchman's English was good, only slightly tinged with an accent.

'If you hadn't been busy,' Matthias retorted, 'I'd have spent the night strapped to a corpse.'

'And now?'

'I feel tired, a little bruised but very hungry.'

'Then come.'

Santerre sprang to his feet. He slapped some water over his face, carelessly drying himself with a rag, which he then flung into a corner. He led Matthias out of the chamber and down the narrow, spiral staircase. Matthias still felt confused. Everything was happening so fast but Santerre was going ahead of him, shaking his head, as if he knew Matthias wanted to question him.

'Remember what Bonaventure said,' he called out over his shoulder. '"If speech is a gift from God, silence is a virtue."'

They stood aside as a group of scholars, bachelors in their shabby brown gowns, bustled up the stairs. Each carried a small bundle; on their belts were strapped ink horns and a sheaf of quills in a small pouch. They nodded at Santerre and Matthias but, as usual, left these two alone. Usually this never bothered Matthias but now he realised that his life in Oxford was really no different from that at Tewkesbury. He was a stranger in a foreign land, like a boy who stands in the middle of a ring and watches other children play around him.

'Stop dreaming!' Santerre called from the foot of the stairs.

Matthias hurried on. The lane outside smelt sweet after the dank fetidness of the hall. The sun was strong, the air clear and crisp. Dung-collectors had taken the refuse from the day before and the streets and alleyways were still empty. Only the occasional, heavy-eyed apprentice, laying up the stalls or taking down the fronts of the shops, was to be seen as Matthias and Santerre hurried across Broad Street and into a side door of the Silver Wyvern. The taverner came out, Santerre whispered to him, the man nodded and handed over a key.

'The third chamber on the first gallery,' he declared. 'I'll send food up immediately.'

Santerre took Matthias up. The chamber was clean – lime-washed walls, fresh rushes on the floor. The tables and stools looked as if they had been scrubbed with hot water and the lattice window was open, allowing in the clear, flower-scented air from the garden below. A tapster brought up cups of watered wine and two trenchers with strips of roast beef in garlic pepper sauce, small bread loaves and pots of honey and butter.

'Why this?' Matthias asked.

'Why not?' Santerre replied, sitting Matthias at the other side of the table. 'I arranged it last night. You and I need to have words.'

Matthias took his horn spoon from his wallet and polished it absent-mindedly on his sleeve.

'About what?'

The Frenchman's eyes held his. 'You know full well, Matthias! Master Ambrose Rokesby, lecturer in Philosophy and self-styled authority in Theology. He has been making complaints about you.'

Matthias groaned. 'Rokesby is a lecher and a lecturer,' he mocked back. 'I have challenged him in the schools.'

'Yes, I know, about his theory on Lucifer and the fallen angels.'

Santerre grinned. Matthias noticed how white and even his teeth were. He liked the Frenchman's cleanliness. Matthias could never understand why so many scholars believed dirt and foul odours were the leading characteristics of learning. Rokesby was one of these, with his fat, unshaven face, slobbery mouth and eyes, which always betrayed a heavy night's drinking. Rokesby had clawed his greasy hair in rage when Matthias had dared to draw him into disputation over his commentary on Aquinas' dissertation on the fall of Lucifer.

'You shouldn't have said it!' Santerre reminded him.

'All I said,' Matthias replied, biting into a piece of meat, 'was that Hell was not a place but a state of mind and that Lucifer probably thought he was in Heaven even when he was in Hell.'

'Rokesby says that's heresy,' Santerre teased back. His face became grave. 'More importantly, that fat little turd-ball has been making deliberate enquiries with the archivist in Duke Humphrey's library. In the Blue Boar yesterday evening, Rokesby was maliciously speculating on your unnatural interest in the Devil and all his works.'

'I am a scholar,' Matthias retorted.

'Even when it comes to reading books which are on the University Index? Men like the Bohemian, John Hus?'

'Hus was a great scholar.'

'The Church says Hus was a heretic. Here, in England, they say Wycliffe, and his followers the Lollards, are no different. Rokesby hints that you are a Lollard.'

Matthias closed his eyes and groaned. Santerre was correct: the Lollards had been persecuted for their emphasis of Scripture, their rejection of the power of the priests as well as a greater part of the Church's teaching on Hell and Purgatory. If Rokesby persisted in his allegations, Matthias might have to appear before the Chancellor's Court.

'We should leave.'

Matthias looked up in surprise. Santerre had a piece of bread in his hand, looking at it carefully, his face tense, eyes watchful.

'We should leave,' the Frenchman repeated. He put the bread down. 'Matthias, how many years have you known me?'

'Over three, ever since I came to Oxford.'

'That's right. I am Henri de Santerre. My family owns châteaux and fertile vineyards in the Loire Valley. I have studied at the Sorbonne in Paris and now here in Oxford.'

Matthias nodded. The Frenchman often talked about his family estates, the sunshine, the vines, the brown-skinned girls.

'A new life,' Santerre said. 'Come to France with me, Matthias. I have wealth enough for both of us.'

'Was that why you were looking for me last night?' Matthias asked.

'Why, of course. Also because Rokesby has threatened you.'

Matthias pulled a face. He pushed away the trencher. He no longer felt hungry.

'Rokesby is a lecher born and bred. He sits in the Blue Boar and watches Amasia like a cat does a mouse and, when he can, it's a hand up her dress or clutching her breast like someone would grasp an apple.' Matthias got to his feet, walked to the window and stared down at the garden. 'Agatha's dead,' he said, not turning his head. 'You know her, the little, blonde-haired girl who could dance like a firefly. She was murdered out in Christ Church Meadows.'

'Yes, so I have heard.' Behind him, Santerre refilled the goblets. 'Rokesby was talking about it last night—'

'He can talk away,' Matthias interrupted testily. 'But it brings back memories.' He looked over his shoulder. 'What do you know about me, Frenchman?'

Santerre pulled a face.

'I mean, really know about me?' Matthias insisted. 'You've hired a chamber here because Rokesby is about to start a persecution. You want me to flee with you to France.'

'Not flee,' the Frenchman contradicted. 'Last autumn I gained my bachelor's. Where I study, or what I do is a matter of my own concern. I intend to leave in the summer anyway.'

Matthias' heart skipped a beat. He hadn't known that and, to be honest, the Frenchman was the only real friend he had. He went back to staring at the herb garden below him.

'I was born in the village of Sutton Courteny in Gloucestershire,' Matthias told him. 'My parents died when I was young. Baron Sanguis, the local lord, became my guardian. He sent me to the abbey schools of Tewkesbury and Gloucester.'

'And then you came to Oxford?'

'Yes, I came to Oxford. I am fluent in Latin and Norman French. I even know some Greek. I can converse with a clerk or a courtier. I am considered a good scholar. I can sing with the best of them, whether it be the '*Veni Creator Spiritus*' or one of the goliard songs of Provence. I can play the rebec and the lyre. Sometimes I drink too much.' His voice fell to a whisper. 'But that's not me.'

'Then who are you?'

Matthias returned to the table and sat down. He drank deeply from the cup, then began to tell Santerre everything that had happened at Sutton Courteny. The Frenchman sat still as a statue, ignoring both the food and the wine. Matthias, however, kept slurping at his cup: sometimes he'd stop, his voice choked with emotion, tears rolling down his cheeks. He spoke in short, harsh sentences about the hermit, the battle of Tewkesbury, the Preacher and the arrival of Rahere the clerk. At the end, when he came to describe the events of All-Hallows Eve 1471, Matthias closed his eyes, trying to curb the panic in his stomach. He was aware that his face had become damp with sweat whilst his hands felt cold and clammy. He paused in mid-sentence.

'And what happened then?'

Matthias opened his eyes. He steadied himself against the table. Santerre had moved away. He was standing with his back to him, staring down at the garden. The Frenchman looked round and smiled.

'Finish the story, Matthias.'

'I don't really know. God be my witness, Santerre. I don't really know. Rahere gave me something to drink, a heavy opiate. When I awoke I was in Baron Sanguis' manor house. The old lord and his son came to see me. I could tell from their faces, as well as those of the servants, that something horrifying had happened. I wanted to go back but Baron Sanguis refused. He said the village was deserted, his tenants would not return there. They had petitioned and he had agreed fresh plans for a new village.'

Matthias filled his wine cup. He was drinking so fast, he was glad the wine was heavily watered. He pushed some meat into his mouth but found it difficult to chew or swallow.

'I was kept a prisoner in the manor. Oh, I was given everything I wanted: toys, books, a tutor. The sheriff came from Gloucester. I remember it was a few days before Christmas. He and a thin-faced scribe asked me what I could remember and I told him about my father and other parishioners huddling into the church. However, they never told me what they knew. It was only later, well after Candlemas, the gossip began to seep through.'

He smiled thinly. 'Apparently on All Saints' Day, the first of November, Baron Sanguis and his men had ridden down to the church. They went through the village, it was deserted. Quite a few had fled. Those who'd remained . . .' Matthias shook his head. 'They said it was dreadful. A corpse here, a corpse there, all killed by accidents, caused by the storm they said. My father's house was empty. In the churchyard, every cross and tombstone had been hurled down. Some of the graves looked as if they had been disturbed.'

'And the church?' Santerre asked.

'Oh, the church housed the real horrors. The windows were shuttered, the doors locked and barred.' Matthias closed his eyes. 'No, one window had been forced, a small aperture leading into the sacristy. One of Baron Sanguis' men got in. They heard him screaming, so terror-struck he could hardly turn the key in the lock or lift the bars. Once inside they found out why: at least two dozen people must have taken refuge there, men and women; all had wounds to their heads or chests. The church stank of blood. In places it ran ankle-deep down the nave. The corpses were strewn about, some had drawn knives or tried to hide but the killers had hunted each down.'

'And yourself?'

'I was rolled up in a blanket in one of the transepts, deeply asleep. At first they thought I was dead or in some deep swoon. They found my father just near the sanctuary.' Matthias looked up. 'He was the parson. I am, Monsieur Santerre, the by-blow of a priest. He had died quickly, a swift blow from an axe to his head.'

'And who was responsible?'

'They said it was Rahere the clerk. They claimed the storm must have turned his wits, unhinged his mind. But how could one man kill so many people?'

'What happened to him?'

'Oh, he had left the church by the window. A tinker found his body in the woods. He was a mass of wounds from head to toe. Some of my father's parishioners had resisted.' Matthias paused. 'Do you know, Santerre, I have never been back there.'

'And since then?'

'I live my life. I learnt very quickly to take each day as it comes and not to dwell on the past. If I did, I'd become madcap or witless.'

Santerre turned. He leant against the wall and crossed his arms.

'And what do you believe now?'

'I don't really know. I attend Mass but I feel as if I am watching someone else pray. I listen to the priests talking about the goodness of God and then I think of my parents: Christina a broken reed, my father wandering drunkenly round the graveyard. I remember those corpses, lives snuffed out like candle wicks.' Matthias paused. 'When I go out to the streets or ride through the fields, I really do envy the people I pass. They live their lives, they marry, they are happy in what they do.'

'Self-pity is dangerous!'

'Oh, it's not self-pity. I am more confused, that's one of the reasons I came to Oxford. Perhaps, in a place of learning, I'd find the answers but I still don't know what happened at Sutton Courteny or why. Baron Sanguis never really talked about it. The sheriff sent letters to London yet everyone seemed determined to forget it as quickly as possible.'

'But you can't?'

'No, I can't.' Matthias sipped at the wine cup. 'And that's when I come to life. My mind quickens. My will takes a purpose. Something happened at Sutton Courteny, something outside our ordinary experience. I want to know what. I don't believe that spirits are little imps or Satan is a goat with cloven hooves and a black cloak. They are fables to frighten children. Only one thing I have found, the legend of the incubus, a spirit who can move from body to body, take over a personality, work through that individual.'

'Possession?'

'Perhaps. My father left me some texts, scribbled jottings he pushed into my hand the night he died. I think he knew the truth. One of the quotations is from St John. It talks about Christ promising that, if someone loves Him, He and His Father will come and make Their home in him.' Matthias shrugged. 'If God can make a home in our hearts, fill our souls, why can't some other spirit?'

'But the murders?' Santerre asked.

'Now that is a mystery. Except in one respect. Nature teaches that, if I wish to live, I must eat and drink. The Church teaches that, if I am to live spiritually, I must eat the Body of Christ and drink His Blood. What happens, Santerre, if this incubus must kill, must drink human blood? A diabolical reflection of the Church's teaching?'

'And you think that's what happened to Agatha?'

'Yes, yes, I do.' Matthias gnawed his lip. 'All this is conjecture,' he sighed. 'Sometimes, I think I can't understand any of it, especially when I look at myself. Why was I singled out by the hermit and the clerk?'

'So why not leave with me?' Santerre sat down and leant

across the table. He grasped Matthias' hand. 'Start again, Matthias, leave these dreams, these nightmares behind.'

Matthias got to his feet and stretched. He came back and gripped Santerre by the shoulder.

'I have never told anyone what happened to me in Sutton Courteny. If I did, they'd either laugh or think I'm a madcap or worse, report me to the Church authorities. I thank you for last night and the offer you made this morning. But why should I flee? Because Rokesby muttered his threats? Or a girl is killed in Christ Church Meadows?'

'Listen!' Santerre replied. 'If this so-called incubus has now returned to haunt you, if I accept your theory he now possesses someone else, what happens if this person is Rokesby?'

'Impossible!' Matthias retorted.

'Is it?' Santerre asked. 'He seems to know a great deal about you. What you read. Where you go. He takes a deep interest in your affairs.'

'That's because he lusts after Amasia and I made fun of him in the schools.' Matthias rubbed his mouth and stared out of the window. He'd rejected Santerre's proposition out of hand, but might there be some truth in it?

'It could even be me,' Santerre joked.

'I don't think so.' Matthias walked to the door. He opened it and stared down the gallery. 'I have known you, what, three years? I've seen you take the Sacrament at Mass. That's one thing I do remember. The hermit never took the Sacrament and, on reflection, neither did Rahere.'

'When the clerk died,' Santerre asked, 'what would have happened to this being?'

'I don't know. The philosopher Albertus Magnus said an incubus must, within a certain period of time, find lodgings elsewhere, rather a homespun way of putting it. Yet, even of that I am not too sure.' Matthias leant against the door. 'According to Aquinas, literally thousands upon thousands of angels fell with Lucifer. We know from the gospels that one possessed man had so many demons in him, he took the name of Legion. This does not fit what I know: one being moving from the hermit and, in time, to Rahere, then to someone else.' Matthias breathed in. 'What I intend to do is continue to live each day as it comes. Agatha was murdered but I am totally innocent of her death. Rokesby is different.

172

I cannot allow him to stir up trouble against me. What hour is it, Santerre?'

'By now, no later than ten.'

Matthias stroked his bruised face. 'I've drunk a little too much and I'm sore from last night's manhandling. I'm going to return to my chamber and sleep. Rokesby will be in the schools now but, this afternoon, he will be back in his lodgings. Where are they?'

'I don't know,' Santerre replied. 'But I'll find out.' He looked anxious. 'What are you going to do?'

'I am going to confront Rokesby. I am going to challenge him and, if possible, make my peace with him.'

'And the murder of the girl?'

'What can I do,' Matthias shrugged, 'except see what happens?'

It was late afternoon when the Frenchman shook Matthias awake.

'You'd best come,' he smiled. 'I have found out where Rokesby lives. He has a chamber not very far from here. It's on the corner of Vinehall Street, near Peckwater's Inn. I saw him stagger in there less than an hour ago, carrying more ale in his belly than a brewer's barrel. Are you sure you wish to meet him?'

Matthias got off the bed and followed Santerre down the ladder. He sat on the stool, pulled on his boots and splashed water over his face.

'*Carpe diem!*' he quipped. 'Seize the day! It will only fester. Rokesby is arrogant. He can be mollified.'

They left the hall and made their way along the High Street, pushing through the throngs of students who, the morning schools now finished, clustered round the open doors of taverns or strolled past the stalls, much to the anxiety of their owners. These watched the ragged-arsed students, notorious for their light fingers and skill at stealing. On the corner of Vinehall Street Lane, one such student had been caught. A furious quarrel was brewing between proctors and beadles of the University and a group of traders, who clamoured for the students to be taken immediately to the Bocardo, the city gaol. The fray stirred up the usual deep-seated animosity between town and gown. Other students began to gather, rusty swords and daggers pushed in their belts, whilst the traders were shouting at their apprentices to arm themselves with quarterstaffs and clubs. Pickpockets and foists looked for easy takings. A group of whores, their saucy faces garishly painted, their gaudy dresses causing a swirl of colour, also drew near for, when tempers rose, passion provided easy custom.

Santerre pushed his way through, turning to grasp Matthias' belt as the two became separated.

'Whatever you decide, Englishman,' he joked. 'I think it's time I left this city. I really wish you'd come with me.'

They reached the bottom of the lane. Santerre led Matthias down a small alleyway and across a weed-strewn court-yard. An old woman was sitting on a stool, sunning herself, munching on her gums. She pointed to a staircase.

'You'll find Master Rokesby in his chamber,' she shrilled. 'Supposedly studying but drunk as a sot!'

They thanked her and climbed the stairs. Rokesby's door was half-open. The chamber inside smelt stale; manuscripts lay piled on the floor. Dust-covered hangings draped the walls, soiled clothing lay thrown about. The room was well furnished, the stools and chests finely made, but it looked as if it hadn't been cleaned for months. Rokesby sat at a table beneath the window. He was dozing, head falling forward. Matthias coughed. He didn't wish to startle this lecturer, who had a foul temper and nasty ways. Matthias coughed again.

'Master Rokesby!' Santerre shouted. 'We have come to see you!'

Rokesby jumped and stirred. His ale-sodden face was unshaven. He blinked bleary-eyed.

'Who is it?' he muttered.

'Matthias Fitzosbert, Domine. I've come to speak to you.'

Rokesby, wheezing and puffing, got to his feet. He reminded Matthias of a toad: he had a malevolent look on his face and kept wetting his lips.

'What do you want?'

'Why, sir, I've come to make my peace.'

Rokesby smirked. He undid the points of his hose and, waddling across the room, picked up a chamber pot and noisily pissed into it. Matthias chose to ignore such an obscene insult. Rokesby finished relieving himself, put the chamber pot down then walked across, tying his points up. His eyes

174

were clearer now though Matthias could smell the stale odour of ale.

'So, the priest's brat has come to speak to me? Eh?' Rokesby poked Matthias in the chest. 'Clever little boys should keep their mouths shut or get their bottoms smacked. Yes, that's what I should do.' He scratched his cheek. 'I should birch you in public. A warning against insolence and questioning your betters. After all, that's what they do to heretics, isn't it?'

'I'm no heretic,' Matthias replied hotly.

'Yes you are. I know a lot about you, Master Fitzosbert. Come from Gloucester, do you? Patronised by the powerful Baron Sanguis, eh? Well, Sanguis is powerful no longer, is he?' He poked his head forward and clasped his hands behind his back, like some angry school teacher berating a dullard. 'Baron Sanguis was a Yorkist. Now that was all well and good but where are the Yorkists now, eh? Where is the great King Edward? Died of apoplexy, he did, three years in his grave. And where are his sons, the Princes?' Rokesby lifted his hand up and snapped his fingers. 'Gone like a mist on a summer's day.' He wetted his lips. 'And the great Clarence? Murdered by his brother, Richard of Gloucester.' Rokesby widened his eyes. 'And we know what happened to him.'

Matthias stared at this wicked little man with his malicious, greasy face.

'What is all this to me?' Matthias declared.

'I know,' Rokesby snapped. 'Your patron, Baron Sanguis – his son fought for Richard III at Bosworth and was killed for his treason! Baron Sanguis' name is not popular at the court of Henry Tudor. There are many who would be delighted to hear that his protégé at Oxford was dabbling in heresy and the occult.'

'Shut up, you pig's turd!'

Rokesby's eyes slid to Santerre. 'Ah, so the Frenchman has found his tongue. Master Matthias' bum boy, eh?'

Santerre stepped forward. 'What do you want with my friend? Why do you harass him?'

'Oh, I'll stop him!' Rokesby bit his lip as if he'd said too much. 'For a night with Amasia. A juicy little morsel, eh? How does she perform in bed? Oh, I'd love to see her bouncing, those long legs, her hair flying. They say she squeals a lot.'

Matthias would have turned on his heel but Santerre grasped him by the sleeve.

'Do you know, Master Rokesby,' the Frenchman sneered, 'the girls at the Blue Boar talk about you? They say how small your member is.' Santerre waggled his little finger. 'And now I've seen you piss, I can see they were exaggerating.'

Rokesby's face suffused with rage. He drew the dagger from his belt and lunged at Santerre. The Frenchman caught his wrist, twisted it and plucked the knife from his fingers but he didn't stop there. He grasped Rokesby by the jerkin, pulled him forward and, with one sweeping cut, slit the lecturer's belly. It happened so quickly Matthias couldn't object.

Santerre held the knife up before Rokesby's startled eyes then dropped it. Rokesby, clutching his stomach, staggered forward. He went to say something but coughed blood and slumped to one knee. Santerre kicked his leg. Rokesby keeled over on to the dirty rushes, body twitching. Matthias stared horrified.

'God save us, Santerre!' he muttered. 'We'll both hang for this!'

'No we won't.' Santerre smiled down at the corpse. 'He was a pig and he died like one. It will be days before they find his corpse and we'll be gone.'

He pulled Matthias out of the room, slamming the door, and, holding Matthias by the arm, hustled him down the stairs.

They hurried back through the late afternoon crowds to Exeter Hall. Matthias found himself numb, unable to speak. All he could remember was Rokesby's sneering face, the quick, deft way Santerre had killed him.

Once back in their chamber Matthias climbed up to his bed in the loft and sat, head in hands. Rokesby had been correct. Sanguis had supported the usurper Richard III and any influence the Baron had at court had died at the Battle of Bosworth the previous August. The good Baron still sent Matthias monies but he was old, grieving over his son and wary of the new Tudor King calling him to account. Matthias cursed his own selfishness but he knew that, apart from Sanguis, no one else could help him.

He glanced down. Santerre had taken his flute from a coffer and, as if nothing had happened, piped some music. The

Frenchman paused then played notes Matthias had never heard before. The tune abruptly changed; Matthias stiffened. The playing was sweet, fluid, the same song he had heard the hermit sing on that dreadful day when the peasants of Sutton Courteny had burnt him to death.

12

'Why?' Matthias sat opposite Santerre. The Frenchman kept his face turned away. 'Who are you?' Matthias' mouth and throat felt dry. He fought hard to control his panic, the cold sweat which broke out on his body. 'Who are you?' he repeated.

'*Oh, Creatura bona atque parva!*'

Matthias couldn't stop the tears. The voice was the same, an accurate echo from his childhood, of sun-filled glades, of his father's house and church. The lonely Tenebral, a dove flying against the blue sky.

Santerre turned his head. Matthias knew he was not dreaming: the same face, but the eyes were different. He'd glimpsed that look in the hermit and Rahere the clerk; brooding, gentle as if the soul behind it wished to say something but couldn't find the words.

'Don't call me that!' Matthias blurted out. 'Just answer me, why?'

'Because I love you.'

'In the body of a man?'

'"The flesh profiteth nothing, it is the spirit which quickens,"' Santerre replied, quoting from the Scriptures. 'Do you really think love is a matter of the flesh? There's more to it than what hangs between the thighs.' He touched his head. 'It's in the brain, it's in the soul!'

'Why me?'

'In time I'll tell you.'

Matthias calmed himself. Santerre was holding his gaze, not just to tell him something but, like the hermit, to soothe, to lull any anxieties.

'I saw you take the Eucharist.'

'How long ago is that, Matthias?' Santerre smiled. 'We've known each other for years.'

178

Matthias glanced away.

'You are a murderer, an assassin.'

Santerre remained unperturbed.

'Life breeds on life. The hawk kills the dove, the fox the rabbit, the lords of the soil whomever and whatever they wish. You saw that at Tewkesbury, Matthias. Men taken out and killed just because they fought for another prince. Or Baron Sanguis – you'd take his money but where does that come from, Matthias? From the blood and sweat of others.'

'Those villagers,' Matthias retorted, 'my father and the rest.'

'I could do nothing against them. They brought it on themselves.' Santerre's face became hard. 'I came to their village and, though they did not know it, my presence brought prosperity. They turned on me. I, who had done them no harm.'

'You killed Fulcher's daughter.'

'True.' Santerre's face relaxed. 'What is it you say, Matthias? How does that prayer go? Remember this, my soul, and remember it well. The Lord thy God is One and He is holy . . .'

'What has that to do with it?' Matthias objected to the prayer being quoted back at him.

Santerre raised both hands, fingers splayed. 'The Ten Commandments, Matthias. Ten in all. "Thou shalt have no other gods before me", that's the first one. Yet, what do your priests do but build false idols of wealth and power? They take God's name in vain. They preach obedience but don't practise it themselves.'

'And does that excuse you?'

'No, Matthias, but it explains what I do. When I kill I have to.' Only now did Santerre's eyes fall away. 'I need the sustenance, it's the price I have to pay.'

'You broke God's law.' Matthias' curiosity was now quickened. He realised that, for the first time since Sutton Courteny, he could question the presence which had shattered his childhood.

'Two things matter in life, Matthias. Only two things: love and the will. Everything else is mere chaff in the wind. I love you and one day, if you come with me, I will explain all the reasons why.' He leant forward, eyes bright. 'Come, Matthias, leave this shabby place. France, Italy, the nations

179

to the east or west across the great unknown. Empires, sights, knowledge which will dwarf the dusty scraps of parchment you pore over here.'

'Why didn't you force me?' Matthias taunted back.

'Two things, Matthias, love and the will. I can kill you. I can make you laugh, I can make you cry, I can make you bleed. I can make you happy, I can make you sad.' His eyes filled with tears. 'I could have all the power in Heaven and on earth. However, there is one thing, Matthias, you cannot force another being to do: you cannot make them love you. Even God Himself has that limitation.'

'You talk of God, you talk of the Scriptures,' Matthias retorted, getting to his feet. 'You talk of love and you talk of the will but you don't tell me why. Not a month passes but I think of my father, of Christina, of the others at Sutton Courteny!'

'Why do you make excuses for them?' Santerre's voice grew angry. 'Parson Osbert was a priest. Yes? He took a vow to be celibate, to be chaste. He broke that vow. He broke God's law. He lay with a woman. He committed fornication. What's the difference, scholar, between breaking the seventh Commandment, "Thou shalt not commit adultery", and the sixth, "Thou shalt not kill"? Why blame me but not him?'

'He loved Christina.'

Santerre smiled. 'And so we agree. Love is an excuse. Love is the reason. I love you, Matthias Fitzosbert.' Santerre's face softened. 'I did not wish Parson Osbert's death; there were things he knew. He rushed at me, I had no choice.'

'Choice?' Matthias retorted. 'You chose to kill those villagers!'

'They persecuted me,' Santerre replied. 'It wasn't revenge. Love thwarted is much deeper, more vibrant, more passionate than any anger, hatred or revenge.'

Matthias leant against the wall. He felt calmer, more resolute.

'I asked who you are?'

'I am the Rosifer,' Santerre replied slowly. 'The Rosebearer, the Rose Carrier, a being of light who chose to love that which I should not. I paid the price. I fell from Heaven for love: was exiled for love, desperate for that love—'

'If you are so powerful,' Matthias interrupted, 'why not use your power on me?'

'Oh come, come, Matthias,' Santerre was now enjoying himself, 'I have seen you debate in the schools. I have talked about love and will. Love needs to be loved back, that's even God's great weakness. Love has to be given freely. Love that is not given freely cannot be love. Oh, I can impress, perform magical tricks, show my power. Twice I have come into your life,' he continued. 'Once when you reached the age of reason, a seven-year-old boy, and now. You are a man, past your twenty-first year, yet I have never really left you, Matthias. I have always been close.'

'Again why?' Matthias asked.

'That is for you to find out. A matter of time.'

'That's why you killed Rokesby, wasn't it?' Matthias came back and sat on his stool. 'You knew that I would provoke him?'

Santerre shrugged. 'Rokesby sealed his own death warrant. You are finished here, Matthias.'

'And you call that freedom?'

Santerre shrugged, his fingers going to his lips.

'I had no choice. It was to protect you. Rokesby was more dangerous than you think. He could have destroyed you. Matthias, you are an innocent. You are naïve. You are still the little boy who scampered along the lanes to Tenebral. Don't you realise?' He got to his feet and crossed to the window, jabbing his finger in the direction of the street below. 'Haven't you realised, Matthias, the people you move amongst? You condemn me for what I am and for what I do yet, all around you, loathsome beings coil and turn like hissing snakes. You made a fool of Rokesby. You, a scholar, brought a master into disrepute. He would have hounded you, persecuted you and, if the opportunity presented itself, totally destroyed you.' Santerre picked up his war belt and strapped it about his waist. 'Greater love than this, Matthias, no man hath, that he lays down his life for his friend.'

'What do you mean?'

Santerre shrugged. 'You ask questions, Matthias, but now is not the time for me to answer them. I beg you, do this one thing for me.' Santerre picked up Matthias' cloak and hood. 'You know the Golden Lyre tavern on the road to Holywell?'

Matthias nodded.

'Go there and wait for me. If you stay here, you'll die. Ask the tavern master for Morgana.' Santerre grinned. 'A lovely name from a fabulous legend. Morgana is my friend. You must do whatever she asks.'

Matthias went to refuse.

'Go, please!' Santerre urged. 'Leave or be taken!'

Matthias took the cloak, put his hand on the latch then turned.

'You killed my father, yet here I stand discussing matters as if we were involved in some disputation at the schools.'

'Parson Osbert's death is not on my hands,' the Frenchman replied. 'He wanted to die. Remember, Matthias, he wanted to die. I had no choice.' He pushed Matthias gently through the door. 'What do you want, Matthias?' he whispered. 'Eye for an eye, tooth for a tooth, life for a life? You know that won't solve anything. Whatever you think, I am your friend. I ask you to do this one thing for me.' He closed the door quickly behind him.

Matthias stumbled down the stairs. When he reached the bottom he realised how quiet the Hall had become until he remembered the great fair being held at nearby Abingdon. He went out into the street. He felt as if he were in a dream, pushing by people, more concerned at what he had learnt than anything around him, yet at the same time the sights and sounds around him appeared magnified. A blind hawker on a corner, his eyes two black holes, his face grained with dirt, clothed in rags, shouted in a singsong voice about the gewgaws he had for sale. An old whore, being caught by a University bailiff, was placed across the stocks, her great, fat buttocks exposed for a birching. Two boys played with a badger, teasing it with a piece of meat. An apothecary's shop, the stall in front covered with pots of ointments; from the longer pole at the top dangled the dried skins of frogs, newts, toads and other small animals. From a casement window a young man's voice beautifully carolled the love song '*Je t'aime, je pense*'.

At last Matthias found the Golden Lyre, a spacious hostelry which served the busy road leading to and from Oxford. As soon as he mentioned the name Morgana, the tavern master became cringingly servile, ushering Matthias like a lord up the winding stairs to a door on the second gallery. The woman who opened it was breathtakingly beautiful: flaming red hair piled up high on her head, covered decorously with a fine gauze veil. Her dress was of pure lambswool, sea-green in colour, tied high at the throat by a white fringe, a golden chain round her slim waist. Her face was heart-shaped, skin like ivory, full red lips and eyes the colour of amber, slightly slanted, full of mischief.

'Why, Matthias,' her voice was soft, slightly stumbling, 'I was told to expect you.'

A touch on his hands, soft and cool, and he was inside the chamber, the door closing behind him. She moved away from him, languorously, every movement elegant, like a dancer. She gestured at the window seat in a small bay which overlooked the back of the tavern. He sat down on the cushions, still bemused, and accepted the goblet of white wine she pushed into his hands. The chamber was the best the tavern could offer, the woodwork black and gleaming, the plaster white as snow. Coloured cloths hung on the walls, a red and gold tester covered the broad four-poster bed.

'Santerre,' Matthias began, 'Santerre told me to come, to wait here.' Matthias couldn't stop stammering, the woman was studying him so closely.

'There's no hurry,' she replied smilingly. 'You are to wait. Just for a short while.' She clinked her own goblet against his. 'To better days, Matthias.'

He drank. The wine was cool, fresh in his mouth and tongue. A memory stirred.

'I saw you,' he gasped. 'I saw you years ago in a small alehouse.'

She laughed deep in her throat and came to sit beside him. Matthias grew embarrassed. He regretted so impulsively obeying Santerre's request.

'You have not aged.' He found it difficult to speak; he drank deeply from the goblet.

'What is age? What is time, Matthias?' Morgana replied.

Matthias felt his eyes grow heavy.

'I have waited so long for this,' she continued. 'To meet you.'

Matthias looked at the cup.

'Aye, the wine is drugged,' she replied coolly. 'You are to sleep, Matthias. You have to: that's why Santerre did what he did today. Rokesby was to have you murdered. He knew you better than you thought. Whilst the other students were at Abingdon, Santerre included, secret Matthias, quiet Matthias, would stay and study. The assassins will come but it's not you they'll find. It will be Santerre.' She touched his brow. Again coolness, as if his hot skin were being dabbed with ice-cold water. '*Monseigneur* wants to show you how much he loves you.'

Matthias tried to rise but she pushed him back as if he were a child. The cup rolled out of his hands, his head went forward and he fell into a deep sleep.

When he awoke he was lying fully clothed on the bed. He felt refreshed, relaxed. For a few moments he stared up at the tester until he realised where he was and what had happened. He struggled to rise, the curtains of the bed were pulled back and Morgana was beside him.

'Sleep on,' she urged. 'Tomorrow morning, at first light, we are to go.'

'Go where?'

'For a while, Sutton Courteny.'

Matthias lay back on the bed. He glanced down at his feet, his boots were still on. He got off the bed.

'Matthias, what are you doing?'

'Relieving myself. I also need something to eat and drink.'

He was through the door before she could stop him. He heard her calling his name but Matthias continued down the stairs. He guessed it must be just before midnight. He hurried through the streets, brushing aside the beggars and drunks. He felt refreshed and alert after his deep sleep but resentful of the opiate; it awoke memories of the church at Sutton Courteny, sleeping whilst terrible events occurred. Matthias paused at the corner of the Turl from where he could watch the main doorway of Exeter Hall. Something had happened: a proctor stepped through the gateway and had a few words with the two men-at-arms posted outside. Matthias drew back into the shadows. As he had come from the Golden Lyre, he'd passed soldiers wearing the livery of the city. They'd been busy putting chains up across the streets leading to the gates and postern doors of Oxford. They had not bothered him. Matthias now realised that they were more intent on stopping and examining people leaving the city rather than those coming in.

Matthias slipped along an alleyway, keeping to the shadows, until he reached the Blue Boar tavern. He waited at the back near the piggery. Sure enough, after a while, Amasia came out carrying a bucket of slops. He called her name and she came over, reluctantly at first but, when Matthias identified himself, she put the bucket down and, running across, pushed him back into the shadows.

'Matthias Fitzosbert.' Her face was pale, eyes staring. Matthias could see she had been weeping. 'Santerre is dead!'

Matthias closed his eyes. Was that planned? he thought. Would it have been Santerre who turned up at the Golden Lyre or someone else?

'He was found murdered in your room,' Amasia hurried on. 'Two other corpses as well. I learnt of this from gossip: the news is spreading through the city.'

'Who are the others?' Matthias asked.

'Hired killers, or so they think, former soldiers. God knows, there's enough hiding out in the woods between here and Woodstock.' She grasped his hand. 'Matthias, they are saying you are responsible.'

'Me, hire killers?'

'No. They say it's connected with the death of Rokesby. He, too, has been found stabbed in his lodgings. An old woman saw you and Santerre go up there earlier today. The Chancellor's men have seized Rokesby's papers. They found information about you. Dantel,' Amasia referred to a student they both knew, 'he says warrants have been issued for your arrest.'

Matthias stared up at the stars, cursing his own foolishness. He now regretted leaving Santerre and, if he tried to return to the Golden Lyre, he would be arrested.

'Can you hide me?' He gripped Amasia's shoulders. 'I swear I am innocent of all their deaths! I – I can't tell you what is happening.' He held her close and stroked her hair. 'Amasia, I swear by all that is holy, I am not responsible for Rokesby's death or that of Santerre!'

'But they are saying Rokesby suspected you of heresy, of dabbling in the black arts. The taproom has been full of such gossip.'

'Can you hide me?'

Amasia turned and pointed to an outside stair.

'Go up there,' she said. 'It will take you on to the top gallery near my room. I'll go ahead and unlock the door.'

She hurried back into the tavern. Matthias waited, then climbed the rickety staircase. He tapped on the door, no answer. He tapped again.

'There he is!'

He whirled round: in a dim pool of light below stood the tavern keeper, joined by scullions and tapsters. They had all armed themselves with staffs, swords, daggers, one even wielded a spit iron. Beyond the door he heard the patter of feet: Matthias realised Amasia had betrayed him. He hurried down the steps but the tavern master and his throng hastened forward, blocking any escape. Matthias' hand fell to the hilt of his dagger. One of the tapsters lifted a bow, an arrow notched to the string. Beyond him Matthias could see Amasia, her face turned away.

'You are a lying bitch, Amasia! Couldn't you have at least tried?'

'She'll share the reward!' tavern master Goodman shouted. 'She knows who gives her bed and board!' The man licked his lips and raised the lantern he carried. 'Amasia is mine now, master scholar. She'll have other duties from tonight.' He walked forward, a long stabbing dirk in his hand. 'Now you can take your belt off and come quietly or we'll kill you. Dead or alive your head is worth the same.' He nodded to the people behind him. 'But the boys here say you were a good customer.'

Matthias undid his belt and let it drop. The mob closed in. He was kicked and punched. His hands were thrust behind his back, tied, and he was led in triumph through the taproom where he was pelted with bits of meat, and out into the dark alleyway beyond. He was cuffed and shoved through the streets, down Broad Place to the entrance of a huge, forbidding house with steel bars over its arrow slit windows, the Bocardo, the city prison.

Its gaoler took custody of Matthias, thrusting the tavern master and his gang back out of the gates, shouting they would have to apply to the Justices for the reward. Once they were gone, the gaoler and the turnkeys had their turn: a punch to the face, blows to the stomach. Matthias winced and groaned but held his tongue. He knew that scholars were the favourite prey of such men. He was then stripped of his boots, jerkin and wallet. Cold and beaten, Matthias was led through a maze of passageways, down rotting steps and into the dungeons beneath the house. An iron-barred, steel-covered door was thrown open and he was thrust inside.

The cell was dank, cold and smelt like a midden-heap; no windows, no furniture, whilst the straw and rushes on the floor were black and slimy: they sometimes moved and shifted as rats scurried across. The only light was a small grille in the door which gave a view back down the torch-lit gallery to where the gaoler sat behind a table.

Matthias cleared a space in the corner and crouched down, wrapping his arms round his chest. He tried to make sense of the day's happenings. Santerre taking him to that tavern, the meeting with Rokesby, that beautiful, mysterious woman at the Golden Lyre. Matthias realised that it had been planned. On the one hand he resented Santerre but, on the other, knew that this being, whoever or whatever it was, had taken upon itself to protect him. Rokesby had been full of venom. It would only have been a matter of time before Matthias had been either attacked, beaten or even killed, or hauled before the Chancellor's court to answer God knows what charges.

He dozed for a while. The passageway was quiet. The gaoler eventually brought in a mess of pottage to eat. He said Matthias was their only guest in the condemned felon's row and did Matthias feel fortunate?

'Can I have a candle?' Matthias asked.

'Of course you can.' The gaoler's sallow face creased into an ingratiating smile. 'And perhaps some wine, some venison and a soft four-poster bed?'

The gaoler waddled off down the corridor, laughing to himself, shoulders shaking. He sat down on his chair.

'This is not one of your halls, young sir!' he yelled. He picked up a piece of parchment. 'The Justices will sit tomorrow and then you'll hang!'

Matthias went back to his thoughts. He knew he would not be missed at the University. Santerre had been his only friend. He refused even to contemplate dying on the gallows at Carfax, the crossroads at the centre of Oxford. Nevertheless, as the night drew on, despair bit into his soul. What hope could he have?

187

Just after dawn, one of the University proctors, a pasty-faced, sandy-haired young man, came down to visit him. The man was apparently terrified of the gaolers, so timid and nervous he bleated a few questions at Matthias and then scurried out. Matthias was given a piece of coarse rye bread and a stoup of brackish water. From his cell he could faintly hear the bells of the city and he reckoned it must have been just after nine when the gaoler and turnkeys took him out of his cell and pulled a hood over his head. He was hustled out of the Bocardo. Feet cut and scarred by the cobbles, Matthias was hoisted up and tossed like a sack into a cart. Jolted and bruised he was thrown about. Now and again he would strain his ears but all he could hear were the cries and shouts of the hawkers, the faint murmur of the crowd. Matthias closed his eyes and prayed. Not so much for life but that he wouldn't end it slowly strangling at the end of a rope, being jeered and hooted by some mob in the market place.

At last the cart stopped. The mask was removed and he was bustled through the porch of St Mary's church. The benches had been cleared from the nave: a large table set up before the rood screen, and behind this sat the three Justices. At a desk on either side of them were two scriveners. The crowds had been allowed in and people were flocking up the transepts to get a good view of the proceedings. Soldiers and bailiffs from the city were busy putting up a cordon of long pieces of white rope. Matthias had to wait for a while. The gaolers on either side of him whispered cold comfort, that the three Justices who would try him were not known for their mercy or tolerance. The sandy-haired proctor came up and offered his help. Matthias took one look at the watery eyes, dripping nose and slack mouth. He shook his head.

'I'll defend myself,' he declared.

At last the court bellman walked up the nave tolling his bell.

'Hear ye! Hear ye!' he bawled. 'All ye who have business before His Majesty's Justices of Oyer and Terminer, sitting in the King's city of Oxford, draw close!'

'That's you, my boy,' the gaoler whispered.

One of the scriveners stood up. 'Bring forward the prisoner!'

Matthias recalled the trial of the Preacher at Sutton Courteny. As he walked through the nave he looked at the crowd but saw little pity there. To them it was a mummers' show and what happened to Matthias was of little interest. About three yards from the Justices' bench the gaolers stopped. Matthias studied the men who were to try him for his life: cold, implacable merchants, dignitaries from the city. They would hold their commission directly from the King. The one on Matthias' right looked as if he were asleep, head cradled in his hand; the Justice on his left was busy studying a document, a long piece of parchment. The principal Justice, white-haired, sharp-nosed, with eyes as hard as glass, looked Matthias from head to toe.

'This should not take long,' he began. 'Your name?'

'Matthias Fitzosbert.'

'How do you plead?'

'How can I? I don't know what I am accused of?'

This brought guffaws of laughter from the transept. All three Justices now moved in their throne-like chairs. Matthias knew that, whatever he said, they had already reached their verdict.

'Are you,' one of them called out, 'a clerk in minor orders?'

'No, I am not.'

'So, you can't plead benefit of clergy?'

Matthias shrugged.

'Oh, for God's sake, read out the indictment!'

One of the clerks stood up and in a loud voice began to read the charges. Matthias' heart sank. Whoever had prepared the case had done so hastily and found the easiest way was to accuse Matthias of everything. Heavy reliance was placed on certain writings found in Rokesby's chamber: Matthias Fitzosbert was a traitor, being a secret supporter of the usurper Richard III, later killed at Bosworth. He was a heretic, a sorcerer and an occultist, not accepting the authority and wisdom of Holy Mother Church. He was a conspirer, a leader of a secret coven, a felon and a murderer, responsible for not only the murder of John Rokesby, Master of Arts and lecturer in the city of Oxford, but also of Henri Santerre, student and scholar in the said university! At last the clerk finished. The Justice in the centre seat folded his hands and leant forward.

'Well, Fitzosbert, now how do you plead?' He raised his eyebrows.

'I did not kill Santerre.'

'Does that mean you are guilty of the rest?'

'I did not say that.'

'You did not deny it.'

'I deny everything.'

'Dearie, dearie me!'

The Justice on Matthias' left picked up a piece of parchment.

'Is it true that you have read books on Lucifer and Satan, and have studied the trials of witches and warlocks?'

'Yes, I have but . . .'

'And were you present when Master Rokesby was killed?'

'Yes, yes, I was . . .' Matthias flailed his hands. 'What is the use?' he cried. He turned to the left and stared at the people thronging the transept. 'I am innocent but I have been found guilty so why should I provide sport for others?'

The crowd fell silent. Matthias looked to the right: a movement caught his eye. A figure stepped out from behind one of the pillars: a woman muffled and cowled but the hood was pushed back for a few seconds. Matthias recognised the flame-red hair of Morgana. She moved away. Another face caught Matthias' attention, a small, squat, square-jawed, clean-shaven man, his hair tonsured like that of a priest. He was dressed in a dark blue robe lined with squirrel fur. He was staring at Matthias differently from the rest, as if fascinated by what he saw. He, too, stepped back into the crowd.

'Matthias Fitzosbert!'

He looked towards the Justices: all three now had a square of black silk covering their heads. Matthias went cold. He had heard how Henry Tudor was issuing commissions, allowing Justices to investigate, judge and sentence but he never knew that his case would be despatched with such alacrity.

'Matthias Fitzosbert, are you listening to us?' The Chief Justice spoke. 'We have examined the evidence and we have heard what little defence you can offer. In our view the charges are proven. You are a traitor, a heretic and a murderer. We sentence you to be burnt to death at Carfax within the octave of this sentence being delivered!'

Matthias' jaw dropped. To be burnt! To be lashed to that blackened stake. He recalled the hermit burning in Sutton Courteny. He closed his eyes and swayed. The gaolers held him fast.

'God have mercy on your soul!' the Justice added. 'Take him away!'

13

Matthias was returned to the Bocardo. Being a condemned felon, he was loaded with chains before being thrown into the back of the cart. The sentence had been so harsh, even the hardened gaolers felt sorry for him.

'If you can find some money,' the chief gaoler declared, sharing a loaf of bread with him, 'we'll buy a bag of gunpowder and tie it round your neck. The heat then blows your throat apart and you die quicker, better that, than feeling your flesh bubble and your eyes turn to water.'

'Or,' his assistant added. 'If you pay us, when the smoke gets really thick, one of us here can come through and strangle you.'

Matthias burst out laughing, throwing his head back he guffawed until the tears ran down his dirty face. The gaolers stared impassively. Such solemn looks on their villainous faces only made matters worse – Matthias found he couldn't stop laughing. He realised how long it had been since he had laughed so heartily and so deeply.

'I am sorry,' he gasped, popping the rest of the bread into his mouth, 'but here I am, gentlemen, about to die a horrible death for crimes I did not commit. The only comfort I am offered is a bag of gunpowder or a garrotte string. I do thank you,' he added hastily seeing their annoyance. 'I am very grateful.' He stared at a point over their heads. 'But I've got a feeling I will not die.'

'Why?' The turnkey became aggressive. He drew back, remembering that Matthias was supposed to have magical powers. 'You don't think you'll get a pardon, do you? I doubt it.'

Matthias leant against the wall. 'I agree, I don't think I'll get a pardon.' He smiled at his gaolers. 'But we'll see.'

He later regretted his remarks. The chief gaoler was now

deeply suspicious. Matthias was manacled and the gaoler kept the cell door open whilst sitting down at the end of the torch-lit passageway watching his prisoner intently. The chains fastened to his gyves were long and loose. Matthias was able to move round the cell and drive off the snouting, sleek-coated rats when they became too bold. Nevertheless, as one day passed into another, Matthias began to despair. He did his best to counter this by going back to his childhood and sweet memories of Christina and Osbert. However, it was the hermit who intruded into his thoughts: showing him the foxes; freeing the dove in the ruined church; riding back with him from Tewkesbury.

On the third evening after Matthias was sentenced the gaoler, perhaps to keep the prisoner subdued, was generous with the wine. Matthias slept, though his mind was plagued by nightmares. He was back in Tenebral, standing in the nave of the ruined church. The sky above was red, as if scored by the flames from a great fire. A group of men were riding up the path, their destriers black as night, heads and faces covered by chain-mail coifs. All around him came a loud chanting, as if an army were intoning the Dies Irae, the sequence from the Mass of the dead. The riders moved slowly, the banners they carried fluttering in the wind. Their leader, his face hidden behind a helmet on which a falcon stood, wings outstretched, stopped. He put his steel gauntlet on Matthias' shoulder, squeezing it tightly; his other hand went to lift the visor. Matthias struggled to turn his face away. At the same time he wanted to cover his ears from the sombre chanting which was growing louder. He opened his eyes: the gaoler was shaking him vigorously, the torch he carried crackling, sending out acrid fumes.

'Master Fitzosbert, oh Lord be thanked! I thought you were dead. You have a visitor. A priest has come to shrive you.'

Matthias struggled back against the wall and stared down the passageway. In the poor light he made out the man he had seen in St Mary's church just before he had been sentenced.

'Do you want a priest?' the gaoler asked. He crouched down. 'It can help. When it comes to being taken out, you'll not be so fearful.'

The gaoler withdrew as the priest came into the cell. As he did so, he dropped a coin into the gaoler's hand.

'Lock the door,' he muttered. 'A man's confession is between him and God.'

The door slammed shut, the key turned. The priest, despite his fine, woollen robes, sat down on the rushes next to Matthias.

'It's good of you to come,' Matthias declared.

The priest stared coolly back. Matthias studied his visitor. A youngish man, his auburn hair was neatly tonsured. Close up, his face was not pleasant: the square jaw was offset by narrow, close-set eyes and a rather spiteful cast to the thin lips, as if the man disapproved of everything he saw and heard.

'Father, are you really here to shrive me?' Matthias asked. 'And, if you are, how do I know you are a priest?'

'My name is Richard Symonds. I am a priest of Oxford.'

The man undid his cloak, revealing his long, black cassock as well as a small silver cross on a copper chain round his neck. He opened the large pouch on his belt and drew out a letter. The turnkey had lit the cresset torch in the cell. Matthias, with a rattle of chains, studied the document carefully. It was a licence, signed and sealed by the Bishop of London, giving one Richard Symonds the faculty to preach, celebrate Mass and hear confessions in London and in the counties of Oxford and Berkshire.

'You have a parish, Father?'

'No, I am a tutor in Lord Audley's household.' His voice dropped to a whisper. 'And you are right, I am not here to shrive you. I come to ask for your help.'

Matthias lifted his hands in a jangle of chains.

'Father, I'm dirty, unshaven and, in about four days, I'm going to be burnt to death. How can I help you?'

'I was at your trial. They said you were a Yorkist.'

'They also said I was an assassin and a sorcerer.'

'But you do have powers, don't you?'

Symonds' head came forward, his eyes gleaming, lips parted. Matthias wondered if the priest were not a little insane: something about the eyes, that slight tilt to the head. A secretive man, Matthias thought, constantly engaged in subtle schemes.

'Father, if I had such powers, I wouldn't be sitting here.'

'She said you'd be diffident.'

Matthias' heart skipped a beat.

193

'Who said that?'

'Morgana. She approached me after the trial. She said you were a Yorkist, not a murderer, a man of great power.'

'What do you propose?' Matthias asked wearily. 'And speak low, for the turnkey is very suspicious.' He smiled weakly. 'He thinks I'll sprout wings and fly away.'

'Oh, don't worry about him. He's already searched me and is richer by two coins.'

Symonds edged a little closer. 'I shall speak and speak quickly. Edward IV of blessed memory died three years ago. Two years later his brother Richard of Gloucester, having assumed the crown, was defeated at Market Bosworth, by Henry Tudor.'

'And I understand George, Duke of Clarence, the third brother,' Matthias added drily, 'died rather mysteriously in the Tower. As did Edward IV's two boys, the Princes. People said they were murdered by their Uncle Richard so that is the end of the House of York.'

'I cannot speak for any of them,' Symonds replied. 'The fate of the Princes is a mystery but Henry Tudor is a usurper.' He drew himself up, his eyes glittering: a fanatic, Matthias thought, a man obsessed with a cause.

'The Yorkists are dead,' Matthias declared. 'And the power of Henry Tudor is more than manifest. You saw it at my trial.'

'One Yorkist prince still lives,' Symonds whispered dramatically. 'Edward of Warwick, Clarence's son.'

The doings of kings and princes did not interest Matthias but he tried to recall what Baron Sanguis had told him.

'He's in the Tower!' Matthias exclaimed. 'Warwick was kept prisoner by his Uncle Richard as well as Henry Tudor.'

'He's an imposter,' Symonds snapped. 'The true Warwick has escaped. He has the support of Yorkist lords and he is safe in a house outside Oxford.' Symonds clapped his hands. 'I intend to take him to Dublin. The Irish lords led by the Earl of Kildare will rise in revolt to support him. Other English lords, including de la Pole, Earl of Suffolk, and my Lord Lovell will join us there. His aunt Margaret, Duchess of Burgundy, will supply us with mercenaries and gold.'

'So, why do you need me? A scholar about to be burnt to death?'

'Morgana says you are a man of great power. You will aid our cause, a talisman for our success.' The priest got to his feet. 'You really have little choice in the matter, do you?'

Matthias shook his head. 'Any fate is better than burning.'

'I shall return tomorrow night.'

'I'll be waiting,' Matthias replied drily, 'my face shaved, my saddlebags packed.'

The priest smirked, sketched a blessing in the air and shouted for the turnkey.

Matthias spent the night speculating on whether Symonds was insane or just foolhardy. Late the following evening, Amasia came: she, too, bribed the gaoler: he leered at Matthias and said he would keep the door to the cell open. Amasia's face was hidden in the shadow of her hood. She sat in a corner of the cell well away from him.

'Why have you come?' Matthias snapped. 'To gloat? To say you are sorry? You might as well go to the execution ground and spit in the flames!'

'*Oh, Creatura bona atque parva!*'

Matthias' head jerked back. It was Amasia's voice, low and sweet, but the words and the tone were that of the hermit.

'Do not get excited.' Amasia turned her face and whispered. 'The oaf at the end of the gallery is watching us. I know what you are going to ask. How and why?' Amasia played with a tendril of her hair. 'When a soul dies, Matthias, it's like light from a candle, it travels so quickly, so far, so fast. The journey lasts for eternity. I am different: I am locked in the same moment of eternity because of my will, because of my love. All I see, all I deal with, is the eternal now. Imagine,' her voice was low and soft, 'imagine, Matthias, you are back at Sutton Courteny. There are houses all along the street. You can go into any of them and do whatever you like – eat, drink. So it is with me.'

'And Amasia?' Matthias asked. 'The girl I knew?'

'Some people,' she replied, 'because of their strength and the spiritual state of their souls, can resist me, like a powerful householder can bar the windows and doors against an intruder. Others? I can slip in like a thief in the night. They have weakened their spirit. Remember the words of the gospel, Matthias: "What shall it profit a man, if he shall gain the whole world, and lose his own soul?" Have you ever

195

wondered, Matthias, how you can lose something which is eternal?' Amasia glanced quickly down the gallery and leant across. 'It's so easy, Matthias. Amasia lost her soul when she betrayed you.' She smiled. 'Remember the gospels, Matthias? When Judas Iscariot betrayed Jesus, Satan entered.'

'Why not possess me?' Matthias taunted.

Amasia's head went back.

'Why not me?' Matthias repeated, shuffling his chains. He sat back when he glimpsed the turnkey stand and stare down. 'You can't, can you?' Matthias whispered. 'Someone, something is blocking you.'

Amasia lifted her head. Her cheeks were wet with tears.

'There are those around you,' she whispered. 'You see battles on earth, the same is true of the spirit world, an eternal war between the lords of the air, yet it's not just that, Matthias. I do not want to enter you. Control is not love: power and love are as far apart as east and west.' She wiped her eyes. 'I want you to know that.'

'If I had stayed with Morgana, where would we have fled?'

'Only heaven knows,' Amasia laughed softly as if savouring the joke. 'But now, rather than control events, like a swimmer in a river, I must flow with them. I knew Rokesby was going to hurt you, that's why he had to die first. I knew the city authorities would try to arrest you, so Morgana was waiting for you. Now the silly priest, Richard Symonds, he is the key to the door.'

'Don't you have that power?' Matthias mocked.

'I have answered that, Matthias. You cannot control the will,' she continued, 'unless the will is handed over to you: that is another matter.'

'You quote Scripture!' Matthias retorted.

'Why not?' Again the smile. 'Evil men can quote it and use it to justify their actions.'

'What's going on there?' The gaoler was glaring down the passageway.

'I must be going,' Amasia said. 'We shall meet again, Creatura.'

For the rest of the day Matthias remained tense and watchful, at the same time trying to hide his emotions from the gaoler.

'They are getting the stake ready at Carfax,' the fellow declared. 'Cleaning the cobbles, the faggots and brushwood have been dried.' He closed one eye and stared at Matthias. 'You should thank God,' he added, 'and pray it doesn't rain. It can take hours to get the fire burning.'

On these words of comfort, he spun on his heel and went back to his table.

It was well after curfew and the gaoler was settling down for another night's drinking when Matthias heard voices at the end of the passageway, followed by the clink of coins and the sound of footsteps. The door was swung open and Symonds came in. He was dressed in a cassock, with a stole over his shoulders, a small, lighted candle in his hand.

'Close the door!' Symonds shouted. 'And pray look after my good sister!'

The gaoler obeyed with alacrity.

'He's well paid,' Symonds declared.

The priest blew the candle out. He undid the silver pyx he carried but, instead of a host, it contained a strange-looking key.

'The work of a master locksmith,' he explained, slipping the key into the gyves and manacles. In a trice they were loose. Symonds then sat back against the wall. He took a small wineskin from beneath his cloak, took a swig and offered it to Matthias. The claret was full and strong and warmed his belly. For a while he just sat and stretched, flexing his muscles, letting the blood run free. Symonds also gave him some bread, cheese and smoke dried ham. Matthias ate these ravenously. He heard a sound, a small scream, from the end of the passageway.

'What is that?' he asked between mouthfuls.

'I would think it's Mistress Morgana doing her duty,' Symonds sneered.

The sounds at the end of the gallery ceased. There was a low groan and the cell door swung open. Morgana, her hair slightly dishevelled, her dark smock and cloak covered with pieces of straw, was smiling down at Matthias. In one hand a dagger, bloody to the hilt, in the other a set of keys.

'I think it's time we left.'

Symonds grasped Matthias by the arm and pushed him out into the passageway. He picked up the gaoler's cloak and tossed it at Matthias. Its owner, his hose still down at his ankles, sprawled on the mattress, throat slashed from ear to ear.

'There are other gaolers,' Matthias muttered.

'Aye, and they'll be asleep,' Symonds mocked. 'Nothing like a small tun of wine, the best claret from Bordeaux with a small dose of valerian to ease people's worries.'

They went up the steps and into the hallway. The few gaolers who did night duty were fast asleep round the table, cups and jugs knocked over as they sprawled in their drunken sleep. As they approached the side door, a soldier lurched out of a chamber. Symonds, who carried a thick ash cane as a walking stick, clubbed the man savagely on the side of the head. They quickly went through the keys. The door swung open. They crossed a small yard, passed through a wicket gate and into an alleyway.

'No one ever escapes from the Bocardo.' Symonds stopped and grinned wolfishly at Matthias. 'Nothing more than a disused house really.'

'Horses?' Matthias asked.

'Not here,' Symonds scoffed.

He made to go: Morgana caught Matthias' hand.

'Matthias, we'll meet again.' She smiled through the darkness. 'You shouldn't have left me at the Golden Lyre.'

'I had no choice,' Matthias replied. 'I had to see what would happen.'

She kissed him gently on each cheek.

'Watch Symonds,' she whispered. 'Mad as a March hare.' She put her arms round his neck and hugged him close. 'If he threatens you, threaten back.' And she slipped away into the darkness.

Symonds, who had gone further down the alleyway, gestured angrily.

'Come on! Come on!' he hissed.

Matthias followed him through a tangle of dark alleyways stinking to high heaven. Scavenging cats fled whining before them. Now and again from the back garden of a house a watch dog would howl or throw itself against the gate. The occasional beggar, huddled in the shadows, pleaded for alms.

Symonds deliberately kept well away from the student quarter. They reached the end of the High Street, entered the old

Jewish cemetery, down a hill, splashing across the Cherwell, the water refreshingly cool against Matthias' chapped legs. Still Symonds hurried on. At last they were in the countryside, the trackway they followed lit by a hunter's moon. Matthias stopped and stared up at the stars. A clear, beautiful night, the breeze soft and sweet. Matthias closed his eyes and thanked God he had escaped.

'Come on! Come on!' Symonds urged again.

At last they left the trackway, crossed an open field and into a copse. Men, masked and hooded, gathered round Matthias, stripping him of his clothing. Another brought a leather bucket and a rag.

'Wash and clean yourself.' The voice was rough.

Matthias did so. Without a by-your-leave, another seized his hair and began to cut it. Matthias did not object as the dirt from the gaol was washed away. Saddlebags were brought, he was given a fresh change of clothing, leather riding boots, a war belt with sword and dagger, and a woollen cloak and cowl.

No one spoke. Symonds sat on a stump of a tree watching him. Food was produced and then horses brought. Symonds clasped the hands of those who had helped him. They led the horses across the fields, back on to the lane, and began a wild ride through the night. It was well after dawn before Symonds eventually agreed to stop for a while to refresh their horses.

The ride proved to be exhausting. They paused now and again to eat, drink or relieve themselves. The only thing Matthias learnt was that they were riding north-west. In the late afternoon they changed horses at a roadside tavern. Symonds kept riding even when darkness fell. Matthias protested but Symonds, reining in, shook his head.

'No, we can't sleep out. We are expected. Just a little further.'

'Where are we going?' Matthias asked.

'To Twyford Grange. That's all I'll tell you.'

Night had fallen by the time they reached the grange, an old, rambling manor house surrounded by lonely fields. The pathway up to it was overgrown, its curtain wall crumbling. Most of the windows were shuttered and those on the ground floor were cracked and dusty. A taciturn manservant took their horses. Another led them into the hall where Symonds introduced Matthias to Elizabeth Stratford, a distant kinswoman of the Yorkist Lord Francis Lovell.

The lady of the manor was tall, angular, her face like yellowing parchment, yet her eyes were bright and friendly, lips parted in a welcoming smile. She extended one vein-streaked clawlike hand for Matthias to kiss and laughed quite merrily when she caught Matthias studying her old-fashioned dress and veil.

'I have seen the years, young man,' she said. 'The hand you kissed has been held by them all: Henry V, his hapless son, the Yorkist lords.' Her eyes grew sad. 'All shadows now, gone into the dark. Come.' She beckoned Matthias into the light provided by a candle wheel which hung on a chain from the ceiling. 'So, you are Symonds' friend, are you?' She studied him closely. Her eyes became guarded, as if she had glimpsed something over Matthias' shoulder.

'Are you a magus?' she asked. 'A sorcerer?'

'My lady, I am a scholar down on his luck and no more. And, with the exception of the good priest here, probably the loneliest man in the kingdom.'

'Is that true, Matthias Fitzosbert?' The old lady stepped back two or three paces. She was studying him anxiously from head to toe. 'When we met over there,' she pointed to the darkness beyond the ring of light, 'I really thought you were what you claim to be but, in the light, I can see that is not so.'

'What do you mean, my lady?' Symonds, his face excited, stepped forward. 'Do you see his power?'

'Yes, yes, I do.'

Lady Elizabeth turned on her heel, walked along the passageway and into the small hall.

'They say Lady Stratford has second sight, that she is fey,' Symonds whispered excitedly. He, too, stopped and looked over Matthias' shoulder. 'I can see nothing.'

'She has a fanciful imagination,' Matthias replied tersely. 'Nothing more and nothing less.' He heard a cough and looked up.

Lady Elizabeth had reappeared in the doorway and was staring at them. Matthias mumbled his excuses and they both followed her into the hall. This also must have seen better days: the hearth was full of cold ash, the drapes, banners and pennants hanging from the beams were dusty and slightly ragged. Cobwebs hung on the shields and weapons, fastened to the walls above the dull, cracked wainscoting. Yet the rushes underfoot were clean and the small table which had been set up in the centre was covered with a white linen cloth. Matthias caught savoury odours from the kitchen. They washed their faces and hands at the lavarium. Lady Elizabeth plucked at Matthias' sleeve and led him away.

'I heard what you said, Master Fitzosbert.' She smiled with her lips but her eyes were hard. 'When you stepped into that pool of light, just for a moment, I glimpsed a shape behind you, the face of a knight, though he was dressed in a long garb like that of a monk.'

The sweat on the nape of Matthias' neck turned cold.

'Just for a moment.' Lady Elizabeth repeated. 'And a hand on your shoulder.' She tapped his boiled leather jacket. 'You are a powerful man, Matthias Fitzosbert, though I suspect you don't realise it.'

'Aren't you afraid?' Matthias teased as she led him to the table.

'No I am not, because I mean you no ill.' Her voice dropped to a whisper. 'I only hope the same can be said for Symonds.'

'Edward!' Symonds exclaimed.

Matthias turned. A youth dressed in a dark burgundy gown which fell just beneath the knee came into the hall. He moved quietly, his feet encased in soft buskins. He bore no arms in the embroidered, leather belt clasped round his waist. His fingers were covered in rings, a silver chain round his neck partly hidden by the stiff white cambric shirt which stretched up to his chin. He had russet hair, neatly cropped just above his ears, a smooth, round face, smiling eyes, but looked weak-mouthed, rather ingratiating, eager to please. Symonds went down on one knee. He almost dragged the young man's hand to his lips.

'Matthias, Matthias, you should kneel,' Symonds whispered. 'This is your prince, Edward, George of Clarence's son who has escaped from the Tower. He intends, with God's help, to seize the throne which is rightfully his.'

Matthias knelt, only too eager to hide his confusion.

Warwick came across: his hand was small, soft and smelt fragrantly of perfume. Matthias kissed the ring, Edward gripped his hand and raised him to his feet.

'You are most welcome, Master Matthias.' Edward of Warwick embraced him and, standing on tiptoe, gave him the kiss of peace on each cheek. He stood away, face smiling. 'I have read Master Symonds' letters on you.' He clapped his hands shyly. 'You are most welcome. When I come into my own you, Master Fitzosbert, will sit at my council table.'

Matthias kept his face impassive though his heart sank. Edward of Warwick was personable, graceful, charming but those watery blue eyes, that ingratiating smile? Would he be any threat to the powerful Tudor? Matthias studied him. Was he really Clarence's son? Nephew of the powerful Edward IV and Richard III? Or some imposter trained to play the part? A cat's-paw for the disaffected? Edward of Warwick grinned across at Symonds and Lady Elizabeth. Matthias could see the old lady had reached her decision: she did not think much of this Yorkist princeling.

'Well, shall we eat?'

Again that childish clapping of the hands. Edward of Warwick almost skipped to the table. Matthias glimpsed the contempt in the old woman's eyes and wondered if the prince were fully in his wits.

Symonds was apparently the master. It was he who guided Edward to the throne-like chair at the top of the table. He whispered instructions on how to use his napkin and only filled his goblet with a quarter of wine, the rest water.

The meal was pleasant enough. Matthias now felt the full effects of his escape and long ride. His body ached, his eyes grew heavy. He ate the jugged hare and picked at the venison in its mushroom sauce whilst listening to Symonds describe what help and assistance they would receive in Ireland and amongst the English lords. At every such pronouncement, Edward of Warwick would shake his head vigorously, but he seemed more concerned with filling his stomach than winning the crown of England. He seemed to have totally forgotten about Matthias. After the meal was finished, servants cleared the platters and trenchers. More candles were brought in. Lady Elizabeth ordered the servants to leave the room. Before they left, one of them brought a silver casket and placed it on the table beside her.

'We shall study the cards,' she announced.

Matthias looked at her expectantly.

'Do you wish to?' she asked the prince.

'Oh yes, oh yes.' Edward of Warwick clapped his hands.

Lady Elizabeth opened the casket and took out the cards. They were large, square with gold backing. She kept them face downwards and slid them across the cloth. One for Edward, one for Symonds, one for Matthias.

'Turn them over.' She looked at Symonds. 'You first.'

The priest did so. He gasped and slid the card back towards the woman. Matthias saw the picture: the figure of death, a skeleton wearing a suit of black armour. He rode a white horse and carried a purple standard with a white rose upon it. Skull and crossbones adorned the reins of the horse's bridle. The horse rode across various people, not caring about their rank or position: a king lay outstretched, crown fallen away: a bishop with his hand held up in prayer: a maiden, her face turned away.

'Superstition!' Symonds snapped.

Edward of Warwick turned his over. He smiled and held the card up: an angel appearing from the clouds, a halo of golden hair around its young face. He was blowing a mighty trumpet from which a white banner hung, emblazoned with a red cross.

'Judgment!' Lady Elizabeth declared. 'And you, Master Fitzosbert?'

Matthias knew little about the tarot and he wondered if Lady Elizabeth was merely teasing him. He smiled.

'And my card, my lady? What will it be? The Devil?'

'Turn it over!' Lady Elizabeth glanced at Symonds. 'You shouldn't be frightened. Master Symonds and my Lord of Warwick have drawn Death and Judgment yet we are all subject to those.'

'Turn it over! Turn it over!' Warwick cried.

Matthias did so slowly. He smiled as he held it up. The card depicted a charioteer in splendid armour of the ancient world.

'Conflict!' Lady Elizabeth cried. Her eyes held his. 'A terrible struggle, Master Matthias, and you stand at the centre of it!'

14

The following morning Symonds, Matthias and Edward of
Warwick left the grange and continued their journey west.
Matthias had considered Warwick to be a fool but the young
prince proved to be a hardy horseman, brave, determined and
a good companion. He would slow down if Matthias' horse
fell behind and, when they stopped to eat or drink, made
sure Matthias was served before him. Matthias was touched
by the youth's simple generosity. Symonds, however, was
surly. The playing of the tarot cards had unsettled him and
he resented his protégé's liking for Matthias. Now and again
they would stop at other lonely houses or taverns for fresh
horses, provisions and a change of clothing. They entered
Lancashire, the countryside becoming harsher, the weather
betraying the first signs of the end of summer.

As they rode, Matthias became unsettled. His stomach
hurt and he complained of gripping pains in his back and
head. He grew feverish and, by the time they reached the
Lancashire coast, Matthias couldn't care whether he lived or
died. His body was racked with pain, covered in sweat, whilst
his stomach couldn't keep down either food or drink. He was
aware of the smell of the sea, salt and fish, a cold breeze, clouds
scurrying against the darkening sky. He was in a taproom
where men, some heavily armed, sat and discussed the tides
and winds. Matthias realised a cog was waiting offshore to
take them to Dublin. He stumbled outside to be sick, falling
to his knees, retching until his stomach hurt. He was aware of
Edward of Warwick coming out, pulling him to his feet, but
Matthias' legs felt weak. The night sky whirled above him.

'Bring him in! Bring him in!' a voice called.

'Has he got the pestilence?' another asked.

'Examine his armpits and groin for buboes. If he has the
Death, cut his throat!'

Matthias blinked, his mouth was dry. He could feel someone stripping his clothes off, hands punching into his armpits and groin feeling for the telltale buboes, the first signs of the plague.

'No,' a voice declared. 'He hasn't the plague but he is weak and fevered.'

'Kill him!' another voice shouted. 'Cut his throat! He can't be left here!'

Matthias heard Edward of Warwick's voice high in protest. A cup was forced to his lips: his mouth was full with a bittersweet drink and he slipped into a fever-filled sleep.

Matthias did not know whether he was alive or dead, awake or asleep. Images came and went: he was on a sheet being taken across slippery sands and tossed unceremoniously into a bumboat. The creak of oars and the nauseous pitching which seemed to go on for ever. He was being raised up, laid out on a deck, sailors cursing, men shouting orders . . . a stinking darkness, which smelt like a jakes, rats scurrying by him. Edward of Warwick bending over, dabbing his face with a cool rag.

Matthias tried to croak his thanks. More of the bittersweet potion was poured into his mouth. He let slip of his reality, grateful for the darkness. Dreams, deep in his soul, rose to torment his mind.

He was in the church at Tenebral, examining the runes on the wall. The air was thick with a fragrant perfume. White doves fluttered all around him. The sunshine was strong until a dark shape blotted out the sky. Matthias looked up. A hawk, black and massive, covered the sun. It was hurtling down, talons outstretched. Matthias cried out but, as the hawk drew closer, it changed in shape: the Preacher, dressed in black from head to toe, his head still twisted from the gallows rope, eyes like burning coals and mouth frothing yellow spittle, hands like claws stretched out to kill. Matthias screamed. The hermit appeared but this time in the shape of a woman with soft brown hair, red chapped skin and light green eyes. He could now smell incense: a drink was forced between his lips. The dreams disappeared. Matthias slept on.

When he awoke Matthias could hardly believe it. No horse pounding beneath him. No lonely manor house or shabby tavern by the seashore. No pitching bumboat or dank, fetid hold. He lay in a broad four-poster bed in a white-washed chamber.

The room was neat and tidy, the floor tiled and polished. A huge crucifix hung on the wall opposite. Chests and stools and other pieces of furniture lay around the room. To his left a fire burnt vigorously in the mantled hearth. Braziers full of glowing charcoal stood in each corner. Matthias moved his hands and feet. He felt weak and tired. He glimpsed the bell on the table beside him. He stretched out to grasp it but it fell to the floor with a crash. Matthias fell back against the bolsters and drifted into sleep. He heard voices, the accent musical, the words lilting.

'He's been awake, that's good!'

Some more potion was pushed between his lips. He tried to open his eyes. All he could do was blink, then drift away. When he awoke again, two people sat by his bed watching him.

'Matthias Fitzosbert?'

The woman was the same woman as in his dreams. She had soft, brown hair, light green eyes, her skin was red-chapped; a strong face full of life and vitality. The man beside her was dark-haired, narrow-faced, one eye covered by a patch, the other bright with life. He had a twisted, sardonic look.

'Well, well, my boy,' the man said. 'Matthias Fitzosbert. We thought you were going to sleep until the last trumpet.' Despite the man's looks, the voice was warm and welcoming.

'How long?' Matthias muttered.

'Have a guess, my boyo.' He grasped Matthias' hand. 'My name is Thomas Fitzgerald. I am a bastard son, or so they say, of one of the Kildares. I am a poet, a soldier, a courtier, a lover of beautiful women and a drinker of red wine.'

'He's also a terrible boaster,' the woman laughed. 'Goodness, if hot air could make gold coins we'd all be princes! My name is Mairead. He thinks I'm his woman. Now, child,' her fingers brushed Matthias' face, 'guess how long you have been asleep?'

Matthias shook his head.

'Well, today is the last day of September.'

Matthias' jaw sagged. He realised he had been ill for at least six weeks.

'Whatever it was,' Mairead continued, 'it was a terrible sickness. We've treated you like a babe and you've slept like one. But, the angels be my witness, you've said some strange things.'

Matthias stiffened and stared at these two strangers.

'Now, boyo.' Fitzgerald got to his feet, throwing his cloak over his shoulder. Beneath, he was dressed in a leather surcoat which reached down to mid-thigh, with black, woollen hose pushed into boots. His clothes were shabby but the war belt wrapped around his waist was of good shiny leather, three daggers hung from it in embroidered pouches. 'Don't be frightened.' Fitzgerald smiled down at him as he picked at a piece of food through his finely set teeth. 'You are in good hands. This is a chamber in the palace of no less a person than the Archbishop of Dublin. Elsewhere is your good friend master Richard Symonds, priest.' The good eye winked slowly. 'And, of course, your prince, the noble Edward of Warwick, soon to be crowned King of England, Ireland, Scotland and France, has his own princely chambers.'

'Tush, Thomas, keep your voice down,' Mairead whispered. She smiled at Matthias. 'Symonds is a snake in the grass,' she declared, 'but young Edward is a fair boy.'

'What's happening?' Matthias asked.

'Ireland's always been for the House of York.' Fitzgerald walked round the bed and sat on the other side. 'Symonds was right to bring his prince here.'

Matthias noticed how Fitzgerald stumbled on the word 'prince'.

'Now the great lords of Ireland have pledged their swords. Kildare, Ormond and the rest. The Church, too, has promised its aid. But it's too late to go campaigning now. The sea is rough. There'll be nothing in England to feed our horses or men.'

'So?' Matthias asked.

'So, my boy, they'll wait for a while,' Fitzgerald continued. 'Not only for the weather but a fleet.'

'A fleet?'

Fitzgerald smiled lazily. 'What's the use of fighting for the English Crown if the English don't help? The Yorkist lords are gathering but they are in the Low Countries. Francis Lovell, John de la Pole, Earl of Lincoln, the son of the Earl of Suffolk.' Fitzgerald tapped his chest. 'That's where I and the beautiful Mairead come in. I am a mercenary,' he whispered with mock fierceness. 'A cutter of throats and a ravisher of women—'

'He's also a liar,' Mairead interrupted, leaning over to

smooth the woollen coverlet. 'I have known this boy, Master Matthias, since he was a babe. He sells his sword to the highest bidder. We are from the retinue of John de la Pole, envoy to the prince here in Dublin. There will be a fleet here soon from the Low Countries. The English lords, their retinues—'

'And, more importantly,' Fitzgerald interjected, 'a thousand landsknechts.'

'What?' Matthias asked.

'Mercenaries,' Fitzgerald explained. 'Born killers, like myself, under their leader, Martin Schwartz. They are a gift from Margaret, Duchess of Burgundy, sister to the once great Edward IV, beloved aunt of our noble prince who now resides here in such opulent splendour.'

'For God's sake, keep your voice low!' Mairead whispered.

Matthias struggled up to rest against the bolsters. Fitzgerald and Mairead hastened to help him, and Matthias caught her perfume, soft and cloying.

'I've always wanted a child,' Mairead said.

Fitzgerald grinned down at Matthias and patted his hand. 'You are her child, you know. A good physician is Mairead. She knows the herbs and potions. She should be a physician.' His face grew solemn. 'Instead they call her a witch.'

'Prince Edward told us to look after you,' Mairead declared. 'Gave us twenty pounds sterling, he did and offered us another thirty if you survived. A lovely boy, but you don't believe he's Warwick, do you?'

Mairead looked at Fitzgerald. The mercenary got up and walked to the door. He opened it, looked out, then closed and locked it.

'There's no one there,' he said, 'and the walls are thick.' He sat on his stool next to Mairead. 'Matthias – I can call you that, can't I? – I am going to tell you the truth because, you know, never once in your rantings or ravings did you ever mention the House of York. So, I think the Cause means as much to you as it does to me.' He winked at Matthias. 'One day you'll have to tell us why you are here. Now I am a ruffian born and bred. I lost my eye in a fray outside Arras but my ears and wits are as sound as any. Edward of Warwick is still in the Tower of London.' He smiled at the surprise on Matthias' face. 'I have listened to the gossip in de la Pole's circle. Edward of Warwick is a cat's-paw: the son of an Oxford tradesman, his real name is Lambert Simnel. He's a figurehead for the Yorkists. If they depose Henry Tudor, I am sure some nasty accident will occur so de la Pole, Earl of Lincoln, can claim the throne.'

'How many people know this?' Matthias asked.

'A few, but suspicion is spreading. The Tudors have taken the real Warwick out of the Tower and paraded him through the streets of London.' Fitzgerald shrugged. 'But we'll see . . .'

'Why are you here?' Mairead asked Matthias, stretching over to straighten the bolsters behind him.

'It's a long story. Symonds regards me as a talisman. As for the rest, I have no choice. If I am ever caught in England, I'll be hanged as a traitor, a murderer or a heretic.'

'By Queen Mab's paps!' Fitzgerald grinned. 'What on earth did you do?'

Matthias shrugged.

'You told us some,' Mairead declared, 'when you were in a fever. You mentioned names: Christina.' She closed her eyes. 'Your father, Osbert, Santerre and two nameless ones, the hermit and the Preacher.'

Matthias studied both these people. Despite the warmth of the bed his stomach pitched in fear. Why were they really helping him? What proof did he have that the Dark Lord, the Rosifer, the being who refused to leave him alone, might not now possess one of these.

Mairead must have caught his suspicion.

'One day,' she said, rising to her feet, 'you can tell us. For the moment you'd best rest.'

Over the next few weeks Matthias regained his strength. Fitzgerald and Mairead were the perfect companions but Matthias did not relax his suspicions. Edward of Warwick came to visit him. Despite what Fitzgerald had told him, Matthias still regarded him as a prince.

Symonds, however, had changed. He no longer wore the dark fustian robes of a priest but those of an elegant courtier. He was dressed in a quilted jacket with rounded neck and cuffs, the hem edged with fur, a chapron on his head, velvet hose and piped patterned shoes studded with precious stones. He would swagger in, thumbs pushed into the brocade belt, and talk grandly about what help they would receive and which Irish chieftains were with them.

As the year drew to a close and Matthias recovered full

health, he began to wander the Archbishop's palace, a grand spacious affair with its polished high ceilings, long wooden galleries, comfortable parlours and chambers. At Edward of Warwick's childish insistence, Matthias also attended council meetings and discovered that Symonds was not as foolish as he thought. English exiles, former Yorkists, were now flooding into Dublin. They brought their horses and armour, sometimes two or three men-at-arms. However, the real source of strength were the Irish chieftains who fascinated Matthias: tall, raw-boned men, skin cut and scored by the biting wind, their faces half-covered by luxuriant moustaches and beards. Proud warriors who dressed in a mixture of native fashion but sometimes imitated the worst excesses of court fops. Loud-mouthed and quarrelsome, generous and open-handed, their tempers could change at a drop of a coin. If they thought their honour had been besmirched, their hands would fall to their daggers and they'd scream at each other in Gaelic. Fitzgerald played a vital part in keeping all parties happy. Matthias could understand why John de la Pole had sent him to Dublin. Fitzgerald was a mercenary but he understood the Irish customs and keen Gaelic sense of honour. Time and again, at council meetings or banquets in the Archbishop's chamber, Fitzgerald would intervene to placate some chieftain or turn a potential knife fight and blood feud into laughter and ribaldry. Outside, in the archbishop's grounds, Matthias would glimpse the wild kerns or tribesmen who made up the retinues of these great chieftains.

'They fight like the very devils,' Fitzgerald said, as he and Matthias watched them out on the frost-covered lawn, feasting on the mutton and beef the aged and venerable Archbishop had provided from his kitchens. 'But that's the trouble,' Fitzgerald continued with a sigh. 'Look at them, Matthias! Naked as the day they were born. They carry shield and stabbing dirk. They cover their bodies with blue and red paint but that's no protection against men-at-arms, mounted knights or the deadly arrows of massed bowmen.'

'But we'll get help in England?' Matthias asked.

Fitzgerald turned, clicking his tongue, his good eye bright with mischief. 'Oh, boyo, you might know your books and sing a hymn in Latin yet you know nothing about politics. You babble like a bairn. I'll tell you what will happen.' Fitzgerald closed the leaded window door and drew closer to Matthias on the window seat.

'We'll land in England and march inland. Henry Tudor and his general, John de Vere, Earl of Oxford, will march north to meet us. Both sides will send out letters, emphasising their royal authority, ordering everyone to flock to their standards. The truth is, boyo, nobody will really jump until they're sure which side is winning.'

'And if we lose?'

Fitzgerald's face became grave. 'Then God help us. We are a foreign army, would be defeated rebels in enemy country. Henry Tudor will show us little mercy.' He slapped Matthias on the leg. 'But, if we win, it will be London Town, fine houses with deep cellars, silver cups and golden rings. We will feast like kings. And the women, Matthias, eh? I'd love to strip those plump, soft-skinned, overfed wives of the London merchants. I bet they'd squeal.' He stopped talking as Mairead came down the gallery towards them. 'But don't ever tell Mairead that,' he whispered. 'She'd cut my balls off!'

A few days later Mairead pronounced Matthias fully recovered.

'It must have been gaol fever,' she declared. 'Some rotten malignancy disturbed your humours. Now I think you are well enough to visit the city.' She kissed Matthias on each cheek. 'And, if you want,' she whispered. 'I can show you the sights.'

Matthias just grinned but never took her up on the offer. He liked Mairead but sensed her saucy flirtation was dangerous. Fitzgerald might swagger and talk about the ladies but he had a passion for the woman which might turn to a fierce, brooding jealousy.

Matthias was given fresh clothes and robes from the wardrobe: a new war belt with a shiny steel sword and a dagger with a long, ornate handle. He decided to see the city for himself and began to wander out. Winter had set in. Rain constantly fell, turning the muddy trackways and paths of the city into a quagmire. On the one hand Dublin was like any great town – the brooding castle, the fine elegant cathedral, the spacious mansions of the merchants and the lords. Cheek by jowl with these were the mean, mud-packed cottages of the poor, the tradesmen, the artisans. Dublin was also a border city. A busy port, merchants and traders from all over Europe thronged there. The air was thick with the smells and stench of the different ships which came into the harbour. Hanse merchants brushed shoulders with Flemings, Burgundians and Spanish. The English, too, were there, though they kept to themselves. The entire city knew about the presence of Edward of Warwick. Fitzgerald's words proved prophetic: none of the visiting English wished to show his allegiance publicly.

To the west Dublin was protected by the pale, an area directly under English rule. Beyond this, in the misty glens, lived the great tribes and fighting clans. Fitzgerald had warned Matthias to be careful and he could see why. These tribesmen came swaggering in, their long hair tied back with coloured clasps and brooches, their bodies almost naked except for breech clouts, boots and multi-coloured cloaks around their shoulders. They looked fierce with their sharp pointed teeth, faces painted in various garish colours. Some of them came to the markets which filled the narrow alleyways and streets of the city. Others arrived to be hired by Edward of Warwick. A good number also came looking for trouble and easy pickings. Once the day was done, the taverns and alehouses would fill with these men, who would challenge each other to drinking contests that might end in vows of eternal friendship or the most bloody and violent of knife fights.

Matthias, in his dark, sober clothes and carrying the seal of Fitzgerald, which offered him the protection of the great Irish lords, was safe enough. He went through the city to divert himself, and to be alone, reflect on what might happen. He wondered whether, if Symonds' projected invasion ever took place, he might slip away: perhaps back to Sutton Courteny and take counsel with Baron Sanguis. Matthias even began to speculate on whether the Rosifer, the Dark Lord, had forgotten him, until one memorable night during the second week of Advent.

Matthias had been sent to deliver a message from Edward of Warwick to a powerful lord who had a mansion overlooking the River Liffey. It was a personal, confidential matter, and Edward of Warwick had insisted that only Matthias should deliver it. As he'd made his way back through a narrow alleyway which led to the spacious grounds of the cathedral, a group of ruffians suddenly stepped out of the shadows. They were not Gaels or any of the tribesmen but sailors from some ship, and they were armed with sword, club and dagger. Their leader, a burly, bald-headed fellow, stepped forward and, jabbering in a patois Matthias couldn't understand, pointed to the war belt he wore and his boots, indicating that Matthias hand them over. He stepped back, hand on the hilt of his sword. The rifflers followed, laughing and mocking his attempts at defending himself.

Then abruptly they stopped. Matthias could just about make out their faces in the light of a pitch torch which burnt on the side of an entrance to a house. Their ribaldry disappeared. They looked, wide-eyed and gape-mouthed, at someone behind him. Matthias felt a cold breeze, a tingle at the back of his neck. He wanted to look round but dare not, fearing some trick. The assailants, however, started to move backwards. One dropped his club and made a hasty sign of the cross. They all turned on their heels and fled into the night. Matthias, slightly shaken, turned round. The alleyway was empty but, swirling amongst the fetid smells, came the sweet smell of a rose garden in full bloom under a summer's sun.

'Are you there?' Matthias called softly. 'Tell me, are you there?'

He went back down the alleyway, hardly daring to wonder what had terrified that group of ruffians so badly. He stepped into an alehouse, nothing more than a small, mean room, the floor covered with smelly rushes. It owned a few rickety stools and makeshift tables. In the corner, near the vats and barrels, stood the ale master. Matthias needed a drink, his throat and mouth were parched. He was also embarrassed at returning and showing his fear to Symonds and the others. A girl came across. She was dressed in a ragged smock, her feet bare. She reminded Matthias of Mairead with her dancing eyes and merry mouth.

'Ale, please.'

The girl nodded and brought it back in a not-too-clean blackjack. Matthias sat in the corner and cradled the drink, sipping it carefully, savouring its tangy sweetness.

In the far corner an old crone, warming her knees near the fire, was being tormented by two sallow-faced youths who insisted on tickling her bare neck with a dirty piece of straw from the floor. The old lady screeched in annoyance, muttering curses. The youths came back, their faces flushed with drink. They tickled the woman again. The old crone got up and shook her stick at them but this only made matters worse. She appealed to the pot-bellied ale master but he just smiled weakly back, shrugged and returned to caressing the hair of the young slattern who had served Matthias. The tormenters returned to their task until Matthias, upset by the old woman's screechings, walked across, drawing his sword and dagger. The youths stopped their baiting, shouted abuse and disappeared through the door into the night. Matthias filled the old lady's tankard, tossing a coin at the slattern. He took the tankard back and pushed it into her hands.

'Sit down, Mother,' he said.

Her wizened, lined face broke into a smile. She supped at the ale, the white foam catching the hairs on her upper lip. She muttered her thanks. Matthias resheathed his sword and dagger and collected his cloak. He was about to leave when the old woman called out, pointing her finger at him.

'What is it, Mother?' Matthias called.

She said something but he couldn't understand it.

'I am sorry,' he apologised. 'I am English.'

Again the cracked smile. 'You are well protected.' Her voice was halting, the words clipped.

Matthias patted the hilt of his sword.

'No, no, not that.' The old woman pointed as if someone were standing beside Matthias. 'He protects you.'

Matthias tried to hide his unease.

'They say I am a witch.' The old woman narrowed her eyes. 'You really can't see him, can you? Cowled and hooded he is, but he has a beautiful face, except for the eyes.' She was now staring at a point beyond Matthias. 'Like coals they are! Burning coals! He's smiling at me.' The old woman crouched back on her stool. 'And the teeth,' she added. 'He is the Dearghul!'

'The what?' Matthias asked.

'The Drinker of Blood, Englishman!'

Matthias swallowed hard, realising what, as he had suspected, had frightened the ruffians who had attacked him earlier. The old woman now had her back to him. She looked slyly over her shoulder.

'You shouldn't worry, Englishman. He's gone now but the Dearghul never leave you alone!'

15

Matthias returned to the Archbishop's palace. Fitzgerald and Mairead were waiting for him.

'Are you well?' she asked anxiously. 'You look pale.'

'The cold always has that effect on me,' Matthias retorted.

He excused himself, went up to his chamber and prepared for bed. He left a candle, hooded and capped, burning on the table beside him. As he lay staring at the flickering flame, Matthias wondered when the Rose Demon would manifest itself. He vaguely recalled his dreams, the nightmare of his delirium, and reflected on what had happened since he had fled Oxford.

'That's what I've become,' he murmured to himself, 'a spectator: I watch my own life but I do not live it.'

He recalled his childhood prayer as he drifted into sleep. When he woke the candle was out. The chamber was clothed in darkness. The windows, firmly shuttered, kept out any moonlight or sound from the courtyard below. Matthias lay listening to the darkness. He felt something on the coverlet, moving over his leg. Matthias cursed the rats which plagued the Archbishop's palace. The rat did not flee. Instead Matthias felt it running backwards and forwards across his legs, squeaking loudly in the darkness. He half-propped himself up, his fingers scrabbling for the tinder. After some difficulty he removed the candle cap and lit the wick. The rat was still there, so he sat up, holding out the candle. The rat was long and black, its head turned away, its sleek body nestling in the folds of the coverlet. Matthias kicked his feet and shouted. The rat turned its head. Matthias stared in horror. Instead of the pointed nose it had human features: face, small and shrunken; glittering eyes, sharp nose and harsh mouth. Matthias screamed and kicked; when he looked again, the rat was gone.

For a while Matthias sat on the edge of the bed, his body drenched in sweat. He didn't know whether he had been dreaming or, half-asleep, had seen some phantasm. He took a cloth and dried his face and neck. He started to shiver. The fire had died and so had the glowing brazier in the corner – not even a wink of red, as if it had been drenched with water. The room grew freezing cold. Matthias heard a sound near the door, as if someone were moving quietly in the darkness – a footfall, the creak of leather. Matthias lunged across the bed and grasped his war belt. He pulled this across and, taking out his sword, picked up the candle. He ignored the cold, which was like a savage biting wind blowing through the chamber. Holding the candle out in front of him, Matthias edged across the room, his eyes fixed on the pool of light. He turned slightly sideways, his sword out ready for any secret assault or hidden attack. Still, the sound came of someone shuffling near the door. Matthias reached the place, his body soaked in sweat, his chest heaving. He moved the candle backwards and forwards. He could see nothing nor detect anything undisturbed.

Matthias was about to go back to his bed when he stopped, rigid as a statue. Whoever was in the room was now behind him, breathing noisily. Matthias turned. He glimpsed a dark shape. He held the candle up and stared in horror: Rahere the clerk was standing there but no longer the court fop. His hair was streaked with grey, his face was haggard, his skin covered with pustules, red-rimmed eyes and lips soaked with blood. On his neck, where the dirty shirt opened at the throat, Matthias could see suppurating lacerations, as if the man had been clawed by a bear or a wolf. Matthias took a step backwards.

'In God's name,' he whispered, 'who or what are you?'

Rahere stepped closer. His upper lip curled like that of a dog about to attack: his teeth were long and white, the eyeteeth drooping like those of a mastiff.

'You.' The voice was low, throaty and full of hate. 'Taken before my time!' A hand came up, fingers long and dirt-stained. 'Called before my time I was, because of you!'

Matthias lashed out with his sword. As he did so the candle fell from his hand, the flame was extinguished. Matthis could smell putrefaction. Filled with terror as well as anger at being

216

haunted and hounded, he seized his sword in two hands, striking out and screaming abuse. Fitzgerald and Mairead, blankets wrapped round their shoulders, burst into the room. Matthias stopped. He drove the point of his sword into the wooden planks of the floor and stood there clasping the hilt, chest heaving, eyes glaring.

'Now, now, boyo!'

Fitzgerald came forward slowly as Mairead lit candles round the room and opened the shutters.

'Come on, boyo.' Fitzgerald gestured at Matthias' sword. 'Let it drop. We are friends!'

Mairead rushed by him and, crouching down, loosened Matthias' fingers from round the sword hilt. Matthias let it go. He slumped down to the floor. Mairead put her arms round him, rocking him gently like a baby.

'What's the matter, love?' she whispered.

'There was someone here,' Matthias replied. 'Frightening, the stench of the grave.'

'Tush, that's nonsense,' she whispered. 'There's no one here. And, as for the stench, Matthias, I thought you had a woman here. Can't you smell the perfume?'

'The room smells like a summer's day,' Fitzgerald declared.

Matthias stood up and stared round the chamber. Apart from cuts to the wood caused by his sword, the candle lying on the floor, he could see nothing out of place. Then he caught the fragrance, the sweet heady smell of roses.

'I am sorry,' he muttered. 'I must have been dreaming.'

'Oh, boyo, that's not good enough.' Fitzgerald went across to the hearth and, scraping aside the ash, he took some kindling, a few of the dried logs and soon the fire was burning merrily. Matthias glanced towards the brazier. It was lit and glowing, though he was certain that when he had woken up the charcoal had been cold and bare. He sat on the stool before the fire. Mairead and Fitzgerald joined him, one on either side. Mairead served them wine.

'You didn't have a dream,' she said. 'Matthias, you were awake. You were terrified. What is it?'

Matthias, not shifting his gaze from the fire, told them slowly and haltingly about the events of Sutton Courteny; the silence of the intervening fourteen years; Santerre, the Bocardo, Symonds and his flight to Dublin. They heard him

217

out. When he had finished Matthias turned and smiled at Mairead.

'You think I'm mad, don't you? Madcap, witless, leaping about like a March hare?'

Mairead shook her head and gently caressed his cheek.

'Here in Ireland, Matthias, we believe in magic. The Devil walks the country lanes and misty glades. The hidden glens and dark woods are full of beings we cannot see but who take an active interest in the affairs of men. There is the banshee,' she continued, 'a grotesque, red-haired woman with a disfigured face and protruding teeth. She dresses in white and haunts dark and lonely places. If you see her or hear her terrible wail it's a sign of approaching death.' She glanced across at Fitzgerald. 'They say she's been heard recently in Dublin, howling like a moonstruck wolf.' She shook her head. 'I do not think Symonds' venture will meet with success.'

'What is the Dearghul?' Matthias asked.

He told them about the incident the previous evening. Mairead smiled bravely but Matthias could tell she was frightened whilst Fitzgerald sat uneasily on his stool.

'They are the blood drinkers,' Mairead replied slowly, her eyes never leaving his. 'The Undead. Tell him, Thomas!'

Fitzgerald hawked and spat into the flames.

'I was born in Ireland,' he began. 'The Dearghul, as the bonny Mairead says, are the Undead. Now, I thought they were childish stories to frighten the weak-minded as well as keep the children in their beds. According to these legends, the Dearghul are Strigoi or vampires. If you get bitten by one they draw blood from your body and replace it with their own. To all intents and purposes you die but, when darkness falls, those who have been given this new, macabre life rise from their graves and look to spread themselves.' He shrugged. 'Those are the legends. Now, sixteen years ago, with no wars in Ireland and Edward IV strong in England, I travelled to France but there was peace there. I joined the Swiss, giving my sword against the Burgundians and, when that war ended, I travelled further east. I joined a party of Teutonic knights, Crusaders moving south towards Greece to fight against the Turks.' Fitzgerald scratched at his chin and played with the black patch over his eye. 'We crossed the Danube and entered Transylvania. Oh, boyo.' He looked at Matthias. 'You think

Ireland is dark and full of woods. Transylvania is a land full of shadows, deep valleys, the sides of which are covered in the darkest and thickest of forests; wild, noisy rivers; a land of perpetual night. The prince of that country, or Voivode as they call themselves, was Vlad Tepes, Vlad the Impaler. He was more popularly known by his nickname "Drakulya", Son of the Dragon. He hired our swords.'

Fitzgerald stretched out his hands towards the flames. 'We did not stay there long. Drakulya's soul must have been made in Hell. Never once did he show any compassion to prisoners, and to those who opposed him, he was cruelty itself. His palace at Tirgoviste was surrounded by a forest of stakes, and on each stake were impaled alive men and women, Turk and Christian, Greek and Arab, anyone who opposed his will. Now, for me he had little time, but Drakulya became very fond of our leader, a young German knight, Otto Franzen. Otto was a brave warrior – he feared nothing – a superb horseman, a redoubtable fighter. Drakulya said we could all leave if we wanted to, but Otto, he begged to stay.' Fitzgerald sipped from his cup. 'The young German refused. He was sickened by the bloodshed, by the soul-crushing terror of Drakulya's court. We made to leave. Drakulya could not stop us. Then Otto fell ill, not a fever or some sickness, just a weakness. Drakulya sent his best physicians. We were kept well away but Otto died. It was too far for us to take his body back home. Drakulya became all courteous and kind. He promised us that Otto would be buried in a princely cemetery outside his own chapel at Tirgoviste, so we agreed.'

Fitzgerald rolled the wine cup between his fingers. 'Five days later we left Tirgoviste. I remember riding down the narrow, cobbled streets towards the city gates. There must have been thirty or forty of us: a long trail of pack animals and sumpter ponies. Drakulya had given each of us a purse of coins and provisions for our journey.' Fitzgerald paused.

'Go on,' Mairead urged.

'Now, it was late in the day when we left, the heart of winter. Darkness was already falling. Voivode Drakulya paid us the supreme compliment of being present at the gates of his city as we left.' Fitzgerald held a hand up. 'Heaven is my witness, I don't lie. I was on the outside of the group. The path leading down was steep. I could see the gates were open.

The thoroughfare on either side was packed with Drakulya's troops. Torches had been lit and placed on iron stands. From where I rode I could see the Voivode himself, surrounded by his officers. As I passed him I looked. At first I couldn't believe it. Drakulya sat on his horse smiling bleakly at us: the man next to him, pale as a ghost, with dark rings round his eyes, was our former commander, Otto Franzen.' Fitzgerald wiped his mouth on the back of his hand. 'He was alive, staring at us with soulless eyes. I saw him. Others saw him. A man whom we had seen die, whom we had coffined and buried. Yet, what could we do? We were taken so much by surprise, we were through the gates and they were slammed behind us. A year later we heard that Drakulya had died, been killed in an ambush. According to the stories, his headless corpse was taken across to the Island of Snagov and laid to rest there. A short while later it was decided to move his corpse to a more fitting tomb but when they opened the grave, there was nothing there.' Fitzgerald breathed in noisily. 'Every so often I dream. I wonder if Otto Franzen still rides those dark, shadow-filled valleys; he and others, following their murderous, bloody-handed, undead prince. So yes, Matthias Fitzosbert, I believe your story but, as Heaven is my witness, I do not know how I can help you!'

'You should tell him,' Mairead said.

Fitzgerald looked as if he were going to refuse.

'Tell me what?' Matthias insisted.

'Two things.'

'Tell him!'

Fitzgerald got to his feet. He refilled his wine goblet, then placed his hand on Matthias' shoulder.

'There have been deaths in the city,' he told him. 'Strange murders. Mostly young women, night-walkers, slatterns, maids: their throats punctured, their bodies drained of blood, as you would squeeze juice out of a grape.'

'So the Rose Demon's here?'

'Possibly,' Mairead said.

'But who?' Matthias asked.

'Have you ever suspected,' Fitzgerald sat down on a stool, 'our noble Edward of Warwick or, more possibly, his mentor, Richard Symonds?'

Matthias wrapped the blanket round his shoulders more

tightly. He felt cold again. He was now certain that the presence he had met in Oxford was here in Dublin. But what could he do?

'There's nothing,' Matthias declared, 'nothing at all I can do. If I go to a priest, I'll be arrested as a heretic or a warlock.' He glanced at his two companions. 'Aren't you frightened?' he mocked bitterly. 'Aren't you terrified of me?'

'I am afraid of nothing,' Fitzgerald retorted, 'nothing that walks on legs.'

'The second thing?' Matthias asked. 'You said there were two things?'

'Ah yes.' Fitzgerald got to his feet. 'Richard Symonds has been talking about you. Dark hints about your secret powers. Time and again he reminds our young prince of your debt to him. It may be time he comes to ask that you repay it.'

Fitzgerald and Mairead then left. Matthias kept the candles alight, crossed himself and climbed into bed. He accepted he could do nothing, except pray and wait.

The next morning Matthias went to Mass in a chantry chapel of Dublin Cathedral. The priest who celebrated it reminded him of his father. Matthias abruptly realised that, in his imprisonment and flight from Oxford, he had lost the list of quotations his father had provided. On his return to his chamber he took a piece of parchment and wrote them down from memory. When he had finished, Matthias studied his scrawled words: these might provide a key to the mystery which confronted him. He also speculated on why he had experienced such harrowing hauntings the previous night. Was this a sign the Rose Demon was close? Or was it something he was to experience throughout his life?

Matthias returned to his duties. Christmas was approaching and the weather had turned cold and bleak, the clouds heavily massed, grey and lowering, bubbling with the threat of violent winds and drenching rain. All preparations for the invasion now came to a halt. The Irish lords had promised what they could. Edward of Warwick would now have to wait until spring arrived and the English exiles sailed from Flanders with whatever help they could provide. News still came from England. Tudor again paraded the boy who, he claimed, was the real Edward of Warwick, through the city of London. Symonds openly scoffed at this, dismissing it as a sign of the usurper's growing anxieties. So confident did Symonds become that he and young Edward were often closeted for hours, detailing arrangements of what would happen once they had seized the English crown.

Symonds also worked hard to keep Matthias well away from the young prince, sending him through the city with messages, treating him no better than a lackey. Matthias did not object. He was already forming secret plans that, if and when the invasion should sail, he would leave the Yorkist rebels as swiftly as possible.

Symonds' hold over the young prince became more apparent. By the feast of the Epiphany, six days into the New Year, Matthias no longer received invitations to join council meetings. Fitzgerald and Mairead were elsewhere, so he was left to kick his heels, though he suspected it was only a matter of time before Symonds moved against him openly. The Archbishop's palace was now a hotbed of intrigue with masked and cowled messengers coming at all hours of the day and night. Sentries stood at every doorway, guards patrolled the grounds. Symonds began to issue letters talking of 'Judas men' spies, possibly assassins, with designs on the young prince's life.

On the Feast of Saints Timothy and Titus, towards the end of January, Symonds summoned Matthias to a meeting in his opulent chamber at the other end of the palace. Symonds, swathed in furs, slouched in a throne-like chair, stretching beringed fingers towards a roaring fire. Servants and lackeys stood in the shadows ready to satisfy his every whim. Matthias was made to sit on a stool opposite. Symonds studied him for a while. Matthias gazed coolly back. In the few months since arriving in Dublin, Symonds had changed: his face was fleshy and reddened by the banquets and feasts he had attended. Veins, high in his cheeks, were an eloquent witness to his nightly carousing. Symonds sucked noisily on his teeth and snapped his fingers.

'Clear the room!' he ordered. 'All of you outside!'

Symonds waited until the door closed behind them. He jabbed a finger at Matthias.

'I am rather disappointed with you. I brought you to Dublin because I thought you were for the House of York. You should help our cause but what do I have? Nothing but a sickly man who spends most of his time closeted with Fitzgerald and his trollop!'

'I did not ask you to bring me,' Matthias returned. 'And I did not wish to be sick. As for Master Fitzgerald and Mairead, they are my friends.'

'Are they now?' Symonds leant forward. 'Are they now, Master Fitzosbert?' His lips curled. 'You have no friends! I brought you because of that woman Morgana. On reflection I wonder who you really are. A Judas man, eh? One of the Welsh usurper's snivelling spies?'

Matthias made to rise.

'If you leave, I'll have you killed!' Symonds snapped.

Matthias sat down on the stool but his fingers drummed on the hilt of the dagger pushed into his belt. Symonds smiled.

'In a few days it will be February,' he said. 'The weather will change: the sea will be less choppy, the winds not so rough. We wait impatiently for de la Pole's fleet to sail from Flanders.' He banged the arm of his chair. 'And the fleet must come. Now, in Ireland they claim . . .' He paused and stared at one of the rings on his finger. 'They say with the right sacrifice the elements can be placated.' He glanced at Matthias.

'What are you asking?' Matthias asked impatiently.

'I was a priest,' Symonds sneered, 'but I no more believe in such nonsense than you do, Master Fitzosbert! You and your haunting nightmares! Oh, I've heard of them! Yours won't be the first Black Mass I've attended.'

Matthias' heart sank: from his studies in Oxford he knew about such blasphemous rituals.

'And,' Symonds continued, 'it won't be the last!'

'You wish me to participate in secret rites? The Black Arts? Aren't there sorcerers and wizards enough in this rain-soaked isle?' Matthias protested.

'Oh, I could fill the cathedral with charlatans,' Symonds retorted. 'But you are different, aren't you, dear Matthias? I have had you followed. Why did those ruffians not attack you? And, in that tawdry alehouse the old witch who talked to you about the Dearghul? And those nightmares which woke the palace?' Symonds pursed his lips and glared at Matthias. 'Do you think I'm a fool?' he hissed. 'People are talking, Matthias! Here we are in an old, draughty palace, the latrines are frozen, the rushes cannot be changed. Why is it that servants say your chamber smells so richly, like a rose garden on a summer's afternoon?'

Matthias realised that Symonds not only resented him but feared him. He viewed him as a practitioner of the Black Arts and was probably terrified that Matthias might use these to exert influence over Edward of Warwick.

'Now, I'll tell you what will happen.' Symonds stared up at the rafters. 'Today is Thursday. At the beginning of February, you and I will meet again. There are some old ruins at the east end of the cathedral grounds. People say they once belonged to the Druids, the ancient priests who lived here before St Patrick arrived. Let me see these powers of yours. Let us call on the Dark One and see what assistance can be given.'

'This is foolishness!' Matthias protested.

'No, Master Fitzosbert, this is politics. I intend to topple Tudor from his throne.' Symonds' eyes gleamed with fanaticism. 'I, as Archbishop of Canterbury, will, one day, place the crown of Edward the Confessor on this prince of York in the Abbey of Westminster. If I have to make a compact with hell to achieve it, then so be it.' He gestured with his fingers. 'You are dismissed!'

Matthias was halfway through the door.

'Oh, Matthias,' Symonds grinned round the chair, reminding Matthias of a gargoyle, 'accidents can happen. You should be careful you are not abducted by some English merchant and taken back to London or Oxford!'

Matthias left the chamber. In the gallery outside he met Mairead and Fitzgerald, who had recently returned to the palace. He was so angry at what had happened, he just brushed by them and spent the rest of the day in his own chamber wondering what to do. There were knocks on the door but he refused to answer. Later in the evening he asked a servant to bring him up some food. He drank deeply and, when he awoke, darkness was falling, the palace was quiet and he was bitterly cold. He built up the fire, stripped and went to bed. This time he slept peacefully, slipping into a dream.

Matthias had never experienced the like before. He knew he was dreaming but he couldn't, he didn't want to wake up. He was on the corner of Magpie Lane in Oxford, on a bright summer's day. People were milling around him. He could hear their chatter and smell the odours of the city. He felt a pang of homesickness as he walked down the lane. Then the dream changed: he was in a small garden and, by the pealing of the bells, he knew it was evening in Oxford. The garden was small, protected by a high, red-brick wall. There were herb beds, small grassy patches. In an arbour Richard Symonds was sitting, a book in his lap.

'Stay and watch,' a voice murmured. '*Oh, Creatura bona atque parva.* Just stay and watch!'

It grew darker still. The sky was beautiful, the stars like precious stones on a dark blue cushion. Symonds, however, was unaware of the beauty of the evening. He was now impatient, walking up and down the path. He opened a brown, metal-studded gate in the wall and went through an alleyway. Matthias followed. Out in the streets there was great excitement. A man, wearing the royal livery, carried a pennant which displayed a red dragon breathing fire. Matthias recognised the livery of Henry Tudor. Symonds, his discomfort obvious, went back into the garden, slamming the gate.

Time moved quickly. Night fell, a hunter's moon above the city. Symonds was still there. He carried a goblet of wine and a trencher of food. Abruptly the gate opened, a man came in, sandy-haired, face unshaven, a cut just beneath his left eye. He was apparently injured elsewhere, for he stumbled and Symonds helped him to a turf seat. The man threw off his brown serge military cloak. Matthias, glimpsing the blood on the man's shirt, drew closer. The man was wearing a ring bearing an insignia; a red wyvern rampant on a field of argent. He was talking to Symonds, clutching his stomach as he did, apparently begging for help.

Symonds nodded sympathetically. He went back into the house and came back out with a goblet of wine. The man on the turf seat was lolling, head down. He took the cup and drank. Matthias stared in horror: as the man lifted his head to drain the cup, Symonds came behind him, a long, thin, Italian stiletto in his hand and, with one swift cut, he slashed the man's throat from ear to ear. Matthias turned away. When he looked again, the darkness was fading, the sky was already streaked with gold. Symonds was in the far corner of the garden. He had dug a deep trench into which he tossed his victim's corpse. He kicked the dirt over, carefully pressing the soil so it looked as if no grave had been dug there.

Matthias' eyes flew open. Outside in the gallery he heard footsteps: servants and retainers, hurrying hither and thither, bringing coals, preparing the household for a new day. Matthias sat up in bed. Despite his many cups of wine, he felt refreshed and clear-headed. He caught the faint smell of roses. Was that his dream? Was he still in that garden? And why had he dreamt so clearly, every detail so finely etched? It was like turning over the pages in a Book of Hours. What had happened was simple to understand: the warm August day, the excitement in the streets and the messenger bearing the pennant of Henry Tudor, showed that Matthias had been shown a scene in Oxford shortly after Henry's victory over Richard III at Market Bosworth in August 1485. But the man who had been murdered? Matthias got up. Absent-mindedly he shaved and washed, then went down to the refectory where Mairead and Fitzgerald were breaking their fast.

'You seem in better humour than you did yesterday,' Mairead teased.

'I have something to ask you.' Matthias slipped on to a bench opposite. 'Fitzgerald, you've lived amongst the Yorkist exiles?'

'Aye, I have.'

'Can you recall any lord or knight whose arms were – ah yes—' Matthias narrowed his eyes, 'a red wyvern rampant on a field of argent?' Matthias filled his cup with beer. 'Could you find out who bore such arms?'

'I don't have to,' Fitzgerald grinned back. 'They belong to Lionel Clifford, a knight banneret of John de la Pole, Earl of Lincoln.'

'Is he dead?'

'Wasn't when I met him in Tournai. He was drinking and wenching as good as the rest.' Fitzgerald must have glimpsed the disappointment in Matthias' face. 'Mind you, it's a mystery about his father, Henry.'

'Why?'

'Well, he fought with Richard III at Bosworth. Sir Henry Clifford was a Yorkist through and through. We know that he left the battlefield and was last seen on the outskirts of Oxford but after that,' Fitzgerald shrugged, 'not a trace. Why do you ask?'

'No reason,' Matthias replied. 'But look, Fitzgerald, how much longer are we to stay here?'

Fitzgerald knew better than to question Matthias further and allowed the conversation to turn to the growing expectancy about the arrival of the fleet from Flanders.

When he could, Matthias left the refectory and made his way directly to Symonds' chamber. The former priest was sitting enthroned in his great four-poster bed, resting against the silken bolsters piled high around him, a fur-trimmed robe about his shoulders. He lifted his head when Matthias came in and grinned.

'Ah, Fitzosbert, so you've come to give me your answer!'

'I don't like your threats.' Matthias sat on the edge of the bed, pleased to see the alarm flare in Symonds' eyes. 'Oh, I wouldn't call your bullyboys. You wouldn't want anyone to know what I do. Well, apostate priest,' he continued, 'I do look forward to John de la Pole arriving in Dublin. I understand that Sir Lionel Clifford will be in his retinue?'

Symonds' face paled.

'I will tell you a story,' Matthias continued, 'about how his father fled from Bosworth. He made his way to what he thought was the house of a Yorkist sympathiser. The priest, Symonds, had a small tenement and garden near Magpie Lane.'

The ex-priest was now gaping at him.

'A beautiful August evening,' Matthias continued. 'Henry Clifford is wounded: he looks for sympathy, solace, a place to hide but Symonds is a lick-spittle coward. He gives Sir Henry Clifford wine, then cuts his throat. I'll say that when they return to England, they should examine the far corner of his garden. They'll find a deep trench and in it, the corpse of Sir Henry thrown there like a bag of dog's bones.'

Matthias got to his feet. 'Now I've written that down,' he declared. 'If something happens to me, copies of my story are to be delivered to Sir John de la Pole and Sir Lionel Clifford.' Matthias grinned and gave a mocking bow. 'So, you see, sir, I have power and I have used it. I do not wish to talk to you again on these matters!'

16

The winter months quickly passed. The weather changed, cool breezes, clear skies: a strong sun burnt up the soggy mud-caked lawns of Dublin. The chieftains and their clansmen swarmed back into the city. Matthias, like Fitzgerald and Mairead, was caught up in the excitement and preparations for war. At last the fleet came from Flanders bringing the English lords John de la Pole, Earl of Lincoln, Francis Lovell, coffers full of gold from Margaret of Burgundy and, more importantly, over a thousand mercenaries led by their commander, Martin Schwartz. The latter poured into Dublin, a fearsome sight. They wore heavy sallets with eye-slits which protected most of their faces; breastplates, and hard-boiled leather leggings. Each man carried a sword, dagger and a heavy steel-stained crossbow with bolts which could crack hardened armour plate. They were also experts in the pike and the lance, redoubtable on foot as well as horse. These and the retinues of de la Pole and Lovell now filled the grounds of the Archbishop's palace.

De la Pole was a square, thickset man, grim-faced, hard-eyed, his chin and forelips cleanly shaved. He soon took over command of the Yorkist forces mustered there. Lovell was lean and sallow-faced, long black hair falling down to his shoulders; he reminded Matthias of Rahere the clerk. Lovell had been a confidant of Richard III, a member of his secret council. Both he and de la Pole had little time for Symonds and his protégé.

'It's obvious,' Fitzgerald commented as he, Mairead and Matthias sat under an oak tree. They were sharing a jug of ale, watching the soldiers set up camp, treating the Archbishop's orchards as if they were their own personal property. 'It's obvious,' Fitzgerald repeated, for he loved to pontificate on military matters, 'that our young prince is only a figurehead.

Once these matters are brought to a successful conclusion, Symonds and Edward of Warwick will soon disappear.' He lowered his voice as he refilled their cups. 'I have taken close counsel with my Lord of Lincoln: Tudor still parades Edward of Warwick in London.'

'It's a wild scheme,' Mairead declared. 'Thomas, my boy, and you, Matthias, we should leave, slip away. Let the witless lead the madcaps. All this will end in blood and tears.'

Fitzgerald just laughed and returned to his drinking, but Mairead's words set Matthias thinking. There was now tension in the Yorkist camp. The retainers of Lovell, wearing the livery of a white greyhound on a square padlock, and those displaying the golden lions of Lincoln, now swaggered through the galleries and corridors of the Archbishop's palace. Fitzgerald breathlessly reported how de la Pole had now made himself master of the young Edward, and Symonds was nothing more than a confidant. The ex-priest could not object. De la Pole, because he was of Yorkist descent, soon won over the allegiance of the Irish chieftains. The Earl also controlled the gold given to him by Margaret of Burgundy, not to mention Schwartz, his principal military adviser. A more rigorous discipline was imposed. Weapons were collected and piled in warehouses down near the harbour. Ships, cogs and herring-boats were impounded. The invasion fleet began to muster.

Matthias kept to himself or talked to Fitzgerald and Mairead. Since his dream he had experienced no other phenomena, though he had heard from whispers in the sculleries and kitchens, as well as a few guarded comments from Mairead, that the strange murders were still occurring in Dublin. Corpses had been found, their throats punctured, drained of blood. Matthias, however, felt helpless: the Rose Demon could inhabit any one of the people he knew and, apart from Mairead and Fitzgerald, there was no one he could confide in.

At the beginning of May 1487, Warwick was crowned King Edward VI in Christ Church Cathedral, Dublin. It was a splendid ceremony, the nave and sanctuary filled with banners, the Mass celebrated by two archbishops and twelve bishops. The crown was placed on the young man's head. He received the holy chrism and was loudly proclaimed as

Edward VI, King of Ireland, England, Scotland and France. The crowded nave, packed with mercenaries, the followers of Lincoln, Lovell and the Irish chieftains, roared its approval. Afterwards banquets were held, toasts given, alliances and friendships proclaimed to be eternal. A few days later the ships, cogs, herring-boats and fishing smacks were loaded up with provisions and arms.

At the beginning of June the Yorkist army embarked on the ships which had collected in the city harbour. Matthias secured a place in the flagship, the *Sainte Marie*, a massive cog which bore most of the commanders. He felt as if he were in a dream: the small fleet standing out in the harbour, emblazoned with flags and pennants; the golden lions of de la Pole; the leopards and lilies of England; the colourful, makeshift banners of the Irish lords. Thanks to Schwartz, everything moved in an orderly fashion. Ships turned and made their way out of the harbour, sails dipping three times in honour of the Trinity.

By the time dusk fell, they were out into the open sea, picking up brisk winds heading for Peil Castle on the Isle of Foudray in Lancashire. The crossing was smooth and uneventful. The Yorkist commanders were beside themselves with joy. There was no sign of the Tudor ships and, on their second day out, they made a landfall, the cogs slipping into a natural harbour. At first confusion reigned as horses, supplies and men were unloaded. There were mishaps and accidents but, by 7 June 1487, the Yorkist army was disembarked, formed its line of march and headed deep into Lancashire. Matthias rode with Fitzgerald; Mairead kept close.

'She's got a soft spot for you.' Fitzgerald drew his horse back and grinned at Matthias. 'But she's also worried, as am I. You've been very quiet, Matthias Fitzosbert. In Dublin you almost became a recluse. What happened between you and Symonds, eh?'

Matthias shrugged. 'I don't trust him and he doesn't trust me.'

'And that's what I want to speak to you about.' Fitzgerald leant closer and gestured at the clouds of dust which now rose on either side of the army. 'It's a beautiful day. You are back in England, the grass is green. The honeysuckle, cowslip, daisy and the rose are in full bloom. So, why do you choke dust in the middle of a rebel army?' Fitzgerald grasped Matthias' wrist. 'You're going to slip away, boyo, aren't you?'

Matthias stared back.

'One dark night you'll fasten on your war belt and, without a word to me or Mairead, you'll be over the hills and miles away.'

'Something like that,' Matthias grudgingly conceded. 'Thomas, you've been a good friend yet you are a mercenary, a fighting man, and I, in truth, am still a prisoner. I am only here because Symonds thought I could help him. If we win, I'll be turned out to fend for myself. If we lose, I'll hang quicker than the rest.' He gathered the reins in his hands. 'I, too, have a life to lead, things to do.'

'Don't go,' Fitzgerald warned.

He pulled Matthias' horse out of the column of march. For a while they sat and watched the horsemen, the carts, sumpter ponies, Schwartz's men striding along, their long pikes over their shoulders, their sallets hanging on their backs. Behind these trotted thousands of wild Irish tribesmen, nothing more than a disorderly mass kept in check by Schwartz's officers and their own chieftains.

'I'm going to tell you, boyo.' Fitzgerald was now sitting very close, his leg brushing that of Matthias. 'So far we've had the devil's own luck. We've crossed the sea and we've disembarked. The sun is strong.' He gestured to the fields on either side. 'Long, cool grass, clear brooks and streams.' He pointed to the small copses and woods which dotted the landscape. 'Don't be fooled by all this, Matthias. Where are the English lords who were supposed to join us? Where are the peasants? The yeomen flocking to our banners?' He gestured at the Irish. 'And how long do you think they'll obey orders?'

'What are you saying, Fitzgerald?'

The mercenary pointed to the far distance.

'Somewhere over there, Tudor's armies are waiting. They have castles, men-at-arms, bowmen, supplies and, above all, they are led by one of the best generals in Europe, John de Vere, Earl of Oxford. He was fighting Yorkists when you were piddling your breeches. Soon the pillaging, the raping and the robbing will begin. I tell you this, Matthias, any stranger found wandering by himself will be regarded as a rebel. The peasants

231

will hate you and, if you are captured, you'll die slowly, not in a matter of hours but days, even weeks. I know, I have fought in these wars. Have you ever seen a living man trussed and bound and fed to hogs? Or turned like a piece of meat over a slow-burning fire? And then there's Symonds! Heaven knows what you said to him, Matthias, but he hates and distrusts you. He considers you a Judas man, a Tudor agent. You are watched more closely than you think. So, stay close to me and Mairead.' He spurred his horse. 'And let tomorrow take care of itself!'

Later that day the army camped in open fields. Within a matter of hours, fires were lit, pavilions set up, whilst men-at-arms foraged to make bothies, small, tent-like structures made of branches woven together. Stolen cattle and sheep were slaughtered. The air grew thick with burning meat and the smell of horse dung and the fetid smells from the latrines, which had been hastily dug by the side of a stream. So far the rebel host was in good mood. Guards were set but, for the rest, it was like a fair or carnival.

Matthias decided to ride round the camp. He made his way through the horse lines, past the outlying sentries. He was going downhill when he heard a sound behind him. He reined in and looked round: through the trees at the top of the hill he saw horsemen shadowing him. Matthias shrugged and rode back to camp, remembering Fitzgerald's warning.

The march continued. The army struggled out, sending up clouds of dust as it wound its way through the country lanes. Fitzgerald's words proved prophetic: as they moved away from the coast and began to reach outlying farms and villages, burning and looting took place. Plumes of black smoke rose to the sky. De la Pole did his best to keep order, and when the army came upon a farmstead pillaged by some of the Irish kerns, the entire group of perpetrators was rounded up. The next morning the army had to march past the makeshift scaffolds set up on either side of the road where two dozen corpses, naked except for their loin cloths, twitched and twirled in the early morning breeze.

Eventually they climbed the hilly ridge of the Pennines, open moorland, gorse and heather turning purple under the warm summer sun. They saw nothing except hunting kestrels, petrels, crows and ravens, which circled noisily over their line of march. Supplies began to run out, the scouts had to forage even further, and sometimes they would march and not see a stream or well to slake their thirst. The heat grew oppressive, the rebels' pace slowed, and the household marshals had to impose even more ruthless discipline. Arms were taken out of the carts and, because no one knew where the Tudor army was, they had to be ready at a moment's notice to form in columns and fight a pitched battle. The scouts and spies informed their leaders of two armies moving slowly north to meet them: the first under John de Vere, Earl of Oxford; the second under Henry Tudor himself.

Matthias rode with Fitzgerald and Mairead just behind the banners of the principal commanders. They grew too tired to talk or even speculate on what might happen. At last, to their relief, they crossed the Pennines.

A few more men joined them under Lord Scrope of Masham. The leaders took counsel with him and decided to advance on York, only to be driven off by a hail of arrows from the citizens.

De la Pole decided to continue south. His army now numbered some eight thousand men, and scouts were bringing in news by the hour. The Tudor army was close, marching towards Nottingham. King Henry had been joined by Lord Strange, but morale in the royal camp was low. De la Pole decided to press on and, on the morning of 15 June, the news arrived that the armies were so close, it would only be a matter of hours before they met in pitched battle.

That evening, the rebel army breasted a hill and saw beneath them, snaking through the fields, the broad glittering River Trent as it wound its way past the small village of East Stoke towards Newark. De la Pole, Schwartz and Lovell went out to inspect the lie of the land. When they arrived back, cursitors were sent out along the army of march. The place had been chosen. De la Pole had decided to fight, putting his army on a ridge with the Trent protecting his rear and right flank. Camp was pitched late at night.

Matthias, exhausted and wondering what the next day would bring, hobbled his horse and, taking his blankets, chose a spot and fell immediately asleep.

He was awoken before dawn by Fitzgerald kicking his boot. Mairead stood smiling down at him.

'This is the day, Matthias.' She pulled a face. 'Break your fast, then it's—'

'Each man to his post,' Fitzgerald finished.

Matthias got to his feet. He felt cold and aching. He rubbed his arms and stared round: a thick river mist now covered the camp. The sound of the horses neighing, the clatter of arms, the shouts of the marshals shattered the silence. Campfires were lit, the smell of oatmeal drifted through the air.

'Do you want a priest?' Mairead asked.

Matthias walked away. He stared down the hill where the mist swirled. He reflected on what Mairead had asked. He fought hard to curb the rage boiling within him. On this day he might die, and what had been his life? His childhood had been shattered, his youth and upbringing overshadowed by a secret which hung over him like a black cloud. Now it had returned and brought him here in the middle of a cold, damp field. What did it matter if de la Pole and Symonds won today?

'Do you know, Mairead,' Matthias said, coming back, 'I believe in the Good Lord but I do wonder whether He believes in me.'

He saw the tears in her eyes. She put her arms round his neck and kissed him on each cheek.

'Come on,' she whispered. 'What is life anyway, Matthias, but the throw of dice? And, if we are to die, let's do it on full bellies!'

Fitzgerald came over. Mairead stood back and the Irishman clasped Matthias' hand.

'We'll be in the centre. Stay close to me, Matthias, whatever happens.'

They went to one of the fires where Mairead begged bowls of oatmeal. Fitzgerald wandered off and brought back some wine. After he had eaten Matthias felt better. Mairead kissed him goodbye.

'I'll be in the rear with the baggage train.' She grinned, her fingers ran softly down his cheek, her lower lip quivered. 'Perhaps, Matthias,' she whispered, 'the next time the wheel of life turns, we will meet again.' And, with no more words, she ran off.

'She's a great lass.' Fitzgerald linked his arm through Matthias'. 'Today's a dying day.'

He took Matthias over to one of the armourer's carts. One of the marshals handed over a boiled leather breast-plate and a heavy steel sallet, which covered the top half of Matthias' face.

'Don't wear any colours,' Fitzgerald whispered. 'If things go wrong . . .'

The mist was lifting, the air was rent by the sound of trumpets and war horns. The army was on the move. Fitzgerald led Matthias over to where the standards were grouped on the brow of the hill: Lincoln's, Lovell's, the Kildares of Ireland, the royal arms of England. Edward of Warwick sat on a white palfrey. He was already accoutred for battle; wearing the silver armour the Archbishop of Dublin had bought him, now covered with a gorgeous blue, red and gold surcoat. Beside him sat Symonds, in the armour of a knight. The former priest had grown even fatter so he looked like a bloated toad. His resentment at being excluded from the military preparations was more than obvious. Lincoln, Schwartz and Lovell stood to one side, surrounded by officers and messengers. Behind them the Swiss and German mercenaries were taking up position: line after line, their tall pikes readied, their faces protected by sallets, many of which sported brilliant plumes of feathers.

As the sun strengthened, Matthias could see the rest of the army taking up position under the direction of marshals: these waved their white wands and moved up and down the ranks, accompanied by trumpeters and young boys beating on tambours. Fires were extinguished, carts rolled away. Matthias caught the excitement of thousands of men preparing for bloodshed – the neigh of horses, the clatter of arms, the shouts of the marshals and the persistent screaming of trumpets. Scouts and cursitors came riding up the hill, their horses covered in a white foam. They slipped from the saddle and hastened to tell their commanders what they had seen. The enemy was on the move and Matthias heard the distant sound of enemy trumpets.

He followed Fitzgerald to the brow of the hill. The mist had nearly lifted: behind the line of trees, which screened the road leading to Nottingham, Matthias glimpsed the first colours of the enemy.

Lincoln mounted his destrier, a great black war horse, and rode along the ranks.

'Good news!' he shouted. 'The enemy is advancing in two battles. De Vere, Earl of Oxford, is leading the first but a gap has appeared between him and his master. Our army is divided into three battles.' He flung his hand out. 'On our right, my own. In the centre Schwartz and his Germans.' He turned his horse and came back. 'To the left our Irish allies.'

The Irish were massed, sitting at a half-crouch. Most of them were naked except for breech clouts and robes. Some wore sandals. All were armed with shield and broad cutting sword. Many of them had daggers pushed into a piece of cloth round their waists. Lincoln's orders came faintly on the breeze.

'Keep to your positions. Do not move until ordered! God will be with us!'

A roar of approval greeted his words like a low roll of thunder. Again the trumpets brayed and the battle line moved to the brow of the hill. Matthias stared down, his stomach pitched with excitement. Oxford was moving fast.

'He did the same at Bosworth,' Fitzgerald whispered. 'I hope to God de la Pole knows what he's doing!'

'Is Tudor far behind?' Matthias asked.

'A good distance,' Fitzgerald replied. 'One of my men brought the news.'

Matthias could see Oxford's banners in the centre, a golden burst of sun on a blue background. Three lines of men: archers, men-at-arms and mounted knights. Matthias knew nothing about strategy. All he could remember was that dreadful fight in Tewkesbury Abbey but even he sensed something was wrong. Oxford was moving too fast, too confidently. There was no pausing, no issuing of challenges, just these three lines marching steadily towards them. Their trumpets blew. Large standards were unfurled, great banners which flapped in the morning breeze, displaying the personal arms of Tudor and those of England. Another trumpet blast from the enemy. Two great pennants, one black, the other red, were also displayed. Oxford's message was simple: the royal banners had been unfurled, the black and red ones proclaimed that no quarter would be shown, no prisoners taken, any man found bearing arms would be killed.

A group of Irish, unable to control their excitement, ignored the shouts of their officers and burst down the hill, a tight knot of men, screaming and cursing, charging straight for the enemy banners. Matthias watched the Irish leaping over the tussocks of grass, waving their swords. Twelve enemy archers stepped forward. They knelt. Matthias heard the order to loose faintly on the breeze, followed by a sound like a rushing wind. The arrows found their mark and the Irish fell as the shafts took them in face, throat or chest. In a twinkling of an eye, a group of men, full of life and fury, were turned into twitching, moaning bundles on the dew-fresh grass.

More trumpet calls, sharp and challenging. Oxford's men came on at a faster pace. The trumpeters of the rebel army shrilled their defiance back. Oxford's archers stopped and began to mass. Bows lifted, the sky suddenly became dark with falling shafts. Most of their fire was directed at Schwartz's mercenaries, who lifted their shields. Some of the arrows found their marks: men came out of the ranks screaming, clutching at arrows in their necks or legs, blood spouting like water from a fountain. Matthias heard the drum of hooves. Lincoln was moving, his whole battle swinging down to take Oxford's left flank and roll the entire column up. The orderly formation crashed into the enemy and the slope of the hill was turned into a heaving sea of fighting men. Oxford's men fought bravely. As Lincoln's force closed, the archers found their bows of little avail. Swords were drawn, the men hastily forming themselves into circles or squares. Oxford's knights were also caught by the suddenness and fury of Lincoln's charge. Banners waved and fell. In the rising clouds of dust Matthias glimpsed Lincoln's banner as the Earl and his household knights aimed like a sword, searching for de Vere and the other royalist commanders. The grassy slope turned to a russet brown. Horses went down screaming and kicking. Men staggered, clutching the most dreadful wounds. Yet the dust made it impossible for Matthias to see clearly what was happening. He glanced around but Fitzgerald had disappeared. One of Schwartz's officers ran up, gesticulating, pointing down the hill.

'They are breaking!' Schwartz cried. 'De Vere's men are beginning to flee!'

His words were cut off by a huge roar from his left. Matthias hurried over. The Irish, unable to control their excitement, had disobeyed their commanders and were now running downhill en masse to join in the battle. Schwartz cursed, shaking his fist, screaming at his own men to hold firm. Slowly Oxford's columns were now being rolled up and pushed further down the hill, leaving behind them a carpet of dead and wounded men and horses.

Matthias stared down at where the fiercest fighting had taken place. If he half-closed his eyes, he could pretend that it was a sea of coloured flowers rather than men twisting and turning in mortal agony. Here and there a horse tried to raise itself up, a man staggered to his knees. A group of Oxford's archers threw down their swords and tried to surrender but they were surrounded by a group of Irish, who slaughtered them to a man. The screams and yells were terrible.

Schwartz and his mercenaries remained impassive though Matthias sensed their concern. Both flanks of the rebel army had now disappeared and, despite messages from Lincoln or the pleas of his own officers, Schwartz refused to advance. Messengers on foot and horse kept galloping up the hill.

Then Matthias heard it in one of those rare moments of silence: the sound of trumpets, clear and vibrant. Schwartz beckoned him and his other officers over. The German's thickset face was covered in a sheen of sweat. A nervous tic had appeared high in his cheek.

'Those trumpets,' he declared. 'It's Tudor's army!'

Matthias looked round: the foot of the hill was now covered by a heavy cloud of dust, which completely cut off sight of the entire approach Oxford had made.

'We can't see anything,' one of Schwartz's officers declared.

'I don't have to,' Schwartz retorted. 'Every man to his position!'

Matthias slipped away to the back. He could glimpse the baggage train where the servants, women and camp followers now sheltered. Should he go down there? Find Mairead and flee? He heard a roar and hurried back to the brow of the hill.

The battle had now shifted dramatically. Lincoln's men were pouring back up the hill. The Irish, too, had broken. Wide-eyed, many of them cut and bruised, they dropped their arms. The dust cloud shifted. Matthias' heart went to his throat. Oxford's men had reformed and, behind them, rank after serried rank, were men-at-arms wearing the insignia

238

of England. To his left and right, horsemen and men-at-arms were moving fast to cut off and surround the rebel army. Schwartz, however, a hardened professional, rapped out an order. The mercenaries moved forward as one man, their pikes lowered, the ranks on the side and the back turning to form a huge square defended by long pikes and shields. Schwartz also tried to impose some order on those in retreat, beating them with the flat of his sword but they pushed and shoved by him. A mercenary officer yelled at Matthias, offering him protection within their ranks. Matthias shook his head. He could not see Fitzgerald. He was determined to reach the baggage train and snatch Mairead before the rout turned into a massacre. He ran as fast as he could, not caring about those around him. One of Lincoln's men, bruised and cut about the face, had stopped to throw away his armour.

'Symonds and the Prince are taken!' he yelled. 'De la Pole's dead! Lovell's fleeing for his life!'

Matthias ran on. So far the enemy had been held, the baggage train looked safe. He heard horsemen galloping behind him and stared round in horror. These were not Lincoln's men but royal sergeants-at-arms, clubbing and hacking the fleeing rebels. Matthias turned but he felt a terrible blow on the back of his head and sank into black unconsciousness.

When he awoke, his head threatening to split with the pain, he was being dragged across the ground. A royal archer held each of his arms.

'Water,' he gasped.

He was flung to the ground. Someone kicked him in the ribs. He stared up. At first he could only see shapes above him. It was cold and dark.

'Water,' he gasped again. His throat and mouth were parched. 'For Jesus' sake, pity!'

One of the figures crouched down. 'You poor bastard. You might as well drink before you hang. You are a rebel, aren't you?'

'I'm no rebel,' Matthias gasped. 'I had no choice.'

The archer pushed his face closer. 'That's what they are all saying.'

'What's happened?' Matthias asked.

'The rebels have been defeated. Now is the hour of judgment.'

The water was taken away. Matthias was hustled to his feet. He stared around unbelievingly. The battlefield was now bathed in moonlight. Dead carpeted the ground as far as he could see. The night was still shattered by screams and groans of dying men or the pathetic whinnies of wounded horses. Cowled figures moved amongst piles of bodies. Those rebels too wounded to be moved had their throats cut, a loud rasp followed by a terrible gurgling cough. The victorious soldiers were also looking for arms, stripping the dead of any clothing or valuables they could find.

Matthias was pushed to the brow of the hill. From every side he glimpsed the camp fires burning merrily. His blood ran cold. Makeshift gallows had been set up. These were now laden with hanged men, some still twitching. Worse still, stakes had been driven into the ground and bodies had been impaled on them. Whether this had been done when they had been alive, Matthias didn't know and didn't want to ask. The cadavers were twisted, contorted, dark shapes held up against the night sky. As he was dragged further down the hill and into the enemy camp, Matthias could see why the makeshift gallows had been built: the branches of every available tree seemed to hold hanged men.

Camp was still being set up, tents and pavilions erected, spluttering pitch torches lashed to poles driven into the ground. Men in half-armour, their faces and hands still stained with blood, slipped across Matthias' path. Somewhere a woman was screaming, a child crying and Matthias' heart sank as he thought of the baggage train and Mairead. He was dragged down the main thoroughfare of the camp. At the centre, a scene reminiscent of Tewkesbury greeted him. A large trestle table had been set up: behind this sat the royal commander and from the banner flying directly behind his chair, Matthias realised the man in the centre, thin-faced and silver-haired, was de Vere, Earl of Oxford. On either side of him sat one of his principal commanders. Prisoners were being pushed forward. A clerk would whisper in de Vere's ear and the Earl would rattle out a few words. The prisoner was then either pushed towards the large execution cart or taken to the stockades which, one of Matthias' guards whispered, lay on the other side of the Newark to Nottingham road. Matthias' turn soon came and he was pushed forward into the pool of light around the table. De Vere glanced up.

'Who are you?'

'Matthias Fitzosbert.'

'Why are you here?'

'Symonds made me.'

'Why?'

'He thought I had Yorkist sympathies.'

'What are you by profession?'

'A scholar.'

'Are you now?'

A scribe came and whispered into de Vere's ear. The Earl's face became hostile.

'You were in Dublin? You were one of the imposter's close councillors?'

'As was I. The boyo's innocent.'

Thomas Fitzgerald sauntered into the torchlight. Unlike the men around him, he wore no armour, just a simple jerkin open at the neck, his hose pushed into soft leather boots. He grinned at the surprise on Matthias' face and made a mocking bow.

'Thomas Fitzgerald at your service, known to his Grace the King and the Earl of Oxford as The Knave.' His smile widened. 'The joker in the pack: their principal spy in the imposter's court.' Fitzgerald turned to de Vere. 'This man was my principal help and assistant. He's no traitor.'

'Where's Mairead?'

Fitzgerald glanced at him. '*Oh, Creatura bona atque parva,* she's dead, gone before I could get to her.'

Matthias stared in dismay. 'You could have saved her!' he hissed.

'What is this?' de Vere snapped.

'You bastard!' Matthias shrieked. 'I was never party to what you did.'

Fitzgerald leant across and, bringing his gauntleted hand back, smashed Matthias on the side of the head. Matthias fell. He heard de Vere's voice, Fitzgerald shouting, but the pain was too much and he lapsed into unconsciousness.

PART III

1487–1489

A Rose in Winter
Bears the highest price.

Martial's Epigrams

17

Matthias regained consciousness in a small, lime-washed cell. He threw back the blankets and staggered to his feet. The chamber was so narrow, if he stretched out his hands he could touch both walls. He peered through the arrow slit window. He was in a castle. The bailey below was busy with grooms leading horses in and out of the stables. A line of geese waddled past guided by a girl with a stick. Somewhere a dog was baying mournfully. Matthias stared down at himself. He was still in the clothes he had worn before the battle, but his belt and boots were gone. A cracked pitcher of water stood in the corner. Dried bread and cheese on a tin plate were being gnawed by rats. Matthias lifted the water, sipped greedily then threw the rest over his plate.

The door opened. Two men came in. The first was stooped and balding, with a thin pinched face and the screwed up eyes of one who had difficulty seeing. He was dressed in a grey, dusty gown, the sleeves folded back; his long fingers were covered in ink. His companion was a typical soldier, burly, thickset, his fair hair cropped so close Matthias at first thought he was bald. He was dressed in a boiled leather jacket, stained and blackened with sweat; dark blue, woollen hose and tight leather boots on which spurs jangled and clattered as he walked. He looked at Matthias and winked. His leathery, weather-beaten face broke into a grin.

'John Vane,' he introduced himself. 'Master-at-arms. This is Master Winstanley, royal clerk.'

'Where am I?' Matthias felt unsteady on his feet. He went back and sat on the bed.

'You are in Newark Castle, brought here late last night.'

Matthias recalled Fitzgerald's blow to his face. He felt the side of his head.

'You are a mystery, Master Fitzosbert.' Winstanley came

over and peered down at him. 'Some say you are a rebel. Others that you are loyal and true. Anyway, his Grace the Earl of Oxford has decided that you won't hang. Clerks are too valuable to be strung up like rats!'

'Where's Fitzgerald?' Matthias asked. 'What's happened?'

'Fitzgerald! Fitzgerald!' Winstanley shrugged. 'I don't know where Fitzgerald is or who he is! The royal army is moving south. People like me and Master Vane are left to clean up the mess.'

'You have received a pardon.' Vane thrust a small parchment scroll into Matthias' hands. 'But on one condition.'

Matthias undid the parchment. He read the copperplate lettering. The small blob of wax at the end bore the personal insignia of the Earl of Oxford. Matthias sighed and closed his eyes. The letter proclaimed that he, Matthias Fitzosbert, be pardoned for all crimes on one condition, that he serve no less than three years as castle clerk at Barnwick on the Scottish march.

'It's better than hanging, lad,' Vane said quietly. The master-of-arms chewed the corner of his mouth. 'God knows I've seen enough hangings to last me ten lifetimes. I have to take you to Barnwick. I'm also taking provisions and money for the garrison.' He crouched before Matthias. 'Now look, lad, I don't know who you are or what you've done. Really, I don't give a damn.' He tapped the piece of parchment. 'This is a second chance. I advise you to take it. Now, we are leaving in two hours, just after noon. I can truss you like a pig and if you try to escape,' he touched the side of Matthias' neck, 'I'll cut your throat. That will be the end of the matter. But you look a bonny lad, you've got honest eyes – give me your word you won't cause me trouble and I'll give you a sword belt, your own horse and treat you as one of the lads.'

Matthias gave his word.

'Good!' Vane got to his feet. He extended his hand.

Matthias clasped it: he held on, squeezing the fingers tightly.

'Who are you?' Matthias whispered. 'Are you really John Vane?'

'Of course I am.' The soldier pulled his hand away. 'I think you've had one too many knocks on the head, lad. I was born John Vane and I will die John Vane but, if you want, you can think of me as the great Cham.' The man-at-arms wrinkled his nose. 'But if you are going to travel with me I want you to bathe. You stink like a pig pen!'

He and Winstanley left. A short while later a servant brought in a leather bucket full of warm water. Matthias stripped and washed, cleaning himself with a rag and rubbing some oil the servants also brought into his skin.

Vane came into the room and tossed a pile of clothes and a good set of riding boots upon the bed. A bleary-eyed, bald-pated man accompanied him: he cut Matthias' hair and expertly shaved the stubble from his face. Matthias found the clothes fitted him. They were musty but clean. Vane gave him a war belt with a sheath for the small broadsword and dagger also provided.

'You don't look like a rebel now,' Vane smiled. 'Come on.'

They went down to the castle refectory. Vane introduced Matthias to the rest of the soldiers, nine men in all: grizzled veterans, men-at-arms looking forward to the journey north as a break from the boring routine of garrison duty. They left Newark a little later than planned, Vane's nine companions, with Matthias in the centre, riding ahead of the three great lumbering carts which accompanied them. On the outskirts of Newark, six archers, dressed in stained Lincoln green, joined them, their specific responsibility to guard the carts. The rest of the day's travelling was taken up in good-natured banter between these and Vane's men.

They journeyed through narrow, country lanes. Matthias still felt unreal. He could hardly accept that the same bright sun, these green fields, the blue sky filled with wispy clouds were the same as he had marched under with the rebel army. They camped out in the open that night, on a small hill overlooking a field of waving corn. One of the archers trapped and skinned some rabbits. Another foraged for herbs. The savoury smell abruptly reminded Matthias of the hermit in that lonely, deserted church at Tenebral. The soldiers accepted him as part of their company but, when Vane remarked that Matthias had marched with the rebels, they took a closer interest.

'Did you really think he was Edward of Warwick?' one of the men-at-arms asked, his mouth full of meat.

'No.' Matthias shook his head. 'To tell you the truth, I don't know what I thought.'

'Just like us,' another shouted. 'You march where your bloody officers tell you to and, if you're lucky and you don't get killed, then you march somewhere else.'

'Were you there?' Matthias asked Vane.

'The battle at East Stoke? No. We were left at Newark to guard the bloody castle.'

He persuaded Matthias to tell them what had happened. Matthias sat under the stars, the night breeze cooling the sweat on his brow as he relived, once again, that bloody fight. He tried not to think of Fitzgerald or Mairead. He gave no hint of why he had really been there.

'Thousands died you know,' Vane declared. 'They say the burial pit was as long and as broad as a castle bailey, the bodies stacked like faggots of wood.'

'And the Irish?' another asked.

'Aye, the poor bastards!' Vane shook his head. 'You heard what happened, Matthias?' He didn't wait for an answer. 'Oxford's bullyboys pinned them against the Trent. It was just like Michaelmas except instead of sheep and cows it was men. They say the blood was ankle-deep in places. The rebel leaders were killed except Lovell, who escaped. No one knows where he is. Symonds, being a priest, has been locked up, immured for life in some lonely monastery. The imposter, Lambert Simnel, has confessed to being the son of an Oxford carpenter. The King – he's a sly one – wouldn't make him a martyr. Lambert's now cleaning out the royal stables.'

The rest of the men began to joke about the imposter. Matthias got up and walked into the clump of trees. What did they mean to me anyway? he thought. He recalled the cards Lady Stratford had dealt that night they were fleeing from Oxford. Symonds had come to judgment whilst the so-called 'young prince' had been forced to face the truth. Matthias smiled. He was glad the young man had suffered no greater indignity and, remembering his skill with horses, he was probably happier in the royal stables than he was with Symonds.

Matthias thought of Dublin and the hundreds of widows amongst the clans, waiting for their men who would never return. He mourned Mairead and cried quietly for her: if only he had reached the baggage train! He closed his eyes: Fitzgerald was there, grinning at him, as he had before de

Vere's tribunal in that blood-stained camp. Matthias wondered when the Rose Demon had taken full possession. He had no doubt that Fitzgerald had always been a spy but Matthias, for the life of him, couldn't recall any abrupt change or suspicious circumstances. The mercenary had struck him, not out of anger but to keep Matthias quiet. If he'd gone on talking, shouting curses, de Vere would have probably hanged him out of hand.

Matthias opened his eyes and stared up through the branches. An owl hooted, low and mournful. A night bird fluttered in the branches above him. Where was Fitzgerald now? Where was the Rose Demon? He glanced back over his shoulder. Vane and the others stretched out before the camp fire. Might one of them house this terrible being now pursuing him? Matthias was beginning to understand it. The Demon could not control him but he could, when he wanted, intervene to protect him. But why not protect Mairead? Or did the Demon want no one in Matthias' life to distract him? He sighed and went back to the campfire. Whatever, he ruefully concluded, three years in a lonely castle on the Scottish march would give him time to think and reflect.

The next morning they reached the Great North Road, a busy thoroughfare with pedlars, packmen, tinkers, wandering friars, scholars, beggars and peasants. The road also carried grim testimony to the royal victory at East Stoke. At every half-mile, for at least a hundred miles, scaffolds and gibbets had been set up: from each hung rotting cadavers. Corruption fouled the air; so great was the stink under the summer sun, Vane ordered the soldiers to leave the highway and use country lanes and trackways.

'The Tudor intends there will be no more Yorkist revolts,' he commented. 'The news of his victory will soon be known to everyone.'

They continued their journey: progress was slow but Vane didn't really care.

'The longer we take,' he joked, 'the more time we can enjoy ourselves. Up to Barnwick by the end of July, it will be September before we dawdle back to Newark. Who knows?' he added. 'We may even avoid another battle!'

They made their way to York, skirting the city, going up towards the moors. The weather remained good, with only an occasional shower. Matthias used the time to calm his soul and soothe his mind. He decided his best course of action was to accept things as they were, not complain and wait for the Rose Demon to make its presence felt. The moors they now crossed were a vast sea of gorse and purple heather, grass turning brown under a searing sun; curlew and snipe whirling above them. Now and again they passed a farm but large, fierce-looking dogs kept them well away. Sometimes there would be a break in the land, a small village clustered around a narrow church. They bought supplies but the villagers were unwelcoming and, most evenings, they slept out under the stars. The weather changed slightly as they travelled north, the breeze colder, brisker, tugging at their hoods and cloaks. One sumpter pony damaged a leg and had to be destroyed, its baggage piled high in one of the carts. Vane became more vigilant.

'We are into the war lands,' he explained. 'James III of Scotland, not to mention the Douglases, often launch cattle raids. They always choose the moors, especially in summer. A small army could march for days and remain undetected.'

In the end Vane's precautions were not necessary. Late one afternoon Matthias reined in and exclaimed in surprise at the long range of disused and derelict buildings, a wall of small forts stretching to east and west as far as he could see.

'What is that?' he asked. 'Where does it begin? Where does it end?'

'The Romans built it,' Vane explained. 'They say it stretches from sea to sea. We'll shelter there tonight, tomorrow we'll be at Barnwick.'

They entered the ruins of one of the castles. Matthias found the sprawling, crumbling walls fascinating and marvelled at the genius which had built it. The horses were hobbled and put out to grass; sentries patrolled the crumbling walls, fires were lit. Matthias thought the men would be happy with some place to shelter but Vane explained how, like sailors, soldiers were suspicious: they feared the ghosts and demons which haunted here.

'Just like Barnwick,' he added enigmatically.

'What do you mean?' Matthias asked.

'You'll see!'

Vane picked up a water bottle and splashed some water on his head and face, wiping it off with his hands.

'I served at Barnwick. I used to belong to the household of Richard III.' He grinned slyly. 'Oh yes, I've served them all. Just like a dance, you must know when to change your partner. Anyway, I was up there in 1482 – a little trouble with some of the black Douglases. I tell you this, the cattle up here must get dizzy: Scotland, England, Scotland, England – around here, thievery and poaching are a way of life and having your roof burnt about your head an occupational hazard. Anyway, it's a sprawling affair, Barnwick. It has a large Norman keep, four towers, one on each corner: it's the north tower you have to watch. They say a demon dwells there.'

'Go on,' Matthias urged. He smiled to hide his anxiety. 'After all, if I'm to spend three years there . . .'

'Well, the castle was built, you know how it is, little bits added here and there. According to one story, in 1320 a Lord Andrew Harclay was betrothed to Maude Beauchamp. One day he discovered his betrothed and a young squire making love in a bedchamber high in the tower. Now Harclay was an evil man. He was feared as a warlock as well as a brigand. He showed no mercy to either. According to legend, he immured both Maude and her lover in the walls of the north tower. They say their ghosts, or some other presence, haunts there. It's a frightening place: strange blue lights have been seen, terrible cries heard, candlelight but no candles. Footfalls but no one walks and a terrible moaning, as if some soul is in the last agonies.'

'Did you see all this?' Matthias asked.

'At first I thought it was children's tittle-tattle. One night, however, I was on the north tower – me and two other lads, archers from Barnsdale: good, true Yorkshiremen, thick in the arm and thick in the head. I tell you this, after that night, they didn't accept life for what it was. We were on the tower wondering if the Scots were going to show us their bare arses. Then we heard it, a sound like a wolf howling on the stairs below. We unbolted the trapdoor but it wouldn't move.' Vane slurped from the wineskin. 'We thought someone was playing a joke. There was a crack in the trapdoor. One of my lads looked through it. He saw a face staring up at him: yellow with age, crumbling teeth, eyes like molten coins, lips which bubbled blood. He was so terrified that if we hadn't restrained him, he would have thrown himself over the parapet. The howling began again and the trapdoor began to lift. All three of us flung ourselves on it, praying to every saint we knew. A terrible smell seeped out, like that of corpses piled high on a battlefield. A voice whispered like a wind. We caught the words: "Let me through, let me through, let me kiss the stars once more!"

'The trapdoor moved, as if an army were pushing beneath it. A hand came out, the nails scored, skin like cracked leather. I didn't know if we were dreaming, but by then I knew it wasn't some joke by one of the garrison.' Vane wiped the sweat from his face as he recalled the nightmare. 'We thought the rest of the garrison must surely have heard the clamour and our screams but the tower is high.' Vane sighed. 'I nearly died that night of fright but the second lad, Ralph, he was blessed with common sense. Whatever was in that tower broke off trying to get at us for a while. Ralph took his bow and, using flames from the beacon, loosed fire arrows into the air. The Constable at the time, Hubert Swayne, raised the alarm. Soldiers came up.' Vane leant closer. 'Do you know something, Matthias? They heard nothing; they detected nothing except for a terrible smell of corruption on the stairs. That was the last time guards were ever set on the north tower. Since then I have had my soul shriven twice a year. I take the Sacraments and, when I hear these clever jacks say there's no God in Heaven, I can at least tell them that there's a devil in Hell.' He drank some wine. 'A new constable's at Barnwick, Humphrey Bearsden. He's a good soldier, tight-lipped but kind-hearted.'

'Anyone else I should know?'

'Well, Father Hubert, the chaplain, I think he's still there. He knows about the north tower. He's a very holy man. Oh yes, and there's Bearsden's sergeant-at-arms, a Scotsman, at least by birth, Malcolm Vattier, a burly brute but one of the best swordsmen I have ever met. Anyway, do you know what I saw today?'

Vane, to lessen the tension, talked about the different wild flowers he had glimpsed. Matthias listened. He had taken a liking to this rough, grizzled soldier's fascination with the beauty of the cowslip and how it could be distinguished from the false oxlip. Or his insistence that bog pimpernel and bethany, if grown properly, could be used for wounds and scratches.

Matthias looked up at the starlit sky and watched a shooting star, a flash of light charging across the heavens. Vane was just about to describe the virtues of St John's wort when there was a stir amongst the sentries: shouts and cries to someone to stop and proclaim himself. Vane sprang to his feet, wrapping his war belt on.

'It's all right,' one of the soldiers called.

An old man, his hood pushed back, stepped into the firelight. Thin-faced, his skin lined and seamed, mere tufts of hair on his almost bald head but the owner of a luxuriant white beard and moustache. He had good stout boots and the robe he wore was serge cloth, bound round the waist by a rope through which a long Welsh stabbing dagger was pushed. In one hand he carried a thick staff, in the other a tattered, leather bag. He sat down without a by-your-leave and glared at Vane.

'What the bloody hell are you doing here? Eh? Do you have some jam? Or some honey? A piece of honey would be really nice.'

'Aye, we've got twenty pounds of it,' Vane joked back. 'Don't you know who we are, old man? We carry the King's commission. Who gave you the right to blunder into our camp and start asking for honey?'

'I couldn't give a donkey's fart for you,' the old man replied. 'I serve the King of Heaven. My name's Pender. I live here. You are in my house.' He waved his hand airily. 'All of this is mine.'

'You are a hermit?' Vane asked.

'Yes, I am a hermit. I came here for peace and quiet, to pray to God. I might as well have stayed in bloody Durham. Tinkers, traders, pedlars, soldiers from Barnwick. Not to mention Scots, English, outlaws and wolf's-heads. You'd think all the world and his sister were here. I went to Castleton to beg. I got bugger all. I've come back.' He glared suspiciously at Vane. 'I come back to find half the royal army camp here.'

Matthias got up and went to their stores. He took out a small, dried loaf and a jar of honey which they had bought in one of the villages. He brought these back and pushed them into Pender's hand.

'Be our guest,' he offered.

Vane leant across and threw two pennies on the ground before Pender.

'We'll pay honest rent,' he joked.

The change in Pender was wondrous. He gave a broad toothless grin, pocketed the pennies, ripped off the piece of linen that covered the jar of honey, stuck his fingers into the honey and began to lick it. Every so often he closed his eyes and rocked backwards and forwards.

'Oh, beauteous taste! Truly the psalmist is right when he says sweeter than the honeycomb!' Pender tore at the bread. 'Blessed be the Lord God!' he intoned. 'And blessed be you in all your bodily functions!' He opened one eye. 'Are you, to crown my pleasure, to give me some wine?'

Vane filled one of their pewter cups and handed it across. The hermit crossed himself, sketched a blessing in the air and continued to fill his stomach. Afterwards he burped and smiled beatifically.

'Lovely!' he breathed. 'Welcome guests all.'

'How long have you lived here?' Vane asked.

'Oh, a good score of years and a few more.' Pender patted the crumbling brickwork. 'This is my palace, my church!'

'You are not frightened?' Matthias asked. 'Of the loneliness?'

The hermit peered across. 'Sometimes! Sometimes at night I hear sounds: cries and calls, dark shapes moving in the heather outside, and they are not Scots. During the day, especially late in the afternoon, I sit in a place like this with my back to the wall. I hear the clink of the armour, the legionaries and, on the breeze, their Latin tongue: orders and commands being shouted.'

The nape of Matthias' neck turned cold.

'I am not being fanciful,' Pender continued, his eyes now watching Matthias intently. 'Ghosts and spirits walk here, still hung between Heaven and earth.'

'Who destroyed this?' Vane asked.

'Some say the weather,' Pender joked. 'But I've had dreams. When this wall stood firm and Rome's legions walked the parapets, it would take more than the weather to cast these stones down. There are legends,' he continued. 'Further down the wall stands a ruined temple. On its wall a huge rose has been carved.' His eyes never left Matthias, who swallowed hard and gazed back. 'There are also strange rune marks scratched in the masonry. Some say they tell a story of the wall's destruction but no one can really make them out or understand them. According to local lore, when the legions left, the soldiers here did not receive the order to depart so they went on guarding, as if there were an empire still left to guard. Now, in the ancient days, to the north were two great peoples who ruled the glens of Scotland. The Picti, or Painted People, and the Caledones. They were united into one army by a famous war chief whose emblem was a rose wound round a staff.'

Matthias stiffened: this ancient legend was connected to his own life, his own experience of that strange force, the sinister Dark Lord who had haunted him all his years.

'If the legend is to be believed,' Pender continued, 'the great Rose Lord fell in love with a Roman lady, daughter of a commander on the wall. He asked for her in marriage. The Roman refused so the Rose Lord brought his great army south and, in one terrible night, annihilated the soldiers of Rome. Every man was killed and the fortifications levelled. For a while the Picts and the Caledones lived on the wall, honouring their great leader but he, on finding the love of his life had been killed in the attack, mysteriously disappeared. His great army broke up and drifted away.' Pender stared into the fire. 'That's only legend. Nevertheless,' he added in a matter-of-fact voice, 'at night the ghosts of all who died here still house themselves in the shadows and corners.' He hitched his cloak around him. 'So, kind though you be, sirs, I hope you are gone by the morrow.'

The hermit wrapped himself up in his cloak and lay down near the fire, resting his head on the tattered, leather bag he carried.

Vane got up, saying he would check on the sentries. Matthias lay down on the ground and stared up at the stars. Who was this Rose Demon? He glanced across the fire. Pender lay there, eyes open, staring at him.

'You should sleep,' the hermit murmured. 'You've nothing to fear. I can see around you those sent to guard you.'

Matthias pulled himself up.

'Nothing but shadows,' the hermit whispered. 'That's all I see.' He grinned. 'And you've got nothing to lose but your soul!'

18

Barnwick Castle was built on the brow of a hill which gently sloped away into a wild sea of tangled grass, flowers, purple heather and gorse which stretched up towards the Scottish border.

'It looks solitary,' Vane observed as they reined in, 'but any Scottish army which wants to plunder the northern march will have to either take it or bypass it. Both would be difficult, especially the former.'

As they rode along the white, dusty track up through the great gateway into the castle, Vane pointed out its principal features: two encircling walls, a broad moat fed by underground springs. The outer wall had small towers along it, whilst the inner wall was built slightly higher. The top was crenellated so, even if an enemy did take the gateway, they would find themselves trapped between two lines of fire. The wooden drawbridge they crossed was good and solid. The soldiers on guard in the dark, sombre gatehouse were well turned out, vigilant but not fussy or overweening. The outer bailey had houses built against the walls; small cottages, workshops, a smithy, forge and stables. The inner bailey was approached by a smaller gateway protected by a heavy, wooden and steel portcullis. A foursquare keep dominated the inner bailey. This soared up against the blue sky. It was built of heavy grey ragstone and looked older than the rest of the castle. Vane explained that this had been built earlier than the rest.

The inner bailey was surprisingly quiet. Some geese and pigs wandered about, chickens pecked at the hard-packed earth, a few soldiers lounged in the shade. One of these came across to take their horses and explained that the rest of the garrison were in the chapel. Matthias remembered it was the Feast of St Peter and St Paul, a Holy Day of Obligation. He asked Vane about the castle.

'The Constable's quarters,' the sergeant-at-arms explained, pointing across to a small two-storey house at the far end of the bailey. 'Solar and parlour on top, hall below.' He lowered his voice. 'Remember, Sir Humphrey Bearsden is a stickler for duty. Everything has to be kept in order, be it one's duty to the King or to God. Ah well,' he added, 'let's make ourselves busy.'

Vane ordered his own soldiers and those lounging about to unload the carts and sumpter ponies: all provisions were to be taken across to the hall. The money he kept with him.

Matthias wandered off. Looking up at the great keep, he studied the north tower and recalled Vane's story. In the golden ripeness of a summer morning it looked nothing out of the ordinary. Somewhere deep in the keep a bell began to toll, followed by the faint sound of voices and footsteps. The door to the keep, which was reached by steep steps, was flung open. Children, laughing and chattering, ran down into the yard to continue their games. Their mothers and women of the garrison streamed out, chattering noisily, after them their menfolk. The Constable and his party came next: they stood at the top of the steps, staring down at Vane and his men whilst one of the sentries went up and explained their arrival.

'You are very welcome,' the leading man shouted down.

He was tall, his silver hair coifed so it fell thick on the nape of his neck, his military-style moustache and beard neatly clipped. He strode quickly down to clasp Vane's hand. Pleasantries were exchanged, introductions made, questions asked about the journey. Sir Humphrey turned to Matthias.

'So you are our new clerk? Good. The last one, Fitzwalter, died of a fever: he was old and doddery.' Bearsden's light blue eyes crinkled in pleasure. 'You look neither. You are not only a member of this garrison but also my family. I am a widower,' he continued. 'Have been for years.'

'Oh, don't tell them your life story, Father!'

The voice was low but carried. Matthias glanced back towards the steps. The young woman coming down moved elegantly, hand clasping a blue samite dress so she wouldn't trip. Matthias glimpsed a red clocked stocking and a well-turned ankle above the smart, brown-berry leather shoes.

'My daughter, Rosamund.' Bearsden must have seen Matthias stiffen. 'It's a lovely name,' he laughed. 'My wife wanted to call her Catherine but she was so small and pink, I thought of a rose bush, hence her name: "Rose of the World".'

'And it suits her,' Matthias replied.

'Why, sir, are you a flatterer?'

Rosamund nestled closer to her father, slipping her arm through his. She was small, petite, with pale creamy complexion, dark blue eyes, long eyelashes and rosebud mouth. She reminded Matthias of a little doll: her hair, dark brown, was covered by a white wimple which was held in place by a circlet of gold cord, a silver bracelet dangled from one wrist.

'We have a courtier at last, Father.' Her eyes opened wide.

Matthias changed his opinion. This was no demure maid; her eyes danced with mischief. Matthias realised she was studying him carefully to imitate him later. So he bowed stiffly as two more people joined them. The first was Malcolm Vattier, the burly, squat sergeant-at-arms of the castle. Square-faced, his red beard, moustache and hair closely cropped, Vattier looked fierce with a deep, purple scar running under his left eye. He was dressed in a leather jerkin, the sleeves cut off, which emphasised the muscular bulge of his arms and his thickset neck. The sword in his war belt looked as if it could fell an ox, yet Vattier moved quickly as a cat. He didn't shake his hand but bowed and studied Matthias from head to toe, his light green eyes betraying no emotion.

'You are a clerk?' Vattier's voice was slightly guttural.

'So they say,' Matthias replied.

'Well, they are mistaken.' Vattier suddenly stretched out one great hand and squeezed Matthias' shoulder. 'You are a swordsman, not an archer or a lancer, but a swordsman.'

'How can you tell, Vattier?' Rosamund quipped.

'It's in the eyes.' Vattier let his hand fall and stepped back. 'It's in the eyes and the way he moves his head.'

Matthias felt embarrassed: he was only too pleased when Sir Humphrey introduced Father Hubert, the chaplain. He took an immediate liking to the small, cheery-faced friar with his lined face, kindly eyes, badly cropped hair: his chin and cheeks were clearly scarred by clumsy attempts to shave. The friar squeezed Matthias' fingers, his soft, brown eyes twinkling with pleasure.

'I'm glad you are here, Matthias,' he said.

'Come on, let's eat,' Sir Humphrey said.

He led the visitors and his own party across the bailey and into the hall. This was a long, barn-like room, the beams painted black, the walls above the wooden panelling of white plaster and lime-washed to keep away the flies. Bright cloths, banners and pennants gave the room some colour. The large windows on either side were open, the wooden shutters thrown back to allow the sunlight to stream through. The tables and benches beneath were cleaned and polished. The scrubbed stone floor had no matting or rushes. No dogs lounged about, only a hawk, a hood covering its face, moved up and down its perch, the jesses on its legs jingling like fairy chimes. Sir Humphrey took them up to the dais, shouting orders to the servants: these scurried in from the scullery behind the screens, bringing large platters of dried meat, cheese and honey.

Father Hubert said the grace and they sat down around the table. Matthias kept silent. Sir Humphrey and the rest now turned to Vane, asking him questions about the King, the recent civil war and the royal victory at East Stoke. Vane chattered back, apparently on good terms with Sir Humphrey and the others. Matthias kept his eyes down, concentrating on the food. When he glanced up, Rosamund was no longer staring at him but imitating the way he sat, morosely popping pieces of food into his mouth. He blushed, drained his tankard and said he wished to take some air.

Matthias went out and wandered round the inner bailey, finding out the small warren behind the hall; the well-kept herb gardens; the bakehouse and fleshing room. The castle seemed a well-ordered community. Matthias accepted this would be his life for at least three years and found he didn't really care. After the turmoil of Oxford and Dublin, the frenetic and suspicious atmosphere of the Pretender's court, Barnwick would be an attractive alternative.

But Matthias also wondered how long it would last. How long before the Rose Demon made its presence felt? He wandered the keep, going up a narrow, spiral, stone staircase; a gaunt, bleak place with stark rooms and narrow galleries. Servants and soldiers passed him by, some smiled, others looked curiously at this stranger. He heard Vane calling him below.

'I'm glad you left,' the master-of-arms explained when Matthias rejoined him. 'It gave me a chance to describe who you were and why you had been elevated to this exalted position.'

'Will they trust me?' Matthias asked.

'Oh, they'll trust you! Look around, Matthias. Where can you go?' Vane clapped him on the shoulder and drew him closer. 'Matthias, I'm leaving tomorrow morning. I'm glad I met you. You were no trouble on our journey north. You are a good companion. I think you have many secrets but that's your business. Let's go back to the hall. Sir Humphrey is going to celebrate our arrival as well as my early departure tomorrow.'

Matthias found that he was soon accepted as one of the castle garrison. No one seemed really to care that he had fought against the King. As Vane, quite the worse for drink later in the day, commented: 'Everyone has secrets whilst both myself and Sir Humphrey have fought for both York and Lancaster.'

Vane left the following morning. Matthias stood in the gatehouse and watched them go until he could glimpse nothing but a faint cloud of dust.

Sir Humphrey came looking for him. The previous evening Matthias had slept in the hall. The Constable now showed him quarters in the east tower of the great keep: two spacious chambers adjoining each other, one for sleeping, the other for working. Matthias was then taken on a quick tour of the castle. Sir Humphrey spoke in quick, clipped sentences. He explained the routine, the hours for meals, the time of morning Mass. What should be done on Sundays and Holy Days. How Matthias would be paid four times each year as well as receive fresh robes at Christmas and Easter.

Matthias soon settled down. The regular routine of the castle was soothing: up just before dawn, Mass, work, then they'd all assemble in the hall to break their fast. They'd eat again early in the afternoon and work until dusk. Matthias' duties were varied. Sometimes he'd sit in his tall, high-backed chair crouching over a sloping desk, transcribing letters, documents and reports for Sir Humphrey. At other times he'd carry out inventories of the castle stores, provisions, arms, the muster rolls, the salaries, the profits of crops, the purchase of fodder for the stables. He also took care of manuscripts, making sure that the archives were kept in good order, the chests regularly washed and cleaned, that everything was arranged in chronological order and that proper returns were made at Michaelmas, Hilary, Easter and midsummer. Such duties were not onerous.

Matthias soon found Sir Humphrey asking his advice on this or that. Father Hubert also had proved himself to be a good friend. He'd question Matthias closely about his studies at Oxford, the treatment of manuscripts and gently ask favours, such as Matthias examining the chapel lectionary and missals and repairing their calfskin covers.

The rest of the garrison accepted him for what he was, a principal retainer to Sir Humphrey. Vattier, however, continued to watch him constantly. At first Matthias was rather wary, believing Vattier knew him from somewhere else. However, three weeks after his arrival, the man-at-arms leant across the supper table.

'You would make a good swordsman, Matthias.'

Matthias held his unblinking gaze. 'So you keep saying, Master Vattier.'

'Tomorrow morning,' the sergeant-at-arms replied, 'you must prove me right.'

Matthias glanced along the table. Rosamund stared back, round-eyed, an impish glee in her eyes. He swallowed hard and returned to his food. That young woman was making him distinctly uncomfortable. Whenever they met, Matthias would catch her studying him intently. Sometimes he thought she was making fun of him but, now and again, he glimpsed a sad glance. Rosamund was kind enough. She brought some flowers for his chamber or arranged for pots of herbs to be placed in the small chancery. Sometimes she would come there, sit on the window seat, ask him a few questions then abruptly get up and leave. Matthias wondered if she was strange, slightly fey. Sir Humphrey openly adored her. Father Hubert called her strong-willed, ruthlessly determined but a very pious girl, a dutiful daughter.

'She is strange, mind you,' the priest commented one morning after Mass.

'What do you mean?' Matthias asked.

'Well, she's a charitable, kind-hearted girl. If anyone falls

261

sick, she always offers help and sympathy but, Matthias . . .' the priest shook his head, 'as for you, I don't know.'

Matthias pushed away his trencher. He had now been three weeks in the castle. Sir Humphrey trusted him; Father Hubert did; Vattier seemed intent on making him a swordsman but had Rosamund glimpsed his true nature? For a moment Matthias felt a wild surge of rage at the forces which had brought him to this: a stranger amongst strangers, with little choice or control over his life.

The next morning, when the other soldiers came to exercise in the outer bailey, shooting at the butts or riding with lance at the quintain, Matthias strolled out to join them. Vattier's ugly face cracked into a grin.

'At last! At last!'

He threw Matthias a leather corselet and told him to pick up a rounded shield and blunted sword. The clerk did so. Immediately Vattier attacked, abrupt and sudden. For a while Matthias just held up his shield and lunged wildly back with his own sword. He felt like dropping both and running away but others were coming across to watch.

'Calm down,' Vattier whispered, grinning over his shield rim.

Matthias stepped back. Vattier lunged again. Matthias parried. Gradually, as if the clash of weapons were some eerie music and the fight a dance which he did not know but liked, Matthias settled down. He watched Vattier's eyes, memorising his feints, thrusts and parries. He felt cold but, at the same time, enjoyed the violence. Vattier began to represent all the hate and enmity from his past. The sergeant-at-arms was now the gaoler from the Bocardo; Symonds smirking at him; Fitzgerald laughing and clapping him on the shoulder. He took great pleasure in the clash of sword, of steel clashing against steel. The laughter and raillery of the soldiers died away. Matthias fought clumsily but there were occasions when Vattier was wary. At last the sergeant-at-arms stood away, throwing his own sword on to the ground.

'Enough for today,' he said, then grinned at the soldiers. 'I have won my wager, he is a swordsman!'

The men-at-arms and archers shuffled forward to hand over their well-earned pennies. They went away glowering. Vattier came up.

'Matthias, you may not be a good horseman, a good singer, a good clerk or even a good man. You do, however, have the makings of a superb swordsman. Don't ask me why, it's just like dancing. Some can, some can't, you can. Train every morning!'

Matthias did so. The savagery of the exercise yard made him relax and purged the evil humours in his blood. He enjoyed the competition, the rivalry. Vattier taught him all he could so Matthias could move quickly, either to disarm or strike a wounding or killing blow. By the beginning of September, when the weather was set to change and the gorse and grassland round the castle began to die, Matthias had won a name for himself.

'You have a fury in you,' Sir Humphrey declared as they sat at supper one night. 'I can see that, Matthias.' The Constable leant across and filled his wine cup. 'But I wonder what it is?'

A few days later Matthias was in the castle chapel on the second storey of the great keep. He sat on the floor, his back to a pillar. Father Hubert had asked him to look at the binding of the Bible, perhaps persuade Sir Humphrey to have it re-covered. Matthias, however, was really studying the verses from Genesis which his father had written on that scrap of paper so many years ago.

'A swordsman, a scholar and now a man of prayer.'

Rosamund had softly entered. She was staring down at him.

'You mock too much, my lady.' Matthias turned the pages. 'And a jest, like a jug of wine, eventually runs out.'

'Matthias the miserable.'

He glanced up. Red spots of anger were high in her cheeks.

'Fitzosbert the Grim. Why are you so grim, Fitzosbert? Why do you walk around like a man burdened with all the cares of the world?' Rosamund walked up and down in front of him.

Matthias laughed as he recognised a perfect parody of himself. She stopped her pacing.

'So, there's wine left in the jug yet, Matthias?'

Rosamund sat down opposite. She opened a small linen napkin and nibbled at some marzipan. Again she imitated him, popping the pieces into her mouth as Matthias did at table. She did it so solemnly, so accurately, that he bellowed with laughter. She glowered back.

'Why do you bother me, my lady?'

'I like you, Fitzosbert, I really do! I have never met a man I like so much as you, Matthias!'

His jaw dropped in amazement. He was used to tavern wenches, the directness of slatterns like Amasia. Rosamund gazed back.

'I like you very, very much, Matthias,' she repeated. 'And all you can do is crouch like a dog with its tongue lolling.' She popped more marzipan into her mouth. 'And, before you think it, never mind say it, I'm not a wanton. I'm a maid, a virgo intacta. I am seventeen years of age. My hand has been asked in marriage five times. The last one was a knight who owned lands in Scarsdale. He was youngish, elegant and he walked like this.'

She got up and did a mincing walk up and down the chapel. Matthias smiled. She imitated the man in such detail: the slight swagger, the hand half-raised, fingers splayed. Matthias had seen fops and court gallants do the same and the look on her face, slightly deprecating, eyes half-closed, was accurate too. She stopped, bunched her skirts up and held herself slightly backwards.

'He had the most incredible codpiece. I told Father he should marry one of our mares!'

Matthias couldn't hold his laughter back. Rosamund crouched beside him, her face now serious. He went to grasp her hand, she knocked it aside, popped a piece of marzipan into his mouth, then punched him gently on the jaw.

'Don't say it, Matthias. Don't say anything to me you don't mean. Don't go away thinking I'm some lady in a tower who dies to be free. I love my father. I love this castle. I love the wild countryside around. I have heard the songs of troubadours and I have listened to courtly praises. I've met men who want to play cat's-cradle with me in some window seat or bower. It just makes me giggle. It's good to see you smile. Now, open your mouth.'

Matthias obeyed, another piece of marzipan was put in.

'So, don't say anything,' she whispered, 'unless you mean it. I have liked you, Matthias, from the very moment I met you. I could say more but I won't.'

And then she was gone. Matthias just sat dumbstruck. He wished she'd come back, he really did. For those few minutes, everything in the past seemed to have gone. He was just a young man, most fortunate in being teased by a lovely woman. She had said she liked him but Matthias had glimpsed the passion in her eyes. He realised how little he did know about women. He got to his feet, absent-mindedly put the Bible back on the altar and wandered out. Father Hubert passed him on the stairs.

'Do you think it can be bound?'

'Yes, it's very nice, Father, isn't it?'

The chaplain looked at him strangely. Matthias realised he hadn't been listening to the question. He went on down, then wandered around the castle. He wanted to see Rosamund but there was no sign of her so he went and lay down on his bed, staring up at the roof beams as if he had never seen them before.

That night at supper Rosamund came down dressed in a dark green samite gown with lace fringes round the neck and cuffs. Her wimple was of pure white gauze. Matthias had never seen anyone so lovely. She sat eating moodily but, when she caught his eye, she winked slowly, followed by such a mischievous grin, Matthias wondered if she were just teasing him. His heart lurched. He couldn't take that. He wanted to see her again. He wanted her to crouch before him. She could poke fun as long as she stayed. After supper, however, she rose quickly, the back of her hand against her forehead.

'I feel a little hot and feverish,' she whispered.

Sir Humphrey glanced at her.

'But tomorrow,' she cooed, 'I'll be better.'

Another slow wink for Matthias, the Devil's own grin, and Lady Rosamund Bearsden swept from the hall.

Matthias did not sleep much that night. He could think of nothing but Rosamund, her beauty, her directness. On one occasion he felt a chill. Her name, Rosamundi: could the Rose Demon be here?

The next morning at Mass he felt guilty. Rosamund took the host as usual. Afterwards Matthias engaged in such a furious bout of sword fighting that Vattier threw his hands up in dismay and conceded defeat.

Matthias, covered in sweat, went back into the keep, up to his own chamber. The door was slightly ajar. His heart leapt in his throat. He pushed the door aside carefully.

'No, it's not her.' Father Hubert was sitting on his bed. 'Come on, Matthias.' He gestured at the stool opposite. 'Close the door and sit down.'

Matthias did so. 'What do you want, Father?'

'You've already told me. I said, "It's not her" and you didn't even bother to ask me who. I'm talking about our Rosamund.'

'What about her?'

'She loves you deeply, Matthias. I could tell that the first day we met. Didn't you see her? She went pale.' The priest leant closer, his face full of concern. 'I've known her since she was . . . well, since I baptised her. She can be a wilful minx, a tease, but she's as honest as the day is long. She is a woman of absolute determination. If she sets her mind on something then it will happen. She has told me she loves you. She loves you deeply, Matthias Fitzosbert.' He shook his head. 'And she doesn't know I am here. I always knew this would happen. Rosamund is not some summer butterfly. When she hates, she hates. When she fights, she fights. I have always said that if she loves, God help the man she chooses. Now, Matthias, you must not play with her affections. This is no "kiss me in the stable", or some tumble in the straw. Do you understand me?'

Matthias, fighting hard to control the elation within him, nodded. Father Hubert looked down at the floor, stubbing it with the toe of his sandal.

'You are a good man, Matthias, honourable and truthful.' He glanced nervously towards the door. 'But there are two other matters I have to tell you.' He paused to choose his words. 'You have heard about the legends of the north tower?'

'Yes.'

'Well, they are not legends. That tower is haunted! Sir Humphrey keeps the door locked. On one occasion I did bless it but, I think, it will need more than a blessing to make reparation for the terrible evil committed there.'

'Father, what has that got to do with me?'

'Well, the tower has been quiet for a number of years, but

266

recently there have been stirrings, faint noises; lights glimpsed through the windows.'

'And?'

'They occurred the first night you arrived here and have done so ever since.'

'Why do you blame me, Father?'

'Ah well, that brings me to the second matter!' He cleared his throat. 'Do you remember, Matthias, a few days ago you were sitting in the small garden on the far side of the hall? A beautiful, sunny day. You had a piece of parchment over your lap, smoothing it down with a pumice stone. Well, I went into the hall. I was thirsty. I took a cup of buttermilk and went and stood by the window to ask if you wanted to share it.'

'Of course, I remember!'

'You were not alone,' the priest said. 'Matthias, believe me, I am not a fool. Since I was a child I have had second sight.' He scratched his balding pate. 'Sometimes I see things which . . . well, I'd prefer if I didn't. A hooded person was sitting next to you. His cloak was black as night, the cowl pulled up. At first I thought it was someone from the garrison but, strange, I hadn't seen him when I first came in, and why sit like that on a hot summer's day? I stared at that figure. I couldn't see any hands or face. I went cold with fear yet, at the same time, through the window, came this rich thick smell of roses. I have never smelt the like before. I put the buttermilk on the table. I was going to call out but, when I glanced up, the figure was gone.'

Matthias got to his feet. 'I can't answer that, Father. All I can say is that I try to be a good man.' He went across to the door and turned. 'But, if you want your answer regarding Rosamund, I love her as much as she does me.'

Matthias went down the steps, both elated and concerned at what the priest had told him. He went across to the small scriptorium where Sir Humphrey kept his keys, each neatly tagged on its hook. The key to the north tower was large and brassy. Matthias took this and hurried down. Thankfully, no one was about. Sir Humphrey had gone hawking; the soldiers were preparing for another day's routine. Matthias entered the keep and unlocked the iron-studded door leading to the north tower. He pushed this open, went through, then locked it behind him. He stood for a moment staring up the spiral stone steps. He sniffed. Nothing but must and mildew. It was colder than the rest of the keep, perhaps because of its position, and that the windows were shuttered and barred. He climbed the steps, stopping at each level. The doors to the small chambers stood open. They were bare, gaunt and swept clean, not a stick of furniture. Matthias walked into one. He went across, pulled up the bar on a shutter and opened it. He stared out across the wild heathland beyond the castle walls. A party of horsemen rode there, Sir Humphrey's favourite hawk soaring in the breezes above them. He closed the shutter.

'Help me! Oh, please help me!' A woman's voice, low and pleading.

Matthias' spine tingled. 'Who's there?' he called.

'*Aidez-moi!*' The woman lapsed into Norman French. '*Aidez-moi maintenant! Priez pour mon âme!* Help me now! Pray for my soul!'

Matthias walked to the door.

'Piss off, clerk!' This time the voice was male, guttural. 'Go away! Leave us alone! Why do you bring the seigneur here?'

Matthias stood in the entrance to the chamber. The door, half-open, swung as if to smash into him. He stepped sideways. The door abruptly stopped moving as if some invisible hand had gripped it. Matthias continued on down the stairs. It was now biting cold as on a harsh winter's day. He refused to be cowed.

'Plead for us!' The woman's voice was low, soothing. 'Please, plead for us!'

Matthias glimpsed something out of the corner of his eye. He turned and stared open-mouthed: a young woman's face was forming in the wall as if some invisible sculptor were carving quickly. He glimpsed high cheekbones, parted lips, wide staring eyes and, beside it, another face, as if the plaster on the wall were bubbling under some tremendous heat. This second face was like that of a gargoyle, harsh and cruel, with pointed nose and slobbering lips. Matthias retreated down the steps. Despite a feeling of wild panic, he moved carefully. He sniffed. The stench was terrible, like that from an open coffin or a sewer full of putrid dirt. There was a sound behind him, he whirled round. A man stood there. His pasty white face, popping eyes and parted lips reminded Matthias of the face being formed on the wall. He was dressed like a priest in a black mantle from neck to toe. Matthias' hand fell to his dagger. The man was coming towards him, not climbing the steps but gliding slowly.

'Get ye gone!'

Matthias nipped his thigh. Was he asleep? In the space behind this awful figure which moved so slowly, so smoothly towards him, were others: Rahere the clerk, the Preacher, Santerre, Amasia, Fitzgerald but not Mairead. There were others, he couldn't make out their faces: a host from Hell, their staring eyes full of blood. Matthias opened his mouth to scream but his throat was dry, his tongue clove to the top of his mouth. Then suddenly he felt warm. The sweet smell of rosewater filled the stairway. The phantasms retreated and vanished like puffs of smoke swirling up into the air.

19

Matthias and Rosamund were betrothed within the week and, on 18 October, the Feast of St Luke the Evangelist, they were married in the castle chapel by Father Hubert. Matthias' courtship had been impulsive and passionate. The deep love between the new clerk and the Constable's daughter was the worst kept secret in the castle. Once Rosamund knew Matthias felt the same, she was too headstrong, too impulsive, too honest to assume the role of the coy, simpering maid. She just sat through every meal smiling at Matthias. He, in turn, stared rapturously back, much to the exasperation of Sir Humphrey and everyone else. Where Matthias went Rosamund followed. If she didn't, he would go looking for her.

Matthias was frightened by his experiences in the north tower but, there again, or so he reasoned, he was growing accustomed to such manifestations. He was also ruthlessly determined not to let such phenomena interfere in his new-found happiness. And Matthias was happy; for the first time in his life, so he told a mystified Father Hubert, he knew what happiness really was. He confessed as much, quietly pointing out that happiness was thinking of the other and not about one's self. Rosamund was, truly, all he could think about. She was like no one he had ever met, so honest, so direct, so lovely. When he was away from her, Matthias felt he was incomplete. For the first time since his traumatic childhood days, he felt reconciled, deeply at peace. If Rosamund was by his side then whom should he fear? He would go down to the gates of Hell and back. He was happy at Barnwick. He had proved himself to be a very good clerk. There were worse careers than promotion in the royal service. He said as much to Sir Humphrey when the Constable decided to confront him just before Michaelmas.

The Constable was anxious but secretly pleased with the match. He had taken close counsel with Father Hubert and they had both reached the same sensible conclusion. Rosamund, for the first and only time in her life, had fallen deeply in love. She was as smitten by Matthias as he by her. The Constable confessed that he knew little about this intelligent young clerk but what he did he liked.

'If he leaves,' Sir Humphrey confided, 'Rosamund's heart will break. I know her.'

The priest nodded solemnly. 'More importantly, Sir Humphrey,' Father Hubert replied, 'we live in a castle, and two young people, their passions running hot . . . ?'

'Better to marry than to burn,' Sir Humphrey joked, quoting St Paul.

'I can only report what I see,' the old priest declared. 'Sir Humphrey, I am well past three score years. I know the human soul. I have seen sin and virtue. Matthias Fitzosbert is a good man. He is mysterious but he is good. More importantly, he loves your daughter.'

Sir Humphrey had been convinced. So, when Matthias blurted out his passion, the Constable sat in his high-backed chair, listening carefully. He agreed, and glancing at his daughter's face so radiant with happiness, he forced back the tears, for in that moment he remembered her mother and his own hot passion so many years ago.

After that meeting Matthias felt as if he were in Heaven. Every day seemed golden. He could only control his excitement and elation by hacking with his sword at poor Vattier or riding like a demon from hell across the heathland. His joy was shared by the entire garrison. Everyone wished him and his bride every happiness. Golden days, as Sir Humphrey had proclaimed: the weather was good, the harvest would be rich and the truce with the Scots seemed to be holding.

The wedding day itself was a glorious climax to this happiness. Matthias, in a jerkin and hose of dark murrey bought him by Vattier, and a white cambric shirt which was the gift of Father Hubert, met Rosamund at the chapel door. He swore his vows, gazing into her eyes, before leading her by the hand up to the two prie-dieus placed before the altar. After the nuptial Mass his bride was snatched away, Matthias was seized by the men of the garrison, led by Sir Humphrey, and taken to the hall where everyone drank deeply and, much to Father Hubert's embarrassment, exchanged ribald stories and sly comments accompanied by nudges and winks.

In the evening a great banquet was held. Matthias and Rosamund sat at the high table, served by Sir Humphrey and Vattier. The rest of the garrison, men, women and children, thronged the tables below the dais and drowned out the poor musicians Sir Humphrey had hired specially from Carlisle. The evening wore on. Matthias made sure his wine was generously watered. He felt so happy he dare not turn and glance at Rosamund. Sometimes, as he watched the people laugh, joke and dance, or smelt the sweet odours from the kitchen and buttery, he thought he was having one of his dreams. Surely he would be punched, nipped or kicked awake and find himself lying in some squalid room or filthy cell.

Outside the sun began to set. Matthias wondered if it was time he and his bride left their guests to their pleasures, when the door to the hall was thrust open. Two soldiers came running in, faces white, eyes staring. They searched out Sir Humphrey, drawing him aside, whispering to him, gesturing towards the door. The laughter and talk died, the music subsided. Sir Humphrey, his face grave, came over to the high table.

'Matthias, Vattier, Father Hubert, you'd best come with me! No, Rosamund, you stay. Look after the guests, tell them all is well.'

The Constable led his party out into the keep. Even as he followed, Matthias' head cleared of the wine fumes. His happiness was tinged by dread. As soon as he entered the keep, he heard the cries and groans echoing along the gallery of the north tower. One of the soldiers took a pitch torch out of its iron holder, but he was trembling so much that Matthias grabbed it from him and led the rest of them on. Sir Humphrey swore under his breath. Father Hubert began chanting a prayer. The stone passageway was icy cold, filled with the rottenness of decay yet it was the shrieks and cries behind the locked door to the north tower which chilled their blood.

'It began about an hour ago,' one of the soldiers whispered. 'At first I thought it was some joke. Listen now!'

They all did. The groans and screams stopped.

'Oh Lord save us!'

Father Hubert grasped Matthias' arm and pointed to the bottom of the door. A ghostly blue light glowed there.

Matthias went to grasp the latch but Sir Humphrey knocked him away. As he did so a woman's voice could be heard.

'Oh please, oh in God's name, no! Oh please stop!'

This was followed by the sound of scraping and hammering, as if someone were building something behind the door. Again the woman's voice, her heart-wrenching pleas for mercy, echoed out. This turned into deep-bellied laughter of someone who had grown witless, or like a mad dog howling at the moon. This devilish chorus – the woman's pleas, the mocking laughter – grew, interspersed with periods of silence. By straining his ears Matthias could hear the man talking, muttering to himself, filthy curses, vows of vengeance. The gallery was now so cold, Father Hubert was rubbing his arms trying to keep warm. One of the soldiers, unable to bear the tension, simply fled the keep.

'Let me go in,' Matthias said.

Sir Humphrey held him back.

'You are my son-in-law,' he smiled bleakly. 'Not now, Matthias, not on this, your wedding night—'

'This has happened before,' Father Hubert broke in. He glanced at Matthias. 'It will happen again. It can wait!'

Matthias agreed. The light under the door vanished. There was silence from the stairwell beyond so they turned and left the keep.

When they returned to the hall, Matthias refused to tell Rosamund what had happened. Instead he went round his guests, filling their wine cups, trying to forget what he had witnessed. He drank a little himself, and the wine settled his stomach and soothed his mind.

A trumpeter amongst the musicians blew long melodious blasts on his horn, then Matthias and Rosamund were led from the hall up to their nuptial bed in Rosamund's chamber beside the solar. The sheets on the new four-poster bed had been turned back, the bolsters piled high. The guests drank one last toast to the bride and groom and left.

Matthias and Rosamund sat on the edge of the bed. Matthias put his hand gently round her waist and pulled her closer. He whispered softly in her ear, tickling her face with the tip of his tongue. She laughed and turned away, pulling at the laces on her white satin dress. Matthias grasped her fiercely and they fell back on the bed.

For the next few days the wedding revelry continued. Matthias and Rosamund lived in their own dreamlike world. They had married on a Monday and Sir Humphrey declared the rest of the week a holiday. The newly wedded couple were left alone, allowed to wander the castle by themselves or, better still, take horses from the stable and ride recklessly over the heathland. Sometimes they filled the saddlebag with bread, cheese and other food wrapped in linen cloths, took a wineskin and rode out to some lonely copse where they could sit and talk or lie quietly in the grass, arms around each other.

On the Sunday, Matthias took Rosamund down to the wall, the ruins where he and Vane had sheltered the night before they had arrived at Barnwick. There was no sign of the old hermit Pender. Matthias, remembering what he had been told, searched the ruins carefully. At last, he found what he was looking for, a carving above a hearth: a man dressed in a cloak standing on a rose in full bloom. Beneath the rose were the strange marks or runes such as he had seen in the deserted church at Tenebral.

'What is it, love?' Rosamund came shyly beside him, slipping her hand through his. She saw how pale her husband's face had become. 'Matthias, what is it?'

Matthias ran his fingers over the carving. Rosamund tugged at his arm.

'Matthias Fitzosbert!'

'Yes, Rosamund Fitzosbert!'

'What is it?' Her sweet eyes held his. 'Matthias, I am no fool, I know you have a secret. Father Hubert knows. I am confident it's nothing evil, nothing wicked.' She grasped his face between her hands. 'The haunting in the north tower? Father Hubert told me about it. I know that it has increased since you arrived. When you came, you were Matthias the Miserable.' She grinned. 'Fitzosbert the Grim. Now you leap for happiness like a child into its mother's arms. What is it, Matthias? Why did you bring me down to the wall? Yes, it's beautiful. The autumn sun is still strong, the ground is firm but, for the last hour, you have searched like a miser who has hidden a bag of gold but can't remember where he has put it. Yet, now you've found it, your face is pallid.' She moved her hand and wiped the sweat from his forehead. 'What is it, Matthias Fitzosbert? What passion drives you?' Her hand fell away. 'You sleep deeply but you talk and you mutter about men called Rahere, Santerre.' She blinked furiously. 'And a woman called Mairead. Was I wrong, Matthias Fitzosbert?'

'Wrong in what?' he asked.

'I'll never stop loving you,' she continued. 'The fires of Hell can freeze and the world will crack before Rosamund stops loving Matthias.' She squeezed his fingers. 'But do you love me, Matthias? Love me enough to tell me your great secret?'

Matthias kissed her on the brow. 'We have some bread and some wine,' he murmured. He took his cloak and placed it on the ground. 'Sit and listen, Rosamund.'

He ensured the horses were hobbled, took off the saddlebag and returned. She was kneeling, sitting back on her heels. Matthias laid out the cloth, filled the two pewter cups, then sat beside her, his back to the wall. He stared up at a white cloud the size of a man's hand.

'I have told you something about my life,' he began, 'but there is something else. So, listen carefully.' He paused. 'And then you'll realise why I am Fitzosbert the Grim.'

Matthias talked for over an hour. As he did so, the cloud, no bigger than his fists, filled out across the sky. Rosamund never interrupted. Sometimes Matthias would pause, drink some wine or just close his eyes to reflect. He tried to tell her everything. Sometimes the account raised fears in his own soul. Once he did glance at Rosamund's face. He was alarmed to see how the colour had drained, her eyes were half-closed, lips slightly parted. When he finished, the silence grew oppressive. Rosamund hardly moved.

'Now you know why Fitzosbert is the Grim,' Matthias joked.

'Did you ever think I housed this being?' Rosamund arranged the folds of her dress. 'Whatever he, whatever it is, Matthias, he loves you: that's why Santerre died. He was trying, in his own way, to show how much you meant to him. It's true isn't it?' she continued in a rush. 'And what better way than to possess my mind, my soul?'

'As God is my witness,' Matthias whispered, 'your name disturbed me but never once . . .'

'Why not?' Rosamund snapped.

'I'm not really sure,' Matthias replied. 'But the Demon can only enter where there's a pathway in. Some moral, some spiritual weakness like an enemy forcing its way through a gap in a castle wall. You have no weakness, Rosamund. You are pure as candlelight and burn as strongly. Secondly, the little I do know, the little I have discovered, is that it would not be acceptable. The Rose Demon wants me to accept him, a free act of will, a final decision. He will not force me.'

'But isn't that what he's doing?' Rosamund faced him squarely. 'He pursues you, he is forcing you to accept him.'

'I don't think so,' Matthias replied. 'I freely accepted the friendship with the hermit and that of Rahere.'

'You were only a child!'

'Children make choices, Rosamund. Imperfect, mistaken but they are still choices. The same is true later on. I chose Baron Sanguis' patronage. I chose to go to Oxford. I chose Santerre as my friend. I chose to alienate Rokesby. I accepted Symonds' help. I stayed with the rebels.' Matthias spread his hands in a gesture of despair. 'Yes, at times I feel my life is not my own. But is anybody's? Would you have been different, Rosamund, if your mother had lived?' he asked. 'And, you forget, if what has happened had not happened to me, how would we have ever met? Once you begin to unravel the past nothing remains.' He got to his feet. 'How do I know?' he continued. 'What might have happened to me without the Demon? Would I have spent my days as the bastard son of a village parson, digging the soil, worrying about the price of corn, or a leak in my thatched roof? True, I blame the Rose Demon for the evil in my life. A theologian might argue that he is also the author of my good fortune.'

'Does that include me?' Rosamund moved a tendril of hair from her face.

'No, it doesn't, that's my point. I have made choices, Rosamund. I married you because I love you, not because of any invisible force or lord of the air. I just love you. You are the beginning and the end of my life.' He crouched down beside her. 'And you?'

'If I did not love you, Matthias, if I did not trust you

completely,' her eyes held his, 'I would say you were a madcap, witless, yet I have seen the pain. I can see the shadows in your eyes.' She grasped his hand. 'And I tell you this, Fitzosbert the Grim. Neither Heaven nor Hell, nor height nor breadth, no power on earth or beyond will ever stop me loving you.' She touched his lips. 'I believe what Father Hubert says, what you say. Every person born on this earth has their own demon to fight. And you are right: it is a matter of the will – some give in, some don't. Whatever comes, Matthias,' her nails dug into his hands, 'I will be with you!'

'You must keep it a secret,' Matthias whispered, folding her into his arms. 'No one must know. To you I can speak the truth, others will not understand.'

Matthias gazed up at the sky. The clouds were massing to block out the sun. Shadows crossed the ruin. The breeze had turned chill. Somewhere a bird called low and haunting as nature mourned the passing of the year. Matthias pressed Rosamund fiercely to him. One thought had occurred, one he dare not share with her. He was being watched by that Dark Lord, that Duke of Hell, the Rose Demon, so what would happen now? Would the demon resent Rosamund? And, before he could stop it, Matthias began to pray, not to God – only halfway through did he stop in shock – he was praying to the Rose Demon! He was begging that invisible being not to lay his hand, or turn his power, against this, the love of his life. He recalled Parson Osbert and intoned the prayer, whispering, 'Remember this, my soul, and remember it well. The Lord thy God is One and He is holy.'

Rosamund pushed him away.

'Do you pray often, Matthias? I mean, we all sketch the sign of the cross, babble our Paternosters or Ave Marias. We stick our tongues out and take the Eucharist but do you really ever pray?'

Matthias glanced down. 'No,' he whispered. 'God forgive me, Rosamund, I don't. I pray as you say. I also become full of self-pity, and yet is my lot any worse than anyone else's? The thousands of Oxford's troops slaughtered on the banks of the Trent? Or Mairead, probably ravished before her throat was cut? Or Amasia, who probably died in some hapless accident? Or Agatha, who danced so well?' He lifted Rosamund to her feet. 'Or the poor ones, the little people of the soil, slaughtered and exploited in their thousands by the great barons?' He gripped her hands. 'Aristotle said nature is where the strong survive, the weak are helpless. I often wonder why God doesn't intervene. We might believe in him but does He really believe in us?'

'I pray.' Rosamund's answer was direct. 'I pray and I mean it. God does intervene.' She fought back her tears. 'If there wasn't a God, I wouldn't have met you.'

Matthias found he could not answer that. He crouched down and neatly folded the pieces of linen which had held their food.

'We must go,' he muttered. 'The weather is changing.'

Rosamund went behind him, putting her hands over his eyes.

'I'll never change,' she whispered. 'Remember that, Fitzosbert the Grim. I shall pray for both of us.'

They returned to the castle. Matthias felt himself purged, shriven, absolved. He had told Rosamund the truth and recognised she loved him all the more for that. Never once in the succeeding days did she refer to his story again but became more determined to build her life around him. Sir Humphrey, the ever-doting father, talked of extending the hall, of constructing special quarters for Rosamund and her husband.

Matthias, once the week of celebration was over, returned to his duties. There was parchment to prepare, skins to be treated, quills to be fashioned, ink to make. Accounts and letters had to be drawn up, stores checked. The change in the weather made itself felt: heavy, lowering clouds; biting winds. Sir Humphrey declared the castle well provisioned, the truce against the Scots was holding and life went on as before.

'Indeed,' the Constable announced, 'we will celebrate All-Hallows and, in a few weeks when Advent comes, we must collect the holly and ivy. This Christmas,' he declared, 'will be one to remember.'

Matthias, sitting at his desk, tensed. He had always been wary of the feast of All-Hallows. In his youth he had, on that date, kept well away from others, greatly relieved when All-Hallows Eve, that dreadful anniversary of what had happened at Sutton Courteny, had come and gone.

On the day in question he woke tense and stiff, finding it difficult to concentrate. He was so abrupt and evasive that Sir Humphrey looked askance whilst Father Hubert wondered if he was coming down with a fever. Only Rosamund, sitting next to him at table, remained quiet and, when she could, gently stroked the back of his hand.

'It's just the change in the weather,' he murmured.

'Unless, dear Matthias,' she replied, 'you're already sickening of the marriage state!'

He tried to joke back yet, for the rest of that day, he could not shake off a sense of foreboding, of quiet menace. He did not join the rest for supper in the hall but retired to his own chamber. He lit a candle beneath the crucifix which hung on the wall and, kneeling on the small prie-dieu beneath it, prayed for God's protection, and that He'd bring those who had died at Sutton Courteny so many years ago to a place of peace and light. He lay down on the bed, pretending to leaf through a Book of Hours, studying the fine cursive script and jewel-like pictures. He was not surprised when, after a while, he heard a distant clamour, shouts of alarm, followed by pounding footsteps on the stairs outside. Vattier, still wearing his conical helmet and dressed in leather brigandine as captain of the night watch, burst into the room.

'Master Matthias, you'd best come! Sir Humphrey and Father Hubert are outside the north tower!'

Matthias put his boots on and followed the sergeant-at-arms. The bailey was pitch-dark, lit only by cresset torches, which flickered and danced where they had been placed away from the biting night breeze. Soldiers had gathered at the foot of the steps. Vattier pushed through these, ignoring their murmuring, and led Matthias up into the gallery. At first the silence was so intense Matthias thought there had been some misunderstanding. Sir Humphrey and Father Hubert were sitting in a window embrasure. The lighted candle Sir Humphrey held in his hand made their faces look drawn and grey. Matthias looked towards the door leading to the north tower. He felt the cold but could see no light or detect any vile odour, nor any of the usual manifestations associated with this haunting. He was about to ask why they had brought him, when the most heart-rending screams came from the tower. These were followed by a man singing. At first Matthias thought it was the chanting of a monk until it turned into a loud, foulsome ranting, a macabre mimicking of the Divine Office: curses, foul epithets, obscene remarks.

'It started within the hour,' Father Hubert whispered. 'I really do think I should go in.'

Matthias shook his head. 'No, Father, I will.' He smiled down at both of them. 'Vattier can guard the door. Now is not my wedding night.'

'In which case . . .' Father Hubert got to his feet. He brought from beneath his cloak a small, silver pyx which contained the consecrated host. It shimmered and glittered in the candlelight. Without asking, he thrust this into a small pocket inside the lining of Matthias' jerkin. He also took the small, wooden cross he wore round his neck and looped the rough cord over Matthias' head. 'These will protect you,' he whispered.

Matthias blessed himself and walked down the gallery. Vattier came with him. The sergeant-at-arms carried a torch. When they reached the door he thrust this into Matthias' hand. Vattier's face was covered in a sheen of sweat, like a man sick with the fever.

'Against sword and buckler,' he whispered, 'I have no fear. But, in God's name, Master Matthias, what is this?'

'I don't know.' Matthias' reply was clipped. 'But lock the door behind me. Only open it at my command.'

Vattier turned the key in the lock, the door swung open. Matthias stepped into the small alcove. He lifted the torch and saw the stairs twisting away up into the darkness. It was bitterly cold but he could detect nothing else. He walked up the stairs, carefully reciting a prayer. He reached the first gallery and stepped into the deserted room as he had done before. This time the door slammed quickly behind him. Matthias spun round.

'In God's name, who are you?' he called.

'In God's name, who are you?' The reply was low and mocking. 'How dare you interfere in my pleasures?'

'No pleasure!'

This time it was a woman's voice, low and tired. Matthias lifted the torch. He could see nothing though he felt a presence, a feeling of sadness, of quiet despair.

'I speak to the woman,' he called out. 'Who are you?'

'Maude. My name is Maude.'

'And why are you here?'

'Tied here. Tied by sin. Unforgiven. No atonement. No reparation.'

'Maude who?' Matthias decided it was best if he talked as he would to strangers, not dwell upon the evil, sinister atmosphere.

'Maude Beauchamp.'

'Why are you held here?'

'I committed a terrible sin. Unfaithful, led to murder. Imprisoned in darkness.'

'And can you leave?'

'In time, yes, when reparation is done. I'd love to continue my journey.'

'Where to?' Matthias asked.

'Out of the darkness. Sometimes I can see the light, just a pinprick, like a star in the sky—'

'She's frightened of you, you whoreson bastard!' the man's voice interrupted, harsh, malicious. Matthias caught a hint of fear.

'Aren't you frightened?' Matthias retorted quickly.

He felt something rush at him out of the darkness. He was pushed, staggering back against the wall, almost dropping the torch. Matthias gasped for breath even as the man's voice screamed.

'I didn't mean it! I didn't mean it! I am sorry.' The voice was now wheedling, importunate.

'Then why are you frightened?' Matthias gasped.

'Oh, Matthias. Creatura.' The man's voice was still wheedling.

'Why do you call me that?'

Matthias stood staring into the darkness. He heard a gasp, like a dog which had run far and fast and was now lolling, mouth open, jaws slavering. The sound made his flesh creep.

'You know why.' The man's voice was soft. 'You carry something sacred but I cannot name that—'

'Oh, please help me!' the woman's voice cut across.

'She's frightened of you.' The man's voice rose as if to drown the woman's. 'She knows about the Dark Lord. She's frightened that she will be hurt even more.'

'What must I do?' Matthias asked.

'Piss off, just piss off!'

'Masses, prayers.' The woman's voice came as a whisper.

Matthias stood for a while but no other voices came. The room grew warm as if braziers had been wheeled in, full of burning charcoal.

'Matthias! Matthias!' Vattier's voice echoed up the steps. 'Matthias, are you all right?'

Matthias went out of the chamber and down the steps. Vattier stood in the doorway, sword drawn. Matthias pushed him outside and slammed the door shut. He walked back to the priest and handed over the crucifix and pyx. Even as he did so, the murmuring and the clattering from the north tower began again.

'There's nothing we can do,' Matthias declared, 'at least for the moment. But in two days' time it will be the Feast of All Souls. Yes?'

Father Hubert nodded.

'The day the Church specially sets aside to pray for the dead. We'll come back then, Father. You and I in the evening, after sunset. We'll offer a Mass for the repose of the soul of Maude Beauchamp.'

20

Two days later, on the Feast of All Souls, Vattier helped Matthias set up an altar in one of the chambers in the north tower: a wooden table, two oil lamps at each end, a crucifix, cruets, a missal, chalice and paten. Matthias also arranged for sconce torches to be lit and placed in the wall. The sergeant-at-arms moved nervously. Matthias could understand why. Now and again they'd hear the quick intake of breath as if some being stood in the shadows watching them intently.

Rosamund had wished to be present but Matthias refused.

'It's best not,' he explained. 'The little I know, and from what I have read, such occasions can go wrong.'

Father Hubert readily agreed to help.

'It's only just and right,' he declared. 'I am a priest: these manifestations and phenomena come from a soul in distress. How can I refuse?'

Sir Humphrey arranged for guards to be placed in the gallery outside the north tower, hand-picked men under the command of Vattier. Matthias gave them strict instructions not to open the door unless they heard his voice or that of Father Hubert. He and the chaplain arrived just before sunset. They watched the sky and, once the weak sun had dipped behind a thick ridge of clouds, Father Hubert began to vest. The oil lamps were lit. Father Hubert, and Matthias acting as his altar boy, approached the altar, bowed to the crucifix:

'*In nomine Patris et Filii et Spiritus Sancti. Amen.* Brothers and sisters in Christ. I, Father Hubert Deverell, priest of the chapel at Barnwick, do, by the powers given to me through ordination, offer this Mass for the repose of the soul of Maude Beauchamp and ask Christ, in His infinite goodness, to lead her to a place of repose and light!'

'Oh, piss off, you vile, scurrilous priest!'

Father Hubert stepped back.

'Just ignore it,' Matthias whispered.

'I therefore call upon St Michael, St Gabriel, St Raphael,' the chaplain continued, 'leaders of the heavenly host, to come out and meet this soul and take it to such a place. Let her not fall into the hands of the enemy, the evil one, the son of perdition!'

'Shut up! Piss off! Leave her alone. Why are you here, Hubert? Who are you to be praying for anybody?' The voice dropped to a wheedle. 'Don't you remember Ursula? Don't you remember how much you used to lust after her?'

Father Hubert bowed his head, shoulders shaking, tears running down his face.

'She was a girl,' he whispered, 'so many years ago.'

'So what, Father?' Matthias retorted. Matthias raised his head and sniffed: the vile stench was back, as if someone had suddenly opened a great sewer. The flames of the torches began to dip. 'Continue!' Matthias hissed. 'For the love of God, Father, you must continue!'

'I will go unto the altar of God, to the God who gives joy to my youth,' the priest intoned. He pressed on and as his voice became stronger, the stench disappeared and the torches revived. Throughout the Mass, even though Father Hubert was now shaking, the sweat pouring down his face, the interruptions continued. Shouted obscenities and clattering on the stairs outside, giggling and, at one time, the walls broke out in a dark, oozing mud. None of these phenomena lasted long. The consecration was reached, host and chalice elevated and the manifestations subsided. Matthias, now and again, heard a woman sobbing but not in distress, rather like someone crying tears of joy or thanksgiving. At that part of the canon of the Mass where the priest had to name the dead soul, the clatter on the stairs outside grew intolerable: running up and down, clashing chains, hammering on the walls. Father Hubert had to pause and sit down.

'I feel sick,' he whispered.

Matthias told him to rest, and went outside. He stared up into the darkness and, abruptly, as if the thought had been whispered to him, he felt an urge to call on the Rose Demon: to bid for his power, his help. He closed his eyes and leant against the wall. So intense was this desire that he had to bite his lip.

'Go away!' he whispered.

'Why?' the man's voice shouted, as if from the top of the tower. 'Where has she gone? I am all alone!'

'Can't you go with her?'

Matthias opened his eyes. Father Hubert was now standing beside him.

'I can't go,' the voice rasped. 'Lost in darkness. I will not go! I will not forgive! I will not ask for mercy!'

'Then,' Father Hubert asked, 'are we never to be rid of you?'

'Not until they come for me, until this place is reduced by fire.'

Father Hubert walked slowly back into the room and, without any coaxing from Matthias, continued with the Mass. He took the Eucharist and gave Matthias the host and the chalice. When he had finished, he sat back on the small stool, staring through the doorway. Matthias was deeply concerned by the look on the priest's face. He had aged and sat like a broken man, chest heaving, eyes flitting round the room as if he could barely sense where he was.

'What is it, Father?' Matthias came up beside him.

The priest smiled gently. He tugged at a lock of Matthias' hair.

'I think we were successful, Matthias. The tortured soul who dwelt here has moved on. But the other?' He shook his head. 'There is nothing you or I can do any more.'

The priest's words proved prophetic. In the days following the Feast of All Souls, the strange manifestation in the north tower subsided. The cost to the old priest, however, was great. He collapsed one morning in the chapel, just after saying Mass, and was carried to his bed. Matthias found there was nothing he could do.

'Don't send for a physician.' Father Hubert grasped his hand. 'Matthias, I was born to be a priest. I have tried to live my life as a priest. I am going to die as a priest.' His head went back on the bolster. 'I'm at peace with God, with my fellow man. I have nothing to take with me.' He coughed. 'I am only sorry I am leaving my friends.'

Matthias studied the old priest's drooping eyes, the sheen of sweat on his head, his rapid breathing. He immediately sent for Sir Humphrey, Rosamund and Vattier. They came at once. Sir Humphrey brought his Book of Hours and, apart from Vattier who couldn't read, they passed round, reciting prayers and psalms. The old priest lay silent, eyes closed. Only by touching the faint pulse in his neck did Matthias learn he was still with them. The hours passed. It was night before Matthias advised all three of them to leave, that he would stay by the bed and watch. Sir Humphrey and Vattier went. Rosamund remained but, when her eyes began to close and her head drooped, Matthias whispered she should leave. She had hardly left, her footsteps faint down the gallery, when Father Hubert turned, his eyes open, staring fixedly at Matthias.

'I'm going now,' he whispered.

Matthias made to rise but the priest's hands caught his arm.

'Stay with me, Matthias. We'll all meet again merrily in Heaven. I shall pray for you, Matthias. I have dreamt about you. You face such a hideous struggle but when it comes, the time of testing . . .' The breath in the priest's throat rattled. He paused. 'When it comes,' he continued weakly, 'the time of testing, I shall be with you.'

His fingers slipped away. Father Hubert gave one sigh, his head slumping to the side. Matthias leant over. There was no longer any blood beat in the neck. The flesh was already growing cold. Matthias closed his eyes, whispered the requiem for this good little priest and sent for the others.

Three days later, a priest came from one of the outlying villages. He sang the requiem in the castle chapel and Father Hubert's corpse, wrapped in a sheet, was buried in the small cemetery in a far corner of the outer bailey. His death created gloom and despondency in the castle. The priest had been respected and popular. For weeks afterwards, little mementoes were placed on his grave. A collection was made amongst the garrison for a special cross to be carved and Father Hubert's name be inscribed upon it. The general mood was not helped as the weather grew worse: dark, lowering clouds, bitter winds.

At the beginning of December, just as the garrison prepared for Christmas, the snow began to fall. At first, it was only small flurries, but by Christmas Eve it started to lie and there was no break in the clouds. Matthias, together with Sir Humphrey and Rosamund, celebrated a quiet Christmas. Father Hubert's death still affected them and it didn't seem right for no Christmas Mass to be sung or prayers to be said.

'It's the same in every castle,' Sir Humphrey declared as they sat before the fire in the solar, sipping mulled wine. 'It will take months before we get a suitable replacement.' He smiled at Matthias. 'It will mean plenty of letters to the abbots and priors of local monasteries.'

'I wish he was here.' Rosamund, wrapped in a fur robe, cradled the wine cup in her hands.

'Don't we all.' Sir Humphrey gently brushed her hand.

'Especially today,' she continued. 'Christ's birth. I would have liked to ask him.'

'Ask him what?' Matthias stared curiously at Rosamund. Over the last two or three weeks she had become secretive, rather withdrawn, though happy enough. Now she sat dreamy-eyed.

'I'd ask him,' she replied slowly, 'to baptise our child.'

Matthias nearly fell out of his chair. Sir Humphrey sat as if he had been pole-axed.

'You?' Matthias couldn't comprehend it. Here, in the solar with the flames merrily crackling round the logs, the windows and doors sealed, the air fragrant with the herbs thrown on the fire and the braziers. He felt as he had on his wedding day, an excitement which made him want to either sit and revel in it or jump to his feet and dance.

'Don't you ever ask?' Rosamund teased. 'Don't you know a woman's courses should come every month and I've missed mine for a second time!'

'But we've only just got married!'

Rosamund threw her head back and cried with laughter. She grasped Matthias' hand and kissed her bemused husband on the cheek.

'What did you expect?' she whispered. 'Some people go to bed to sleep, Matthias Fitzosbert.'

'I think you'd best take care of your father,' Matthias, embarrassed, whispered back.

Sir Humphrey was still staring, mouth gaping: his face lit with pleasure. He put his cup down and hugged Rosamund: he shook Matthias' hand so vigorously, the young man thought it would fall off. Sir Humphrey did a little dance then, pacing up and down the chamber, still shaking his head.

'I've got to tell someone,' he declared and, spinning on his heel, walked out of the room.

'He'll tell everyone,' Rosamund whispered.

He did. Within the hour, Vattier and others of the garrison found some excuse to come up to the solar, their faces bright with smiles. Rosamund was kissed, Matthias' hand ached with being clasped so much.

Matthias himself couldn't believe it. For the remaining few days of the year he kept pestering his wife: 'Are you sure? Are you well?'

Eventually she threatened to box his ears if he didn't shut up.

The New Year was greeted with joy and acclamation. The news of Rosamund's condition was soon known to everyone in the castle. Sir Humphrey, ever genial and generous, could not be restrained in organising celebrations. Even the weather became more clement, the snow stopped falling, the clouds began to break. A weak sun turned the inner and outer baileys into pools of muddy slush. Sir Humphrey and Matthias insisted on following Rosamund around, terrified that she'd slip on a stair or fall on the ice, badgering her to stay indoors and sit by the fire.

On the day after the Epiphany, matters changed again. A sentry on the great gateway chilled the castle by blowing three warning blasts on the war horn: the agreed signal that some danger was approaching. Sir Humphrey and Matthias were chatting in the Chancery. They seized their war belts and hurried out to see what was the matter. Vattier met them at the door of the gatehouse.

'Riders,' he said. 'Some distance away. Two of them but they are coming as fast as they can. I've ordered the drawbridge to be raised and the portcullis dropped.'

'Only two?' Matthias interrupted.

'They may be scouts!' Vattier snapped. 'We can take no chances!'

In the end the riders proved to be messengers. Sir Humphrey and Matthias took them to the solar.

'We are from Lord Henry Percy. My name is David Deveraux.' The principal messenger took out a scroll of parchment from his wallet. He handed this to Sir Humphrey who, in turn, gave it to Matthias. 'This is Bogodis, my squire.'

Matthias studied the two men. Deveraux was tall, fair-haired, chubby-faced, clean-shaven and clear-eyed. He was fidgety, nervous.

'My feet are like blocks of ice,' he protested.

Sir Humphrey waved them to stools in front of the fire. Deveraux took off his cloak, pulled off his boots and sighed. Bogodis was small and dark: crooked-faced, one eye much lower than the other, thin-nosed, a perpetual sneer on his lips. He kept fingering the dagger stuck in his belt and was as restless as his master. Sir Humphrey served them some wine and shouted for a servant to bring platters of food from the kitchen.

Matthias undid the scroll; it was a letter from Henry Percy, Earl of Northumberland, giving safe conduct to his faithful squire Deveraux. Matthias studied the red seal bearing the imprint of the Percy lion. He tossed the letter on to a table and walked across to stand behind Sir Humphrey.

'We've travelled far and fast,' Bogodis declared, rubbing his feet. 'The truce with Scotland is over.'

Sir Humphrey groaned.

'As you know,' Bogodis continued, 'King James III is having trouble with his barons. They have hanged his favourites in Edinburgh and brought the King to book. King James hopes to unite the country in a war against the "auld enemy". He's sent out writs ordering levies. The great nobles are bringing their men in. They could be over the border within days.'

'At the dead of winter?' Sir Humphrey exclaimed.

'They are on the move already,' Deveraux spoke up. 'We have seen the banners of James's principal commander, the Black Douglas.'

'And what advice does the Lord Percy give?' Sir Humphrey asked.

Deveraux shrugged. 'Be on your guard. Keep the draw-bridge up, the battlements manned. Don't send parties out into the countryside, they could be ambushed.'

'And you?' Matthias asked.

He had taken an immediate dislike to both men but couldn't understand why, which made him feel guilty. Perhaps he just resented them as outsiders. They were intruders, bringing harsh news into the castle, reminding Matthias that there was a world beyond the walls: cold, bloody and threatening. Bogodis looked up at him.

'We have ridden hard and long,' he retorted. 'We are tired, our horses spent. Sir Humphrey, if you will, a few days to rest and then we'll continue.'

'There are other riders out,' Deveraux added. 'We are to do what we can, then return.'

Sir Humphrey thanked them and beckoned Matthias into the Chancery. The Constable sat on a stool and rubbed his face.

'I don't like this,' he whispered. 'It's the dead of winter. The roads are clogged with mud. Snow covers the moors.'

'Could a Scottish raiding party move south so quickly?' Matthias asked anxiously.

'Oh yes,' Sir Humphrey replied. 'The snow melts and there are trackways and byways. They have done it before. Have you ever seen Scottish horses, Matthias? Stout little garrons, they are half-wild and roam the glens. Our snow-covered moors will be little problem for them. All we can do is pray that the snow returns. What we need is it laying thick and fast. For the rest?' He got to his feet. 'I'll tell Vattier no patrols are to be sent out. We'll keep a watch.'

In the end the sky fully cleared. The sun, weak though it was, melted the snow even further round the castle. Matthias' anxiety deepened as the tenor of the castle changed. Stores had to be carefully counted, armaments readied, a constant watch by day and night. On the Feast of St Hilary, as Matthias was breaking his fast with Rosamund and Vattier, he heard the distant braying of the war horn and the alarm being raised. He told Rosamund to go back to their chamber, and followed Vattier out up into the high tower of the gatehouse. He didn't need the guards' explanation, a dark plume of smoke stained the horizon.

'God help us!' Vattier breathed. 'There's a farm burning out there. The bastards are coming!'

Vattier again sounded the war horn. The children stopped playing in the outer and inner baileys and were led away by their white-faced mothers. Soldiers tumbled out of their lodgings, fully armed. Vattier and Matthias went down to check the drawbridge was up and the portcullis down and locked. They continued their long vigil.

On the following day, just before noon, Matthias glimpsed small, dark figures on the horizon. At first they reminded him of ants creeping down a white-washed wall, just a few at first. Leaning over the battlements he strained his eyes against the whiteness of the landscape and made out horse and riders. He tried to calm the churning in his stomach. Within the hour there were more. Soon, a dark mass of horse and foot were moving slowly but inexorably towards the castle. They fanned out, reminding Matthias of the horns of a bull: on each wing, horsemen; men-at-arms in the centre; carts behind a dark, seething mass.

Every man stood to arms and, by late in the afternoon, the enemy had gathered across the frozen moat. They included mounted men-at-arms and a whole mass of lightly armed foot soldiers dressed in a motley collection of rags, braids and cloaks. Matthias recalled the Irish that had fought at East Stoke, with their rounded shields and long stabbing dirks. Slowly, the Scots force, under the brilliant banners of its commanders, fanned out along the moat and pitched camp. Tents and pavilions were set up: bothies made out of branches and pieces of wood, for the common soldiers. Fires were lit and Matthias caught the stench of burning meat. He also heard the faint cries and taunts of the enemy. Now and again, the lightly armed men would come down to the edge of the water to shriek insults in a tongue Matthias couldn't understand.

'They are well provisioned,' Sir Humphrey remarked. 'See the carts, Matthias. They would have left Scotland empty, but between here and the border lie solitary farms. These have been plundered for food, fodder for their horses, wood for their kindling. When they need more, they'll simply send out foraging parties.'

'But why here?' Matthias asked. 'Sir Humphrey, Barnwick is guarded by a gatehouse and walls, not to mention a stout garrison. The Scots have no siege weapons. All we have to do is sit here and wait.'

Sir Humphrey took his helmet off and scratched the back of his neck.

'I know, Matthias. That's bothering me.' He crouched down and drew a line in the dirty snow. 'These are the English defences along the Scottish march,' he explained. 'A line of strong castles, fortified garrisons. The Scots very rarely attack us because, as you say, that takes siege equipment. However, there's always the chance the Scots may take one castle, punch a hole in the line of defence and continue south. They could do so quickly, ravage the lands in the south where they are least expected and then retreat back into Scotland before the Warden of the northern march can muster his levies.'

'Why don't they just go round us?' Matthias asked.

'That's dangerous,' Vattier broke in, helping Sir Humphrey back to his feet. 'Once they pass us, we know where they are going. We can send warnings and, when the Scots return, the rest of the castles would amass a force and be waiting for them.'

Matthias looked down at the sprawling camp, listening to their faint cries, watching the flames of the fires grow stronger. The Scots had already set up picket lines, riders being despatched back from where they had come.

'The other castles don't know they are here,' Sir Humphrey explained. 'And, even if they did, they daren't send for help.' He gestured at the enemy. 'This may only be a raiding party, more waiting further north, looking for one of the castles to weaken itself.' Sir Humphrey leaned over the battlements. 'I wonder what he wants?'

Matthias followed his gaze. A knight, his face hidden by a conical helmet, his great cloak flapping behind him, rode slowly down to the edge of the moat and stared up at the castle. He turned, raising one hand, and shouted. Six archers ran forward.

'Oh, for the love of God!' Vattier shouted. 'Down!'

Sir Humphrey pushed Matthias beneath the crenellations. He heard a whirring noise which awoke nightmares from the battle of East Stoke: the arrows came flying over the battlements, smashing against stone or falling aimlessly into the bailey below.

Matthias peered over the battlements. The six archers, followed by the horseman, were now going back to the Scottish camp. Sir Humphrey clicked his fingers, told Matthias and Vattier to join him and went down to the gatehouse.

'Now, that's a surprise,' Vattier grinned.

'Yes, it is.'

Sir Humphrey stamped his foot, squeezing his nose, a common gesture whenever he was perplexed or worried.

'I don't understand it,' he muttered. 'First those Scots can no more break in here than I can fly. They can stay out there and rot till the Second Coming. Secondly, the Scots are not the best archers but they have master bowmen with them. Perhaps twenty, maybe even thirty?'

'Longbows and arrows can't take a castle,' Matthias remarked.

'No,' Sir Humphrey sighed, 'but they can divert us and make sure we keep our heads down. Vattier, let the men know.'

Despite Vattier's warnings, the Scottish longbow men had some luck with their targets, the occasional sentry who forgot or was too rash. On the second day of the siege, one was killed, an arrow straight through his cheek: another was knocked off the parapet and later died of his injuries.

The mood in the castle grew sombre. The hard-packed earth in the cemetery was again dug up and sheeted corpses interred, a cross above them. Women and children wailed for the dead men. Sir Humphrey called constant meetings to discuss the situation: the Scots sat outside, waiting and watching.

'Father is at a loss,' Rosamund declared, as she and Matthias lay in bed one night. 'He cannot understand what the Scots want: he wonders whether he should sally out and drive them off.'

Matthias could not agree. He spent hours in the gatehouse staring down at the Scottish camp. He reckoned their force outnumbered the garrison's by at least three to one and, as Vattier said, what happened if there were others in the vicinity?

After the first week, days of frayed temper and sleepless nights, Sir Humphrey relaxed, poking fun at what the Scots intended.

'There's nothing we can do,' he declared. 'Just wait and see. Perhaps they'll become tired and wander off elsewhere.'

Matthias wasn't so sure. He felt a presentiment of danger, a silent threat or menace. He was uneasy whenever the two messengers, Deveraux and Bogodis, were in the vicinity. Work in the Chancery came to a standstill. Instead Matthias became more involved in the defence of the castle, going out at night to the sentries, taking great care when he peered over the battlements to ensure the Scots were not attempting some new strategy. On Candlemas Eve he had done such a duty.

Then he returned to his own chamber, lit a candle and stared down where Rosamund was sleeping peacefully like a babe, her hands cupped under one cheek. He heard a knock on the door. Sir Humphrey came in. He glanced towards the bed and beckoned at Matthias, who grabbed his boots and followed him out into the gallery.

'What is it?' Matthias asked.

'I don't know.' Sir Humphrey was clearly agitated.

Matthias put his boots on, wrapped his cloak round him and followed Sir Humphrey down the steps and across the inner bailey towards the keep.

'Sir Humphrey, what is it?' Matthias insisted, grabbing him by the arm.

The Constable turned. His lower lip quivered: in the light from the torch he had taken from an iron bracket, his face looked aged and lined.

'It's Anna,' he murmured, naming a kitchen slattern with a reputation for teasing the soldiers.

'For God's sake, man, what about her?'

'She went missing early this afternoon.'

'And?'

Sir Humphrey just pulled his arm away. He walked on so fast Matthias had to run to catch up with him. The Constable entered the keep. He went down some narrow steps leading into a maze of dungeons and storerooms. Two guards, each carrying a torch, stood within the doorway at the bottom of the steps. One of them had been sick: he was wiping his mouth on the back of his hand. Sir Humphrey led Matthias along the icy-cold, musty passageway and into a room where barrels and casks were stored. Even before he pulled a barrel aside, Matthias glimpsed the pair of bare feet sticking out from behind it. Sir Humphrey gestured with his hand and turned away.

Matthias knelt down. He recognised Anna. The young woman lay, her smock pulled above her knees, her legs twisted strangely. Her head was turned sideways, long, lustrous hair covered her face and neck. Matthias moved the hair and turned the head towards him. Anna stared sightlessly up. Matthias looked at her throat. He closed his eyes and groaned. The girl's bare shoulders were bruised, and on either side of her windpipe were two great jagged holes.

21

Matthias was too frightened, too tongue-tied to offer any explanation. He just advised Sir Humphrey that the corpse be removed and stumbled back to his own chamber. He did not sleep that night but slouched in a chair. The Rose Demon was back, incarnated in some person in the garrison: the macabre killings had begun again. The night seemed to stretch like an eternity. He just sat and waited for Rosamund to wake and, when she did just after daybreak, he told her in clipped sentences what he had seen the previous evening. Rosamund sat up, her back against the bolsters, her long hair flowing down over her shoulders. She was so calm, so unperturbed, Matthias was surprised.

'Of course I expected it,' she snapped crossly. 'Matthias, do you think I am a numbskull? When you told me, that day we went to the wall, I knew then this being would not leave us alone. The question is who? And why now?'

'Deveraux or Bogodis?' Matthias asked. 'They are strangers here. Until now everything has been quiet.'

'They are sinister,' Rosamund replied. 'I know you don't like them. They are shifty, secretive and certainly deserve watching, but we'll have to see.'

The news of Anna's death soon spread amongst the garrison. Matthias felt a slight shift in feelings towards him, dark looks whilst muttered conversations abruptly stopped whenever he appeared. Even Sir Humphrey seemed a little cold. Rosamund was blunt.

'Matthias, Matthias,' she put her arms round his neck and kissed his cheek, 'people have memories. The hauntings in the north tower, the death of Father Hubert, the appearance of the Scots and now this. They put it down to you, but it will pass as all black moods do. You wait and see!'

In the end she was wrong, terribly so. Matthias was accustomed to take guard duty in the late afternoon. He went up into the gatehouse. By now he was bored with the Scots so he and the two guards sat down, their backs to the wall. The soldiers, wrapped in their cloaks, dozed, protected against the cold biting wind. Matthias simply crossed his arms and thought about Anna's death. He tried to piece together what had happened, wondering if he should advise Sir Humphrey to send Deveraux and Bogodis out of Barnwick.

He heard someone climbing the steps and thought a servant, or perhaps one of the soldier's women, was bringing food and drink. He heard his name called and looked up. Rosamund was coming towards him. She had a small bowl wrapped in a towel, he could see the steam curling up from it. She was wearing a bright red shawl across her shoulders, pulled up to protect her neck and the back of her head. It was like a dream. She was smiling at him: so happy to see her husband, she had forgotten about the Scots. She was walking directly in line to a gap between the crenellations. Matthias moved, he knew the bright red cloth would present a target but, even as he scrambled to his feet, he heard the death-bearing whirr in the air. A yard-long shaft with its plume of black feathers struck Rosamund full in the chest. She stopped, eyes closing, head down. The bowl dropped from her hands. The other two soldiers sprang to their feet, crossbows at the ready. They loosed back but the damage was done. Matthias could only squat and stare down at Rosamund, horror-struck, as the blood snaked out of the corner of her mouth.

'Rosamund! Rosamund!'

Her face was white as alabaster. She coughed and opened her eyes. One of the soldiers was already running downstairs, shouting for Sir Humphrey. Matthias lay down beside her; putting his arm beneath her shoulder, he lifted her up as if they were in their bed. He couldn't believe, he couldn't accept what was happening.

'Rosamund, my sweet.' He pulled her towards him. Her mouth opened. He kissed her on the lips. Already they were cold. 'Rosamund!' he screamed.

She opened her eyes, the lashes fluttering like a butterfly's wings.

'I love you, Matthias Fitzosbert. I have always loved you. I always will. Don't you believe that?' She paused, coughing on her own blood. 'I'll always . . .' she gasped. He hugged her close. '. . . I'll always be with you.'

Her body shuddered. When he looked down, her eyes were half-closed, lips slightly parted. He felt for the blood pulse in her neck but it was gone. There was clattering on the steps. Sir Humphrey was beside him on all fours like a dog. He crouched like a child, hands to his mouth and began to sob.

Matthias couldn't accept it. He tugged at the arrow, felt his wife's wrists, then a blackness came over him. He was up, screaming at the sky and ran to the battlements shouting obscenities, filling the air with his curses. He tried to take a crossbow from one of the soldiers. Men were struggling with him. He was pushed down to the ground. A soldier he knew to be called Dickon was pressing him down. The fellow only had one eye, the other was just a white piece of flesh. Matthias called him a devil. He struggled, trying to get to his feet until a blow to his head knocked him unconsciousness.

Matthias spent the rest of the day a captive in his own chamber. The guard outside kept filling his wine cup, refusing to let him leave. Sir Humphrey came up, Matthias saw his mouth move but couldn't understand what he was saying.

The next morning he bathed and shaved to attend the paltry ceremony in the small graveyard. He watched his wife's body being committed to the earth. He knelt by the grave but found he couldn't pray and, when he looked up, Sir Humphrey was kneeling on the other side, glaring balefully at him.

'You are cursed, Matthias Fitzosbert,' he muttered. 'I curse the day you came to Barnwick. You are devil's spawn! If it were not for Rosamund, I'd execute you now and send you back to Hell!'

The Constable staggered to his feet, his face sodden with drink. 'You have one more day in Barnwick,' he rasped. 'Tomorrow I'll drive you out of the castle. What the Scots do to you,' he threw his head back and spat at Matthias, 'I couldn't give a fig!'

Matthias stayed by the grave. He couldn't believe this small stretch of ground contained his heart, his soul, his life. Dickon came over and offered him a cup of hot posset. Matthias drank it greedily and stumbled back to his chamber. Everyone he met avoided him. People drew apart. He heard a woman curse. An urchin picked up a piece of ice and flung it at his head.

He reached his chamber and, for a while, he paced up and down talking to himself. Sometimes he'd punch the side of his head. He was asleep, he was sure of it. This was a nightmare and soon he'd wake up, Rosamund would come in and begin her inevitable teasing. The more he paced, the greater the pain. Rosamund's hair brush, a wimple she had tossed on a chair, two rings from her fingers and, on the window seat, a small jerkin she had been making for their child. Matthias could stand it no more. He fell to his knees and howled like a dog. He took the cross from the wall and ground it beneath the heel of his boot. As he did so he mocked his childhood prayer.

'Remember this, my soul, and remember this well. There is no God, neither in the heavens above nor in the earth beneath!' He raged, shouting obscenities, and then lay curled on the floor, staring blindly around him.

'Are you here?' he whispered. 'Are you, the Rose Demon, here? If you are, I call upon you. I do call upon you!'

He heard a knock on the door. A soldier pushed it open, Matthias told him to piss off. The soldier left hurriedly. Matthias scrambled to his feet. He felt clear-headed, strong and certain. He took his war belt and wrapped it around his waist. He went out of the chamber, telling the guard that he wished to take the air. For a while he walked up and down the bailey. A bell rang for the evening meal but Matthias ignored it. He looked for Deveraux and Bogodis, but those who would meet his eye simply shook their heads. He went into the kitchens. The cooks and slatterns avoided his gaze. They worked lacklustrely, chopping pieces of meat, cutting bread and cheese and laying them out on trenchers. Matthias, feeling the effects of the wine, sat down on a stool.

'Has anyone seen Bogodis and Deveraux?' he yelled.

All he could see were blank glances. Matthias drew his knife. He went up to the chief cook and pressed the tip of his dagger into the man's soft, quivering jowls.

'I asked a question. The two messengers who came here, Deveraux and Bogodis, where are they?'

'I don't know, sir,' the man bleated. 'Sir Humphrey . . .'

Matthias let the dagger fall away. He closed his eyes and tried to think. No one would help him. He opened his eyes and smiled, the dagger came back under the cook's chin.

'Vattier will help. Where is he?'

'He's gone a-courting,' one of the maids behind him murmured. 'You know he's sweet on Caterina, the maid who cleans the chambers.'

'Oh yes.' Matthias grinned. 'And where does he do his courting?'

'I saw them in the keep.'

Matthias pushed by the cook. He ran out of the kitchens, across the ice-covered bailey and down the steps to the dungeons beneath the keep. Someone was there: the door was open and sconce torches had been lit along the draughty passageways.

Matthias tiptoed along. He heard a sound from a storeroom and paused. He drew both sword and dagger. The door was open. A candle burnt on the ledge. Peering through the gloom, he glimpsed a pair of legs, Caterina's long, red hair. The rest was hidden by the man leaning over her as if he were kissing her neck. Matthias moved softly towards him. The man's head came up like a guard dog sensing danger.

'*Ah, Creatura bona atque parva!*'

Vattier got slowly to his feet and turned to face him.

The sergeant-at-arms looked no different though the light was poor. Matthias stepped back. Vattier followed him into the pool of light shed by the thick tallow candle.

'Always the same,' Matthias murmured. 'Except for the eyes!'

'The poet said the eyes are windows of the soul.'

'You pursued me here,' Matthias retorted. 'Why?'

'I haven't pursued you.'

Matthias held himself steady. It was Vattier talking, his lips moving, his hands spread in a gesture of peace, but Matthias watched the eyes, bright and searching: that same soft look he had glimpsed in the hermit or when Rahere had bent over him to explain some point.

'I am here, Matthias, to protect you. I can't leave you alone. Can a mother forget her babe? Can a lover the beloved?'

'You brought me misery,' Matthias accused.

'Did I now, Matthias? Or did you call on me? I have

been here before, long before you were ever born. That old, babbling hermit Pender told you, did he not?'

'What do you want?'

'I love you, Matthias.'

'If you love me, why did Rosamund die?'

'Matthias. I am not the Lord God. I did not want her death. I have no power over the will, over the individual actions of every man and woman. You were warned, all of you.' Vattier closed his eyes. 'I did what I could, Matthias. Believe me, I did what I could.'

Matthias moved sideways and glanced round him. The body of the maid was slumped on the floor.

'And Caterina is dead. She died giving life: to drink blood is the price I must pay.' Vattier breathed in deeply.

'Sir Humphrey is a fool,' he went on. 'He should never have allowed Deveraux and Bogodis in, but his mind is fuddled, always fuddled.'

'What do you mean?'

'It's too late, Creatura. Every man makes choices. Every man has an intellect and a will. Sir Humphrey has made his.'

'You were jealous of Rosamund?'

Vattier stepped closer. 'Creatura—'

'Don't call me that!'

'You must leave here. You must keep yourself safe.'

'Leave me alone!' Matthias hissed, stepping back. 'Tell me now you'll leave me alone!'

'Creatura, I cannot. I cannot stop, nor can you. The will is immutable, determined. Its choices are made.'

'I have made my choice.'

Vattier shook his head. 'Not now, Creatura, now is not the time.'

Matthias heard an uproar outside, the sound of shouting and screaming. Vattier stretched out a hand.

'Come, Creatura, come with me. They are all dead.'

'Why, what's happening?'

Matthias moved to the doorway, the sound of shouting had grown. He could hear the clatter of swords.

'The Scots are in the castle,' Vattier said softly. 'I told you, Sir Humphrey was a fool. Time and again I'd prick your suspicions. I can make you think, Creatura, but I can't make you decide. Bogodis and Deveraux are spies,' he continued.

'They are not messengers from the Percys. They are traitors. Sir Humphrey should have sent them away immediately.'

Mathias stared at him aghast.

'They are spies,' Vattier repeated. 'And, while the garrison supped, they took care of the guards in the gatehouse. The drawbridge has been lowered, the portcullis raised. The Scots are in.'

Matthias, despite his own fears, closed his eyes and groaned. Of course, Bogodis and Deveraux had been their outriders. The Scots had come, sat down and waited until their men were accepted. Vattier was right. Sir Humphrey had been foolish and so he would pay the price.

'Now you have called on me, I can help. I shall, in the future, send you warnings.'

'There is no future!' Matthias whispered.

'Come with me,' Vattier urged.

Matthias felt a sudden spurt of blind rage. He brought his sword back and gave a cutting bow. Vattier swerved aside.

'I'll kill you!' Matthias whispered hoarsely. 'You could have helped us.'

'I could not, until you called!' There were tears in Vattier's eyes.

'Then draw your sword,' Matthias hissed. 'If you love me, draw your sword.'

Vattier did so. Matthias closed: a hacking blow with the sword, a thrust of the dagger, but Vattier blocked this and stepped back. Outside the screams and clamour were growing. Matthias didn't care. Rosamund was dead. His world was shattered and Vattier, whoever he was, would pay the price. Again he closed, hacking blows, thrusting with his dagger. Vattier used all his skills to dance aside. Matthias heard footfalls outside but still he pressed on. Vattier was looking over his shoulder. Matthias refused to turn. A voice shouted: 'Not that one!' There was a click, Vattier was running towards him. The crossbow bolt took the sergeant-at-arms full in the throat. He collapsed to his knees, gave a loud sigh and fell gently sideways.

Matthias whirled round. Armed men stood at the doorway, crossbows at the ready. Deveraux stood in front. They thronged in. One of them knocked the sword from Matthias' hand. Deveraux kicked Vattier's corpse.

301

'So, you are fighting amongst yourselves now?'

'Sir Humphrey, where is he?' demanded Matthias.

'He's dead.' A knight in chain mail came into the room, the sword he held bloody to the hilt. He took off the heavy sallet which covered most of his face. 'Lord George Douglas,' he introduced himself.

Matthias stared at the man's ruddy, stubbly features under the glistening mop of red hair. His face was as pale as the underbelly of a landed fish, a cruel, warlike face; crooked nose above thin lips, eyes which hardly blinked. Douglas scratched an unshaven cheek and gestured with his head.

'The garrison have surrendered.'

'Bogodis?' Deveraux asked.

'He's dead. Sir Humphrey killed him.' He glanced at Matthias. 'You must be his son-in-law?' Douglas sat down on a cask. 'I tried to save Sir Humphrey, God knows I did, but he refused my terms and fought like a madman!' Douglas looked round. 'So, what's been happening here?'

'We've been entertaining traitors,' Matthias snapped.

A soldier went to seize Matthias' arm but Douglas shook his head.

'Get out, all of you. Deveraux, you stay. Tell the garrison they can take what they carry and piss off! If they are not gone by dawn, I'll hang every one of them.'

Douglas waited until the soldiers had left the cellar, then got to his feet.

'I'm not a freebooter,' he continued. 'I am here in the service of his Most Esteemed Grace James III of Scotland.' Douglas' voice was scornful.

Matthias recalled Sir Humphrey's remarks about the ineptitude of the present Scottish king. But Sir Humphrey was dead! The heat of the battle drained from him, Matthias felt cold, tired and sick at heart. He sat down, back to the wall, staring through the doorway.

'We came south.' Douglas too sat down. He picked up a piece of rag to clean his sword. 'The weather suited us and Barnwick was chosen. I might as well tell you, because you are going nowhere; well, at least not for the moment. We couldn't take Barnwick by storm, but by stealth was another matter. Are you interested in what I'm saying, Englishman?'

Matthias kept staring at the doorway. 'I couldn't care,' he

replied, 'whether I live or die. You, my Lord Douglas, and your strategies do not concern me.'

'Oh, but they do, my bonny lad. You see I'm going to continue south, go on a pilgrimage to Castleden Priory.'

'And add blasphemy and sacrilege to your crimes?'

Douglas grinned wolfishly. 'We will not harm a hair on the brothers' heads. We are simply going to collect what they have.'

Again Matthias recalled Sir Humphrey's words: how the Warden of the northern march kept armaments, particularly gunpowder, stored in certain houses across the border.

'We are going to borrow it,' Douglas continued, 'use it for our own purposes.' He glanced at Deveraux. 'You did good work.'

The traitor smirked. Douglas got to his feet.

'I told a lie, mind you, Sir Humphrey didn't kill Bogodis.'

'Then who?'

'I did.'

Douglas thrust his sword straight into Deveraux's stomach, turned and pulled it out. The man stumbled towards him at a half-crouch, the blood spouting out between his fingers. Douglas struck again, a killing blow to the neck. Deveraux crashed to the ground.

'Two things I never trust,' Douglas leant down and cleaned his sword on the man's corpse, 'are mercenaries and traitors.' He grinned at Matthias. 'And they both know a little too much about you. Ah well, let's see what is happening.'

He called his soldiers back. Matthias' hands were tied, though loosely. He was bundled out into the inner bailey, now a scene of carnage with bodies lying everywhere. Already the Scots were preparing a funeral pyre. Matthias asked to search out Sir Humphrey. He begged Douglas for the pitiful, scarred corpse to be buried next to that of his daughter. The Scottish lord shrugged but agreed. Matthias was given the help of two archers to hack the hard-packed earth. Sir Humphrey's corpse, wrapped in his military cloak, was interred, the earth kicked back over it. Matthias stared at the two pathetic mounds of soil, the sole reminder of what had been halcyon days. He found he couldn't cry. He was glad that Bogodis and Deveraux were dead. If the Douglas hadn't killed them, he would have done so himself.

The soldiers then imprisoned Matthias in an outhouse. The rest of the garrison, those who had survived, were now being herded out through the gateway across the drawbridge, driven off by their conquerors with the flats of their swords.

The next morning a group of Scots, led by Douglas himself, took the best horses and galloped south. A large party was left behind under the command of one of the master bowmen. He immediately ordered the portcullis to be lowered, the drawbridge raised. The castle was scoured for any supplies. Matthias felt as if he were dreaming. All traces of Sir Humphrey, Rosamund, the people he had worked and played with, were ruthlessly swept away. The Scots weren't harsh but hostile. Matthias' cords were cut and he was allowed to wander wherever he wished.

'You can try to escape,' the master bowman declared. 'You'll either break your neck or freeze in the moat. Or, if you wish, we can use you for target practice.'

Matthias didn't bother to answer. He spent most of his day wrapped in his cloak in the cemetery, staring at the mounds of earth, quietly mourning Rosamund and the child they never had. He was also puzzled by Vattier and what he had told him. Apparently the Rose Demon could not influence or direct events as he wished. On reflection, Matthias realised that Sir Humphrey had acted most foolishly. He should never have allowed Deveraux and Bogodis to stay. He could have sent a letter along the border to another castle or at least kept those two spies under close watch.

Matthias returned to his chamber: this had been looted. All the chests, Rosamund's jewellery and clothes had long disappeared, and the Scots were beginning to dismantle the great four-poster bed. Anything and everything of value was being taken into the outer bailey whilst the Scots scoured the castle for carts.

'What will you do?' Matthias asked the master bowman.

The lean-visaged villain smirked in a display of yellow, cracked teeth.

'Och we'll take it all with us. You don't think we are going to leave Barnwick as we found it? You wait and see.'

Matthias went to the north tower of the keep. So far, no manifestations or phenomena had been reported by the Scots. Matthias climbed the steps and went into the chamber where he and Father Hubert had celebrated the Mass. The floor was still spattered with candle grease. Matthias found he was no longer frightened. After Rosamund's death nothing concerned him. He pulled the shabby shutters away and stared out over the frozen moorland. A bird flew by. Matthias recalled the Scottish archer's threats.

'So what?' Matthias murmured. 'Perhaps it's best.'

He could throw himself over the battlements and finish it all: life, the fear of death, the pain and hurt. Surely God wouldn't mind? After all, what did it matter? Matthias stood, running his hand along the dust-covered ledge. The more he reflected, the more his conviction grew. He'd decided to leave when the door to the chamber slammed shut. Matthias caught at the latch but the door was locked as if someone was holding fast to the other side. In frustration Matthias threw his weight against it and hammered so hard, pain shot through his arms. Exhausted, he slipped down the wall and sat staring at the pale ray of sunlight coming through the arrow slit window. He dozed.

When he awoke, a sweet, soft fragrance, the same perfume Rosamund had worn, filled the room. The fragrance was so heavy, it was as if she were sitting close to him. Matthias recalled their wedding night, her passionate embraces, the air sweet with the rich cream she had rubbed on her arms, neck and body. Matthias put his hands out as if, in some way, he could touch, grasp, hold her. The sunlight grew stronger and the air filled with the smell of incense, as if Mass were being celebrated and the thurible were throwing out sweet smoke.

Matthias got to his feet and went to the door. This time it opened easily. He went out on to the stairwell and caught a flurry of colour, bottle-green, as if Rosamund were running ahead of him. He charged down the steps and out into the bailey but there was nothing, only a group of Scottish soldiers lounging against the wall. These stared curiously. Matthias walked into the outer bailey and up the steps to the battlements. He had no real desire or firm conviction to throw himself over but he was curious. He wanted to see what would happen.

He reached the top, the biting wind caught at his face and hair. Matthias leant over the battlements and stared down. Far below him, the moat was still frozen hard. Matthias raised his foot; there was a ledge there. It would be so easy to climb on, to stand for a few seconds before falling like a stone.

'Matthias! Matthias!'

He whirled round, mouth gaping. Rosamund was calling him as she often did but, in the yard below, only Scots moved about.

'Matthias, come down! You are to come down now!'

Matthias rubbed his eyes. He could see no one even looking at him. The figures below were intent on carting out any valuables, curtains, drapes, chests and coffers. Matthias looked over the battlements. The drop was dizzying. He felt sick. He gingerly went down the steps and back across into the cemetery. Despite the weak sunlight he was freezing cold. He knelt beside Rosamund's grave, digging his fingers in the dirt as hot, scalding tears ran down his cheeks.

'Are you with me, Rosamund? Are you truly with me?'

He heard a sound behind him and looked round. Nothing. Only a piece of parchment, blown away from some plundered coffer, skittered across the earth. Matthias caught it: the writing was cramped, small and faded. He recognised Rosamund's hand. It must have been written months ago, before she declared her love for him.

'Matthias,' he read, 'amo te, amo te, Matthias. Matthias, I love you. Matthias, I love you.' The same words were written time and again.

On the bottom of the page Rosamund had drawn a face with a miserable expression. Matthias smiled. He kissed the scrap of parchment, folded it carefully and put it inside his jerkin. He then got to his feet and left the graveyard.

Early next day Lord George Douglas and his party were seen approaching. His commander in the castle breathed a sigh of relief and danced a jig.

'Thank God! Thank the Guid Lord!' he shouted. 'If the English had known what happened,' he clapped Matthias on the shoulder, 'the hunter would have become the hunted and I couldn't face being besieged in Barnwick until Easter. It was all a gamble before the refugees from here could raise a warning. My Lord of Douglas is a bonny lad!'

The portcullis was raised and the drawbridge lowered. Douglas and his party entered. They had now brought with

them a string of carts. Some were empty, others full of armaments, crossbows, arbalests, lances, buckets full of arrows,
swords, halberds, even a pile of chain-mail jerkins and leather
sallets. One cart was full of gunpowder: barrels and tuns
stacked on top of each other and covered with a canvas
cloth.

Lord George Douglas came to a stop. He threw Matthias
his reins. Matthias let them drop. The Scotsman made a face
and dismounted.

'I am your prisoner, not your servant,' Matthias declared.

'That's obvious,' Douglas replied.

'Then why am I here? Why wasn't I released with the
rest?'

Douglas narrowed his eyes and, grasping Matthias by the
shoulders, walked him away from the others.

'I have a task for you, Fitzosbert,' he murmured. 'Deveraux
told me what had happened here: the young girl who was
mysteriously killed and, above all, the hauntings in the north
tower. Are you fey? Do you have the second sight?'

'I am a clerk, I am cold, I am hungry and I want to
leave!'

Douglas' hand fell to his dagger hilt. 'I asked you a question, Englishman. I did give your father-in-law honourable
burial.'

'I don't know what I am. I don't know what I have,'
Matthias replied. 'But the north tower is haunted.' He pointed
to a cart full of gunpowder. 'You are going to use some of that
here, aren't you?'

'Of course! We are leaving this afternoon. We dare not stay
here any longer. I would like to destroy Barnwick completely,
leave not one stone upon another. However, that would take
too long and I haven't got the powder, so I am choosing what
I should destroy. The gatehouse will go. Some of the outer
and inner walls and, as a favour to you, Englishman, I'll store
powder in the base of the north tower.'

Orders were rapped out, the plunder was hoisted into the
carts, the Scots sweeping the castle again to make sure they
had missed nothing. Five of Douglas' soldiers were engineers,
one a master of ordnance. The gunpowder was placed at
certain strategic points: the gatehouse, the north tower, two
postern gates as well as the hall and solar. Matthias didn't care.

In a way he was glad that rooms where he had experienced such happiness would never again be used by anyone else.

Late in the afternoon Douglas' party left. Scouts were sent out before them because the Scots now feared the English might have learnt what was happening and organised another force. As they left, the engineers fired the long fuses.

When they were some distance away, the troops stopped beneath bare-branched trees. Matthias stared back at Barnwick. He glimpsed the north tower, the empty gatehouse and his eyes filled with tears. He kept whispering, 'Rosamund! Rosamund!'

Suddenly there was a fierce explosion. Parts of the castle seemed to lift, then collapse in thick clouds of dust. The horses whinnied and pranced about, tossing their heads at the thunder which rolled towards them. The Scots cheered as tongues of flame flared up from the castle. Matthias crossed himself. He heard a cawing from the trees and stared up. Two figures, all in black, sat in the branches glaring down at him: the Preacher and Rahere, pallid-faced, red-eyed. Matthias blinked and stared again. They were only ravens. They cawed fiercely at the tumult and, spreading their great dark wings, soared off up into the sky.

22

Five days later Douglas and his party reached Edinburgh. They had travelled across the wild heathland, past small villages and hamlets. The children and dogs came running out to watch them whilst their parents stood in the doorways and glanced dourly at these fighting men. Eventually they struck east towards the coast, before moving inland to where Edinburgh crouched on its great crag. It looked a princely town but, once within its gates, Matthias found it not very different from London, which he had visited on a number of occasions. The great high street stretched in a herringbone with dark alleys and lanes running off it. Some of the houses had three or four storeys with glazed or painted windows. Others were poor cottages made of wattle and daub, and covered in thatch. They passed the kirk, the Tolbooth and courthouse, across the main market place where the dismembered limbs of traitors were displayed. The crowds swirled about. Rich merchants and their wives in velvets and damask rubbed shoulders with the poor, garbed in coarse linen, wooden clogs on their feet. It was a busy, tumultuous place with different markets in various parts of the city: the fishers, the clothiers, the blood-covered stalls of the fleshers and butchers. Douglas and his party had to force their way through, using whips and the flats of their swords. As in London, the commoners were not so easily cowed, and Douglas and his men, even though they'd loudly proclaimed a successful foray into England, were cursed and spat at.

At last they broke free of the city and entered the palatial grounds of the Abbey of Holyrood. They crossed gardens and fields where lay brothers worked busily on the land, past fisheries and orchards, laundries, outhouses, barns and granges, then into the great cobbled yard which divided the abbey from the small palace which adjoined it. Here, retainers, wearing the black and scarlet of the royal household, came out to meet them, grooms and ostlers, supervised by men-at-arms in quilted jackets.

Douglas snapped his fingers and ordered Matthias to follow him into a flat-stoned passageway. The galleries and entrances to every room were guarded by knight bannerets all wearing the livery of the red lion rampant of Scotland. Holyrood was a close, secretive place. Despite the wooden wainscoting, the coloured cloths on the walls, the beautifully polished oak furniture, the broad sweeping stairs and clean, well-lit galleries, the palace was a military camp with armed men thronging about. Time and again Douglas was stopped and, before he entered the royal chambers, he reluctantly had to surrender his sword and dirk to a royal archer, who also searched him for any hidden weapons. Douglas scarcely greeted anyone, whilst those he and Matthias passed stared askance or looked away. They were ushered into a small waiting chamber opulently furnished with cushioned seats round the wall. More guards thronged here. Douglas told Matthias to wait: an archer opened a door and led the Scottish lord into the royal presence.

Matthias must have kicked his heels for an hour. No one approached; now and again the archers would stare but mainly they chose to ignore him. Nevertheless, Matthias realised that they had him in custody: both the entrance to the royal chamber and the door which they had just come through were locked and guarded.

At last the door to the royal chamber was thrown open. Douglas came out and beckoned Matthias forward. The chamber they entered was hot and stuffy, the windows shuttered. A fire burnt fiercely under a mantled hearth. Pitch torches flickered on the walls whilst a table in the centre of the room was covered with lighted candles. The man standing in the far corner talking softly to a handsome peregrine, perched hooded on the great wooden stand, came out of the shadows. Douglas poked Matthias in the ribs.

'He might not be your king,' he whispered, 'but he is Christ's anointed.'

Matthias went on one knee. The hand he kissed was covered in precious stones; it was also cold and clammy.

'You are welcome, Englishman.' The voice was low, devoid of any accent.

Matthias got to his feet. James III of Scotland was of medium height. His red hair was hidden under a black velvet cap that was decorated by a huge gleaming amethyst. The King's face was covered in freckles, his moustache and beard were straggly. He had watery blue eyes, a loose-lipped mouth, from which his tongue kept flickering out to one side as if to lick an open sore. A weak man, Matthias thought, frightened of Douglas.

'You are most welcome.'

The King tried to sound courteous and calm but Matthias sensed his tension. James studied Matthias as if he hoped to glimpse something else.

'So, you are Fitzosbert, an English clerk?'

'Yes, Your Grace.'

'And do you have secret powers?' The King was staring open-eyed as if Matthias might sprout wings and fly round the chamber.

'I think he has, Your Grace,' Douglas gruffly interrupted. 'And, knowing Your Grace's interest in such matters, I thought it best to bring him to you.'

'Yes, yes, quite.' James waved his hand. 'You, my Lord of Douglas, will retire.'

'Your Grace, I'd best stay with you.'

'Ach, tush man!' James's voice became plaintive. 'The man's not armed and I've always been told,' James's eyes became mean, his mouth twisted into a vicious smile, 'that it will be a Scot who kills me.' He pushed his head forward. 'You are not Scots, are you, Fitzosbert?'

'I am of English stock, sire.'

Matthias was glad to see Douglas, the author of his present troubles, so summarily dismissed.

'Come now, come on.' James clapped his hands like a child, his voice growing high and plaintive. 'My Lord of Douglas, I am not your prisoner.'

'I shall stay outside, sire.' Douglas deliberately turned his back on the King as a gesture of contempt.

The King looked over Matthias' shoulder, waiting until the door was closed. He then grasped him by the arm and pushed him to sit in front of the fire.

'Sit there, man.' The King went to a small table where he poured two goblets of wine. He gave one to Matthias and sat down beside him. 'I know what you are thinking, Englishman, but, God be my witness, I trust nobody. I pour my own wine. I even cook my own food. I trust none of them, not even my own son.' The King sipped at his wine. 'My queen's dead. My boy hates me. As for those nobles,' the King started to cry, to Matthias' astonishment, the tears rolling down his cheeks, 'I had a great friend, young Cochrane, but they hanged him. Throttled him with a silken cord! Now they want to hang me.' He wiped the tears from his cheeks. 'Douglas is a leading wolf of the pack, busy on his raid into England, wasn't he? Och aye.' The King nodded. 'I've heard all about that. Went to collect gunpowder, did he? Now he comes trotting into my presence with an Englishman. Do you, Fitzosbert, have magical powers?'

'No, Your Grace, I do not!'

'Not a bit?' The King held up a little finger.

'No, sire, I am a clerk, a scholar of Oxford. I was at Barnwick—'

'Tush, man, I don't want to know your life.' The King waved a hand. 'I ask you again.' He put his cup down on the floor and drew a long Italian stiletto from the sleeve of his gown.

Matthias froze as this madcap king pricked his neck, just beneath his left ear.

'You are telling me you have no powers? None whatsoever?' He leant closer. 'I have a mirror, you know,' James whispered. 'And if a Black Mass is offered in the room, and you say the Lord's Prayer backwards, you can see the future. Can't you tell me the future, Matthias Fitzosbert?'

'I know two things, sire,' Matthias replied, not daring to move his head.

'About the future?'

'Yes, sire.'

'So, you do have powers?'

'I can tell you two things from the future,' Matthias repeated. 'You are going to die and so am I.'

The King stared unbelievingly at him, then he giggled like some old maid, fingers over his mouth. He dropped his hand, the dagger disappeared back up the sleeve of his gown. James struck Matthias gently on the shoulder.

'You answered well, Englishman.' His smile faded. 'If you had replied any different, I'd have hanged you.'

Matthias let out a deep sigh.

'So, you say you are a clerk?'

Matthias answered his questions and realised that, beneath the madness, James was weak and suspicious, with a deep interest in the sciences, particularly the work of bookbinders and parchment-makers.

They sat and chatted for a while. Matthias didn't really understand if the King was genuinely interested or just wanted to make Douglas kick his heels for as long as possible. An hour passed. James turned the conversation to Barnwick. When Matthias mentioned the haunting of the north tower and Douglas' destruction of it, the King beat a fist against his spindly thighs.

'He shouldn't have done that! He shouldn't have done that! I would have liked to have visited such a place.' James leant closer. 'They say this abbey is haunted,' he whispered, 'by a monk who didn't say his Mass properly. I have spent many a night sitting on my arse in that cold place but I've glimpsed nothing but moonbeams and rats. What hour is it?'

'Sire, I don't know. It must be late in the afternoon.'

'Is it now, is it now?' the King murmured, his fingers to his lips. 'I must go to the abbey and say my prayers.' He glanced slyly at Matthias. 'I've still got Cochrane's body here, you know,' James declared, referring to his dead favourite. 'I had him embalmed and laid out in a splendid coffer. I hear Mass, then I talk to Cochrane about all of my troubles. I'll ask him about you. I know he'll agree I shouldn't hang you. You don't like the Douglas, do you?' James grasped Matthias' wrist. 'So you can stay with me.'

The King got to his feet, tossing the rest of his wine on to the fire. He walked to the door and threw it open.

'Ah, Douglas, I didn't think you'd wait, man.'

Lord George came into the room, biting his lip in anger. He was followed by the captain of the guard.

'Take this Englishman.' The King pointed to Matthias. 'No, I don't want him hanged. Give him a chamber here in the household. He'll have three marks a month and fresh robes at Easter. He can eat at the royal board. I've got to go to church now.'

The King went to leave but paused in the doorway.

'Oh, Douglas, the plunder from Barnwick: I'm your king so, by law and ancient custom, I'll have half of it.'

Douglas bowed stiffly from the waist but the King had already left, shouting at his guards to follow.

The royal officer led Matthias and Douglas out of the King's chambers and up some stairways. Matthias was shown into a small, white-washed room. The captain of the guard gestured round.

'This is yours, Englishman.' He grasped Matthias by the shoulder. 'I'll get servants to bring sheets and blankets for the bed. I'll also give you some advice, lad. Never anger the King. Never contradict him. If you do,' he snapped his fingers, 'as sure as my name's Archibald Kennedy, he'll have you hanged!'

The captain left. Douglas closed the door and leant on it.

'So, what do you think of our king?'

Matthias sat down on a stool and stretched his legs. He felt weak after such a fraught meeting.

'A most gracious prince, my lord.'

'Spare me your sarcasm, Englishman. The man's as mad as a moonstruck hare. You know he'll kill you?'

'My life is in God's hands, my lord.'

'He'll kill you.' Douglas played with the hilt of his dagger. 'One day he'll remember how you were brought into the royal presence by one of the hated Douglases and you'll die.'

'So, why did you bring me here?'

'Well, Englishman, if the King doesn't kill you, I will.'

Matthias stared at this wolf amongst men.

'Or else what, my lord?'

'Well . . .' Douglas opened the door and glanced down the gallery.

'Well, my lord? I am sure there must be something else.'

'You can kill the King!'

The words were softly spoken but Douglas' face was hard.

'He might not be my king,' Matthias replied, 'but remember, my lord, he is the Lord's anointed.'

Douglas ignored Matthias' mimicry of his own words.

314

'But the Lord has taken His hand away from him, as He did from Saul and bestowed His favour on David.'

'And, of course, you have this new David?' Matthias taunted. 'The King's young son?'

'The boy is a bonny lad. He has great favour, is well liked and respected by the lords spiritual and temporal, not to mention our many bonnet lairds. James III is mad. The Exchequer's empty, the kingdom's weak. He pours good gold and silver into one madcap scheme after another. We have tried to teach him the true paths. We hanged six of his favourites but still he hasn't learnt.'

'So, you organised a foray into England?' Matthias replied. 'To collect arms and munitions as well as an Englishman whom the King might be interested in?'

'You'll be given many an opportunity.'

Matthias rubbed his face. Was there no end to this? To be the tool and instrument of power-hungry men?

'Do it as you wish,' Douglas continued. 'The knife, a cup of poison.'

'And if I do?' Matthias spat the words out. 'If I do this for you, Lord George Douglas, who destroyed my life and brought me here, an exile amongst strangers?'

'You'll be loaded with honours and returned to the border,' Douglas replied.

Aye, Matthias thought, pigs will fly and fish will walk on dry land.

'Think about it.' Douglas forced a smile. He stepped out of the room, closing the door quietly behind him.

Matthias sat staring at the wall. He didn't really care about what Douglas had said. He searched his mind. What did he feel? A deep anger at Rosamund's death? Yes, and a growing hatred for the men who had caused it. He stayed in the chamber until Archibald Kennedy came back.

'The King's waiting for ye. He wishes you to sup with him.'

Matthias followed the soldier back to the chamber where he had first met the King. James was more relaxed: one of the shutters had been opened. The King waved him to a stool on the other side of a small table which was covered with trenchers and bowls full of meat, bread and fruit. The King blessed himself and, chattering about how he would like to develop the Abbey of Holyrood, invited Matthias to eat. The

King watched Matthias put food on his trencher and begin to eat. He had hardly done so when the King stretched across, knocked his hand away and took the trencher for himself whilst Matthias was given his plate. The same occurred when the wine was poured. Matthias realised that, whether he liked it or not, he was the King's food-taster. James watched him, narrow-eyed.

'Why did Douglas bring you here, Englishman?'

'Oh, it's quite simple, Your Grace. He wishes me to kill you.'

James threw his head back in a loud neighing laugh, spitting food from his mouth.

'Englishman, you jest!'

'Your Grace, I do not.'

'Och aye!' The King sighed, wiping his fingers on his gown. 'I could have you hanged for that.' He sighed again. 'But you are telling the truth, aren't you?'

Matthias stared into those hard, cunning eyes full of madness. He stretched across to take a small manchet loaf but the King knocked his hand away.

'Don't eat that!' he whispered. 'It's poisoned!'

Matthias swallowed hard. His appetite abruptly died.

'I poisoned that myself,' the King continued. 'I heard your conversation with the Douglas. The chamber you were given has a false wall. In one of the beams there are two holes. You can look through or put your ear to them.'

'Archibald Kennedy was there all the time, wasn't he?' Matthias asked.

'Och aye.' James smiled. 'Douglas wants me dead.'

'Why don't you kill him? It is treason to plot against you, the King.'

The King rubbed his hand together. 'I'd love to,' he whispered hoarsely. 'I'd love to see that arrogant red head on the end of a pike but not here, not now. If I kill the Douglas his clan would be swarming through Edinburgh. They'd burn the abbey and the palace to the ground and I would disappear into some dark pit.' He smiled again. 'If ye hadn't told me the truth, I would have let you eat that poison. But come on, have some more wine. Tell me about Oxford!'

So began Matthias' bizarre life at the Scottish court. Sometimes the King would forget him and Matthias would wander the dusty galleries or go into the great abbey. He'd sit at the base of a pillar and listen to the rhythmic chant of the monks in their stalls or stare up at the stained-glass windows, where angels blew golden trumpets to raise the dead and demons danced on an ocean of fire. The abbey walls, too, were decorated with gorgeous multi-coloured scenes from the Bible. Matthias got to know each and every one of them, and the memories of those paintings at Tewkesbury flooded back: the golden summer day, the hermit staring at a painting, tears streaming down his face.

Matthias did try to escape. One morning he slipped out of a small postern gate and crossed the great meadow which ran down to one of the curtain walls round the abbey. He thought no one would notice. He was halfway across when he heard the whirr of arrows and two long shafts smacked into the soft earth on either side of him. Matthias turned round. Kennedy stood at the top of the hill: the master bowman beside him was notching another arrow to his string. Matthias shrugged and walked slowly back.

On other occasions he was closeted with the King; James was a madcap, seething with rage at the humiliation foisted upon him by his great barons. He was superstitious and, at other times, deeply religious. Matthias would sometimes sleep in the same chamber or sit at his right at banquets in the great refectory. He would taste every morsel of food and cup of wine placed before the King.

Matthias was also invited into the royal chapel where Cochrane, the King's long-dead favourite, lay embalmed in an open casket. James had a special chair placed at the head of this. He would sit for hours stroking his dead favourite's face, playing with the tendrils of the hair, cooing softly or talking about affairs of state. James would then quietly listen, as he put it, 'for Cochrane's good counsel'.

Douglas had left the court. When he returned, he never approached Matthias but just stared angry-eyed, fingers tapping the hilt of his dagger. Matthias would shrug and glance away. He felt safe enough and, after his walk through the long meadow, never again attempted to escape. He didn't pray or put his trust in God. He simply reached a decision that, if an opportunity to escape presented itself, he would seize it.

The months passed, a wet winter turned into a glorious

spring. James spent more hours closeted in the royal chapel crooning and murmuring over Cochrane's corpse. When he returned to his private chambers, he became immersed in letters, all written in a secret hand, to his 'friends and trusted counsellors throughout Scotland'.

One day, at the beginning of May, Matthias found the King beside himself with excitement.

'It's war!' he whispered across the table. 'It's now or never, Englishman! Cochrane has given me his advice! I am to take the field. Do you agree?'

'Your Grace knows best,' Matthias replied.

'I have got to look for a cause,' the King replied.

A few days later he was given this. A group of Douglas' allies, the Humes, wild, border bonnet lairds, arrived in a clatter of hooves and clash of armour at the palace demanding an immediate audience with the King. James, dressed in his finest regal robes, met them in the throne room, his royal guards all about him, Matthias being relegated to a shadowy corner. At first Matthias couldn't understand what was happening. The Humes, dressed in half-armour, their long, red hair falling down to their waists, stood arrogantly before the King and shouted for their rights.

'The revenues of Coldingham Priory,' their leader insisted, 'belong to the Humes. They are ours by right and ancient privilege!'

'Nothing is yours by right or privilege,' James tartly retorted.

The Humes repeated their demands. James, bored, rose to his feet, clapped his hands as a sign that the audience was over and swept out of the throne room.

Within a week the Humes and their confederates the Douglases were up in arms. James became frenetic with excitement. His allies, the Huntleys and Crawfords, brought their retinues to Edinburgh. More royal troops arrived and the King began to move: his napery, his salt cellars, tapestries and curtained beds, spinning wheels, towels, combs, mirrors, chests and coffers were piled on to carts. The King, now the warrior, constantly marched about in half-armour, brought specially from Milanese craftsmen. James saw himself as a new Robert Bruce, full of military oaths and what he would do after his great victory. Matthias was given a coat of chain mail, a conical helmet, a war belt and a rounded shield.

'You'll be my squire, Englishman,' James smiled at him. 'You'll stand by me in the fray. If you don't, my good man Kennedy has orders to slash your throat from ear to ear.' He grasped Matthias' arm. 'That's the advice Cochrane gave me.'

Matthias glanced at the captain of the royal guard. Kennedy winked back.

'God knows how this will end,' he whispered later to Matthias, 'but Cochrane has also told him how to fight this war.'

At the end of May James, astride a snow-white palfrey, the saddle and harness of burnished leather edged with silver, led his royal army out of the grounds of Holyrood, down through the stinking wynds of Edinburgh. They paused at the great open space before St Giles' Cathedral where the priests blessed them. The royal army then continued. James had a body of archers and men-at-arms who wore coats of mail. These soldiers were well armed with bows and arrows, broadswords and daggers, but the rest were bare-footed clansmen, dressed in loose plaids and saffron-dyed shirts, and they carried little except a stout dagger in their belts, a spear and shield. Nevertheless, what they lacked in armour they made up in courage and determination. They did not care a whit about the King but were eager for war, to burn, pillage and, above all, wreak vengeance on their deadly enemies the Humes and the Douglases.

The King moved to Blackness on the Firth of Forth. His army caught sight of the enemy mustering in the distance. They, too, carried the royal banner of Scotland, having amongst their ranks the King's eldest son. James's courage now cooled. He refused to give battle but marched his troops further west. Kennedy told Matthias that he thought they were going for Stirling to seek protection behind its fortified walls. The King's enemies moved faster and, when the royal army tried to cross Sauchieburn, a river which snaked its way across Stirling Plain, they found their way blocked by the Humes and Douglases and a greatly swollen rebel army.

James, Matthias in tow, rode up and down the lines of his troops, exhorting them to stand and fight, interfering in the commands and orders of his captains. The royal forces were not fully deployed when the rebel army moved with incredible

319

speed. Matthias stared unbelievingly at the great line of horse and foot which raced towards them. This was no Tewkesbury or East Stoke but a wild rush of men. Most of James's soldiers simply turned and fled: the levies from Edinburgh and other towns were the first to leave the field. The King, watching the flight of his troops from a nearby hill, panicked, took his helmet off and, turning his horse, left the field. Most of his bodyguard had been deployed in the line of battle and, as the King began his wild ride, Matthias realised only he and Kennedy were left to guard him. Behind them the roars of battle, the cries and shrieks of dying men faded as the King rode away.

They crossed a small stream, driving their horses up the wet slippery bank, and were about to pass a mill when James's palfrey, unused to such mad gallops, slipped and rolled, tossing the king. He managed to extricate himself but, in doing so, hurt his legs. He lay gasping, screaming for Cochrane and beating his gauntleted hand on the ground like a spoilt child who has been deprived of a toy. Then he groaned and, clutching his side, fell back on the ground.

'Englishman,' Kennedy dismounted, 'see if there is any pursuit.'

Whilst he crouched beside his king, Matthias turned his horse's head and rode back to the top of the bank. He took his helmet off, allowing the breeze to cool the sweat on his face. He pulled back the mailed coif and drank from the waterskin slung over his saddle. He didn't give a fig about James or the pursuers and, for some time, his attention was caught by a small white cloud no bigger than a man's hand. He stared at it, lost in a reverie: the sky, the cloud, the warm sun reminded him of that day at the wall when he had told Rosamund about his past.

'Englishman, are you asleep?'

Matthias shook his head, splashed some water over his face and stared across the heathland. At first he could see nothing but, straining his eyes, he glimpsed colour behind a copse of trees and saw some riders emerge. Half a dozen, these fanned out as they rode towards them. Behind them came another party. Matthias tried to make out the colours. He glimpsed a banner, green and white. The breeze blew more strongly, the riders turned direction and he saw the black and gold banner of Lord George Douglas.

'There are pursuers!' Matthias shouted. 'And they are coming fast.' He trotted his horse down. 'What now?'

Kennedy had grasped the King by the shoulder and was lifting him up from the ground. A faint trickle of blood snaked out of the corner of the King's mouth. His face was white. He was grasping his side.

'He has broken a rib, bruised something inside.' Puzzlingly, Kennedy smiled up at Matthias. 'Who's leading the pursuit?'

'Lord George Douglas.'

'Aye,' the King muttered, opening his eyes. 'He has pursued me in life, he will pursue me to the death.' He grasped Kennedy's arm. 'Archibald man, kill him.' He pointed at Matthias. 'We'll take his horse.'

'Sire,' the Scottish captain dabbed at the King's face with a rag, 'you cannot be moved.'

The King stared at him wildly. 'But, for God's sake man, if we stay the Douglas will take my head!'

'Get him some water!' Kennedy ordered.

Matthias offered the small leather bottle.

'Ach no,' the King groaned. 'Bring me fresh from the burn!'

Matthias ran up the bank, grasped his helmet and went down to the burn. He filled his helmet with water and looked up. Douglas and his party were drawing closer. He heard a faint shout as they glimpsed him running back up the bank. He went to kneel by the King. Kennedy snatched the helmet from his hand and poured the water over the King's face.

'Are they drawing closer?' Kennedy asked.

'For God's sake, yes, man!' Matthias retorted.

'Kill him,' the King murmured. 'Kill the Englishman and fetch me a priest!'

Kennedy drew his dagger. Matthias didn't know whether to spring at him or jump away. He caught a look in the Scotsman's eyes, gentle, kindly: then the dagger was brought down. One swift thrust into the exposed throat of King James III of Scotland, who wriggled and choked as Kennedy held the dagger firm, all the time his eyes staring at Matthias.

'Go on, Creatura! Go on now!'

'Why?' Matthias asked, getting to his feet.

'Win or lose, the King had given orders for your death but his soul was ours. Go on, Creatura, ride like the wind.' He pointed to his own horse and the longbow looped over the saddle horn. 'I have unfinished business with the Lord Douglas!'

23

At Lanercost Priory outside Carlisle, the chronicler transcribing local events during the second half of the year of Our Lord 1488 was as mystified as anyone by the strange stories brought by travellers, journeymen and packmen when they stayed in the guest house on the far side of Lanercost church. Brother Simon, the chronicler, avid for information, greedy for scandal and gossip, scratched his balding head and would spend a long time, pen poised, wondering how to record such mysterious events. True, Barnwick Castle had been destroyed in a Scottish raid in the winter of that year: the keep had been fired, the gatehouse demolished, any wooden building burnt to the ground whilst parts of the wall were brought to terrible ruin by the Scots marauders. The Warden of the Scottish march, too fearful of what might be happening in Scotland, left the place neglected. The castle became the haunt of ravens, owls, foxes, badgers and other wild animals which roamed the desolate heathland between Scotland and England.

Occasionally some traveller would stay there, taking shelter amongst the ruins, lighting a fire, cooking food and sleeping till dawn. However, they all felt that they were not alone. They would talk of footfalls in the darkness, the sound of someone moving around them. Of a dark shape or a figure glimpsed briefly in bright moonlight. In the morning the travellers would be only too willing to leave. Brother Simon listened to their stories and wove an embroidered tale of the ruins being haunted by a coven of ghosts.

Such stories helped Matthias. He had reached Barnwick early in August 1488, having successfully eluded Scottish patrols. He slipped over the border and, on one golden-filled summer day, arrived back at Barnwick. He had changed during those weeks since he'd fled the battle at Sauchieburn. He had been hunted by men and dogs. He knew, from the small villages and hamlets he passed through, that huge rewards had been posted for an Englishman, a devilish traitor, responsible for stabbing the Lord's anointed, King James III, as well as the cowardly murder of Lord George Douglas. The latter, according to common report, had been 'hurrying to help his king when a mysterious bowman, no less a person than the Englishman Matthias Fitzosbert, had sent a longbow shaft deep into Douglas' neck, killing him instantly'. Matthias, disguised, his hair long and straggly, half his face covered by a moustache and beard, had secretly rejoiced at the news. He was innocent of spilling any royal blood but pleased that Lord George Douglas, who had shattered his own life, had, at last, received his just reward.

Matthias had not immediately fled to the border: that would have been a mistake. Instead, he had ridden to and fro across Scotland, lying low until the hunt died down and the Scottish Council became more concerned about who would control the young King rather than the death of his feckless father and a Douglas laird. Matthias had eventually crossed the Tweed, striking south-east, following the rugged Northumbrian coast before turning west. He was well armed and the horse he rode was a sturdy garron.

Now and again he'd stop to do some work on a farm or in a village where he would obtain free food or a few coins. He did not know what to do or where to go. He knew he should visit Barnwick, but after that? Matthias considered the problem many a lonely night and found he really didn't care. Something had died in him. He was ruthless, determined not to become the cat's-paw of any man, yet on that August afternoon when the ruined towers of Barnwick came into sight, Matthias sat stock-still in the saddle and cried for what might have been.

He rode on. The moat had been filled in with bricks, rocks and boulders from the ruined walls. The gatehouse was shattered. Local farmers and peasants had already plundered the ruins for stones and wood for their own barns and granges. Steel and iron from the portcullis had long been stripped. The outhouses in the castle baileys had simply vanished. The keep still stood but the north tower was a pile of shattered masonry. Of the hall, parlour and solar, only blackened timbers remained.

Some of the soldiers' quarters, built into the small towers along the inner wall, were still usable. Matthias stabled his horse in one of them. He collected fodder, drew water from the well and made himself at home. He snared rabbits in the warren and, armed with bow and arrow, went out on the heathland to shoot quail and pheasant.

For the first two days Matthias found it impossible to go to the cemetery. When he did, he was astonished to discover that the grave had been carefully tended: the tumulus of soil neatly raked and weeded. The cross still stood secure and, at the other end of the grave, a small rose bush grew. The flowers, small and delicate, were white as snow. Matthias knelt down. He must have stayed for hours quietly sobbing. When he had finished, he lay down on his back staring up at the sky watching the day die. He poured his heart out, as if Rosamund were still alive, lying in his arms beside him. He told her about Scotland, about its mad king whose dreadful death he had witnessed; the intervention of the Rose Demon and his own long desperate flight to the border. When the wind stirred he caught the sweet smell of the roses and, on one occasion, just before he drifted into sleep, the faint fragrance of his dead wife's perfume.

After that Matthias decided to stay at Barnwick: the grim life of a hermit had its own rewards. He was free of any responsibilities, of any duties. He had no one to care for but, there again, no one to bother him. He revelled in the silence and resented any intruders. Even when the weather changed, the winds turning harsh and the snow lying thick over the castle ruins, Matthias wouldn't have exchanged it for the warmest, most luxurious of chambers in some royal palace.

Matthias spent some of his day hunting for food. Now and again, though very rarely, he would travel to one of the outlying farms or villages to beg, buy or work for bread, flour and other necessities. After a while he became accepted for what he claimed to be: a hermit, supposedly a man of God, though never once did he pray. He tended Rosamund's grave and, when spring came, built a small mausoleum, using bricks and other materials he found in the castle. No one ever approached him and there were no mysterious phenomena. Matthias rejoiced. He had forgotten the world and perhaps the world had forgotten him? The local farmers told him, with some relish, how the stories were spreading that Barnwick was haunted. Matthias smiled grimly and did his best to encourage such local legends and lore.

Barnwick became a place most people avoided. One spring afternoon, however, Matthias was unexpectedly aroused from his afternoon slumber by terrible screams from the far side of the castle. He rose quickly, strapped on his war belt, took his crossbow and bolts and went to investigate. He crossed the inner bailey and peered through a gap in the wall to where the gatehouse had been. At first he couldn't make out what was happening. Four men, dressed in a motley collection of rags and leather, guarded their captives. Two children lay on the ground, their hands and feet bound. Matthias couldn't distinguish whether they were boys or girls. The three other prisoners were adults: the man had been stripped, his hands and feet bound and now he was being hoisted on a rope over a timber. A small fire had been lit beneath his feet. The two others, naked as they were born, were women. One was middle-aged, the other a young lass, probably sixteen or seventeen summers old. The women, pricked with daggers, were being made to dance whilst the children sobbed and the man screamed a mixture of pain and defiance.

Matthias studied the scene carefully. There were about six horses and two sumpter ponies. He realised that some merchant's party, foolishly travelling by themselves, had been attacked by outlaws. The victorious wolf's-heads were now intent on enjoying their ill-gotten gains. Matthias wondered whether he should intervene. But why should he? The moorlands were haunted by outlaws, men who feared neither God nor man. Matthias did not wish to incur their enmity. Then a wolf's-head went over and kicked one of the children lying on the ground. Matthias could stand no more. He slipped a bolt into the groove of his arbalest and walked out of his hiding-place. An outlaw caught sight of him and waved drunkenly. They were all the worse for drink.

'It's the hermit!' another shouted. He lumbered forward, his cruel, unshaven face flushed with wine. 'We caught them out on the moors, sitting there, feasting themselves.'

'Christ Jesus, help us!' The man hoisted on the beam stared beseechingly at Matthias. He was young, his beard and moustache finely trimmed but his face was grey with exhaustion and fear, his eyes almost starting out of his head. The two women clung to each other whilst the pathetic bundles on the grass just sobbed and moaned.

The outlaws did not regard Matthias as a threat.

'There's enough for five.' One of the outlaws gestured to the pile of clothes, the bundles, saddlebags and sumpter ponies. 'What we'll do,' he continued, 'is have our pleasure and then,' he pointed to the children, 'they can be taken to one of the western ports and sold. The horses are good stock.'

Matthias studied the outlaws. One was old and grizzled but the others were young and vicious. They reminded Matthias of a group of stoats closing for the kill. None of them could stand upright. They had drunk much and, so secure in this desolate place, believed they could take their time over this villainy. Matthias felt ashamed that they should regard him as one of them.

'Come on!' the outlaw leader urged. 'There's enough for you!'

The older woman broke free, her long, jet-black hair falling down her back. She ran and grasped Matthias' leg and stared beseechingly up at him.

'Help us!' she pleaded.

Matthias glanced away. The woman's fingers dug deep into his thigh.

'For the love of the Good Lord,' she begged, 'have pity!'

Matthias shook her away. 'There are four of them and one of me.'

He smiled wolfishly at the outlaw leader, who was growing wary of this tall, silent hermit, the crossbow he carried and the great war belt strapped round his waist.

'She asks for pity,' Matthias mocked. 'What is that? I'll go and get my cup and join you.'

He turned his back. As he did so, he brought back the cord of the crossbow, looping it over the catch. The outlaws guffawed at the woman's screams. They were still laughing when Matthias spun round: the crossbow bolt took the outlaw leader in the side of the head, digging deep into his skull, and then, sword and dagger drawn, Matthias was amongst them.

327

They were so drunk, so taken by surprise that Matthias easily despatched two of them: the last was more agile, his cold, hard eyes and long nasty face more wary. Matthias and he circled each other. The male prisoner screamed in agony at the flames, which now licked the soles of his feet. Matthias shouted at the woman to kick the fire away: as he did so, the outlaw closed. Matthias swerved, the dagger skimmed his ear. Again they parted, continuing to circle in a half-crouch.

'Why?' the outlaw hissed.

'I changed my mind,' Matthias taunted.

The outlaw came in a rush. Matthias stepped aside: he caught the man deep, just beneath the rib cage, withdrew his sword and watched as the outlaw slumped to his knees, screaming at the terrible rent in his side. Matthias came behind. Dropping his dagger, he grasped the hilt of his sword and, with two hands, took the outlaw's head in one cutting slice. Around him the young woman was screaming; the two children sobbed uncontrollably, their faces buried deep in the dirt as they tried to hide from any sight or sound of what was happening.

Matthias cut the captured man down: he was bruised, still terrified, the soles of his feet were slightly scorched but otherwise he'd suffered no serious injuries. Matthias then moved to the children, a young boy and girl. He cut their bonds and gently stroked their hair. He calmed them, assuring them that all was well and that he intended no injury. He went round the outlaws. Three were dead, one was grievously wounded. Matthias cut his throat and dragged all four corpses out of sight. The women had seized their clothing and gone elsewhere. The man, still acting like a dream-walker, had to be dressed by Matthias: he then sat on the ground, one arm round each of his children. The women returned. Matthias used some of the wine to bathe their bruises and cuts. As darkness fell, he cooked food and made them all drink deeply of the wine.

A full day passed before they began to recover from their shock, the mother first. She gathered her family together, talking to them softly, reaffirming Matthias' assurances. Every so often she would grasp Matthias' fingers and squeeze them.

'My husband is a merchant,' she whispered. 'We were on a pilgrimage to York.' Her face now looked comely, her hair tied decorously back. 'We slept in one morning. We became separated from our party and then stopped to eat. The outlaws struck.'

Matthias gently stroked her cheek. 'Did the outlaws harm you or your daughter?'

'No, they found the wine. They were evil!' She spat the words out. 'Demons from hell!'

Matthias nodded and walked away. He knew about demons.

Two days passed. The man introduced himself as Gilbert Sempringham, a prosperous clothier.

'I did a stupid thing,' he confessed. 'I thought it was safe.'

'It is,' Matthias reassured him. 'You were just unlucky. Never ever do it again. Never leave the roads, never go on to the moors.'

At last the Sempringhams recovered from their shock. The children first, so absorbed in the present, they viewed the outlaws' attack as a horrid nightmare to be quickly forgotten. Sempringham's wife, Margaret, was a calm, common sense woman. Elizabeth, the daughter, comely, rather shy, spent most of the time gazing adoringly at Matthias as if he were some gallant knight errant clothed in silver armour rather than a wild-haired hermit. Matthias enjoyed their company. Then Master Gilbert said it was time they should leave, and would Matthias accompany them back to the nearest village? He quickly agreed. The fear and terror in young Elizabeth's eyes at the prospect of the family being alone again and the beseeching look Mistress Margaret gave him could not be resisted.

'What do we do with the outlaws' corpses?' the merchant asked. The corpses still lay where they had fallen.

'They lived Godless. They died Godless,' Matthias retorted. 'Let them lie Godless!'

He led the Sempringhams out of Barnwick and on to the road to the nearest village. Again Master Gilbert importuned Matthias to stay with them and he agreed. The following morning he arranged for the family to join another party of merchants making their way south to York. When he said he'd go no further, the Sempringhams, their eyes filled with tears, gathered round him in the small cobbled yard of the tavern where they had stayed the night.

'I'd best leave you now,' he said.

Mistress Margaret caught at his hand. 'I have talked to the landlord. He says there's a hermit out at Barnwick. It's you, isn't it?'

'Yes, I suppose it is.'

Master Sempringham pushed a bag of silver into his hands.

'No,' he warned as Matthias made to refuse. 'After what you have done, sir, it would be a grave insult. Please.'

'What is your name?' Elizabeth asked.

Matthias stared across at the tavern sign: the Two Brothers.

'My name is Cain,' he replied. He stared at these people, so homely, leading ordinary lives, deeply attached to each other. 'I am cursed by God,' he continued. 'I bear His mark.'

'Surely not?' Mistress Margaret put her arms round his neck and, standing on tiptoe, kissed him on each cheek. 'God will reward you,' she whispered. 'And we will never forget.'

Matthias made his farewells, collected his horse and rode out across the moorland. A slight mist was creeping in. He dismounted and stood stroking the muzzle of his horse, half-listening to the shriek of a curlew. He did not want to go back to Barnwick. Rosamund's small tomb was built and the outlaw attack had shattered his peace. Others from the gang might come and they would certainly seek vengeance. Moreover, Matthias had enjoyed the company of the Sempringhams. He should rejoin the world of men, but go where? What should he do? He stared at the leather bag hanging on his saddle horn. He had weapons and a few pathetic possessions. He'd ride south, perhaps visit London.

Matthias travelled south. He kept well away from the main trackways and paths. The journey was an uneventful one. He reached Colchester ten days later, where he stayed at the Golden Fleece tavern and hired a barber to shave his face and cut his hair, closely cropped like that of a soldier. He bought new clothes in the marketplace – sober, dull attire – and then continued his journey. Two days later he arrived at St Giles, Cripplegate, and entered London.

At first Matthias found it difficult. So many people of different sorts: madcaps, beggars, white-eyed Abraham men dancing their mad jigs along the streets. Merchants and lawyers in their wool and samite robes. The gaudily decked whores, the courtiers in their taffeta; the city toughs and bravos with their tight hose and protuberant codpieces. These walked narrow-eyed, fingers constantly tapping the hilt of their swords or daggers. The streets were dirty and packed. People moved in shoals round the stalls, which sold everything from Spanish herbs to cloths from Bruges. Fights broke out. Apprentices touted for custom, bailiffs and beadles stood in the doorways of churches and shouted their messages. Iron-wheeled carts crashed and lumbered across the cobbles. Funeral processions wound their way to the city cemeteries.

Matthias grew so dizzy he had to dismount. He stood for a while in a tavern yard, sipping at a tankard of ale to calm his stomach and soothe his wits. A party of sheriff's men ran by the gateway crying, 'Harrow! Harrow!' in pursuit of a felon against whom the hue and cry had been raised. On the corner of St Martin's Lane, just near the Shambles, an execution was being carried out: a rogue who had killed a shopkeeper was now being hanged from the sign of his victim's shop. The crowds gathered round to watch him kick in his death throes. Matthias pushed his way through. He wondered if anyone would be interested in him. In law he'd received a pardon after East Stoke but, there again, he had not served his three years at Barnwick.

Matthias made his way up, past the grim, stinking prison of Newgate. He turned right after Cock Lane into the great expanse of Smithfield. The open area in front of St Bartholomew's was fairly desolate. A group of beggars chattered beneath the huge gallows in the centre. A woman knelt before the great blackened stake where people were burnt, hands clasped, sobbing quietly to herself. Two rogues, caught selling bogus relics, had their hose removed, were tied back to back and forced to wander until darkness fell and their crime was purged. A madman ran up, a dribble of white foam coming out of the corner of his mouth. He was dressed in a dirty linen robe with a cord round his waist.

'Have you heard?' he screamed. 'The Great Whore has returned to Babylon! Her dragon has been seen in the skies! The moon will turn to blood! The stars will fall from Heaven! The Antichrist is now on his way. Have you seen him?'

A long, sharp dagger appeared from the sleeve of his gown.

'Have you seen him?' he threatened.

'Yes,' Matthias replied soothingly, 'I have. He's been taken to Newgate.'

'Thank you, thank you, brother.' The madman ran off, brandishing the knife in his hand.

A whore slipped silently up beside him, her hand going out to stroke his genitals.

'A fine cock there,' she murmured. 'And all fit for the crowing!'

'I have a loathsome disease,' Matthias replied, 'which will rot your stomach and turn you blind.'

The whore screamed an obscenity and ran off. Matthias paused and glanced around. A long line of gong carts trundled out of Little Britain, the area behind St Bartholomew's. They had just emptied the public jakes: the breeze wafted the stench, Matthias covered his mouth and nose. He glimpsed a tavern sign, the Bishop's Mitre, and made his way across. He was tired, rather disturbed by his abrupt arrival in London so he bargained with the landlord for a stable for his horse and a narrow, dank garret for himself.

Matthias spent his first two days in London eating, drinking and sleeping. Then he asked the taverner for his advice and went to St Paul's to stand by the '*Si Quis*' door where merchants, traders, noblemen and lawyers came to hire servants and maids. The place was thronged: the great central aisle full of people waiting to be hired. Matthias paid a scrivener to write a short description of his name and his skill as a clerk. Matthias pinned this to his tunic and walked around the great tomb of Duke Humphrey but, though some expressed an interest, no one would hire him. He carried no letters of accreditation and was reluctant to discuss his recent service at Barnwick.

The days passed. Matthias' supply of silver dwindled. He lost his garret but the landlord agreed, in return for Matthias doing tasks around the tavern, that he could sleep in the stable. Matthias eventually had to sell his horse and saddle but he kept his arms. He tired of walking St Paul's and spent more time out in the graveyard where the thieves and rogues of London sheltered from the sheriff's men.

One day, about a month after his arrival in London, Matthias was sitting with his back to the wall sunning himself. He was wondering if he should leave and go back to

Baron Sanguis when someone tapped his foot. He raised his head, shading his eyes, and peered up at a grizzled-faced, one-eyed man.

'God save us both, if it's not Master Matthias Fitzosbert!' The fellow crouched down. Matthias studied the narrow-seamed face, the white eye covered by a milky film, the other dancing with mischief. The man was dressed in a soiled ragged shirt, tattered leather jacket and hose. He wore two right boots of different size but Matthias noticed the sword and dirk pushed in the waistband were sharp and clean.

'Do I know you, sir?'

'Dickon,' the fellow replied. 'Don't you remember, Master? The gatehouse at Barnwick? I served as an archer there. I held you down the day . . .' the good eye began to flutter, '. . . the day young Rosamund was killed.'

Matthias closed his eyes and sighed. 'Of course!' He looked at the man. 'So, what have you been doing?'

Dickon shrugged. 'Well, when we were driven out of Barnwick, I thought that's it: no more soldiering for Dickon boy! I travelled south, a little bit of fighting here, a touch of robbery there.' Dickon was now peering at him carefully. 'I've never forgotten you, Master Fitzosbert. Even now I still tell my friends about the north tower of the keep. Do you remember it?'

'If I have to.'

'You seem down on your luck.' Dickon sat beside him.

'I'd say that was a fair assessment of my situation.'

Dickon patted him on the thigh. 'I thought you were dead.' He shifted, his good eye studying Matthias. 'But, of course, the likes of you don't die, do they? Do you have any money?' he continued.

Matthias flicked his empty wallet. 'I have what you see. And, as for food, I'd give my right arm for a meat pie and a tankard of ale.'

Dickon scrambled to his feet. 'Come on!' he urged. 'I have someone who would like to meet you.'

Matthias stayed where he was. 'Who is he?'

'Henry Emloe. He's a . . .' Dickon grinned, 'he's a merchant, a trader. You'll get more than a meat pie and a blackjack of ale from him.'

Matthias glanced round the graveyard: the tawdry stalls, the

333

mummers and the jackanapes. Perhaps it might be best to stay rather than go, cap in hand, to Baron Sanguis. He scrambled to his feet and followed Dickon out along Bowyers Row, past Blackfriars. They crossed the Fleet river and entered the tangled maze of alleyways which surrounded the great convent of Whitefriars. Matthias had never been here before. It was a small town in itself: a ward dominated by thieves, cutthroats and wolf's-heads. The great-storeyed houses were shabby and dilapidated. They rose up so close together, the lanes and alleys beneath narrow and gloomy. Ramshackle bridges stretched from one house to another. The doorways to the taverns were thronged with beggars, men and women who had good reason to hide from the law. There were no stalls, but hawkers and garishly dressed journeymen pushed their wheelbarrows around, piled high with goods and trinkets they had filched from the markets in Cheapside. Whores, guarded by their pimps, called out salacious invitations. Every so often Dickon and Matthias were stopped and asked their business. The men were some of the most depraved Matthias had ever seen: their faces showed their souls were steeped in villainy. Some bore the mutilations of previous punishments: brand marks upon their faces, slit noses and lips, their hair was often long to conceal cropped and clipped ears. A few had lost a hand or a foot. Nevertheless, they were all well armed and watchful over who passed along their respective street or alleyway. Dickon did not carry or show any pass, he simply murmured Emloe's name and these self-appointed guardians slunk back into the darkness.

Dickon brought Matthias to a house standing at the mouth of an alleyway which led down to the river. The house was four-storeyed with wooden plaster. The paint was peeling, falling like flakes into the small, overgrown garden which stood in front of it. Dickon went down the uneven pathway and rapped hard at the knocker shaped like a grinning skull. The door opened, Dickon beckoned Matthias inside.

At first, because the passageway was so gloomy, Matthias had to blink and place his hand against the wall to get his bearings. The passageway was long. The wainscoting on either side was of black shiny wood: the strip of plaster above painted purple. A few candles, also purple, burnt in bright steel holders but they created more shadow than light.

'Come on! Come on!' Dickon whispered.

Matthias followed him deep into the house. They passed chambers, then went up a broad stairway, its woodwork also painted a glossy black. Matthias felt he was entering a house of death. The drapes which hung on the walls and galleries were all sombre, sometimes lined with silver silk. However, despite the poor light and the shabby exterior, the house was opulently furnished. Woollen rugs woven together covered most of the floor and deadened any sound. Heavy drapes covered walls and doorways. The tables and benches were all carefully sculptured and, again, painted black. Matthias was about to express his concern when Dickon turned abruptly, finger to his lips.

'The walls have ears,' he murmured. 'And I mean what I say!'

They walked on. Matthias stopped to examine a painting, a man ladling out silver coins in a counting house, beside him two young women, the tops of their dresses cut low to expose full ripe breasts. Matthias pretended to be fascinated but he noticed a movement and realised that there were eyelets in the picture to allow others to peer out. Again Dickon hoarsely urged that he should hurry. Matthias was about to follow when out of the shadows stepped a man, his face hidden by a hood pulled well over his head. A sword peeped out from beneath his cloak and he carried a cudgel. Matthias bowed sardonically at this sinister, silent guard and hurried on.

The second gallery was much the same. Matthias was led into a small chamber. It had a window open: this offset the dark funereal cloths on the wall and the silver death's-head placed in the middle of a shiny table which stood in the centre of the chamber. Matthias went to the window and stared out as Dickon closed the door behind him. He glimpsed the dark swirling waters of the Thames and watched as a seagull skimmed lazily over the surface. He heard a sound and turned.

The man who stood in the doorway was very tall and angular. His black hair was closely cropped well above his ears; his long, narrow face had a lantern jaw and protruding spiky nose, thin bloodless lips and eyes as dead as pieces of glass. He was dressed like a priest, in a black gown from neck to toe, his hands hidden up the sleeves of his habit. The man bowed.

'I am Henry Emloe,' he declared softly. 'Welcome to my house. You wish some wine?'

And, before Matthias could answer, Emloe brought his hand up and clicked his fingers. Emloe continued staring at Matthias, as if memorising every single feature. A servant bustled in, his face hidden by a hood. He placed a silver tray bearing a jug and goblets on the table and scurried out. Emloe poured the wine himself. It came thick and red, swirling out like blood. He passed a cup to Matthias and toasted him.

'Welcome to my house, Matthias Fitzosbert.'

Emloe's eyes betrayed no emotion, still and glassy like those of a corpse. He sipped at his wine.

'Dickon told me about Barnwick.' The words slipped out, Emloe hardly moving his lips, talking in a guttural manner, as if that were the only exertion he could afford.

'A frightening time,' Matthias replied.

Emloe gave a crooked smile, turning his face sideways. 'You'll find London,' he taunted, 'is just as full of demons!'

24

Matthias entered Emloe's household. He had a few pricks of conscience but shrugged these off, muttering that beggars can't be choosers and, if wishes were horses, no man would walk. He was given a chamber in one of the galleries. Dickon said this was a mark of honour, most of Emloe's retainers slept in the outhouse behind the gloomy mansion. Now and again Emloe entertained Matthias in a small hall below stairs. His cooks and scullions served up the most delicious meals. Once or twice they were alone, on other occasions they were joined by whores, city courtesans and Emloe's henchmen.

Matthias soon learnt Emloe was a king of Whitefriars. He ruled by fear, with a finger in the profits of every housebreaker, foist, pickpocket and counterfeit man. Above all, he traded in stolen goods, sometimes returning these to the rightful owners for a heavy price. Or, if that was too dangerous, transporting them across to the stews in Southwark to be sold in the shabby night markets.

Emloe never interrogated Matthias, at least not outright; a question here, a question there; a tart observation or a wry comment. Yet within two weeks Emloe had created a patchwork picture of Matthias' life. He treated Matthias most courteously, as did those around him. On occasions, however, Emloe would let Matthias witness his justice, summary and ruthless. A foist who refused to hand over his profits was brought into the cobbled yard behind the house, his hands spread out on the fleshing table: three fingers were neatly sliced off, the stumps smeared with boiling hot pitch. A courtesan who had rebuffed one of Emloe's clients had her cheeks nicked with a dagger. Two ruffians who mistakenly attacked one of Emloe's acquaintances coming in from the city abruptly found themselves arrested and handed over to the sheriff's men. Matthias observed and took careful note and, apart from Dickon, he kept to himself. He never asked questions and found he was never entrusted with a task he could conscientiously refuse. Clothes, food, a chamber were provided, as well as a regular supply of silver which he entrusted to a Cheapside goldsmith. Matthias' duties were comparatively light. He would stand on guard when Emloe met mysterious, cowled figures from the city. Matthias would guide them to and from Emloe's house, carry messages to different parts of the city and, on one occasion, even as far as Canterbury. Emloe seemed to trust him except in one matter. Matthias, like the rest of the henchmen, was strictly excluded from the top gallery of the house. The stairs to this were guarded. Even Dickon, who revelled in gossip and collected as much tittle-tattle as he could, was unable to enlighten Matthias about what happened there.

Over the weeks Matthias discovered a little about his new lord. Emloe was a former priest who had been defrocked for certain nefarious practices. What was abundantly clear was that Emloe now had nothing to do with the Church or religion.

'He's an excommunicant,' an elderly priest of a small parish near the Temple confided to Matthias. 'Cut off from the Church now, and cut off from Heaven after death.' He leant closer. 'And the same goes for those who walk with him. He's a warlock, a necromancer, a raiser of the dead. He communes with spirits.'

Matthias, who had been accosted by the priest while out on one of Emloe's errands, at first rejected the accusation as scurrilous gossip. Dickon was more forthright.

'He's a master of the black arts,' the one-eyed archer whispered, 'and has been known to carry out the gibbet rites in cemeteries.'

They were sitting in a small tavern which overlooked the Thames where it curved to go down to Westminster.

'So, why do you stay with him?' Matthias asked.

'I don't intend to,' Dickon confided. 'Like you, Master Fitzosbert, I have got no place to go, no hearth I can call my own.' The archer wetted his lips. 'But it won't always be so. Like you, I have been salting away the pennies and, when I have enough, I'll be gone.'

Matthias listened, nodding wisely. He wasn't too sure

whether Dickon was a friend or a spy. He was coldly amused that Dickon had apparently followed him and knew that he was banking money with a goldsmith.

That was the last time Matthias saw Dickon alive. Three days later his drenched corpse, throat slashed from ear to ear, his face twisted into the rictus of his last agony, was wheeled on a hand barrow from the riverside into the yard behind Emloe's house. Emloe himself came down to pay his respects. An old woman was hired to dress the corpse. Emloe even bought a shiny coffin and led a line of paid mourners up to St Thomas' church. Emloe always prided himself that he looked after his kin in both life and death. Others whispered differently – that Dickon had held back certain monies and was punished.

By the middle of October Matthias had had enough. He tried not to provoke any suspicion but laid careful plans to take what monies he had banked, buy a good horse and ride as fast as he could to Gloucester. Emloe, however, kept him busy, almost as if the defrocked priest could read his thoughts. One day Matthias was summarily invited to Emloe's chamber.

'I see you are restless,' the man began brusquely. 'Do you want to leave us, Matthias?'

'Perhaps it's time I went my own way,' he replied guardedly. 'I have family elsewhere,' he lied. 'There are other things to do.'

Emloe nodded vigorously in agreement. He opened the small coffer on the table and took out a fistful of silver which he thrust into Matthias' hand.

'Then go. Don't let me keep you. But do me one favour, Matthias. Stay until the first week of November, after the month's accounts have been done. After that,' he smiled sarcastically, sketching a blessing in Matthias' direction, 'you can go with my benediction.'

Matthias agreed. Nevertheless, due to what both the priest and Dickon had told him, Matthias became more watchful as the eve of All-Hallows approached. On the festival of Samhain, witches and warlocks came into their own: if Emloe were a warlock, it would certainly be celebrated by the likes of him. Memories of what had happened at Sutton Courteny and in the north tower of Barnwick came flooding back. Matthias was pleased when, on the day in question, Emloe kept him busy sending him on this minor errand or that. Matthias decided to spend the evening away from his master in some tavern or alehouse. However, when he'd finished his last task, visiting a blacksmith in Bride Lane who owed Emloe money, he found six of his master's henchmen waiting for him in the cobbled street outside. They were all dressed in black leather jerkins and armed to the teeth. Their leader, a Portuguese named Roberto, stood, legs apart, slapping heavy leather gloves against his thighs.

'Matthias, you are to come with us.'

'Why?' Matthias stood with his back to the wall.

Roberto's men fanned out in a semi-circle around him.

'You are to dine with the Master.' The Portuguese's sallow face broke into a smile. 'You are to be his guest.'

'I had other plans.'

'Well, they can wait, can't they?' His smile faded. 'Now, Matthias.' The Portuguese stumbled on his name, which provoked a snigger from his companions. Roberto flushed and his hand fell to the hilt of his sword. 'You are to come or you are to be brought.' He shrugged. 'I don't really care.'

'How can I refuse such an invitation so prettily delivered?' Matthias gave a mock bow and walked quickly down the alleyway, forcing Roberto and the rest to break into a run to keep up with him.

Emloe was waiting for him in the hall. The table had been laid out: silver plates, golden goblets, a jewel-encrusted salt cellar. Matthias was waved to a seat. Others joined them: Emloe's principal henchmen, including Roberto, and some whom Matthias didn't recognise. The meal was eaten in silence. Afterwards Emloe led his guests upstairs and into the top gallery. Armed guards stood about. A door was unlocked and Matthias entered a long, low, sombre chamber. The walls were covered in purple drapes. The floorboards and ceiling were painted black as elsewhere in the house. The candles fixed in sconces around the wall were of pure beeswax and gave off the most fragrant of perfumes. At the far end was a dais with a small altar covered in black and silver linen cloths. Matthias' eyes grew accustomed to the gloom: the cross on the altar was upturned.

He tried to push his way back to the door but Emloe's henchmen blocked his path. The defrocked priest had now taken off his black robe; beneath were the alb and surplice of a celebrant dressed for Mass: these, however, were of a deep purple with golden stars and silver pentangles sewn on them.

'My dear Matthias, you are to stay.' Emloe tossed his employee's cloak to one of his assistants. He seized Matthias' chin between his forefinger and thumb and squeezed gently. 'You have powers, Matthias. Whether you concede to it or not. I, who am skilled in such matters, have sensed the presence around you. You are one of the chosen.' Emloe's voice thrilled with excitement, his eyes coming to life. 'Tonight is the Feast of All Witches. If we make the sacrifice, because of you, the demon will be raised.'

Matthias struggled but his hands were pinioned behind him, lashed together with a silken cord. He was forced to kneel and watch as more torches were lit and Emloe intoned the blasphemous ritual. Matthias heard the muttered words and glimpsed the purple candles lit on either side of the altar. He kept his head down now and, for the first time in months, muttered a short prayer. A cock crow was followed by the smell of freshly spilt blood, incense and heavy wine. At last the ritual was over. Emloe's henchmen squatted around the room, chanting phrases or responses when required.

Matthias opened his eyes. The muscles of his face and the back of his neck ached with pain. He grimaced and tried to stretch himself to ease the cramps. His body was damp with sweat yet the room had grown cold, reminding him of the north tower at Barnwick. Emloe and his henchmen were excited and expectant. The bloody remains of the cock, strewn over a silver platter on the altar, were quickly cleared away. Someone complained of the cold; another pointed out that some of the candles had gone out. Charcoal braziers were brought into the room and placed along one side. They blew hot and merry but still Matthias couldn't stop shivering. New cloths were laid on the altar. The most exquisite mirror, about two feet high and the same across, held fast in a frame of golden snakes which coiled and writhed around each other, was also put in a special stand on the altar. This glowed as it caught the light from the candles and brazier.

Emloe walked round the room, sprinkling incense as he chanted softly to himself. He then knelt on a red-gold tasselled cushion before the altar. Head pulled back, he stared up into the mirror. A blasphemous prayer was offered, the others joined in. Matthias tried to keep his eyes closed but found he couldn't. The mirror drew him on and he found himself falling into a trance as he watched the lights dance in the pure glass. There was silence. Emloe began a chant again, a blasphemous litany to Satan and all the armies of Hell. The lights in the mirror dimmed. Smoke curled there. Matthias' throat went dry with fear; he found it difficult to swallow. He struggled at his bonds and his fingers caught a knot less tight than the rest. He plucked at it, working it loose. The mirror was now clear again: the lights danced and then the reflection rippled like the smooth surface of a lake. Emloe stopped his chanting and held his hand up for silence. The others watched, gasping in appreciation. Matthias worked the cord loose. He kept his hands behind him despite the pain in his arms and shoulders.

'Le Seigneur is replying!' Emloe's voice was high with excitement. 'Le Seigneur has deigned to look at us!'

The chanting began again. The mirror became black as if someone had thrown a cloak over it. Matthias watched intently. The darkness began to move, shift like fire smoke. A head appeared, lifting upwards, its eyes glowed, its mouth, half-open, had a small snake of blood running out of one corner, a ghoulish creature. Matthias shivered and closed his eyes as he recognised the Preacher. Other faces appeared, equally terrifying. Rahere the clerk, his arrogant, handsome features now twisted and leering. Santerre with his mocking eyes, Fitzgerald sneering. Emloe and his companions sat back on their heels staring in disbelief. The faces were frightening, disembodied heads, lips moving and cursing, eyes full of malevolence.

Emloe crowed softly with pleasure, already seeing himself as a great magus. Matthias recognised the danger signs. The Rose Demon was making his presence felt. Suddenly the braziers began to crackle, sparks began to fly up. Matthias shook his gaze from the mirror. The sparks grew more plentiful, combining in the air to make small balls of fire, rising like bubbles from a cauldron. These grew larger. One caught the mirror. It shattered. Other small balls of fire circled the room. Matthias saw one pass in front of his eyes: he recognised in it the tortured face of Amasia. The crackling braziers were now shooting out sparks, small tongues of flame. Emloe stood up, hands outstretched. He was still crowing in triumph when some of the fire caught at an arras on the wall. In seconds this was engulfed by a sheet of flame. Other sparks hit Emloe's henchmen, setting fire to clothes.

Matthias sprang to his feet. He reached the door and fled out into the gallery. The guards ran to stop him but he knocked them aside, and by the time he reached the top of the stairs the fire had distracted them. Matthias ran down to his own chamber. He picked up his war belt, took what coins he had from his secret hiding-place and continued his flight. From the noise around him, the fire was spreading quickly. Matthias slipped through the kitchen, out by a postern door and into an alleyway. The curfew bell had long sounded and he could see the beacon light glowing from the steeple of St Mary Le Bow. Matthias ran up the alleyway. No one accosted him. Shadows moved from doorways but, when Matthias was recognised as one of Emloe's henchmen, he was allowed safely on his way.

He spent the night out at Smithfield, sleeping beneath the hedgerows. The following morning he returned to the Bishop's Mitre in Smithfield where he broke his fast and rehired his small garret.

Only when he was there, wrapped in blankets lying on the small pallet bed, did Matthias accept the full horror of what had happened. He slept fitfully, slipping in and out of dreams: of darkened chambers, glowing arrows of fire, men turned to human torches, dark shapes, the haunting voice of the hermit and those faces he had glimpsed in the balls of flame. Matthias got up late in the afternoon. He felt dull-headed, his stomach rather queasy. He understood what had happened during the Satanic rites the night before. Emloe, like any sorcerer, believed he could control the Powers of Darkness where, in fact, they were mocking his puny efforts. The ghosts of those possessed by the Rose Demon still hung around Matthias and, when provided with the opportunity, malevolently involved themselves in the affairs of men.

'I am not alone,' he whispered. 'I must remember that. I am never alone.'

Matthias went down to the taproom. He studied the hour candle in the inglenook above the fireplace and realised it was much later than he thought, between four and five in the afternoon. He hurried out, back through the city gates past Newgate, pushing his way through the market crowds to the goldsmith's shop which stood within the shadows of the hospital of St Thomas of Acon. Matthias was resolved to withdraw all his monies, buy a fresh horse and put as much distance between himself and London as possible. Nevertheless, he moved cautiously. He stepped into the hospital doorway and watched the crowds. A wild beggar, claiming he was St John the Baptist, came bounding along: in one hand a wooden cross, in the other a burning brand. He was screaming and yelling that Satan was in the city and, like Nineveh of old, the citizens should repent and don sackcloth and ashes. The crowd shifted and made a path to let him through. Matthias' heart sank: at least half a dozen of Emloe's bullyboys were watching the entrance to the goldsmith's.

Matthias cursed his own stupidity at leaving it so long. He slipped back down an alleyway. He stopped at the alehouse which stood in Paternoster Row, just next to St Paul's Cathedral. Matthias raged at himself and the obstacles placed in his path. Emloe must have survived the previous night: he was apparently more concerned about getting his hands on Matthias again than he was about any damage caused to his sinister mansion.

Matthias drank more than he had intended. When he lurched out of the tavern, it was dark: the stalls had been put away, only the hucksters and the tinkers tried to interest him in their gewgaws. Whores called out from the doorways. Somewhere a child cried and two women burst out of a doorway, hitting and kicking each other. The debtors from the Fleet, chained together and sent out to beg for alms, were now being rounded up. As he passed the cemetery of St Paul's, Matthias paused and listened to a choir of beautiful-voiced boys singing the acclamation '*Christus Vincit*'. Matthias threw them a penny. He walked along Eel-Pie Alleyway and stopped: further down a group of men were struggling. One broke free.

'I am a Franciscan!' the man yelled. 'I collect for the poor! I am Christ's good priest!'

The three rifflers, however, closed again, tugging at the pouch on his girdle. The friar, a small, wiry individual, broke

344

free and ran towards Matthias. He grasped his arm, his small, nut-brown face soaked in sweat.

'I am a friar,' he gasped. 'I am unarmed.' And then, as if it were an after-thought, 'I am also very small.'

Matthias, still full of ale, grinned good-naturedly back.

'On your way!' The three rifflers now blocked his path.

Matthias stared at them.

'On your way!' the middle one repeated.

Matthias' hand went to his sword. He gazed at their ugly faces and the rage he felt for Emloe surged against these night birds blocking his path.

'Well, well, well.' Matthias took a step backwards, pulling the Franciscan with him. 'Never have I seen three such ugly gallows carrion.'

His assailants attacked. Matthias had his sword and dagger out. He caught the leading assailant a savage gash in the side of his neck. The other two closed: Matthias' sword took one in the thigh whilst he struck with his dagger at the other. He heard the Franciscan scream and turned, just in time, to meet a fourth assailant who seemed to appear from nowhere and came at him, dagger up. Matthias ducked, stabbing out with his sword but the blade took him in the shoulder. The pain made him yell and, losing all control, Matthias lashed out with his sword.

'They've gone! They've gone!'

Matthias calmed down. The pain in his shoulder was searing. He crouched against the wall of a house, gasping for breath. Two of his assailants lay on the cobbles in spreading pools of blood.

'The other two have gone,' the Franciscan remarked. 'For a while you were just beating the air.' He helped Matthias to his feet. 'That was good of you.'

He prised the sword and dagger out of Matthias' hand and pushed them back into their scabbards. Matthias swayed, the cobbles seemed to shift. The pain in his shoulder now reached the back of his neck. He felt sick and weak.

'You'd best come with me,' the Franciscan murmured.

He put Matthias' arm round his neck. They hobbled out of the alleyway past the Chancellor's Inn and along to Greyfriars.

'My name is Father Anthony,' the Franciscan gasped as he helped Matthias through the small postern gate, up through the darkened, sweet-smelling garden and into the cloisters. 'I am infirmarian and almoner.'

Matthias paused and stared down at his benefactor. The friar's round, kindly face was wreathed in concern.

'You'd best come with me,' Father Anthony murmured. 'If that dagger were dirty, the wound might not be clean!'

He helped Matthias along stone-paved corridors and stopped to ring a small bell. Other brothers appeared, heavy-eyed from their slumbers. They helped Father Anthony take Matthias along the cloister and into a small, white-washed chamber. They threw a canvas sheet over a small trestle bed and laid Matthias down. His boots and war belt were removed, then his jerkin and his shirt. He struggled but a cup was held to his lips. He tasted a bittersweet potion and fell into a deep sleep.

When Matthias awoke, sunlight filled the chamber. A vacuous-faced lay brother looked down at him. The man muttered something. His voice seemed far off, as if he were speaking down a tunnel. Again the cup was forced between Matthias' lips. He felt for the wound in his shoulder but it was numb. He gazed at the stark crucifix on the far wall. For some strange reason he thought he was back at his father's church in Sutton Courteny and then he fell asleep again. This time he dreamt. Nothing frightening: he was chasing a goose along the village street. It ran into the Hungry Man tavern where Agatha Merryfeet was dancing barefoot on the table. Matthias gazed around, recognising his father's parishioners.

'I must go home,' he declared. 'Father and Mother will be anxious.'

'Then, if you have to go, you should,' John the bailiff declared.

'Run like the wind!' Piers the ploughman shouted from the inglenook. 'Run as fast as you can, Matthias. Your father is waiting.'

Fulcher the blacksmith helped him to the door. Joscelyn the taverner pushed a piece of sweet bread into his hands. Matthias ran down the street and up the path to his house. The door was open, but when he went into the kitchen it was cold and dark. The windows were broken, the ceiling open to the night sky. Parson Osbert was sitting in his favourite chair but he was cloaked and cowled.

'Father.' Matthias went towards him.

Parson Osbert looked up, his kindly face was sad, his eyes seemed to search Matthias' soul.

'Father, what are you doing here?'

'I am dead, Matthias.'

Matthias crouched down beside him.

'Father, do you sleep when you die?'

Parson Osbert shook his head. 'No, you don't sleep, Matthias, you travel.'

'And where have you been, Father? I've missed you. I've missed Christina. I want my mother!'

Parson Osbert smiled. 'She travels ahead of us, Matthias. I cannot yet continue.'

'Why? Where have you been, Father?'

'I have visited every monastery, every friary in the world. I kneel in front of their altars and pray for you and for me.'

'Why, Father? What is wrong?'

'You'll know soon enough, Matthias.'

His father got up and walked towards the door.

'Come back! Come back!' Matthias shouted.

He tried to follow but he couldn't. Someone was holding him back. He opened his eyes. Father Anthony was staring down at him, brown eyes smiling.

'Matthias, Matthias,' he whispered, 'you were having a dream.'

Matthias lay back against the bolsters.

'How long have I been asleep?'

'Three days.' Father Anthony pulled up a stool and sat beside the bed.

Matthias pulled his shoulder and felt a slight twinge of pain.

'Oh, don't worry about that.' The friar patted his hand. 'It was deep but small. We've cleaned and tended it.' The friar chewed the corner of his lip. 'We gave you a potion to make you sleep but we thought something else was wrong. You seemed unwilling to wake.' He patted his hand. 'You had a bellyful of ale but you must have been very, very tired.'

Matthias stretched his legs. 'I feel very, very hungry,' he grinned.

The friar left and returned with a tray bearing a bowl of steaming broth, small chunks of bread, a dish of vegetables and a goblet of watered wine. The savoury smell whetted

Matthias' hunger. He ate ravenously and shame-facedly asked for more.

'Of course! Of course!'

More food was brought. Matthias ate. He felt tired again and dozed for a while but, when he awoke, felt stronger. He spent the next two days in bed and found he couldn't forget the dream about his father. The Franciscan seemed fascinated by him and, whenever his duties allowed, he'd slip into the chamber to chat about the affairs of the Friary. Slowly, gradually, he also began to probe as to where Matthias was from and what he was doing in that alleyway.

'You had strange dreams, Matthias. The things you talked about . . .'

Matthias smiled and shrugged.

'Are you a soldier?' the Franciscan asked.

Matthias told him about Barnwick.

'And Rosamund?'

Matthias fell silent and, though he tried, he could not stop the tears brimming.

'She's dead, isn't she?'

'Yes, Father, she died.'

Matthias leant his head back against the wall and, eyes on the crucifix, told this Franciscan everything. Father Anthony listened intently. Now and again, he'd scratch his small white moustache and beard or run his fingers slowly up and down the side of his nose.

'You're hearing my confession, Father.'

'Yes, I know I am.'

Matthias then continued. Occasionally the Franciscan would ask Matthias the same question: in that situation, whatever it was, be it Emloe or his bloody confrontation with the outlaws in the ruins of Barnwick, what did Matthias want? What did he wish? Matthias sometimes had to pause as he sifted amongst his memories.

'You remind me of the hermit,' he declared, half-jokingly. 'He always said it was the will that matters. What you really wanted, rather than your actual acts.'

'And that is true,' Father Anthony replied. 'Do you believe in God? Do you believe in the Lord Jesus?'

'I don't know,' Matthias replied. 'As I live, Father, I don't really know and, sometimes, I don't really care. I, Matthias

Fitzosbert, am a parson's son. I trained to be a clerk and I have served as a soldier. As a man I love books and libraries. I like green fields, good food and a goblet of wine. I would love to go fishing or for a walk in the meadow. I wish I had friends, a place I could call my own. I am ordinary and I wish to be ordinary but life, the Rose Demon or whatever, will not leave me alone. I want to be free. I want to be free of all these shadows: the likes of Emloe, Fitzgerald, Douglas.' Matthias put his face in his hands. 'I try to break free but, whenever I do, I am always dragged back. So, Father,' he looked at the friar, 'that is my confession. What is my penance?'

Father Anthony lifted his hand and recited the words of absolution, making the sign of the cross over Matthias' head.

'Your penance is your life,' he murmured. 'This crisis, Matthias, is your life. You cannot escape it!'

25

Father Anthony gazed beseechingly at Matthias.

'One day,' he said, 'you must make a choice. You can either accept this Rose Demon, and whatever his love means to you, or you can continue this struggle, this savage battle against bitterness, heartbreak and sorrow.' He smiled wanly. 'So far you seem to have made the right choice but, at a certain time, in a certain place, you must make the final choice.'

'Is that all my life means?' Matthias spat the words out.

'Yes. There will be no Matthias Fitzosbert the clerk, the family man, the husband, the father. No Matthias the bibliophile, the scholar, the man who likes fishing or collecting apples on the dew-soft grass of an orchard. Oh, you will eat and you will drink, you will sleep, you may love, you may fight but the constant theme in your life will be this terrible struggle.

'Why?' Matthias pulled himself up on the bed. He flailed his hands. 'Why me?'

'Why not?' Father Anthony replied. 'Do you think you are alone? Don't you ever think that someone like myself would like to be a father, a lover, a poet, a troubadour? Do you know what it's like to wake in the early hours and be alone? To do good and be attacked in an alleyway? To pray into the darkness and get no reply?'

Matthias leant over and gently stroked the friar's cheek.

'I am sorry,' he apologised.

'Such self-pity is no sin,' the friar replied. 'Even Christ protested that he hadn't got a home to call his own or a pillow to lay his head on! It only becomes a sin when you wallow in it and make it a way of life.'

'So, what should I do?' Matthias asked.

'Accept each day as it comes but try and plan for the future. Your association with the Rose Demon seems to begin with

Hospitallers. The hermit claimed to have been one and, you say, he met another Hospitaller in Tewkesbury who fought for the House of Lancaster.'

'Yes, that's true.'

'Now, across Smithfield,' Father Anthony continued, 'lies the Priory of St John of Jerusalem, the Mother House of the Hospitaller Order in England. I will write you a letter of introduction to Sir Edmund Hammond, the present Grand Master, a saintly man, shrewd and trustworthy. Tell your tale to him. God knows what other secrets the Priory may hold.'

Matthias agreed.

'I can provide you with new clothes,' Father Anthony continued. 'I have also checked your purse; you have little money.'

'A goldsmith in Cheapside holds £120 sterling,' Matthias explained, 'but the shop is watched by Emloe's gang.'

'That can be resolved.' The friar got to his feet. 'I will bring parchment and quill. You write out a letter handing over the entire amount held by the goldsmith to our Friary.' He smiled. 'In return, we will raid our coffers and give you that amount before you leave.'

Two days later Matthias, dressed in new clothes, a stout leather money belt wrapped around his waist, accompanied Father Anthony across the cloisters and into a little side chapel. It was no more than a white-washed cell. A small altar stood against the far wall: a statue of the Virgin and Child on one side and, on the other, a life-size effigy of St Anthony of Padua holding the Baby Jesus.

'This is a chantry chapel,' the friar explained, 'where I say Mass. Often my duties prevent me from joining the brothers in the main church.'

He genuflected to the crucifix and took Matthias across to kneel first before the statue of the Virgin, where he lit a candle, and then before the statue of St Anthony of Padua.

'He is my patron,' the friar declared. 'Anthony of Padua was one of St Francis' first disciples, a great preacher, a formidable scholar. He was gentle to all, a mystic with a profound love of God and the incarnate Lord. He's a wonder worker. Anything you ask him is never refused.'

Matthias stared up into the carved, serene face of this most famous Franciscan. The sculptor had carved an angelic, smooth-faced young man, the tonsure carefully cut, the eyes almost liquid in their gentleness. In one hand he carried a lily, in the other the Baby Jesus. Matthias found it difficult to believe that praying in front of this statue could help him, but he humoured the friar and, for a while, knelt then crossed himself and got to his feet.

'I must be going,' he said briskly. 'I thank you for your kindnesses.'

The friar caught him by the sleeve. 'I shall remember you at Mass every day, Matthias. Each evening I shall come and talk to St Anthony about you. I know you don't believe, Matthias, but, at the appointed time, when the battle lines are drawn, if you keep faith, if you fight the good fight, help will come.'

A few minutes later, Matthias, Father Anthony's good wishes still ringing in his ears, left Greyfriars. He kept to the alleyways and side streets and made his way across Farringdon, past the Bishop of Ely inn towards the great gatehouse of the Priory of St John of Jerusalem. Matthias felt strange to be away from the harmonious atmosphere of the Franciscans. He did his best to avoid the people thronging round the market stalls or pouring into Smithfield because it was Execution Day and the death carts were bringing the usual batch of prisoners for execution. Every so often he would stop and look round but no one was following him. The soldier on duty at the Priory gate waved him in: a servitor sitting in the garden beyond, trying to catch the last of the autumn sun, took Father Anthony's letter. They went across an enclosed courtyard where fountains splashed, through a maze of tiled corridors and up a broad, wooden staircase to the Commander's quarters.

For a while Matthias just kicked his heels in a small vestibule. He refused the watered wine and sweetmeats offered and went to look out of the window at the clipped box hedges and neatly laid out herb gardens of the Priory. He saw the trees were beginning to lose their leaves and realised how little notice he took of the seasons. Despite the sun, autumn was turning into winter and Matthias idly wondered what other horrors would be waiting for him before the year ended. He doubted whether the Hospitallers could help him. He had already resolved to collect his few belongings from the Bishop's Mitre and return to Baron Sanguis. Perhaps the old manor lord could . . .

'Matthias Fitzosbert?'

He turned. The man standing in the doorway was of middle stature, silver hair swept back over his head to lie thick around the nape of his neck. His face was burnt dark by the sun, his moustache and beard were neatly clipped in a military fashion. Matthias couldn't reckon his age. He was struck by the sheer intensity of the man's gaze.

'Matthias Fitzosbert?' he repeated, hitching the heavy furred robe closer round his shoulders.

'Yes, sir!'

The Hospitaller smiled and held out his hand.

'I am Sir Edmund Hammond.' He patted the robe. 'I am sorry I am swaddled like a baby but I spent most of my years in Cyprus and Malta. London will be the death of me.'

'You seem to know me, sir.'

The Hospitaller opened his mouth to reply but paused and instead beckoned Matthias into a small, wooden panelled chamber. The windows were shuttered, a fire roared under the canopied hearth and chafing dishes, full of hot coals, stood around the room. A servitor came in and, under Sir Edmund's directions, moved high-backed chairs in front of the fire. A small table was set between, and cups, brimming with white wine, were served and placed there. Sir Edmund waited until the servant closed the door behind him.

'I know it is very hot,' he smiled. 'If you want, Matthias, take off your sword belt and jerkin; come and sit down.'

Matthias obeyed. For a while the Grand Master just sipped at his wine, cradling the cup between his fingers.

'I don't know you, Matthias Fitzosbert,' he began. 'But I know of you. The execution of Sir Raymond Grandison at Tewkesbury eighteen years ago, the consequent massacre at Sutton Courteny, not to mention the death by burning of Sir Raymond's brother, Otto. Oh yes,' he caught the surprise in Matthias' face, 'they were brothers, Hospitallers. As young knights they were given a most sacred task to carry out before Constantinople fell to the Turks. They failed. The Rose Demon Father Anthony alludes to in his letter was, by their mistake, once again released into the world of men. Sir Raymond spent the rest of his life scouring Europe. He discovered that the Rose Demon was in England, so he tied his fortunes to those of Margaret of Anjou and the House of

Lancaster.' The Hospitaller sipped from his wine. 'You know what happened to him. His brother, Otto, decided to live a life of reparation as a hermit out on the rock of Masada above the Dead Sea in Palestine. Otto disappeared. He was later seen in England, but there's no doubt that by then the Rose Demon had become incarnated in him. He was the hermit the villagers of Sutton Courteny burnt to death.' He sighed. 'I suspect that the royal clerk Rahere was also possessed.'

Matthias put his wine cup down. He felt a thrill of excitement. For the first time ever, he was talking to someone who regarded the Rose Demon as a matter of fact, as a great danger which must be confronted.

The Hospitaller was watching Matthias closely. 'I am only telling the little I know. The existence of the Rose Demon is one of the great secrets of our Order. There's someone who knows more. Someone you may later meet. First I want to hear your story, from the beginning until now.'

Matthias forgot about the cloying warmth of the room. This time he told his life story in precise tones. He described scenes from his life as he would a painting or a carving. Now and again he would pause to sip at the wine or answer the occasional question. When he had finished, Sir Edmund sat, elbows propped on the arms of the chair, his fingers rubbing the side of his temple. He did not look up. Matthias sensed the Hospitaller was frightened, as if Matthias had said something which was most important though its significance was lost on him.

'You should go back.' The Hospitaller Commander got to his feet. His face was grey, his tone harsh. 'You should go back to Sutton Courteny.'

'Why?' Matthias asked. 'You said there was someone else who might help?'

'There is, but not now. You cannot see her.' The Commander walked across to a side table to refill his goblet. He came back and gingerly did the same for Matthias as if the old soldier wished to keep his distance. 'There is a great mystery about what you have told me. First, did Parson Osbert ever keep a record?'

Matthias recalled the small, black and gold Book of Hours or breviary his father always carried. Sometimes he would make notes there, sermons or thoughts which occurred to him. Matthias rubbed his mouth. Strange, after his mother's death Matthias couldn't remember his father either holding or using the breviary.

'You also say the hermit carved runes, strange marks on the wall in the derelict church at Tenebral?'

'Yes,' Matthias replied.

'Go back there and copy them down,' the Hospitaller commanded. 'You are a clerk. Take quill and parchment. Copy them as accurately as you would a charter or a letter and, when you have done this, return here. If possible, try to find any record of your father's past.' Sir Edmund gazed at Matthias, as if he couldn't really decide who the clerk was or claimed to be. 'That is all the help I can give,' he concluded. 'At least for the time being.'

He did not shake Matthias' hand. Indeed, the Hospitaller seemed eager to get him out of his chamber, away from the Priory as swiftly as possible. Matthias felt angry and embarrassed but the Hospitaller's advice did not conflict with what he had already decided.

The sun was setting, the evening turning cold, so he walked briskly across Smithfield and into the musty, darkened taproom of the Bishop's Mitre.

Matthias informed the landlord that he would be leaving that evening before the curfew sounded. He settled his account and followed the landlord out into the courtyard. Matthias inspected the horseflesh kept in the stables and brought out a sturdy, berry-brown mount which seemed sound of wind. Matthias checked the horse's mouth and feet and declared himself satisfied, though he did not question the landlord too closely on where the horse came from. More haggling followed before Matthias was able to buy back the saddle and harness he had sold to the taverner when he had first arrived in the city. The fellow, pleased at making such a profitable sale, offered Matthias, free of charge, a small garret for the night.

'You can also have a free meal and break your fast tomorrow,' he urged. 'It will be far better than riding dark, windswept roads.'

Matthias agreed. He trotted his new horse around the cobbled yard to make sure that he had spent his silver well, checked the saddle and harness and returned to the taproom.

He had supper with the rest at the common board and went up to his garret where he carefully packed his saddlebags, lay down on his bed and fell into a dreamless sleep. He woke late the next morning, more refreshed and determined to leave as soon as possible. He ate bread and cheese in the taproom and, hiring a razor and a jug of hot water, returned to his garret to finish his preparations. The landlord was not as jovial as the night before but Matthias ignored that. He carefully shaved and was about to dry himself when the water in the bowl rippled and moved. Matthias stared, fascinated, at the shapes which appeared, as if he were looking through a window or staring into a mirror. The scene was commonplace. He recognised the stable in the yard below. He saw the berry-brown horse he had bought and his saddle and harness on a peg in the wall above the stall. Two men were talking to the landlord. They turned. Matthias' heart skipped a beat: he recognised Roberto and another of Emloe's henchmen. They had their war belts on. The landlord said something, they nodded then separated, going into the shadows at each end of the stable. Matthias touched the water and the scene disappeared. He dried his hands and face, put his war belt on, picked up the saddlebags and his small arbalest.

When he crossed the taproom, the landlord refused to meet his gaze but turned his back. Matthias went out. He placed his saddlebag and cloak on the ground, set a bolt in the groove of the crossbow, pulling back the cord, and walked into the darkened stable. He heard a sound from his right: the assassin came at a run. Matthias loosed the crossbow and the bolt took the man full in the chest, sending him crashing back against the stalls. The horses reared and neighed. Matthias turned, throwing the crossbow at Roberto's head as he slipped silently towards him. It missed, the Portuguese moving sideways. Matthias drew his sword and dagger and stood back.

'Leave!' he pleaded. 'Roberto, I don't want your death. Go back and tell Emloe we are finished!'

'Master Fitzosbert, you know I cannot do that. An order is an order.'

'Please!' Matthias begged.

Roberto rushed in, sword and dagger snaking out. Matthias countered, they drew apart. Again they closed in a clash of steel but the Portuguese was an indifferent swordsman.

Matthias was able to block and, with one counterparry, thrust his dagger deep into Roberto's belly. He pulled it out. Roberto staggered, bending over double, coughing on his own blood and fell with a groan to the ground. Matthias collected his cloak and saddlebag, then saddled his horse. As he left the stable, the landlord came running out, all a-fluster.

'Lackaday! Lackaday!' he cried. 'What's happening here?'

'You are a liar,' Matthias declared, swinging himself into the saddle. He gathered the reins. 'You can send for the sheriff but then he might want to know why two assassins were waiting in your stables. Or you can send a courier to Master Emloe but he will ask why I expected to find his two men waiting for me. All in all,' Matthias turned his horse's head, 'you are in for a very interesting day.'

Matthias left the city, riding up Aldersgate. After Charterhouse the houses became sparser, the crowds less dense. By noon he was out in the open countryside, taking the road west. He rode hard and fast, stopping occasionally to rest, feed and water his horse. At night he sheltered in a wayside tavern, the occasional friary and, on one occasion, slept in a small copse.

Five days after leaving London, he glimpsed the spire of Tewkesbury Abbey and, a short while later, urged his horse up trackways and passageways he remembered from boyhood days. Matthias felt the bitter sweetness of nostalgia as certain landmarks brought back memories of Parson Osbert or Christina. He avoided Sutton Courteny and Tenebral but took a more circuituous route to Baron Sanguis' manor house. This was much decayed. The curtain wall had gaps in it. The gates hung askew. No soldiers stood on guard. Matthias glimpsed only a few servants, whilst the outlying barns and granges looked dilapidated. The manor house was no better: the paths leading to it were choked with weeds. The gardens had not been tilled, the windows were all shuttered and the paint on the front door was cracked and peeling. A servant answered his knock. Matthias asked for Taldo the seneschal.

'He's dead,' the old man replied mournfully. 'All are dead.'

'And Baron Sanguis?'

'Who are you?'

'A friend from London.'

'Then you'd best come in. Baron Sanguis has few friends now.'

The old manor lord was crouched on a chair before a fire in his shabby solar. Matthias was shocked by his appearance. Sanguis' face was lined and seamed. He was rheumy-eyed, his hair fell in greasy locks and for a while he just peered at Matthias, who wondered if the old man's wits were wandering.

'I am Matthias Fitzosbert,' he repeated. 'You remember, my lord, Parson Osbert's son? I came here often as a boy. You gave me sweetmeats.'

The old man's fingers flew to his lips.

'Has the devil come again?' he asked, staring blankly at Matthias. 'They say the devil flew down to Sutton Courteny. He killed the entire village. My lands are cursed, my family's cursed. My boy was killed at Bosworth and the new King in London has never forgiven me.' He gripped the arm of his chair with his rheumatic fingers. 'I was the King's good servant,' he pleaded as with himself. 'I fought under York's banner.' He scratched his unshaven chin. 'But Satan crept in to Sutton Courteny and my fortunes changed. You say you are Matthias Fitzosbert. No, he died with the rest. You can't be. They are all dead!'

Matthias bowed and made his way back to the door.

'Wait!'

He turned. The old manor lord was now standing up, hands outstretched.

'You are not to go there,' he warned. 'Stay well away from Sutton Courteny. The place is thronged with ghosts.'

The old servant was waiting outside in the hallway.

'His wits have wandered?' Matthias asked.

'Sometimes,' the fellow replied dourly. 'Yet he speaks the truth. It's common legend how Satan swept into Sutton Courteny and everything changed. The old lord's right. I heard him shouting. You should not go there.'

Matthias collected his horse and left the manor. For a while he became lost but he remembered the forest trackways and found the path leading to the woods. He reached Tenebral late in the afternoon. Sharp memories flooded back. Nature was busy reclaiming its own. The houses were more ruined, some had disappeared altogether. Bushes and brambles now choked doorways and windows, and crept over walls to cover gardens.

Matthias dismounted and hobbled his horse. He searched out the place where the hermit had taken him to see the young foxes but this was all hidden by gorse and bramble so Matthias returned to what had been the old high street and made his way up to the ruined church. Part of the wall had now crumbled, the lych-gate had disappeared, but the church, with its ruined doorway and nave open to the sky, had changed little. Matthias made his way carefully down the path. He stopped and looked over his shoulder. He remembered his father standing there that terrible morning when they had reached Tenebral and Matthias believed Parson Osbert was going to kill him.

'I am sorry,' Matthias murmured. 'I am truly sorry.'

He entered the church and made his way up into the sanctuary. He expected to see the rose on the wall much faded but the colours were as fresh and as vigorous as if they had been painted the day before. Matthias exclaimed in surprise at how beautiful and exquisite, how precise had been the hermit's work. The rose was large and red; the golden centre still glowed like a sun whilst the silver stem had all the freshness of a dewy spring morning. Matthias crouched down and studied the runes written in column after column beneath the rose. He touched the lettering and wondered what they meant. Why had the hermit taken so much time, so much care with these?

He went out and brought back his horse. As he led the animal into the overgrown cemetery and through the doorway of the church, it abruptly became restive, shaking its head, rearing and Matthias had to stroke it and speak softly to it. He cut some of the wild grass from the cemetery and created a makeshift stall. He then unsaddled his horse and took the harness and his saddlebag up into the sanctuary.

He reckoned he had a few hours of daylight. Matthias started copying the runes as faithfully and as quickly as he could. He did not want to reflect on what this place meant to him, how it had changed and shattered his life. He had reflected and thought enough. Since leaving Oxford, apart from his time with Rosamund, he had wasted his life over too much brooding. He required answers and assistance. If he brought this information back to the Hospitallers, perhaps some solace, some comfort, or at least some explanation, would be given.

He crouched, using the saddlebag as a rest, his pieces of parchment spread out over it. Matthias quickly drew the rose and faithfully copied the symbols inscribed beneath it. He had to rest, his neck and arms becoming cramped and tired.

He stared up at the darkening sky and wondered about what had happened just before he had left London. The Rose Demon had come to his assistance once again. If it had not been for that vision, Emloe's men would either have taken him prisoner or killed him. Matthias got up and walked vigorously the length and breadth of the church, stretching his arms, easing the cramp. He went out and stood in the doorway. Daylight was fading. The breeze had turned sharp and cold. He looked further down the ruined village and glimpsed the first faint tendrils of a mist creeping in.

Matthias decided to stay the night. He collected some brush-wood, made a fire and took out the food he had bought on his journey to Sutton Courteny. He lit a second fire beneath the markings on the wall. He worked as faithfully as he could until, fearful he might make some mistake, he decided he would finish the task in the morning. He went down and checked his horse. The animal seemed to have lost its early fears.

Matthias heard a sound. He spun round. Two figures stood in the sanctuary, grey shapes, cloaked and hooded. Matthias could not make out their faces or who they were.

Matthias felt no fear but walked back. He drew his sword, not knowing whether these were phantasms or real. The figures turned and he realised they'd had their backs to him. They started to move towards him – not a run or charge but gliding swiftly across the ruined church floor. Matthias held his sword up. As they came towards him they parted. He glimpsed features hidden deep in a hood, pasty white with black-rimmed eyes. Matthias recognised one of the assassins he had killed in the Bishop's Mitre. Swerving abruptly, he glanced at the other and recognised the corpse-like face of Roberto. A rush of cold wind wafted a smell of rottenness with them. By the time he had recovered his wits, the phantasms had disappeared.

Matthias stood in the centre of the church, chest heaving. He wiped the sweat from his brow and stared around but he could neither see nor hear anything untoward. He crouched down, gasping for breath, forcing himself to relax and soothe his mind. The occurrence reminded him of that journey back to Sutton Courteny, when he had sat on the saddle of the hermit's horse and seen that line of ghosts coming towards him. Of course it was dusk, the same time of day as then. The visions were not threatening, apart from a malevolent glance, and did no injury. He went and sat on the cracked steps of the sanctuary. He recalled a lecture he had attended at Oxford, the words of a Master, 'The dead, for a while, always stay with us.' But why did he see such phantasms? And would he see any more?

Matthias returned and built up a fire. He decided after all to continue his copying but this time more slowly, more carefully. He gasped when he reached one line. By now he recognised that these signs made up words, with gaps between them. He already suspected he had copied his own name but now he was certain that he had copied that of Rosamund. There were nine symbols in all. The hermit had carved a small flower and, in the poor light, Matthias believed this was the shape of a rose. He put the parchment and quill down, carefully screwing on the top of the small ink pot. He sat chewing on the bread and meat he had laid out. Now and again taking mouthfuls from the wineskin.

'How could that be?' he asked. 'How could the hermit have known about Rosamund?' He stared up. The sky was overcast, no stars, no moon. 'How could that be?' he murmured again. 'When these symbols were written I was only a child!' He threw more wood on to the fire, watching it snap and break: the hungry flames danced high.

'Matthias, is that you?'

He scrambled to his feet. The voice came from the far end of the church as if someone were standing in the doorway. Matthias took a burning brand from the fire and walked down.

'Matthias, is that you? Why do you trouble me?'

He stopped, holding the burning ember out in front of him as far as he could.

'Matthias!'

The voice became more insistent. A woman's voice. Matthias' mouth went dry. At first he couldn't place it, but that slight stumble with the letter M.

'Amasia!' he called.

'Just ignore her!' A voice spoke from behind.

Matthias spun round. He held the torch up and, for a few seconds, glimpsed the grinning face of Santerre. Matthias returned to the fire. He threw more wood on and sat for a while, hands over his ears. He must have crouched for an hour whilst voices from his distant past, those who had been caught up in this deadly game, shouted his name through the darkness.

26

By midnight the voices had stopped. Matthias was left in peace. He slept fitfully and, when he awoke, a thick mist had swirled up the nave of the ruined church. Matthias built up the fire, broke his fast on the sparse rations left, then finished copying the runes from the wall. After he had finished, he saddled his horse and rode back to the manor to buy fresh supplies. The servant he had met the day before was generous in the portions he allocated, wrapping them up in linen cloths.

'We have few visitors here.' His watery eyes smiled. 'Baron Sanguis still does not know who you are.'

'What will happen?' Matthias asked, gazing round the dusty, cluttered kitchen.

'I doubt if the old lord will survive the winter. And the royal lawyers are waiting. He'll hardly be cold in his grave when the Exchequer officials arrive to claim all this for the Crown.'

Matthias thanked him and left. He took the pathway to Sutton Courteny. The mist still hung thick, deadening all sound. Matthias soon found himself in the woods. Memories flooded back: how he used to run and play here before the hermit ever arrived. The night the soldiers attacked him: the hermit's intervention and how, as a boy, he'd run, lungs fit to burst, to warn the hermit of what the villagers were planning.

Matthias was in Sutton Courteny before he knew it, the hanging stone looming up before him. The gibbet, which soared above it, still stood firm. A piece of rope, the strands decaying, danced in the morning breeze. Matthias rode on. He stopped outside the Hungry Man tavern. He dismounted and looked through where the sturdy front door had once hung. He couldn't stop the tears flowing. The last time he had been here was on that dreadful night when the storm had broken.

Matthias walked on. He felt as if he were a ghost walking through the Valley of Death. He could remember everything as it was and yet, despite the mist, see so precisely what it had become. The blacksmith's house, the crumbling forge; the prosperous tenement of John the bailiff, its roof long disappeared, the gardens around it overgrown. No sound broke the silence except the slither of his boots and the creak of harness. Now and again the horse would slip on the mud-soaked cobbles, the sound echoing along the high street. Matthias half-expected to see someone come out of the house and greet him, yet everywhere he looked was ruin and decay. Weeds sprouted in the high street and Matthias wondered where the survivors had gone.

As he approached the church, Matthias' sense of nostalgia was replaced by one of quiet dread. The silence had grown oppressive, with not even the creak of a door or the call of a bird. He stopped outside the lych-gate. The headstones and crosses were flattened as on the night of the massacre. The church, however, looked untouched, even the tiles on the roof had not been pillaged. The wooden door in the main porch hung slightly askew. This was powerful testimony to how the local villagers must regard Sutton Courteny as a place of dread, not even worth entering to plunder what remained.

Matthias, the reins gathered round his hand, walked on up to the house. Everything was as it should be. Oh, the horn in the windows had long gone, tiles had slipped from the roof, the garden was overgrown, but if he half-closed his eyes the mist would lift, the sun would come out and he'd find Christina in the buttery or his father dozing in his chair before the fire.

However, when he entered his childhood home, he found it bleak and desolate. The furniture had long gone, probably taken by the survivors, the rooms were gaunt and empty. He crouched by the parlour hearth and ran his fingers through the cold, soggy dust. This was probably the remains of the last fire his father had ever made. Matthias stared towards the niche where the skull had been. All he glimpsed were shards of bone as if someone had taken a club and smashed it to pieces. He went carefully upstairs: the chambers were barred and equally desolate. Someone had lit a fire in his room, the walls were black and scorched. In his parents' chamber, all was gone except for a cross daubed in faded red paint, beside it, the words 'Jesus miserere'. Matthias sensed the intensity with which the unknown painter had done this. Was it his father, or had one of the survivors come and taken what they wanted, then left a memento of how God had abandoned the place?

Matthias tried hard not to scream in protest at the way his life had been shattered. He went downstairs and sat in the parlour, his back to the wall. If he could only turn back the years. He recalled the words of the Hospitaller and tried to concentrate on where his father might have hidden his Book of Hours, his breviary or, perhaps, a letter, a memorandum which might explain the tragedy of those last few hours of his childhood. Matthias closed his eyes. Where would his father hide such documents? On that last All-Hallows Eve he'd gone to the church to comfort the parishioners who had fled there. Matthias racked his brains. He could not remember his father carrying anything. All he could recall was Parson Osbert's face, his kindly eyes, the attempts at reconciliation.

Matthias went out into the old cemetery. He checked on his horse and went across to where the death house stood. It was covered in creeping lichen and the shutters over the small window had long disappeared. Matthias peered through this. He almost screamed: standing in the gloom was the Preacher glaring malevolently at him. He was dressed in the same rags as when they had hanged him on the gibbet. Matthias recoiled. He looked again, there was nothing. He walked across the cemetery towards the church.

'Matthias! Matthias!' The voice was like a hiss.

He stopped. The Preacher was now standing beneath the overhanging branches of a yew tree. He was dressed in black from head to toe, his face a liverish white, his eyes pools of glaring malevolence. The phantasm bared his teeth, like a dog ready to attack, in a hiss of air, a long-drawn-out breath of hatred. Matthias stood rooted to the spot. His hand went to his dagger. He couldn't tear his eyes away. At the same time he was aware of other shapes, shrouded in grey, appearing around the cemetery. Although used to such phenomena, Matthias couldn't control his sense of dread. He closed his eyes. When he looked again, there was only the mist curling its tendrils above the cemetery. Somewhere in a tree a bird began to chatter. Matthias ran to the door of the church. The porch was dank, dark and musty. He pushed with all his might and slammed the old door shut behind him.

Matthias, trying to control his breathing, walked down the nave, gloomy as a grave, except for the faint rays of light pouring through the arrow slit windows. He paused and leant against a pillar. The church was greatly changed. Someone had burnt down the rood screen. The altar, too, had gone. The pulpit had been overthrown. Wood lay piled in one of the transepts as if someone had taken an axe and smashed the benches. All the statues were gone. No crucifix hung on the walls. It was like a long-disused barn from which both God and man had fled.

Matthias collected bits of wood, took them into the sanctuary and built a small fire. He sat for a while warming himself then, taking an ember from the fire, walked back down the nave. He carefully studied the floor and pillars. There were cuts and marks, dark splashes on the pillars and walls. Matthias surmised these must be blood stains from the massacre. He stamped his feet and blew into his hands. The church was much colder than he had realised. He returned to the fire and remembered he had left his saddlebags in the house so he went back for these, crossing the cemetery at a run. He found them just within the doorway of the priest's house, and hurried back.

He could see nothing untoward except, when he returned to the church, some of the dark stains he had glimpsed before were now glistening. Matthias stared at the pools of blood trickling along the paved stone of the nave. He returned to the sanctuary, accepting he would not be allowed to escape unscathed from this ghost-ridden place. Nevertheless, he was determined he would not leave empty-handed. He ate some food and drank a little wine. He went back to his childhood days, to his father celebrating Mass here.

'Yes,' Matthias spoke into the darkness, 'there was a place where he hid things. The little silver pyx he used to take the viaticum to the sick. The oils and chrism he needed for baptisms and marriages.' Matthias drank more from the wineskin. 'That's it. Father always complained about how thieves would enter village churches and steal such valuable items.'

Christina had laughed at this and asked why he didn't keep it in the house. Parson Osbert had shaken his head. He claimed such sacred objects should always be kept in a holy place. Matthias got to his feet and walked slowly round the sanctuary. He examined the small lavarium built in the wall where his father used to wash his fingers during Mass before he touched the sacred species. There was nothing. Matthias scrutinised the bricks in the wall, searching vainly for one that might be loose. He knelt down and closed his eyes.

'Please,' he prayed. 'Some sign!'

Daylight was fading. The church was growing darker and he grew more desperate in his searches. On hands and knees, Matthias crawled across the paving stones but these held firm and secure. He recalled his father saying there was no crypt beneath the church. Matthias' hands and knees became sore from crawling, his eyes hurt. He returned to the fire and bit into the cheese he had bought from the old manor steward, yet he'd lost his appetite and he wondered if his search were a wasteful, dangerous task. He stared down the church, trying to ignore the pools still glistening on the floor. Where else would his father hide anything? Taking a firebrand to light his way, he went down the nave, through a narrow door into the small bell tower. The steps were wet and mildewed; somewhere above there must be a crack in the walls or tiles through which the rain and snow had poured in over the years.

Matthias climbed, moving carefully until he reached the small gallery where his father had stood to summon the parishioners to Mass. The bell rope had long rotted away. Matthias lifted the firebrand and stared at the wooden pegs around which the rope had once been wrapped. These were driven into a wedge of wood fixed into the wall. Matthias pulled and tugged at these; they held firm.

He gave up in disgust and was about to go down the steps when he noticed a small grille built into the base of the wall. Matthias crouched down. He used his dagger and hacked away. The grille came loose. Moving the dying firebrand to give him light, Matthias pushed his hand into the aperture and dug around. From the outside it looked like a simple drain hole but the cavity within was much larger. Matthias sighed as his fingers touched something hard. He drew out the silver pyx, now covered in dirt, then two small phials where the chrism and oil had been kept. He searched again. His hand brushed something hard. He pulled this out. In the poor light he could see the leather bag was engrained with dirt, the cord round the neck frayed. When he cut them loose, his father's Book of Hours slipped into his hand. Leaving everything except his dagger, Matthias grasped the book and ran down the steps, back into the nave. He built the fire up and, in its warm glow, started to turn over the pages.

The book was made up of stiff pages of parchment stitched together and held between two pieces of very thin wood covered with leather. The book contained psalms and readings from the scriptures. On some pages the carefully curved letters had faded, the small jewel-like miniature paintings grown indistinct. In many of the margins Parson Osbert had written his own commentary in a tidy cursive hand; at the back, the blank folio pages had been covered with jottings and notes. Matthias read through these, trying to ignore the memories they evoked, the homilies his father had planned on the special saints' days of the parish. He found what he was searching for at the very back. It carried the date, the Feast of the Holy Cross, September 1471. At first Matthias thought his father had simply copied out the 'Confiteor', the 'I Confess' which every priest recited before Mass. The writing was hasty, the letters ill-formed. Matthias kept moving the book, trying to make out each word.

I, Parson Fitzosbert, confess to Almighty God, the Blessed Virgin Mary, to all the angels and saints and to you my brothers and sisters that I have sinned exceedingly, in thought, word and deed. I have sinned against my God and my Church by becoming handfast to a woman. I have broken my vow of celibacy and chastity. God, in turn, has punished me most grievously. Christina, my wife, is dead. The boy she bore is no flesh of mine. Christina has sinned and confessed as much. She lay with the man in whose death I had a hand: the hermit of Tenebral. Yet, he deserved to die, not only for his terrible sins and what he was, but what he did in making her betray me.

The writing then faltered. Matthias closed the book. He gripped it firmly between his hands. He couldn't think about

368

anything except his father yelling at him, cursing him, rejecting him. Christina's strange behaviour, the way she fell ill the day the hermit was tried and executed. Matthias couldn't stop shivering. He heard sounds outside, horsemen were approaching. All he could do was sit by the fire, his arms wrapped across his chest.

'Fitzosbert! Matthias Fitzosbert!'

He didn't move.

Again, 'Matthias! Matthias Fitzosbert!' The voice was harsh.

Matthias glanced up at a window. Darkness had fallen. The riders outside were approaching the church. A horse neighed, followed by screams and the sound of swords being drawn. Someone was hammering at the main door but Matthias ignored it. Again, screams, horses rearing and neighing in terror, then silence. Matthias didn't move. He didn't care. When those grey shapes he had glimpsed in the cemetery thronged at the back of the church and moved like clouds towards him, he glared back in defiance. The fire began to die. The church was intensely cold. He could not make out the shapes, corpses in their shrouds. The lost, earthbound souls of the dead villagers, faces grey as the shrouds they wore, eyes dead, came and went like puffs of smoke. Matthias felt no fear. Why should he? His father had hinted at the reason for Christina's collapse and his own soul-breaking rage. Christina had been seduced by the hermit: both she and Osbert believed Matthias was the child of this adulterous liaison.

'What am I?' Matthias called into the darkness. 'Man or demon?'

Was that why he had the second sight? Why he brought chaos and terror to everyone in his life? His parents had died because of him. This village had been devastated because of him. Santerre, Amasia, that long line of dead. Outside a chanting had begun as ghostly choristers assembled in the darkness. Matthias heard the words of the Dies Irae: 'Day of wrath, oh day of mourning, see fulfilled the heavens' warning. Heaven and earth in ashes burning.' Knocking then began on the walls and doors: ghostly voices calling his name. Matthias kept drinking the wine. Verses from Psalm 91 kept running through his tired brain:

You will not fear the terror of the night.
Nor the arrow that flies by day.
Nor the Plague that prowls in the darkness.
Nor the scourge that lays waste at noon.

Matthias staggered drunkenly to his feet.

'I don't fear them!' he shouted. 'Because I am them! I am the terror of the night! I am the arrow that flies by day! The Plague which prowls in the darkness and the noonday scourge!'

His words echoed round the church. Outside silence fell. The chanting stopped. The knocking on the doors and the pattering along the walls ceased. In the dying light of the fire, Matthias noticed the pools of blood drying up.

'I can do no more,' he muttered.

And, lying down on the floor, he curled up like a child and fell into a drunken sleep.

He woke stiff and cold the following morning. His limbs ached, he had a terrible pain in his head and his mouth was dry. He staggered to the window and peered out. The mist had lifted. The grass sparkled under a weak November sun. Matthias went down and opened the door. A corpse sprawled there: the side of the man's head had been dashed against the iron studs of the door. Matthias felt his neck, there was no blood pulse. He turned the body over: sightless eyes, a horrible wound in the side of the head, the blood congealing on the door and steps.

'One of Emloe's men,' Matthias muttered.

He laughed wildly. Emloe's men must have followed him here. Of course, the warlock must have surmised that Matthias would return to Sutton Courteny. Matthias stumbled across the cemetery. Another corpse lay like a broken toy over a graveyard slab. The head was twisted like that of a hanged man, as if someone had come behind him and snapped his neck. At the lych-gate the third corpse was a mass of bruises, his face disfigured into a bloody mass. Matthias didn't know how the other two had died but his third would-be assassin must have been holding the horses. Something had sent them mad with terror and, rearing up, lashing out with their hooves, they had pounded this man into the ground. Now all was quiet. The graveyard grass was covered in a thick white hoar frost. No sound broke the silence. Of the horses, Matthias could find no trace.

He returned to the priest's house. His own mount was safe and secure where he had put it in the ruined stables behind. Matthias stroked its muzzle. He released the cord and took it on to the high street.

'Go on,' he urged, striking its rump. 'Go on, I won't need you any more!'

The horse, puzzled, made to stay. Matthias drew his dagger and pricked it gently on the rump.

'Go on!' he yelled. 'Go on! No one will come here!'

The horse, now frightened, galloped further down the street then stopped. Matthias, who had already decided what to do, went into the small herb garden. He stopped for a while to clear his head and stared around. This was where Christina grew her herbs: camomile, briony, bogbean, hound's tongue, comfrey, sorrel, basil and thyme. The garden was a tangle of weeds but, in the far corner, Matthias found what he was looking for. His mother had always warned him to keep well away from this tall, green, perennial herb with its much branched stems and bell-like leaves, deadly nightshade. Christina and the other villagers had used this in very small doses for stomach upsets but, in any quantity, it brought death. Matthias cut a few of the stems. He took these to the church and ground both stem and leaf. Matthias took what was left of his wine, poured it into the small metal cup he carried and put the nightshade in, stirring it constantly with his finger. Matthias had no other thoughts in his head. He felt unreal as if watching himself in a dream. He did not want to go on. How could he? How could he accept that he was a bastard child, the cause of so much death and terror? He glanced down the church and recalled the deaths of the villagers.

'If they could come back,' he whispered, 'they'd all vote for my execution.'

In his mind's eye he saw Father Hubert and Father Anthony's kindly faces, then Rosamund as on the day she had come to the top of the tower, bringing food, only seconds before the arrow had struck her.

'And you,' he whispered. He lifted the wine cup in a silent toast and took a sip. His mouth caught the acrid taste. 'Not here!' he whispered. 'I'll go where all felons die!'

He staggered out of the church and, holding the wine cup steady, made his way down towards the hanging stone. Now and again he would stop outside some desolate house.

'Don't worry!' he shouted. 'Justice has been done and will be seen to be done! I'll be with you soon!'

He reached the gibbet and sat on the stone. He stared back up the street. His horse still stood there gazing forlornly at him. He looked the other way, along the track into the woods to Tenebral. He caught a flash of colour.

'If it's Emloe's men,' he whispered, 'they are welcome to my corpse.'

He lifted the cup and drank. Closing his eyes he heard the sound of hoof beats and his name being called. He drank again, shaking the last dregs into his mouth. The first pains caught him in the belly but then he felt himself seized. Gazing up, he stared into Morgana's beautiful face, her red hair hidden in a fur-edged cowl.

'Open your mouth!' Her eyes were hard as glass. 'Open your mouth, you stupid man!'

Someone else came behind, an arm tight around his throat. Matthias gasped. Morgana was pushing something into his mouth, like the quill of a pen, scratching the back of his throat. Matthias' belly and chest felt like a sea of fire. Yet he still vomited. He broke free, crouching on the ground like a dog as the spasms shook him, emptying his stomach. Again he was seized, the feather pushed down, scouring his throat. The pain in his stomach and chest was intense. A cup, forced between his lips, poured in a sweet, sticky substance: his head was held back forcing him to swallow. Again he retched. Once more he was forced to drink and, just when he thought he could bear it no longer, Matthias slipped into unconsciousness.

Now and again he would wake. He was on his horse, Morgana riding in front of him. Somebody else was riding close alongside. Matthias' limbs felt heavy. He had no strength, his throat was so dry, parched by a raging thirst. He slipped into unconsciousness again.

The next time he awoke he was in a chamber, white sheets pulled up to his chin. Matthias could feel warming stones against his feet and, when he moved his hands, he found they were gloved, his body was coated with sweat.

'Drink a little of this.' Morgana was holding his head up, allowing him to sip at the delicious water.

He fell asleep again. Every so often he would wake fitfully. A tall, serene-faced woman with a creamy complexion, large soulful eyes, full red lips and hair as black as a raven, sat next to him. She would feed him thin gruel, soups, watered wine, or ground meat as if he were a baby.

At last Matthias woke fully, it was dark. He stared round. The room was comfortable and clean. He was in a large four-poster bed. There were tables on each side, and coffers and chests stood around the room. A thick woollen drape covered the windows and, on one wall, a woven tapestry showed Adam and Eve in the garden of Eden. Matthias pulled himself up. He felt very weak, clammy. A dog barked and there were footsteps on the stairs. The door opened and the tall, raven-haired woman came into the room. She was dressed in a dark red gown, a sky-blue cloak pulled over her shoulders. Her face was slightly pinched with the cold but she smiled and clapped her hands.

'So, you are awake, Matthias!'

'How long have I been here?'

'Don't you remember?' The woman came and sat on the edge of the bed. She took his hand. Matthias realised that she was not only soothing him but checking to see if there was any fever or hotness. 'You were brought here at the end of November. Another year has come since then.'

Matthias gaped.

'It's the twelfth of January 1490,' she laughed. 'And you, Matthias, have been very sick.' She leant over and tapped him on the forehead. 'In body as well as mind.'

'Morgana?'

'Oh, she's gone.'

'Who is she?'

'Why, the Master's handmaid. As I am.'

'And who is the Master?'

'Matthias, Matthias!' She smiled slyly at him. 'The Seigneur is the One we worship.'

'You are a witch?'

'Yes. If you were a church official, you would call me a witch. I am also a physician and, as you will see, a very good cook.'

'But I've been asleep for two months!' Matthias exclaimed.

'What did you expect?' she snapped. 'The deadly night-shade is a most potent poison. Did you dream?'

Matthias shook his head. 'If I did,' he murmured. 'I can't remember.'

'Good,' she replied and grasped his hand more firmly.

'Matthias, nightshade is a deadly plant and the body must purge that. However, you were sick of another fever. Something snapped in your mind. If you hadn't slept and taken the potions I gave you, your wits would have wandered. I made you sleep and now,' she got to her feet, 'I will make you strong.'

'What is your name?' Matthias asked.

She came over and kissed him gently on the brow.

'I go by many names,' she murmured. 'But you can call me Eleanor. There is only me and my maid, Godwina. You are on a small farm not far from the Tewkesbury-to-London road.' She drew back. 'My orders are quite simple. You are not to leave here until you are well and strong. Once you are, you may go where you wish.'

'Have you met the Master?'

She shrugged. 'Like you, Matthias, he comes and goes where he wishes. What form he takes is up to him.'

Matthias spent three months at the farm, getting stronger every day. Eventually he was able to walk downstairs and enjoy the spring sunshine. His horse was well stabled and looked after. His saddlebags contained everything, including the etchings he had made at the church in Tenebral. Matthias realised the madness had passed. During his stay with Eleanor he came to accept the tragedy of his parents' death and also accepted that he had not caused it, drawing strength from Parson Osbert's attempt at reconciliation on that dreadful night.

For the rest, he was left alone, no dreams, no phantasms, no visions. Eleanor tried to seduce him, even sending up young, buxom Godwina, but Matthias rejected both. He thought of Rosamund constantly and found he could not lose himself in the love of another woman.

At the same time Matthias had secret fears which he himself would hold. If he was the son of the Rose Demon, his conception the fruit of love between his mother and an incubus, then what about his own seed? He idly wondered if Eleanor knew his secret. Was this the reason she pressed her warm, strong body against his, her arms going round his neck, her lips searching his? She was not insulted by his rejection but a coldness grew between them. When Matthias decided to leave, just after Easter, she made no attempt to stop him. Matthias was determined to return to London. He refused to tell Eleanor but his mind was set on meeting, once again, with the Commander of the Hospitallers.

PART IV

1490–1492

Remember a rose at full bloom is a rose about to die.
Old Spanish saying

27

For the year 1490, the Chronicler of St Paul's in London
could only shake his head at the way God had visited the sins
of the people upon their heads. The sweating sickness swept
into the city, sparing neither rich nor poor, the strong as well
as the weak, the young as well as the old. The hospitals at St
Mary Bethlehem, and elsewhere in the city, were overflowing.
Death carts constantly trundled the streets, trading stopped,
those who could, fled the city, those who couldn't, barred
themselves indoors. Great communal graves were dug out
at Charterhouse and to the north-west of the city. Streets
were chained off, soldiers, masked and muffled, guarded
the entrances. Huge bonfires burnt in every open space for
the doctors believed that fire and smoke would fumigate
the city.

Matthias heard about this as he came through Epping, on
the London road: he stopped for a few days in the small
village of Leighton before riding on. He took a chamber in
a small hostelry in Clerkenwell and, the following day,
presented himself at the Priory of St John of Jerusalem. Sir
Edmund Hammond was a little more cordial than when they
had first met. When he took Matthias up to his chamber, he
rummaged in a chest and brought out a burnished piece of
steel which served as a mirror.

'Master Fitzosbert, it's not my business to pry, but you
seem like a man who has seen his own calvary.' He thrust
the mirror into Matthias' hand.

Matthias held it up and stared at his own reflection. His face
was still olive-skinned but he noticed the furrows around the
corner of his mouth, lines under his eyes and, even though he
was only twenty-six, his hair had pronounced streaks of grey.
Matthias smiled and handed the mirror back.

'My journey, sir, was not just to a place but to the past.'

'A harrowing experience.' Sir Edmund lifted his hand for silence as a servant came in to serve them bread and wine.

Once he had gone, Matthias described his visit to Baron Sanguis, the attack by Emloe's men, their mysterious and brutal deaths.

'I thought as much,' Hammond interrupted. 'The lay brothers noticed the Priory was being watched shortly after you left, and questions were asked.' Hammond spread his hands. 'Before I could stop it, some gave answers to seemingly innocent questions.' Hammond jabbed a thumb to the window behind him. 'It's my view the Priory is still being watched – beggars, tinkers, traders, journeymen, all Emloe's creatures, so you should be careful.'

Matthias described how he was staying at Clerkenwell, that he intended to leave the city as soon as possible. He took out of his saddlebags his father's Book of Hours and handed it over, opening it at the page where Parson Osbert had written that last dramatic Confiteor. Hammond read it, his lips moving soundlessly and, although he tried to disguise it, Matthias sensed his agitation.

'You did say,' Matthias declared, 'that someone here could help? You promised . . .'

Hammond handed the Book of Hours back.

'I cannot help you.' His eyes were very sad. 'I can pray for you, Master Fitzosbert, but I cannot help you carry your cross. I cannot take it away. Yes, there is a woman, an anchorite. Her name is Emma de St Clair, a woman of great piety.' He smiled thinly. 'As well as great age. She has, for the last fifty years, lived in a cell here within the hospital. She spends her days in prayer, meditation and reparation for her sins and those of others. She is the person I mentioned.'

'Does she know about the Rose Demon?' Matthias asked.

Hammond got to his feet. Although it was a sunny day, he pulled the shutters of the windows over, making the room dark, even more stuffy.

'Stay here,' he ordered.

He left, locking the door behind him. He was gone for well over an hour. Matthias sat dozing in a chair, half-listening to the sounds of the Priory and wondering how an old anchorite could help him. His eyes grew heavy.

His head was nodding when he felt a kiss on the side of

his head. For a second Matthias thought it was Christina. He glanced up, the woman's face was old but her eyes were young and vivacious. Dame Emma had slipped into the room, Hammond closing and locking the door behind her. Now she stood calm and serene, her hands clasped together, smiling down at him. She was dressed in white, a veil and wimple around her face, a long gown, which stretched from just beneath her chin to her sandalled feet. A green cord was tied round her waist. In her hands were a large string of Ave Maria beads which she constantly moved, slipping them between her fingers. Matthias sat, gaping up at her.

'Are you so tired, Matthias? Or just overcome by how old I am?'

'Madam.' Matthias scrambled to his feet.

He knelt down as a sign of respect and kissed her on the back of each hand. She stroked his hair, her fingers smoothed the side of his face; they were cool and light.

'It's a long time since a man knelt before me, Matthias Fitzosbert.' She laughed, a bubbling, merry sound like a young lady flirting with a courtier. She cupped her hand beneath Matthias' chin and stared down at him. 'I know what you are thinking, Matthias Fitzosbert. Sir Edmund has spoken of you many a time since your arrival here. He has told me briefly about your journey to Sutton Courteny and what you found.' Her face became grave. 'You are a good man, Matthias. I believe God's grace is strong in you. I can see that in your eyes. You, Matthias, are a man of sorrow but your heart is good and your face is turned towards God. You struggle, you fall but you always get up.' She grinned impishly. 'Like you should now.'

Matthias did so. He was taken by this old woman, with her girlish eyes and soft voice. He could feel the sheer strength of her soul and knew that he had found a friend. Someone who might not be able to help but, at least, would make sense of this terrible world. She sat in Hammond's chair and stared across at him, her fingers playing with a small parchment knife.

'Sir Edmund, as I have said,' she remarked, 'has told me that you have just returned from Sutton Courteny.'

Matthias handed his father's breviary over. She read the

entry, carefully holding the page close up to her eyes. She closed the book, shrugged and handed it back.

'I am not going to ask you to confess to me, Matthias. God knows you must have told your tale a number of times and, though the telling helps,' she pulled a face, 'it does not explain what is happening. So, for once, let me tell you a story. When I have finished, you'll know why I am an anchorite here at the Priory and why there is a bond between us.' She leant back in her chair, staring at a point above Matthias' head. 'I have a woman's vanity,' she began. 'I always have had. Despite my years I like to be complimented.' She closed her eyes and smiled. 'I am ninety years of age, Matthias.' She opened her eyes. 'I was fifteen when the great Henry defeated the French at Agincourt. Well past my thirtieth year when they burnt the Maid at Rouen. However, the only part of my life which interests you is the summer and winter of 1426.'

She breathed in deeply. 'My birth name is Emma de St Clair. My father owned lands along the Welsh march. I had two brothers, William and Martin. They were twins. They became Hospitallers with a vision of fighting God's enemy here on earth. My mother died when I was young. I was spoilt, adored, loved; my every whim satisfied. I would only marry for love and my father hastened to agree. When my brothers, who had not yet entered the Hospitaller Order, decided to make a great pilgrimage through Russia to the city of Constantinople, I begged, I screamed, I wheedled and I flattered until my poor, exhausted father agreed that he and I should accompany them.' She paused, fingering her rosary beads. 'A glorious time, Matthias,' she murmured. 'France had been turned into a battlefield so we journeyed through the Low Countries and across the Rhine. We forded rivers deep and turbulent as the sea, through forests dark as night and across wheatlands which stretched like a golden carpet as far as the eye could see. We visited Cologne, Trier, the great cities along the Danube. We joined other pilgrims; knights, adventurers, scholars, all making their way to the Golden Horn, to the great city of Constantinople.

'One day we were joined by a German knight, Ernst von Herschel. He was as handsome as an angel: tall, face like a hawk, golden-haired, a superb horseman. He flattered me and I flirted with him. I was in seventh heaven. We made our way slowly, stopping at taverns, hostelries, priories and monasteries – a golden summer until we heard about the deaths. In every town and village we stayed someone always died. A young man, or a woman, their corpses found out in the fields or some other lonely place. Always the same marks, their throats bitten deeply, their bodies drained of blood as if it had been sucked out of them like one would claret from a wineskin.' She paused at Matthias' sharp intake of breath. 'We didn't know this until our party began to be stopped and questioned by officials. It was clearly established that the assassin must be one of us, but who?' She closed her eyes, rocking herself gently backwards and forwards.

'We reached Constantinople,' she continued. 'The Emperor received us well. We were given a villa with beautiful gardens in the suburb of the city. The other pilgrims likewise. To cut a long story short, the imperial spies arrested Ernst von Herschel as the assassin responsible for those horrific murders.' She shook her head. 'I know very few details. He was defiant to the end, loudly proclaiming that he could not die. Nevertheless, they struck off his head and placed it on a pole on one of the approaches to the city.

'For the rest of that year all was quiet. My father and brothers became very friendly with a noble family, the Alexiads, cousins to the Emperor. They had a daughter, Anastasia: one of the most beautiful women I've ever met. Yet, despite her looks, her exquisite manners, Anastasia was a merry soul, full of mischief and laughter, ever ready to mock herself. We became firm friends, close sisters. She had a vibrancy I've never met in another human being.' Dame Emma wiped the tears away from her eyes. 'The killings began again: horrid murders, this time young men. The spies came back: the city was watched.'

'Anastasia now housed the Rose Demon?' Matthias asked.

'Oh yes. I couldn't believe it. Even when she was arrested and brought into the imperial presence, she challenged, she questioned, she mocked. Sentence of death was passed against her. She was closely imprisoned. The Alexiads begged for her life. I joined with them. There was an important official, John Nicephorus. He had the Emperor's ear, the power of life and death. I went to him and begged. Nicephorus was a lewd man, dedicated to the pleasures of the flesh.' Dame

Emma's voice trembled. 'He said he'd never slept with a Frankish woman.' Dame Emma paused and picked at the beads wrapped round her fingers. 'God forgive me,' she whispered, 'I slept with him to save Anastasia's life. There would be no public execution, no degradation. An imperial physician was summoned. Anastasia was put into a deep sleep, her body sealed in a casket. The Alexiads paid a fortune to have a chamber beneath the Blachernae Palace especially laid out.'

'Why?' Matthias interrupted.

'The Alexiads argued that Anastasia would slip from a deep sleep into death. No pain, no hurt, no blood. She was their beloved daughter. No expense was spared. A holy priest, Eutyches, argued differently. He said Anastasia should die. If not, her burial chamber should be protected, not only by thick walls and special doors but by holy relics. At the time we didn't know what he meant.' She sighed. 'I thought that would be the end of the matter.'

'But she didn't die?' Matthias asked.

'No, she didn't. In a short while, I'll explain more fully. However, one thing I have learnt is this. The Rose Demon is a powerful spirit. Once it becomes incarnated in someone, it must stay there until that individual dies.' She spread out her fingers. 'You know that. The hermit, Amasia, Fitzgerald, all would have died. The Rose Demon moves on to a new dwelling place.'

Dame Emma rose and went to the side table. She filled two goblets with wine and brought one back for Matthias. She sat and sipped at hers.

'Anastasia never died. When I returned to England I began to do my own studies. I lost all joy in life. Slowly I realised what a terrible thing I had done. My brothers became Hospitallers. Because of my sin in begging for Anastasia's life, I realised reparation would have to be made. One year after my return to England, I took my vows as an anchorite before the Bishop of London and came here.' She put the cup down. 'I became obsessed with what I had done. In 1453 my nightmares became reality. I used to dream of that chamber, of Anastasia in her sarcophagus. When I heard the Turks were besieging Constantinople I went to the Grand Master and confessed everything. My brothers, still alive at the time, took solemn oaths that I was not lying. The Grand Master believed me. A squadron of Knights Hospitallers led by two brothers, Otto and Raymond Grandison, were despatched to Constantinople, ostensibly to help the Emperor. Their real task was to destroy that casket and whatever was in it. The Emperor also knew the terrible secret. Just before the city fell the Grandison brothers, together with the old priest Eutyches, were given orders to destroy the sarcophagus and all that was in it. They did not and Anastasia escaped. Once again the Rose Demon had entered the world of men.' She stared at Matthias. 'The rest you know. It becomes your story not mine.'

'But what does it mean?' Matthias asked. 'Where will it end?'

'I have been privileged,' she replied, 'to study all that is written about angels and demons. What I am going to tell you is not an article of faith but legends handed down from the Jewish into the Christian tradition. I believe your father, on the night he died, gave you certain texts?' She held her hand out. 'Do you have these now?'

Matthias felt deep into his jerkin. He drew out two pieces of parchment. One the scrap he had found at Barnwick with Rosamund's handwriting all over it. He kissed this and put it back into his pocket. The other he handed to Dame Emma. She opened it and read it, nodding understandingly.

'Your father was a learned man,' she declared. 'Now let me put these texts into context. Imagine, Matthias, a creation before the world existed. God and his angels – the latter are beings of pure light and intelligence.' She tapped herself playfully on the wrist. 'I must not forget, Matthias, that you studied in the halls at Oxford but what I am going to tell you has no evidence in scripture.' She picked up the parchment knife. 'Imagine a world of spirits. The angels are beings with intelligence, power and will. God reveals a plan to them. He will create a visible world. He will make man in his own image. More importantly, God will become incarnate. He will take flesh and become one of these beings. You've heard of that theory before?'

'Yes.' Matthias replied. 'The great Anselm in his book *Cur Deus Homo – Why God became Man* proposed an original thesis: how the incarnation of Christ was planned from all eternity: that God would have become incarnate whether man had fallen from grace or not.'

'Precisely,' Dame Emma replied. 'But this decision caused a great revolt in Heaven. One of the greatest beings, Archangel Lucifer, rose in revolt. He would not accept God's plan. According to legend he fell from Heaven and took others with him. We know from Genesis that Lucifer, whom we now call Satan, brought man into his revolt to wage a cosmic and eternal war on God.' She pulled a face. 'This is the staple diet of many sermons.' She tapped the parchment Matthias had given her. 'However, there is this curious verse in Chapter Six of Genesis: "The sons of God saw the daughters of men that they were fair; and they took them wives of all which they chose." According to a Jewish legend, written in the Book of Enoch, one of the fallen angels, the Archangel Rosifer, joined Lucifer because of his love for Eve. He took a golden rose from the gardens of Heaven, a mystical, magical flower, and seduced Eve.'

'Why?' Matthias asked.

'Because of her beauty,' Dame Emma replied. 'Because the Rosifer also wanted to experience what God had planned: the conception of a son. This is what happened at the incarnation when the Virgin Mary accepted God and conceived Christ.'

'The Rosifer wished to imitate this?'

'Yes, he did. Not just as an act of defiance but because of love.' Dame Emma shrugged. 'Some theologians even argue that that was the real cause of the fall of Satan and all his angels. To be like God in everything, in particular his plan to become incarnated, to be fully man.' She picked up the parchment. 'This explains the verse from the prophet Isaiah. Some commentators believe that the prophet is talking about the King of Babylon. Others claim that the verse, "I will exalt my throne above the stars of God", is a reference to Lucifer and his brother the Rosifer: their determination to be like God in all things. Do you understand what I am saying, Matthias?'

'Yes I do, but me?'

'Time and again through history, the Rosifer has tried to conceive a child. The Book of Tobit, Chapter Three, Verse Eight, describes how the young, beautiful Jewess Sarah was the object of the Rosifer's desire, a being we should properly call the Rose Demon. In the Jewish text he is called Asmadeus. So jealous was he of Sarah that any man who tried to have intercourse with her was promptly killed.'

'And the last verse?' Matthias asked. 'The words of Christ: "If anyone loves me, I shall love him and my Father will love him. And my Father and I will come and make our home with him."'

'Ah, I'll explain that in a short while, but what you must accept, Matthias, is that the Rosifer has, and does, love Eve and all her daughters. Some, like Sarah, are more special than others. Your mother, Christina, was his choice.'

'But am I his son?' Matthias asked.

'I don't know. But, Matthias, in God's world, in the realm of the spirit, the intelligence and the will are all that matter. We humans recognise that. I can make you cry, Matthias. I can make you laugh. I can make you weep but I cannot make you love me. The Rosifer loves you. He sees you as his incarnation.' She put the knife down. 'Rightly or wrongly, yet that is not the important matter. What is important to the Rose Demon is that you know who he is, that you accept who he is, and that you love him in return.'

'But the deaths?' Matthias exclaimed. 'The violence?'

'Is your life any different from others', Matthias? Go out on the streets of London. Men, women and children are dying in many barbaric ways. The Rose Demon sees that as a part of life.'

'But why the deaths?'

'Whatever his beauty,' she replied, 'whatever his power, whatever he says, whatever he does, the Rose Demon is a powerful being with his face and will turned against God. He will not be checked. He will not allow anyone to block his way. If people do, if they frustrate him, as happened in Sutton Courteny, they are to be punished.'

'But why the blood-drinking?' Matthias asked.

'Again, a mockery of what God does. Christ came among us and the price he paid was in his own blood: the Rose Demon turns this on its head. If he becomes incarnated in someone, he needs, both physically and spiritually, the blood of others to sustain him.'

'And he can do that?' Matthias asked. 'Move from one being to another?'

'Of course. If the door to someone's soul is open, he can enter. Read the gospels, Matthias. Remember how Judas betrayed Christ. The words used.' She closed her eyes. 'Yes that's it: "And Satan entered Judas." We can all do it, Matthias. That's why your father wrote the last quotation from the gospels about Christ and His Father making their home in any of us. If God the Creator can enter the human soul why can't any other spirit? If we love Christ, if we love our neighbour, God will come to us. If we hate, if we steep our lives in wickedness, we send out a call which the Powers of Darkness will always answer.'

'So, why doesn't he enter me?' Matthias asked.

'Two reasons, I suppose. First, Matthias, whatever you've done, your face is turned towards God. Rosamund saw that: she recognised the goodness in you. As long as your will is turned to the good you are protected. Secondly, the Rose Demon himself wants to be accepted. You can force yourself into someone's house, Matthias, but you are hardly welcome.'

'But look at me,' Matthias declared. 'I am twenty-six years of age. My life has been shattered, my parents died barbarously, as did my neighbours and my beloved wife. I have the smell of death on me. Does the Rose Demon think he will persuade me?'

'Of course.' Dame Emma pointed to a crucifix. 'Read the gospels, Matthias. We know the Devil confronted Christ on two important occasions. The first, when he was in the desert after fasting forty days. Satan thought Jesus would be vulnerable in mind, body and soul. He thought Christ would accept his offer. Christ, of course, refused.'

'And the second occasion?'

'By implication, in the garden of Gethsemane, the night He was betrayed. Jesus was tired, dispirited, full of anguish at Judas' treachery. I am sure Satan would have been waiting for Him amongst the olive groves, ready to tempt, to place another reality before Him.'

'And that will happen to me?' Matthias asked.

Dame Emma blinked back the tears, her eyes full of pity.

'Yes it will, Matthias. At the appointed time, in a chosen place, you will have your own Gethsemane. The offer will be made. The words will be put: "Look at the misery of life,

Matthias. Deny everything and accept me."' Dame Emma leant across and grasped his hand. 'And, whether you like it or not, young man, that is what all your life is about. And, before you ask, I do not know whether this has happened before or might happen again.' She squeezed his fingers and withdrew her hand. 'And don't fuddle your brain or exhaust your spirit by wondering who you are or where you are from! That is not important. What is, is what you do and what you intend to do.'

'These others?' Matthias asked. 'The woman Morgana? The witch Eleanor?'

Dame Emma just waved her hands. 'God knows: they are just puffs of smoke, Matthias. The Rose Demon's helpers and disciples. They are there to help carry out his will. They only pose danger if you let them.' Dame Emma threaded the Ave beads through her fingers. 'You are not a passive observer, Matthias. Don't you realise how, time and again, you could have accepted the darkness? Made choices? Done evil? But you did not!'

'But must I wait?' Matthias asked. 'Could I not give my life in some noble cause? Hide in a monastery?' He smiled. 'Or even join the Hospitallers?'

'Matthias, I am just an anchorite, a woman who tries to pray and do good. I am not a prophet. Nevertheless, I think you could fly to the ends of the earth or hide on the other side of the moon but you cannot escape this. You must pray that the testing time comes soon. I know,' she added softly, 'and so does the Good Lord, that flesh and blood can only take so much.' She paused and sipped from her wine cup. 'Now you went to Tenebral and copied the marks down?'

Matthias rummaged in his saddlebag. He brought out the creased and yellowing roll of parchment he had used at Tenebral. Dame Emma studied this. She rose, complaining about the pain in her joints, and took a large eyeglass from a small table nearby. She pored over the manuscript.

'I've never seen the likes before,' she murmured. 'They are a mixture of Anglo-Saxon runes and Ogham.' She lifted her head. 'The latter's a Celtic sign code, very ancient.'

Matthias told her about his visit to the wall.

'Yes, it's true,' Dame Emma replied. 'Time and again in history, the Rose Demon makes its presence felt. There have been other occurrences. You've heard of the legend of Arthur? Master Caxton's printed edition of the work provoked much admiration, both at court and here, where the knights read such tales avidly. You know the legend about Uther Pendragon and the conception of the mystical King Arthur? Sometimes I wonder if that was the work of the Rose Demon. I've heard similar stories brought back by knights who've served in the eastern marshes or the burning sands of North Africa. They, too, have tales of a mysterious prince, a powerful being and his love for a certain woman.' Dame Emma put the eyeglass down. 'Never believe, Matthias, that Satan and his legions are little black imps. St Thomas Aquinas teaches that there are seven choirs of angels, each more brilliant than the preceding one, and they are led by five archangels. Three of these we know: Michael, Gabriel and Raphael. I suppose the same is true of Hell: Lucifer is a king, the Rose Demon and the Destroying Angel, whom men called Achitophel, are his dukes. Beneath them the barons, counts and the lords of Hellfire.'

'Do you understand what they mean?' Matthias pointed at the parchment.

'No, I don't but there is an abbot, a holy man, a scholar, Benedict Haslett. He's Abbot of the Monastery of St Wilfrid's at Dymchurch on the Romney Marshes. It's a Benedictine house: a lonely, bleak place surrounded by marshes and heathland which stretch down to the sea.' She sipped from her wine cup. 'I will arrange for a letter to be drawn up for you to give him. Benedict is old and venerable, the work may take some time. However, Dymchurch and the Monastery of St Wilfrid's may be a good place for you to hide, Matthias. Give you time to think, to reflect, to plan what to do next.'

'Will I be safe there?' Matthias asked.

'Never depend upon anyone,' she replied. 'Neither me, nor Abbot Benedict nor anyone else. Depend upon yourself, Matthias,' she insisted. 'Keep your heart pure. Take the Sacrament, attend Mass. The Rose Demon can never take the host but, unfortunately, he can work through those who do, who merely worship Christ with their lips and not with their hearts.' She got up, came round the table and stood over him. 'I will pray for you, Matthias,' she continued. 'I shall never forget you but a word of warning. I am housed here, an anchorite, yet Sir Edmund is kind to me. The gossip and chatter of the community, what is happening in the world outside, is full of interest to a garrulous old woman like myself.' Her smile faded. 'We know about Emloe: he is a very evil, wicked man. The sweating sickness may be raging in the city but he will have news of your arrival here. Some old woman begging for alms, some urchin playing with his toy – such may be his spies.' She grasped Matthias' hand and squeezed it. 'I will help you prepare for the journey. Some food, a good night's sleep and there's that letter. Is there anything else I can do?'

'Yes, Dame Emma, there is. In your cell, carve my name and that of Rosamund. Put a heart between them and pray for me.'

28

Even in summer, the Monastery of St Wilfrid's, built amongst the fens and moors of Romney Marsh, which ran down to Dymchurch on the south coast, looked bleak and dour. The trackway leading to the main gate was laid with shingle collected from the nearby beaches: it rattled under Matthias' horse's hooves. He reined in before the main gate and stared up at the grey ragstone buildings before pulling at the bell rope. A small postern door opened. Matthias dismounted and led his horse through into the cobbled yard. Monks, clothed in black, were filing across the yard, answering the bell of the abbey church to attend Divine Office. They stopped and looked towards him. Not one of them smiled or raised his hand in greeting. The guestmaster, Brother Paul, was welcoming enough: a small tub of a man with a merry, red face, his auburn hair closely cropped, his cheeks and chin unshaven. Matthias was sure the guestmaster had been drinking rather deeply when summoned from his chamber.

'Abbot Benedict is in church,' Brother Paul declared, after Matthias had introduced himself. He gestured at the lay brothers dressed in grey, who stood silently behind him. 'These will look after your horses and saddle and, whilst you wait, I may as well show you the monastery.'

They stopped at the buttery for two pots of tangy, highly flavoured ale and small finger slices of bread covered in toasted cheese. Afterwards, licking his fingers, Brother Paul led Matthias around the sprawling monastery. The buildings ringed a central court and cloister garth. On the north was the abbey church, to the west the long ground-floor dormitory with warming chambers below. On the south were the dining-hall or refectory, with more chambers and store rooms below; beyond these were the kitchens. On the south-east corner stood the Abbot's apartments whilst on the east were the Chapter House, parlour and library. Matthias noticed how small streams surrounded the abbey grounds. Brother Paul explained these rivulets provided fresh water and also cleaned the latrines and sewers of the monastery. He then took Matthias round the cloister, which was made up of four covered ways or alleys: little cubicles or carrels were built along there so the monks could take advantage of the daylight to read or write. Brother Paul, wheezing and panting, his fat face covered in a sheen of sweat, led Matthias away from the main buildings. He pointed to a low, grey brick house which stood by itself in the corner of the great encircling wall of the monastery.

'Don't go there,' he warned. 'Brother Roger is kept close confined.' He tapped the side of his head. 'Gone in his wits, he is.' The guestmaster went to go on but the abbey bell began to toll.

'Come,' he said. 'Abbot Benedict will be waiting.'

The Abbot's quarters were a collection of rooms with glass in the windows, carved wooden ceilings, red hangings on the walls, with gold and silver gilt-covered plate and cups on tops of chests and cupboards. Abbot Benedict was seated on a throne-like chair behind a great, broad table. A small fire burnt in the square stone mantel hearth beside him. He rose as Matthias entered. Abbot Benedict was tall and thin, his white hair now a mere circlet round his dome-like head. His severe face was lined and marked with care, yet the eyes were kindly and the grip of his vein-streaked hand was surprisingly strong and warm. He thanked Brother Paul and, when the guestmaster had left, waved Matthias to a chair, offering refreshments. Matthias refused – the ale he had drunk so quickly was beginning to curdle in his stomach.

For a while they chatted about Matthias' journey. Abbot Benedict described the monastery and then courteously asked the reason for Matthias' visit. He handed across the letter Dame Emma had drawn up before he left Clerkenwell. Abbot Benedict picked up a pair of eyeglasses, perched them on the end of his nose, broke the seal and carefully read the letter. Now and again he'd pause and stare at Matthias as if he wished to memorise every detail of his face.

'Your journey was uneventful?' Abbot Benedict rolled up the letter.

Matthias recalled, when he left Clerkenwell, two beggars, standing on the corner of St John Street, who had followed him for a while, watching him carefully before disappearing up some alleyway. He had expected trouble but none had come and his journey south had been uneventful

'Dame Emma says you might have been troubled?' the Abbot explained.

'No, Father. I think the Good Lord sent an angel to guide me.'

Abbot Benedict tapped the letter. 'If this is true, and I am sure it is, then Matthias Fitzosbert, you need a legion of angels to guard you.' He pushed the letter away. 'St Wilfrid's is a strange place, Matthias. In our chapel we have a relic of the great saint. He who worked and preached in these parts. We are of the Benedictine Order. We are pledged to prayer, work and study but,' he rubbed his brow, 'being a monk, Matthias, is no protection against anything. St Wilfrid's is not an ordinary monastery. It belongs to an Order which stretches from Scotland through France, Spain to the eastern marches. In such a great Order,' Abbot Benedict continued slowly, 'we have our saints and we have our sinners.' He smiled grimly. 'St Wilfrid's is where – how can I put it – my Order, in its wisdom, sends those who have sinned, who have broken their vows. It is my task, and that of my prior, Jerome, to bring back these lost souls to a clearer understanding of the monastic life.' He clicked his tongue. 'I tell you this because you may find some of the brothers' behaviour,' he shrugged, 'rather eccentric. Now, today, you can settle in. You may have a chamber in our guest house: feel free to wander the buildings. Dame Emma says that you are a clerk, so any help you can give to Brother John Wessington, our librarian, would be greatly appreciated.

The Abbot rang a small handbell. A lay brother answered. 'Tell Prior Jerome that I would like to see him now,' Abbot Benedict instructed.

A few minutes later, Prior Jerome Deorhan was ushered into the chamber. Matthias rose to greet him and took an immediate dislike to this tall, thickset man. Jerome shook his hand limply: his narrow eyes were unwelcoming, his thin vinegarish face puckered in disdain. Abbot Benedict described how Matthias was a messenger, a trained clerk who would be staying in the monastery for some time as his guest. Prior Jerome was not convinced. He scratched his long rather knobbly nose, his bloodless lips drawn tight in a false smile.

'Why on earth should anyone come to Romney?' he purred. 'Our library is not famous,' the smile became a sneer, 'whilst our house does not enjoy a reputation for hospitality, sanctity or, indeed, anything else.'

'Matthias is my guest,' Abbot Benedict declared sharply and glared determinedly at the Prior.

Matthias could see that there was little love between the two.

'Then he should be shown to his chamber in the guest house.'

The Abbot drummed his fingers on the table. 'I want a further word with him, Prior Jerome. I would be grateful if you would wait outside.'

Prior Jerome, angry at such a rebuke, gave a mocking bow and walked out of the room, slamming the door behind him.

'God forgive me.' Abbot Benedict rested his head in his hands. 'God forgive me, Matthias, but that man has been sent to be a thorn in my flesh. I have prayed and I have fasted. I wish him well but I can't stand the man. He's full of ambition without the talent to match. He is suspicious of everything and everyone. He wants to be Abbot here. He has remembered everything and learnt nothing.' The Abbot glimpsed the puzzlement on Matthias' face. 'Prior Jerome,' he explained, 'was leader of a small house in Salisbury. He had a zeal for the rule and a determination to punish ruthlessly any who had transgressed. He beat some of the brothers. One of them, an old man, nearly died under such discipline. That's why Prior Jerome is here. He is dangerous and you should watch him. Do not tell him why you are here.' He smiled. 'Tomorrow I need to see these runes Dame Emma described. My eyesight is fading, whilst the fire in my brain doesn't burn as fiercely as it once did. As you get older, you realise how the little we men know is written upon water, mere dust, and the wind can blow it away any time it chooses.' He gestured with his hand. 'Prior Jerome awaits.'

Matthias was glad of the Abbot's warning. They were scarcely out of earshot of the Abbot's chamber when the Prior began his questions: what was his name? Where was he from? What was he doing here? Was he a monk? Was he a lay person?

Matthias tried to answer as truthfully and as diplomatically as he could, yet by the time Prior Jerome left him in the simple stark chamber in the guest house he realised he had made an enemy.

Matthias unpacked his saddlebags and laid out the clothing he had bought in London in a small aumbry which stood in a corner of the guest chamber. He hung his cloak and war belt on a peg, washed his hands and face before walking round the monastery. He visited the stables, found everything in order and went into the abbey church. He walked up and down the desolate nave. He knelt outside the sanctuary, sitting back on his heels, staring up at the great crucifix which dominated the high altar and the polished stalls on either side. Above him the bell began to toll. Matthias watched as the monks filed through a side door to sing the Office of the hour. Many of the brothers did not have their hearts in what they sang. The chanting was desultory, some of the brothers dozed, others scratched themselves or picked their noses. A few gossiped and quietly laughed until Prior Jerome, who sat in the Abbot's seat, would beat his white wand on the bench in front of him and glare at the offending party.

The service lasted no longer than half an hour. Matthias was about to leave when Brother Paul hastened up and said he had arranged for food to be taken to the guest chamber. Matthias took the hint. The brothers did not like him wandering where he wanted so he returned to his own room and the rather delicious meal of fish cooked in a white sauce, bread, a bowl of vegetables and a goblet of white wine.

Matthias ate, then slept for a while. He woke later in the day and returned to the church where the whole community had assembled to sing Vespers. Matthias sat with his back to a pillar far down the nave. Abbot Benedict now presided in full pontifical robes. The singing was vigorous, the chanting rising and falling in rhythmic cadence. Matthias listened carefully to the psalms which asked God, as night approached, to guard them against the power of the Evil One. Matthias, distracted, turned to the dangers confronting him. He accepted what Dame Emma had told him. He no longer felt troubled or anxious but calm, like a soldier before a battle: soon, the mist would lift and the enemy clearly show himself. Nevertheless, he heeded Dame Emma's warnings. How long would it be? What was the date? It was now the end of June 1490. If Barnwick hadn't been stormed! If Rosamund were still alive, they would have a child now. Matthias closed his eyes. Someone he could have taught how to fish? Ride a horse? How pleasant it would have been to hold a little hand. This prompted bittersweet memories of the past: he was walking through a field, a small boy, one hand held by Parson Osbert, the other by Christina. They were going to eat and drink down by the mere. They were picking him up and swinging him. He and Rosamund could have done that!

Matthias closed his eyes, breathing deeply. If only she had lived. He slipped back into memories: Rosamund teasing him, imitating him, the way he walked, the way he looked. He felt his foot being tapped and opened his eyes. Abbot Benedict was looking down at him.

'Are you tired, Matthias? Come.' The Abbot helped him up. 'Vespers are finished. Soon the candles will be out.' He stared round the church. 'And all will be dark.'

Matthias shivered. He liked this old abbot, holy and worldly-wise, but, deep in his heart, Matthias wished he was elsewhere. This was not his world.

'Go to bed, Matthias,' the Abbot said kindly. 'And tomorrow we shall begin!'

The next morning Matthias handed over his copy of the Tenebral runes. Abbot Benedict said he would decipher them but it would take time.

'I am a busy man, Matthias,' he explained. 'The decoding of these symbols could take weeks, even months. But, until then,' he spread his hands, 'until I have finished, you are my guest.'

Matthias, despite his reservations, settled down to the tedious round of monastery life. The routine kept the darkness at bay: Matins just after midnight, followed by Prime, the Chapter Mass, the Abbot's high Mass at midday, then, in the afternoon, Matthias helped wherever he could: in the scriptorium, or with the cellarer, chamberlain, sacristan or the keeper of the Galilee Chapel which stood at the west end of the abbey church and housed the relic of St Wilfrid. Matthias even donned the robes of a lay brother, working in the fields or orchards. As long as he kept busy, St Wilfrid's provided a refuge.

He soon became aware of Abbot Benedict's warnings about the monks. In the main they were a cheerful band of rogues. Some were gamblers, others, like Brother Paul, too fond of their ale and wine. A few had anxieties about their past lives or found it difficult to accept the obedience of their rule. In this, Prior Jerome was their nemesis: a harsh disciplinarian, ever ready to criticise and correct. He held the brothers in fear, and when he walked the cloisters or dormitory Matthias glimpsed terror in some of the brother's eyes. The Prior, however, kept well away from Matthias, except for hateful, baleful glances.

One afternoon, when Matthias was sharing a tankard of ale with Brother Paul in the buttery, the guestmaster leant across and tapped the side of his bulbous, fleshy nose.

'Don't worry,' he said in a gust of ale-drenched breath. 'Brother Jerome is suspicious of you, Matthias. He believes you are a spy sent here by the Mother House.' Brother Paul leant back and chortled with laughter. 'Your Latin is so good, he really thinks you are a monk and, if anything happens to Father Benedict, you will take over the running of this monastery.' Brother Paul picked up his stoup of ale and stared across its rim. 'You should be careful, Matthias. Jerome is a son of Cain. I see murder in his eyes!'

Matthias heeded the advice and kept well away from the Prior. To a certain extent, Matthias became lulled by the monotonous routine of the monastery. At first he was wary, watching the community for any sign of the Rose Demon. He took a particular interest in the Eucharist and who partook of the Body and Blood of Christ. Nevertheless, he could detect no one who refused the sacrament or practised any trickery to deceive. Abbot Benedict, meanwhile, was immersed in deciphering the runes. Matthias had to be patient. The Abbot had to send couriers to Oxford and Westminster asking for the loan of precious books to assist him in his task. As they waited for such manuscripts to arrive, Matthias began to tell him the story of his life. The Abbot would sit fascinated. He was not repelled but gave his own commentary, briskly dismissing any of Matthias' fears.

'You are what you are,' he declared tersely. 'Not who begot you. Every soul on earth is created by God and don't you forget that, Matthias. What I want to know is what part these runes play in your mystery. I have never seen the likes before.' His face grew grave. 'I must warn you, Matthias: it may yet take months to decipher the symbols, let alone understand what the hermit wrote.'

Matthias had to accept this. The weeks rolled into months. The weather changed: driving winds, ice-cold sleet and snow, stripped the trees, making the marshlands around the abbey even more gloomy. Sea mists rolled in, thick and clammy, seeping into the cloisters, even into the monastery buildings. Advent came, the galleries and chambers were decorated with evergreens, the church vestments were purple to mark the time of fast and abstinence in preparation for the great Feast of Christmas. This, when it arrived, was celebrated in regal style. The rule of Benedict, fairly lax at the best of times, was virtually ignored during the twelve days between Christmas and Epiphany.

At the end of these holy days, Abbot Benedict proudly declared that he had deciphered some of the symbols.

'Each symbol stands for a letter,' he explained to Matthias as they sat before a roaring fire. 'Soon I'll be able to make out words.'

Matthias' excitement began to mount. He found it hard to disguise his curiosity and determination to see the Abbot at every possible moment. According to Brother Paul, he truly fanned Brother Jerome's suspicions until Matthias, heeding the guestmaster's warnings, only visited the Abbot at night. Outside the weather changed. Spring came, an end to the biting winds and ice-cold rain. Some of the brothers travelled down to the sea ports of Rye and Winchelsea to buy supplies: leather, parchment, seeds for the sowing, materials for the scriptorium and library, tuns of wine from Gascony. Brother Paul invited Matthias to accompany him. Matthias refused, still fearful that Emloe and his men might be hunting for him. His worst fears were realised when, after a journey to Rye, Brother Paul took Matthias for a walk in the cloisters.

'You have no family here?' he began. 'No relations or acquaintances? And yet in Rye?'

Matthias' heart sank. He stopped his pacing and faced the guestmaster squarely.

'I am a stranger here, Brother Paul, and you know that.'

'Not in Rye,' Brother Paul replied. 'Robert Peascod – he's a parchment-maker and ships' chandler – he asked if I knew of a man called Matthias Fitzosbert.' Brother Paul winked and tapped the side of his nose. 'I told him I didn't but asked why I should.' He tugged at Matthias' sleeve and they continued their walking. 'Old Peascod was open and frank. He explained how he and other merchants in the town had been approached by journeymen who, despite their apparent poverty, had offered good silver if they could provide information. So, Matthias, the outside world still takes a deep interest in your wellbeing. Oh, by the way,' he continued, 'Prior Jerome's beginning to whisper. He talks of some connection between you and Brother Roger. You know, our madcap brother.'

Matthias walked away, more to hide his shock and unease. From the gossip in the monastery he'd learnt that Brother Roger had been declared insane and was kept a virtual prisoner, being a danger to himself as well as to others. Brother Paul had darkly hinted that Brother Roger was not so much mad as possessed of an evil spirit. Matthias had kept well away. During his stay at St Wilfrid's, he had experienced no mysterious phenomena, visions or apparitions but he was wary of this possessed monk and kept his distance from that grey forbidding prison just within the monastery walls.

One day, just after dark, he slipped into the Abbot's chambers and told Abbot Benedict about his anxieties.

'I have heard nothing.' The Abbot shook his head. 'But, there again, knowing Prior Jerome, he would want that. You should not be a-feared, Matthias. This is hallowed ground. If poor Brother Roger poses a problem or, more importantly,' he wagged a finger, 'Prior Jerome tries to turn it into a problem, you have my authority to confront them.' He ushered Matthias to a seat. 'But I have good news for you, Matthias. I have begun to translate the messages copied from that wall in Tenebral.' He held a hand up. 'No, still not all of it. It's written in a logical sequence. Different symbols were used and you must decipher each one before you can move on to the next. The writer was very subtle. They are not just Anglo-Saxon runes but a mixture of ancient signs used by civilisations long vanished. The writer was playing a game with any scholar who attempted to decipher them. He deliberately turned some symbols on their head or, to confuse, has used symbols which can stand for one, two or even three letters of our own alphabet. In other sentences he used Greek, both the classical and the Koine, as well as Latin and Hebrew. I haven't done much but I think you'll understand this.' He picked up a piece of parchment and handed it over.

Matthias studied it carefully and his blood ran cold.

1471: Tewkesbury Battle, the Hospitaller dies. Matthias the Beloved watches this. 1471: Christina the Beloved is ill. Matthias, my son; the Preacher has come. The fires burn but I shall return. 1471: the clerk brings vengeance but the Beloved remains.

There were other entries for each succeeding year, 1472, 1473 and 1474 all describing Matthias' whereabouts, predicting exactly what Matthias would be doing. Matthias looked up.

'He knew the future. He could see what was happening.'

Abbot Benedict gazed soulfully across the table at him.

'I don't believe he could see the future, Matthias. I certainly don't think he controlled it – no being under God can do that – but he could predict. Like the pilot of a ship who calls out the depths as he leads his craft through rocky shoals.'

'Why did he write it?' Matthias asked.

Abbot Benedict shrugged. 'As an act of defiance. A last will and testament, only this was about the future rather than the past. Or, there again, he knew that one day you would return. You would try and decipher them and learn that the Rose Demon will never leave you.'

'Can't you hurry on?' Matthias replied.

Abbot Benedict shook his head. 'I've told you, Matthias. It's like peeling an onion, you must take the top layers off first. Any other method and I'll just become lost in a maze of puzzles. Matthias, I appreciate you have been here months, but soon I will reach the end.'

The following morning Prior Jerome, a spiteful look on his face, was waiting for Matthias outside the abbey church.

'You must come with me, Master Matthias.'

'Prior Jerome, I am under no obligation to go anywhere, least with you.'

The Prior stepped closer. In the early morning light, his face looked livid, his breath stank stale.

'Brother Roger has been asking for you,' he whispered, his eyes glittering with malice. 'He says he has messages from your friends, Amasia and Santerre. Who are these, Brother Matthias?' He cocked his head sideways. 'They mean something to you, don't they? Now why should a worthy man like you have anything in common with a mad, possessed monk? More importantly, how does such a person know so much about you?' He stepped back, slipping his hands up the voluminous sleeves of his gown. 'Either you come with me or I will repeat Brother Roger's request to the full chapter.'

'Then you'd best show me,' Matthias retorted. 'I have nothing to fear.'

They walked across the dew-wet grass. Matthias hid his unease as he approached the squat, ragstone building: its iron-studded door was barred and bolted whilst the windows were mere arrow slits, so narrow, a person couldn't even slide his hand through. As he approached, Matthias heard his name being called.

'Come on, Matthias Fitzosbert! Hell awaits. Those who've gone in darkness before us require an answer!'

They reached the door. Prior Jerome pulled back the small wooden flap. Matthias turned away, revolted at the stench which seeped through the grille.

'Oh, don't be like that.' The voice was soft, but the glaring eyes in the unshaven face were full of madness. Brother Roger pressed his lips against the grille and licked the cold iron. 'I have messages for you, Matthias. Santerre stands in the darkness, as do Amasia and others. Fulcher and John the bailiff, Fitzgerald. Aye, and even a king, James Stewart, whose blood was spilt at Sauchieburn. Like children they are, lost in the night! They ask you to free them. They scream into the dark that they were innocent, their lives snatched away, sent unprepared into eternal night. I've drawn a rose,' he whispered, 'a lovely rose, red as the dawn, with a long, green stem. Prior Jerome gave me the paints and each leaf stands for one of your friends.' The mad, crazed face fell back; dirty, long nails scrabbled at the bars. 'Come in, Matthias, come in and meet your friends!'

Matthias pushed the slat of wood across the grille and turned away. On the other side of the door a terrible pounding and screaming broke out.

'You've got to come in! You've got to come in!' The voice

grew so strident it cracked. 'They are your friends yet they've become my guests! They haunt me at night!'

Matthias, however, was striding across the grass. Prior Jerome caught up.

'What is all this?' He caught at Matthias' arm. 'Tut, tut, Brother!'

Matthias grabbed the Prior by the front of his tunic and, drawing his dagger, pricked the side of his neck. Fear replaced malice in the Prior's close-set eyes.

'Stay away from me, you whoreson!' Matthias cursed. He pressed the dagger tip against the Prior's nose. 'Keep that out of my business and out of my affairs!' He pointed back to where Brother Roger still cursed and ranted. 'And leave that poor soul be!' He pushed the Prior away. 'And don't worry about our good abbot. He knows everything about me, as he will about this!'

Abbot Benedict was studying the accounts with his cellarer. He took one look at Matthias' face and quietly asked the monk to leave.

'What is it, Matthias?'

Matthias sat down and, in halting phrases, told the Abbot about Brother Roger's wild rantings and threats.

'Why?' he asked. 'Why do these dead always walk with me? I was not guilty of their deaths. Nor did I ask the Rose Demon to house himself in their souls. My hands are free of any blood or guilt.'

'Matthias, Matthias.' Abbot Benedict came round the desk and stood over him. 'These were souls who were plucked, unprepared, from life. Our theology of life after death is so small, it could be summed up in two or three sentences. Yet death is probably like birth. A baby does not want to leave the womb and, when he does, he is born in blood and pain. He's confused and, perhaps, that's what happens to the dead. These men and women were thrust out unprepared and do not know where they are or what really happened. They blame you. They stay with you because of the strong bond forged between them and you during life. Now, as for Prior Jerome,' the Abbot beat his hands against the desk, 'it's time some other house had the benefit of his expertise.'

Two days later, Matthias was woken by the tolling of the bell. Not the solemn calling to prayer or other duties but the wild clang of a tocsin. He tried to open his door but it had been locked from the outside. In the passageway beyond he could hear the slap of sandals, the shouts of monks. He went to the window but could see little so he sat on the edge of his bed and waited, trying to calm the panic seething within him. He'd spent most of the previous day in the library trying to hide himself in a world of study away from the rantings of Brother Roger and the cold malice of Prior Jerome. In the evening he had dined by himself, but when Brother Paul brought a tray of food across he whispered how the entire monastery knew that Prior Jerome had been summoned to the Abbot's chamber.

'The brothers are beside themselves with glee,' the guest-master informed Matthias. 'The cellarer overheard the Abbot say that, by the end of the week, Prior Jerome will be gone.'

Matthias wondered what had happened. He went across and lifted his clothes from a peg on the wall. His war belt had been removed! Someone had slipped into his chamber during the night and quietly taken it. A key turned in the lock. He whirled round. Prior Jerome, accompanied by four burly lay brothers, all carrying staffs, burst into the chamber. The Prior was grinning cynically. He pushed Matthias back on to the bed.

'Assassin!' he snarled, his finger thrust only inches away from Matthias' face. 'Assassin and son of the Devil!'

Matthias tried to get up but two of the lay brothers seized his arms.

'What's the matter?' he protested.

'Last night, Brother Roger,' Prior Jerome hissed, 'was killed. Some force picked him up and flung him against the wall, dashing his brains out. More seriously, Abbot Benedict has also died. We found him lying on the floor of his chamber.'

'God rest him,' Matthias breathed. 'But—'

'His heart failed him,' Prior Jerome retorted. 'Yet what was the true cause, eh? Are you a warlock, Fitzosbert? Did you silence Brother Roger and Abbot Benedict?' He took a step back. 'The Abbot of St Wilfrid's has his own jurisdiction: the power of the axe and tumbrel, the sword and the gallows. Now Abbot Benedict is dead, those powers are vested in me. You will stand trial, warlock, for your hideous crimes!'

29

Matthias was confined to his chamber. He received no visitors and his only food was bread and water. The cell was closely guarded by three lay brothers. Matthias was only released to relieve himself in the latrines at the far end of the guest house. The lay brothers refused to answer any questions but Brother Paul came down. The guestmaster had lost all his jollity, his eyes were red-rimmed from crying. He managed to gain admission to Matthias' chamber by bringing the bread and water himself, for which he apologised.

'The whole monastery is in uproar,' he declared. 'Two deaths in one night. Brother Roger was madcap. Abbot Benedict's heart seems to have failed him.' Brother Paul leant closer. 'Matthias, your situation is most serious. Prior Jerome is now Acting Abbot. He has the same powers of life and death as any manor lord. He is claiming that you are a warlock, a magician, who brought about the good Abbot's death and that of poor Brother Roger.' He breathed out noisily. 'Both their funerals take place this afternoon.'

'Isn't that too soon?' Matthias asked. 'They've only been dead two days. Prior Jerome's haste to inter them is unseemly!'

Brother Paul looked at him from under lowering brows. 'What are you implying, Matthias?'

'Of Brother Roger's death nothing. Yet I do find it strange that, on the very day the Abbot decided to send his prior to another house, Benedict dies. There are many potions, Brother Paul, to make an old man's heart fail!'

'Is that what you think?' the guestmaster asked.

'Abbot Benedict was my friend. A holy scholar, a man who was going to help me deal with a truly terrible problem.' Matthias picked up the hard rye bread and nibbled at it.

Brother Paul got to his feet. 'Such problems are nothing,' he whispered, 'to what will happen tomorrow. Prior Jerome is convoking a full Chapter meeting. You will be tried on charges of sorcery and black magic.'

'Nonsense!' Matthias sprang to his feet. 'He has no evidence.'

'Hasn't he?' Brother Paul replied. 'Are you prepared to tell the brothers why you are here? Why you visited Abbot Benedict at night? What was so important? Why did Brother Roger mention you? How could a madcap monk know anything of a visitor to our monastery?' He grasped Matthias' hand. 'These are only some of the questions Jerome, in his malice, is whispering among the brothers. He has sown a deadly crop, Matthias. Tomorrow you may well harvest it.'

After Brother Paul left, Matthias sat back on the bed. The full dangers of his situation now confronted him. He'd hoped that Prior Jerome would be only too willing to expel him from St Wilfrid's. Matthias would have collected the parchment, whatever Abbot Benedict had deciphered, packed his belongings and ridden away. He had fully underestimated Jerome's malice. The Prior did have the power of life and death. But would he use it? Would Matthias' troubled life end here in this cold and dank monastery in the middle of Romney Marshes?

Matthias tried to pray but found he couldn't. As the day wore on he also began to feel weak from the poor nourishment he had received. Brother Paul returned at noon with a bowl of meat and some diced vegetables. Matthias ate these greedily and quickly drank a cup of wine. He slept for a while and was awoken by the tolling of the funeral bell. From his cell he heard the faint strains of a Requiem Mass and the chanting of the monks. Matthias got up and, for a while, sat at his desk trying to prepare a defence against Prior Jerome's accusations. In the end he threw his quill down in disgust. What could he say? Who would believe him?

Brother Paul came back late in the evening, bearing a tray of food.

'I insisted on this,' he declared, though he refused to meet Matthias' eyes. 'I pointed out that you were innocent until your guilt was proved.'

Matthias thanked him and pulled the guestmaster closer.

'Brother Paul,' he whispered, 'I am innocent. I cannot tell the brothers why I am here. Even if I did, they would not believe me and it would only make a bad situation worse. You know I am innocent!'

'I will do what I can,' Brother Paul offered. 'Prior Jerome is hated. However, he is wielding his power, making his influence felt. There will be few who will speak for you, Matthias.'

'Tell them not to.' Matthias tried to hide the anger in his voice. 'But if you can, Brother, for friendship's sake, go to Abbot Benedict's chamber. Look for two manuscripts: one bearing strange symbols, the other Abbot Benedict's translation. Don't bring them here. Just keep them safe.'

'Prior Jerome may have already found them.'

Matthias recalled the huge leather-bound tome in which Abbot Benedict had kept the parchments well hidden. He described this to the guestmaster, who said he would see what he could do.

The next morning, just after High Mass, four lay brothers opened Matthias' cell. They bound his hands behind his back, escorted him along the stone passageways and up into the Chapter House. The entire community were seated round the walls on their stone sedilia. Prior Jerome sat in the Abbot's chair, his face a mask of solemnity as Matthias was brought up to the table where the scribes sat. The doors were closed. Prior Jerome led the community in prayer and the mockery of a trial began.

'Matthias Fitzosbert.' Prior Jerome rose from his seat; he came down the steps and stood across the table, confronting him. 'Matthias Fitzosbert, why did you come to St Wilfrid's Monastery?'

'That is no business of yours,' Matthias retorted. 'It was a confessional matter between me and Abbot Benedict. Moreover, I am not a member of this Order, or of this community. You have no power over me.'

'A matter for the confessional?' Prior Jerome stared in mock wonderment at the other assembled monks.

Matthias followed his gaze. Many of the community, eyes down, heads lowered, were not happy with the proceedings but any hopes were dashed as Prior Jerome pulled a document from the sleeves of his gown and held it up.

'A matter of the confessional,' he repeated in a loud, ringing voice. 'But this, dear brothers in Christ, is a letter written from an anchorite in London, in which she insinuates that the bearer, Matthias Fitzosbert,' Prior Jerome stretched his hand dramatically towards Matthias, 'is greatly troubled by a demon.'

'You misquote her words,' Matthias replied hotly. 'Dame Emma is my friend, my counsellor, as was Abbot Benedict.'

'Are you troubled by a demon?' Prior Jerome asked silkily. 'Place your hand on the Bible in front of you and say that you are not!'

Matthias stared back.

'So, why don't you tell us why you were at St Wilfrid's?'

'It is a matter of the confessional.'

'But it isn't,' Prior Jerome insisted. 'It's a matter discussed by this anchorite and our late deceased abbot. Why don't you answer my questions? Why don't you take the oath and say that you are not troubled by a demon? Again, I ask you solemnly, why did you come to St Wilfrid's? Why did poor Brother Roger know you? Why did he claim to have messages for you from deceased friends? Do you commune with the spirits, Master Fitzosbert?' His voice rose to a shout. 'Do you deal with the Powers of Darkness?'

'Nonsense!' Matthias yelled back. He struggled at the bonds which held his hands. 'I am innocent of any crime, either of Brother Roger's death or Abbot Benedict's!'

'I don't think so.' Prior Jerome forced a smile and walked slowly back towards his chair. 'I think, Master Fitzosbert, you are a warlock.'

'Nonsense!' Matthias replied. 'The good brothers here know me. I attend Mass every day. I take the sacrament.'

'Then, if you are such a good Christian,' Prior Jerome turned, 'why not take the oath and give honest answers to honest questions?'

'It does not concern you,' Matthias declared.

'Oh yes it does. Oh yes it does.' Prior Jerome walked back briskly. 'I accuse you, Matthias Fitzosbert, of using your devilish powers to silence Brother Roger.' His eyes smiled maliciously. 'And, because you knew the Abbot was growing concerned at this, you invoked curses and brought about his death.'

Matthias stared back. Prior Jerome had neatly trapped him.

His allegations were nonsensical but, because he would not answer them, he was trapped.

'It stands to reason.' Prior Jerome stretched out his arms and turned slowly to address the assembled community. 'Here we have a man who will not tell us why he is here. Who is known quite intimately to Brother Roger but cannot explain the reason why. Then, in one night, Brother Roger and Abbot Benedict die.'

'You have no jurisdiction over me!' Matthias shouted.

Prior Jerome lowered his arms and smiled. 'Ah, but I do. It says in the rule, and this is accepted by the Crown, that any man who stays in a monastery more than six months and dons the habit of that community, falls within its jurisdiction.'

Some of the older monks nodded in agreement.

'Do you find him guilty?'

Matthias stood, horror-struck, as some of the monks raised their hands and mumbled, 'Aye!' Others, however, kept their hands pushed up the sleeves of their gowns yet Jerome had the majority. He smiled in satisfaction and sat down.

'Sentence will be passed,' he said clearly. 'I have the power of the gallows!'

'Wait!' Brother Paul sprang to his feet. 'Father Prior, with all due respect, there is no evidence connecting this man with either the tragic deaths of Brother Roger or our Father Abbot. Coincidence,' Brother Paul shouted, coming down the steps to stand directly in front of the Prior, 'coincidence is not evidence. Brother Matthias did have secret talks with Abbot Benedict but how do we know they were not confessional matters? Never once did I, or any of our brothers, ever hear our Father Abbot speak disparagingly of our guest here.'

A murmur of agreement ran round the Chapter House. 'Moreover,' Brother Paul added defiantly, 'in this matter you do not have power of life and death, the rule is quite explicit: in between the death of one Father Abbot and the appointment of another, any monk, facing a capital charge, must be reserved for final judgment by the new Abbot.'

This time the chorus of agreement was louder. Matthias closed his eyes and muttered a prayer of thanks. Because this community was drawn up of men who found it difficult to accept the rules, they were also men only too willing to question authority, particularly someone they hated like Prior Jerome. Now they had a spokesman in Brother Paul.

'There is one other matter,' Brother Paul continued. 'When I visited the prisoner in his chamber, I noticed his war belt had gone.' He winked at Matthias.

'What has that got to do with it?' Prior Jerome, who could scarcely control his anger, sat forward, fists clenched on his knee.

'Matthias,' Brother Paul asked, 'where is your war belt?'

'It was taken the morning Abbot Benedict was found dead. My door was locked, my war belt was removed.'

'I did that,' Prior Jerome replied hastily. 'I thought it was best.'

'In which case,' Brother Paul replied tartly, 'you'd already judged our good brother guilty.' Brother Paul took a step forward and spread his feet. His whole body breathed defiance. 'Abbot Benedict is dead,' he declared flatly. 'According to our rule, Prior Jerome, you have authority in this monastery, but your malice towards this man is well known. You have already made up your mind that he is guilty. I know the constitution as well. I appeal to the authority of our Mother House and to the new Abbot. How say ye?'

A chorus of delighted 'Aye!' greeted his declaration.

Prior Jerome sprang to his feet and came down the steps.

'That is true.' He found it difficult to control his breathing. 'But I still have the authority of sentencing. Matthias Fitzosbert will be kept in the same house as Brother Roger. No visitors will be allowed, no food and drink given except bread and water.'

The smiles on the assembled brothers' faces faded. Prior Jerome clapped his hands.

'That is my sentence and it will stand!'

Matthias was hustled out of the Chapter House. The lay brothers, holding him fast by the arms, bundled him through the corridors out across the grounds. Brother Paul caught up with him.

'You heard what Father Prior said,' one of them declared abruptly. 'No one is to speak to him!'

Brother Paul seized Matthias' face between his hands.

'Be careful what you eat and drink!' he whispered. 'Take courage and wait!'

410

He stepped aside and the brothers hurried Matthias on. The door of the small prison house was flung open and he was thrust inside the square, stone box. The dirt and filth left by Brother Roger had been cleaned but the foul odour still remained. There was a cot bed, a small table and a rickety stool, and in the other corner a small recess for the latrine. The arrow slit windows provided little light and, when the door was slammed shut and bolted behind him, the chamber became even more dark and sombre.

For a while Matthias just crouched within the doorway. He found he couldn't stop his trembling. He thanked God for Brother Paul: if Prior Jerome had had his way those same brothers would have hustled him on a cart and taken him out to the gallows which overlooked the marshes. Nevertheless, he accepted that he was still in great danger. It might take months before the new Abbot arrived and anything could happen. He wondered if Abbot Benedict had been poisoned. When the door was flung open and a pewter jug of water and a wooden bowl containing scraps of bread were thrust in, Matthias decided to ignore them. Instead he got up and walked slowly round the prison house. The floor was of paved stone. The white, plastered walls were streaked with dirt. Near the bed Mathias found Brother Roger's drawing.

The rose was crudely drawn. Beneath it, the green stem trailed down to the ground. Each of the bell-shaped leaves had a name scrawled above it: Santerre, Amasia, the Preacher and even some Matthias couldn't recognise. All other traces of the dead monk had been removed: the mattress and the blankets had been replaced, the latrine cleaned. There were no books, nothing to distract him except peering through the narrow arrow slit windows. Bread and water were pushed in. Matthias, tearful of Jerome's malice, crumbled the bread and threw it out of the window then poured the water down the latrine. By the morning of the third day, he was feeling weak and spent most of his time fitfully dreaming on the bed, lost in ghoulish nightmares from his past.

Later that day Matthias was woken by a rap on the door. Brother Paul pushed through the usual tray of bread and water followed by a second one, a bowl of diced meat, hot and covered with a rich, thick sauce, bread, a small jug of wine and marzipan chopped up and wrapped in a linen cloth. Matthias ate ravenously. He felt better, though the panic returned. How long would this go on? If Jerome was so powerful, so malicious, Brother Paul might soon be taken care of. Matthias did not want to die a lingering death or writhe in agony from some deadly poison.

On the following morning, therefore, he was surprised when the door was flung open. Brother Paul and two others came into the prison house. One of them carried Matthias' belongings in a heap: clothes, saddlebag and war belt. These were piled just within the doorway. Brother Paul pushed a small purse of coins into his hands. Looking through the doorway, Matthias glimpsed his horse all saddled and harnessed.

'You are to go now, Matthias,' the guestmaster declared. 'God's judgment has been made known.'

Matthias stared back in puzzlement.

'Prior Jerome had an accident this morning.' One of the other monks spoke up. 'He climbed the tower of the abbey church and, coming down, slipped and broke his neck.'

'The brothers consider this God's judgment,' Brother Paul declared. 'Prior Jerome's accusations against you are false yet the brothers do not wish you to stay. You are to leave immediately. Don't worry,' he pointed to the saddlebags, 'I found the parchments you asked for in Abbot Benedict's room. You will find everything in order. Now, you must be gone. Some of the older brothers wish to bring in the sheriff.' He looked back through the doorway. 'Three deaths in one week, all in mysterious circumstances.' He patted Matthias on the shoulder. 'The sheriff might detain you till he knows more about your past, Matthias. So, it's best if you go now.'

Matthias hurriedly changed. Brother Paul helped him put his belongings into a bundle tied with some cord. These and other possessions were fastened securely to his saddle.

Matthias clasped the guestmaster's hand.

'I cannot thank you enough, Brother Paul.'

'Yes you can.' The guestmaster smiled back. 'Four of the lay brothers are to take you on to whatever road you wish.' He raised his hand. '*Au revoir*, Matthias.'

A short while later, escorted by four burly lay brothers, Matthias left the Monastery of St Wilfrid's. He felt tired and depleted, not sure of what to do. When he came to the

412

crossroads, the lay brothers stopped and looked expectantly up at him.

'Rye or Winchelsea?' one of them asked.

Matthias recalled Brother Paul's warnings about people asking about him in Rye so he turned his horse towards the Winchelsea road.

'Oh.' The lay brother proffered a small, sealed parchment. 'Brother Paul asked us to give you that. You are to go now,' he added flatly, 'and we are to make sure you never come back.'

'Of that,' Matthias declared, 'there is no worry.'

And, digging in his spurs, Matthias cantered along the lonely trackway which wound through fields of ripening corn towards Winchelsea. When he was out of sight he reined in. He ate some of the food and drank a little of the wine he'd been given, then opened the guestmaster's letter.

Brother Paul to Matthias Fitzosbert, greetings. I have not long to live. My body decays. Take the writings from Tenebral. They have little import. They were my memorial to you, *Creatura bona atque parva*. Brother Paul.

Matthias folded the manuscript and stared up at a bird wheeling in the blue sky.

'When?' he murmured. 'When did the Rose Demon come?' Matthias smiled to himself. Of course, he reasoned, now he understood Brother Paul's bold defiance of Prior Jerome: his stalwart defence, the bringing of food and, of course, Prior Jerome's fall. Matthias realised it was no accident. The steps up the tower of the abbey church were steep and sharp-edged. If a man was pushed, he would find it difficult to keep his balance. Such a fall would shatter bone and sinew, as it did for Prior Jerome.

Matthias put the parchment away and continued on his journey.

He arrived in Winchelsea late that evening. Even before he entered the town he caught the salty tang of the sea, the smell of fish mixed with tar. A prosperous place, Winchelsea, with its winding alleys and streets, was a thriving port; the best place, Matthias reasoned, for a man to lose himself. He stabled his horse and took a chamber at the Cog of War inn just within the town walls. He was well supplied with silver and began to plan for the future.

He felt safe enough, and spent the first week wandering the town. He became interested in the different companies of soldiers, wearing no particular insignia, who camped out on the open commons beyond the city walls. One night he went and wandered through the campsites. One banner caught his attention: a golden angel, on a blue background, a shield in one hand, a sword in the other. Matthias, intrigued, drew closer to study it.

'Why the interest, sir?' A figure came out of the darkness.

The standard was set well away from where a group of men squatted round the fire: one of them was idly turning a spit. The air was rich with the sweet smell of roasting rabbit.

'The insignia interested me,' Matthias replied.

'I chose it myself,' the man said proudly. 'St Raphael.' He stretched a hand out. 'My name is Sir Edgar Ratcliffe. I am from Totton in Yorkshire.'

Matthias shook his hand. Ratcliffe was a young man with a strong, boyish face which he tried to hide by growing a luxurious moustache and beard. He was dressed in a leather tunic open at the collar. Beneath this were military black hose pushed into leather riding boots on which spurs clinked merrily.

'There are many such companies,' Matthias declared.

'Aye.' Ratcliffe scratched his close-cropped head. 'It's a miracle how a good idea seems to appeal to so many people.' Ratcliffe played with his leather wrist brace and laughed to himself. 'I am the second son of a second son.' He gazed up at the banner now fluttering bravely in the evening breeze. 'There are no more wars. What's your name?'

'Matthias Fitzosbert.'

'There are no more wars,' Ratcliffe repeated. 'King Henry is desirous of keeping the peace with everyone. The Turks now control Constantinople and Jerusalem, so it's Spain for the likes of us.'

'Spain?' Matthias asked.

At St Wilfrid's he'd heard the gossip of how the Tudor King was growing closer to this powerful kingdom and their warlike king and queen; Ferdinand of Aragon and Isabella of Castile dreamt of uniting their kingdom which, if realised, would turn Spain into the greatest power in Europe.

'Haven't you heard?' Ratcliffe asked. 'Where have you been hiding yourself?'

'In a monastery,' Matthias replied. 'And I'm not joking.'

Ratcliffe looked up at the banner, an adoring look on his face.

'It's the last crusade, Matthias! Ferdinand and Isabella have collected a huge army and moved south to besiege Granada. If that falls, the Moors will be driven from Spain for ever. I have raised the company of St Raphael.' He turned back and pointed to the campfire. 'Twenty mounted men, ten hobelors and the same number of archers, though God knows where those idle buggers have gone. Probably drinking their wages in the nearest tavern.' Ratcliffe poked Matthias in the chest. 'You look like a fighting man. I can tell that from your chest and arms. The pay is not good, a shilling a quarter but there'll be food, comradeship and fair shares of any plunder taken.' He held out his hand again. 'Well?'

Matthias shook it and laughed. 'Sir Edgar, if I decided to go to Spain then it would be with you under the banner of St Raphael. Yes.' He looked up at the standard. 'That would be rather fitting: protection from one of God's great archangels!'

He walked away even as Sir Edgar shouted that they would tarry here a while until all were assembled and then leave for Rye. Matthias raised his hand in acknowledgment and walked slowly back to the tavern. The prospect of fighting with a company of St Raphael, of going to Spain, appealed to him. Such a venture would be godly and take him away from a country where he was no longer welcome. Tewkesbury, Gloucester, Sutton Courteny, Oxford were all closed to him. He doubted if Dame Emma was still alive and he was not too sure of what reception the Hospitallers would give him. He stopped beneath the creaking tavern sign. Emloe and his gang would be waiting for him in London, even elsewhere. Yes, he'd be party to a crusade, to fight for Church and the Cross, whilst Ratcliffe looked a worthy man. Matthias was tired of his own loneliness.

He walked through the inn yard and up the stairs to his chamber. He opened the door and unseen hands pushed him

415

deeper into the room. The door was slammed and bolted behind him. A tinder scraped, candles were lit. Matthias' hand went to his dagger.

'Don't! Just stand there!'

The room was full of shadowy figures. Emloe stepped forward, pulling back his cowl, his arms pushed up the sleeves of his gown, his cadaverous face smiling and welcoming.

'Matthias! We have waited many a week!'

Matthias stared round: there were at least six of them, two were carrying crossbows. He caught the glint of naked steel and heard the clink of chain mail.

'How did you know I was here?'

'Matthias, we have had people waiting at the ports for many a month. You know I have a finger in many pies, take a deep interest in what comes in and out of our kingdom. You weren't at Winchelsea an hour before a messenger was speeding to London.'

'What do you want?'

'Matthias, must I spell it out as if you are a child? That night in my secret chamber.' Emloe stepped closer. 'Never have I seen such power, such a manifestation.' He shrugged one shoulder. 'True, the house was burnt but nothing that cannot be replaced. You, however, Matthias, cannot be replaced. You are more precious to me than the costliest silk or rarest diamonds.' Emloe's voice took on a more mocking tone. 'And we looked for you, here and there. What happened to my riders? Sent into deepest Gloucestershire, they were! It was months before I discovered their rotting corpses round that church!' Emloe's eyes glittered in the gloom. 'What happened, Matthias? Did you release the power?' He wagged a finger. 'Then back and forth to the Hospitallers at Clerkenwell. Tush! Tush! We dare not seize you there.' He spread his hands. 'The good knights cannot be bribed and bought. They have a tendency to smite first and ask afterwards.'

Matthias pulled his cloak around him and glared at Emloe. He was not afraid, just angry, seething with fury. Emloe and the rest – James of Scotland, Fitzgerald, Prior Jerome, men who would not leave him alone – and now what? Trussed and bound, taken back like a puppet to London? Matthias' hand went to the second dagger he wore strapped close to his belt.

He slipped this easily from its pouch. Emloe was revelling in his good fortune.

'So, what is it to be, Matthias? A knock on the head and bundled into some cart? Come back to London! Live like a lord! Wine, gold, any wench you want! A house? Favour at court?' He waggled a finger. 'I've been a good detective, Matthias. There are still warrants out for your arrest! That business at Oxford, and your name was among the list of rebels captured at East Stoke. And what happened at Barnwick? Who did let the Scots into that castle?'

Matthias idly wondered if this was the confrontation Dame Emma had spoken of. Was the Rose Demon here? Emloe smirked, lording it over him.

'I'll come with you,' Matthias declared. 'You want to see the power, Master Emloe?'

The warlock nodded.

'You wish to see the demons rise? So you shall, and here's my hand on it.'

Matthias stepped forward. As he did so, his hand came up, and before Emloe could even move Matthias struck the dagger deep, turning it into the man's stomach. He pulled Emloe close, pushing in the dagger with all his strength.

'Go down,' he whispered. 'And meet the demons!'

Matthias threw Emloe, gagging and choking on his own blood, to the floor.

Figures came out of the darkness but Matthias knocked them aside. He reached the door, fingers pulling at the bolts. Then he was out, racing down the stairs.

'Murder!'

A scullion coming up the stairs was knocked sideways.

'Stop him!' a voice shouted. 'Murder!'

By the time Matthias reached the cobbled yard, he could hear the shouts of 'Harrow! Harrow!', the usual call when the hue and cry were being raised. Matthias raced along the alleyway. At the bottom he stopped and turned. His heart sank. He could see pinpricks of torchlight, people shouting, hurrying towards him. He thought of Sir Edgar Ratcliffe but realised the camp was too far away. He ran on into the marketplace and through the open door of a darkened church.

30

Matthias slammed the church door behind him and stared around. Torches glowed in their iron clasps on the pillars: candles and oil lamps dotted the darkness before statues in the side chapels. Matthias heard the cries of 'Harrow! Harrow!' draw nearer. He pushed close the bolts of the door and walked swiftly up the nave into the sanctuary. He had hardly reached it when a small, balding man, dressed in a priest's gown, came running through a side door. He lifted his spluttering torch and stared at Matthias.

'What is it you want, young man?'

Matthias grasped the side of the altar.

'My name is Matthias Fitzosbert, clerk. I demand sanctuary of Holy Mother Church!'

The priest sighed and lowered the torch.

'Oh, not here!'

Matthias took a silver coin out of his purse.

'Father, you know the law as do I. I demand sanctuary.'

The priest's demeanour changed at the sight of the silver. He pocketed it quickly.

'You can sleep over there,' he declared, pointing to a shadowy alcove. 'I'll bring you some food, wine and blankets.' He scratched his pock-marked nose. 'You say you know the law but so do I. The mayor and bailiffs will come here. You can either surrender to them and stand trial,' he paused, 'or stay here forty days and ask to be exiled. Now, what is your crime, murder?'

Matthias nodded.

'Yes, it always is,' the priest sighed. 'And you are going to tell me it was in self-defence.'

'I did not want the man's death.'

'Well,' the priest stretched out his hand, 'my name is Father Aidan. The sanctuary is yours.' He pointed to a side door. 'I'd be grateful if you didn't urinate or relieve yourself in here. There's a small latrine outside fed by an underground brook. Remember this is God's House and the Gate of Heaven. Keep it clean.'

'Oh, Father?'

The priest turned round. Matthias held out a second silver piece. 'There's another one of these, Father, on two conditions. First, would you collect my baggage from the Cog of War tavern? They won't refuse to hand it over to a priest.'

'And?'

'I don't want any accidents happening to me,' Matthias declared. 'No one slipping in and out of the church.'

'They wouldn't dare!'

'Oh yes they would, Father. These men fear neither God nor man. I killed their leader.'

'Very well.' Father Aidan pointed down the church. 'When I say Mass the front porch will be open, but after I'm gone you can bolt both doors from the inside.' He took the silver coin. 'You and your possessions will be safe.' He paused as he heard the hubbub outside. 'I'll just remind our assembled brethren about the law of sanctuary. If they break it they are excommunicated.' He waved his hand. 'I know, I know. I heard what you said. They fear neither God nor man, but if they break into my church and commit violence, they'll do a merry jig on the town's gallows!'

Father Aidan may have been a mercenary priest but he was true to his word: the crowd assembled outside soon dispersed. He brought the rest of Matthias' belongings from the Cog of War and made his uninvited guest as comfortable as possible.

The next morning, just after Mass, the mayor and bailiff arrived. They stood in the mouth of the rood screen while the town clerk recited in a rushed monotonous fashion Matthias' rights. When he had finished, the Port Reeve stepped forward.

'You murdered a man at the Cog of War. I know, I know,' he raised his voice, 'it was self-defence but there's a whole host of witnesses say it wasn't. So, you've got a choice, my murdering lad! You can surrender to us and, if you do, you'll probably hang, or you can take an oath to leave the country by the nearest port. Now, in normal circumstances, that would be here in Winchelsea but I reckon that's too close to be a fitting punishment,' he continued sonorously. 'So, for you, my bucko, it's Rye. You can't take a horse. You'll have to walk there. You must carry a cross we give you. If you leave the King's highway, you can be slain on the spot.' He shrugged. 'Though the friends of the man you killed will probably take care of that anyway!'

'I know I can't ride a horse,' Mathias retorted, 'but the law doesn't say I can't lead one.'

The Port Reeve stared back, brow puckered at this fine point of law.

'Ah well, who gives a sod? Your horse and saddle are yours.'

The officials left. Matthias sat in the alcove and wondered what to do. He was determined not to wait for forty days before making his move. Father Aidan might be trustworthy but the longer he stayed, the more time Emloe's gang had to plot and collect reinforcements. He recalled Sir Edgar Ratcliffe marching to Rye and made his decision. He rang the small handbell Father Aidan had given him. After a short while the priest, much the worse for wear by drink and still chewing on a chicken leg, knocked on the side door. Matthias let him in. The priest's eyes glittered as Matthias held up another silver coin. He threw the chicken leg out of the door when a second coin appeared.

'Ah no, not yet.' Matthias drew his hand back. 'Father, I intend to leave tomorrow morning just after dawn. I'd be grateful if you would inform the mayor, Port Reeve and bailiffs.'

The priest smiled.

'I also want you to hire two of your burliest parishioners. They are to come well armed and ride behind me until I reach Rye.'

'Agreed,' Father Aidan slurred. 'I'll be honest, I'll be glad to see the back of you. So it's dawn tomorrow! Make sure you are ready. I'll bring some wine and chicken for you tonight. If you are going to walk, you'll need all the strength God and man can give you.'

Once he left Matthias went back to the alcove. He packed his belongings and went through the contents of his saddle-bag. He took out the scrap of parchment he had found at

Barnwick covered in Rosamund's handwriting. He held it to his face and kissed it, then put it inside a pocket of his jerkin. As he did, he noticed how soiled and dirty his clothes had become. He rubbed his unshaven cheek and chin.

'Don't worry,' he murmured. 'If you look like a cut-throat they might leave you alone.'

For a while he dozed, dreaming of Rosamund. When he awoke he felt she was close to him.

'Stay with me!' he whispered. 'Whatever happens, don't leave me!'

He went back to his saddlebag and found the piece of parchment Abbot Benedict had been working on. There was very little new. The old scholar had reached 1486: the words, 'Santerre', 'Exeter Hall' and 'Amasia' had all been deciphered in one long line. Then Abbot Benedict, as if he'd sensed death was close and realised Matthias needed this more than the past, had tried to jump. Matthias saw the name Rosamund. Abbot Benedict had got Barnwick wrong, as he had James Stewart's name: each of these had a question mark beside them. Fitzgerald was translated 'Fitzpatrick'. The other entries were even more vague. A mere collection of letters or words: Castile? Alhambra? Isabella? And a strange phrase: 'Into the west to the "Beautiful Islands".' Matthias realised the old Abbot was anticipating his desire to travel to Spain. At the foot of the page Abbot Benedict had written a series of dates with numbers in brackets beside them: '1471 (7)? 1478 (14)? 1486 (21)? 1492 (28)?' Matthias sat back and stared up at the glittering red sanctuary lamp.

'What do these mean?' he murmured.

Of course, he concluded: when he had been at Oxford he had learnt that seven was a sacred number. It was also agreed that seven, and its multiples, be regarded as decisive stages in a man's life. At the age of seven, a child reached the age of reason, according to the theologians. At fourteen a boy was regarded as a young man: at twenty-one a full adult.

Matthias got to his feet. 'I was just past my seventh birthday when I met the hermit,' he murmured. 'I was fourteen when I was sent to the abbey school. I was past twenty-one when my troubles began in Oxford.'

Matthias paused in his pacing. Now he was in his twenty-eighth year. He recalled the date: mid-July 1491. In February 1492 he'd pass his twenty-eighth birthday. Would this be a decisive time? Would the Rose Demon show his hand? But where? How?

After a while Matthias gave up this speculation and returned to planning what would happen tomorrow. Father Aidan came back with some food. He told Matthias that the Port Reeve had agreed to be here at dawn the following morning whilst two parishioners, in return for another piece of silver, could be persuaded to escort Matthias to Rye.

The following morning, when the church was still dark, Father Aidan escorted Matthias down on to the front porch of the church. The Port Reeve was standing on the steps. A short distance away two burly parishioners sat on tired-looking hacks. Between them stood Matthias' horse, saddled and harnessed. Father Aidan took his baggage down to this. The Port Reeve stuck a crude crucifix and a small scroll of parchment into Matthias' hand and gabbled through a proclamation.

'You, Matthias Fitzosbert, are to journey by foot to the nearest town, the port of Rye. You are not to leave the King's highway. You are safe from malicious attack provided you do not. You are to carry the crucifix at all times. You are to be in Rye, whatever the weather, within five days. You are to declare yourself to the Port Reeve, show him the enclosed proclamation and be on board ship within three days. You are never to return to England without a royal pardon. If you do, you will suffer summary execution. Given at Rye on the Feast of St Mary Magdalene, the twenty-second of July 1491.'

The Port Reeve shoved Matthias down the steps.

'Now piss off!' he shouted. 'And don't come back!'

Matthias, despite such rough handling, shouted his farewell and thanks to Father Aidan. The priest lifted his hand in blessing and Matthias walked off, across the market square and down the narrow thoroughfare to the town gates. Everything was quiet. The sun was beginning to rise but the market horn hadn't been sounded: the houses he passed were shuttered and silent. Here and there a dog barked, beggars and whores scuttled in the shadows. A sleepy-eyed guard opened the gates and, within the hour, Matthias was in the open countryside. Behind him his two guardian angels, coarse-featured, rough-voiced men, trotted slowly, fighting hard to control Matthias' horse.

Matthias walked purposefully. He was glad to be free of the church. The day was a fine one. Birds swooped and warbled above him; on either side fields of golden wheat stretched to the far horizon. By mid-morning Matthias was tired and hungry. He and his guards paused to drink from a small brook and eat some of the bread and cheese Father Aidan had supplied. The two men were very taciturn, uneasy at what they were doing but their mood and faces brightened when Matthias promised them a shilling as soon as they reached Rye. They continued on their journey. One of the guards was hopeful that they could be in Rye that same day and Matthias agreed. The sky was blue, the sun strong, the trackway underfoot made easy going. Matthias thanked God it was summer, for heavy rains turned such trackways into mud-clogging morasses.

Matthias kept up a vigorous walk. As he did so, he tried not to concentrate on the aches in his legs and the dryness in his throat. He thought of Rosamund and the day they went out to the Roman wall: so short a time ago, yet, to Matthias, it seemed an eternity away. He felt a flurry of excitement at leaving England and being free of people who wanted to use him. Once again he recalled his mood before the battle of East Stoke, not frightened or fearful, but waiting. He was not frightened of death. Life was so bitter, what further horrors could it hold for him? He wondered if a time would come when the Rose Demon might leave him alone? Would he be allowed to live a normal life and, if he did, what should he be? Clerk or soldier? Merchant or scholar? Would he ever meet another woman? No one would ever replace Rosamund but life could be lonely and Matthias was tired of being by himself.

They forded a small river, Matthias stopping to bathe his hands and face in the clear water. The countryside then changed, the fields giving way to dark woods on either side. The sunlight was blocked out, the birdsong not so clear, yet Matthias was glad for the coolness. He wondered if they really would be in Rye by nightfall. He walked deeper into the forest, admiring how the sunlight showed up the different shades of green. He stopped to pluck a wild rose growing on the edge of the path. He heard a whirr like the flight of some bird, followed by a cry. He turned round to see both his guards fall from their horses, clutching at the arrows in their chests. Dark shapes slipped from the trees. Before Matthias could even move, these figures drew knives, quickly slitting his guards' throats. Matthias whirled round. Other men, hooded and masked, crept on to the path, forming a ring around him. Matthias held his cross up though he knew the gesture was futile: it was struck from his hand. He was bundled on to his horse and led under the spreading branches of an oak tree. He struggled but his hands were bound behind him. A horseman rode up, his eyes glittering behind his mask.

'Guilty of Emloe's death!' he rasped. 'You'll die the way you should!'

A piece of sacking was put over Matthias' head. A noose tightened round his neck. He dug his feet more firmly into the stirrups. His horse, nervous, shied and reared. Matthias hung on grimly, digging in his knees even as Emloe's gang tried to pull the horse clear and leave him to die of excruciating strangulation. Matthias panicked. He struggled with all his might. Men were shouting. He heard the rasp of steel. His horse reared in agony, then collapsed beneath him. Matthias hung suspended, the noose biting deep into his throat. He heard, as if above the roaring of waves, the sound of horses, and the rope was cut. He fell and hit something lying on the road. The sacking was pulled off, the cord round his neck swiftly cut. For a while he just lay gasping and retching. The cords binding his hands were also sliced. He realised he was lying on the corpse of his horse.

'Bastards!' he muttered. 'He was a brave animal!'

'Aye,' a voice said. 'If he hadn't fought back, we wouldn't have been in time.'

Matthias rolled over and stared into the smiling face of Sir Edgar Ratcliffe. He struggled to his knees. The corpses of Emloe's men littered the trackway and, by the sounds from the trees, others were being hunted and killed deep in the woods.

'Nothing like a bit of exercise for my lads,' Ratcliffe smiled, helping Matthias to his feet.

For a while Matthias let himself be tended: one of Ratcliffe's retainers bathed his neck and wrists with coarse wine. Another took him to sit beneath the trees, from where he watched his horse being lifted and the saddle taken off. Eventually Ratcliffe's men, with bloody swords and daggers, returned on to the trackway. Sir Edgar came and squatted before Matthias.

'I am sorry we couldn't save your friends,' he retorted. 'But we came as fast as we could. Your messenger said that she knew we were leaving today and that she was frightened you would be attacked.' Ratcliffe dug into his purse and brought out three pure gold coins. 'There's nothing like a pretty face and a bag of gold coins to spur on a knight errant.' He turned. 'Did you get the bastards?' he shouted.

A blond, surly-faced young man dressed in a black leather jerkin and red hose came swaggering across, thumbs pushed into his war belt. He had a cast in one eye which made him look sly.

'City bullyboys,' he declared. 'They really should have kept to the alleyways. Two or three got away but the rest . . .' He pointed back to where Ratcliffe's men were now stripping the dead. 'They are as dead as those. Anyway, who's he?'

'I've told you,' Ratcliffe replied. 'A friend of mine. He's the one the young lady told us about.'

The man hawked and spat, then swaggered back to join the plundering. Ratcliffe narrowed his eyes and watched him go.

'Gervase Craftleigh,' he said, 'my lieutenant. He'd like to command this troop. A good fighting man, but mean-spirited and choleric.'

'What are you talking about?' Matthias asked. 'What young lady?'

'Oh.' Ratcliffe pulled back his chain mail coif and wiped the sweat from his face. 'We heard rumours about your little trouble in Winchelsea. Ah well, I thought, that's the end of that: we've lost a good recruit. Then this morning, just before dawn a beautiful, red-haired woman came to our camp. Matthias,' Ratcliffe shook his head, 'she was exquisite: hair like fire, creamy skin, eyes full of life. She was with a man. It was dark, I couldn't make out his features. Anyway, she said that you were leaving Winchelsea today but that she feared for your safety. Well, to cut a long story short, she offered me a small purse of gold and kissed me on each cheek, so we struck camp and marched as quickly as we could. We could see you were in difficulties.' He gestured back to the road. 'Thank God for your horse. He was rearing and kicking until the bastards killed the poor brute. What was it all about?'

Matthias told him about Emloe and his gang, depicting it as a blood feud. Ratcliffe heard him out and got to his feet.

'Well,' he sighed, 'I've done what I came to do.' He looked up at the sky. 'We are going to camp out under the stars tonight: you are welcome to stay.'

'Can I still join your company?' Matthias asked.

Ratcliffe pulled a face. 'Matthias, we've signed articles. We are now a full free company, nothing can be decided without a full vote of the council. We'll do that tonight.'

Matthias was given one of the horses from Emloe's gang. The soldiers stayed for a while to drag the corpses from the road, Ratcliffe insisting that they gave them some sort of decent burial. By the time they had finished, it had grown dark. They continued their journey through the woods and camped in the lee of a small hill. For a while all was bustle: horse lines were set up, a latrine dug, campfires lit, whilst some of Ratcliffe's men went hunting, bringing back a pheasant and a couple of rabbits. These were quickly prepared for roasting. Coarse wine was served, everyone sitting round the campfire congratulating themselves on a good day's work. Matthias gathered they were not only richer by the gold from Morgana, for it must have been she, but Emloe's men had also provided horseflesh, armour, clothing, not to mention the contents of the purses.

'Well, gentlemen?' Ratcliffe got to his feet, clapping his hands. 'The man we saved wants to join us. I offered him a post before we all sealed articles and left Winchelsea. Now, this time tomorrow, he could well be on board our transport and sailing with us to Spain.'

A chorus of approval greeted his words.

'We've all done good work today. So, perhaps before we continue, it's only right to give thanks to God and our protector, St Raphael.'

'St Raphael! St Raphael! St Raphael!'

The cry was taken up. Sir Edgar recited a Paternoster, an Ave, a Gloria and, in a fine tenor voice, launched into a Latin hymn to Raphael, the great archangel who stood before God's throne. The rest of the company joined in: a fine harmonious sound which filled the silence of the night. Matthias realised that, in the main, he was in the presence of good men who regarded themselves as soldiers of Christ. He closed his eyes and said his own quiet prayer that he would be allowed to join them.

'Well,' Sir Edgar declared once the hymn was finished, 'Matthias Fitzosbert, is he a member of our troop or not? I say he is.'

The matter would have gone smoothly enough, the men already chorusing their 'Ayes', when Gervase Craftleigh sprang to his feet.

'No!' he cried.

The rest looked at him in silence.

'I say no!'

'Why?' Ratcliffe queried.

'We are all fighting men,' Craftleigh declared pugnaciously. 'We all know each other – well, to a certain extent – but who is this Fitzosbert? He's a felon. He killed a man in Winchelsea and took sanctuary in a church. We did say,' he added to a chorus of 'Ayes' and nodding heads, 'that no felon would be allowed into the company of St Raphael.' He smiled maliciously at Ratcliffe. 'We have no place for him. Thank God we lost no men in our recent fight. Oh, and by the way, when will the gold the red-haired woman brought be distributed?'

'When I say,' Ratcliffe replied calmly.

'Why not now?'

'According to the articles,' Ratcliffe reminded him, 'all booty is distributed on a monthly basis. Those same articles also placed great trust in me. I am a knight and God's own warrior, Master Craftleigh, I am no thief.'

Craftleigh, however, remained unabashed.

'Well,' he said, 'my vote is against Fitzosbert on two counts: he is a stranger and a murderer.'

'I killed in self-defence!' Matthias shouted.

'In which case,' Craftleigh sat down, 'why didn't you stand trial?'

'You know the reason.' Ratcliffe intervened. 'The dead man was the leader of those assassins we killed on the road.'

'Why did you kill him?' Craftleigh glared at Matthias.

'It's a long story,' he replied. 'And not your business to know.'

'Are you sure?' Ratcliffe asked quietly.

Matthias got to his feet. 'Take your vote!' he said.

He wandered off down the hill, bathing his hot face and hands in a small brook. He heard the hum of conversation behind him, then silence. He splashed more water over his face. He turned at the sound of footsteps. Sir Edgar Ratcliffe crouched beside him. His lips smiled, but his eyes were sad.

'The lads voted against you, Matthias. They would have taken you but Craftleigh is a troublemaker. He knows the famous articles, and so far the men—' he shrugged – 'they are still not too sure that I am truly their leader.' He patted Matthias on the shoulder and got up. 'But you can keep the horse and we'll take you into Rye. I am sorry I cannot do any more.'

Matthias stared up in the star-strewn sky. A full moon bathed the meadow and hillside in a silvery light. The cool water looked inviting. He saw a fish snaking amongst the reeds. He watched it curl and turn. His eyes grew heavy, he lay back on the grass and drifted off to sleep.

He began to dream immediately. He was lying in the camp, the fire was burning low. Across the red-hot embers Sir Edgar Ratcliffe, head back, mouth open, was sleeping like a baby. Matthias saw a shape move towards him. His hand went to his dagger, a thin Italian stiletto he always carried. He fumbled with his war belt but the dagger pouch was empty. In the dying light of the fire he saw Craftleigh lift a dagger – it was Matthias' own – and with both hands plunge it into the chest of the sleeping Ratcliffe.

'No!' Matthias sat up.

The night breeze was cold. Looking over his shoulder, he could see Ratcliffe and his company preparing for the night. Matthias scrambled to his feet and went back to the fireside. His saddle and belongings were piled high: he picked up his war belt, the stiletto was missing. He glanced up; Ratcliffe was watching him curiously.

'Sir Edgar, may I have a word, please?' He took the knight out of earshot of the others. 'My dagger's gone,' he declared.

Ratcliffe shrugged. 'Matthias, I saved your life. I can't account for every single item of your belongings.'

'No, it was stolen,' Matthias whispered hoarsely. 'I've had a dream, Sir Edgar. Tonight Craftleigh intends to kill you. He will stab you with my dirk. You will die and I will hang. Craftleigh will have the gold as well as the company of St Raphael.'

Ratcliffe, face tensed with rage, pushed Matthias away.

'You are a liar!' he hissed. 'Perhaps Craftleigh is right. You've lost your dagger and now you try to blacken a man's name and besmirch his reputation.'

'Sir Edgar, listen . . .'

Ratcliffe was striding off through the darkness. Matthias returned to the campfire. He took a small arbalest and loaded it. Someone pushed a cup of wine into his hand. He sipped it, it tasted a little bitter but he finished it, put the cup down and stretched out, resting his head on a saddle. He felt drowsy and, try as he might, he could not keep his eyes open.

He was roughly awoken by Ratcliffe. All around was uproar. Matthias pushed Ratcliffe away and half-raised himself. It was still dark. Men were running and shouting. Across the fire lay a corpse with a crossbow bolt embedded deep between the shoulder blades. Ratcliffe pulled Matthias to his feet. Someone threw wood on to the fire. Matthias glimpsed Craftleigh's face, eyes staring, a trickle of blood snaking out of the corner of his mouth. A few inches from his splayed fingers lay Matthias' dagger. Ratcliffe clasped Matthias' hand.

'How did you know?' he asked.

Matthias still felt heavy-headed: his mouth was dry, his throat parched.

'I meant to stay awake,' he declared. 'Someone gave me a cup of wine . . .'

'I did.' An archer came forward. 'Craftleigh filled it and told me to give it to you. He said it would help drown your sorrows.'

'I watched you drink it,' Ratcliffe said. 'Then you were asleep within minutes. I called your name. I even came across and shook you.' He grinned. 'I might as well have tried to rouse the dead. I began to wonder. The cup was still beside you. How, I thought, could a man make such an allegation then fall so quickly into a deep sleep? I told an archer to hide in the shadows. If he saw any danger during the night, he was to loose.'

'I saw a figure move.' The crossbow man stepped into the firelight. 'Craftleigh was so quick, so silent. I saw the glint of steel, so I loosed.' He hawked and spat into the flames. 'He was a murdering bastard!'

'Comrades,' Ratcliffe put his arm round Matthias' shoulders, 'may I introduce the newest recruit to our company, Matthias Fitzosbert.'

A loud cheer rang out. Sir Edgar shook Matthias' hand.

'You can take Craftleigh's armour and weapons. His horse is good as well. Thomas!' He shouted at an archer. 'Take Craftleigh's corpse and bury it amongst the trees. The rest, catch what sleep you can!'

Matthias returned to his makeshift bed.

The next morning he felt better, more able to receive the congratulations of Ratcliffe and the others. By noon they were in Rye, clopping through the cobbles of the winding streets down to the quayside. Ratcliffe had already signed indentures with the captain of a cog, the *St Anthony*. Later in the day, the entire company and its horses were taken out by barge to the waiting ship. Just before dusk the captain gave the orders to weigh anchor. The ship turned slowly, its great loose sail filling with wind. Three times, the ship's banners were dipped in honour of the Trinity, whilst Sir Edgar led his company in their hymn to St Raphael. Matthias, standing on the poop, watched the retreating white cliffs of England. In his heart he knew he'd never see or set foot on that land again.

31

'Three whores have been murdered in the last month.'

The Castilian captain knelt down and covered the corpse of a sallow-skinned girl, her black hair spread out like a fan around her head. The sheet was dirty but at least it protected her from the flies which, despite winter, still plagued the great Catholic army outside the Moorish city of Granada.

Matthias murmured a prayer and walked back along the street, past the stables which could house a thousand horses and on to the edge of the great no man's land, the Vega, brown-scorched earth which stretched from the camp of Ferdinand and Isabella up to the soaring walls and formidable gates of Granada. Matthias fought to control his own thoughts. He looked up at the city: above its soaring, rambling walls rose the Alhambra, the great Moorish palace, a place of mystery and power in the centre of the city. Matthias had heard the stories about its stately gardens and arching fountains, its intricate mosaic rooms and beautifully tiled floors; its chambers which seemed to open endlessly from one sun-filled courtyard to another. Beyond Granada, through the early morning mist, rose the snow-capped ridges of the Sierra Nevada.

Matthias sat down, his back to a tree. He and Sir Edgar had been in Spain for almost four months. It was now December 1491. Matthias could hardly believe that he was so far from home, part of a crusading army, tens of thousands of men from Castile, Aragon, León, France and the Low Countries. He and Sir Edgar had joined up with another English contingent under Lord Rivers: young men, fired by an ideal, determined to place the silver cross of Castile on the ramparts of Granada and end Moorish power in Spain for ever.

For the first few weeks Matthias had been fascinated. Both King Ferdinand and Queen Isabella had joined the army: he had glimpsed them either riding through the camp or seated on their thrones before the great high altar when solemn Mass was sung on Sundays and Holy Days. Matthias had been caught up in the excitement of this great crusading army. So determined were the Catholic monarchs to take Granada, they had built a small city to house their army, quarrying rock and masonry to build the town of Holy Faith; a potent warning to the Muslims that the besiegers would never give up until Granada was theirs.

Matthias had witnessed the daring deeds, the life and death struggle between the Catholic monarchs and their Moorish enemy. A Muslim champion, Yarfel, had galloped close into the Castilian encampment and hurled his spear at the royal quarters. It bore an insulting and obscene note for Isabella, Queen of Castile. In revenge a Castilian soldier, Puljar, had led fifteen companions through a poorly guarded gate into Granada's central mosque. The knights had, in whispered voices, rededicated the mosque to the Virgin Mary and left a note, pinned by a dagger to the main door, with the words 'Ave Maria' scrawled across it.

Matthias had also become used to the camp's routine. He and the rest had soon recovered from a turbulent voyage down the Bay of Biscay and the exhausting march from Cádiz across southern Spain to the Catholic camp.

Shortly after All-Hallows, Matthias had heard rumours: young women, whores, camp followers had been found barbarously murdered, their throats pierced, their cadavers drained of blood. Matthias had kept his own counsel, but this morning, the corpse he had just glimpsed had been found where the English had their quarters. One look had convinced Matthias the Rose Demon had returned.

'Ever the dreamer, eh, Matthias?'

Sir Edgar Ratcliffe stood over him. His face had soon burnt brown under the Spanish sun, his beard and moustache were more luxuriant. Sir Edgar, however, still had the easy charm and good-natured camaraderie which had first attracted Matthias.

'You saw the whore?'

'Aye I did,' Mathias replied.

Sir Edgar sighed and sat down beside him.

'I knew her.' He caught Matthias' sharp glance. 'Not in the

carnal sense.' Ratcliffe grinned. 'But she was a merry girl and could dance wildly like a gypsy.'

Matthias nodded and stared across the Vega at the green silver-edged banner floating above the main gateway of Granada. Matthias had wondered if Sir Edgar could be trusted yet. There again, even as late as yesterday, he and the English knight had shared the Sacrament together at a Mass celebrated by Lord Rivers' chaplain.

'Are you waiting for him?' Ratcliffe abruptly asked. 'It should happen about now.'

Matthias looked back at him, puzzled.

'Yarfel!' Ratcliffe exclaimed.

'Oh yes,' Matthias nodded. 'Him! Someone should accept his challenge.'

Matthias studied the heavily fortified postern door built into one of the side towers near the main gate of Granada. Every morning a trumpet would blow and the huge Moorish champion, head protected by a spiked helmet, his chain mail covered by a flapping red cloak, would ride his great black destrier out of Granada and issue his challenge to single combat. This had begun a month earlier. At first the challenge had been quickly accepted. Time and again some knight from the Spanish army had ridden out, pennants snapping bravely on the end of his spear. Each time Yarfel had been victorious. A superb horseman, a skilled swordsman, he had ridden back into Granada with his enemy's head stuck on his lance. The rules of chivalry forbade a general assault upon him. However, his constant daily mocking and easy victories had so dispirited the Spanish army that Queen Isabella had issued a written order that no one, on pain of death, was to accept the challenge. No one was even to watch when he rode out, but Matthias ignored the decree.

Every morning he came to the same place and studied the Moorish champion: his posture, the way he guided his horse with his knees, the speed with which he lifted his sword and the manner in which his weapons seemed as much part of his body as his arm or leg. Slowly, as each day passed, Matthias began to wonder. He had been accepted by Ratcliffe's company and enjoyed their lazy comradeship, the good-natured banter of the camp. He was fascinated by Spain, its freezing nights, the searing heat of the day; the gorgeous panoply of the great lords, the sultry-eyed beauty of their women, the heavy wine, the wild stamping dances and that gypsy music which fired the heart and filled the nights with melodious, twanging sounds.

'A land of rocks and saints,' Lord Rivers described Spain.

Nevertheless, Matthias never forgot why he was here. As the weeks passed he wondered where his great chivalrous idea would lead him. He had imagined great battles, men storming crenellated walls, bloody hand-to-hand fights. Instead, nothing but the boring routine of the military camp, until Yarfel had come out of the gates and issued his challenge. Matthias had brooded. Was this the place, he wondered, where he would die? In between Granada and the Catholic camp, defending the honour of the Cross and reputation of a Spanish queen?

A shrill trumpet blast stirred him from his reverie. Despite Ferdinand and Isabella's instructions, knights, squires and soldiers gathered at the gates or climbed on to the parapets of the makeshift walls of their camp. The postern gate in the city walls opened. Another trumpet blast and the Moorish champion rode out. The early morning sun flashed and gleamed on his armour and helmet. His great cloak billowing out behind him, he rode within the bowshot of the Spanish camp and issued his challenges. He spoke in the lingua franca, the patois of the soldiers, calling them cowards, the sons of bitches, women in men's clothing. He ridiculed Isabella as a yellow-haired strumpet and, punning on her name, called her a new Jezebel, a witch, a virago. The Spanish soldiers returned this abuse with vigour but Yarfel simply laughed as his horse pranced up and down.

'It's a wonder no one shoots him,' Matthias murmured. 'A master bowman could plant a shaft in his neck or pierce that chain mail.'

'And bring dishonour on us all!' Ratcliffe snapped. 'A man, whom we could not kill in fair fight, but secretly murder. That is not the way, Matthias, the code of chivalry!' He turned in exasperation to the young Englishman, but started in surprise for Matthias was gone.

Sir Edgar shrugged and continued to watch the Moor ride up and down. Ratcliffe could not understand Fitzosbert: a quiet, moody man constantly lost in his own thoughts, though a good Christian. Fitzosbert regularly prayed and attended

Mass, took the Sacrament and, every week, was shrived by a priest. Nevertheless, though they had shared a long and dangerous voyage, followed by a dusty, throat-parching march, Matthias was as much a stranger to Sir Edgar as he was on the first day they had met.

The English knight returned to studying the Moorish champion, grudgingly admiring how the man now made his horse cavort and dance. Sir Edgar was distracted by shouting behind him, men running, a horse's hooves. He turned and stared in astonishment as Matthias, dressed in his chain mail suit, a sallet upon his head, cantered through the gateway: shield on one arm, the reins wrapped round his wrist, his long stabbing sword held aloft. Spanish soldiers ran along on either side in a half-hearted attempt to stop him. Matthias reined in and smiled at Ratcliffe's astonishment.

'I decided yesterday,' he said.

Ratcliffe grabbed the bridle of Matthias' horse, gesturing angrily at the Spaniards to back away.

'This man is English,' he shouted. 'He is under my command.'

The Spaniards shrugged and stepped back.

'For God's sake, Matthias!' Ratcliffe seized Matthias' knee. 'All you are carrying is a wooden shield, a sword, chain mail which has seen better days, and a helmet I wouldn't even piss in!'

Matthias moved his sword and shield to the other hand. He took off the helmet and let it fall with a clang at Ratcliffe's feet.

'Sir Edgar, you are right. If the Moor didn't kill me the stench from that would.'

'Yarfel is a champion,' Ratcliffe whispered hoarsely. 'And you know about the royal command. No man is to accept his challenge on pain of death.'

Matthias gently grasped Ratcliffe's hand.

'Don't you realise, Sir Edgar, I have to? I must prepare for death as any man.' He gave a lopsided smile. 'Look at him, Sir Edgar!'

Ratcliffe looked out where Yarfel, alerted by the clamour around the gate, was now sitting on his horse, staring in their direction.

'He'll kill you,' Ratcliffe retorted.

'Haven't you read the Scriptures?' Matthias replied. 'And David went up against Goliath and the Lord was with him.'

'But is the Lord with you?' Ratcliffe dug his fingers more tightly into Matthias' knee.

'I don't know. But, if he isn't, the Spanish soon will be!'

Matthias dug his spurs into his horse and galloped down the small escarpment on to the great open plateau. As in a dream he could hear the cries and shouts from the Spanish camp for the news had already spread. Men in their thousands were streaming through the walls or gates. He looked back: Ratcliffe was now surrounded by officers from the royal household. He heard a trumpet blast from Granada and glanced up. The battlements and towers were crowded, people clustered like ants to see the Christian fool who dared to pick up their champion's challenge. Matthias heard their yells and faint mocking laughter: he did not look the part in his battered chain mail, tattered leather saddle and simple wooden shield. He grasped his sword more carefully, calming his horse. For a while Yarfel chose to ignore him. He rode his destrier towards the Spaniards clustered all along the walls and edge of their camp. The Moor was speaking fast. Matthias only understood a few words but he gathered that Yarfel was mocking him, taunting the Spanish that was he the best that they could send out? The Moorish champion stood high in his stirrups. He now deigned to notice Matthias pointing his sword towards him. He kept uttering one word, which was taken up by the Moors lining the battlements. At last Matthias understood it. They were calling him a scarecrow. Rocks and pieces of offal and dirt were thrown from the battlements. They had no hope of hitting him, the gesture was more a sign of the soldiers' disdain than an attempt to hurt.

Matthias closed his eyes. He thought of Rosamund. They were alone in their chamber. She was sitting in a chair, teasing him, trying to keep her face straight whilst her eyes danced with mischief. She held a book in her hand, one of those chivalrous romances she loved to read and then make fun of. The fire in the hearth burnt merrily. Outside it was snowing. Matthias felt that, if he could only walk towards her, if he could put his arms around her once more, he would not be on barren, sun-scorched Spanish earth awaiting his death but warm and secure in their chamber at Barnwick.

'That was heaven,' Matthias whispered. 'Oh Rosamund.' He fought back the tears. 'I miss you. I am so lonely. I can do no more.'

A loud roar made him open his eyes. He glanced towards the Spanish camp. The entire army was now assembled, watching what he was doing. He glimpsed the pennants and banners of the royal household. So far no Spaniard had dared to ride on the field to stop him and Matthias knew they would not. Deep in their hearts, the soldiers wanted Yarfel's challenge answered and couldn't care whether Matthias lived or died. The Moorish champion turned his horse and, sword extended, saluted someone above the main gateway of the city. Matthias, his mind still full of Rosamund, watched the Moor canter towards him. Matthias controlled his horse, dropping his sword down as a gesture of peace. The Moor followed suit and reined in. Matthias gently spurred his horse forward. The Moor took off his pointed helmet, pushing back the chain mail coif: his face was olive-skinned, dark, beautiful eyes, a finely cut moustache and beard round a soft, sensuous mouth. The Moorish champion, eyes unblinking, spoke slowly in Spanish. Matthias shook his head uncomprehendingly.

'By what name are you called?' The Moor lapsed into the lingua franca.

'I am Matthias Fitzosbert. I am English.'

'Matthias Fitzosbert?' The Moor's eyes smiled as his tongue tripped over the strange-sounding names. 'You are a long way from home, Inglese. Is it your fate to die under a foreign sun?'

'My fate is in God's hands,' Matthias retorted. 'I care not if I live or die.'

The words were out before he could stop them. The Moor edged his horse closer, his face puckered in concern.

'You are not frightened of death?'

Matthias stared down and watched the sun glint on the Moor's sword.

'I am sorry.' He lifted his head. 'I did not mean that. It's not so much death I fear. I simply do not care if I have to leave this life.'

'Is that why you are here?' Yarfel put his helmet back on: both men were now impervious to the growing clamour from either side.

'I don't know,' Matthias replied. 'It is God's will.'

'Allah il Allah.' Yarfel replied. 'Our fates are written.'

He gathered up his reins and galloped back sixty yards before stopping and turning. Yarfel held his sword up, turning once again to salute the rose-red walls of Granada. Matthias grasped his reins. The weight of the shield in his left arm was hurting him and, despite the cries from the Catholic encampment, he dropped it on the ground. He watched Yarfel prepare for battle. The sun was growing stronger. A heat haze now swirled across the open expanse.

Now Yarfel was moving at a canter. Matthias crossed himself and urged his horse forward. As they approached, both men spurred their horses into a charge. Matthias, reins in his left hand, his sword slightly out, kept his eyes on the Moor. He forgot about the sun, the hard ground underneath, the breeze cooling the sweat on his brow: his world had shrunk to that man charging towards him. Matthias remembered what he had learnt. Yarfel expected Matthias to pass him in a cloud of dust and a clash of swords. Matthias intended different. He let the reins slip, guiding his horse by his knees; he now held his sword with two hands. Yarfel moved, as he'd expected, a little to Matthias' right and Matthias moved with him. They met: Matthias' horse crashing into Yarfel's. Matthias felt himself lifted from the saddle up in the air then crashing to the earth, a bone-jarring fall, but he rolled and, ignoring the searing pain in his left leg, struggled to his feet, sword out. Yarfel also had been pitched from the saddle. The Moor had lost his helmet but he was ready for battle: curved scimitar out, legs apart, he waited for Matthias to charge.

As the dust settled and the spectators saw what was happening, a great roar rose from the Spanish camp. Yarfel had never been dismounted: he often despatched his opponent within a few minutes of the initial charge. Matthias edged closer. The Moor was watching him intently. Matthias prayed and realised he was praying to Rosamund. In a sense he wasn't here. He was in the outer bailey at Barnwick Castle, learning the tricks and turns of a professional swordsman. He coughed and lowered his head as if there was dust in his eyes. Yarfel charged. Matthias stepped sideways. Swords clashed, Matthias twisted his and cut deep into the Moor's right arm. Yarfel stepped away. This time Matthias moved in slashing and jabbing with his sword, forcing the Moorish champion backwards. Despite the heat and the dust, the pain in his leg from his fall, Matthias felt cold. Yarfel's sword did not bother him; that winking flashing piece of steel was not to be feared. He must watch the Moor's eyes. Yarfel glanced away, a quick momentary look and Matthias closed. Instead of swinging from the right Yarfel brought his sword up in an attempt to slash Matthias' chest. Matthias moved, not sideways, but backwards. The Moor lost his footing. Matthias had seen others do this: a blow given too quickly, too strongly and for a few seconds the right side of the neck was exposed. Matthias' sword sliced through the air: a slashing, deep-boned cut which finished the fight. The Moor turned, his face contorted in agony. He staggered, knees buckling. He went to speak but his eyes rolled in his head and the blood frothed out of his mouth. He crashed to his knees and sprawled out on the ground.

Matthias felt no elation. He stared in disbelief. It had been so quick, so effortless. That was not what should have happened. He looked towards Granada. As he did so, the Catholic camp burst into cheering which rose to the heavens. An entire line of Crusaders now rushed forward. Men brandishing swords and shields as the trumpets of the Catholic army began to bray their defiance. Soon he was not alone. People were pressing about him. Someone kicked the fallen Yarfel and Matthias screamed his protest. Sir Edgar Ratcliffe was there, a friend amongst the sea of faces. Matthias begged Ratcliffe to show respect to Yarfel's corpse. The Englishman agreed. He spoke quickly in French, much-used here, to a Spanish officer standing behind him. The man nodded. Matthias' legs grew weak. He resheathed his sword and turned to look for his horse.

'I really should ride away,' he muttered. The sweat grew cold on his skin. 'I shouldn't be here.' He took a step forward, the sky seemed to move, whirl around, and Ratcliffe caught him as he fainted.

When Matthias awoke, he looked towards the mouth of the tent and saw it was dark. Men were clustered there chattering excitedly in Spanish. He pulled himself up. Ratcliffe came out of the shadows, put an arm round his shoulders and lifted a wineskin to his lips.

'Well, well, my boy!'

His words reminded Matthias of Fitzgerald. He looked up sharply but Sir Edgar smiled.

'Don't be alarmed, Matthias. When you fell from your horse, you received a blow to your head. Didn't you feel it?'

'No.'

'You defeated the champion,' Ratcliffe whispered, pulling him up and raising the bolsters to support him. 'So quickly. I didn't know we had a Lancelot amongst us!'

A figure blocked the entrance to the tent. He spoke in Spanish and Ratcliffe replied. The man came forward and crouched beside Matthias.

'I am the Duke of Medina-Sidonia,' he began slowly. 'I can speak your tongue.' His grizzled face broke into a smile. 'I learnt it on an embassy to your fog-bound island.' He opened his pouch, took out a small, jewelled cross and placed it carefully around Matthias' neck. 'You broke their Majesties' command. You picked up the Moor's challenge but God was with you. Their Majesties have been kind enough to send you this, a token of their affection and esteem.' He also took a small scroll of parchment and a heavy jingling purse from his pouch. 'This is a pass which will give you permission to go wherever you wish. It commands all officers of the Crown to assist you in your passage and provide you with every sustenance and comfort. You are to be regarded, here in Spain, as their Majesties' most loyal servant.' The man rose and bowed stiffly. 'When Granada falls, and fall it will, you are to ride in triumph with other members of the royal household.'

Matthias spent the next few days recovering from his bruises. Ratcliffe fussed around him like a mother hen, carefully arranging that those who came to see the English champion did not stay too long. The tent Matthias found himself in was the gift of a Spanish bishop. Other presents arrived: silken cloths, fruit, cooked dishes, wine. Matthias asked for these to be distributed amongst the company of St Raphael.

After a while the excitement subsided. Concerns were taken up by news that the rulers of Granada, fearful of the city being starved to death or taken by storm, had sent out envoys to enquire about an honourable surrender.

Matthias was left to his own devices and noticed how Ratcliffe's attitude was changing. As Matthias cleaned some equipment, or sat round the campfire with the rest of the company, he would catch Sir Edgar watching him from the corner of his eye, studying him carefully. At length, one night just after they had celebrated Christmas, Matthias went to his usual place outside the camp, staring up at the stars, wondering what he would do next. He glimpsed the pinpricks of light along the battlements or from windows along the walls. Granada would fall. The Spanish kings would take possession of this last city in Moorish hands but what would he do? Ratcliffe was talking of leading his men north into France, then east to join the Teutonic knights or even the Hospitallers in the Middle Sea. A twig snapped behind him; Matthias whirled round.

'It's only me!' Ratcliffe came and sat beside him. 'They say it's a beautiful city.' He began pointing towards the battlements. 'A veritable treasure house.'

'Why have you come, Edgar?'

Ratcliffe chewed on the corner of his lip.

'I watched you fight, Matthias,' he replied slowly. 'God forgive me, I was already whispering your Requiem.'

Matthias sensed he was smiling.

'Then I saw you charge. Your horse colliding with that of the Moor. Everything was covered in a curtain of dust. When it settled and I saw you standing, sword out, ready to fight, I thought, God is with that man.'

'And?'

'You were so fast,' Ratcliffe continued. He plucked at a piece of the dried grass and held it between his lips.

'What are you implying, Sir Edgar? What is this about?'

The English knight faced him squarely, his eyes no longer tender but hard and certain.

'Don't you realise, Matthias? Here you are, nothing more than an Englishman at arms. You rode out on a sorry-looking horse without helmet and shield, yet you killed a Moorish champion: a man who had slain, in open combat, some of the best knights of Castile and Aragon. You despatched him in minutes like a farmer would a pig.' He shrugged and sat, head half-cocked, listening to the faint strains of a guitar, the stamp of feet and the cries and shouts of the soldiers, encouraging some woman in her mad, passionate dance.

'I was injured,' Matthias replied churlishly. 'And all soldiers have luck.'

'I haven't forgotten,' Ratcliffe replied, 'on the road to Rye: you warned me about Craftleigh. I thought it was just a presentiment, a premonition?'

'And now?'

'When you fell unconscious and were brought back to the camp, the Spanish had Yarfel's body removed. You didn't kill him outright.' He paused and Matthias' blood ran cold. 'He was taken to the Santa Hermanda. You know who they are? The Holy Brotherhood, the military arm of the Inquisition. They have doctors, physicians, leeches, they are also headed by one of the most powerful men in Spain, the Dominican, Tomas de Torquemada. He's confessor to Queen Isabella. Yarfel regained consciousness, just for a short while. He said something strange. He called out your name, Matthias, then he added something in Latin.'

Matthias stiffened.

' "*Creatura bona atque parva*," the Moor whispered. He said it again. A few seconds later he was dead.' Ratcliffe chewed on the grass blade. 'Torquemada came to see me. He had been by Yarfel's bedside hoping to elicit information about the state of the garrison in Granada. He wondered why a Moor should call out your name and what was the meaning of these words? Torquemada,' Ratcliffe continued slowly, 'is a dangerous man. He passionately believes in the *limpieza de sangre*, the purity of the Spanish blood. He sees Spain as a great Catholic kingdom. He argues constantly with their Majesties, so Lord Rivers has told me, that, when Granada falls, the purity of the Spanish blood must be maintained. Spain is to be purged of all Moriscos, the Conversi, those Muslims who have converted to Catholicism, as well as Jews, schismatics, heretics and,' he looked up at the star-strewn sky, 'those guilty of dabbling in the black arts.'

'Are you accusing me of being a warlock?' Matthias snapped, getting to his feet.

'No, Matthias, I am not. I am giving you a warning.' Ratcliffe also scrambled to his feet. 'When Granada falls, do not stay too long in Spain. Indeed, if you have incurred the interest of Master Torquemada, I strongly suggest that you leave Spain as quickly as you can, whilst you can.'

'But I am leaving with you?' Matthias knew his words sounded half-hearted.

Ratcliffe lifted a hand. 'Are you, Matthias?' he asked softly. 'Do you really want to come? You are a man searching for death, Matthias. God knows what nightmares you suffer and only God knows what happened out there in that terrible fight. You are, in truth, an uncommon man. I do not believe your destiny lies with me or the company of St Raphael.' He let his hand drop. 'We will see you out of Spain, but after that . . .' He shrugged and walked off into the darkness.

Matthias stared up at the sky.

'Even then,' he murmured, 'the Rose Demon must have suspected what I was doing. Was he so close?'

Matthias heard a sound behind him. He glimpsed a figure stride off. In the fading light of a flickering torch, Matthias recognised the black and white robes of a Dominican monk.

32

On 2 January 1492, so all the Chroniclers of Europe wrote, God manifested his glory to his people when Boabdil, the last Moorish king of Granada, surrendered his city to Ferdinand and Isabella and secretly left his palace by the door of the Seven Sighs. The main gates to the city were thrown open and, with banners flying and trumpets braying, the Catholic army passed into the streets of Granada.

Matthias Fitzosbert, on a specially caparisoned destrier, rode in the long snaking column of the splendidly arrayed household of Ferdinand and Isabella. The sun had barely risen but already the townspeople, Christian, Moor and Jew, had flocked out to greet their new rulers. Ferdinand and Isabella had promised the citizens their lives and freedom whilst the strictest instructions had been issued against pillaging or the molestation of any of Granada's inhabitants.

Matthias rode alongside Sir Edgar Ratcliffe, his own anxieties forgotten, as he stared in wonderment at this jewel of a city: cool, porticoed basilicas, marble villas, squares washed by fountains, gardens neatly laid out behind terraced walls and, everywhere, a mixture of fragrant smells: precious oils from the perfume quarter, the mouth-watering odours from the kitchens and cook shops and, above all, the great puffs of incense coming from the censers swung by the priests who walked either side of the cavalcade. The sun rose higher and, despite the season, Matthias found it hot, his skin turning clammy beneath his leather hauberk.

At last they climbed a hill and entered the splendid Alhambra Palace. Many of the household remained outside but Matthias and Sir Edgar were allowed to follow the monarchs into the Hall of Justice. Matthias stared in wonderment at the lacy walls, painted ceilings, scintillating domes, brilliantly coloured tiles and silken gold mosaics. The palace was composed of interconnecting courtyards, each a perfect marble square enclosed by ivory-coloured columns and ornamental arches.

The Te Deum was sung at the centre of this palace. For the first time ever Matthias could study close up the two Spanish monarchs: long-nosed, heavy-jowled, russet-haired Ferdinand, with the face and eyes of a crafty fox; Isabella, skin like alabaster, her golden, grey-streaked hair gathered up under an elegant laced veil. With her perfectly composed face, high cheekbones, half-closed eyes, her hands joined devoutly in front of her, she reminded Matthias of a picture of the Virgin Mary he had once seen in an Oxford church. Memories of England flooded back and Matthias, standing in a porticoed corner of the Lion Court, felt a wave of homesickness. This was a strange world of glaring sunshine, savage, beautiful countryside, mysterious people, golden halls, silver-draped chambers, a place of opulence, of exotic tapestries, blood-red wine, meat and fruits piled high on golden platters. Matthias half-closed his eyes: it was also a place of danger and mystery. Here, in the Alhambra, or so he had been told, was the Room of Secrets, with its whispering alcoves which magnified and echoed every sound. According to Lord Rivers, a former sultan had beheaded over two score princes there and then washed his feet in their blood as it seeped across the marble floor.

Matthias opened his eyes. The great Lion Hall was now packed with soldiers, courtiers and priests gathered in a horseshoe fashion behind Ferdinand and Isabella, who knelt on cushions. They all watched two friars place up against the marble wall a gaunt, black cross on which an ivory-bodied Christ writhed in his final torments. The hall fell quiet. When suitable silence had been observed, there was a bray of trumpets from outside and the whole assembly broke into wild cheering as the signal that the great silver cross of Castile had, at last, been placed on the highest peak of the Alhambra Palace. Chamberlains and knight bannerets of the royal household now began to clear the hall. Matthias gazed round. Despite the clamour, the gorgeous colours, the jubiliation, the cries of triumph in a number of languages, he was sure he was being watched. His eyes swept the room: in the far corner a Dominican was watching him. The man was short and squat, his head neatly tonsured, his face was heavy, the nose aquiline but the friar's eyes seemed to burn: even though they stood yards apart, Matthias felt the Dominican was probing his very soul.

'Who is that?' he whispered gruffly.

Ratcliffe followed his gaze. 'The former Prior of Segovia,' he murmured. 'Confessor to Queen Isabella, about whom I have spoken. As you may know, he has been keeping you under strict surveillance during the last few days.'

Finally it was the turn of Matthias and Ratcliffe to leave. The English knight grasped Matthias' elbow and, when they left the Alhambra, took him across to a small wine shop. The place was full of roistering soldiers. In the small garden beyond, a small patch of faded green, intersected by pebble-dashed paths, Ratcliffe sat Matthias down. A young boy, eager to please, dressed in ragged leggings and a tattered linen shirt came up and jabbered at them, his eyes dancing with merriment. Ratcliffe laughed and tossed him a coin, demanding wine.

'Not water!' He shouted as the boy scampered away. '*Nualla aqua!*'

A few minutes later, a podgy woman brought two pewter cups of dark-red wine and a platter of brown bread smeared with butter and honey. She served them quickly, not raising her head. She took the coin Ratcliffe offered and waddled away.

'They don't know whether to be glad or sad.' Ratcliffe leant back against the hard brick wall, moving to ease the cramp in his thighs.

'Aren't they pleased?' Matthias asked. 'That Granada is Spanish and Catholic?'

'Granada was an island in itself,' Ratcliffe answered. 'A city of opulence, luxury, carefree in all matters. If it hadn't been for a group of fanatics, Boabdil would have surrendered as soon as the Catholic standards appeared over the hill. Granada is a place, Matthias, where Christian, Jew, Moor, as well as a few faiths you've never even heard of, lived in easy amity. Now all has changed. Granada is Catholic, the Santa Hermanda, the Inquisition and, above all, Tomas de Torquemada are here. Rumours are rife. Ferdinand and Isabella are pragmatic: they need the Moorish craftsmen and they depend heavily upon the Jewish bankers.'

'But Torquemada?' Matthias asked.

'Ah yes.' Ratcliffe lowered his voice and made a sign to Matthias to do so. He stared round the garden. 'Be careful, Matthias. They say that Torquemada even pays the birds, the mice and the rats to bring him information. Torquemada is a zealot. He not only sees a united Catholic Spain but, as I have said, a kingdom free of Moor and Jew. He has already accused Ferdinand and Isabella of selling the Church, like Judas sold Christ, for the sake of money and peace.'

'He said that!' Matthias exclaimed.

'Torquemada and his Inquisition answer to no one but God. Even the Pope in Rome fears him. He has Isabella's soul in the palm of his hand and, like a child with a toy, Torquemada knows how to use it!'

'And?'

Ratcliffe sipped at his wine, savouring its rich sweetness. 'It's better than the vinegar we've got in camp,' he observed. 'Lord Rivers has been given the honour of accompanying certain nobles from Granada to Madrid. He has asked for the company of St Raphael to join him. I have agreed. We leave tomorrow morning before first light.' He knocked the dust from his jacket. 'If you wish, and I advise you to do so, you may come with us.'

Matthias stared across the garden. Somewhere in the tavern a man was singing a lusty, merry song. Matthias realised he was in danger, that he was under surveillance by the Holy Brotherhood. Yet he didn't really care. Those dying words of Yarfel showed that, whatever he did, he was like a swimmer in a fast-flowing river: however hard he struggled, the current would always have its way. He closed his eyes. He'd always been fleeing: from Oxford, from Barnwick, from Scotland, from London, from St Wilfrid's, from Emloe's men. He opened his eyes.

'I'll stay,' he declared.

'In which case,' Ratcliffe put his cup down and stood up, 'I suggest you find quarters in the city here.' He pointed to the cross the Spanish Queen had sent Matthias. 'You have the royal warrant to do what you want and go where you will. I shall arrange for whatever the company owes you to be left in trust with Hidalbo, a Spanish merchant. He has a house just within the gateways of Holy Faith city, near the sign of the Bull.'

Matthias got to his feet. 'I don't want it, Edgar.' He saw the surprise in the man's face. 'My horse is stabled in the Alhambra. I paid a groom to guard that and my saddlebags. What I want, what I need, is in them: the rest you can keep.'

Matthias liked this English knight but he knew any hope of camaraderie, of a deeper, more lasting friendship was gone for ever. He stretched out his hand.

'I shall not return tonight. God be with you, Sir Edgar.'

'Is that how it is, Matthias?'

'That's how it is, Edgar. You are a good soldier, a loyal friend. In the last few months you have been my brother. However, I cannot tell you about my past or what haunts me and it's best if I continue alone. The company of St Raphael do not need me and I do not need them.'

Sir Edgar clasped his hand and embraced him. They exchanged the kiss of peace. Sir Edgar left, walking purposefully across the garden and into the tavern without a backward glance.

Matthias sat down on the bench and picked up his wine cup. He stared down at Sir Edgar's, fighting hard against the self-pity which threatened to engulf him. He closed his eyes.

'Why?' he whispered. 'Why don't you come, Rosifer. Why not now?'

The sun was warm on his face. Matthias leant back and dozed. His mind slipped into dreams of Barnwick and Rosamund: such dreams occurred frequently, more insistently. He felt himself shaken and opened his eyes. The little boy was staring at him sadly, pointing to his cup and chattering. Matthias shook his head.

'No, I've had enough wine.'

He pressed a coin into the boy's hand, got to his feet and went back into the courtyard to the Alhambra where he collected his horse. The city was now packed with soldiery but their mood was happy. Archers, wearing the silver cross of Castile, were massed at every corner, bows in hand, arrows notched under the watchful eye of royal knights, their sole duty to maintain law and order. The wine shops were full: some men slept in the cool shade of trees or, taking off their boots, sat and dangled their feet in the fountains. Every so often royal couriers, messengers, as well as heralds bringing proclamations, would enter the streets or gallop by on foam-flecked horses.

Matthias wandered into the Jewish quarter. He crossed a square and entered a more wealthy area. Here, officers from the royal army, English, French, Spanish and German, were negotiating with householders for chambers. Matthias turned his horse, meaning to go back to the taverna he had left, when a woman came out of a house, tripping down the outside steps. Matthias stared in astonishment. She was dressed resplendently in a rich crimson velvet skirt covered with layers of brocade: a matching mantilla, decorated with stars, covered her shoulders, whilst her head was protected from the strong sun by a broad-brimmed black hat from which a white plume danced in the breeze. Matthias only caught the side of her face but he recognised the cheek and mouth, the fiery red hair peeping out just above her ear.

'Morgana!' he called. 'Morgana!'

Some passing soldiers stopped and stared in astonishment. Matthias, recovering from his surprise, hurried down the street after the woman, pulling his horse behind him. He entered a square, roughly cobbled, with traders' stalls around all four sides. He hurriedly mounted his horse; standing up in the stirrups, he looked over the heads of the crowd and glimpsed the woman again. She was standing on the far edge beneath a goldsmith's sign at the mouth of an alleyway. Matthias hastened across. He had to dismount, pushing his way through the traders and people milling about. A journeyman ran up offering a bejewelled baldric. Matthias pushed him aside.

When he reached the goldsmith's sign he stopped and looked around. There was no sign of Morgana. He went down an alleyway and glimpsed her, or at least her cloak, just as she entered a taverna. Matthias followed. There was an alleyway leading down the side of the inn, and he took his horse along and into the stable yard. A groom lazing in the sun got up. Matthias threw him the reins, pressed a coin in his hands and explained that he would receive another if he looked after the horse. The boy pulled a face and Matthias hurried off. Inside, the taverna was cool, with a high ceiling: a large, spacious room with wine vats and tuns at one end, just outside the kitchen door. The rest of the room was taken up with roughly hewn tables and makeshift stools: hams and other pieces of meat hung from the rafters to be cured, giving the air a spicy tang. The customers looked up as Matthias blundered through the doorway. He stood, narrowing his eyes against the gloom.

'Morgana!' he called.

The landlord came over, a small tub of a man, wiping bloody fingers on his dirty apron. Matthias asked him, using the lingua franca, about a red-haired woman he'd glimpsed coming in. The taverner spread his hands, shaking his head.

Matthias stared around: there were stairs leading to the upper storeys but a soldier blocked the way, dead drunk. The cup in his lap had spilled, the wine staining his hose. Matthias was sure Morgana had come in here. He stared back at the doorway: there was a small porch leading into it. Had she just stepped in there and left immediately?

Matthias hurried back to the stable yard. The boy was still holding his horse but now he stood rigid with fright.

'What's the matter, lad?'

Matthias turned to the gateway. A group of riders blocked the entrance. They were dressed completely in black, masks of the same colour covering their faces. They were armed, and on his front each wore a silver embroidered cross. They sat like a cluster of ravens. Matthias pressed a coin into the boy's hand.

'Go on, lad!' he murmured.

The boy needed no second bidding but fled screaming into the taverna. Matthias mounted his horse and made to leave: the line of horsemen never stirred.

'Out of my way, sirs!' Matthias' hand went inside his pouch. He pulled out the scroll given to him by Isabella. 'I have the Queen's warrant – *la Reina Isabella!*'

One of the black-garbed riders spurred his horse forward.

'You are Matthias Fitzosbert?' A black-gloved hand snatched the parchment from his hand. The man's voice was muffled behind his mask. He spoke the lingua franca. 'You are Matthias Fitzosbert?' he repeated.

'I am. Stand aside!'

'Matthias Fitzosbert, we are soldiers of the Holy Inquisition. You are under arrest!'

'On what charge?'

'That is not necessary.'

Before Matthias could even gather his reins, the other horsemen clustered around him. Hands scrabbled at his war belt, sword and dagger were plucked from their sheaths, his reins were seized and, with these terrifying, black-garbed men surrounding him, Matthias was led off through the streets of Granada.

The square which he had recently crossed was now empty. Traders and their customers had fled at the sight of the Inquisition. Another party of horsemen were waiting for them. Two carried great, black, flapping banners, on which silver crosses were embroidered. The two parties met and continued up, past the Alhambra, along cobbled trackways. Matthias tried to discover where he was going but no one replied. The horsemen had no trouble getting through the streets. Even though Granada was freshly taken, the terror of the Inquisition preceded them. Townspeople fled, even the soldiery, the hidalgos, the nobles, the foreign mercenaries hastily cleared away.

The party stopped at a crossroads. Before he could object, a black mask was pulled over Matthias' head, his hands were tied by silken cords to the saddle horn and the journey continued. Matthias found it difficult to control his horse: the inside of his thighs became sore, his back stiff as he tried to keep his position. He heard different sounds which always died whenever the Inquisition passed. The hood was hot and stifling and, just when Matthias thought he could bear it no longer, he heard gates being opened, the sound of horse hooves, clattering on the cobbles and he was dragged unceremoniously from the saddle. He was pushed up some steps, through a door and the mask was taken off.

Matthias expected a dungeon but the room was large, cavernous and airy. A window, its shutters thrown back, looked out over a pleasant, tree-shaded garden. It was large enough to allow in sunlight and fresh air but too small for a man to force his way through. The cords round Matthias' hands were cut and his captors left, the key of the door being turned behind them. Matthias stared around. He was genuinely surprised. The white walls had been given a fresh coat of lime wash against flies and insects. The floor was of polished wood and covered with rugs: the bed was large and soft, the sheets crisp, the bolsters as white as driven snow. On a table stood a jug of cool sherbet and a bowl of fruit, some of which Matthias had never seen before. There was a shelf of books just to the left of the doorway. Matthias wandered over: there was a copy of the Bible, a few tracts and treatises of some theologians, prominently Bonaventure and Albertus Magnus.

Matthias sat in the low-backed, cushioned chair placed under the window. As he became accustomed to the room, he smelt the fragrance of resin, sandalwood and incense. He went across and filled a small, jewel-rimmed pewter goblet. The sherbet tasted delicious, washing his mouth, slaking the dust from his throat.

He heard the key turn and a little, dark-browed man came in. He was dressed in a grey robe with a cord round the waist.

'My name is Miguel Vincessors.' He spoke the lingua franca slowly. 'I am your servant. Oh dear!' His hand went to his lips. He hurried out of the doorway and brought back a crucifix which he placed on a hook on the wall. 'Are you comfortable?' He gabbled on, not waiting for an answer.

Matthias smiled at this little mouse of a man with his constant twitching nose and blinking eyes.

'You'll eat before sunset. You like meat? Lamb nicely cut?' He pointed to the fruit bowl. 'The pomegranates are fresh. They have to be cut. Don't eat the skin. Oh, but you haven't a knife, have you?'

The little man hurried off and a bemused Matthias went across to the bed and sat down. He recalled the saying often used by the Spanish soldiers: 'What will be, shall be. A man's fate is written on his forehead.' Matthias wondered what danger he was in. In the camp he'd been so immersed in his own problems, he'd scarcely grown accustomed to the habits, history and customs of Spain. He'd heard horrifying stories of the Inquisition. He glanced up at the beautiful cloth tester above the bed. This was no Bocardo, no filthy, rat-infested dungeon. Matthias was on the verge of falling asleep when the door opened again. Two Dominicans padded quietly into the room. The younger, dark-faced one, stood near the door, his hood pulled across his head, his hands up the sleeves of his gown. The other was Torquemada. He walked over and smiled down at Matthias, now sitting on the edge of the bed. He was smaller than Matthias had thought but of stout stature: his olive-skinned face was freshly shaved, his mouth was soft, the dark eyes gentle.

'Are you comfortable, Matthias Fitzosbert?' He smiled apologetically, clicked his fingers, gesturing at Matthias to remain as he was whilst the younger Dominican moved a chair from the table across for his master to sit on.

'There.' Torquemada smiled and breathed out noisily. 'I am so tired. My bones—' He stopped. 'I cannot speak English.' He changed from lingua franca to Latin. 'You are an Oxford scholar?'

Matthias nodded.

'You understand Latin?'

'Almost as well as English,' Matthias retorted.

Torquemada rocked backwards and forwards, clapping his hands gently. He chuckled softly, his soft eyes dancing with merriment.

'I've always wished to visit England,' he replied. 'There's a growing alliance between our two countries but they say England is cold: the mists seeps into the bones. A fairy island.'

Matthias watched him intently.

'A mysterious place. They say Englishmen wear tails.'

'They say many things, Father.'

'Of course they do, of course they do.'

Torquemada fingered the simple cross which hung on a cord round his neck. He stared across at a square oil painting on the wall. Matthias followed his gaze. He'd hardly noticed it before but now he realised it was a scene from the Old Testament: Saul visiting the witch of Endor, who raised the ghost of Samuel. The painting was dark but the fires at the centre seemed to glow with a life of their own, filling the scene with a chilling light, catching the wraithlike figure of Samuel, the staring eyes of Saul and the cruel, hooked visage of the witch. Torquemada glanced at Matthias.

'It is true there are witches in England?'

'Father, I have no knowledge of that.'

Torquemada tapped his sandalled foot against the floor.

'I've only been here a few minutes,' he said. 'But you never asked why you are here.' A podgy finger jabbed towards Matthias' face. 'You've never objected,' Torquemada continued. 'Now why is that, eh? You are an Englishman: you enjoy the special protection of our Queen. You have been plucked from your lawful business, bound, hooded and taken to a place which you do not know, yet you do not object.' Torquemada's face was still gentle: he spoke slowly, enunciating every word. 'Which means,' Torquemada rubbed his hands together, 'you are either guilty of some great crime or you don't care. Now, why shouldn't you care?' His eyes shifted to the window. 'Are you like a leaf ready to be borne by every wind that blows? And, if so, why?'

'What will be, shall be.' Matthias repeated the soldiers' aphorism. 'And a man's fate is written upon his forehead.'

'Is it now?' Torquemada's hands dropped away. 'Every man's fate, Matthias, is in the hands of God.'

'Then, if that is so, Father, I have nothing to fear.' Matthias got up from the bed and walked over to the window, keeping his back to Torquemada. 'I am an Englishman and a soldier, Father. I came to Spain to fight in the cause of the Church. I am innocent of any crime. But what's the use of protesting to people who arrest me and do not tell me the reason why?'

He heard a chuckle and turned round. Torquemada was smiling.

'You are a strange man, Fitzosbert. You killed a Moorish champion and yet that man seemed to know you. What did he mean by "*Creatura bona atque parva*"?' His eyes narrowed. 'It can't be a conspiracy. How could an English mercenary know anything about a Moorish knight like Yarfel? But it is strange, is it not? And those deaths?'

'What deaths?' Matthias asked.

'The young women found with their throats punctured? You remember them?'

Matthias nodded.

'The deaths began when Sir Edgar Ratcliffe and his party arrived outside Granada. Strange, is it not?'

'I have nothing to answer.'

'Have you not? Have you not? Come with me, Matthias.'

Torquemada got to his feet. The other Dominican opened the door and they went out on to the long, polished gallery. The windows on either side were moon-shaped and looked out over a grassy square with a white marble fountain in the centre. Flowers grew in beds on either side, filling the air with their perfume. Down the passageway, standing in shadowy recesses, were soldiers of the Inquisition, the silver cross resplendent on their black liveries. Matthias heard a sound and turned round: two soldiers, their faces masked by tall, black hoods, walked quietly behind him. Torquemada waddled ahead, muttering to himself.

They left the house and went down some outside stairs. The room below was large and lit by cresset torches. Matthias glimpsed figures standing around open braziers. As his eyes grew accustomed to the gloom, he saw these men were stripped half-naked. They chattered softly amongst themselves as they turned red-hot pokers in the blazing coals.

At the far end of the room a stake had been driven into the ground; a man was lashed to this. He was naked except for a breech cloth across his loins: head sagging forward, he was bound by cords across his chest, stomach and legs. His hands were lashed behind him. Torquemada beckoned Matthias across. As he approached, Matthias recoiled in distaste: the man's body was covered in red, bubbling burns where the torturers had pressed the burning, hot steel.

'We have to move quickly,' Torquemada murmured apologetically. 'Their Majesties have given me this house and God's work waits for us in Granada.'

He stretched out a hand and lifted the prisoner's bearded face. Matthias fought hard to control his nausea. One eye had been removed from the socket, leaving a bloody hole, the rest of the prisoner's face was badly disfigured by cuts and lacerations. A trickle of blood ran down the corner of his mouth.

'This is Juan Behahda,' Torquemada explained. 'Juan was, or is, a merchant. We know he worked hard in persuading Boabdil not to surrender Granada to their Majesties. A traitor and a heretic. We have been asking Juan who else was in his coven but,' Torquemada shrugged, tears brimming in his eyes, 'he won't tell us,' he whispered. 'Juan refuses the pardon of Holy Mother Church and, by his actions, has put himself beyond her protection. Matthias, what are we to do with such men? How can they answer for their actions?'

Torquemeda shouted in Spanish across to the torturers. The fellows' answer was short and terse. Torquemada sighed and dabbed at the tears in his eyes.

'*Fiat, fiat*,' he murmured. 'Let it be. Let it be.' He turned to his shadowy companion. 'Brother Martin,' he said softly. 'Hear the man's confession and have him garrotted.'

Torquemada beckoned to Matthias to follow him out of the room and, escorted by the two soldiers, returned to the chamber.

Torquemada closed the door behind him, gesturing at Matthias to sit whilst he filled two goblets with sherbet: taking quick sips from his cup, Torquemada walked round the room shaking his head.

'Juan was an obdurate soul.' He stopped his pacing.

'What are you doing, Father?' Matthias got to his feet. 'Do you think you can frighten me? Do you think the torturers will get the truth? What do you accuse me of?'

'I don't know,' Torquemada replied. His face was a mask of genuine concern. 'I really don't know, Matthias. I've made a careful study: you are a mystery. Sir Edgar Ratcliffe knew little about you though he told me how you saved his life. There is the question of Yarfel. And, even when you were arrested, so I understand, you were searching for a woman?' He put his cup down on the table. 'But what woman, Matthias? Eh? You are a solitary man. How could you know some woman living in Granada? To put it bluntly, Englishman, are you a witch? Are you a warlock?' His face grew serious. 'Are you a member of a coven?'

'I am an Englishman. I am innocent. I also enjoy the Queen's special protection,' Matthias replied.

'Oh yes, so you do.' Torquemada walked to the door. He turned, gave Matthias his blessing and quietly left.

Matthias sat down, trying to control his trembling. Try as he might, he couldn't remove from his mind the picture of that tortured man in the dungeons below. He could imagine the whispered confession, the cords being placed round his neck and tightened with a piece of stick until he strangled to death. Matthias picked at some fruit but found he had no appetite. He could only sit and wait.

Just after sunset, the door was flung open and the black-masked guards seized and bundled him out. Matthias tried to control his fear as the soldiers led him along the galleries, illuminated only by flashes of light from glowing candles or lanterns slung on hooks. However, he was not taken outside but into a small hall. A few torches provided light. The walls were covered in heavy drapes whilst underfoot thick carpet deadened any sound. The windows were shuttered, the air was stuffy and hot but smelt fragrantly of incense. At the far end on a dais seven men sat behind a long, oaken table. Torquemada in the middle, hands joined, smiling benevolently down at him, but the men on either side were hooded and masked. Behind Torquemada, the walls were covered in dark-red drapes with the arms of Castile boldly etched in the centre. From a beam above the table hung a stark, black crucifix. A scribe, who sat on a small bench just beneath the dais, rose and tinkled a small handbell.

The soldiers pushed Matthias forward. He was made to sit on a stool just before the table so he had to stare up at Torquemada. Matthias didn't know whether this was a dream or reality. The Inquisitor General smiled like a benevolent uncle but the sombre-masked judges seemed like figures from the Apocalypse: their very silence and lack of movement a terrifying reminder of the power of the Inquisition. Matthias tried to object, claiming he was an Englishman and innocent of any charges, that he also had the special protection of the Queen. Torquemada swept this aside.

'There are no charges.' He leant forward. 'You may well be innocent. And you still enjoy the protection of our Queen. So?' He sat back in the purple-draped throne-like chair. 'If you are innocent, you have nothing to fear.'

The questioning then began. It was done in Latin. All of the judges spoke softly, eager to clarify their points by lapsing into lingua franca. The questions were always the same. Who was he? Why was he in Spain? Why did the Moorish champion, Yarfel, speak as he did? Did Matthias know any of the women killed so barbarously in the camp? Was he a true son of Holy Mother Church?

Matthias kept his answers short and terse. He did not know Yarfel. He was a Christian fighting for the Church. He had been born a Catholic: he wanted to die a Catholic. He had no woman's blood on his hands. And the woman he had been seeking in Granada?

'She reminded me of someone,' Matthias explained. 'A girl I loved in England,' he lied. 'I was tired, my mind was dazed. The memory plays tricks.'

Matthias kept staring at Torquemada. He couldn't see what impact his answers had on the other judges but Torquemada looked genuinely puzzled. Matthias grew stiff: the ache in his back from his fall grew more intense. He explained this. Torquemada spread his hands and apologised. Matthias was allowed to stand and walk round the room. Refreshments were served: chilled white wine, a dish of sweetened figs and then the trial continued. At the end Torquemada clapped his hands softly as a sign for silence.

'What do you say, brothers?' he said, weaving his fingers together as if in prayer. 'Guilty or innocent?'

One of the judges at the end of the dais stood up, facing down the table at Torquemada.

'Reverend Father,' he said, measuring his words carefully, 'Matthias Fitzosbert appears to be innocent of any charges. His life seems a mystery, like a rose before sunrise, the petals closed tight—'

Matthias stiffened. The judge was speaking in Latin but there was something about his voice, the intonation, the reference to a rose.

'You wax lyrical,' Torquemada broke in. 'Brother Benjamin, what do you propose?'

'Matthias Fitzosbert enjoys the protection of the Queen?' the black-masked judge asked Torquemada.

'Yes he does!'

'He is, therefore, the Queen's subject if he enjoys her protection?'

'Of course!' Torquemada snapped back. 'That is why we have the right to question him!'

'He is a man of great courage,' the judge continued.

Matthias now knew that the Rose Demon was present in the room.

'Their Majesties are looking for officers,' the anonymous judge continued. 'The Genoese, Columbus, and his projected voyage across the Western Seas – Fitzosbert would make an excellent officer for such an expedition.'

The judge sat down. Torquemada stood, his face wreathed in smiles.

'Matthias Fitzosbert,' he declared. 'What do you say?'

Matthias stared back.

'You have appealed to God,' Torquemada declared. 'So,

let God decide. You have a choice. To subject yourself further to the interrogation of the Inquisition or to be the Inquisition's man if, and when, this Columbus sails across the Western Seas.'

'I would rather go than stay!'

'Good!' Torquemada sat down. 'Until then you shall continue to be our guest.'

Matthias turned and stared at the anonymous judge who had intervened. However, in the candlelight, all he could glimpse were eyes glittering behind the sombre mask.

33

Half an hour after sunrise, on 3 August 1492, the 100 ton ship the *Santa Maria*, escorted by its two 60 ton caravels, the *Niña* and the *Pinta*, left its moorings in the port of Palos in southern Spain. They were to sail west across unknown seas in the hope of finding a swifter, more accessible route to Cathay and Cipango. All three ships were well provisioned with water and white wine as well as hard biscuits, olive oil, salt meat and cured fish. Portuguese lentils, chick peas, almonds, raisins and rice had also been stowed to offset the hard diet.

The *Santa Maria*, Christopher Columbus' flagship, was a sluggish, three-sailed cog, heavy-bottomed with a high raised castle in the front and stern. The *Niña* and *Pinta*, each commanded by the Pinzon brothers, Vincente and Martin, were similarly rigged but moved faster in the water.

Matthias Fitzosbert, master-at-arms on board the *Santa Maria*, though not listed among its crew, stood in the stern castle and watched the retreating white buildings of the small Spanish port of Palos. To his right and left (Matthias had not yet grown accustomed to 'port' and 'starboard'), the *Pinta* and *Niña*'s square sails billowed full in the early morning breeze. All three ships were in line, a fine sight as they crossed the bar of the Saltes river and made their way past the friary of La Rabida where the good Franciscan brothers were now being called to the office of Prime by the faint tolling of the bell.

Matthias loosened the lacing of his leather jerkin and spread his feet more firmly. The sky was now streaked with red, the winds were soft. He was growing accustomed to the pitch of the ship ever since he had joined it at the end of June. The previous months had been spent as an enforced guest of the Inquisition. After his dramatic trial by night, Mathias had been left to his own devices, though he suspected there were hidden eyelets and peepholes in his chamber where Torquemada or his officers could keep him under close watch.

At first Matthias had raged against what was happening; not so much the verdict of the court – he had been relieved of the threat of incarceration in the Inquisition's dungeon – but the sheer boredom of each day. He had books, he was allowed to walk in the garden but nothing else happened. It was as if the world had forgotten him. Now and again a physician would call to ensure all was well. If it hadn't been for the servant Miguel, Matthias would have spent most of his time either talking to himself or reading the different works of piety Torquemada's officers delivered to his room. Miguel had been his saviour. An Inquisition spy and certainly Torquemada's creature, nevertheless he had a sardonic view of the world and kept Matthias informed of events in the city and beyond.

By the end of February Miguel had become Matthias' teacher: first in the basic elements of the Spanish tongue then, as Matthias grew more proficient, correcting his use of the language until Matthias found he was able to think in Spanish. Matthias noticed how Miguel, time and again, would deftly turn the conversation to the matters on which Matthias had been tried. Matthias, however, maintained every aspect of orthodoxy. He took the Sacrament on Sunday and Holy Days in a small side chapel. He deliberately showed little interest in Miguel's stories about witchcraft and demons in Spain. It was like a game of chess. Miguel would turn the conversation one way and Matthias would expertly turn it back. The subject which really preoccupied him as the weeks passed was Columbus. Who was he? What were his plans? Miguel would always clap his hands and shake his head.

'Columbus,' he declared, 'is a dreamer, a Genoese. He claims to have secret maps and has been begging their Majesties and Holy Mother Church to fund an expedition across the great unknown Western Ocean. He really believes that, by sailing west, he can find a shorter route to the country of the Great Khan and so open up a lucrative trade in spices and gold, but the man's a fool!'

'Is there anything to the west?' Matthias asked. He recalled Abbot Benedict's reference to the Beautiful Islands.

'There are stories of islands populated by strange people and mythical beasts.'

'What do you believe, Miguel?'

'I don't think the world's flat,' Miguel retorted. 'Everyone knows it's a sphere, otherwise, when you walked along a road,' he smiled triumphantly, 'you wouldn't see the spire of a church rise up on the horizon.' His smile faded. 'Some people believe Columbus is a sorcerer.'

Matthias deliberately stifled a yawn as this funny, rather nervous servant of Torquemada tried to bring the conversation to more topical matters.

At night Matthias was more circumspect. He dreamt scenes from his past and was fearful lest he talk in his sleep and thus provide fresh information for the silent watchers. In the middle of June, however, Torquemada came to visit him. The Inquisitor General was booted and spurred, ready to leave: his attitude to Matthias was one of bored indifference. He handed his English captive a purse of silver.

'In a few days,' he declared, after giving his final benediction, 'you will be released. Soldiers will take you to the port of Palos.' He shrugged. 'After that, you are on your own!' He was about to leave but turned, one hand on the door. 'Of course, you might desert but that would be very foolish. If you are caught, and it would not be hard to hunt for an Englishman in southern Spain, we would certainly meet again. Goodbye, Englishman!' And he slammed the door unceremoniously behind him.

Two weeks later an officer of the Santa Hermanda arrived late in the evening and announced that, tomorrow morning, they would leave. Matthias was to pack and be ready. Matthias was overjoyed but his happiness was soon marred by the long, bone-racking journey under a scorching sun to the small fishing port of Palos. There Matthias had been handed over to Columbus' business partners and Spanish captains, the Pinzon brothers. They were tactful, but cold and distant. Matthias recognised the subtlety of Torquemada. Both men saw him as a mercenary, a creature of the Inquisition.

Columbus himself, who now had the title of Captain General, was even more cold and forbidding. The Genoese was tall, thickset, open-faced, with eyes heavy-lidded under a high, sweeping brow. In many ways he reminded Matthias of Torquemada: a man absorbed by dreams. When the Pinzon brothers introduced Matthias, Columbus hardly raised his eyes from the charts spread out on the table

462

before him. He limply clasped Matthias' hand, said that he should expect no favours, and then dismissed him.

Matthias moved against the ship's rail. He'd also been given clear instructions about his conduct on board ship: the rigging of the sails, the navigation, duties on board were not for him. In the event of any enemy attack he would man the light cannon, four-inch bombards which fired a stone ball, or take one of the crossbows. Matthias chewed on his lip and watched the sailors scurrying like monkeys around the deck. Bare-footed, dressed in drab hose and ragged linen shirts, all were born sailors. They moved with the lightness of a cat despite the pitching deck and the constant sea spray which drenched everything from the huge square sail bearing a resplendent red cross to the small bumboat slung along the side. Matthias hardly knew any of the crew. He'd met the royal representative Escobedo, whilst the barber surgeon, a converted Jew, Louis de Torres, was amiable enough. The rest of the crew, however, regarded him as a foreigner.

'Don't worry,' de Torres had confided. 'I'm here to patch their wounds and, because I am fluent in many tongues, I'm to be Columbus' interpreter for the Great Khan.' He winked, a sign that he no more believed Columbus would meet such a great king than, indeed, any other of the crew did.

'Columbus is a dreamer,' de Torres hissed, 'and every man Jack on board our three ships is only here because they have come from Palos. If it hadn't been for the Pinzon brothers, Columbus would have had to paddle his own boat out into the unknown.'

Nonetheless, despite all this, Matthias had been pleased to be free of Torquemada. The Pinzon brothers kept an eye on him but he'd been allowed to wander the taverns and wine shops which lined the busy quayside. Matthias had caught the excitement caused by Columbus' projected voyage. Many were doubtful, though, secretly, they nursed dreams of finding golden cities and mines rich with silver. Matthias had also kept his ears open for any strange occurrences. He still wondered if it really had been Morgana he'd glimpsed in Granada.

In the end, the days passed in humdrum fashion until on 1 August Matthias had been given his orders that, the next time he boarded the *Santa Maria*, it would be no exercise. He was to check the bombards and ensure that the strings of the

463

crossbows were still dry. Columbus was determined to catch the easterly winds and sail out into the unknown.

'Fitzosbert! Fitzosbert!'

Matthias broke from his reverie. De Torres was standing on the steps of the forecastle beckoning him over.

'The Captain General wishes to see you.'

Matthias looked at the small, monkey-faced man, his friendly eyes and ever-smiling mouth. De Torres scratched his close-cropped hair.

'He's in a temper,' he whispered. 'He's never in the best of moods so watch what you say.'

Columbus' cabin was no more than a dark panelled closet under the stern castle. A small pallet bed in one corner, a collapsible table, a chair and two stools. Columbus was sitting, studying the charts spread over his lap. He was dressed in a light blue shirt, open at the neck. He'd kicked his boots off and his bare feet tapped impatiently on the wooden floor.

'Sit down! Sit down! Sit down!' Columbus wiped the sweat from his brow. He rolled the charts up and gently tapped Matthias on the cheek, forcing his head sideways. 'The Pinzon brothers noticed that!'

'Noticed what?' Matthias replied.

'The rope marks on your neck!'

Matthias nursed the small scar left by the rough handling of Emloe's men on the Winchelsea road.

'Are you a felon, Englishman? A gallows bird?'

'I'm a soldier,' Matthias replied bleakly. He regarded his life as a closed book, especially to this Genoese who studied him in such a hostile manner.

'I know nothing of you.' Columbus leant forward. 'You seem to have an honest face. I received the letter from the Inquisition that you were to come, be part of the crew with the specific duties of master-at-arms. However, you are not on my manifest and I shall not mention you in my log. Most of the crew here are seamen from Palos, about two or three are from gaols elsewhere: people whom the authorities in Spain want as far away from them as possible. You are one of these. I am Captain General. I have the power of life and death over everyone in this fleet. You will carry out my orders and that's all I care about. I don't give a fig about your past or why you are really here. If we return to Spain, Torquemada wishes to meet you again. I expect you to obey my orders. Do you understand?'

'Yes, sir!'

'Good. Your duties are light. Remember: don't try to climb the rigging or mast, you'll only go overboard. I haven't got time for a search. However, you can be part of the forward watch. Each man does four hours every day, sometimes in the morning, sometimes at night. I expect you to be awake when I do my rounds.'

'What are we looking for, Captain General? I mean, we are sailing into the unknown . . .'

Columbus smiled bleakly. 'We are setting sail for the Grand Canaries, no more dangerous than a jaunt along a river. But, when we leave there,' he held his hand up, 'the Portuguese may have men-of-war waiting for me. I'm to give these the slip. Once we are out in the open,' he pushed his face closer, 'it's land, do you understand, Fitzosbert?' Columbus stumbled over Matthias' name. 'For the man who first sights land, there'll be a pension for life.'

Matthias was dismissed. Later in the day he was given his place to sleep in the corner of the forecastle. Matthias' goods were stowed away with the rest. There was no mattress, only a threadbare, rather smelly grey blanket.

In the succeeding days Matthias became accustomed to the humdrum routine of the ship. He was relieved that any sea-sickness soon passed, and his ability to participate in different duties, including a watch, soon made him acceptable to other members of the crew. They drew him into their light-hearted conversations and banter about each other: the sexual exploits of women who lived in the Canaries; of Columbus and their dreams of what they might find out in the unknown ocean. They were a tough group of men, self-sufficient, with little respect for authority, even for the Captain General.

'He'll have to prove himself,' Alonzo Baldini declared. He was a fisherman from Palos who had also served as a pirate. He rubbed his hands. 'What I want to see are these women on the Grand Canaries.' He lowered his voice. 'Do you know that before a virgin is married, she is fattened with milk until her skin is plump as that of a ripe fig. The people there claim that thin maidens are not as good as fat ones.' He licked his lips. 'Once she is fattened she is shown to the groom.'

His voice dropped to a whisper because of Columbus' strict instructions against impure and Godless conversation. 'She's shown naked,' he whispered, 'like a cow at a fair.'

Other members of the crew joined in, making tart observations on what they hoped to do before they left the Canaries. They told Matthias that he should hire the service of a good whore because the women of the Great Khan were too small for Spaniards and not able to cater for their sexual needs.

Matthias half-listened. Staring round the moon-dappled deck, he idly wondered which of these men did not possess their own soul. Was the Rose Demon amongst them? So far he had encountered nothing to provoke any suspicions and he wondered about the old stories he had read in Oxford – could demons cross vast expanses of water? And, if they did reach lands across the Western Seas, would Matthias find peace? A sanctuary from the forces which had pursued him for most of his life?

Six days after leaving Palos, the *Pinta* and *Niña* closed up behind the *Santa Maria*. Following the glow of the brazier which was slung over the flagship's stern, they followed it into the harbour of San Sebastián, which stood on the cliffs overlooking the port on the island of Gomera in the Canaries.

The rest of the day was spent in bringing the ships alongside each other in the harbour. The Pinzon brothers came over to confer with Columbus whilst the crew waited to see what orders would be given. At last, late in the afternoon, Columbus announced that the *Pinta* would be sailing back because of a fault with its rudder whilst he would wait to present his compliments to Lady Bobadilla, the widowed ruler of the Canaries. The crew were, therefore, given leave to go ashore.

Matthias found Gomera a restful place: its white, gleaming buildings, small, cool wine shops, gardens and vineyards and the great, green expanse of the island stretching up to the rim of an extinct volcano. The islanders were an easy, careless, merry group of people who welcomed the ships and the gossip they brought.

They landed at Gomera on 12 August. Matthias spent the first few days wandering round the seaside port. He then went out into the countryside to view the great dragon trees. Huge, red-barked, with strangely arranged branches, these produced a red-coloured resin highly prized as a medicine.

Matthias mixed with the crew, but after a while he grew tired of days and evenings spent in the tavernas carousing and quarrelling with whores. He took to journeying out, going for long walks, climbing the escarpment of rocky ridges and sitting under the cool shade of the trees. Below him sprawled San Sebastián and he could make out the *Santa Maria* and *Niña*, their sails unhooked, as Columbus changed the rigging, eager to catch every breeze once he had set sail into the unknown ocean.

Matthias listened to de Torres or the little fisherman, Frederico Totonaz: their constant chatter about their families, beloved ones, girlfriends, as well as whispers about Columbus being mad, that he was a secret Jew and how he possessed secret information on what would happen across the great ocean. Would they sail into nothingness? And, if there was land, would the women be comely and welcoming? Matthias compared their concerns to his own life. He felt no attraction towards women – sometimes a desire to empty himself, to stroke smooth flesh, to bury his face in a woman's hair – but then he'd think of Rosamund and his desire would fade. Only now and again, particularly in the last weeks of his imprisonment in Granada, had Matthias confronted the problem which clouded his soul. Was he the son of Parson Osbert or the offspring of a demon? Was that possible? If it was, was his soul lost and damned before he was ever born? But, if that was the case, why these constant confrontations? What was at stake? What was the issue?

On the Feast of the Assumption 1492, Matthias sat on the hillside and stared down at Columbus' ships. Despite his coldness, Matthias felt a kinship with the Genoese. The Captain General was an outsider, a stranger, a man driven by a burning ambition. On the voyage from Palos, Matthias had listened to the crew and watched the admiral of the Western Ocean. Columbus was driven by one thought and one thought only: to find out a new route to the Indies, to bring back the treasures of Cathay and Cipango and lay them at the feet of Ferdinand and Isabella. Matthias moved deeper into the shade of a dragon tree. And what would happen if they ever did return? Matthias was totally determined not to fall into the hands of Torquemada yet it seemed that no royal protection could save him from the Inquisition. And what happened if the voyage went wrong? Would Matthias be blamed? Bundled off into some dungeon to be tortured and quietly garrotted? Matthias shifted uneasily. Should he continue this journey? Columbus was determined to sail as soon as all was ready. Matthias knew from the gossip that other ships sailed to and from Gomera. He could travel back to Lisbon, beyond the arm of the Inquisition, and then into France, perhaps Italy?

Matthias rose and made his way slowly down the hill. So immersed in his thoughts, he was oblivious to the warbling of the birds and the beautiful variegated butterflies which moved in clouds from one bunch of flowers to another. He entered the back streets of San Sebastián. It was still early in the afternoon. He felt thirsty so he called into a small taverna. He bought a jug of chilled wine and sat in the corner sipping at it, wondering what to do. He was lost in his own thoughts: sometimes he was back at Barnwick, or waiting on the ridge at East Stoke.

He felt a soft touch on his hand and became aware of a cloying, lingering perfume. He looked up. Morgana was sitting opposite him, her red hair like a gorgeous cloud on either side of her beautiful face, green eyes smiling. She proffered her empty cup.

'Are you going to drink alone?'

Matthias stared at this exquisite witch-woman. Her dress was a low-cut, clinging simple gown fringed with gold: it emphasised her beautiful slender neck and rich lustrous breasts. Matthias noticed the green earrings which hung from either lobe, small balls of flashing light. He filled her cup and glanced round the taverna. The other customers were looking at him curiously.

'Just ignore them, Matthias,' Morgana murmured, her green eyes more catlike than ever. She lowered her head and dabbed at the sweat between her breasts. Her eyes never left his.

'Where do you come from?' Matthias asked. 'How did you get here?'

'Like the breeze,' she smiled, 'I come and go as I wish.'

'And your companion? The man who always escorts you?'

'Oh, he's with you, Matthias. He's on board the *Santa Maria* to protect you. Sailors are superstitious. They do not like strangers or people who act as if their lives are cursed.' Her smile widened. 'Have you not read the Scriptures: the fate of Jonah? We cannot have that happening to you.'

'Who are you?' Matthias asked. 'You say your name is Morgana.'

'I am a servant of the Master,' she replied, her smile fading as she sipped the white wine Matthias had poured. 'I go where he tells me. I do what he orders. I have a special charge for you.'

'I can see that,' Matthias replied tartly. 'I am hounded like a dog from one place to another. Snatched up, imprisoned, bullied and threatened. If you are the breeze, Morgana, I am a dry leaf with no life of my own.'

'Are you?' she teased back. 'Are you really, Matthias? Tell me how different you are from any of the men who serve on the *Santa Maria*. Or those who died at Tewkesbury, at East Stoke, at Barnwick, at Sauchieburn?' Her eyes became hard, like beautiful emeralds, but not vibrant with life or warmth. 'Are you going to sit and wallow in self-pity, Matthias? How do you know your life would have been any different? Or shorter? Or more tragic?'

'Other people know why they live. They have a purpose.'

'Some do,' she replied. 'But so have you, Matthias.' She leant across the table and squeezed his hand.

'Am I his son?' Matthias asked abruptly.

Her face softened. 'You are the Beloved, Matthias. You are his Beloved. He wants you. He wants your love. He wants you to accept him for what he is.'

'And how long must I wait?'

'Love is about waiting, Matthias. Haven't you realised that? There is a time and a place for love to be consummated, to be returned, to be agreed upon. It will come!'

'And what happens if I go?' Matthias asked. 'What happens if I flee?'

'What will be, shall be and a man's fate is written upon his forehead.' Morgana glanced round the room. 'Here we are on the island of Gomera. If you wish, Matthias, you could travel back to Sutton Courteny, and sit in the fields and listen to the nightingales sing. There are many ways of travelling back home. Various paths, strange routes but, in the end, the journey will be about your heart's desire. Matthias, you carry your world within you. You can fly to the dark side of the moon, free from Torquemada, of all those who pursue you – but never free of yourself.'

Matthias heard a commotion on the far side of the room. A

group of young men who had been playing noisily were now looking across at him, arguing loudly amongst themselves. They dismissed him with disdain, their narrow-eyed looks and leering glances were all for Morgana. One of them, a young, arrogant buck, his olive skin scarred by knife wounds to his cheek and neck, unloosed his long, black, oily hair and strutted across the floor like a barnyard cock. He put one hand on Morgana's shoulder, the other on the rough-handled knife pushed into the ragged sash round his waist. He said something to Matthias then spat into the rush-covered floor. Matthias went to rise but Morgana squeezed his hand.

'Look at him, Matthias,' she whispered. 'Speak to him in Spanish. Tell him to return quietly to his seat. Tell him that he is lucky to be alive. This morning he fell from the stern of his fishing boat. If he does not sit down, tomorrow he will drown. Tell him that. Hold his gaze.'

Matthias did so, quietly repeating Morgana's message.

The young man blinked, his jaw sagged. He backed away, his face a mask of fear, and ran from the taverna. His companions watched in astonishment, then followed.

'We'd best go,' Morgana said. 'The day draws on. Soon it will be cool.' She picked up the small wineskin she carried and wrapped the cord round her hand. 'Let's go, Matthias, out into the hills. Go back to that dragon tree under which you sat.'

Matthias followed her out. She took his hand as if they were lovers, strolling along the cobbled street and into the countryside.

'I did see you in Granada, didn't I?' Matthias asked.

'Yes, you did,' she replied. 'I was told to be there.'

'And your companion?' Matthias asked. 'Which member of the crew is he?'

'Oh come, Matthias,' she joked. 'You worry so much. I've told you, sailors are a suspicious group. He is there to guard you, to watch over you night and day. So, who he is, is of no real concern.'

'How long have you been . . . ?'

'You mean as I am now?' Morgana stopped and faced him. With the breeze ruffling her flame-red hair, Matthias had never seen a woman so beautiful. 'I come and go,' she smiled. 'I am older than you think,' she teased. 'Do you not find me attractive, Matthias?'

470

'Yes,' he replied quickly. 'Of course I do.' He glanced at the wild grass at the verge of the track. 'But you are like a butterfly: you move constantly, never still.'

'I will today,' she smiled impishly.

She ran ahead of him, long-legged strides, her hips swaying, then gazed provocatively over her shoulder at him. Teasing and laughing, they left the trackway and climbed the hill, up under the outstretched branches of the huge dragon tree. They lay down in the long, fresh grass. Morgana unstoppered the wineskin and teasingly made Matthias open his mouth. She poured the most delicious drink he had ever tasted, sweet and rich. She kept pouring until he spluttered. Morgana then drew away laughing and, lifting the wineskin, squeezed the wine into her own mouth. Even as she did so, she glanced sideways, teasing and provoking Matthias with her eyes. She put the wineskin down, placed her hand behind his head, kissing the wine back into his mouth. Her tongue wetted his lips, her fingers massaging the back of his neck. Matthias responded greedily until he recalled that day with Rosamund sitting in the ruins of the old Roman wall. He drew away and stared up at the branches above him, watching a multicoloured bird hop along a branch.

'Are you tired, Matthias?' Morgana murmured, nestling up beside him. She traced the contours of his face with her finger; her touch was like silk. 'Sleep,' she whispered. 'Forget your teasing thoughts.' Her voice was low, soothing.

Matthias felt his body jerk as he began to relax. Dreamily he stared up at the bird, watching it intently. Morgana kissed his ear, the side of his face, her fingers ruffling his hair. He drifted into a dreamless sleep and, when he woke, the sky was darkening, the breeze much cooler. He turned. Morgana was lying with her back to him. He stretched out and turned her over. Her eyes were open and staring, her face as white as snow and her neck crusted with blood which had seeped out from the two great wounds on either side of her windpipe. Matthias sprang to his feet. He felt for the knife in his sheath: it was still there. He stared around: darkness was falling, the birds above were mocking in their sweet, plaintive song. Matthias whirled round.

'Who's there?'

No answer, only Morgana's eyes staring sightlessly up at him. Matthias gripped his dagger and fled into the night.

471

34

'Nothing to the north! Nothing to the south!' The lookout's voice was whipped away by the wind.

Matthias, standing on the forecastle of the *Santa Maria*, watched the great waves pitch and break over the bulwarks. On either side of Columbus' ship, the two caravels, the *Niña* and *Pinta*, moved briskly under an easterly wind. Matthias heard Columbus' reply from the stern. As always: 'West ever west! Helmsman, watch my mark!'

Beside Columbus, Raphael Murillo turned the hourglass. Matthias stared up, the sky was darkening, soon it would be night. Columbus would order lanterns to be swung from the stern and one of the bombards fired, a signal to the Pinzon brothers to close up for the night. Matthias never really knew whether Columbus was frightened of losing his fellow captains or fearful that they would steal a march on him. They had left the Canaries well behind them and now, as the Captain General said, they were in the hands of God. Everything depended on Columbus, his maps and charts and, above all, his astrolabe and quadrant which he used for taking the height of the sun at midday and the pole star at night to determine what latitude they were crossing.

Matthias was baffled by such technicalities. He put more trust in what the men said about Columbus, that he navigated by dead reckoning whereby he plotted the position of the ships by the map in his mind.

Matthias leant against the rail and became lost in his own memories. He had fled from the scene of Morgana's murder and gone straight back to the port. The following day he had returned up the hill but had found no trace of her corpse or the wineskin or any blood, no indication that he and Morgana had lain there. Matthias had waited. Perhaps the authorities had discovered the corpse? He'd joined his companions in the tavernas or sitting out on the quayside chatting with the fishermen. He heard nothing, even though some of his companions had learnt about the beautiful, red-haired woman and constantly teased him about her. Matthias wondered who had killed Morgana. Had someone been following them? Was it the Rose Demon's work or someone else's? Matthias shook his head, that would be impossible. He had also closely scrutinised the crew. Morgana had said that he was being watched but by whom? Matthias realised a subtle game was being played with him. It would be virtually impossible to track such a man down. Columbus had left it to the crew where and when they attended Mass whilst, in the tightly enclosed spaces of his three ships, discussion about religion or any disputatious topic was strictly forbidden. And Morgana? Matthias wondered why she had given up her life so easily? Surely this wasn't the thanks the servants of the Rose Demon received? She had been killed yet she'd never struggled or cried out. Her assassin had come like a thief in the night, her death being sprung on her like a trap.

On Wednesday, 5 September, the evening before they sailed, Baldini, Murillo and the rest had persuaded Matthias to come to a party, a wild raucous affair in a ramshackle taverna in an alleyway off the quayside. The wine flowed like water, fresh meats and fish grilled over charcoal, smothered in the vegetable sauce, were served up on trenchers. Each platter had a hunk of soft, white bread to mop the juices up. There had been singing and dancing, the usual tomfoolery before sailors prepared to leave port. Matthias had drunk a little more deeply than he wanted. A young girl had come up and sat on his lap but Matthias had pushed her away. At last the Pinzons and other officers came to take the sailors back to the ships. Matthias was following the rest out of the door; the men were shouting their farewells, blowing kisses at the girls when Matthias heard his name called out.

'Farewell, Matthias! Take care of yourself, Creatura!'

The words were spoken in English. Matthias had stared at the woman through a drunken haze. He had not noticed her before. She had deep olive skin, black hair which fell like a veil, shrouding her beautiful face, her eyes were bold, her mouth pert. She stared at Matthias boldly, lifted one bare shoulder and winked. In that moment the fug cleared from

Matthias' mind. He saw the look in those eyes and knew that, whatever the girl called herself, Morgana's spirit was there. Matthias had returned to the ship baffled. Were other beings spirits in the service of the Rose Demon? At the same time he recognised Morgana's cleverness: her death had removed any thought of flight from his mind and now, whether he liked it or not, Matthias Fitzosbert was committed body and soul to Columbus' great venture and whatever lay waiting for him across this broad, unknown, mysterious ocean.

Matthias walked up and down the forecastle. Now and again he'd stop to check the hourglass placed there and, when the sand ran out, turn it over. He'd watch the glass until midnight, when he'd be relieved and others would take over. Darkness fell. The stars seemed brighter, closer than they did on land. Matthias wondered how far they had sailed. Columbus had been rash in proclaiming that the voyage would be 750 miles. The crew had taken him at his word and, each day, the distance was carefully measured. The excitement of leaving land had now faded. The rigours of ship life were making themselves felt. The water had turned brackish, the wine slightly sour, the biscuits and bread hard, the meat too well spiced and salted. The men crowded each other, the chance to be alone was a luxury. Moreover, despite the strictest instructions, the ship now stank. Men fell ill, vomited and retched, or ran, clutching their stomachs, to the side, as their bowels turned to water. Every day the slops were washed out; buckets of seawater were taken down to sluice the bilges, rats were hunted and killed. As the ships drove on, the crew greedily recalled the luxuries of the Canaries and returned to counting the miles.

'Matthias, Matthias Fitzosbert!' The voice just came out of the darkness.

Matthias walked to the rail and stared down. The sea swelled and broke beneath him. He looked back along the deck: in the faint light of the lantern he glimpsed men sleeping in nooks, crannies and corners, their blankets pulled over them.

'Matthias! Matthias!' The voice was hollow like someone shouting down a funnel. 'Listen now!'

Matthias seized the rail, gripping it. Was he hearing the voice? Or was it in his own mind?

'Listen now! Nothing to the north, nothing to the south! Due west! Due west! We shall meet again!'

'Look!'

Matthias broke from his reverie. On the deck men were stirring themselves, pointing up to the sky. A comet, a falling star, was soaring across the night sky. Members of the crew, Columbus and his officers, now joined Matthias on the foredeck.

'What is it?' someone asked.

'A falling star,' Escobedo replied.

'A comet,' another one observed.

'It's a sign!' Columbus added, eager to seize any opportunity to vindicate himself. 'It's a sign from God! We shall not be disappointed!'

'It's like a rose, isn't it?' De Torres pointed up. 'Look. There's the flower and there's the stem.'

Matthias watched the sign and wondered about that mysterious voice repeating the course the ship was following.

In the succeeding days, he realised how important that voice had been. The ships were now out on a sea that never ended, under a sky which yielded no recognisable horizon. On 19 September soundings were taken but, even with a 200 fathom line, no bottom was found. This drew dark looks but Columbus took comfort when two pelicans flew and rested on the ship's mast, loudly declaring that such birds never fly far from land. The men reckoned that they had sailed far enough but still no land was in sight. They passed through a sea of weed, thick, greeny and slimy, which opened up before the ships then closed in around them.

On 23 September the winds dropped and they became becalmed until a great swell rose to lift the hull, the winds picked up and they sailed on. Now and again, the lookouts, eager to claim the reward, their eyes constantly scouring the horizon, sometimes shouted they had seen land but this was proved to be a figment of their imagination. The crew now began to demand exactly how far they had travelled and, more importantly, how much further they were to go. The Pinzon brothers came across to the *Santa Maria* to pore over Columbus' charts and engage in fierce debate. Columbus stuck to his original order: 'West, west! There'll be no deviation and,' he added, 'if we return empty-handed to Spain, every man will have to face the fury of our royal patrons, Ferdinand and Isabella.'

The crew settled down. They forgot about the brackish water, weevil-ridden food, the stench of the ships, the sheer boredom and terror of such a long voyage. September passed. In October, however, the gloom deepened. Columbus had said that, on their voyage to Cathay and Cipango, they would pass the Island of the Blest discovered by the Irish saint and seafarer St Brendan. No island hove into sight. The men grumbled: if Columbus was wrong about the island couldn't he be wrong about everything else?

On 8 October birds were seen flying south-west. The crew insisted that Columbus changed direction. Gathered on the deck, the men shouted that if birds flew in such a direction towards land, should they not follow? The Pinzon brothers on the *Niña* and *Pinta* came across and supported these cries. A vote was taken. Only two people voted not to change direction: Columbus and Matthias.

'Why not, Englishman?' Columbus called.

'Nothing to the north, nothing to the south,' Matthias repeated the voice he had heard. 'Ever west, Captain General. That was your order and we should keep to it.'

Columbus smiled bleakly but the rest of the crew, led by the Pinzons, were insistent. The *Santa Maria* changed tack.

That night the crew were comforted to hear more birds passing overhead. Four days later a look-out cried that he could see things in the water. A reed and a stick were picked up, as well as a piece of wood around which grass was wrapped. When these were brought aboard the excitement of the crew intensified, for the piece of wood looked as if it had been carved. The gloom lifted. The winds freshened. Escobedo announced that they were now travelling at 7 knots a day. Matthias was teased because he had been against the change in direction. One evening, just after sunset, Matthias was taking the first watch when he heard that mysterious voice again.

'Nothing to the north, nothing to the south! You must sail ever west! Look for the light!'

Matthias stared round: on the far side of the foredeck a

young sail-maker, Diego Yemodes, was squatting, stitching a piece of canvas, but he never looked up.

'Nothing to the north! Nothing to the south! Ever west! Look for the light! Tell Columbus to look for the light!'

'Is everything all right?'

Matthias jumped and turned round. Columbus was standing at the top of the steps staring at him curiously.

'Why did you vote against changing direction, Englishman?'

'I don't know,' Matthias lied, holding the Captain General's gaze. 'I still think it was a mistake to change.'

Columbus nodded and looked up at the night sky.

'I believe you are right.' He turned and went down the steps.

Matthias heard one of the bombards fire, followed by the slap of feet on the deck. Lanterns were lit, signals flashed to the *Niña* and *Pinta*. The *Santa Maria*, sails straining under the wind, changed tack at the shouts of the Captain General, back on the original course, due west.

Matthias forgot about his own anxieties. He felt the ship twist and turn. He heard something bump against the side, and looked over. It was a piece of wood, a branch or trunk. It swirled by so fast Matthias couldn't determine. He went back to his watch. He stared so hard his eyes hurt and then he glimpsed it, a light like that of a wax candle, being moved up and down. He blinked and stared again. He was sure he had seen it. No star, no figment of his imagination or trick of the ocean. Again the light, up and down as if someone were signalling him through the darkness. He left his post and ran down to the deck, hammering on the door of Columbus' cabin. The Captain General came bustling out. He took one look at Matthias' face and went like a monkey up the steps, standing on the bowsprit, holding on to the ropes.

'You saw something?'

'Dead ahead,' Matthias replied. 'Nothing to the north, nothing to the south! Ever west!'

'You are mis— No, I see it!'

Columbus jumped down. He was soon joined on the forecastle by other officers. The rest of the crew were aroused and from across the water came the boom of a bombard. The *Pinta*, too, had seen the light. All three ships now closed up. Sails were furled, strict orders given to hold their position. The whole crew, as if participating in a holy vigil, waited for dawn.

Prayers were offered, the Salve Regina sung: throughout the night the three ships backed and filled under reduced canvas off this unknown shore. Columbus was like a man possessed. The men were impatient, urging Columbus to move closer but, when dawn broke, the Captain General's caution was vindicated. They could see a white shoreline, trees rising up, surf seething along a coral rock which stretched like fangs up out of the sea; these would have torn their ships to shreds if they had tried to sail directly to shore.

Once daybreak had come, the three ships tacked along the coastline looking for a place to anchor. At last they found a bay and slipped in easily. The leadsmen sang out the depths until the signal was given to drop anchor. The men clustered on the deck and stared in wonderment: white sands, wooded hills, even the breeze had lost its salty, tangy taste and now wafted the sweeter smells of fruits and vegetation towards them. Figures were seen slipping in and out of the treeline.

'Savages,' Navarette, one of the most keen-sighted, reported from where he stood, halfway up the main mast. 'Naked as babies, they are.'

All three ships' boats were lowered. Columbus, now dressed in gilded armour, a great cloak round his shoulders and carrying the royal standard of Castile, clambered into his; the Pinzons, carrying the banners of the expedition, a green cross with the initials of the two sovereigns on either side, joined him. Matthias was also chosen to go and he climbed gingerly into the boat.

They reached the shoreline in a matter of minutes. Matthias felt strange to be on dry land again, a sensation not helped by the shimmering, white sands, the glare of the sun and the strange, exotic smells which swept down from the dark green forest which fringed the beach. He helped Baldini pull the boat further up out of the water. Columbus and a number of officers were already planting the standards of Spain into the hot sands before kneeling down. A prayer of thanksgiving was offered and 'this land and all the territories appertaining to it' were claimed in the name of King Ferdinand and Queen Isabella of Spain.

A group of olive-skinnd figures slipped out of the trees and came down the beach. Matthias had heard all sorts of stories about the subjects of the Great Khan: how they were small, yellow, wizened and slant-eyed or had the faces of dogs. They, however, were olive-skinned, with jet-black hair which fell down as far as the nape of the neck, of good stature and very comely. They were naked as the day they were born and reminded Matthias of children as they moved shyly towards the Captain General. Some of the women wore beach clouts, with ivory ornaments round their necks and wrists. Dark-eyed, their high-cheekboned faces slightly turned away, as if they did not wish to look fully at these strange creatures. They jabbered quietly amongst themselves. A beautiful young woman, her hair half-covering her face, pinched her nose and giggled. Matthias smiled. With the wind behind them, the smell of Columbus and his party, not to mention that from the ships, must be highly offensive to these people. They bore gifts, fruit and food he'd never seen, and calabashes full of water. Their leader, a stocky young man, plucked up courage and walked towards Columbus. He touched the Captain General's face and clothes and looked in wonderment at the banners flapping above him.

Columbus whispered instructions to de Torres, who shrugged and began to talk to the natives in English, Spanish, Arabic, French, Hebrew and Aramaic. The leader just looked at him, owl-eyed. Eventually, he did reply, his voice low and guttural. He pointed up to the skies, then at de Torres, who laughed and shook his head.

'I can't understand them fully, sir,' he informed Columbus, 'but he thinks we come from Heaven.'

The man began to talk again. Matthias, who had edged forward to study these people more closely, saw the look of welcome on the man's face being replaced by that of fear. The leader repeated the word 'Caniba', and pointed out in a southerly direction. The word was taken up by his companions. De Torres caught their drift. He shook his head.

'Not Caniba! Not Caniba!' he replied.

Again the man spoke, this time using sign language. Despite the heat Matthias felt a chill go down his back. This young subject of the Great Khan left little to the imagination and Matthias almost knew how de Torres was going to translate it for Columbus.

'He wants assurances that we are not the Caniba,' he

declared. 'They are the great enemies of these people.' He paused as the young Indian intervened and made waving movements with his hand. 'He says they come here in great canoes,' de Torres said slowly. 'They take them prisoner, cut their throats, drink their blood and eat their flesh.'

'They are not armed,' Martin Pinzon spoke up. 'Have you noticed that, sir? They carry no arms.'

Pinzon was correct. Matthias could see no bow or arrow, no sword, daggers, clubs or axes. De Torres drew his sword and held it up so it caught the sunlight. The natives gasped and stared, amazed. He handed the sword to the leader. However, instead of grasping the hilt, the man touched the blade and cut his finger. He stared down in astonishment at the blood welling from the small cut.

'They know nothing of weapons,' Escobedo whispered. 'But Marco Polo, in his journals, says the subjects of the Great Khan are well armed.'

De Torres now sheathed his sword and, when he used a crossbow to bring down a seabird, the natives fell to the sand. Matthias began to wonder. Had they reached Cathay? The great island of Cipango? Or were they somewhere else? Who were these people who acted so innocently? Had they reached a paradise? But, if so, who were the Caniba? Was this a place where both the angels and demons lived? Matthias remembered that mysterious voice: he also wondered who, amongst these people with their childlike faces and innocent ways, had brought Columbus in by showing that mysterious light the evening before? The Captain General, however, had now noticed the small studs of gold in the natives' noses and ears. He pointed at these and excitedly asked de Torres where they were from? The native leader, surprised by Columbus' excitement, shrugged, took the gold from his nose and ears and handed it over. He pointed further south, chattering in his own tongue. Columbus stared round, not even waiting for de Torres to translate.

'We are on the outskirts of Cathay,' he declared. 'Their mines and quarries, from which this gold came, must lie to the south.' He snapped his fingers.

Baldini opened a small chest and Columbus distributed gifts: beads, coins, pieces of cloth and red bonnets. The natives, excited, took them like children seizing toys, only too willing to hand over the small pieces of gold they wore. Columbus then gave strict instructions that the people were not to be harmed or abused in any way.

'They are,' he declared, 'the subjects of their Catholic Majesties.'

After they returned to the ships, those lucky enough to have accompanied the Captain General described what the rest had only seen from afar. Columbus loudly proclaimed he had found the Indies and was determined to sail south. However, late in the afternoon, more of the natives in long dugouts, the oars of which looked like bakers' shovels, came out to greet all three ships. They brought more gifts, strange-looking fruits and small carvings. Columbus allowed some of the people on board and these gazed in wonderment up at the rigging. When the Captain General gave the order for one of the bombards to be fired, the natives caused much merriment by simply jumping overboard but, when they realised the sound meant them no harm, they laughed and splashed in the water like children.

Columbus sent another party ashore. These brought back cotton threads, multicoloured parrots and hooks made out of fishbones. They described strange plants and trees, talked of inner lakes full of fresh water, flocks of birds never seen before, so many they could darken the sun. Villages with huts made out of palm leaves: enormous snakes and other strange creatures. Matthias, like the rest, listened in wonderment. They also discovered the place they had landed was called Guaharini but Columbus rechristened it San Salvador. De Torres was unable to discover what tongue the natives spoke but soon they established a common list of words and left the rest to sign language. Columbus learnt that there were two islands further along the coast much larger than this, called Colba and Bohio. The Captain General was determined to reach these and, in the succeeding days, the *Santa Maria* and its two caravels edged along the coastline.

Columbus still maintained an iron discipline, placing lookouts with strict instructions, for the entire coastline was protected by a long line of cruel-looking reefs which could rip the bottom out of any of his craft. The Captain General soon proved he was a brilliant navigator. Time and again he managed to thread through these reefs into naturally formed harbours and ports. They landed on two more islands which were christened Isabella and Hispaniola. The natives were like those they first met, friendly, unarmed, innocent and eager to please. Sometimes Columbus took a few with him, determined that they would be his scouts who would eventually lead him to the great kingdom of the Khan.

Matthias found the voyage strange. Blue skies, soft white fluffy clouds, gentle breezes and warm sun prevailed. He recalled how, in England, autumn would be giving way to winter, with savage cold winds, driving sleet, dying leaves and iron-grey skies. Matthias was still perplexed, unable to establish what was so special about this place: why the Rose Demon and his followers such as Morgana had been so determined that he come here.

Even the Captain General now suspected that, perhaps, he had not reached the Indies. He took careful note of the fruits, trees, birds and creatures they discovered. Some of these were killed and dried for passage back to Spain but the Captain General still cherished dreams of casks of silver.

They eventually reached Colba, which Columbus renamed Cuba: high mountains soaring up to the sky, strange palm trees. The natives were similar to those they had met earlier, bringing out beds made out of netting, small gold figurines, harpoons and fruit. They listened patiently to Columbus' interminable questions about Golden Cathay, nodding and pointing, as the others had, further south. All of them were friendly and showed no fear of Columbus and his party until the word 'Caniba' was used. In Cuba the daughter of a chieftain came aboard. De Torres questioned her closely. 'The Caniba,' de Torres explained, having listened carefully to the young woman, 'live further to the south.' He paused as the young woman chattered again. 'They paint their faces red and have cords tied along their legs and arms,' de Torres translated. 'They come in long canoes and raid these islands. They take the people and use their flesh as meat: small babies they regard as a delicacy. They show no mercy or compassion.'

Columbus, seated on a chair with the girl at his feet, told de Torres to tell the girl that she need not fear. He, with his bombards, would destroy the Caniba. The young woman listened attentively. Her soft, gentle face, however, remained concerned. She replied slowly, carefully using her fingers to paint pictures in the air.

'You cannot kill them,' de Torres explained to Columbus and the rest. 'They are as many as the grains in the sand. They fear no one.'

A few days later they reached the island of Bohio. Its young cacique or chieftain, who called himself Cuacagnari, showed Columbus and his party some of the terrors of the Caniba. The chieftain, a young man of no more than twenty summers, met them on the beach bringing gifts of fruit and the juice of mastic trees which Columbus recognised as valuable and hoped to take back to Spain. The conversation followed the line of others, de Torres translating. Columbus described the glory of Spain, the power of Ferdinand and Isabella, the strength of their bombards and again asked where was Cathay or Cipango? The cacique listened attentively and again, to Columbus' exasperation, pointed further south. However, he made signs with his hands that they should go no further. He, too, talked of Caniba and brought forward three of his subjects: these had several ugly wounds on their arms and legs, as if a dog had taken great bites out of them though the flesh had healed well. The cacique explained how these people had been captured by the Caniba. They had begun to eat them alive but then they had escaped. Columbus and his party stared in disbelief. When they returned to their ships, the Captain General and the Pinzon brothers debated whether they should sail further south or change tack. A dispute broke out and the following day, without taking his leave, Martin Pinzon and the *Pinta* crew slipped their moorings and left, determined to make their own discoveries. Columbus continued his journey. One morning, towards the end of November, he came to a small island. He fired a bombard for he knew that the news of their arrival had spread the length and breadth of the archipelago. The natives would be expecting him and invariably flocked down to the beach. This time there was no such reception: the beach was empty, the trees, a long, dark forbidding line.

'Fitzosbert! Baldini!' Columbus ordered. 'Take the boat and go ashore!'

Two of the sailors were ordered to go with them as an escort. All four were armed with crossbows, swords and daggers. The boat was beached, the two sailors left on guard. Matthias with Baldini entered the dark line of trees. Matthias was now used to such forests, with their palm trees very similar to those he had seen on the Canaries, gaily coloured birds, strange smells, the chattering clatter of the jungle around him. They found a trackway, Baldini going first. Now and again they'd stop to leave a mark to ensure they did not get lost. They must have journeyed for some time, and the deeper they went into the jungle, the more concerned Matthias became. He suspected they were being watched: he was sure he had seen dark figures slip through the jungle on either side of him.

'I think we should return.' Matthias stopped.

He armed his crossbow. At the same time came the thud of a bombard from the *Santa Maria*, a prearranged signal that something was wrong. Matthias, not waiting for Baldini's agreement, turned and ran back along the trackway. He stopped and looked over his shoulder: Baldini was following him. Matthias also glimpsed something else, a flash of red amongst the trees.

'We are being followed!' he shouted, and ran on.

Because he was on the trackway, he was certain they could move faster than their pursuers. Matthias, drenched in sweat, kept looking to the right and left, fearful lest the pursuers encircle them and cut off their escape. At last he turned a bend and saw the beach stretching out before them. He glimpsed the *Santa Maria*. The two sailors had pushed the boat back into the shallows and were waiting for them. He turned to urge Baldini to run faster but the young Spaniard had stopped, chest heaving. He was smiling, staring strangely at Matthias.

'Come on!' Matthias urged.

'Why, *Creatura bona atque parva*?' The words sounded so strange in this exotic, humid, strange-smelling jungle: a far cry from the greenery of Gloucestershire, the cool darkness of the church at Tenebral. 'These are our friends, Matthias. These are my subjects. I will die to become one of them but you have nothing to fear.'

Matthias heard a shout from behind him. He turned and stared in horror. Two natives had stepped on to the track, blocking his way. Matthias had never seen such fierceness: tall men, darker-skinned than the natives he had met, with cords wrapped high along the calves of their legs. Each carried a club or axe. Their faces reminded him of ghouls, red ochre round the eyes, the cheeks and mouth smeared in white: blue and gold cockatoo feathers pushed into their cropped, matted hair. Matthias took a step forward. Both men were looking past him, eyes on Baldini as if they recognised him.

'Caniba!' Matthias spat out the word.

The leader stepped forward, mouth open, teeth like that of a dog, sharp and jagged. Matthias brought the crossbow up and fired, the shaft hit the man full in the chest. The other leapt forward. Matthias struck him with the crossbow and burst into a run, down the sun-dappled forest path. Behind him he heard a cry, a howl, long and blood-chilling.

The forest became alive with sound. Matthias turned to his left. Dark shapes were now running through the trees but, because of the undergrowth, not as fast as him. He reached the beach. Matthias heard the crash of a bombard, saw a puff of smoke and a stone ball crashed into the jungle behind him. He was now running for the boat. A terrible scream echoed from the forest behind him. He did not know whether it was Baldini or one of his pursuers. His chest ached, his legs felt heavy. He reached the shoreline, the water was cold as he splashed out, arms extended and he was hoisted aboard. One of the sailors was screaming. Matthias heard the twang of a crossbow, oars splashing and the boat pulled away.

Matthias stumbled to his knees and gasped in astonishment. The entire beach was filling with Caniba, armed with spears and clubs, their coloured, jaunty headdresses bobbing in the breeze. These surged down to the water line, shouting their war cries, waving spears and clubs. Matthias kept still as the oarsmen cursed him. The boat was small and narrow and there was a danger that it would be upset.

'To the left!' one of them shouted.

Matthias looked over. Canoes were now being brought down to the water line but, at last, the sailors were out of danger. The boat bobbed against the side of the *Santa Maria* even as Matthias heard the Captain General order the bombards to be fired again. The three men climbed over the rails: the boat was secured, the anchor raised and the *Santa Maria* turned for the open sea.

35

A few weeks later, on Christmas Eve, Matthias crouched at the foot of the mast, feeling the *Santa Maria* rock gently beneath him. The night was silent. Matthias slipped in and out of dreams of former Christmas Eves: he was a young boy in Sutton Courteny. The snow was falling and he and Christina were hurrying up the path to church. They were going to help his father put up the crib in the Lady Chapel, adorn the transepts and rood screen with red-berried holly and the magical ivy. The church bell was tolling. Matthias was given the task of taking the baby Jesus and putting it before the high altar; the statue of the Christ child would not be put in the crib until Christmas morning. Then he was at Oxford, he and Santerre singing in the choir, '*Oh puer natus*'. And, of course, there was Barnwick; Rosamund teasing him, kneeling before Matthias in their chamber, warming the posset cups whilst making Matthias guess what she was giving him for Christmas.

Matthias opened his eyes and looked up at the starlit sky. In a week the year would draw to a close. Since the attack by the Caniba very little had happened. Of Baldini there had been no further sign. Matthias had told the Captain General that his companion had been killed outright. The Captain General pursed his lips and nodded. Baldini's death and the savage foray of the Caniba had clearly shown they were not in Paradise. Many of the crew now loudly protested that they weren't in Cathay. Columbus was openly worried: they had been almost three months amongst the islands and, although he'd collected exotic fruits, plants and animals, there was very little gold or silver.

Martin Pinzon's *Pinta* had been reported further along the coast: the Captain General wondered if Pinzon had discovered anything fresh. He was making plans to go searching for his erstwhile Captain once Christmas had come and gone. So far the *Santa Maria* had not left the waters of the great island of Bohio. Cuacagnari, the local chief, was still friendly, wetting Columbus' appetite for treasure with small gifts such as a statue, a mask all hammered out of purest gold. The young chieftain also talked of lands further to the south, where the palaces were of costly material and the streets paved with gold.

Matthias breathed in deeply and abruptly stopped. He had become used to the heavy perfume of the islands, the strange sweet smells of the plants mixing with the rotting vegetation, and the salty tang from the sea. Yet, for a moment, he was sure he had smelt the heavy fragrance of a rose garden, as if he were back in England on a summer's day. He lay back, mocking his own imagination. Then he caught it again, as if someone had splashed rosewater over his face.

Matthias went cold and stumbled to his feet. Something was wrong. He looked towards the stern castle. He could see no figure against the night sky. The *Santa Maria* bumped as if something were scraping along the bottom of the hull. Matthias scrambled for the alarm bell and rang it. The sound of grinding grew. Matthias looked to starboard: he could see the lights of the *Niña* ahead of him. Men were scrambling to their feet. Columbus came out on deck. Lanterns were lit. Juan Delcrose came down from the stern castle, his eyes heavy with sleep.

'In God's name, what's wrong?' Columbus shouted.

Men were peering over the sides even as Delcrose fell to his knees and confessed he had fallen asleep. Escobedo came scrambling up from the hold.

'We've hit the rocks!' he cried. 'Long and jagged, well below the water line!'

'Where?' Columbus cried.

'In the bows!'

The boat was lowered, desperate attempts were made to move the *Santa Maria* off the gap-toothed reef. However, a wind rose, the swell increased and the *Santa Maria* was driven further on to the rocks. Sailors below reported that the seams were beginning to open so, just before dawn, Columbus gave the order to abandon ship. The crew had planned to spend Christmas Day feasting and junketing. Instead, under Columbus' lashing tongue, the *Santa Maria*,

487

now holed beyond repair, was stripped of all its movables, which were brought to the beach or across to the *Niña*.

Two days later Columbus addressed the crews of both ships. The Captain General stood on a large sea chest, hands on hips, his face grey with exhaustion. He seemed to have aged in a matter of days but his voice was still strong, his chin set in determination.

'There are too many,' he began, 'for the *Niña* to take.' He let his words sink in. 'We have travelled far and discovered much. It is time to return to Spain.' He flung a hand out. 'You saw how little time it took us to reach here. The journey home will be even shorter.' He paused. 'But not all of us will be able to go.' He stilled the murmur with his hand. 'By the powers given to me, I have decided, having consulted with officers, to found a colony here. I shall call it the Villa de la Natividad in honour of Christmas Day. I take the wreck of the *Santa Maria* as a sign from God, on the day his Son became man, that such a town be founded on these islands.' He breathed in deeply. 'The men who shall stay here will continue to search for gold and silver. You will be left well provisioned with food, arms and munitions. The cacique has promised his support.' He smiled bleakly. 'It is not too harsh a sentence: the land is pleasant, the sea warm, the islands well stocked with food, the natives are friendly, and the women . . .' Columbus let his words hang in the air. A shrewd man, he knew that many might prefer such a tempting offer than to be bundled abroad the *Niña* for an arduous journey home.

'And what about you?' a seaman cried.

'I intend to leave on the *Niña* within the next few days. I shall go looking for Pinzon, return to Spain and, within six months, I shall return with new ships, troops and supplies. I have decided that, before we leave, a stockade will be built. The cacique and his men will help build huts. I promise; those who remain will not suffer because they have done so,' Columbus now spoke more slowly, 'when it comes to the sharing out of rewards and honours from their Majesties in Spain. Forty men will remain under the following officers: Diego de Harana, Pedro Guitirres and the Englishman, Matthias Fitzosbert.' Columbus jumped down from the chest. 'Who else will volunteer?'

Men leapt to their feet. Matthias, sitting with his back to a palm tree, closed his eyes and groaned. He knew the wrecking of the *Santa Maria* had been no accident. Even Columbus suspected treachery but that seemed incredible. Delcrose was one of Columbus' principal supporters, a superb seaman and part owner of the *Santa Maria*. He confessed to falling asleep, claiming he had never felt so exhausted. Such a tiredness swept over him that he failed to ensure the *Santa Maria* kept in line with the *Niña* and so it had drifted upon the coral reef.

Matthias knew different. He recalled the sweet, heady smell of the roses and quietly resigned himself to the way the game was being played out.

The last week of the year was used by Columbus to build a stockade on a promontory overlooking the coral-edged sea. Trees, and wood from the wreck, were prepared to build a small stockade whilst, within the enclosure, the cacique's men helped build huts, showing Columbus and his officers how they were to be laid out. One small gate was built into the side of the stockade, not far from a ready supply of water. The other looked out towards the forest and was protected by the bombards taken from the *Santa Maria*. Two huts were set aside for arms and provisions. A makeshift parapet walk was set up and a small tower.

Columbus had the men assembled, solemnly proclaimed the colony's new name, gave de Harana and Guitirres his last orders, then he and the rest, having taken leave of the cacique, embarked on the *Niña*. Just before the ship left, with the natives assembled along the shoreline and the men of the newly founded garrison standing on the promontory, Columbus ordered the *Niña* to fire shot into what remained of the wreck of the *Santa Maria* – a farewell to his newly founded colony, as well as a harsh reminder to the natives of the power of Spain.

By 4 January Columbus had gone. He had taken no notice of Matthias, not even explaining why he had been chosen, though Matthias sensed the reason. Columbus did not trust him. He had been foisted on the Captain General by the Inquisition. He was the first to have seen the light on the first night they reached land. He had also been with Baldini, the only man Columbus had lost on the voyage, and been on deck when the *Santa Maria* had hit the rock.

Matthias had few regrets. If he returned to Spain what would wait for him? And if he tried to desert, Columbus might then seize the opportunity to use him as an example to others. He found the two officers, Guitirres and de Harana, just as cold: in the days following Columbus' departure, Matthias was not included by the officers in their deliberations. Indeed, the two men seemed more concerned about vying with each other than maintaining any discipline in the newly founded colony. Matters were allowed to drift. No exercise or arms drill was held. No roster of duties established, whether it be guard duty or keeping the small colony clean. Within a week the place was stinking and the men grew more accustomed to wandering down to the villages or sleeping out in the jungle. Disputes broke out, particularly over women, who seemed fascinated by these new arrivals, 'the men from Heaven'. Matthias objected but de Harana just shrugged.

'Oh Englishman!' De Harana filled his wine cup and glanced bleary-eyed at Matthias. 'We have food, we have water. The natives are amenable.'

'We should send out scouts,' Matthias replied.

'Oh yes.' De Harana slurped from the cup. 'Your friends the Caniba. Pity about poor Baldini, eh?' He lurched to his feet, breathing wine fumes into Matthias' face. 'You are our master-at-arms,' he slurred. 'You are a good runner. We saw that the day Baldini was killed.'

'It wasn't my fault!' Matthias snapped.

'Well, it's not mine either!' de Harana jibed. 'As I said, you are the master-at-arms and I'm your superior officer. Go out and scout!'

Later that day Matthias took a water bottle, some food wrapped in a ragged cloth, a war belt, an arbalest and slipped out of the stockade. He kept to the coastline.

Matthias was more pleased to be by himself than intent on spying out possible dangers. He sensed something was about to happen but accepted there was little he could do. He continued walking, keeping the sea to his right.

When night fell he camped out in the open, finding a small cave on the edge of the trees overlooking the sea. Matthias collected some dried wood, struck a tinder and sat staring out into the darkness. That night he dreamt once more of Barnwick and, when he awoke, he felt stiff and slightly cold, for the fire had gone out. Matthias went to the cave mouth, stretched, then gasped. Last night the sea had been calm, the waves breaking like a dull thunder on the rocks of the coral reef below him.

Now it shimmered in the early morning sun and seemed to be full of long, high-beached canoes streaming towards the shoreline. Matthias crouched, straining his eyes. He counted and reckoned there must be at least 60 canoes; each bore 20 to 30 Caniba warriors, their gaudy headdresses flapping in the morning breeze. They were moving past him, turning in towards the shore somewhere to the north. Others followed and Matthias realised this was not some raid but a war horde on the move. He hurried back and reached Natividad late in the afternoon and demanded a meeting with de Harana and Guitirres. Both men listened contemptuously.

'They know Columbus has left,' Matthias concluded. 'The ships have gone. I think they had been invited here. The men must be brought back, the fortress prepared. With a stout defence we could drive them off.'

'A stout defence could drive them off,' Guitirres slurred. 'I agree, Englishman, there's nothing the natives fear more than Spanish steel or a bombard stone tearing them limb from limb. I am taking a troop of men out of the stockade tomorrow morning. De Harana here agrees the men need to be kept busy. We need supplies and the natives have said there's gold.' His eyes gleamed in their creases of fat. 'There are mines further inland. We'll pile the treasure so high the Captain General will have no need for a beacon when he returns.'

Matthias protested but de Harana and Guitirres were adamant. They were bored: it might be months before Columbus returned and, like their Captain General, the officers were determined to return to Spain as wealthy men.

The following morning Guitirres led forty of the men out. Matthias was ordered to accompany him. The Englishman's heart sank at the lack of organisation. The troops straggled out in a line. They were even allowed to bring their native women, and he strongly suspected that many of the water bottles contained wine. No scouts or flankers were sent out ahead. Guitirres left just after dawn. Matthias kept to the rear of the column. Now and again he would leave the track and go off into the jungle. He found nothing to confirm his fears that the Caniba were following them.

Just before noon they stopped at the mouth of a small valley, a pleasant open space, the land cultivated by a nearby village whose smoke they could glimpse. While the

491

men rested, Matthias went ahead, following the small brook which wound its way along the valley floor. The fields were deserted. Matthias stopped and studied the dark line of the jungle on either side. He could see nothing untoward. The march continued. Matthias expected to be greeted by some of the villagers but the valley remained silent. Even Guitirres became slightly suspicious.

'For the love of God!' Matthias snarled. 'At least send scouts out ahead!'

Guitirres shrugged, glanced bleary-eyed, turned his back and went after his men. Matthias stopped by the brook, opened his jerkin and began bathing his face and neck with cool water. He heard a cry and glanced up. The column had stopped. From the line of trees on their right had appeared a long column of Caniba. Silent, menacing, they advanced down the slope towards the valley floor. More of them followed. The Spaniards gazed in astonishment as this phalanx of warriors, so unlike the natives they'd met, marched slowly towards them. Their chiefs preceded them; warriors armed with clubs and axes, their headdresses adorned by the brilliant plumage of parrots and other wild birds. Matthias stood up, slipping a bolt into the arbalest. Guitirres was shouting orders but the men appeared stunned. Some of the Indian women were screaming, tugging at their would-be protectors, pointing back down from where they had come.

'Fall back!' Matthias screamed.

To his horror he heard a loud ululating war cry come from the trees behind him. He whirled round. A second horde of Caniba were now streaming from the jungle on their left. As they did so, the column of Caniba to Matthias' right shouted their war cry and raced towards the small, chaotic Spanish force. All order and any hope of defence broke down. Guitirres tried to form his men into a circle but this proved fruitless, and the men streamed back towards Matthias. They pushed and shoved each other, splashing through the small brook, some even dropped swords and spears in their haste to get away. Matthias drew his sword and tried to stop the deserters but they pushed by him. The group which had stayed round Guitirres were soon overwhelmed. The Caniba burst amongst them, axe and club falling, their short stabbing spears thrusting in and out. Matthias watched in horror as a Caniba took one of the young Indian girls away from the group and, with one quick cut, slashed her throat and, kneeling down, burrowed his face into her bloody neck.

Some of the Spaniards were also not being killed but were clubbed and pulled away, hands and feet tied. A few Spaniards broke through, fighting coolly with sword and spear whilst others kept firing their arbalests, yet the Caniba seemed to have no fear. These, too, were overwhelmed and already the Caniba were in hot pursuit of those who had fled. Matthias stood his ground. He loaded the arbalest and, taking shelter behind a palm tree, loosed whenever he could. A few Spaniards joined him in an attempt to protect their fleeing comrades, yet it was a desolate fight. Matthias looked to his left and right: the Caniba were now entering the jungle in an attempt to outflank and encircle him, whilst others pursued the rest of the small force back to the stockade which, Matthias knew, despite the bombard, would soon be overrun.

The massacre in the middle of the valley now ended. The Caniba reorganised and streamed up to where Matthias and a few Spaniards still maintained their futile defence. Matthias kept loading and firing his arbalest. As he did so, Caniba broke out from the trees on the left and right, engulfing Matthias and his small party in a ferocious hand-to-hand fight. Matthias, his back to a tree, sword and dagger in his hand, cut and thrust. His body was soaked in sweat, his arms ached yet he felt cold and composed. The fight seemed to represent his entire life but now he could see his enemy and give blow for blow, thrust for thrust. The air rang with the screams and groans of his dying companions. They had seen what had happened to the rest; no man wished to be taken alive.

Matthias noticed something extraordinary. The Caniba now surrounded him, a party of at least thirty, but he had received no wound, though they could have killed him easily. Time and again warriors came in, their fierce faces gaudily painted in red and white. They seemed more determined to disarm him than deliver any killing blow. Eventually, Matthias, by sheer power of numbers, was forced away from the tree. In one wild rush the Caniba surrounded him, catching at his arms and legs. Matthias lashed out. He felt a blow to his head: the branches of the palm tree above whirled and he lapsed into unconsciousness.

When he awoke, Matthias was lying in a small glade. A Caniba, his ferocious face daubed in war paint, was bathing the wound on his head, talking to him softly, though the words were guttural and harsh. Matthias tried to rise but others appeared and pressed him gently back on to the ground. Matthias stared to the left and right. Through the trees he could just about glimpse the valley, and saw Caniba warriors dragging away the dead. He sniffed the breeze, his stomach curdled, he caught the smell of woodsmoke and, beneath that, burning flesh, a sickly sweet odour. He stared up at the warrior.

'Kill me!' he whispered.

'Canabo! Canabo!' he said and thrust a finger into Matthias' stomach. 'Cacique Canabo!'

He narrowed his eyes and Matthias, despite the pain in his head, understood that he was to be taken to their chief, the cacique Canabo. The warrior allowed Matthias to drink from a calabash of water and threw the rest over his face. Matthias continued to lie there. Any attempt to turn over or get to his feet was gently but firmly repulsed. Looking around, Matthias saw the legs and feet of his captors. Now and again the Caniba came and stared down at him. Others arrived, chieftains by their gaudy, multicoloured headdresses and the necklaces of polished coral slung round their necks. Matthias was dragged to his feet and pushed back into the valley. He stopped in amazement: the valley floor was now thronged with the Caniba army. They were camped in small groups along the hillside. Of the Spaniards or their women, there was no sign. Every corpse had disappeared, all weapons had been collected. Only a splash of blood on the grass, a piece of clothing or scraps of armour bore witness to the desperate fight which had occurred there.

Matthias, his arms held gently by the Indian chieftains, was pushed along the edge of the brook. They passed a group of Caniba who were busy raping one of the Indian women they had captured. The woman had been gagged, her body stretched out on the ground and her conquerors were taking it in turns to kneel down between her outstretched legs. Again Matthias smelt the stench of burning flesh. He saw at the far end of the valley long columns of smoke rising from cooking fires. He thought the chieftains would be taking him there but, pulling him by the sleeve, they led him up a gentle slope into the

494

jungle, along a path which led into a glade. All the weapons of Guitirres' column were piled here: crossbows, swords, daggers, spears, armour, clothing, boots and war belts. At the far end of the glade, beneath the outspread branches of a palm tree, sat the cacique Canabo enthroned on a small, wooden chair. On either side of him, sitting cross-legged, were his chieftains. Matthias was pushed across and made to kneel before the cacique. Canabo was a young, thickset warrior. His face was long, sharp-nosed, with black, unblinking eyes: unlike the rest, who sat in ominous silence, he wore no war paint, and only a single white plume adorned his headdress. The tooth of some animal hung on a piece of cord round his neck, and on either side of his nose was a small nugget of gold on a pin.

'Where are my companions?' Matthias spoke in Spanish. 'Why were we attacked?'

Canabo shifted in his seat. He stared at Matthias and smiled. The chieftain's face relaxed, lips parted, his eyes, studying Matthias carefully, were now not so lifeless.

'Are you really concerned about them, *Creatura bona atque parva?*' The cacique spoke in Spanish. 'What are they to you, Matthias?' Now he spoke in English.

Matthias heard gasps from the chieftains around him. They gazed in wonderment at their leader, who could not only defeat the 'men from Heaven' in open battle but even speak their tongue. Canabo got up. Like the rest, he was naked except for a loin cloth around his waist. He lowered his firm muscular body down, sitting cross-legged, indicating that Matthias do the same. The chieftains watched solemnly. They could not understand their cacique showing such honour to a defeated man but, over the past few weeks, they had been astonished by the transformation in their leader and if he wanted the life of this white man, then so be it. Matthias settled himself. Canabo issued an order. A small gourd was thrust into Matthias' hand.

'Drink, Matthias,' Canabo ordered. 'We took it from Guitirres' body.'

Matthias tasted the wine. It was delicious, cleaning his mouth and throat, warming his belly. Canabo accepted a similar gourd and sipped at it carefully, his eyes never leaving Matthias.

'So, we have come to this, Matthias.' He took the gourd from his lips. 'You have come a long way.'

495

'Why?' Matthias asked. 'Why have you pursued me? Who are you?'

'I am the Rosifer,' Canabo answered. 'Pure spirit, intelligence and will.' His eyes took on a faraway look, reminding Matthias of the hermit sitting in the church at Tenebral. 'Before the world ever began, Matthias,' Canabo continued, 'before matter came into being, only the angels existed. Only they occupied Paradise and looked upon the face of God. That was in the beginning. Aye, Lucifer, Michael, Gabriel and Raphael, all of us archangels and leaders of the heavenly hosts. Then a new creation was planned.' He paused and smiled. 'I am going to use the language of your books because the human heart does not comprehend the beauty that once existed. God created His own image in flesh. We were to serve these and then the divine plan unfolded. God Himself intended to take flesh and become one of His creation. In Himself, all that was created, both visible and invisible, would become one. Lucifer and others rebelled at this, withdrew from Heaven and created their own.'

'And you fell with him?' Matthias asked.

'What I did is not contained in your books.' The answer was short and terse. 'But I saw the divine plan: to create flesh and to love that flesh.' His voice fell to a whisper. 'To create another being, Matthias! To be like God, that was my dream!' Canabo stopped and closed his eyes. 'In Eve that dream became a hunger, a lasting ambition, to fall in love with this image of God in flesh, to beget through her other images of the divine.' Canabo plucked a blade of grass and held it up between his fingers. 'I, the Rosebearer, God's own gardener, the keeper of Paradise. I took my ambition in the form of a rose and offered it to Eve, to seduce her, to give her powers so that she and I would be one.' Canabo opened his eyes and stared up through the interlacing branches at the sky. 'That was my sin,' he declared. 'Not one of rebellion but one of love as well as ambition. When Eve fell, I fell with her through time and space.' He let the grass fall from his fingers. 'God has offered me eternal pardon and I eternally refuse. I love the daughters of men and my desire to be with them, to be one, to create is an eternal hunger.' Canabo paused and sipped from the wine gourd. 'I wish to be like God,' he whispered. 'To become incarnate in flesh.'

'And you can't,' Matthias replied bitterly. 'You can only

possess: the bodies of the Preacher, Rahere, Santerre and the rest. Empty houses!'

'Empty houses,' Canabo replied. 'I could never have taken possession if they had not willed it.' Canabo leant across and touched Matthias gently on the cheek. 'I have to be close to you, Matthias, my beloved, my son.'

Matthias felt his stomach clench. He gently removed Canabo's hand from his cheek.

'I am not your son,' he replied. 'I am the son of Parson Osbert and Christina.'

'You are my son, the Beloved,' Canabo retorted, his eyes hard and shining. 'Christina was my second Eve. In her I found fulfilment, the conception of you. Love and will uniting in another being: that being, Matthias, is you. You are part of me.'

Matthias stared back. 'You really believe that, don't you?' He shook his head. 'But it's a lie! You cannot beget. You have no authority. You do not have the power to create souls.'

Canabo breathed in, nostrils flaring.

'And did you think I'd respond?' Matthias declared. 'Did you plot my life on the walls of Tenebral church?'

'The future is like a river,' Canabo replied. 'You, Matthias, can only see either bank but I can see the way it flows.'

'But why?' Matthias asked. 'Look at me! Exiled from my own home. Hunted, harried, threatened and persecuted!'

'Is that my fault?' Canabo replied. 'Has it not been explained to you? How different is your life from millions of others? I had to let you go, Matthias. I had to let you feel and drink deeply from the cup. Yes,' he leant forward, eyes gleaming, 'reflect on your life, your world: what meaning does it have? The rich get richer, the fat gorge themselves, the hunter kills the hunted. Tell me, what does that have to do with the will of God and the law of Christ? I had to let you experience life, Matthias: to reflect, to bring you to a point where you could see the empty glories of the world, the power and pomp of princes, the hypocrisy of the Church, the greed of human kind.'

'For what?' Matthias asked.

'To accept me, *Creatura bona atque parva*. To accept me for what I am.' He stretched out a hand. 'To love me for what I am.'

'And if I refuse?'

'I am making the same offer to you,' Canabo replied, 'which the great Lucifer made to Christ at Gethsemane: to forsake the world of man, to leave them to their power struggles, to the darkness which they create. Just to leave. And yet I offer more,' he added. 'To come with me, Matthias, become part of me, to drink the blood, to live for ever, to travel the face of the earth. Never to know death, no more hardship, no more persecution, to live like kings and ride in glory.' He paused and gestured around. 'Soon we can leave here, travel south, Matthias, to great kingdoms you have never even thought of, to be accepted as gods: you and me, the Rosifer and his Beloved.'

'And if I refuse?' Matthias repeated.

'There is a time, Matthias, when love will meet. As streets on a corner, there is an inevitability, a final decision has to be made. You have reached that, here, in what that fool Columbus thought Paradise, your decision must be made.'

'You must know it,' Matthias replied.

Canabo shook his head. 'I can see you walk. I can tell which direction you will take. I can guess the motives and thoughts of others, Matthias, but your mind, your will, they must always be yours. If they are not, how can your love be free?'

Matthias bowed his head and closed his eyes. The Rosifer had told him much of what he had suspected. He had been brought here specially, allowed to taste the world and all its joys and sorrows but a decision was to be made. He admired the cunning, as well as the subtlety of the Rosifer. Matthias had tasted the wine of life and it was bitter. Images filled his mind: Emloe's sneering face; Ratcliffe's rejection; Symonds, full of ambition and pride. The carnage of East Stoke; the cold cruelty of Torquemada. Everywhere, each place he had gone, the Rosifer had protected him. The images faded. Matthias suddenly recalled Barnwick but, try as he might, Rosamund's face escaped him.

'Where are you?' he whispered.

Then suddenly he felt he was back in Sutton Courteny. It was a summer's day. He was a child, walking hand in hand with Parson Osbert and Christina. He was holding their hands, they were crossing the great meadow, going down to sit by the mere where they would enjoy the day and wait until the shadows grew longer. Osbert and Christina were laughing as they swung him between them. They let go. He was running across the meadow but he was a man now, not a child, someone was coming towards him: Rosamund, her hair unbraided, her dress flapping in the breeze. A child, he could not make out the face, was running with her; they were calling his name. The image changed: he was home, in the parlour with Father Hubert. The friar was sitting at the base of a statue of St Anthony, he was teaching him his prayer, the one he used to say every night before he fell asleep. Matthias opened his eyes. Canabo was staring at him.

'What is your answer, Matthias?'

'Remember this, my soul and remember it well.' Matthias held Canabo's gaze. 'The Lord thy God is One and He is holy. And thou shalt love the Lord thy God with all thy mind, with all thy heart and with all thy strength.'

'That is no answer, Creatura.'

'It's the only one I can give,' Matthias whispered. 'When I was a child and met you at Tenebral, you showed me the foxes and we ate roast rabbit. You held my hand, I thought you were God incarnate: such warmth, such friendship, yet when you are a child, you think like a child.'

'I loved you too, Creatura, and still do.'

'But, when you are a man,' Matthias continued remorselessly, 'you enter a different world.'

'That is why I waited, Creatura.'

'Only when I met Rosamund,' Matthias continued, 'did I come to know what love really was. I loved her. I still do. I always will. If I had not met her,' he shook his head, 'my answer could well be different.'

'Creatura.' Canabo stretched his hands out in supplication.

'I don't love you,' Matthias replied. 'And you are right. I've drunk the chalice of the world and its dregs have made me sick. Let me go,' he beseeched. 'Release me!'

Canabo looked at him. Matthias hardened himself to the pleading in his eyes.

'If you really love me,' Matthias persisted, 'if you still do, let me go!'

Canabo bowed his head. When he lifted it, tears welled in his eyes.

'The lords of the air,' he declared softly, 'have said this is the time, the demand has been made, your reply has been witnessed.' He shook his head. 'Oh, Creatura . . .'

Turning, Canabo muttered something to one of his companions. The warrior rose and brought back a small gourd filled with wine. Canabo sniffed it and handed it to Matthias.

'Drink, Creatura,' he whispered. 'Do you remember that day at Tenebral?'

Matthias lifted the gourd. He toasted Canabo and drank deeply to fortify himself. He did not know what was coming and he was fearful lest his body betray him. Canabo was staring at him, a strange, faraway look in his eyes. Matthias felt the wine and what was in it flow through his body. He lurched forward, a terrible numbness spreading from his stomach.

'I am dying!' he gasped. He held his hand out. 'Not alone, please!'

'Oh, Creatura!' Canabo was sobbing. He grasped Matthias' hand. 'Go, Creatura!' he whispered. 'Run like the wind. No objection will be made at your passing.'

But Matthias couldn't hear him. The gourd slipped from his fingers; his hands had lost their feeling. He felt a stiffness in his body, a difficulty in breathing and he was oh so tired. He closed his eyes, head falling forward. He was lying on the grass near the old Roman wall. Rosamund was bending over, shaking him, kissing his face. Matthias sighed, one last gasp and his soul went out to meet hers.

Later that day the great cacique Canabo sat on a promontory overlooking the sea and watched the water turn a bloody red in the rays of the setting sun. Behind him, in the shattered fortress of Natividad and in the trees beyond, his warriors feasted on the flesh of their enemies. Now and again they would look at their leader sitting so alone, and talk in wonderment about his new powers and his love for the white man who had drunk the poisoned wine and been allowed to die so quickly. The corpse of that young white man had not been desecrated. Canabo had placed it in a canoe, lit a funeral pyre and his warriors had pushed it out into the open sea. Canabo had watched the fire burn until the charred canoe, and all within it, sank quietly beneath the ocean. All the time Canabo wept. He cried for Matthias, for himself, for what might have been, and for the lost golden rose gardens of Heaven.

AUTHOR'S NOTE

The historical events, as described in this novel, are based on fact: the battle of Tewkesbury, the quarrel between the Lancastrian commanders. In the abbey today you can still see signs of the desperate struggle put up by the Lancastrians who fled for sanctuary there. The Prior of the Hospitallers was one of those who faced summary execution in Tewkesbury market place, for the Yorkists were determined on the destruction of the Lancastrian House, both root and branch. In 1485 the only remaining champion of the House of Lancaster, Henry Tudor, made his successful bid at Bosworth though, within two years, he had to face Lambert Simnel's conspiracy, which culminated in the bloody battle of East Stoke.

James III of Scotland was as described, a weak man who dabbled in sorcery and black magic. An ineffectual king and a poor soldier, he died mysteriously at Sauchieburn, stabbed to death by a man he thought was a priest.

The fall of Granada, in January 1492, brought Spain to the rank of a premier power in Europe. It also unleashed the terrors of Torquemada, who was determined 'to cleanse the new Spanish kingdom of any impurity'.

Columbus' voyage to the New World is based on an edition of his own journal. Columbus did report seeing a strange light, like that of a candle being lifted and raised, the night the ship first sighted land. His voyage round the islands of San Salvador, Cuba and Haiti was a desperate search to vindicate his own arguments that a voyage across the great Western Ocean would bring him to Cathay and Cipango. The 'Caniba' were held in great awe and terror, a fierce warlike people who were eventually wiped out by the Spanish colonists. When Columbus returned, in 1493, Natividad was no longer, undoubtedly the work of these Caniba.

The symbolism of the rose is a major theme in medieval art,

literature and architecture. The flower itself has always held a mystical significance. The idea of possession by a demon also played a major part in medieval thought and the Rosifer, or Rose Demon, is simply a development of such an idea.